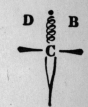

BOLT
BY
DICK FRANCIS

A QUESTION OF PRINCIPLE
BY
JEFFREY ASHFORD

THE CAPE MURDERS
BY
DOLORES WEEKS

Published for the
DETECTIVE BOOK CLUB ®
by Walter J. Black, Inc.
ROSLYN, NEW YORK

BOLT
Copyright © 1986
by Dick Francis

A QUESTION OF PRINCIPLE
Copyright © 1986
by Jeffrey Ashford

THE CAPE MURDERS
Copyright © 1987
by Dolores Weeks

THE DETECTIVE BOOK CLUB ®
Printed in the United States of America

BOLT

BY

DICK FRANCIS

How can Roland de Brescou win when amoral Henri Nanterre is free to use any tactics while Roland must follow his old-world code of honor?

G. P. Putnam's Sons Edition $17.95

A QUESTION OF PRINCIPLE

BY

JEFFREY ASHFORD

Dennis Rickmore faces an agonizing dilemma. If he testifies against his despised brother-in-law, will he be upholding a principle . . . or getting even?

St. Martin's Press, Inc. Edition $13.95

THE CAPE MURDERS

BY

DOLORES WEEKS

In light of Owen Wentworth's wheeling and dealing, his murder was not entirely unexpected. He was the first to die . . . but not the last. The Islanders are soon forced to consider the chilling possibility that a maniac is on a rampage.

Dodd, Mead & Co. Edition $15.95

BOLT

BY

DICK FRANCIS

Published by special arrangement with G. P. Putnam's Sons.

for
Danielle and Holly
both born since
Break In

1

Bitter February, within and without. Mood to match the weather; raw and overcast, near to freezing. I walked from the weighing room to the parade ring at Newbury races trying not to search for the face that wouldn't be there, the intimately known face of Danielle de Brescou, to whom I was formally engaged, diamond ring and all.

Winning the lady, back in November, had been unexpected, an awakening, deeply exciting . . . happy. Keeping her, in the frosts before spring, was proving the merry devil. My much-loved dark-haired young woman seemed frighteningly to be switching her gaze from a steeplechase jockey (myself) to an older richer sophisticate of superior lineage (he was a prince) who hadn't even the decency to be bad-looking.

Unmoved as I might try to appear on the surface, I was finding the frustration erupting instead in the races themselves, sending me hurtling over the fences without prudence, recklessly embracing peril like a drug to blot out rejection. It might not be sensible to do a risky job with a mind two hundred miles from one's fingertips, but tranquilizers could come in many forms.

Princess Casilia, unaccompanied by Danielle, her husband's niece, was waiting as usual in the parade ring, watching her runner, Cascade, walk round. I went across to her, shook the offered hand, made the small bow, acknowledging her rank.

"A cold day," she said in greeting, the consonants faintly thick, vowels pure and clear, the accent only distantly reminiscent of her European homeland.

"Yes. Cold," I said.

Danielle hadn't come. Of course she hadn't. Stupid of me to hope. She'd said cheerfully on the telephone that she wouldn't be coming to stay this weekend, she would be going to a fabulous Florentine gathering in a hotel in the Lake District with the prince and some of his friends, where they would listen to lectures on the Italian Renaissance given by the Keeper of the Italian paintings in the Louvre, and various other things of that sort. It was such a great and unique opportunity, she was sure I'd understand.

It would be the third weekend in a row she'd been sure I would understand.

The princess looked distinguished as always, middle-aged, slender, intensely feminine, warm inside a supple sable coat swinging from narrow shoulders. Normally bareheaded, dark smooth hair piled high, she wore on that day a tall Russian-type fur hat with a huge up-turning fur brim, and I thought fleetingly that few could have carried it with more style. I had ridden her string of twenty or so horses for more than ten years and I tended to know her racegoing clothes well. The hat was new.

She noted the direction of my glance and the admiration that went with it, but said merely, "Too cold for Cascade, do you think?"

"He won't mind it," I said. "He'll loosen up going down to the start."

She wouldn't mention Danielle's absence, if I didn't. Always reticent, sheltering her thoughts behind long eyelashes, the princess clung to civilized manners as if to a shield against the world's worst onslaughts, and I'd been in her company enough not to undervalue her chosen social façades. She could calm tempests with politeness, defuse lightning with steadfast chit-chat and disarm the most pugnacious adversaries by expecting them to behave well. I knew she would prefer me to keep my woes to myself, and would feel awkward if I didn't.

She did, on the other hand, understand my present predicament perfectly well. Not only was Danielle her husband's niece, but Litsi, the prince currently diverting Danielle to a fifteenth-century junket, was her own nephew. They were both currently guests under her Eaton Square roof, meeting from breakfast to dinner . . . and from dinner to breakfast, for all I really knew.

"What are our chances?" the princess asked neutrally.

"Pretty good," I said.

She nodded in agreement, full of pleasant hope, the prospect of winning real enough.

Cascade, despite an absence of brains, was a prolific winner of two-mile 'chases who had shown his heels in the past to every opponent in that day's field. Given luck he would do it again; but nothing's certain, ever, in racing . . . or in life.

Prince Litsi, whose whole name was about a yard long and to my mind unpronounceable, was cosmopolitan, cultured, impressive and friendly. He spoke perfect idiomatic English with none of his aunt's thickened consonants, which was hardly surprising as he'd been born after his royal grandparents had been chased off their throne, and had spent much of his childhood in England.

He lived now in France, but I'd met him a few times over the years when he'd visited his aunt and escorted her to the races, and I'd liked him in a vague way, never knowing him well. When I'd heard he was coming again for a visit I hadn't given a thought to the impact he might make on a bright American female who worked for a television news agency and thirsted for Leonardo da Vinci.

"Kit," the princess said.

I retrieved my attention from the Lake District and focused on the calmness in her face.

"Well," I said, "some races are easier than others."

"Do your best."

"Yes."

Our prerace meetings over the years had developed into short comfortable interludes in which little was said but much understood. Most owners went into parade rings accompanied by their trainers, but Wykeham Harlow, trainer of the princess's horses, had altogether stopped going to the races. Wykeham, growing old, couldn't stand the incessant winter journeys. Wykeham, shaky in the memory and jerky in the knees, nevertheless still generated the empathy with horses that had put him straight into the top rank from the beginning. He continued to send out streams of winners from his eighty-strong stable, and I, most thankfully, rode them.

The princess went indomitably to the races in all weathers, delighting in the prowess of her surrogate children, planning their futures, recalling their pasts, filling her days with an unflagging interest. Over many years she and I had arrived at a relationship that was both formal and deep, sharing intensities of success and moments of grief, understanding each other in easy accord at race meetings, parting to unconnected lives at the gate.

Unconnected, that is to say, until the previous November when Danielle had arrived from America to take up her London posting and ended in my bed. Since then, although the princess had undoubtedly accepted me as a future member of her family and had invited me often to her house, her manner to me, as mine to her, had remained virtually unchanged, especially on racecourses. The pattern had been too long set, and felt right, it seemed, to us both.

"Good luck," she said lightly, when the time came for mounting, and Cascade and I went down to the start with him presumably warming up from the canter but as usual sending no telepathic messages about his feelings. With some horses a two-way mental traffic could be almost as explicit as speech, but dark, thin, nippy Cascade was habitually and unhelpfully silent.

The race turned out to be much harder than expected, as one of the other runners seemed to have found an extra gear since I'd beaten him last. He jumped stride for stride with Cascade down the far side and clung like glue round the bend into the straight. Shaping up to the last four fences and the run-in he was still close by Cascade's side, his jockey keeping him there aggressively although there was the whole wide track to accommodate him. It was a demoralizing tactic that that jockey often used against horses he thought frightenable, but I was in no mood to be overcrowded by him or by anybody, and I was conscious, as too often recently, of ruthlessness and rage inside and of repressed desperation bursting out.

I kicked Cascade hard into the final jumps and drove him unmercifully along the run-in, and if he hated it, at least he wasn't telling me. He stretched out his neck and his dark head toward the winning post and under relentless pressure persevered to the end.

We won by a matter of inches and Cascade slowed to a walk in a few uneven strides, absolutely exhausted. I felt faintly ashamed of myself and took little joy in the victory, and on the long path back to the unsaddling enclosure felt not a cathartic release from tension but an increasing fear that my mount would drop dead from an overstrained heart.

He walked with trembling legs into the winner's place to applause he certainly deserved, and the princess came to greet him with slightly anxious eyes. The result of the photo-finish had already been announced, confirming Cascade's win, and it appeared that the princess wasn't worried about whether she had won, but how.

"Weren't you hard on him?" she asked doubtfully, as I slid to the ground. "Too hard, perhaps, Kit?"

I patted Cascade's steaming neck, feeling the sweat under my fingers. A lot of horses would have crumbled under so much pressure, but he hadn't.

"He's brave," I said. "He gives all he's got."

She watched me unbuckle the girths and slide my saddle

off onto my arm. Her horse stood without moving, drooping with fatigue, while Dusty, the traveling head-lad, covered the brown dripping body with a sweat-sheet to keep him warm.

"You have nothing to prove, Kit," the princess said clearly. "Not to me. Not to anyone."

I paused in looping the girths round the saddle and looked at her in surprise. She almost never said anything of so personal a nature, nor with her meaning so plain. I suppose I looked as disconcerted as I felt.

I more slowly finished looping the girths.

"I'd better go and weigh in," I said, hesitating.

She nodded.

"Thank you," I said.

She nodded again and patted my arm, a small familiar gesture that always managed to convey both understanding and dismissal. I turned away to go into the weighing room and saw one of the Stewards hurrying purposefully toward Cascade, peering at him intently. Stewards always tended to look like that when inspecting hard-driven horses for ill-treatment, but in this particular Steward's case there was far more to his present zeal than a simple love of animals.

I paused in midstride in dismay, and the princess turned her head to follow my gaze, looking back at once to my face. I met her blue eyes and saw there her flash of comprehension.

"Go on," she said. "Weigh in."

I went on gratefully, and left her to face the man who wanted, possibly more than anything else on earth, to see me lose my jockey's license.

Or, better still, my life.

* * *

Maynard Allardeck, acting as a Steward for the Newbury meeting (a fact I had temporarily forgotten), had both bad and good reasons to detest me, Kit Fielding.

The bad reasons were inherited and irrational and therefore the hardest to deal with. They stemmed from a feud between families that had endured for more than three centuries and had sown a violent mutual history thick with malevolent deeds. In the past, Fieldings had murdered Allardecks, and Allardecks, Fieldings. I had myself, along with my twin sister, Holly, been taught from birth by our grandfather that all Allardecks were dishonest, cowardly, spiteful and treacherous, and so we would probably have gone on believing all our lives had Holly not, in a Capulet–Montague gesture, fallen in love with and married an Allardeck.

Bobby Allardeck, her husband, was demonstrably not dishonest, cowardly, spiteful or treacherous, but on the contrary a pleasant well-meaning fellow training horses in Newmarket. Bobby and I, through his marriage, had finally in our own generation, in our own selves, laid the ancient feud to rest, but Bobby's father, Maynard Allardeck, was still locked in the past.

Maynard had never forgiven Bobby for what he saw as treason, and far from trying for reconciliation had intensified his indoctrinated belief that all Fieldings, Holly and I above all included, were thieving, conniving, perfidious and cruel. My serene sister, Holly, was demonstrably none of these things, but Maynard saw all Fieldings through distorted mental pathways.

Holly had told me that when Bobby informed his father (all of them standing in Bobby and Holly's kitchen) that Holly was pregnant, and that like it or not his grandchild would bear both Allardeck and Fielding blood and genes, she'd thought for an instant that Maynard was actually going to try to strangle her. Instead, with his hands literally stretching toward her throat, he'd whirled suddenly away and vomited into the sink. She'd been very shaken, telling me, and Bobby had sworn never to let his father into the house again.

Maynard Allardeck was a member of the Jockey Club, racing's ruling body, where he was busy climbing with his monumental public charm into every position of power he could reach. Maynard Allardeck, acting as Steward already at several big meetings, was aiming for the triumvirate, the three Stewards of the Jockey Club, from among whom the Senior Steward was triannually elected.

For a Fielding who was a jockey, the prospect of an Allardeck in a position of almost total power over him should have been devastating: and that was where Maynard's good and comprehensible reasons for detesting me began, because I had a hold over him of such strength that he couldn't destroy my career, life or reputation without doing the same to his own. He and I and a few others knew of it, just enough to ensure that in all matters of racing he had to be seen to treat me fairly.

If however he could prove I had truly ill-treated Cascade, he would get me a fine and a suspension with alacrity and joy. In the heat of the race, in the upsurge of my own uncontrollable feelings, I hadn't given a thought to him watching on the stands.

I went into the weighing room and sat on the scales, and then returned to just inside the door to see what was going on outside. From the shadows, I watched Maynard talking to the princess, who was wearing her blandest and most pleasant expression, both of them circling the quivering Cascade, who was steaming all over in the freezing air as

17

Maynard had commanded Dusty to remove the netlike sweat-sheet.

Maynard as always looked uncreased, opulent and trustworthy, an outer image that served him very well both in business deals, where he had made fortunes at others' expense, and in social circles, where he gave largely to charity and patted himself on the back for good works. Only the comparative few who had seen the mean, rough, ruthless reality inside remained cynically unimpressed.

He had removed his hat in deference to the princess and held it clasped to his chest, his graying fair hair brushed tidily into uncontroversial shape. He was almost squirming with the desire to ingratiate himself with the princess while at the same time denigrating her jockey, and I wasn't certain that he couldn't cajole her into agreeing that yes, perhaps, on this one occasion, Kit Fielding had been too hard on her horse.

Well, they would find no weals on Cascade because I'd barely touched him with the whip. The other horse had been so close that when I'd raised my arm I found I couldn't bring my whip down without hitting him instead of Cascade. Maynard no doubt had seen my raised arm, but it was legs, feet, wrists and fury that had done the job. There might be whip marks in Cascade's soul, if he had one, but they wouldn't show on his hide.

Maynard deliberated for a lengthy time with pursed lips, shakes of the head and busy eyes, but in the end he bowed stiffly to the sweetly smiling princess, replaced his hat carefully and stalked disappointedly away.

Greatly relieved, I watched the princess join a bunch of her friends while Dusty with visible disapproval replaced the sweat-sheet and told the lad holding Cascade's bridle to lead him off to the stables. Cascade went tiredly, head low, all stamina spent. Sorry, I thought, sorry, old son. Blame it on Litsi.

The princess, I thought gratefully as I peeled off her colors to change into others for the next race, had withstood Maynard's persuasions and kept her reservations private. She knew how things stood between Maynard and myself because Bobby had told her one day back in November, and although she had never referred to it since, she had clearly not forgotten. I would have to do more than half kill her horse, it seemed, before she would deliver me to my enemy.

I rode the next race acutely conscious of him on the stands: two scampering miles over hurdles, finishing fourth. After that I changed back into the princess's colors and returned to the parade ring for the day's main event, a three-mile steeplechase regarded as a trial race for the Grand National.

Unusually, the princess wasn't already in the ring waiting, and I stood alone for a while watching her sturdy Cotopaxi being led round by his lad. Like many of her horses he bore the name of a mountain, and in his case it fitted aptly, as he was big, gaunt and craggy, a liver chestnut with splashes of gray on his quarters like dirty snow. At eight years old, he was coming satisfactorily to full uncompromising strength, and for once I really believed I might at last win the big one in a month's time.

I'd won almost every race in the calendar, except the Grand National. I'd been second, third, and fourth, but never first. Cotopaxi had it in him to change that, given the luck.

Dusty came across to disrupt the pleasant daydream. "Where's the princess?" he said.

"I don't know."

"She'd never miss old Paxi." Small, elderly, weather-beaten and habitually suspicious, he looked at me accusingly, as if I'd heard something I wasn't telling.

Dusty depended on me professionally, as I on him, but we'd never come to liking. He was apt to remind me that, champion jockey or not, I wouldn't get so many winners if it weren't for the hard work of the stable-lads, naturally including himself. His manner to me teetered sometimes on the edge of rudeness, never quite tumbling over, and I put up with it equably because he was in fact good at his job, and right about the lads, and besides that I hadn't much choice. Since Wykeham had stopped coming to the races, the horses' welfare away from home depended entirely upon Dusty, and the welfare of the horses was very basically my concern.

"Cascade," Dusty said, glowering, "can hardly put one foot in front of the other."

"He's not lame," I said mildly.

"He'll take weeks to get over it."

I didn't answer. I looked around for the princess, who still hadn't appeared. I'd wanted particularly to hear what Maynard had said to her, but it looked as if I would have to wait. And it was extraordinary that she hadn't come into the ring. Almost all owners liked to be in the parade ring before a race, and for the princess especially it was an unvarying routine. Moreover she was particularly proud and fond of Cotopaxi and had been talking all winter about his chances in the National.

The minutes ticked away, the signal was given for jockeys to mount, and Dusty gave me his usual adroit leg-up into the saddle. I rode out onto the course hoping nothing serious had happened, and had time, cantering down to the start, to look up to where the princess's private box was located, high on the stands, expecting anyway to see her there watching with her friends.

The balcony was, however, deserted, and I felt the first twinge of real concern. If she'd had to leave the racecourse suddenly I was sure she would have sent me a message, and I hadn't been exactly hard to find, standing there in the paddock. Messages, though, could go astray, and as messages went, "Tell Kit Fielding that Princess Casilia is going home" wouldn't have rated as emergency material.

I went on down to the start thinking that no doubt I would find out in time, and hoping that there hadn't been sudden bad news about the frail old chairbound husband she traveled home to every evening.

Cotopaxi, unlike Cascade, was positively bombarding me with information, mostly to the effect that he was feeling good, he didn't mind the cold weather, and he was glad to back on a racecourse for the first time since Christmas. January had been snowy and the first part of February freezing, and keen racers like Cotopaxi got easily bored by long spells in the stables.

Wykeham, unlike most of the daily press, didn't expect Cotopaxi to win at Newbury.

"He's not fully fit," he'd said on the previous evening. "He won't be wound up tight until Grand National day. Look after him, now, Kit, won't you?"

I'd said I would, and after Cascade I doubly meant it. Look after Cotopaxi, look out for Maynard Allardeck, bury Prince Litsi under the turf. Cotopaxi and I went round circumspectly, collectedly, setting ourselves right at every fence, jumping them all cleanly, enjoying the precision and wasting no time. I did enough stick-waving to give an impression of riding a flat-out finish, and we finished in un-disgraced third place, close enough to the winner to be encouraging. A good workout for Cotopaxi, a reassurance for Wykeham and a tremor of promise for the princess.

She hadn't been on her balcony during the race and she didn't appear in the unsaddling enclosure. Dusty muttered obscurely about her absence and I asked around in the weighing room for any message from her, with no results. I changed again to ride in the fifth race, and after that, in street clothes, decided to go up to her box anyway, as I did at the end of every racing afternoon, to see if the waitress who served there might know what had happened.

The princess rented a private box at several racecourses and had them all decorated alike with colors of cream, coffee and peach. In each was a dining table with chairs for lunch, with, beyond, glass doors to the viewing balcony. She entertained groups of friends regularly, but on that day even the friends had vanished.

I knocked briefly on the box door and, without waiting for any answer, turned the handle and walked in.

The table as usual had been pushed back against a wall after lunch to allow more space, and was familiarly set with the paraphernalia of tea: small sandwiches, small cakes, cups and saucers, alcohol to hand, boxes of cigars. That day they were all untouched, and there was no waitress pouring, offering me tea with lemon and a smile.

I had expected the box to be otherwise empty, but it wasn't.

The princess was in there, sitting down.

Near her, silent, stood a man I didn't know. Not one of her usual friends. A man of not much more than my own age, slender, dark-haired, with a strong nose and jaw.

"Princess . . ." I said, taking a step into the room.

She turned her head. She was still wearing the sable coat and the Russian hat, although she usually removed outdoor clothes in her box. Her eyes looked at me without expression, glazed and vacant, wide, blue and unfocused.

Shock, I thought.

"Princess," I said again, concerned for her.

The man spoke. His voice matched his nose and jaw, positive, noticeable, full of strength.

"Go away," he said.

2

I went.

I certainly didn't want to intrude uninvited into any private troubles in the princess's life, and it was that feeling that remained with me to ground level. I had been too long accustomed to our arm's-length relationship to think her affairs any of my business, except to the extent that she was Danielle's uncle's wife.

By the time I was walking out to my car I wished I hadn't left as precipitously without at least asking if I could help. There had been an urgent warning quality in the stranger's peremptory voice that had seemed to me at first to be merely protective of the princess, but in retrospect I wasn't so sure.

Nothing would be lost, I thought, if I waited for her to come down to return home, which she must surely do in the end, and made sure she was all right. If the stranger was still with her, if he was as dismissive as before, if she was looking to him for support, then at least I would let her know I would have assisted if she'd needed it.

I went through the paddock gate to the car park where her chauffeur, Thomas, was routinely waiting for her in her Rolls-Royce.

Thomas and I said hello to each other most days in car parks, he, a phlegmatic Londoner, placidly reading books and paying no attention to the sport going on around him. Large and dependable, he had been driving the princess for years, and knew her life and movements as well as anyone in her family.

He saw me coming and gave me a small wave. Normally, after I'd left her box, she would follow fairly soon, my appearance acting as a signal to Thomas to start the engine and warm the car.

I walked across to him, and he lowered a window to talk. "Is she ready?" he asked.

I shook my head. "There's a man with her . . ." I paused. "Do you know a fairly young man, dark-haired, thin, prominent nose and chin?"

He pondered and said no one sprang to mind, and why was it worrying me.

"She didn't watch one of her horses race."

Thomas sat up straighter. "She'd never not watch."

"No. Well, she didn't."

"That's bad."

"Yes, I'd think so."

I told Thomas I would go back to make sure she was OK and left him looking as concerned as I felt myself.

The last race was over, the crowds leaving fast. I stood near the gate where I couldn't miss the princess when she came, and scanned faces. Many I knew, many knew me. I said goodnight fifty times and watched in vain for the fur hat.

The crowd died to a trickle and the trickle to twos and threes. I began to wander slowly back toward the stands, thinking in indecision that perhaps I would go up again to her box.

I'd almost reached the doorway to the private stand when she came out. Even from twenty feet I could see the glaze in her eyes, and she was walking as if she couldn't feel the ground, her feet rising too high and going down hard at each step.

She was alone, and in no state to be.

"Princess," I said, going fast to her side. "Let me help."

She looked at me unseeingly, swaying. I put an arm firmly round her waist, which I would never have done in ordinary circumstances, and felt her stiffen, as if to deny her need for support.

"I'm perfectly all right," she said, shakily.

"Yes . . . well, hold my arm." I let go of her waist and offered my arm for her to hold on to, which after a flicker of hesitation she accepted.

Her face was pale under the fur hat and there were trembles in her body. I walked with her slowly toward the gate, and through it, and across to where Thomas waited. He was out of the car, looking anxious, opening a rear door at our approach.

"Thank you," the princess said faintly, climbing in. "Thank you, Kit."

She sank into the rear seat, dislodging her hat on the way and apathetically watching it roll to the floor.

She peeled off her gloves and put one hand to her head, covering her eyes. "I think I . . ." She swallowed, pausing. "Do we have any water, Thomas?"

"Yes, madam," he said with alacrity, and went round to the trunk to fetch the small refreshment box he habitually took along. Sloe gin, champagne, and sparkling mineral water, the princess's favorites, were always to hand.

I stood by the car's open door, unsure how much help she would consider receiving. I knew all about her pride, her self-control, and her self-expectations. She wouldn't want anyone to think her weak.

Thomas gave her some mineral water in a cut-glass tumbler with ice tinkling, no mean feat. She took two or three small sips and sat staring vaguely into space.

"Princess," I said diffidently, "would it perhaps be of any use if I traveled with you to London?"

She turned her eyes my way and a sort of shudder shook her, rattling the ice.

"Yes," she said with clear relief. "I need someone to . . ." She stopped, not finding the words.

Someone to prevent her breaking down, I guessed. Not a shoulder to cry on but a reason for not crying.

Thomas, approving the arrangement, said to me prosaically, "What about your car?"

"It's in the jockeys' car park. I'll put it back by the racecourse stables. It'll be all right there."

He nodded, and we made a brief stop on our way out of the racecourse for me to move the Mercedes to a safe spot and tell the stable manager I'd be back for it later. The princess seemed not to notice any of these arrangements but continued staring vaguely at thoughts I couldn't imagine, and it wasn't until we were well on the way to London in the early dusk that she finally stirred and absentmindedly handed me the glass with the remains of bubbles and melted ice as a kind of preliminary to talking.

"I'm so sorry," she said, "to have given you trouble."

"But you haven't."

"I have had," she went on carefully, "a bad shock. And I cannot explain . . ." She stopped and shook her head, making hopeless gestures with her hands. It seemed to me all the same that she had come to a point where assistance of some sort might be welcomed.

"Is there anything I can do?" I said neutrally.

"I'm not sure how much I can ask."

"A great deal," I said bluntly.

The first signs of a smile crept back into her eyes, but faded again rapidly. "I've been thinking . . ." she said. "When we reach London, will you come into the house and wait while I talk to my husband?"

"Yes, of course."

"You can spare the time? Perhaps a few hours?"

"Any amount," I assured her wryly. Danielle had gone to Leonardo and time was a drag without her. I stifled in myself the acute lurch of unhappiness and wondered just what sort of shock the princess had suffered. Nothing, it seemed now, to do with Monsieur de Brescou's health. Something perhaps worse.

While it grew totally dark outside we traveled another long way in silence, with the princess staring again into space and sighing, and me wondering what to do about the tumbler.

As if reading my thoughts Thomas suddenly said, "There's a glass-holder, Mr. Fielding, located in the door below the ashtray," and I realized he'd noticed my dilemma via the rear-view mirror.

"Thank you, Thomas," I said to the mirror, and met his amused eyes. "Very thoughtful."

I hooked out what proved to be a chrome ring like a

toothmug holder, and let it embrace the glass. The princess, oblivious, went on staring at uncomfortable visions.

"Thomas," she said at length, "please will you see if Mrs. Jenkins is still in the house? If she is, would you ask her to see if Mr. Gerald Greening would be free to come round this evening?"

"Yes, madam," Thomas said, and pressed buttons on the car's telephone, glancing down in fractions while he drove.

Mrs. Jenkins worked for the princess and M. de Brescou as secretary and all-round personal assistant and was young, newly married and palely waiflike. She worked only weekdays and left promptly at five o'clock, which a glance at my watch put at only a few minutes ahead. Thomas caught her apparently on the doorstep and passed on the message, to the princess's satisfaction. She didn't say who Gerald Greening was, but went quietly back to her grim thoughts.

By the time we reached Eaton Square, she had physically recovered completely, and mentally to a great extent. She still looked pale and strained, though, and took Thomas's strong hand to help her from the car. I followed her onto the pavement, and she stood for a moment looking at Thomas and myself, as we stood there lit by the street-lamps.

"Well," she said thoughtfully, "thank you both."

Thomas looked as always as if he would willingly die for her besides driving her carefully to and from the races, but more mundanely at that moment walked across the pavement and with his bunch of keys opened the princess's front door.

She and I went in, leaving Thomas to drive away, and together walked up the wide staircase to the second floor.

The ground floor of the big old house consisted of offices, a guest suite, a library and a breakfast room. It was upstairs that the princess and her husband chiefly lived, with drawing room, sitting room and dining room on the second floor and bedrooms on three floors above. Staff lived in the semibasement, and there was an efficient elevator from top to bottom, installed in modern times to accommodate M. de Brescou's wheelchair.

"Will you wait in the sitting room?" she said. "Help yourself to a drink. If you'd like tea, ring down to Dawson . . ." The social phrases came out automatically, but her eyes were vague, and she was looking very tired.

"I'll be fine," I said.

"I'm afraid I may be a long time."

"I'll be here."

She nodded and went up the next broad flight of stairs to the floor above, where she and her husband each had a private suite of room, and where Roland de Brescou spent most of his time. I had never been up there, but Danielle had described his rooms as a minihospital, with besides his bedroom and sitting room, a physiotherapy room and a room for a male nurse.

"What's wrong with him?" I'd asked.

"Some frightful virus. I don't know exactly what, but not polio. His legs just stopped working, years ago. They don't say much about it, and you know what they're like, it feels intrusive to ask."

I went into the sitting room, which had become familiar territory, and phoned down to Dawson, the rather august butler, asking for tea.

"Certainly, sir," he said austerely. "Is Princess Casilia with you?"

"She's upstairs with Monsieur de Brescou."

He said, "Ah," and the line clicked off. He appeared in a short time, bearing a small silver tray with tea and lemon but no milk, no sugar and no biscuits.

"Did we have a successful afternoon, sir?" he asked, setting down his burden.

"A win and a third."

He gave me a small smile, a man nearing sixty, unextended and happy in his work. "Very gratifying, sir."

"Yes."

He nodded and went away, and I poured out and drank the tea and tried not to think of buttered toast. During the February freeze, I had somehow gained three pounds and was in consequence having a worse than usual battle against weight.

The sitting room was comfortable with flowered fabrics, rugs and pools of warm lamplight, altogether friendlier than the satins and gilt of the very French drawing room next door. I switched on the television to watch the news, and switched it off after, and wandered around looking for something to read. I also wondered fleetingly why the princess had wanted me to wait, and exactly what help it was that she might find too much to ask.

Reading materials seemed to be a straight choice between a glossy magazine about architecture in French and a worldwide airline timetable, and I was opting for the second when on a side table I came across a folded leaflet that announced "Master Classes in a Distinguished Setting," and found myself face to face with Danielle's weekend.

I sat in an armchair and read the booklet from front to back. The hotel, with illustrating photographs, was described as a country house refurbished in the grand manner, with soul-shaking views over fells and lakes and blazing log fires to warm the heart indoors.

The entertainments would begin with a reception on the Friday evening at six o'clock (which meant it was in progress as I read), followed by dinner, followed by Chopin sonatas performed in the gold drawing room.

On Saturday would come the lectures on "The Masters of the Italian Renaissance," given by the illustrious Keeper of Italian paintings in the Louvre. In the morning, "Botticelli, Leonardo da Vinci, Raphael: Master Works in the Louvre," and in the afternoon, "Giorgione's *Concert Champêtre* and Titian's *Laura Dianti*: the Cinquecento in Venice," all to be accompanied by slides illuminating points of brushwork and technique. These lectures, the leaflet said, represented a rare privilege seldom granted outside France by probably the world's greatest expert in Italian Renaissance art.

On Saturday evening there would be a grand Florentine banquet especially created by a master chef from Rome, and on Sunday visits would be arranged to the Lakeland houses of Wordsworth, Ruskin and (if desired) Beatrix Potter. Finally, afternoon tea would be served round the fire in the Great Hall, and everyone would disperse.

I seldom felt unsure either of myself or of my chosen way of life, but I put down the leaflet feeling helplessly inadequate.

I knew practically nothing of the Italian Renaissance and I couldn't reliably have dated da Vinci within a hundred years. I knew he painted the *Mona Lisa* and drew helicopters and submarines, and that was about all. Of Botticelli, Giorgione and Raphael I knew just as little. If Danielle's interests deeply lay with the Arts, would she ever come back to a man whose work was physical, philistine and insecure? To a man who'd liked biology and chemistry in his teens and not wanted to go to college? To someone who would positively have avoided going where she had gone with excitement?

I shivered. I couldn't bear to lose her, not to long-dead painters, nor to a live prince.

Time passed. I read the worldwide air timetables and found there were many places I'd never heard of, with people busily flying in and out of them every day. There were far too many things I didn't know.

Eventually, shortly after eight, the unruffled Dawson reappeared and invited me upstairs, and I followed him to the unfamiliar door of M. de Brescou's private sitting room.

"Mr. Fielding, sir," Dawson said, announcing me, and I walked into a room with gold-swagged curtains, dark-green walls and dark-red leather armchairs.

Roland de Brescou sat as usual in his wheelchair, and it was clear at once that he was suffering from the same severe shock that had affected the princess. Always weak-looking, he seemed more than ever to be on the point of expiring, his pale yellow-gray skin stretched over his cheekbones and the eyes gaunt and staring. He had been, I supposed, a good-looking man long ago, and he still retained a noble head of white hair and a naturally aristocratic manner. He wore, as ever, a dark suit and tie, making no concessions to illness. Old and frail he might be, but still his own master, unimpaired in his brain. Since my engagement to Danielle I had met him a few times, but although unfailingly courteous he was reclusive always, and as reticent as the princess herself.

"Come in," he said to me, his voice, always surprisingly

strong, sounding newly hoarse. "Good evening, Kit." The French echo in his English was as elusive as the princess's own.

"Good evening, monsieur," I said, making a small bow to him also, as he disliked shaking hands: his own were so thin that the squeezing of strangers hurt him.

The princess, sitting in one of the armchairs, raised tired fingers in a small greeting, and with Dawson withdrawing and closing the door behind me, she said apologetically, "We've kept you waiting so long . . ."

"You did warn me."

She nodded. "We want you to meet Mr. Greening."

Mr. Greening, I presumed, was the person standing to one side of the room, leaning against a green wall, hands in pockets, rocking on his heels. Mr. Greening, in dinner jacket and black tie, was bald, round-bellied and somewhere on the far side of fifty. He was regarding me with bright knowing eyes, assessing my age (thirty-one), height (five foot ten), clothes (gray suit, unremarkable) and possibly my income. He had the look of one used to making quick judgments and not believing what he was told.

"The jockey," he said in a voice that had been to Eton. "Strong and brave."

He was ironic, which I didn't mind. I smiled faintly, went through the obvious categories and came up with a possibility.

"The lawyer?" I suggested. "Astute?"

He laughed and peeled himself off the paintwork. "Gerald Greening," he said, nodding. "Solicitor. Would you be kind enough to witness some signatures to documents?"

I agreed, of course, reflecting that I wouldn't have expected the princess to ask me to wait so long just for that, but not protesting. Gerald Greening picked up a clipboard that had been lying on a coffee table, peeled a sheet of paper back over the clip and offered a pen to Roland de Brescou for him to sign the second page.

With a shaky flourish, the old man wrote his name beside a round red seal.

"Now you, Mr. Fielding." The pen and the clipboard came my way, and I signed where he asked, resting the board on my left forearm for support.

The whole two-page document, I noticed, was not typed, but handwritten in neat black script. Roland de Brescou's name and mine were both in the same black ink. Gerald Greening's address and occupation, when he added them at the bottom after his own signature, matched the handwriting of the text.

A rush job, I thought. Tomorrow could be too late.

"There isn't any necessity for you to know what's in the document you signed," Greening said to me easily, "but Princess Casilia insists that I tell you."

"Sit down, Kit," the princess said, "it'll take time."

I sat in one of the leather armchairs and glanced at Roland de Brescou, who was looking dubious, as if he thought telling me would be unproductive. He was no doubt right, I thought, but I was undeniably curious.

"Put simply," Greening said, still on his feet, "the document states that notwithstanding any former arrangements to the contrary, M. de Brescou may not make any business decisions without the knowledge, assent, and properly witnessed signatures of Princess Casilia, Prince Litsi"—he gave him at least half his full name—"and Miss Danielle de Brescou."

I listened in puzzlement. If there was nothing wrong with Roland de Brescou's competence, why the haste for him to sign away his authority?

"This is an interim measure," Gerald Greening went on. "A sandbag affair, one might say, to keep back the waters while we build the sea-wall." He looked pleased with the simile, and I had an impression he had used it before.

"And, er," I said, "does the tidal wave consist of anything in particular?" But it had to, of course, to have upset the princess so much.

Gerald Greening took a turn around the room, hands, complete with clipboard, clasped behind his back. A restless mind in a restless body, I thought, and listened to details about the de Brescous that neither the princess nor her husband would ever have told me themselves.

"You must understand," Greening said, impressing it upon me, "that M. de Brescou is of the ancient regime, from before the revolution. His is a patrician family, even though he himself bears no title. It's essential to understand that for him personal and family honor is of supreme importance."

"Yes," I said, "I understand that."

"Kit's own family," the princess said mildly, "stretches back through centuries of tradition."

Gerald Greening looked slightly startled, and I thought in amusement that the Fielding tradition of pride and hate wasn't exactly what he had in mind. He adjusted my status in his eyes to include ancestors, however, and went on with the story.

"In the mid-nineteenth century," he said, "M. de Brescou's great-grandfather was offered an opportunity to contribute to the building of bridges and canals and, in consequence, without quite meaning to, he founded one of France's great construction companies. He never worked in it himself—he was a landowner—but the business prospered hugely and with unusual resilience changed to fit the times. At the beginning of the twentieth century, M. de Brescou's grandfather agreed to merge the family business with another construction company whose chief interest was roads, not canals. The great canal-building era was ending, and cars, just appearing, needed better roads. M. de Brescou's grandfather retained fifty percent of the new company, an arrangement that gave neither partner outright control."

Gerald Greening's eyes gleamed with disapproval as he paced slowly round behind the chairs.

"M. de Brescou's father was killed in the Second World War without inheriting the business. M. de Brescou himself inherited it when his grandfather died, aged ninety, after the Second World War. Are you with me so far?"

"Yes," I said.

"Good." He went on pacing, setting out his story lucidly almost as if laying facts before a fairly dim jury. "The firm that had merged with that of M. de Brescou's grandfather was headed by a man called Henri Nanterre, who was also of aristocratic descent and high morals. The two men liked and trusted each other and agreed that their joint business should adhere to the highest principles. They installed managers of good reputation and sat back and . . . er . . increased their fortunes."

"Mm," I said.

"Before and during the Second World War, the firm went into recession, shrinking to a quarter of its former size, but it was still healthy enough to revive well in the

1950s, despite the deaths of the original managing friends. M. de Brescou remained on good terms with the inheriting Nanterre—Louis—and the tradition of employing top managers went on. And that brings us to three years ago, when Louis Nanterre died and left his fifty-percent share to his only son, Henri. Henri Nanterre is thirty-seven, an able entrepreneur, full of vigor, good at business. The profits of the company are annually increasing."

Both the princess and her husband listened gloomily to this long recital, which seemed to me to have been a success story of major proportions.

"Henri Nanterre," Greening explained carefully, "is of the modern world. That is to say, the old values mean little to him."

"He has no honor," Roland de Brescou said with distaste. "He disgraces his name."

I said slowly, to the princess, "What does he look like?"

"You saw him," she said simply. "In my box."

There was a brief silence, then the princess said to Greening, "Please go on, Gerald. Tell Kit what that . . . that wretched man wants, and what he said to me."

Roland de Brescou interrupted before he could speak, and, turning his wheelchair to face me directly, said, "I will tell him. I will tell you. I didn't think you should be involved in our affairs, but my wife wishes it . . ." He made a faint gesture with a thin hand, acknowledging his affection for her. ". . . and as you are to marry Danielle, well then, perhaps . . . But I will tell you myself." His voice was slow but stronger, the shock receding in him too, with perhaps anger taking its place.

"As you know," he said, "I have been for a long time . . ." He gestured down his body, not spelling it out. "We have lived also a long time in London. Far away from the business, you understand?"

I nodded.

"Louis Nanterre, he used to go there quite often to consult the managers. We would talk often on the telephone and he would tell me everything that was happening. We would decide together if it looked sensible to go in new directions. He and I, for instance, developed a factory to make things out of plastic, not metal, nor concrete. Things like heavy drainpipes that would not crack under roads, nor corrode. You understand? We developed new plastics, very tough."

He paused, more it seemed through lack of breath than of things to say. The princess, Greening and I waited until he was ready to go on.

"Louis," he said eventually, "used to come to London to this house twice a year, with auditors and lawyers—Gerald would be here—and we would discuss what had been done, and read the reports and suggestions from the boards of managers, and make plans." He sighed heavily. "Then Louis died, and I asked Henri to come over for the meetings, and he refused."

"Refused?" I repeated.

"Absolutely. Then suddenly I don't know any longer what is happening, and I sent Gerald over, and wrote to the auditors . . ."

"Henri had sacked the auditors," Gerald Greening said succinctly into the pause, "and engaged others of his own choice. He had sacked half the managers and was taking charge directly himself, and had branched out in directions that M. de Brescou knew nothing about."

"It's intolerable," Roland de Brescou said.

"And today?" I asked him tentatively. "What did he say at Newbury today?"

"To go to my wife!" He was quivering with fury. "To

40

threaten her. It's . . . disgraceful." There weren't words, it seemed, strong enough for his feelings.

"He told Princess Casilia," Gerald Greening said with precision, "that he needed her husband's signature on a document, that M. de Brescou did not want to sign, and that she was to make sure that he did."

"What document?" I asked flatly.

None of them, it seemed, was in a hurry to say, and it was Gerald Greening, finally, who shrugged heavily and said, "A French government form for a preliminary application for a license to manufacture and export guns."

"Guns?" I said, surprised. "What sort of guns?"

"Firearms for killing people. Small arms made of plastic."

"He told me," the princess said, looking hollow-eyed, "that it would be simple to use the strong plastics for guns. Many modern pistols and machine-guns can be made of plastic, he said. It is cheaper and lighter, he said. Production would be easy and profitable, once he had the license. And he said he would definitely be granted the license, he had done all the groundwork. He had had little difficulty because the de Brescou et Nanterre company is so reputable and respected, and all he needed was my husband's agreement."

She stopped in a distress that was echoed by her husband.

"Guns," he said. "I will never sign. It is dishonorable, do you understand, to trade nowadays in weapons of war. It is unthinkable. In Europe these days it is not a business of good repute. Especially guns made of plastic, which were invented so they could be carried through airports without being found. Of course, I know our plastics would be suitable, but never, never shall it happen that my name is used to sell guns that may find their way to terrorists. It is absolutely inconceivable."

I saw indeed that it was.

"One of our older managers telephoned me a month ago to ask if I truly meant to make guns," he said, outraged. "I had heard nothing of it. Nothing. Then Henri Nanterre sent a lawyer's letter, formally asking my assent. I replied that I would never give it, and I expected the matter to end there. There is no question of the company manufacturing guns without my consent. But to threaten my wife!"

"What sort of threats?" I asked.

"Henri Nanterre said to me," the princess said faintly, "that he was sure I would persuade my husband to sign, because I wouldn't want any accidents to happen to anyone I liked . . . or employed."

No wonder she had been devastated, I thought. Guns, threats of violence, a vista of dishonor: all a long way from her sheltered, secure and respected existence. Henri Nanterre, with his strong face and domineering voice, must have been battering at her for at least an hour before I arrived in her box.

"What happened to your friends at Newbury?" I asked her. "The ones in your box."

"He told them to go," she said tiredly. "He said he needed to talk urgently, and they were not to come back."

"And they went."

"Yes."

Well, I'd gone myself.

"I didn't know who he was," the princess said. "I was bewildered by him. He came bursting in and turned them out, and drowned my questions and protestations. I have

42

not . . ." She shuddered. "I have never had to face anyone like that."

Henri Nanterre sounded pretty much a terrorist himself, I thought. Terrorist behavior, anyway: loud voice, hustle, threats.

"What did you say to him?" I asked, because if anyone could have tamed a terrorist with words, surely she could.

"I don't know. He didn't listen. He just talked over the top of anything I tried to say, until in the end I wasn't saying anything. It was useless. When I tried to stand up, he pushed me down. When I talked, he talked louder. He went on and on saying the same things over again . . . When you came into the box I was completely dazed."

"I should have stayed."

"No, much better that you didn't."

She looked at me calmly. Perhaps I would have had literally to fight him, I thought, and perhaps I would have lost, and certainly that would have been no help to anyone. All the same, I should have stayed.

Gerald Greening cleared his throat, put the clipboard down on a side table and went back to rocking on his heels against the wall behind my left shoulder.

"Princess Casilia tells me," he said, jingling coins in his pockets, "that last November her jockey got the better of two villainous press barons, one villainous asset stripper and various villainous thugs."

I turned my head and briefly met his glance, which was brightly empty of belief. A jokey man, I thought. Not what I would have chosen in a lawyer.

"Things sort of fell into place," I said neutrally.

"And are they all still after your blood?" There was a teasing note in his voice, as if no one could take the princess's story seriously.

"Only the asset stripper, as far as I know," I said.

"Maynard Allardeck?"

"You've heard of him?"

"I've met him," Greening said with minor triumph. "A sound and charming man, I would have said. Not a villain at all."

I made no comment. I avoided talking about Maynard whenever possible, not least because any slanderous thing I might say might drift back to his litigious ears.

"Anyway," Greening said, rocking on the edge of my vision, and with irony plain in his voice, "Princess Casilia would now like you to gallop to the rescue and try to rid M. de Brescou of the obnoxious Nanterre."

"No, no," the princess protested, sitting straighter. "Gerald, I said no such thing."

I stood slowly up and turned to face Greening directly, and I don't know exactly what he saw, but he stopped rocking and took his hands out of his pockets and said with an abrupt change of tone, "That's not what she said, but that's undoubtedly what she wants. And I'll admit that until this very moment I thought it all a bit of a joke." He looked at me uneasily. "Look, my dear chap, perhaps I got things wrong."

"Kit," the princess said behind me, "please sit down. I most certainly didn't ask that. I wondered only . . . oh, *do* sit down."

I sat, leaning forward toward her and looking at her troubled eyes. "It is," I said with acceptance, "what you want. It has to be. I'll do anything I can to help. But I'm still . . . a jockey."

"You're a Fielding," she said unexpectedly. "That's what Gerald has just seen. That something . . . Bobby told me you didn't realize . . ." She broke off in some confusion.

She never in normal circumstances spoke to me in that way. "I wanted to ask you," she said, with a visible return to composure, "to do what you could to prevent any 'accidents.' To think of what might happen, to warn us, advise us. We need someone like you, who can imagine . . ."

She stopped. I knew exactly what she meant, but I said, "Have you thought of enlisting the police?"

She nodded silently, and from behind me Gerald Greening said, "I telephoned them immediately Princess Casilia described to me what had happened. They said they had noted what I'd told them."

"No actual action?" I suggested.

"They say they are stretched with crimes that have actually happened, but they would put this house on their surveillance list."

"And you went pretty high up, of course?"

"As high as I could get this evening."

There was no possible way, I reflected, to guard anyone perpetually against assassination, but I doubted if Henri Nanterre meant to go that far, if only because he wouldn't necessarily gain from it. Much more likely that he thought he could put the frighteners quite easily on a paralyzed old man and an unworldly woman and was currently underestimating both the princess's courage and her husband's inflexible honor. To a man with few scruples, the moral opposition he expected might have seemed a temporary dislodgeable obstinacy, not an immovably embedded barrier.

I doubted if he were actually at that moment planning accidents. He would be expecting the threats to be enough. How soon, I wondered, would he find out that they weren't?

I said to the princess, "Did Nanterre give you any time

scale? Did he say when and where he expected Monsieur to sign the form?"

"I shall not sign it," Roland de Brescou murmured.

'No, monsieur, but Henri Nanterre doesn't know that yet."

"He said," the princess answered weakly, "that a notary would have to witness my husband signing. He said he would arrange it, and he would tell us when."

"A notary? A French lawyer?"

"I don't know. He was speaking in English to my friends, but when they'd gone he started in French, and I told him to speak English. I do speak French of course, but I prefer English, which is second nature to me, as you know."

I nodded. Danielle had told me that as neither the princess nor her husband preferred to chat in the other's native tongue, they both looked upon English as their chief language, and chose to live in England for that reason.

"What do you suppose Nanterre will do," I asked Greening, "when he discovers four people have to sign the application form now, not just Monsieur?"

He stared at me with shiny eyes. Contact lenses, I thought inconsequentially. "Consequences," he said, "are your particular field, as I understand it."

"It depends then," I said, "on how rich he is, how greedy, how power-hungry, how determined and how criminal."

"Oh, dear," the princess said faintly, "how very horrid this all is."

I agreed with her. At least as much as she, I would have preferred to be out on a windy racetrack where the rogues had four legs and merely bit.

"There's a simple way," I said to him, "to keep all your family safe and to preserve your good name."

"Go on," he said. "How?"

"Change the name of the company and sell your share."

He blinked. The princess put a hand to her mouth, and I couldn't see Greening's reaction, as he was behind me.

"Unfortunately," Roland de Brescou said eventually, "I cannot do either without Henri Nanterre's agreement. The original partnership was set up in that way." He paused. "It is of course possible that he would agree to such changes if he could set up a consortium to acquire the whole, with himself to be at its head with a majority vote. He could then, if he wished, manufacture guns."

"It does seem a positive solution," Gerald Greening said judiciously from the rear. "You would be free of trouble, monsieur. You would have your money out. Yes, certainly a proposal to be considered."

Roland de Brescou studied my face. "Tell me," he said, "would you personally follow that course?"

Would I? I thought. Would I, if I were old and paralyzed? Would I if I knew the result would be a load of new guns in a world already awash with them? If I knew I was backing away from my principles? If I cared for my family's safety?

"I don't know, monsieur," I said.

He smiled faintly and turned his head toward the princess. "And you, my dear? Would you?"

Whatever answer she would have given him was interrupted by the buzz of the house's intercom system, a recent installation that saved everyone a lot of walking. The princess picked up the handset, pressed a button, and said "Yes?" She listened. "Just a minute." She looked at her husband, saying, "Are you expecting visitors? Dawson says two men have called, saying they have an appointment. He's shown them into the library."

Roland de Brescou was shaking his head doubtfully when there was an audible squawk from the handset. "What?" asked the princess, returning it to her ear. "What did you say, Dawson?" She listened but seemed to hear nothing. "He's gone," she said, puzzled. "What do you suppose has happened?"

"I'll go and see, if you like," I said.

"Yes, Kit, please do."

I rose and went as far as the door, but before I could touch it it opened abruptly to reveal two men walking purposefully in. One unmistakably was Henri Nanterre: the other, a pace behind, a pale sharp-featured young man in a narrow black suit, carrying a briefcase.

Dawson, out of breath, appeared with a rush behind them, mouth open in horror at the unceremonious breaking of his defenses.

"Madam," he was saying helplessly, "they simply ran past me . . ."

Henri Nanterre rudely shut the door on his explanations and turned to face the roomful of people. He seemed disconcerted to find Gerald Greening there, and he took a second sharp look at me, remembering where he'd seen me before and not particularly liking that, either. I guessed that he had come expecting only the princess and her husband, reckoning he had softened them both up enough for his purpose.

His beaky nose looked somewhat diminished against the darker walls, nor did his aggression seem as concentrated as it had been in the smaller box, but he was still forceful, both in his loud voice and in the total rejection of the good manners he should have inherited.

He clicked his fingers to his companion, who removed a single beige-colored sheet of paper from the briefcase and handed it to him, and then he said something long and clearly objectionable to Roland de Brescou in French. His target leaned backward in his wheelchair as if to retreat from unpleasantness, and into the first available pause said testily, "Speak English."

Henri Nanterre waved the paper and poured out another lengthy burst of French, drowning de Brescou's attempts to interrupt him. The princess made a helpless gesture with her hand to me, indicating that that was exactly what had happened to her also.

"Nanterre!" Gerald Greening said peremptorily, and got a glance but no pause in the tirade. I went back to the armchair I'd occupied before and sat down there, crossing my legs and swinging my foot. The motion irritated Nanterre into breaking off and saying something to me that might have been *"et qui êtes-vous?"* though I couldn't be sure. My sketchy French had mostly been learned on the racecourses of Auteuil and Cagnes sur Mer, and chiefly consisted of words like *courants* (runners), *haies* (fences) and *piste* (track).

I stared mildly at Nanterre and went on swinging my foot.

Greening took the opportunity of the brief silence to say rather pompously, "Monsieur de Brescou has no power to sign any paper whatsoever."

"Don't be ridiculous," Nanterre said, at last speaking English, which like many French businessmen, he proved to know fluently. "He has too much power. He is out of touch with the modern world, and his obstructive attitude must cease. I require him to make a decision that will bring new impetus and prosperity to a company that is ageing and suffering from out-of-date methods. The period of road-building is over. We must look to new markets. I have found such a market, which is uniquely suited to the plastic materials we are accustomed to make use of, and no stupidly old-fashioned ideas shall stand in the way."

"Monsieur de Brescou has relinquished his power to make solo decisions," Greening said. "Four people besides yourself must now put their names to any change of company policy."

"That is absolutely untrue," Nanterre said loudly. "De Brescou has total command."

"No longer. He has signed it away."

Nanterre looked flummoxed, and I began to think that Greening's sandbags might actually hold against the flood when he made the stupid error of glancing smugly in the direction of the downturned clipboard. How could he be so damned silly, I thought, and had no sympathy for him when Nanterre followed the direction of his eyes and moved like lightning to the side table, reaching it first.

"Put that down," Greening said furiously, but Nanterre was skimming the page and handing it briskly to his pale acolyte.

"Is that legal?" he demanded.

Gerald Greening was advancing to retrieve his property, the unintroduced Frenchman backing away while he read and holding the clipboard out of reach. "*Oui,*" he said finally. "Yes. Legal."

"In that case . . ." Nanterre snatched the clipboard out of his grasp, tore the handwritten pages off it and ripped them across and across. "The document no longer exists."

"Of course it exists," I said. "Even in pieces, it exists. It was signed and it was witnessed. Its intention remains a fact, and it can be written again."

Nanterre's gaze sharpened in my direction. "Who are you?" he demanded.

"A friend."

"Stop swinging that foot."

I went on swinging it. "Why don't you just face the fact that Monsieur de Brescou will never let his company sell arms?" I said. "Why, if that's what you want to do, don't you agree to dissolve the existing company, and with your proceeds set up again on your own?"

He narrowed his eyes at me, everyone in the room waiting for an answer. When it came, it was grudging, but clearly the truth. Bad news, also for Roland de Brescou.

"I was told," Nanterre said with cold anger, "that only if de Brescou applied personally would I be granted the facility. I was told it was essential to have the backing of his name."

It struck me that perhaps someone in the French background didn't want Nanterre to make guns, and was taking subtle steps to prevent it while avoiding making a flat and perhaps politically embarrassing refusal. To insist on a condition that wouldn't be fulfilled would be to lay the failure of Nanterre's plans solely and neatly at de Brescou's feet.

"Therefore," Nanterre went on ominously, "de Brescou will sign. With or without trouble." He looked at the torn pages he was still grasping and held them out to his assistant. "Go and find a bathroom," he said. "Get rid of these pieces. Then return."

The pale young man nodded and went away. Gerald

Greening made several protestations, which had no effect on Nanterre. He was looking as though various thoughts were occurring to him that gave him no pleasure, and he interrupted Greening, saying loudly, "Where are the people whose names were on the agreement?"

Greening, showing the first piece of lawyerly sense for a long time, said he had no idea.

"Where are they?" Nanterre demanded of Roland de Brescou. For answer, a Gallic shrug.

He shouted the question at the princess, who gave a silent shake of the head, and at me, with the same result. "Where are they?"

They would be listening to the sweet chords of Chopin, I supposed, and wondered if they even knew of the agreement's existence.

"What are their names?" Nanterre said.

No one answered. He went to the door and shouted loudly down the hallway. "Valery. Come here at once. Valery! Come here."

The man Valery hurried back empty-handed. "The agreement is finished," he said reassuringly. "All gone down the drain."

"You read the names on it, didn't you?" Nanterre demanded. "You remember those names?"

Valery swallowed. "I didn't, er . . ." he stuttered. "I didn't study the names. Er . . . the first was Princess Casilia . . ."

"And the others?"

Valery shook his head, eyes wide. He as well as Nanterre saw too late that they had thrown away knowledge they might have used. Pressure couldn't be applied to people one couldn't identify. Bribes and blandishments could go nowhere.

Nanterre transmitted his frustration into an increase of aggression, thrusting the application form again toward Roland de Brescou and demanding he sign it.

Monsieur de Brescou didn't even bother to shake his head. Nanterre was losing it, I thought, and would soon retire. I was wrong.

He handed the form to Valery, put his right hand inside his jacket, and from a hidden holster produced a black and businesslike pistol. With a gliding step he reached the princess and pressed the end of the barrel against her temple, standing behind her and holding her head firmly with his left hand under the chin.

"Now," he said gratingly to de Brescou, "sign the form."

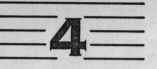

4

Into an electrified atmosphere I said plainly, "Don't be ridiculous."

"Stop swinging that foot," Nanterre said furiously.

I stopped swinging it. There was a time for everything.

"If you shoot Princess Casilia," I said calmly, "Monsieur de Brescou will not sign the form."

The princess had her eyes shut and Roland de Brescou looked frail to fainting. Valery's wide eyes risked popping out altogether and Gerald Greening, somewhere behind me, was saying "Oh, my God," incredulously under his breath.

I said, my mouth drier than I liked, "If you shoot Princess Casilia, we are all witnesses. You would have to kill us all, including Valery."

Valery moaned.

"Monsieur de Brescou would not have signed the form,"

I said. "You would end up in jail for life. What would be the point?"

He stared at me with hot dark eyes, the princess's head firm in his grip.

After a pause that lasted a couple of millennia, he gave the princess's head a shake and let her go.

"There are no bullets," he said. He shoved the gun back into its holster, holding his jacket open for the purpose. He gave me a bitter glance as if he would impress my face on his memory forever and without another word walked out of the room.

Valery closed his eyes, opened them a slit, ducked his head and scuttled away in his master's wake, looking as if he wished he were anywhere else.

The princess with a small sound of great distress slid out of her chair onto her knees beside the wheelchair and put her arms round her husband, her face turned to his neck, her shining dark hair against his cheek. He raised a thin hand to stroke her head, and looked at me with somber eyes.

"I would have signed," he said.

"Yes, monsieur."

I felt sick myself and could hardly imagine their turmoil. The princess was shaking visibly, crying, I thought.

I stood up. "I'll wait downstairs," I said.

He gave the briefest of nods, and I followed where Nanterre had gone, looking back for Gerald Greening. Numbly he came after me, closing the door, and we went down to the sitting room where I'd waited before.

"You didn't know," he said croakily, "that the gun was empty, did you?"

"No."

"You took a terrible risk." He made straight for the tray of bottles and glasses, pouring brandy with a shaking hand. "Do you want some?"

I nodded and sat rather weakly on one of the chintz sofas. He gave me a glass and collapsed in much the same fashion.

"I've never liked guns," he said hollowly.

"I wonder if he meant to produce it?" I said. "He didn't mean to use it or he'd have brought it loaded."

"Then why carry it at all?"

"A prototype, wouldn't you say?" I suggested. "His plastic equalizer, demonstration model. I wonder how he got it into England. Through airports undetected, would you say? In pieces?"

Greening made inroads into his brandy and said, "When I met him in France I thought him bombastic but shrewd. But these threats . . . tonight's behavior . . ."

"Not shrewd but crude," I said.

He gave me a glance. "Do you think he'll give up?"

"Nanterre? No, I'm afraid he won't. He must have seen he came near tonight to getting what he wanted. I'd say he'll try again. Another way, perhaps."

"When you aren't there." He said it as a statement, all the former doubts missing. If he wasn't careful, I thought, he'd persuade himself too far the other way. He looked at his watch, sighing deeply. "I told my wife I'd be slightly delayed. Slightly! I'm supposed to be meeting her at a dinner." He paused. "If I go in a short while, will you make my apologies?"

"OK," I said, a shade surprised. "Aren't you going . . . er . . . to reinstate the sandbags?"

It took him a moment to see what I meant, and then he

said he would have to ask M. de Brescou what he wanted.

"It might safeguard him as you intended, don't you think?" I said. "Especially as Nanterre doesn't know who else to put pressure on." I glanced at the Master Classes leaflet that still lay on the coffee table. "Did Danielle and Prince Litsi know their names had been used?"

He shook his head. "Princess Casilia couldn't remember the name of the hotel. It didn't affect the legality of the document. Their assent at that stage wasn't necessary."

A few steps down the road, though, after Nanterre's show of force, I reckoned it was no longer fair to embroil them without their consent, and I was on the point of saying so when the door quietly opened and Princess Casilia came in.

We stood up. If she had been crying, there was no sign of it, although she did have the empty-eyed look and the pallor of people stretched into unreality.

"Gerald, we both want to thank you for coming," she said, her voice higher in pitch than usual. "We are so sorry about your dinner."

"Princess," he protested. "My time is yours."

"My husband asks if you could return tomorrow morning."

Greening gave a small squirm as if jettisoning his Saturday golf and asked if ten o'clock would suit, and with evident relief took his departure.

"Kit . . ." The princess turned to me. "Will you stay here in the house, tonight? In case . . . just in case . . ."

"Yes," I said.

She closed her eyes and opened them again. "It has been such a dreadful day." She paused. "Nothing seems real."

"Can I pour you a drink?"

"No. Ask Dawson to bring you some food. Tell him you'll sleep in the bamboo room." She looked at me without intensity, too tired for emotion. "My husband wants to see you in the morning."

"Fairly early," I suggested. "I have to be at Newbury for the first race."

"Goodness! I'd forgotten." Some of the faraway look left her eyes. "I didn't even ask how Cotopaxi ran."

"He was third. Ran well." It seemed a long time ago. "You'll see it on the video."

Like many owners she bought videotapes of most of her horses' races, to watch and re-enjoy their performances over and over.

"Yes, that'll be nice."

She said goodnight much as if she hadn't had a gun aimed closely against her head half an hour earlier, and with upright carriage went gently away upstairs.

A remarkable woman, I thought, not for the first time, and descended to the basement in search of Dawson, who was sitting, jacket off, in front of the television drinking beer. The butler, slightly abashed by having let the uninvited guests outrush him, made no demur at checking with me through the house's defenses. Window locks, front door, rear door, basement door, all secure.

John Grundy, the male nurse, he said, would arrive at ten, assist Monsieur to bed, sleep in the room next to him, and in the morning help him bathe, shave and dress. He would do Monsieur's laundry and be gone by eleven.

Only Dawson and his wife (the princess's personal maid) slept in the basement, he said: all the rest of the staff came in by day. Prince Litsi, who was occupying the guest suite on the ground floor, and Miss de Brescou, whose room was beyond the princess's suite, were away, as I knew.

His eyebrows shot up at the mention of the bamboo room, and when he took me by lift to the floor above the princess and her husband, I could see why. Palatial, pale blue, gold and cream, it looked fit for the noblest of visitors, the bamboo of its name found in the pattern of the curtains and the pale Chinese-Chippendale furniture. There was a vast double bed, a dressing room, a bathroom, and an array of various drinks and a good television set hidden behind discreet louvered doors.

Dawson left me there, and I took the opportunity to make my regular evening telephone call to Wykeham, to tell him how his horses had run. He was pleased, he said, about Cotopaxi, but did I realize what I'd done to Cascade? Dusty, he said, had told him angrily all about the race, including Maynard Allardeck's inspection afterward.

"How is Cascade?" I asked.

"We weighed him. He's lost thirty pounds. He can hardly hold his head up. You don't often send horses back in that state."

"I'm sorry," I said.

"There's winning and winning," he said testily. "You've ruined him for Cheltenham."

"I'm sorry," I said again, contritely. Cheltenham, two and a half weeks ahead, was of course the top meeting of the jumping year, its races loaded with prestige and prizes. Wykeham liked above all to have successes there, as indeed did I and every jump jockey riding. Missing a winner there would serve me right, I supposed, for letting unhappiness get the better of me, but I was genuinely sorry for Wykeham's sake.

"Don't do anything like that tomorrow with Calgoorlie," he said severely.

I sighed. Calgoorlie had been dead for years. Wykeham's memory was apt to slip cogs to the point that sometimes I couldn't work out what horse he was referring to.

"Do you mean Kinley?" I suggested.

"What? Yes, of course, that's what I said. You give him a nice ride, now, Kit."

At least, I thought, he knew who he was talking to: he still on the telephone called me often by the name of the jockey who'd had my job ten years earlier.

I assured him I would give Kinley a nice ride.

"And win, of course," he said.

"All right." A nice ride and a win couldn't always be achieved together, as Cascade very well knew. Kinley however was a white-hot hope for Cheltenham, and if he didn't win comfortably at Newbury the expectations could cool to pink.

"Dusty says the princess didn't come into the ring before Cotopaxi's race, or see him afterward. He says it was because she was angry about Cascade." Wykeham's old voice was full of displeasure. "We can't afford to anger the princess."

"Dusty's wrong," I said. "She wasn't angry. She had some trouble with . . . er . . . a visitor in her box. She explained to me after . . . and invited me to Eaton Square, which is where I am now."

"Oh," he said, mollified. "All right, then. Kinley's race is televised tomorrow," he said, "so I'll be watching."

"Great."

"Well then . . . Goodnight, Paul."

"Goodnight, Wykeham," I said.

Wryly I telephoned to the answering machine in my own house, but there was nothing much in the way of messages, and presently Dawson returned with a supper of chicken soup, cold ham and a banana (my choice).

Later, together, we made another tour of the house, meeting John Grundy, a sixty-year-old widower, on his way to his own room. Both men said they would be undisturbed to see me wandering around now and then in the small hours, but although I did prowl up and down once or twice, the big house was silent all night, its clocks ticking in whispers. I slept on and off between linen sheets under a silk coverlet in pajamas thoughtfully supplied by Dawson, and in the morning was ushered in to see Roland de Brescou.

He was alone in his sitting room, freshly dressed in a city suit with a white shirt and foulard tie. Black shoes, brilliantly polished. White hair, neatly brushed. No concessions to his condition, no concession to weekends.

His wheelchair was unusual in having a high back—and I'd often wondered why more weren't designed that way—so that he could rest his head if he felt like dozing. That morning, although he was awake, he was resting his head anyway.

"Please sit down," he said civilly, and watched me take the same place as the evening before, in the dark-red leather armchair. He looked if possible even frailer, with gray shadows in his skin, and the long hands that lay quiet on the padded armrests had a quality of transparency, the flesh thin as paper over the bones.

I felt almost indecently strong and healthy in contrast, and asked if there were anything I could fetch and carry for him.

He said no with a twitch of eye muscle that might have been interpreted as an understanding smile, as if he were accustomed to such guilt reactions in visitors.

"I wish to thank you," he said, "for coming to our defense. For helping Princess Casilia."

He had never in my presence called her "my wife," nor would I ever have referred to her in that way to him. His formal patterns of speech were curiously catching.

"Also," he said, as I opened my mouth to demur, "for giving me time to consider what to do about Henri Nanterre." He moistened his dry lips with the tip of an apparently desiccated tongue. "I have been unable to sleep . . . I cannot risk harm to Princess Casilia or anyone around us. It is time for me to relinquish control. To find a successor . . . but I have no children, and there are few de Brescous left. It isn't going to be easy to find any family member to take my place."

Even the thought of the discussions and decisions such a course would lead to seemed to exhaust him.

"I miss Louis," he said unexpectedly. "I cannot continue without him. It is time for me to retire. I should have seen . . . When Louis died . . . it was time." He seemed to be talking to himself as much as me, clarifying his thoughts, his eyes wandering.

I made a nondescript noise of nothing much more than interest. I would have agreed that the time to retire was long past, though, and it almost seemed he caught something of that thought, because he said calmly, "My grandfather was in total command at ninety. I expected to die also at the head of the company, as I am the chairman."

"Yes, I see."

His gaze steadied on my face. "Princess Casilia will go to

the races today. She hopes you will go with her in her car."
He paused. "May I ask you to defend her from harm?"

"Yes," I said matter-of-factly, "with my life."

It didn't even sound melodramatic after the past evening's events, and he seemed to take it as a normal remark. He merely nodded a fraction and I thought that in retrospect I would be hotly embarrassed at myself. But then, I probably meant it, and the truth pops out.

It seemed anyway what he wanted to hear. He nodded again a couple of times slowly as if to seal the pact, and I stood up to take my leave. There was a briefcase, I saw, lying half under one of the chairs between me and the door, and I picked it up to ask him where he would like it put.

"It isn't mine," he said, without much interest. "It must be Gerald Greening's. He's returning this morning."

I had a sudden picture, however, of the pathetic Valery producing the handgun application form from that case, and of him scuttling away empty-handed at the end. When I explained to Roland de Brescou, he suggested I take the case downstairs to the hall, so that when its owner called back to collect it, he wouldn't need to come up.

I took the case away with me but, lacking de Brescou's incurious honesty, went up to the bamboo room, not down.

The case, black leather, serviceable, unostentatious, proved to be unlocked and unexciting, containing merely what looked like a duplicate of the form that Roland de Brescou hadn't signed.

On undistinguished buff paper, mostly in small badly printed italics, and of course in French, it hardly looked worth the upheaval it was causing. As far as I could make out it wasn't specifically to do with armaments, but had many dotted-line spaces needing to be filled in. No one had filled in anything on the duplicate, although presumably the one Valery had taken away with him had been ready for signing.

I put the form in a drawer of a bedside table and took the briefcase downstairs, meeting Gerald Greening as he arrived. We said good mornings with the memory of last night's violence hovering, and he said he had not only rewritten the sandbags but had had the document properly typed and provided with seals. Would I be so good as to repeat my services as witness?

We returned to Roland de Brescou and wrote our names, and I mentioned again about telling Danielle and Prince Litsi. I couldn't help thinking of them. They would be starting about now on "The Master Works of Leonardo . . ." Dammit, dammit.

"Yes, yes," Greening was saying, "I understand they return tomorrow evening. Perhaps you could inform them yourself."

"Perhaps."

"And now," Greening said, "to update the police."

He busied himself on the telephone, reaching yesterday's man and higher, obtaining the promise of a CID officer's attentions, admitting he didn't know where Nanterre could be found. "Immediately he surfaces again we will inform you," he was saying, and I wondered how immediately would be immediately, should Nanterre turn up with bullets.

Roland de Brescou, however, showed approval, not dismay, and I left them beginning to discuss how best to find a de Brescou successor. I made various preparations for the day, and I was waiting in the hall when the princess came down to go to the races, with Dawson hovering and Thomas, alerted by telephone, drawing smoothly to a halt outside. She was wearing a cream-colored coat, not the sables, with heavy gold earrings and no hat, and although she seemed perfectly calm she couldn't disguise apprehensive glances up and down the street as she was seen across the pavement by her three assorted minders.

"It is important," she said conversationally as soon as she was settled and Thomas had centrally locked all the doors, "not to let peril deter one from one's pleasures."

"Mm," I said noncommittally.

She smiled sweetly. "You, Kit, do not."

"Those pleasures earn me my living."

"Peril should not, then, deter one from one's duty." She sighed. "So stuffy, don't you think, put that way? Duty and pleasure so often coincide, deep down, don't you think?"

I did think, and I thought she was probably right. She was no mean psychologist, in her way.

"Tell me about Cotopaxi," she commanded, and listened contentedly, asking questions when I paused. After that, we discussed Kinley, her brilliant young hurdler, and after that her other runner for the day, Hillsborough, and it wasn't until we were nearing Newbury that I asked if she would mind if Thomas accompanied her into the meeting and stayed at her side all afternoon.

"Thomas?" she said, surprised. "But he doesn't like racing. It bores him, doesn't it Thomas?"

"Ordinarily, madam," he said.

"Thomas is large and capable," I said, pointing out facts, "and Monsieur de Brescou asked that you should enjoy the races unmolested."

65

"Oh," she said, disconcerted. "How much . . . did you tell Thomas?"

"To look out for a frog with a hawk's nose and keep him from annoying you, madam," Thomas said.

She was relieved, amused and, it seemed to me, grateful.

Back at the ranch, whether she knew it or not, John Grundy was sacrificing his Saturday afternoon to remain close to Roland de Brescou, with the number of the local police station imprinted on his mind.

"They already know there might be trouble," I'd told him. "If you call them, they'll come at once."

John Grundy, tough for his years, had commented merely that he'd dealt with fighting drunks often enough, and to leave it to him. Dawson, whose wife was going out with her sister, swore he would let no strangers in. It seemed unlikely, to my mind, that Nanterre would actually attempt another head-on attack, but it would be foolish to risk being proved wrong with everything wide open.

Thomas, looking all six foot three a bodyguard, walked a pace behind the princess all afternoon, the princess behaving most of the time as if unaware of her shadow. She hadn't wanted to cancel her afternoon party because of the five friends she'd invited to lunch, and she requested them, at my suggestion, to stay with her whatever happened and not to leave her alone unless she herself asked it.

Two of them came into the parade ring before the first of her two races, Thomas looming behind, all of them forming a shield when she walked back toward the stands. She was a far more likely target than de Brescou himself, I thought uneasily, watching her go as I rode Hillsborough out onto the course: her husband would never sign away his honor to save his own life, but to free an abducted wife . . . very likely.

He could repudiate a signature obtained under threat. He could retract, kick up a fuss, could say, "I couldn't help it." The guns might not then be made, but his health would deteriorate and his name could be rubble. Better to prevent than to rescue, I thought, and wondered what I'd overlooked.

Hillsborough felt dull in my hands and I knew going down to the start that he wouldn't do much good. There were none of the signals that horses feeling well and ready to race give, and although I tried to jolly him along once we'd started, he was as sluggish as a cold engine.

He met most of the fences right but lost ground on landing through not setting off again fast, and when I tried to make him quicken after the last he either couldn't or wouldn't, and lost two places to faster finishers, trailing in eighth of the twelve runners.

It couldn't be helped: one can't win them all. I was irritated, though, when an official came to the changing room afterward and said the Stewards wanted to see me immediately, and I followed him to the Stewards' Room with more seethe than resignation, and there, as expected, was Maynard Allardeck, sitting at a table with two others, looking as impartial and reasonable as a saint. The Stewards said they wanted to know why my well-backed mount had run so badly. They said they were of the opinion that I hadn't ridden the horse out fully or attempted to win, and would I please give them an explanation.

Maynard was almost certainly the instigator, but not the spokesman. One of the others, a man I respected, had said for openers, "Mr. Fielding, explain the poor showing of Hillsborough."

He had himself ridden as an amateur in days gone by, and I told him straightforwardly that my horse had seemed not to be feeling well and hadn't been enjoying himself. He had been flat-footed even going down to the start and during the race I'd thought once or twice of pulling him up altogether.

The Steward glanced at Allardeck and said to me, "Why didn't you use your whip after the last fence?"

The phrase "flogging a dead horse" drifted almost irresistibly into my mind but I said only, "I gave him a lot of signals to quicken, but he couldn't. Beating him wouldn't have made any difference."

"You appeared to be giving him an easy ride," he said, but without the aggression of conviction. "What's your explanation?"

Giving a horse an easy ride was an euphemism for "not trying to win," or even worse, for "trying not to win," a loss-of-license matter. I said with some force, "Princess Casilia's horses are always doing their best. Hillsborough was doing his best, but he was having an off day."

There was a shade of amusement in the Steward's eyes. He knew, as everyone in racing knew, how things stood between Allardecks and Fieldings; Stewards' inquiries had for half a century sorted out the fiery accusations flung at Maynard's father by my grandfather, and at my grandfather by Maynard's father, both of them training Flat racers in Newmarket. The only new twist to the old battle was the recent Allardeck presence on the power side of the table, no doubt highly funny to all but myself.

"We note your explanation," the Steward said dryly, and told me I could go.

I went without looking directly at Maynard. Twice in two days I'd wriggled off his hooks, and I didn't want him to think I was gloating. I went back fast to the changing room to exchange the princess's colors for those of another owner and to weigh out, but even so I was late into the parade ring for the next race (and one could be fined for that also).

I walked in hurriedly to join the one hopeful little group without a jockey, and saw, thirty feet away, Henri Nanterre.

5

He was standing in another group of owners, trainer and jockey, and was looking my way as if he'd been watching my arrival.

Unwelcome as he was, however, I had to postpone thoughts of him on account of the excited questions of the tubby enthusiastic couple whose dreams I was supposed to make come true within the next ten minutes; and anyway, the princess, I hoped, was safely surrounded upstairs.

The Dream, so named, had been a winner on the Flat and was having his first run over hurdles. He proved to be fast, all right, but he hadn't learned the knack of jumping: he rattled the first three flights ominously and put his feet straight through the fourth, and that was as far as we went. The Dream galloped away loose in fright, I picked myself up undamaged from the grass and waited resignedly for wheels to roll along to pick me up. One had to expect a fall every ten or eleven rides, and mostly they were easy, like that, producing a bruise at worst. The bad ones turned up perhaps twice a year, always unexpected.

I checked in with the doctor, as one had to after every fall, and while changing for the next race made time to talk to the jockey from the group with Nanterre: Jamie Fingall, long a colleague, one of the crowd.

"French guy with the beaky nose? Yeah, well, the guvnor introduced him but I didn't pay much attention. He owns horses in France, something like that."

"Um . . . Was he with your guvnor, or with the owners?"

"With the owners, but it sounded to me like the guvnor was trying to sweet-talk the Frenchie into sending him a horse over here."

"Thanks, then."

"Be my guest."

Jamie Fingall's guvnor, Basil Clutter, trained in Lambourn about a mile down the road from my house, but there wasn't time to seek him out before the next race, the three-mile 'chase, and after that I had to change again and go out to meet the princess in the parade ring, where Kinley was already stalking round.

As before, she was well guarded and seemed almost to be enjoying it, and I didn't know whether or not to alarm her with news of Nanterre. In the end I said only to Thomas, "The frog is here. Stay close to her," and he gave a sketchy thumbs-up, and looked determined. Thomas looking determined, I thought, would deter Attila the Hun.

Kinley made up for an otherwise disgusting afternoon, sending my spirits soaring from depths to dizzy heights.

The rapport between us, established almost instantly during his first hurdle race the previous November, had deepened in three succeeding outings so that by February he seemed to know in advance what I wanted him to do, as I knew what he wanted to do before he did it. The result was racing at its sublime best, an unexplainable synthesis at a primitive level and undoubtedly a shared joy.

Kinley jumped hurdles with a surge that had almost left me behind the first time I felt it, and even though every time since I'd know what was going to happen, I hadn't outgrown the surprise. The first hurdle left me gasping as usual, and by the end I reckoned we'd stolen twenty clean lengths in the air. He won jauntily and at a canter and I hoped Wykeham, watching on the box, would think it "a nice ride" and forgive me Cascade. Maynard Allardeck, I grimly thought, walking Kinley back along the path to the unsaddling enclosure, could find no vestige of an excuse that time to carp or cavil, and I realized that he and Kinley and Nanterre among them had at least stopped me brooding over Botticelli, Giorgione, Titian and Raphael.

The princess had her best stars in her blue eyes, looking as if guns hadn't been invented. I slid to the ground and we smiled in shared triumph, and I refrained with an effort from hugging her.

"He's ready for Cheltenham," she said, sticking out a glove to pat lightly the dark hide. "He's as good as Sir Ken."

Sir Ken had been an all-time star in the 1950s, winning three Champion Hurdles and numerous other top hurdling events. Owning a horse like Sir Ken was the ultimate for many who'd seen him, and the princess, who had, referred to him often.

"He has a long way to go," I said, unbuckling the girths. "He's still so young."

"Oh, yes," she said happily. "But . . ." She stopped abruptly, with a gasp. I looked at her and saw her eyes widen as she looked with horror above my right shoulder, and I whipped round fast to see what was there.

Henri Nanterre was there, staring at her.

I stood between them. Thomas and the friends were behind her, more occupied with avoiding Kinley's light-hearted hooves than with guarding their charge in the safest and most public of places.

Henri Nanterre momentarily transferred his gaze to my face and then, with shock, stared at me with his mouth opening.

I'd thought in the parade ring that since he'd been watching me, he'd found out who I was, but realized in that second that he'd thought of me then simply as the princess's jockey. He was confounded, it seemed, to identify me from the evening before.

"You're . . ." he said, for once at a loss for loud words. "You . . ."

"That's right," I said. "What do you want?"

He recovered with a snap from his surprise, narrowed his eyes at the princess, and said distinctly, "Jockeys can have accidents."

"So can people who carry guns," I said. "Is that what you came to say?"

It appeared, actually, that it more or less was.

"Go away," I said, much as he'd said it to me a day earlier up in the box, and to my complete astonishment, he went.

"Hey," Thomas said agitatedly, "that was . . . that was . . . wasn't it?"

"Yes, it was," I said, looping the girths round my saddle.

"Now you know what he looks like."

"Madam!" Thomas said penitently, "where did he come from?"

"I didn't see," she said, slightly breathless. "He was just in there."

"Fella moves like an eel," one of her friends said; and certainly there had been a sort of gliding speed to his departure.

"Well, my dears," the princess said to her friends, laughing a trifle shakily, "let's go up and celebrate this lovely win. And Kit . . . come up soon."

"Yes, Princess."

I weighed in and, as it was my last ride of the day, changed into street clothes. After that I made a detour over to the saddling boxes because Basil Clutter, as Jamie had told me, would be there, saddling up his runner for the last race.

Trainers in those places never had time to talk, but he did manage an answer or two, grudgingly, while he settled weight cloth, number cloth and saddle onto his restless charge's back.

"Frenchman? Nanterre, yes. Owns horses in France, trained by Villon. Industrialist of some sort. Where's he staying? How should I know? Ask the Roquevilles, he was with them. Roquevilles? Look, stop asking questions, ring me tonight, right?"

"Right," I said, sighing, and left him sponging out his horse's mouth so he should look clean and well-groomed before the public. Basil Clutter was hard-working and always bustling, saving money by doing Dusty's job, being his own traveling head-lad.

I went up to the princess's box, drank tea with lemon,

and relived for her and the friends the glories of Kinley's jumping. When it was time to go she said, "You will come back with me, won't you?" as if it were natural for me to do so, and I said, "Yes, certainly," as if I thought so too.

I picked up from my still parked car the overnight bag I habitually carried with me for contingencies, and we traveled without much trouble back to Eaton Square where I telephoned to Wykeham from the bamboo room. He was pleased, he said, about Kinley, but annoyed about Hillsborough. Dusty had told him I'd made no show and been hauled in by the Stewards for it, and what did I think I was doing, getting into trouble two days in a row?

I could strangle Dusty, I thought, and told Wykeham what I'd told the Stewards. "They accepted the explanation," I said. "Maynard Allardeck was one of them, and he's after me whatever I do."

"Yes, I suppose he is." He cheered up a good deal and even chuckled. "Bookmakers are taking bets on when— not whether—he'll get you suspended."

"Very funny," I said, not amused. "I'm still at Eaton Square, if you want me."

"Are you?" he said. "All right then. Goodnight, Kit."

"Goodnight, Wykeham."

I got through next to Basil Clutter, who told me the Roquevilles' number, and I caught the Roquevilles on their return from Newbury.

No, Bernard Roqueville said, he didn't know where Henri Nanterre was staying. Yes, he knew him, but not well. He'd met him in Paris at the races, at Longchamp, and Nanterre had renewed the acquaintanceship by inviting him and his wife for a drink at Newbury. Why was I interested? he asked.

I said I was hoping to locate Nanterre while he was in England. Bernard Roqueville regretted he couldn't help, and that was that.

A short lead going nowhere, I thought resignedly, putting down the receiver. Maybe the police would have better luck, although I feared that finding someone to give him a finger-wagging for waving an empty gun at a foreign princess wouldn't exactly have brought them out steaming in a full-scale manhunt.

I went downstairs to the sitting room and discussed Hillsborough's fall from grace over a drink with the princess, and later in the evening she, Roland de Brescou and I ate dinner together in the dining room, served by Dawson; and I thought only about twenty times of the Florentine Banquet up north.

It wasn't until after ten, saying goodnight, that she spoke about Nanterre.

"He said, didn't he, that jockeys have accidents."

"That's what he said. And so they do, pretty often."

"That wasn't what he meant."

"Perhaps not."

"I couldn't forgive myself if because of us you came to harm."

"That's what he's counting on. But I'll take my chance, and so will Thomas." And privately I thought that if her husband hadn't cracked instantly with a gun to his wife's head, he was unlikely to bend because of a whole barrage pointed at ours.

She said, remembering with a shiver, "Accidents would happen to those I liked . . . and employed."

"It's only noise. He won't do anything," I said encouragingly, and she said quietly that she hoped not, and went to bed.

I wandered again round the big house, checking its defenses, and wondered again what I'd overlooked.

In the morning, I found out.

I was already awake at seven when the intercom buzzed, and when I answered, a sleepy-voiced Dawson asked me to pick up the ordinary telephone as there was an incoming call for me. I picked up the receiver and found it was Wykeham on the line.

Racing stables wake early on Sundays, as on other days, and I was used to Wykeham's dawn thoughts, as he woke always by five. His voice that day, however, was as incoherently agitated as I'd ever heard it, and at first I wondered wildly what sins I might have committed in my sleep.

"D—did you hear what I s—said?" he stuttered. "Two of them! T—two of the p—princess's horses are d—dead."

"Two?" I said, sitting bolt upright in bed and feeling cold. "How? I mean . . . which two?"

"They're dead in their boxes. Stiff. They've been dead for hours . . ."

"Which two?" I said again, fearfully.

There was a silence at the other end. He had difficulty remembering their names at the best of times, and I could imagine that at that moment a whole roll-call of long-gone heroes was fumbling on his tongue.

"The two," he said in the end, "that ran on Friday."

I felt numb.

"Are you there?" he demanded.

"Yes . . . Do you mean . . . Cascade . . . and Cotopaxi?"

He *couldn't* mean it, I thought. It couldn't be true. Not Cotopaxi . . . not before the Grand National.

"Cascade," he said. "Cotopaxi."

Oh, no . . . "How?" I said.

"I've got the vet coming," he said. "Got him out of bed. I don't know how. That's his job. But two! One might die, I've known it happen, but not two . . . Tell the princess, Kit."

"That's your job," I protested.

"No, no, you're there . . . Break it to her. Better than on the phone. They're like children to her."

People she liked . . . Jesus Christ.

"What about Kinley?" I asked urgently.

"What?"

"Kinley . . . yesterday's hurdle winner."

"Oh, yes, him. He's all right. We checked all the others when we found these two. Their boxes were next to each other, I expect you remember . . . Tell the princess soon, Kit, won't you? We'll have to move these horses out. She'll have to say what she wants done with the carcasses. Though if they're poisoned . . ."

"Do you think they're poisoned?" I said.

"Don't know. Tell her now, Kit." He put his receiver down with a crash, and I replaced mine feeling I would burst with ineffectual anger.

To kill her horses! If Henri Nanterre had been there at that moment I would have stuffed his plastic gun down his loud-voiced throat. Cascade and Cotopaxi . . . people I knew, had known for years. I grieved for them as for friends.

Dawson agreed that his wife would wake the princess and tell her I had some sad news of one of her horses, and would wait for her in the sitting room. I dressed and went down there, and presently she came, without makeup and with anxious eyes.

"What is it?" she asked. "Which one?"

When I told her it was two, and which two, I watched her horror turn to horrified speculation.

"Oh, no, he couldn't," she exclaimed. "You don't think, do you . . ."

"If he has," I said, "he'll wish he hadn't."

She decided that we should go down to Wykeham's stable immediately, and wouldn't be deterred when I tried to persuade her not to.

"Of course I must go. Poor Wykeham, he'll need comforting. I should feel wrong if I didn't go."

Wykeham needed comforting less than she did, but by eight-thirty we were on the road, the princess in lipstick and Thomas placidly uncomplaining about the loss of his free day. My offer of driving the Rolls instead of him had been turned down like an improper suggestion.

Wykeham's establishment, an hour's drive south of London, was outside a small village on a slope of the Sussex Downs. Sprawling and complex, it had been enlarged haphazardly at intervals over a century, and was attractive to owners because of its maze of unexpected little courtyards, with eight or ten boxes in each, and holly bushes in red-painted tubs. To the stable staff, the picturesque convolution meant a lot of fetching and carrying, a lot of time wasted.

The princess's horses were spread through five of the courtyards, not filling any of them. Wykeham, like many trainers, preferred to scatter an owner's horses about rather than to clump them all together, and Cascade and Cotopaxi, as it happened, had been the only two belonging to the princess to be housed in the courtyard nearest the entrance drive.

One had to park in a central area and walk through

archways into the courtyards, and when he heard us arrive, Wykeham came out of the first courtyard to meet us.

He looked older by the week, I thought uneasily, watching him roguishly kiss the princess's hand. He always half flirted with her, with twinkling eyes and the remnants of a powerful old charm, but that morning he simply looked distracted, his white hair blowing when he removed his hat, his thin old hands shaking.

"My dear Wykeham," the princess said, alarmed. "You look so cold."

"Come into the house," he said, moving that way. "That's best."

The princess hesitated. "Are my poor horses still here?"

He nodded miserably. "The vet's with them."

"Then I think I'll see them," she said simply, and walked firmly into the courtyard, Wykeham and I following, not trying to dissuade her.

The doors of two of the boxes stood open, the interiors beyond lit palely with electric light, although there was full daylight outside. All the other boxes were firmly closed, and Wykeham was saying, "We've just left the other horses here in their boxes. They don't seem to be disturbed, because there's no blood. That's what would upset them, you know . . ."

The princess, only half listening, walked more slowly across to where her horses lay on the dark-brown peat on the floor of their boxes, their bodies silent humps, all flashing speed gone.

They had died with their night rugs on, but either the vet or Wykeham or the lads had unbuckled those and rolled them back against the walls. We looked in silence at the revealed dark sheen of Cascade and the snow-splashed chestnut of Cotopaxi.

Robin Curtiss, the tall and gangling boyish vet, had met the princess occasionally on other mornings, and me more often. Dressed in green protective overalls, he nodded to us both and excused himself from shaking hands, saying he would need to wash first.

The princess, acknowledging his greeting, asked at once and with composure, "Please tell me . . . how did they die?"

Robin Curtiss glanced at Wykeham and me, but neither of us would have tried to stop him answering, so he looked back to the princess and told her straight.

"Ma'am, they were shot. They knew nothing about it. They were shot with a humane killer. With a bolt."

6

Cascade was lying slantwise across the box, his head in shadow but not far from the door. Robin Curtiss stepped onto the peat and bent down, picking up the black forelock of hair that fell naturally forward from between the horse's ears.

"You can't clearly see, ma'am, as he's so dark, but there's the spot, right under his forelock, where the bolt went in." He straightened up, dusting his fingers on a handkerchief. "Easy to miss," he said. "You can't see what happened unless you're looking for it."

The princess turned away from her dead horse with a glitter of tears but a calm face. She stopped for a minute at the door of the next box, where Cotopaxi's rump was nearest, his head virtually out of sight near the manger.

"He's the same," Robin Curtiss said. "Under the forelock, almost invisible. It was expert, ma'am. They didn't suffer."

She nodded, swallowing, then, unable to speak, put one hand on Wykeham's arm and with the other waved toward the arch of the courtyard and Wykeham's house beyond. Robin Curtiss and I watched them go and he sighed in sympathy.

"Poor lady. It always takes them hard."

"They were murdered," I said. "That makes it harder."

"Yeah, they sure were murdered. Wykeham's called the police, though I told him it wasn't strictly necessary. The law's very vague about killing animals. But with them belonging to Princess Casilia, I suppose he thought it best. And he's in a tizzy about moving the bodies as soon as possible, but we don't know where he stands with the insurance company . . . whether in a case like this they have to be told first . . . and it's Sunday . . ." He stopped rambling and said more coherently, "You don't often see wounds like these, nowadays."

"What do you mean?" I asked.

"Captive bullets are old hat. Almost no one uses them now."

"Captive bullets?"

"The bolt. Called captive because the killing agent doesn't fly free of the gun, but is retracted back into it. Surely you know that?"

"Yes. I mean, I know the bolt retracts. I saw one, close to, years ago. I didn't know they were old hat. What do you use now, then?"

"You must have seen a horse put down," he said, astonished. "All those times, out on the course, when your mount breaks a leg . . ."

"It's only happened to me twice," I said. "And both times I took my saddle off and walked away."

I found myself thinking about it, trying to explain. "One moment you're in partnership with that big creature, and maybe you like him, and the next moment he's going to die . . . So I've not wanted to stay to watch. It may be odd to you, especially as I was brought up in a racing stable, but I never have seen the gun actually put to the head, and I've always vaguely imagined it was shot from the side, like through a human temple."

"Well," he said, still surprised and mildly amused, "you'd better get educated. You of all people. Look," he said, "look at Cotopaxi's head." He picked his way over the stiff chestnut legs until he could show me what he wanted. Cotopaxi's eyes were half open and milky, and although Robin Curtiss was totally unmoved, to me it was still no everyday matter.

"A horse's brain is only the size of a bunched fist," he said. "I suppose you know that?"

"Yes, I know it's small."

He nodded. "Most of a horse's head is empty space, all sinuses. The brain is up between the ears, at the top of the neck. The bone in that area is pretty solid. There's only the one place where you can be sure a bolt will do the job." He picked up Cotopaxi's forelock and pointed to a small disturbance of the pale hairs. "You take a line from the right ear to the left eye," he said, "and a line from the left ear to the right eye. Where the lines cross, that's the best . . . more or less the only . . . place to aim. And see? The bolt went into Cotopaxi at that exact spot. It wasn't any old haphazard job. Whoever did this knew exactly what to do."

"Well," I said thoughtfully, "now you've told me, I'd know what to do."

"Yes, but don't forget you have to get the angle right as well as the place. You have to aim straight at the spot where the spinal cord and the brain meet. Then the result's instantaneous and, as you can see, there's no blood."

"And meanwhile," I suggested ironically, "the horse is simply standing still letting all this happen?"

"Funnily enough, most of them do. Even so, I'm told that for short people it's difficult to get the hand up to the right angle at the right height."

"Yes, I'm sure," I said. I looked down at the waste of the great racing spirit. I'd sat on that back, shared that mind, felt the fluid majesty of those muscles, enjoyed his triumphs, schooled him as a young horse, thrilled to his growing strengths.

I made my way back to the outside air and Robin Curtiss followed me out, still matter-of-factly continuing my education.

"Apart from the difficulty of hitting the right spot, the bolt has another disadvantage, which is that although it retracts at once, the horse begins to fall just as quick, and the hard skull bones tend to bend the bolt after a lot of use, and the gun no longer works."

"So now you use something else?"

"Yes," he nodded. "A free bullet. I'll show you, if you like. I've a pistol in my car."

We walked unhurriedly out of the courtyard to where his car was parked not far from the princess's Rolls. He unlocked the trunk, and in there unlocked an attaché case, and from it produced a brown cloth, which he unwrapped.

Inside lay an automatic Luger-type pistol, which looked ordinary except for its barrel. Instead of the straight narrow barrel one would expect, there was a wide bulbous affair with a slanted oval opening at the end.

"This barrel sends the bullet out spinning in a spiral," he explained.

"Any old bullet?"

"It has to be the right caliber, but yes, any old bullet, and any old gun. That's one big advantage, you can weld a barrel like this onto any pistol you like. Well, the bullet leaves the gun with a lot of short-range energy, but because it's going in a spiral, almost any obstruction will stop it. So if you shoot a horse, the bullet will stop in its head. Mostly, that is." He smiled cheerfully. "Anyway, you don't have to be so accurate, as with a bolt, because the wobbling bullet does a lot more damage."

I looked at him thoughtfully. "How can you be so sure those two were killed with a bolt?"

"Oh, with the free bullet you get powder burns at the entry, and also blood coming down the nose, and probably also from the mouth. Not much, sometimes, but it's there, because of the widespread damage done inside, you see."

"Yes," I said, sighing, "I see." I watched him wrap up his gun again and said, "I suppose you have to have a license for that."

"Sure. And for the captive bullet also."

There must be thousands of humane killers about, I reflected. Every vet would have one. Every knackers' yard. A great many sheep and cattle farmers. The huntsman of every pack of hounds. People dealing with police horses . . . the probabilities seemed endless.

"So I suppose there are hundreds of the old bolt types lying around out of date and unused?"

"Well," he said, "under lock and key."

"Not last night."

"No."

"What time last night, would you say?"

He completed the stowing and locking away of his own pistol.

"Early," he said positively. "Not much after midnight. I know it was a cold night, but both horses were stone cold this morning. No internal temperature. That takes hours ... and they were found at half six." He grinned. "The knackermen don't like fetching horses that have been dead that long. They have difficulty moving them when they're stiff, and getting them out of the boxes is a right problem." He peeled off his overalls and put them in the trunk. "There'll have to be post-mortems. The insurance people insist on it." He closed the car trunk and locked it. "We may as well go into the house."

"And leave them there?" I gestured back toward the courtyard.

"They're not going anywhere," he said, but he went back and shut the boxes' doors, in case, he said, any owners turned up for a nice Sunday look-round and had their sensibilities affronted. Robin's own sensibilities had been sensibly dumped during week one of his veterinary training, I guessed, but he didn't need a bedside manner to be a highly efficient minister to Wykeham's jumpers.

We went into Wykeham's house, ancient and rambling to match the yard, and found him and the princess consoling themselves with tea and memories, she at her most sustaining, he looking warmer and more in command, but puzzled.

He rose to his feet at our appearance and bustled me out of his sitting room making some flimsy remark about showing me where to make hot drinks, which I'd known for ten years.

"I don't understand," he said, leading the way into the kitchen. "Why doesn't she ask who killed them? It's the first thing I'd want to know. She hasn't mentioned it once. Just talks about the races in that way she has, and asking about the others. Why doesn't she want to know who killed them?"

"Mm," I said. "She suspects she knows."

"What? For God's sake then, Kit . . . who?"

I hesitated. He looked thin and shaky, with lines cut deep in the wrinkled old face, the dark freckles of age standing out starkly. "She'd have to tell you herself," I said, "but it's something to do with her husband's business. For what it's worth, I don't think you need worry about a traitor in your own camp. If she hasn't told you who she thinks it is, she won't tell anyone until she's discussed it with her husband, and they might decide to say nothing even then, they hate publicity so much."

"There's going to be publicity anyway," he said worriedly. "The ante-post cofavorite for the Grand National shot in his box. Even if we try, we can't keep that out of the papers."

I rattled about making fresh tea for Robin and myself, not relishing any more than he did the fuss lying ahead.

"All the same," I said, "your main worry isn't who. Your main worry is keeping all the others safe."

"Kit!" He was totally appalled. "B—bloody hell, K—Kit." He was back to stuttering. "It w—won't happen again."

"Well," I said temperately, but there was no way to soften it, "I'd say they're all at risk. The whole lot of her horses. Not immediately, not today. But if the princess and her husband decide on one particular course of action, which they may do, then they'll all be at risk, Kinley, perhaps, above all. So the thing to do is to apply our minds to defensive action."

"But Kit—"

"Dog patrols," I said.

"They're expensive . . ."

"The princess," I remarked, "is rich. Ask her. If she doesn't like the expense, I'll pay for them myself." Wykeham's mouth opened and closed again when I pointed out, "I've already lost the best chance I ever had of winning the Grand National. Her horses mean almost as much to me as they do to her and to you, and I'm damned well not going to let anyone pick them off two by two. So you get the security people here by tonight, and make sure there's someone about in the stable the whole time from now on, patrolling all the courtyards night and day."

"All right," he said slowly. "I'll fix it . . . If I knew who'd killed them, I'd kill him myself."

It sounded extraordinary, said that way, without anger, more as an unexpected self-discovery. What I'd wished I could do in fury, he proposed as a sane course of action; but people say these things, not meaning them, and he wouldn't have a mouse's chance physically, I thought regretfully, against the hawklike Nanterre.

Wykeham had been a Hercules in his youth, he'd told me, a powerhouse on legs with the joy of life pumping through his veins. "Joy of life," he'd said to me several times, "that's what I have. That's what you have. No one gets anywhere without it. Relish the struggle, that's the way."

He'd been an amateur jockey of note, and he'd dazzled and married the daughter of a mediumly successful trainer whose horses had started winning from the day Wykeham stepped into the yard. Now, fifty years on, with his strength gone, his wife dead and his own daughters grandmothers, he retained only the priceless ability to put the joy of life into his horses. He thought of little besides his horses, cared for little else, walked round at evening stables talking to each as a person, playing with some, admonishing others, coaxing a few, ignoring none.

I'd ridden for him from when I was nineteen, a fact he was apt to relate with complacency. "Spot 'em young," he'd told sundry owners. "That's the thing. I'm good at that." And he'd steadfastly given me, I sometimes reflected, exactly what he gave his charges; opportunity, trust and job-satisfaction.

He had trained a winner of the Grand National twice when I'd been at school, and in my time had come close, but it was only recently I'd realized how deeply he longed for a third slice of glory. The dead horse outside was for all of us a sickening, dragging, deflating disappointment.

"Cotopaxi," he said intensely, for once getting the name right, "was the one I would have saved first in a fire."

The princess and I traveled back to London without waiting for the police, the insurers or the slaughterer's men. ("So horrid, all of that.")

I'd expected her to talk as usual chiefly about her horses, but it was of Wykeham, it seemed, that she was thinking.

"Thirty-five years ago, before you were born," she said, "when I first went racing, Wykeham strode the scene like a Colossus. He was almost everything he says he was, a Hercules indeed. Powerful, successful, enormously attractive. Half the women swooning over him with their hus-

bands spluttering . . ." She smiled at this memory. "I
suppose it's hard for you to picture, Kit, knowing him only
now, when he's old, but he was a splendid man. He still is,
of course. I felt privileged, long ago, when he agreed to
train my horses."

I glanced in fascination at her serene face. In the past I'd
seen her often with Wykeham at the races, always defer-
ring to him, tapping him playfully on the arm. I hadn't
realized how much she must miss him now he stayed at
home, how much she must regret the waning of such a
titan.

A contemporary of my grandfather (and of Maynard Allardeck's father), Wykeham had been already a legend to
me when he'd offered me the job. I'd accepted, almost
dazed, and grown up fast, mature at twenty from the demands and responsibility he'd thrust on me. Hundreds of
thousands of pounds' worth of horseflesh in my hands all
the time, the success of the stable on my shoulders. He'd
given me no allowances for youth, told me in no uncertain
terms from the beginning that the whole enterprise rested
finally on its jockey's skill, cool head and common sense,
and told me if I didn't measure up to what was needed, too
bad, but bye bye.

Shaken to my soul I'd wholeheartedly embraced what he
offered, knowing there weren't two such chances in any
life, and it had worked out fine, on the whole.

The princess's thoughts were following my own. "When
Paul Peck had that dreadful fall and decided to retire," she
said, "there we were at the height of the season with no
stable jockey and all the other top jockeys signed up else-
where. Wykeham told me and the other owners that there
was this young Fielding boy in Newmarket who had been

riding as an amateur since he'd left school a year earlier . . ." She smiled. "We were very doubtful. Wykeham
said to trust him, he was never wrong. You know how
modest he is!" She paused, considering. "How long ago
was that?"

"Ten years last October."

She sighed. "Time goes so fast."

The older the faster . . . and for me also. Time no longer
stretched out to infinity. My years in the saddle would end,
maybe in four years, maybe five, whenever my body
stopped mending fast from the falls, and I was far from
ready to face the inexorability of the march of days. I intensely loved my job and dreaded its ending: anything
after, I thought, would be unutterably dreary.

The princess was silent for a while, her thoughts reverting to Cascade and Cotopaxi.

"That bolt," she said tentatively, "I didn't like to ask
Robin . . . I really don't know what a humane killer looks
like."

"Robin says the bolt type isn't much used nowadays," I
said, "but I saw one once. My grandfather's vet showed
me. It looked like an extra-heavy pistol with a very thick
barrel. The bolt itself is a metal rod that slides inside the
barrel. When the trigger is pulled, the metal rod shoots
out, but because it's fixed inside to a spring, it retracts
immediately into the barrel again." I reflected. "The
rod . . . the bolt . . . is a bit thicker than a pencil, and
about four inches of it shoots out into . . . er . . . whatever
it's aimed at."

She was surprised. "So small? I'd thought, somehow,
you know, that it would be much bigger. And I didn't
know until today that it was . . . from in front."

She stopped talking abruptly and spent a fair time concentrating on the scenery. She had agreed without reserve to the dog patrols and had told Wykeham not to economize, the vulnerability of her other horses all too clearly understood.

"I had so been looking forward to the Grand National," she said eventually. "So very much."

"Yes, I know. So had I."

"You'll ride something else. For someone else."

"It won't be the same."

She patted my hand rather blindly. "It's such a waste," she said passionately. "So stupid. My husband would never trade in guns to save my horses. Never. And I wouldn't ask it. My dear, dear horses."

She struggled against tears and with a few sniffs and swallows won the battle, and when we reached Eaton Square she said we would go into the sitting room for a drink "to cheer ourselves up."

This good plan was revised, however, because the sitting room wasn't empty. Two people, sitting separately in armchairs, stood up as the princess walked in; and they were Prince Litsi and Danielle.

"My dear aunt," the prince said, bowing to her, kissing her hand, kissing her also on both cheeks. "Good morning."

"Good morning," she said faintly, and kissed Danielle. "I thought you were returning late this evening."

"The weather was frightful." The prince shook my hand. "Rain. Mist. Freezing. We decided yesterday we'd had enough and left early today, before breakfast."

I kissed Danielle's smooth cheek, wanting much more. She looked briefly into my eyes and said Dawson had told them I was staying in the house. I hadn't seen her for three weeks and I didn't want to hear about Dawson. Around the princess, however, one kept raw emotions under wraps, and I heard myself asking if she'd enjoyed the lectures, as if I hoped she had.

"They were great."

The princess decided that Prince Litsi, Danielle and myself should have the drinks, while she went upstairs to see her husband.

"You pour them," she said to her nephew. "And you, Kit, tell them everything that's been happening, will you? My dears . . . such horrid troubles." She waved a hand vaguely and went away, her back straight and slender, a statement in itself.

"Kit," the prince said, transferring his attention.

"Sir."

We stood as if assessing each other, he taller, ten years older, a man of a wider world. A big man, Prince Litsi, with heavy shoulders, a large head, full mouth, positive nose and pale intelligent eyes. Light-brown hair had begun to recede with distinction from his forehead, and a strong neck rose from a cream open-necked shirt. He looked as impressive as I'd remembered. It had been a year or more since we'd last met.

From his point of view I suppose he saw brown curly hair, light-brown eyes and a leanness imposed by the weights allocated to racehorses. Perhaps he saw also the man whose fiancée he had lured away to esoteric delights, but to do him justice there was nothing in his face of triumph or amusement.

"I'd like a drink," Danielle said abruptly. She sat down, waiting. "Litsi . . ."

His gaze lingered my way for another moment, then he turned to busy himself with the bottles. We had talked only on racecourses, I reflected, politely skimming the surface with postrace chit-chat. I knew him really as little as he knew me.

Without inquiring he poured white wine for Danielle and Scotch for himself and me.

"OK?" he said, proffering the glass.

"Yes, sir."

"Call me Litsi," he said easily. "All this protocol . . . I drop it in private. It's different for Aunt Casilia, but I never knew the old days. There's no throne anymore. I'll never be king. I live in the modern world . . . so will you let me?"

"Yes," I said. "If you like."

He nodded and sipped his drink. "You call Aunt Casilia 'Princess,' anyway," he pointed out.

"She asked me to."

"There you are, then." He waved a large hand, the subject closed. "Tell us what has been disturbing the household."

I looked at Danielle, dressed that day in black trousers, white shirt, blue sweater. She wore the usual pink lipstick, her cloudy dark hair held back in a blue band, everything known and loved and familiar. I wanted fiercely to hold her and feel her warmth against me, but she was sitting very firmly in an armchair built for one, and she would only meet my eyes for a flicker or two between concentrations on her drink.

I'm losing her, I thought, and couldn't bear it.

"Kit," the prince said, sitting down.

I took a slow breath, returned my gaze to his face, sat

down also, and began the long recital, starting chronologically with Henri Nanterre's bullying invasion on Friday afternoon and ending with the dead horses in Wykeham's stable that morning.

Litsi listened with increasing dismay, Danielle with simpler indignation.

"That's horrible," she said. "Poor Aunt Casilia." She frowned. "I guess it's not right to knuckle under to threats, but why is Uncle Roland so against guns? They're made all over the place, aren't they?"

"In France," Litsi said, "for a man of Roland's background to deal in guns would be considered despicable."

"But he doesn't live in France," Danielle said.

"He lives in himself." Litsi glanced my way. "You understand, don't you, why he can't?"

"Yes," I said.

He nodded. Danielle looked from one of us to the other and sighed. "The European mind, I guess. Trading in arms in America isn't unacceptable."

I thought it was probably less acceptable than she realized, and from his expression Litsi thought so too.

"Would the old four hundred families trade in arms?" he asked, but if he expected a negative he didn't get it.

"Yes, sure, I guess so," Danielle said. "I mean, why would it worry them?"

"Nevertheless," Litsi said, "for Roland it is impossible."

A voice on the stairs interrupted the discussion: a loud female voice, coming nearer.

"Where is everyone? In there?" She swept into view in the sitting-room doorway. "Dawson says the bamboo room is occupied. That's ridiculous. I always have the bamboo room. I've told Dawson to remove the things of whoever is in there."

Dawson gave me a bland look from over her shoulder and continued on his way to the floor above, carrying a suitcase.

"Now then," said the vision in the doorway. "Someone fix me a 'bloody.' The damn plane was two hours late."

"Good grief," Danielle said faintly, as all three of us rose to our feet. "Aunt Beatrice."

7

Aunt Beatrice, Roland de Brescou's sister, spoke with a slight French accent heavily overlaid with American. She had a mass of cloudy hair, not dark and long like Danielle's, but white going on pale orange. This framed and rose above a round face with round eyes and an expression of habitual determination.

"Danielle!" Beatrice said, thin eyebrows rising. "What are you doing here?"

"I work in England." Danielle went to her aunt to give her a dutiful peck. "Since last fall."

"Nobody tells me anything."

She was wearing a silk jersey suit—her outdoor mink having gone upstairs over Dawson's arm—with a heavy seal on a gold chain shining in front. Her fistful of rings looked like ounce-heavy nuggets, and a crocodile had passed on for her handbag. Beatrice, in short, enjoyed her cash.

She was clearly about to ask who Litsi and I were when the princess entered, having come downstairs, I reckoned, at record speed.

"Beatrice," she said, advancing with both hands out-stretched and a sugar-substitute smile, "what a delightful surprise." She grasped Beatrice's arm and gave her two welcoming kisses, and I saw that her eyes were cold with dismay.

"Surprise?" Beatrice said, as they disengaged. "I called on Friday and spoke to your secretary. I told her to be sure to give you the message, and she said she would leave a note."

"Oh." A look of comprehension crossed the princess's face. "Then I expect it's down in the office, and I've missed it. We've been . . . rather busy."

"Casilia, about the bamboo room . . ." Beatrice began purposefully, and the princess with dexterity interrupted her.

"Do you know my nephew, Litsi?" she said, making sociable introductions. "Litsi, this is Roland's sister, Beatrice de Brescou Bunt. Did you leave Palm Beach last evening, Beatrice? Such a long flight from Miami."

"Casilia . . ." Beatrice shook hands with Litsi. "The bam—"

"And this is Danielle's fiancé, Christmas Fielding." The princess went on obliviously. "I don't think you've met him either. And now, my dear Beatrice, some tomato juice and vodka?"

"Casilia!" Beatrice said, sticking her toes in. "I always have the bamboo room."

I opened my mouth to say obligingly that I didn't mind moving, and received a rapid look of pure steel from the princess. I shut my mouth, amazed and amused, and held my facial muscles in limbo.

"Mrs. Dawson is unpacking your things in the rose room, Beatrice," the princess said firmly. "You'll be very comfortable there."

Beatrice, furious but outmaneuvered, allowed a genial Litsi to concoct her a bloody mary, she issuing sharp instructions about shaking the tomato juice, about how much Worcestershire sauce, how much lemon, how much ice. The princess watched with a wiped-clean expression of vague benevolence and Danielle was stifling her laughter.

"And now," Beatrice said, the drink finally fixed to her satisfaction, "what's all this rubbish about Roland refusing to expand the business?"

After a frosty second of immobility, the princess sat collectedly in an armchair, crossing her wrists and ankles in artificial composure.

Beatrice repeated her question insistently. She was never, I discovered, one to give up. Litsi busied himself with offering her a chair, smoothly settling her into it, discussing cushions and comfort and giving the princess time for mental remustering.

Litsi sat in a third armchair, leaning forward to Beatrice with smothering civility, and Danielle and I took places on a sofa, although with half an acre of flowered chintz between us.

"Roland is being obstructionist and I've come to tell him I object. He must change his mind at once. It is ridiculous not to move with the times and it's time to look for new markets."

The princess looked at me, and I nodded. We had heard much the same thing, even some of the identical phrases, from Henri Nanterre on Friday evening.

"How do you know of any business proposals?" the princess asked.

"That dynamic young son of Louis Nanterre told me, of course. He made a special journey to see me, and explained the whole thing. He asked me to persuade Roland to drag himself into the twentieth century, let alone the twenty-first, and I decided I would come over here myself and insist on it."

"You do know," I said, "that he's proposing to make and export guns?"

"Of course," she said. "But only plastic parts of guns. Roland is old-fashioned. I've a good friend in Palm Beach whose husband's corporation makes missiles for the Defense Department. Where's the difference?" She paused. "And what business is it of yours?" Her gaze traveled to Danielle, and she remembered. "I suppose if you're engaged to Danielle," she said grudgingly, "then it's marginally your business. I didn't know Danielle was engaged. Nobody tells me anything."

Henri Nanterre, I thought, had told her a great deal too much.

"Beatrice," the princess said, "I'm sure you'll want to wash after your journey. Dawson is arranging a late lunch for us, although as we didn't know there would be so many . . ."

"I want to talk to Roland," Beatrice said obstinately.

"Yes, later. He's resting just now." The princess stood, and we also, waiting for Danielle's aunt to be impelled upstairs by the sheer unanimity of our expectant good manners; and it was interesting, I thought, that she gave in, put down her unfinished drink and went, albeit grumbling as she departed that she expected to be reinstated in the bamboo room by the following day at the latest.

"She's relentless," Danielle said as her voice faded away. "She always gets what she wants. And anyway, the bamboo room's empty, isn't it? How odd of Aunt Casilia to refuse it."

"I've slept in there the last two nights," I said.

"Have you indeed!" Litsi's voice answered. "In accommodation above princes."

"That's not fair," Danielle said. "You said you preferred those rooms on the ground floor because you could go in and out without disturbing anyone."

Litsi looked at her fondly. "So I do. I only meant that Aunt Casilia must esteem your fiancé highly."

"Yes," Danielle said, giving me an embarrassed glance. "She does."

We all sat down again, though Danielle came no nearer to me on the sofa.

Litsi said, "Why did Henri Nanterre recruit your aunt Beatrice so diligently? She won't change Roland's mind."

"She lives on de Brescou money," Danielle said unexpectedly. "My parents do now as well, now that my black sheep of a father has been accepted back into the fold. Uncle Roland set up generous trusts for everybody out of the revenues from his land, but for as long as I've known my aunt she's complained he could afford more."

"For as long as you've known her?" Litsi echoed. "Haven't you always known her?"

She shook her head. "She disapproved of Dad. He left home originally under the heaviest of clouds, though what exactly he did, he's never told me; he just laughs if I ask, but it must have been pretty bad. It was a choice, Mom says, between exile and jail, and he chose California. She and I came on the scene a lot later. Anyway, about eight years ago Aunt Beatrice suddenly swooped down on us to see what had become of her disgraced little brother, and I've seen her several times since then. She married an American businessman way way back, and it was after he died she set out to track Dad down. It took her two years— the United States is a big country—but she looks on persistence as a prime virtue. She lives in a marvelous Spanish-style house in Palm Beach—I stayed there for a few days one spring break—and she makes trips to New York, and every summer she travels in Europe and spends some time in 'our chateau,' as she calls it."

Litsi was nodding. "Aunt Casilia has been known to visit me in Paris when her sister-in-law stays too long. Aunt Casilia and Roland," he explained to me unnecessarily, "go to the chateau for six weeks or so around July and August, to seek some country air and play their part as landowners. Did you know?"

"They mention it sometimes," I said.

"Yes, of course."

"What's the chateau like?" Danielle asked.

"Not a Disney castle," Litsi answered, smiling. "More like a large Georgian country house, built of light-colored stone, with shutters on all the windows. Chateau de Brescou. The local town is built on land south of Bordeaux mostly owned by Roland, and he takes moral and civic pride in its well-being. Even without the construction company, he could fund a mini-Olympics on the income he receives in rents, and his estates are run as the company used to be, with good managers and scrupulous fairness."

"He *cannot*," I commented, "deal in arms."

Danielle sighed. "I do see," she admitted, "that with all that old aristocratic honor, he simply couldn't face it."

"But I'm really surprised," I said, "that Beatrice could face it quite easily. I would have thought she would have shared her brother's feelings."

"I'll bet," Danielle said, "that Henri Nanterre promised her a million-dollar handout if she got Uncle Roland to change his mind."

"In that case," I suggested mildly, "your uncle could offer her double to go back to Palm Beach and stay there."

Danielle looked shocked. "That wouldn't be right."

"Morally indefensible," I agreed, "but pragmatically an effective solution."

Litsi's gaze was thoughtful on my face. "Do you think she's such a threat?"

"I think she could be like water dripping on a stone, wearing it away. Like water dripping on a man's forehead, driving him mad."

"The water torture," Litsi said. "I'm told it feels like a red-hot poker after a while, drilling a hole into the skull."

"She's just like that," Danielle said.

There was a short silence while we contemplated the boring capacities of Beatrice de Brescou Bunt, and then Litsi said consideringly, "It might be a good idea to tell her about the document you witnessed. Tell her the bad news that all four of us would have to agree to the guns, and assure her that even if she drives Roland to collapse, she'll still have to deal with me."

"Don't tell her," Danielle begged. "She'll give none of us any peace."

Neither of them had objected to the use made of them in their absence; on the contrary, they had been pleased. "It makes us a family," Danielle had said, and it was I, the witness, who had felt excluded.

"Upstairs," I said, reflecting, "I've got what I think is a duplicate of the form Henri Nanterre wanted Monsieur de Brescou to sign. It is in French. Would you like to see it?"

"Very much," Litsi said.

"Right."

I went upstairs to fetch it and found Beatrice Bunt in my bedroom.

"What are you doing here?" she demanded.

"I came to fetch something," I said.

She was holding the bright-blue running shorts I usually slept in, which I had stored that morning in the bedside table drawer on top of Nanterre's form. The drawer was open, the paper presumably inside.

"These are yours?" she said in disbelief. "*You* are using this room?"

"That's right." I walked over to her, took the shorts from her hand and returned them to the drawer. The form, I was relieved to see, lay there undisturbed.

"In that case," she said with triumph, "there's no problem. I shall have this room, and you can have the other. I always have the bamboo suite, it's the accepted thing. I see some of your things are in the bathroom. It won't take long to switch them over."

I'd left the door open when I went in and, perhaps hearing her voice, the princess came inquiringly to see what was going on.

"I've told this young man to move, Casilia," Beatrice said, "because of course this is my room, naturally."

"Danielle's fiancé," the princess said calmly, "stays in this room as long as he stays in this house. Now come along, Beatrice, do, the rose room is extremely comfortable, you'll find."

"It's half the size of this one, and there's no dressing room."

The princess gave her a bland look, admirably concealing irritation. "When Kit leaves, you shall have the bamboo room, of course."

"I thought you said his name was Christmas."

"So it is," the princess agreed. "He was born on Christmas Day. Come along, Beatrice, let's go down for this very delayed lunch." She positively shepherded her sister-in-law out into the passage, and returned a second later for one brief and remarkable sentence, half instruction, half entreaty.

"Stay in this house," she said, "until she is gone."

After lunch, Litsi, Danielle and I went up to the disputed territory to look at the form, Litsi observing that his money was on Beatrice to winkle me out of all this splendor before tomorrow night.

"Did you see the dagger looks you were getting across the mousse."

"Couldn't miss them."

"And those pointed remarks about good manners, unselfishness, and the proper precedence of rank?"

The princess had behaved as if she hadn't heard, sweetly making inquiries about Beatrice's health, her dogs and the weather in Florida in February. Roland de Brescou, as very often, had remained upstairs for lunch, his door barricaded, I had no doubt. The princess with soft words would defend him.

"Well," I said, "here's this form."

I retrieved it from under my blue shorts and gave it to Litsi, who wandered with it over to a group of comfortable chairs near the window. He read it attentively, sitting down absentmindedly, a big man with natural presence and unextended power. I liked him and because of Danielle feared him, a contradictory jumble of emotion, but I also trusted his overall air of amiable competence.

I moved across the room to join him, and Danielle also, and after a while he raised his head and frowned.

"For a start," he said, "this is not an application form for a license to make or export arms. Are you sure that's what Nanterre said it was?"

I thought back. "As far as I remember, it was the lawyer Gerald Greening who said it was a government form for preliminary application for a license. I understood that that was what Henri Nanterre had told the princess in her box at Newbury."

"Well, it isn't a government form at all. It isn't an application for any sort of license. What it is is a very vague and general form that would be used by simple people to draw up a contract." He paused. "In England I believe one can buy from stationers' shops a printed form for making a will. The legal words are all there to ensure that the will is properly executed. One simply inserts in the spaces what one wants done, like leaving the car to one's grandson. It's what's written into the spaces that really counts. Well, this form is rather like that. The legal form of words is correct, so that this would be a binding document, if properly signed and properly witnessed." He glanced down at the paper. "It's impossible to tell of course how Henri Nanterre had filled in all the spaces, but I would guess that overall it would say merely that the parties named in the contract had agreed on the course of action outlined by the accompanying documents. I would think that this form would be attached to, and act as page one of, a bulk of papers that would include all sorts of things like factory capacity, overseas sales forces, preliminary orders from customers and the specifications of the guns proposed to be manufactured. All sorts of things. But this simple form with Roland's signature on it would validate the whole presentation. It would be taken very seriously indeed as a full statement of intent. With this in his hands Henri Nanterre could apply for his license immediately."

"And get it," I said. "He was sure of it."

"Yes."

"But Uncle Roland could say he was forced into signing," Danielle said. "He could repudiate it, couldn't he?"

"He might have been able to nullify an application form quite easily, but with a contract it's much more difficult. He could plead threats and harassment, but the legal position might be that it was too late to change his mind, once he'd surrendered."

"And if he did get the contract overthrown," I said reflectively, "Henri Nanterre could start his harassment over again. There could be no end to it, until the contract was re-signed."

"But all four of us have to sign now," Danielle said. "What if we all say we won't?"

"I think," I said, "if your uncle decided to sign, you would all follow his lead."

Litsi nodded. "The four-signature agreement is a delaying tactic, not a solution."

"And what," Danielle said flatly, "is a solution?"

Litsi looked my way. "Put Kit to work on it." He smiled. "Danielle told me you tied all sorts of strong men into knots last November. Can't you do it again?"

"This is a bit different," I said.

"What happened last time?" he asked. "Danielle told me no details."

"A newspaper was giving my sister, Holly, and her husband a lot of unearned bad publicity—he's a racehorse trainer and they said he was going broke—and basically I got them to apologize and pay Bobby some compensation."

"And Bobby's appalling father," Danielle said, "tell Litsi about him."

She could look at me, now, as if everything were the same. I tried with probably little success to keep my general anxiety about her from showing too much and told the story to Litsi.

"The real reason for the attacks on Bobby was to get at his father, who'd been trying to take over the newspaper. Bobby's father, Maynard Allardeck, was in line for a knighthood, and the newspaper's idea was to discredit him so that he shouldn't get one. Maynard was a real pain, a ruthless burden on Bobby's back. So I . . . er . . . got him off."

"How?" Litsi asked curiously.

"Maynard," I said, "makes fortunes by lending money to dicky businesses. He puts them straight and then calls in the loan. The businesses can't repay him, so he takes over the businesses, and shortly after sells off their assets, closing them down. The smiling shark comes along and gobbles up the grateful minnows, who don't discover their mistake until they're half digested."

"So what did you do?" Litsi said.

"Well, I went around filming interviews with some of the people he had damaged. They were pretty emotional stuff. An old couple he'd cheated out of a star racehorse, a man whose son committed suicide when he lost his business, and a foolish boy who'd been led into gambling away half his inheritance."

"I saw the film," Danielle said. "It hit like hammers. It made me cry. Kit threatened to send videotape copies to all sorts of people if Maynard did any more harm to Bobby. And you've forgotten to say," she said to me, "that Maynard tried to get Bobby to kill you."

Litsi blinked. "To kill . . ."

"Mm," I said. "He's paranoid about Bobby marrying my sister. He's been programmed from birth to hate all Fieldings . . . he told Bobby when he was a little boy that if he was ever naughty the Fieldings would eat him."

I explained about the depth and bitterness of the old Fielding-Allardeck feud.

"Bobby and I," I said, "have made it up and are friends, but his father can't stand that."

"Bobby thinks," Danielle said to me, "that Maynard also can't stand you being successful. He wouldn't feel so murderous if you'd been a lousy jockey."

"Maynard," I told Litsi, smiling, "is a member of the Jockey Club and also now turns up quite often as a Steward at various racecourses. He would dearly like to see me lose my license."

"Which he can't manage unfairly," Litsi said thoughtfully, "because of the existence of the film."

"It's a standoff," I agreed equably.

"OK," Litsi said, "then how about a standoff for Henri Nanterre?"

"I don't know enough about him. I'd known Maynard all my life. I don't know anything about arms or anyone who deals in them."

Litsi pursed his lips. "I think I could arrange that," he said.

8

I telephoned to Wykeham later that Sunday afternoon and listened to the weariness in his voice. His day had been a procession of frustrations and difficulties that were not yet over. The dog-patrol man, complete with dog, was sitting in his kitchen drinking tea and complaining that the weather was freezing. Wykeham was afraid most of the patrolling would be done all night indoors.

"Is it freezing really?" I asked. Freezing was always bad news because racing would be abandoned, frosty ground being hard, slippery and dangerous.

"Two degrees off it."

Wykeham kept thermometers above the outdoor water taps so he could switch on low-powered battery heaters in a heavy freeze and keep the water flowing. His whole stable was rich with gadgets he'd adopted over the years, like infrared lights in the boxes to keep the horses warm and healthy.

"A policeman came," Wykeham said. "A detective constable. He said it was probably some boys' prank. I ask you! I told him it was no prank to shoot two horses expertly, but he said it was amazing what boys got up to. He said he'd seen worse things. He'd seen ponies in fields with their eyes gouged out. It was c–c–crazy. I said Cotopaxi was no pony, he was cofavorite for the Grand National, and he said it was b–bad luck on the owner."

"Did he promise any action?"

"He said he would come back tomorrow and take statements from the lads, but I don't think they know anything. Pete, who looked after Cotopaxi, has been in tears and the others are all indignant. It's worse for them than having one killed accidentally."

"For us all," I said.

"Yes." He sighed. "It didn't help that the slaughterers had so much trouble getting the bodies out. I didn't watch. I couldn't. I l–loved both those horses."

To the slaughterers, of course, dead horses were just so much dogmeat, and although it was perhaps a properly unsentimental way of looking at it, it wasn't always possible for someone like Wykeham, who had cared for them, talked to them, planned for them and lived through their lives. Trainers of steeplechasers usually knew their charges for a longer span than Flat-race trainers, ten years or more sometimes as opposed to three or four. When Wykeham said he loved a horse, he meant it.

He wouldn't yet have the same feeling for Kinley, I thought. Kinley, the bright star, young and fizzing. Kinley was excitement, not an old buddy.

"Look after Kinley," I said.

"Yes, I've moved him. He's in the corner box."

The corner box, always the last to be used, couldn't be

reached directly from any courtyard but only through another box. Its position was a nuisance for lads, but it was also the most secret and safe place in the stable.

"That's great," I said with relief, "and now, what about tomorrow?"

"Tomorrow?"

"Plumpton races."

There was a slight silence while he reorganized his thoughts. He always sent a bunch of horses to go-ahead Plumpton because it was one of his nearest courses, and as far as I knew I was riding six of them.

"Dusty has a list," he said eventually.

"OK."

"Just ride them as you think best."

"All right."

"Goodnight, then, Kit."

"Goodnight, Wykeham."

At least he'd got my name right, I thought, disconnecting. Perhaps all the right horses would arrive at Plumpton.

I went down there on the train the next morning, feeling glad, as the miles rolled by, to be away from the Eaton Square house. Even diluted by the princess, Litsi and Danielle, an evening spent with Beatrice de Brescou Bunt had opened vistas of social punishment I would as soon have remained closed. I had excused myself early, to openly reproachful looks from the others, but even in sleep I seemed to hear that insistent complaining voice.

When I'd left in the morning Litsi had said he would himself spend most of the day with Roland after John Grundy had left. The princess and Danielle would occupy Beatrice. Danielle, working evening shifts in her television news company, would have to leave it all to the princess from soon after five-thirty. I had promised to return from Plumpton as soon as possible, but truthfully I was happy to be presented with a very good reason not to, in the shape of a message awaiting me in the changing room. Relayed from the stable manager at Newbury racecourse, the note requested me to remove my car from where I'd left it, as the space was urgently required for something else.

I telephoned to Eaton Square, and as it happened Danielle answered.

I explained about the car. "I'll get a lift from Plumpton to Newbury. I think I'd better sleep at home in Lambourn, though, as I've got to go to Devon to race tomorrow. Will you apologize to the princess? Tell her I'll come back tomorrow night, after racing, if she'd like."

"Deserter," Danielle said. "You sound suspiciously pleased."

"It does make sense in terms of miles," I said.

"Tell it to the marines."

"Look after yourself," I said.

She said, "Yes," on a sigh after a pause, and put the phone down. Sometimes it seemed that everything was the same between us, and then, on a sigh, it wasn't. Without much enthusiasm, I went in search of Dusty, who had arrived with the right horses, the right colors for me to wear and a poor opinion of the detective constable for trying to question the lads while they were working. No one knew anything, anyway, Dusty said, and the lads were in a mood for the lynching of any prowling stranger. The head-lad (not Dusty, who was the traveling head-lad) had looked round the courtyards as usual at about eleven on Saturday night, when all had appeared quiet. He hadn't looked into all the eighty boxes, only one or two whose inmates weren't well, and he hadn't looked at either Cascade or Cotopaxi. He'd looked in on Kinley and Hillsborough to make sure they'd eaten their food after racing, and he'd gone home to bed. What more could anyone do? Dusty demanded.

"No one's blaming anybody," I said.

He said, "Not so far," darkly, and took my saddle away to put it on the right horse for the first race.

We stage-managed the afternoon between us, as so often, he producing and saddling the horses, I riding them, both of us doing a public relations job on the various owners, congratulating, commiserating, explaining and excusing. We ended with a typical day of two winners, a second, two also-rans and a faller, the last giving me a soft landing and no problems.

"Thanks, Dusty," I said at the end. "Thanks for everything."

"What do you mean?" he said suspiciously.

"I just meant, six races is a busy day for you, and it all went well."

"It would have gone better if you hadn't fallen off in the fifth," he said sourly.

I hadn't fallen off. The horse had gone right down under me, leaving grass stains on its number cloth. Dusty knew it perfectly well.

"Well," I said. "Thanks, anyway."

He gave me an unsmiling nod and hurried off, and in essential discord we would no doubt act as a team at Newton Abbot the next day and at Ascot the next, effective but cold.

Two other jockeys who lived in Lambourn gave me a lift back to Newbury, and I collected my car from its extended parking there and drove home to my house on the hill.

I lit the log fire to cheer things up a bit, ate some grilled chicken and telephoned to Wykeham.

He'd had another wearing day. The insurers had been questioning his security, the detectives had annoyed all the lads, and the dog-patrol man had been found asleep in the hay barn by the head-lad when he arrived at six in the morning. Wykeham had informed Weatherbys, the Jockey Club secretariat, of the horses' deaths (a routine obligation) and all afternoon his telephone had been driving him mad as one newspaper after another had called up to ask if it were true that they'd been murdered.

Finally, he said, the princess had rung to say she'd canceled her visit to her friends at Newton Abbot and wouldn't be there to watch her horses, and please would Wykeham tell Kit that yes, she did very definitely want him to return to Eaton Square as soon as he could.

"What's going on there?" Wykeham asked, without pressing interest. "She sounds unlike herself."

"Her sister-in-law arrived unexpectedly."

"Oh?" He didn't pursue it. "Well done, today, with the winners."

"Thanks." I waited, expecting to hear that Dusty had said I'd fallen off, but I'd misjudged the old crosspatch. "Dusty says Torquil went down flat in the fifth. Were you all right?"

"Not a scratch," I said, much surprised.

"Good. About tomorrow, then . . ."

We discussed the next day's runners and eventually said goodnight, and he called me Kit, which made it twice in a row. I would know things were returning to normal, I thought, when he went back to Paul.

I played back all the messages on my answering machine and found most of them echoes of Wykeham's: a whole column of pressmen wanted to know my feelings on the loss of Cotopaxi. Just as well, I thought, that I hadn't been at home to express them.

There was an inquiry from a Devon trainer as to whether I could ride two for him at Newton Abbot, his own jockey having been hurt: I looked up the horses in the form book, telephoned to accept, and peacefully went to bed.

The telephone woke me at approximately two-thirty.

"Hello," I said sleepily, squinting at the unwelcome news on my watch. "Who is it?"

"Kit . . ."

I came wide awake in a split second. It was Danielle's voice, very distressed.

"Where are you?" I said.

"I . . . oh . . . I need . . . I'm in a shop."

"Did you say shock or shop?" I said.

"Oh . . ." She gulped audibly. "Both, I suppose."

"What's happened? Take a deep breath. Tell me slowly."

"I left the studio . . . ten after two . . . started to drive home." She stopped. She always finished at two, when the studio closed and all the American news-gatherers left for the night, and drove her own small Ford car back to the garage behind Eaton Square where Thomas kept the Rolls.

"Go on," I said.

"A car seemed to be following me. Then I had a flat tire. I had to stop. I . . ." She swallowed again. "I found . . . I had two tires almost flat. And the other car stopped and a man got out . . . He was wearing . . . a hood."

Jesus Christ, I thought.

"I ran," Danielle said, audibly trying to stifle near-hysteria. "He started after me . . . I ran and ran . . . I saw this shop . . . it's open all night . . . and I ran in here. But the man here doesn't like it. He let me use his telephone . . . but I've no money, I left my purse and my coat in the car . . and I don't know . . . what to do . . ."

"What you do," I said, "is stay there until I reach you."

"Yes, but . . . the man here doesn't want me to . . . and somewhere outside . . . I can't . . . I simply can't go outside. I feel so stupid . . . but I'm frightened."

"Yes, you've good reason to be. I'll come at once. You let me talk to the man in the shop . . . and don't worry, I'll be there in under an hour."

She said, "All right," faintly, and in a few seconds an Asian-sounding voice said, "Hello?"

"My young lady," I said, "needs your help. You keep her warm, give her a hot drink, make her comfortable until I arrive, and I'll pay you."

"Cash," he said economically.

"Yes, cash."

"Fifty pounds," he said.

"For that," I said, "you look after her very well indeed. And now tell me your address. How do I find you?"

He gave me directions and told me earnestly he would look after the lady, I wasn't to hurry, I would be sure to bring the cash, wouldn't I, and I assured him again that yes, I would.

I dressed, swept some spare clothes into a bag, locked the house and broke the speed limit to London. After a couple of wrong turns and an inquiry from an unwilling night-walker I found the street and the row of dark shops, with one brightly lit near the end next to the Undergound station. I stopped with a jerk on double yellow lines and went inside.

The place was a narrow minisupermarket with a take-away hot-food glass cabinet near the door, the whole of the rest of the space packed to the ceiling with provisions smelling subtly of spices. Two customers were choosing hot food, a third further down the shop looking at tins, but there was no sign of Danielle.

The Asian man serving, smoothly round of face, plump of body and drugged as to eye, gave me a brief glance as I hurried in, and went back methodically to picking out the customers' choices, chapatis and sausage rolls, with tongs.

"The young lady," I said.

He behaved as if he hadn't heard, wrapping the purchases, adding up the cost.

"Where is she?" I insisted, and might as well not have spoken. The Asian talked to his customers in a language I'd never heard; took their money, gave them change, waited until they had left.

"Where is she?" I said forcefully, growing anxious.

"Give me the money." His eyes spoke eloquently of his need for cash. "She is safe."

"Where?"

"At the back of the shop, behind the door. Give me the money."

I gave him what he'd asked, left him counting it, and fairly sprinted where he'd pointed. I reached a back wall stocked from floor to ceiling like the rest, and began to feel acutely angry before I saw that the door, too, was covered with racks.

In a small space surrounded by packets of coffee I spotted the doorknob; grasped it, turned it, pushed the door inward. It led into a room piled with more stock in brown cardboard boxes, leaving only a small space for a desk, a chair and a single-bar electric fire.

Danielle was sitting on the chair, huddled into a big dark masculine overcoat, trying to keep warm by the inadequate heater and staring blindly into space.

"Hi," I said.

The look of unplumbable relief on her face was as good, I supposed, as a passionate kiss, which actually I didn't get. She stood, though, and slid into my arms as if coming home, and I held her tight, not feeling her much through the thick coat, smelling the musky Eastern fragrance of the dark material, smoothing Danielle's hair and breathing deeply with content.

She slowly disengaged herself after a while, though I could have stood there for hours.

"You must think I'm stupid," she said shakily, sniffing and wiping her eyes on her knuckles. "A real fool."

"Far from it."

"I'm so glad to see you." It was heartfelt: true.

"Come on, then," I said, much comforted. "We'd best be going."

She slid out of the oversize overcoat and laid it on the chair, shivering a little in her shirt, sweater and trousers. The chill of shock, I thought, because neither the shop nor the storeroom was actively cold.

"There's a rug in my car," I said. "And then we'll go and fetch your coat."

She nodded, and we went up through the shop toward the street door.

"Thank you," I said to the Asian.

"Did you switch the fire off?" he demanded.

I shook my head. He looked displeased.

"Goodnight," I said, and Danielle said, "Thank you."

He looked at us with the drugged eyes and didn't answer, and after a few seconds we left him and crossed the pavement to the car.

"He wasn't bad, really," Danielle said, as I draped the rug round her shoulders. "He gave me some coffee from that hot counter, and offered me some food, but I couldn't eat it."

I closed her into the passenger seat, went round and slid behind the wheel, beside her.

"Where's your car?" I said.

She had difficulty in remembering, which wasn't surprising considering the panic of her flight.

"I'd gone only two miles, I guess, when I realized I had a flat. I pulled in off the highway. If we go back toward the studio . . . but I can't remember . . ."

"We'll find it," I said. "You can't have run far." And we found it in fact quite easily, its rear pointing toward us down a seedy side turning as we coasted along.

I left her in my car while I took a look. Her coat and handbag had vanished, also the windshield wipers and the radio. Remarkable, I thought, that the car itself was still there, despite the two flat tires, as the keys were still in the ignition. I took them out, locked the doors and went back to Danielle with the bad news and the good.

"You still have a car," I said, "but it could be stripped or gone by morning if we don't get it towed."

She nodded numbly and stayed in the car again when I found an all-night garage with a tow truck, and negotiated with the incumbents. Sure, they said lazily, accepting the car's keys, registration number and whereabouts. Leave it to them, they would fetch it at once, fix the tires, replace the windshield wipers, and it would be ready for collection in the morning.

It wasn't until we were again on our way toward Eaton Square that Danielle said any more about her would-be attacker, and then it was unwillingly.

"Do you think he was a rapist?" she said tautly.

"It seems . . . well . . . likely, I'm afraid." I tried to picture him. "What sort of clothes was he wearing? What sort of hood?"

"I didn't notice," she began, and then realized that she remembered more than she'd thought. "A suit. An ordinary man's suit. And polished leather shoes. The light shone on them, and I could hear them tapping on the ground. How odd. The hood was . . . a woolen hat, dark, pulled down, with holes for eyes and mouth."

"Horrible," I said with sympathy.

"I think he was waiting for me to leave the studio." She shuddered. "Do you think he fixed my tires?"

"Two flat at once is no coincidence."

"What do you think I should do?"

"Tell the police?" I suggested.

"No, certainly not. They think any young woman driving alone in the middle of the night is asking for trouble."

"All the same . . ."

"Do you know," she said, "that a friend of a friend of mine—an American—was driving along in London, like I was, doing absolutely nothing wrong, when she was stopped by the police and taken to the police station? They stripped her! Can you believe it? They said they were looking for drugs or bombs. There was a terrorist scare on, and they thought she had a suspicious accent. It took her ages to get people to wake up and say she was truly going home after working late. She's been a wreck ever since, and gave up her job."

"It does seem unbelievable," I agreed.

"It happened," she said.

"They're not all like that," I said mildly.

She decided nevertheless to tell only her colleagues in the studio, saying they should step up security round the parked cars.

"I'm sorry I made you come so far," she said, not particularly sounding it. "But I didn't want the police, and otherwise it meant waking Dawson and getting someone there to come for me. I felt shattered . . . I knew you would come."

"Mm."

She sighed, some of the tension at last leaving her voice. "There wasn't much in my purse, that's one good thing. Just lipstick and a hairbrush, not much money. No credit cards. I never take much with me to work."

I nodded. "What about keys?"

"Oh . . ."

"The front-door key of Eaton Square?"

"Yes," she said, dismayed. "And the key to the back door of the studios, where the staff go in. I'll have to tell them in the morning, when the day shift gets there."

"Did you have anything with you that had the Eaton Square address on it?"

"No," she said positively. "I cleaned the whole car out this afternoon . . . I did it really to evade Aunt Beatrice . . . and I changed purses. I had no letters or anything like that with me."

"That's something," I said.

"You're so practical."

"I would tell the police," I said neutrally.

"No. You don't understand, you're not female."

There seemed to be no reply to that, so I pressed her no

further. I drove back to Eaton Square as I'd done so many times before, driving her home from work, and it wasn't until we were nearly there that I wondered whether the hooded man could possibly have been not a rapist at all, but Henri Nanterre.

On the face of it, it didn't seem possible, but coming at that particular time it had to be considered. If it in fact were part of the campaign of harassment and accidents, then we would hear about it, as about the horses also: no act of terrorism was complete without the boasting afterward.

Danielle had never seen Henri Nanterre and wouldn't have known his general shape, weight, and way of moving. Conversely, nor would he have turned up in Chiswick when he had no reason to know she was in England, even if he knew of her actual existence.

"You're very quiet all of a sudden," Danielle said, sounding no longer frightened but consequently sleepy. "What are you thinking?"

I glanced at her softening face, seeing the taut lines of strain smoothing out. Three or four times we'd known what the other was thinking, in the sort of telepathic jump that sometimes occurred between people who knew each other well, but not on a regular basis, and not lately. I was glad at that moment that she couldn't read my thoughts, not knowing if she would be more or less worried if she did.

"Tomorrow evening," I said, "get Thomas to drive you to work. He's not going to Devon now . . . and I'll fetch you."

"But if you're riding in Devon . . ."

"I'll go down and back on the train," I said. "I should be back in Eaton Square by nine."

"All right, I guess . . . thanks."

I parked my car where hers stood usually, and took my bag from the trunk, and with Danielle swathed in the rug as if in an oversized shawl we walked round to the front door in Eaton Square.

"I hope you have a key?" she said, yawning. "We'll look like gypsies if you don't."

"Dawson lent me one."

"Good . . . I'm asleep on my feet."

We went indoors and quietly up the stairs. When we reached her floor I put my arms round her, rug and all, again holding her close, but there was no clinging relief-driven response this time, and when I bent to kiss her it was her cheek she offered, not her mouth.

"Goodnight," I said. "Will you be all right?"

"Yes." She would hardly meet my eyes. "I truly thank you."

"You owe me nothing," I said.

"Oh . . ." She looked at me briefly, as if confused. Then she dropped the rug, which she had been holding close round her like a defensive stockade, put her arms round my neck and gave me a quick kiss at least reminiscent of better times, even if it landed somewhere on my chin.

"Goodnight," she said lightly, and walked away along the passage to her room without looking back, and I picked up my bag and the rug and went on upstairs feeling a good deal better than the day before. I opened the door of the bamboo room half expecting to find Beatrice snoring blissfully between my sheets, but the linen was smooth and vacant, and I plummeted there into dreamland for a good two hours.

Around seven-fifteen in the morning I knocked on Litsi's ground-floor door until a sleepy voice said, "Who is it?"

"Kit."

A short silence, then, "Come in, then."

The room was dark, Litsi leaning up on one elbow and stretching to switch on a bedside lamp. The light revealed a large oak-paneled room with a four-poster bed, brocade curtaining and ancestral paintings: very suitable, I thought, for Litsi.

"I thought you weren't here," he said, rubbing his eyes with his fingers. "What day is it?"

"Tuesday. I came back here before five this morning, and that's what I've come to tell you about."

He went from leaning to sitting up straight while he listened.

"Do you think it really was Nanterre?" he said when I'd finished.

"If it was, perhaps he wanted only to catch her and frighten her. Tell her what could happen if her uncle didn't give in. She must have surprised whoever it was by running so fast. She wears trainers to work . . . running shoes, really . . . and she's always pretty fit. Maybe he simply couldn't catch her."

"If he meant a warning he couldn't deliver, we'll hear from him."

"Yes. And about the horses, too."

"He's unhinged," Litsi said, "if it was him."

"Anyway," I said, "I thought I'd better warn you."

I told him about Danielle's handbag being missing. "If it was an ordinary thief, it would be all right because there was no connecting address, but if Nanterre took it, he now has a front-door key to this house. Do you think you could explain to the princess and get the lock changed? I'm off to Devon to ride a few races, and I'll be here again this evening. I'm picking Danielle up when she finishes work, but if I miss the train back, will you make sure she gets home safely? If you need a car, you can borrow mine."

"Just don't miss the train."

"No."

His eyebrows rose and fell. "Give me the keys, then," he said.

I gave them to him. "See if you can find out," I said, "if Danielle told her aunt Beatrice where she works and at what time she leaves."

He blinked.

"Henri Nanterre," I reminded him, "has a spy right in this house."

"Go and break your neck."

I smiled and went away, and caught the train to Devon. I might be a fool, I thought, entrusting Danielle to Litsi, but she needed to be safe, and one short ride in my Mercedes, Litsi driving, was unlikely to decide things one way or another.

For all the speed and risks of the job, jump jockeys were seldom killed: it was more dangerous, for instance, to clean windows for a living. All the same, there were occasional days when one ended in hospital, always at frustrating and inconvenient moments. I wouldn't say that I rode exactly carefully that day at Newton Abbot, but it was certainly without the reckless fury of the past two weeks.

Maybe she would finally come back to me, maybe she wouldn't: I had a better chance right under her eyes than two hundred miles away in traction.

The chief topic of conversation all afternoon on the racecourse as far as I was concerned was the killing of Cascade and Cotopaxi. I read accounts in the sports pages of two papers on the train and saw two others in the changing room, all more speculation and bold headlines than hard fact. I was besieged by curious and sympathetic questions from anyone I talked to, but could add little except that yes, I had seen them in their boxes, and yes, of course the princess was upset, and yes, I would be looking for another ride in the Grand National.

Dusty, from his thunderstorm expression, was putting up with much the same barrage. He was slightly mollified when one of the princess's runners won, greeted by clapping and cheers that spoke of her public popularity. The clerk of the course and the chairman of the board of directors called me into the directors' room, not to complain of my riding but to commiserate, asking me to pass on their regrets to the princess and to Wykeham. They clapped me gruffly on the shoulder and gave me champagne, and it was all a long way from Maynard Allardeck.

I caught the return train on schedule, dined on a railway sandwich, and was back at Eaton Square before nine. I had to get Dawson to let me in because the lock had indeed been changed, and I went up to the sitting room, opening the door there on the princess, Litsi and Beatrice Bunt, all sitting immobile in private separate silences, as if they were covered by vacuum bell jars and couldn't hear each other speak.

"Good evening," I said, my voice sounding loud.

Beatrice Bunt jumped because I'd spoken behind her. The princess's expression changed from blank to welcoming, and Litsi came alive as if one had waved a wand over a waxwork.

"You're back!" he said. "Thank God for that at least."

"What's happened?" I asked.

None of them was quite ready to say.

"Is Danielle all right?" I said.

The princess looked surprised. "Yes, of course. Thomas drove her to work." She was sitting on a sofa, her back straight, her head high, every muscle on the defensive and no ease anywhere. "Come over here"—she patted the cushions beside her—"and tell me how my horses ran."

It was her refuge, I knew, from unpleasant reality: she'd talked of her runners in the direst of moments in the past, clinging to a rock in a tilting world.

I sat beside her, willingly playing the game.

"Bernina was on the top of her form, and won her hurdle race. She seems to like it in Devon, that's the third time she's won down there."

"Tell me about her race," the princess said, looking both pleased and in some inner way still disorientated, and I told her about the race without anything in her expression changing. I glanced at Litsi and saw that he was listening in the same detached way, and at Beatrice, who appeared not to be listening at all.

I passed on the messages of sympathy from the directors, and said how pleased the crowd had been that she'd had a winner.

"How kind," she murmured.

"What's happened?" I said again.

It was Litsi who eventually answered. "Henri Nanterre telephoned here about an hour ago. He wanted to speak to Roland, but Roland refused, so he asked for me by name."

My eyebrows rose.

"He said he knew my name as one of the three others who had to sign business directives with Roland. He said Danielle and the princess were the others: his notary had remembered."

I frowned. "I suppose he might have remembered if someone had told him the names . . . he might have recognized them."

Litsi nodded. "Henri Nanterre said that his notary had left his briefcase in Roland's sitting room. In the briefcase could be found a form of contract with spaces at the bottom for signatures and witnesses. He says all four of us are to sign this form in the presence of his notary, in a place that he will designate. He said he would telephone each morning until everyone was ready to agree."

"Or else?" I said.

"He mentioned," Litsi said evenly, "that it would be a shame for the princess to lose more of her horses needlessly, and that young women out alone at night were always at risk." He paused, one eyebrow lifting ironically. "He said that princes weren't immune from accidents, and that a certain jockey, if he wished to stay healthy, should remove himself from the household and mind his own business."

"His exact words?" I asked interestedly.

Litsi shook his head. "He spoke in French."

"We have asked Beatrice," the princess said with brittle veneer politeness, "if she has spoken with Henri Nanterre since her arrival in this house on Sunday, but she tells us she doesn't know where he is."

I looked at Beatrice, who stared implacably back. It wasn't necessary to know where someone actually was if he had a telephone number, but there seemed to be no point in making her upgrade the evasion into a straightforward lie, which the boldness in her eyes assured me we would get.

The princess said that her husband had asked to talk to me on my return, and suggested that I might go at this point. I went, sensing the three of them stiffening back into their bell jars, and upstairs knocked on Roland de Brescou's door.

He bade me come in and sit down, and asked with nicely feigned interest about my day's fortunes. I said Bernina had won and he said "Good" absentmindedly, while he arranged in his thoughts what to say next. He was looking, I thought, not so physically frail as on Friday and Saturday, but not as determined either.

"It is going to take time to arrange my retirement," he said, "and as soon as I make any positive moves, Henri Nanterre will find out. Gerald Greening thinks that when he does find out, he will demand I withdraw my intention,

under pain of more and more threats and vicious actions."
He paused. "Has Litsi told you about Nanterre's telephone
call?"

"Yes, monsieur."

"The horses . . . Danielle . . . my wife . . . Litsi . . .
yourself . . . I cannot leave you all open to harm. Gerald
Greening advises now that I sign the contract, and then as
soon as Nanterre gets his firearms approval, I can sell all
my interest in the business. Nanterre will have to agree. I
shall make it a condition before signing. Everyone will
guess I have sold because of the guns . . . some at least of
my reputation may be salvaged." A spasm of distress
twisted his mouth. "It is of the greatest conceivable personal disgrace that I sign this contract, but I see no other
way."

He fell silent but with an implied question, as if inviting
my comment; and after a short pause I gave it.

"Don't sign, monsieur," I said.

He looked at me consideringly, with the first vestige of a
smile.

"Litsi said you would say that," he said.

"Did he? And what did Litsi himself say?"

"What would you think?"

"Don't sign," I said.

"You and Litsi." Again the fugitive smile. "So different.
So alike. He described you as—and these are his words,
not mine—'a tough devil with brains,' and he said I should
give you and him time to think of a way of deterring Nanterre permanently. He said that only if both of you failed
and admitted failure should I think of signing."

"And . . . did you agree?"

"If you yourself wish it, I will agree."

A commitment of positive action, I thought, was a lot different from raising defenses; but I thought of the horses, and the princess, and Danielle, and really there was no question.

"I wish it," I said.

"Very well, but I do hope nothing appalling will happen."

I said we would try our best to prevent it, and asked if he would mind having a guard in the house every day during John Grundy's off-duty hours.

"A guard?" He frowned.

"Not in your rooms, monsieur. Moving about. You would hardly notice him, but we'd give you a walkie-talkie so you could call him if you needed. And may we also install a telephone that records what's said?"

He lifted a thin hand an inch and let it fall back on the arm of the wheelchair.

"Do what you think best," he said, and then, with an almost mischievous smile, the only glimpse I'd ever had of the lighter side within, he asked, "Has Beatrice got you out of the bamboo room yet?"

"No, monsieur," I said cheerfully.

"She was up here this morning demanding I move you," he said, the smile lingering. "She insists also that I allow Nanterre to run the business as he thinks best, but truly I don't know which of her purposes obsesses her most. She switched from one to the other within the same sentence." He paused. "If you can defeat my sister," he said, "Nanterre should be easy."

By the following midmorning I'd been out to buy a recording telephone, and the guard had been installed, in the unconventional form of a springy twenty-year-old who had learned karate in the cradle.

Beatrice predictably disapproved, both of his looks and of his presence, particularly as he nearly knocked her over on one of the landings, while proving he could run from the basement to the attic faster than the elevator could travel the same distance.

He told me his name was Sammy (this week), and he was deeply impressed by the princess, whom he called "Your Regal Highness," to her discreet and friendly amusement.

"Are you sure?" she said to me tentatively, when he wasn't listening.

"He comes with the very highest references," I assured her. "His employer promised he could kick a pistol out of anyone's hand before it was fired."

Sammy's slightly poltergeist spirits seemed to cheer her greatly, and with firmness she announced that all of us, of course including Beatrice, should go to Ascot races. Lunch was already ordered there, and Sammy would guard her husband: she behaved with the gaiety sometimes induced by risk-taking, which to Litsi and Danielle at least proved infectious.

Beatrice, glowering, complained she didn't like horse-racing. Her opinion of me had dropped as low as the Marianas Trench since she'd discovered I was a professional jockey. "He's the *help*," I overheard her saying in outrage to the princess. "Surely there are some rooms in the attic."

The "attic," as it happened, was an unused nursery suite, cold and draped in dust-sheets, as I'd discovered on my night prowls. The room I could realistically have expected to have been given lay beside the rose room, sharing the rose room's bathroom, but it, too, was palely shrouded.

"I didn't know you were coming, Beatrice, dear," the princess reminded her. "And he's Danielle's fiancé."

"But *really* . . ."

She did go to the races, though, albeit with ill grace, presumably on the premise that even if she gained access again to her brother, and even if she wore him to exhaustion, she couldn't make him sign the contract, because first, he didn't have it (it was now in Litsi's room in case she took the bamboo room by force) and second, his three cosigners couldn't be similarly coerced. Litsi had carefully told her, after Nanterre's telephone call and before my return from Devon, that the contract form was missing.

"Where is it?" she had demanded.

"My dear Beatrice," Litsi had said blandly, "I have no idea. The notary's briefcase is still in the hall awaiting collection, but there is no paper of any sort in it."

And it was after he'd told me of this exchange, before we'd gone to bed on the previous evening, that I'd taken the paper downstairs for his safekeeping.

Beatrice went to Ascot with the princess in the Rolls; Danielle and Litsi came with me.

Danielle, subdued, sat in the back. She had been quiet when I'd fetched her during the night, shivering now and again from her thoughts, even though the car had been warm. I told her about Nanterre's telephone call and also about her uncle's agreement with Litsi and me, and although her eyes looked huge with worry, all she'd said was, "*Please* be careful. Both of you . . . be careful."

At Ascot it was with unmixed feelings of jealousy that I watched Litsi take her away in the direction of the princess's lunch while I peeled off, as one might say, to the office.

I had four races to ride: one for the princess, two others for Wykeham, one for a Lambourn trainer. Dusty was in a bad mood, Maynard Allardeck had again turned up as a Steward, and the tree of my favorite lightweight saddle, my valet told me, had disintegrated. Apart from that it was bitterly cold, and apart from that I had somehow gained another pound, probably via the railway sandwich.

Wykeham's first runner was a four-year-old ex–Flat racer out for his first experience over hurdles, and although I'd schooled him a few times over practice jumps on Wykeham's gallops, I hadn't been able to teach him courage. He went round the whole way letting me know he hated it, and I had difficulty thinking of anything encouraging to say to his owners afterward. A horse that didn't like racing was a waste of time, a waste of money and a waste of emotion: better to sell him quick and try again. I put it as tactfully as possible, but the owners shook their heads doubtfully and said they would ask Wykeham.

The second of Wykeham's runners finished nowhere also, not from unwillingness, as he was kind-hearted and sure-footed, but from being nowhere near fast enough against the opposition.

I went out for the princess's race with a low *joie de vivre* rating, a feeling not cured by seeing Danielle walk into the parade ring holding on to Litsi's arm and laughing.

The princess, who had been in the ring first, after seeing her horse saddled, followed my gaze and gently tapped my arm.

"She's in a muddle," she said distinctly. "Give her time."

I looked at the princess's blue eyes, half hidden as usual behind reticent lashes. She must have felt very strongly that I needed advice, or she wouldn't have given it.

I said, "All right" with an unloosened jaw, and she briefly nodded, turning to greet the others.

"Where's Beatrice?" she asked, looking in vain behind them. "Didn't she come down?"

"She said it was too cold. She stayed up in the box," Litsi said, and to me, he added, "Do we put our money on?"

Col, the princess's runner, was stalking round in his navy-blue gold-crested rug, looking bored. He was a horse of limited enthusiasm, difficult to ride because if he reached the front too soon he would lose interest and stop, and if one left the final run too late and got beaten, one looked and felt a fool.

"Don't back him," I said. It was that sort of day.

"Yes, back him," the princess said simultaneously.

"Frightfully helpful," Litsi commented, amused.

Col was a bright chestnut with a white blaze down his nose and three white socks. As with most of the horses Wykeham was particularly hoping to win with at Cheltenham, Col probably wouldn't reach his absolute pinnacle of fitness until the National Hunt Festival in another two weeks, but he should be ready enough for Ascot, a slightly less testing track.

At Cheltenham he was entered for the Gold Cup, the top event of the meeting, and although not a hot fancy, as Cotopaxi had been for the Grand National, he had a realistic chance of being placed.

"Do your best," the princess said, as she often did, and as usual I said yes, I would. Dusty gave me a leg-up and I cantered Col down to the start trying to wind up a bit of life-force for us both. A gloomy jockey on a bored horse might as well go straight back to the stable.

By the time we started I was telling him we were out there to do a job of work, and to take a little pride in it, talking to myself as much as him; and by the third of the twenty-two fences there were some faint stirrings in both of us of the ebb turning to flood.

Most of the art of jump racing lay in presenting a horse at a fence so that he could cross it without slowing. Col was one of the comparatively rare sort that could judge distances on his own, leaving his jockey free to worry about tactics, but he would never quicken unless one insisted, and had no personal competitive drive.

I'd ridden and won on him often and understood his needs, and knew that by the end I'd have to dredge up the one wild burst of all-out urging that might wake up his phlegmatic soul.

I daresay that from the stands nothing looked wrong. Even though to me Col seemed to be plodding, his plod was respectably fast. We traveled most of the three miles in fourth or fifth place and came up into third on the last bend when two of the early leaders tired.

There were three fences still to go, with the 240-yard run-in after. One of the horses ahead was still chock-full of running: it was his speed Col would have to exceed. The jockey on the other already had his whip up and was no doubt feeling the first ominous warning that the steam was running out of the boiler. I gave Col the smallest of pulls to steady him in third place for the first of the three fences in the straight. This he jumped cleanly and was going equally well within himself as we crossed the next, passing that jockey with his whip up before we reached the last.

Too much daylight, I thought. He liked ideally to jump the last with two or three others still close ahead. He jumped the last with a tremendous leap, though, and it was no problem after all to stoke up the will-win spirit and tell him that now . . . now . . . was the time.

Col put his leading foot to the ground and it bent and buckled under him. His nose went down to the grass. The reins slid through my fingers to their full extent and I leaned back and gripped fiercely with my legs, trying not to be thrown off. By some agile miracle, his other foreleg struck the ground solidly, and with all his half-ton weight on that slender fetlock Col pushed himself upright and kept on going.

I gathered the reins. The race had to be lost, but the fire, so long arriving, couldn't easily be put out. Come on, now, you great brute, I was saying to him: now's the time, there is one to beat, get on with it, now show me, show everyone you can do it, you still can do it.

As if he understood every word he put his head forward and accelerated in the brief astonishing last-minute spurt that had snatched last-second victories before from seeming impossibilities.

We nearly made it that time, very nearly. Col ate up the lengths he'd lost and I rode him almost as hard as Cascade but without the fury, and we were up with the other horse's rump, up with the saddle, up with the neck . . . and the winning post flashed back three strides too soon.

The princess had said she wouldn't come down to the unsaddling enclosure unless we won, as it was a long way from her box.

Maynard was there, however, balefully staring at me as I slid to the ground, his eyes dark and his face tight with hate. Why he came near me I couldn't understand. If I'd hated anyone that much I would have avoided the sight of him as much as possible: and I did loathe Maynard for what he'd tried to do to Bobby, to brainwash his own son into killing.

Dusty put the sheet over Col's heaving chestnut sides with a studied lack of comment on the race's result, and I went and weighed in with much of the afternoon's dissatisfaction drifting around like a cloud.

I rode the next race for the Lambourn trainer and finished third, a good way back, and with a feeling of having accomplished nothing, changed into street clothes, done for the day.

On my way out of the weighing room, en route to the princess's box, a voice said, "Hey, Kit," behind me, and I turned to find Basil Clutter walking quickly in my wake.

"Are you still looking for Henri Nanterre?" he said, catching me up.

"Yes, I am." I stopped and he stopped also, although almost jogging from foot to foot, as he could never easily stand still.

"The Roquevilles are here today; they had a runner in the first race. They've someone with them who knows Henri Nanterre quite well. They said if you were still interested perhaps you'd like to meet her."

"Yes, I would."

He looked at his watch. "I'm supposed to be joining them in the owners' and trainers' bar for a drink now, so you'd better come along."

"Thank you," I said, "very much."

I followed him to the bar and, armed with Perrier to their port, met the Roquevilles' friend, who was revealed as small and French-looking, with a gamine chic that had outlasted her youth. The elfin face bore wrinkles, the club-cut black hair showed grayish roots, and she wore high-heeled black boots and a smooth black leather trouser-suit with a silk scarf knotted at the back of her neck, cowboy fashion.

Her speech, surprisingly, was straightforward earthy racecourse English, and she was introduced to me as Madame Madeleine Darcy, English wife of a French racehorse trainer.

"Henri Nanterre?" she said with distaste. "Of course I know the bastard. We used to train his horses until he whisked them away overnight and sent them to Villon."

She talked with the freedom of pique and the pleasure of entertaining an attentive audience.

"He's a cock," she said, "with a very loud crow. He struts like a rooster. We have known him since he was young, when the horses belonged to his father, Louis, who was a very nice man, a gentleman."

"So Henri inherited the horses?" I said.

"But yes, along with everything else. Louis was soft-headed. He thought his son could do no wrong. So stupid. Henri is a greedy bully. Villon is welcome to him."

"In what way is he a greedy bully?" I asked.

Her plucked eyebrows rose. "We bought a yearling filly with nice bloodlines that we were going to race ourselves and breed from later. Henri saw her in the yard—he was always poking round the stables—and said he would buy her. When we said we didn't want to sell, he said that unless we did, he would take all his horses away. He had eight . . . we didn't want to lose them. We were furious. He made us sell him the filly at the price we'd paid for her . . . and we'd kept her for months. Then a few weeks later, he telephoned one evening and said horse-boxes would be arriving in the morning to collect his horses. And pouf, they were gone."

"What happened to the filly?" I said.

Her mouth curved with pleasure. "She contracted navicular and had to be put down, poor little bitch. And do you know what that bastard Nanterre did?"

She paused for effect. About four voices, mine included, said, "What?"

"Villon told us. He was disgusted. Nanterre said he didn't trust the knackers not to patch up the filly, pump her full of painkillers and sell her, making a profit at his expense, so he insisted on being there. The filly was put down on Villon's land with Nanterre watching."

Mrs. Roqueville looked both sick and disappointed. "He seemed a pleasant enough man when we met him at Longchamp, and again at Newbury."

"I expect the Marquis de Sade was perfectly charming on the racecourse," Madeleine said sweetly. "It is where anyone can pretend to be a gentleman."

After a respectful pause I said, "Do you know anything of his business affairs?"

"Business." She wrinkled her nose. "He is the de Brescou et Nanterre construction company. I don't know anything about his business, only about his horses. I wouldn't trust him in business. As a man deals with his racehorse trainer, so will he deal in business. The honorable will be honorable. The greedy bully will run true to form."

"And . . . do you know where I could find him in England?"

"I wouldn't look, if I were you." She gave me a bright smile. "He'll bring you nothing but trouble."

I relayed the conversation to Litsi and Danielle up in the princess's box.

"What's navicular?" Litsi said.

"A disease of the navicular bone in a horse's foot. When it gets bad, the horse can't walk."

"That Nanterre," Danielle said disgustedly, "is gross."

The princess and Beatrice, a few feet away at the balcony end of the box, were talking to a tall, bulky man with noticeably light-gray eyes in a big bland face.

Litsi, following my gaze, said, "Lord Vaughnley. He came to commiserate with Aunt Casilia over Col not winning. Do you know him? He's something in publishing, I think."

"Mm," I said neutrally. "He owns the *Towncrier* newspaper."

"Does he?" Litsi's agile mind made the jump. "Not the paper that attacked Bobby?"

"No, that was the *Flag*."

"Oh." Litsi seemed disappointed. "Then he isn't one of the two defeated press barons after all."

"Yes, he is." Lord Vaughnley's attention was switching my way. "I'll tell you about it, some time," I said to Litsi, and watched Lord Vaughnley hesitate, as he always did, before offering his hand for me to shake: yet he must have known he would meet me in that place, as my being there at the end of each day's racing was a ritual well known to him.

"Kit," he said, grasping the nettle, "a great race . . . such bad luck."

"The way it goes," I said.

"Better luck in the Gold Cup, eh?"

"It would be nice."

"Anything I can do for you, my dear fellow?"

It was a question he asked whenever we met, though I could see Litsi's astonishment out of the side of my eyes. Usually I answered that there wasn't, but on that day thought there was no harm in trying a flier. If one didn't ask, one would never learn.

"Nothing, really," I said, "except . . . I suppose you've never come across the name of Henri Nanterre?"

Everyone watched him while he pondered, the princess with rapidly sharpening interest, Litsi and Danielle with simple curiosity, Beatrice with seeming alarm. Lord Vaughnley looked around at the waiting faces, frowned, and finally answered with a question of his own.

"Who is he?" he asked.

"My husband's business partner," the princess said. "Dear Lord Vaughnley, do you know of him?"

Lord Vaughnley was puzzled but slowly shook his big head. "I can't recall ever . . ."

"Could you . . . er . . . see if the *Towncrier* has a file on him?" I asked.

He gave me a resigned little smile, and nodded. "Write the name down for me," he said. "In caps."

I fished out a pen and small notepad and wrote both the name and that of the construction company, in capital letters as required.

"He's French," I said. "Owns horses. He might be on the racing pages, or maybe business. Or even gossip."

"Anything you want specifically?" he said, still smiling.

146

"He's over in England just now. Ideally, we'd like to know where he's staying."

Beatrice's mouth opened and closed again with a snap. She definitely knows, I thought, how to reach him. Perhaps we could make use of that, when we had a plan.

Lord Vaughnley tucked the slip of paper away in an inner pocket, saying he would get the names run through the computer that very evening, if it was important to the princess.

"Indeed it is," she said with feeling.

"Any little fact," I said, "could be helpful."

"Very well." He kissed the princess's hand and made general farewells, and to me he said as he was going, "Have you embarked on another crusade?"

"I guess so."

"Then God help this Nanterre."

"What did he mean by that?" Beatrice demanded as Lord Vaughnley departed, and the princess told her soothingly that it was a long story that wasn't to interfere with my telling her all about Col's race. Lord Vaughnley, she added, was a good friend she saw often at the races, and it was perfectly natural for him to help her in any way.

Beatrice, to do her justice, had been a great deal quieter since Nanterre's telephone call the evening before. She had refused to believe he had killed the horses ("It must have been vandals, as the police said") until he had himself admitted it, and although she was still adamant that Roland should go along with Nanterre in business, we no longer heard praise of him personally.

Her hostility toward me, on the other hand, seemed to have deepened, and on my account of the race she passed her own opinion.

"Rubbish. You didn't lose the race at the last fence. You

were too far back all along. Anyone could see that." She picked up a small sandwich from the display on the table and bit into it decisively, as if snapping off my head.

No one argued with her pronouncement and, emboldened, she said to Danielle with malice, "Your fortune-hunter isn't even a good jockey."

"Beatrice," the princess immediately said, unruffled. "Kit has a fortune of his own, and he is heir to his grandfather, who is rich."

She glanced at me briefly, forbidding me to contradict. Such fortune as I had I'd earned, and although my grandfather owned several chunks of Newmarket, their liquidity was of the consistency of bricks.

"And Aunt Beatrice," Danielle said, faintly blushing, "I am poor."

Beatrice ate her sandwich, letting her round eyes do the talking. Her pale-orange hair, I thought inconsequentially, was almost the same color as the hessian-covered walls.

The sixth and last race was already in progress, the commentary booming outside. Everyone except Beatrice went on the balcony to watch, and I wondered whether a putative million dollars was worth an unquiet mind. "It's nice to be nice," our grandmother had said often enough to Holly and me, bringing us up, and "Hate curdles your brains." Grandfather, overhearing her heresies, had tried to undo her work with anti-Allardeck slogans, but in the end it was she who'd prevailed. Holly had married Bobby, and apart from the present state of affairs with Danielle and other various past hard knocks, I had grown up, and remained, basically happy. Beatrice, for all her mink/crocodile/Spanish-house indulgences in Palm Beach, hadn't been so lucky.

When it came to going home, Beatrice again went with the princess in the Rolls. I had hoped Litsi would join them, as I was detouring to Chiswick to deliver Danielle to the studio, but he took Danielle's arm and steered her and himself, chatting away, in the direction of the jockeys' car park as if there had never been any question. Litsi had his aunt's precious knack of courteously and covertly getting his own way. He would have made a great king, I thought wryly, given the chance.

We dropped Danielle off (she waved to both of us and kissed neither) and I drove the two of us back to Eaton Square. Beatrice, naturally enough, came into the conversation.

"You were shocked," Litsi said, amused, "when she called you a fortune-hunter. You hadn't even thought of Danielle's prospects."

"She called me a bad jockey," I said.

"Oh, sure." He chuckled. "You're a puritan."

"Danielle has the money she earns," I said. "As I do."

"Danielle is Roland's niece," he said as if teaching an infant. "Roland and Aunt Casilia are fond of her, and they have no children."

"I don't want that complication."

He grunted beside me and said no more on the subject, and after a while I said, "Do you know why they have no children? Is it choice, or his illness? Or just that they couldn't?"

"His illness, I've always supposed, but I've never asked. He was about forty, I think, when they married, about fifteen years older than her, and he caught the virus not very long after. I can't remember ever seeing him walk, though he was a good skier, I believe, in his time."

"Rotten for them," I said.

He nodded. "He was lucky in some respects. Some people who get that virus—and thank God it's rare—lose the use of their arms as well. They never speak of it much, of course."

"How are we going to save his honor?"

"You invent," Litsi said lazily, "and I'll gofer."

"Gofer a lever," I said absentmindedly.

"A lever?"

"To move the world."

He stretched contentedly. "Do you have any ideas at all?"

"One or two. Rather vague."

"Which you're not sharing?"

"Not yet. Have to think a bit first." I told him I'd bought a recording telephone that morning. "When we get back, we'll rig it and work out a routine."

"He said he would ring again this evening."

No need to say who "he" was.

"Mm," I said. "The phone I bought is also a conference phone. It has a loudspeaker, so that everyone in the room can hear what the caller's saying. You don't need the receiver. So when he rings, if it's you that answers, will you get him to speak in English?"

"Perhaps you'd better answer, then he'd have to."

"All right. And the message we give is no dice?"

"You couldn't just string him along?"

"Yeah, maybe," I said, "but to fix him we've got to find him, and he could be anywhere. Beatrice knows where he is, or at least how to reach him. If we get him out in the open . . ." I paused. "What we ideally need is a tethered goat."

"And just who," Litsi inquired ironically, "are you electing for that dead-end job?"

I smiled. "A stuffed goat with a mechanical bleat. All real goats must be guarded or careful."

"Aunt Casilia, Roland and Danielle, guarded."

"And the horses," I said.

"OK. And the horses guarded. And you and I . . ."

I nodded. "Careful."

Neither of us mentioned that Nanterre had specifically threatened each of us as his next targets: there was no point. I didn't think he would actually try to kill either of us, but the damage would have to be more than a pinprick to expect a result.

"What's he like?" Litsi said. "You've met him. I've never seen him. Know your enemy . . . the first rule for combat."

"Well, I think he got into all this without thinking it out first," I said. "Last Friday, I think he believed he had only to browbeat the princess heavily enough, and Roland would collapse. That's also very nearly what happened."

"As I understand it, it didn't happen because you were there."

"I don't know. Anyway, on Friday night when he pulled the gun out that had no bullets in . . . I think that may be typical of him. He acts on impulse, without thinking things through. He's used to getting his own way easily because of his hectoring manner. He's used to being obeyed. Since his father died—and his father had customarily indulged him—he has run the construction company pretty well as he likes. I'd say he's quite likely reached the stage where he literally can't believe he can be defied, and especially not by an old, ill man long out of touch with the world.

When Roland rejected him by post, I'd guess he came over thinking 'I'll soon change all that.' I think in some ways he's childish, which doesn't make him less destructive: more so, probably."

I paused, but Litsi made no comment.

"Attacking Danielle," I said. "He thought again that he would have it all his own way. I'll bet it never once occurred to him that she could run faster than he could. He turned up there in a city suit and polished leather shoes. It was a sort of arrogance, an assumption that he would naturally be faster, stronger, dominant. If he'd had any doubts at all, he'd have worn a jogging suit, something like that, and faster shoes."

"And the horses?" Litsi said.

I hated to think of the horses. "They were vulnerable," I said. "And he knew how to kill them. I don't know where he would get a humane killer, but he does deal in guns. He carries one. They attract him, otherwise he wouldn't be wanting to make them. People mostly do what their natures urge, don't they? He may have a real urge to see things die. Wanting to make sure the slaughterers didn't cheat him could be just the only acceptable reason he could give for a darker desire. People always think up reasonable reasons for doing what they want."

"Do you?" he asked curiously.

"Oh, sure. I say I race for the money."

"And you don't?"

"I'd do it for nothing, but being paid is better."

He nodded, having no difficulty in understanding. "So what do you expect next from Nanterre?" he asked.

"Another half-baked attack on one of us. He won't have planned properly for contingencies, but we might find ourselves in nasty spots nevertheless."

"Charming," he said.

"Don't go down dark alleys to meet strangers."

"I never do."

I asked him rather tentatively what he did do, back in Paris, where he lived.

"Frightfully little, I'm afraid," he said. "I have an interest in an art gallery. I spend a good deal of my life looking at paintings. The Louvre expert Danielle and I went to listen to is a very old acquaintance. I was sure she would enjoy . . ." He paused. "She did enjoy it."

"Yes."

I could feel him shift in the passenger seat until he could see me better.

"There was a group of us," he said. "We weren't alone."

"Yes, I know."

He didn't pursue it. He said unexpectedly instead, "I have been married, but we are separated. Technically I am still married. If either of us wished to remarry, there would be a divorce. But she has lovers, and I also . . ." He shrugged. "It's common enough, in France."

I said, "Thank you," after a pause, and he nodded; and we didn't speak of it again.

"I would like to have been an artist," he said after a while. "I studied for years. I can see the genius in great paintings, but for myself . . . I can put paint on canvas, but I haven't the great gift. And you, my friend Kit, are damn bloody lucky to have been endowed with the skill to match your desire."

I was silent; silenced. I'd had the skill from birth, and one couldn't say where it came from; and I hadn't much thought what it would be like to be without it. I looked at life suddenly from Litsi's point of view, and knew that I was in truth damn bloody lucky, that it was the root of my basic happiness, and that I should be humbly grateful.

When we got to Eaton Square I suggested dropping him at the front door while I went to park the car, but he wouldn't hear of it. Dark alleys, he reminded me, and being careful.

"There's some light in the mews," I said.

"All the same, we'll park the car together and walk back together, and take our own advice."

"OK," I said, and reflected that at one-thirty, when I went to fetch Danielle, I would be going alone into the selfsame dark alley, and it would be then that I'd better be careful.

Litsi and I let ourselves in, Dawson meeting us in the hall saying the princess and Beatrice had vanished to their rooms to change and rest.

"Where is Sammy?" I said.

Sammy, Dawson said with faint disapproval, was walking about, and was never in any place longer than a minute. I went upstairs to fetch the new telephone and found Sammy coming down the stairs from the top floor.

"Did you know there's another kitchen up there?" he said.

"Yes, I looked."

"And there's a skylight or two. I rigged a nice little pair of booby traps under those. If you hear a lot of old brass firearms crashing around up there, you get the force here pronto."

I assured him I would, and took him downstairs with me to show him, as well as Dawson and Litsi, how the recording telephone worked.

The normal telephone arrangements in that house were both simple and complicated: there was only one line, but about a dozen scattered instruments.

Incoming calls rang in only three of those: the one in the sitting-room, one in the office where Mrs. Jenkins worked by day, and one in the basement. Whoever was near one of those instruments when a call came in would answer, and if it were for someone else, reach that person via the inter-com, as Dawson had reached me when Wykeham rang the previous Sunday. This arrangement was to save six or more people answering whenever the telephone rang.

From each guest bedroom outgoing calls could be di-rectly made, as from the princess's rooms, and her hus-band's. The house was rarely as full as at present, Dawson said, and the telephone was seldom busy. The system nor-mally worked smoothly.

I explained that to work the new telephone one had simply to unplug the ordinary instrument and plug in the new one.

"If you press that button," I said, pointing, "the whole conversation will be recorded. If you press that one, every-one in the room can hear what's being said."

I plugged the simple box of tricks into the sitting-room socket. "It had better be in here while we are all around. During the day, if everyone's out, like today, it can go to Mrs. Jenkins's office, and at night, if Dawson wouldn't mind, in the basement. It doesn't matter how many calls are unnecessarily recorded, we can scrub them out, but every time . . . if one could develop the habit?"

They all nodded.

"Such an uncouth man," Dawson commented. "I would know that loud voice anywhere."

"It's a pity," Litsi said, when Dawson and Sammy had gone, "that we can't somehow tap Beatrice's phone and record what she says."

"Anytime she's upstairs, like now, we can just lift the receiver and listen."

We lifted the receiver, but no one in the house was talking. We could wait and listen for hours, but meanwhile no outside calls could come in. Regretfully Litsi put the receiver back again, saying we might be lucky, he would try every few minutes; but by the time Beatrice reappeared for dinner the intermittent vigil had produced no results.

I had meanwhile talked to Wykeham and collected the messages off my answering machine, neither a lengthy event, and if anyone had inadvertently broken in on the calls, I'd heard no clicks on the line.

Beatrice came down demanding her "bloody" in a flattering white dress covered in sunflowers, Litsi fussing over her with amiable solicitude, and refusing to be disconcerted by ungraciousness.

"I know you don't want me here," she said bluntly, "but until Roland signs on the dotted line, I'm staying."

The princess came down to dinner, but not Roland, and on our return to the sitting room afterward Litsi, without seeming to, maneuvered everyone around so that it was I who ended up sitting by the telephone. He smiled over his coffee cup, and everyone waited.

When the bell finally rang, Beatrice jumped.

I picked up the receiver, pressing both the recorder and conference buttons; and a voice spoke French loudly into our expectations.

11

Litsi rose immediately to his feet, came over to me and made gestures for me to give him the phone.

"It isn't Nanterre," he said.

He took the receiver, disengaged the conference button and spoke privately in French. *"Oui . . . Non . . . Certainement . . . Ce soir . . . Oui . . . Merci."*

He put down the receiver and almost immediately the bell rang again. Litsi picked up the receiver again, briefly listened, grimaced, pressed the record and conference buttons again, and passed the buck to me.

"It's him," he said succinctly, and indeed everyone could hear the familiar domineering voice saying words that meant nothing to me at all.

"Speak English, please," I said.

"I said," Nanterre said in English, "I wish to speak to Prince Litsi and he is to be brought to the telephone immediately."

"He isn't available," I said. "I can give him a message."

"Who are you?" he said. "I know who you are. You are the jockey."

"Yes."

"I left instructions for you to leave the house."

"I don't obey your instructions."

"You'll regret it."

"In what way?" I asked, but he wouldn't be drawn into a specific threat; quite likely, I supposed, because he hadn't yet thought up a particular mayhem.

"My notary will arrive at the house tomorrow morning at ten o'clock," he said. "He will be shown to the library, as before. He will wait there. Roland de Brescou and Princess Casilia will go down there when he arrives. Also Prince Litsi and Danielle de Brescou will go down. All will sign the form that is in the notary's briefcase. The notary will witness each signature, and carry the document away in his briefcase. Is this understood?"

"It is understood," I said calmly, "but it's not going to happen."

"It must happen."

"There's no document in the briefcase."

It stopped him barely a second. "My notary will bring a paper bearing the same form of words. Everyone will sign the notary's document."

"No, they aren't ready to," I said.

"I have warned what will happen if the document is not signed."

"What will happen?" I asked. "You can't make people behave against their consciences."

"Every conscience has its price," he said furiously, and instantly disconnected. The telephone clicked a few times and came forth with the dialing tone, and I put the receiver back in its cradle to shut it off.

Litsi shook his head regretfully. "He's being cautious. Nothing he said can be presented to the police as a threat requiring action on their part."

"You should all sign his document," Beatrice said aggrievedly, "and be done with all this obstruction to expanding his business."

No one bothered to argue with her: the ground had already been covered too often. Litsi then asked the princess if she would mind if he and I went out for a little while. Sammy was still in the house to look after things until John Grundy came, and I would be back in good time to fetch Danielle.

The princess acquiesced to this arrangement while looking anything but ecstatic over further time alone with Beatrice, and it was with twinges of guilt that I happily followed Litsi out of the room.

"We'll go in a taxi," he said, "to the Marylebone Plaza hotel."

"That's not your sort of place," I observed mildly.

"We're going to meet someone. It's his sort of place."

"Who?"

"Someone to tell you about the arms trade."

"Really?" I said, interested. "Who is he?"

"I don't precisely know. We are to go to room eleven twelve and talk to a Mr. Mohammed. That isn't his real name, which he would prefer we didn't know. He will be helpful, I'm told."

"How did you find him?" I asked.

Litsi smiled. "I didn't exactly. But I asked someone in France who would know . . . who could tell me what's going on in the handguns world. Mr. Mohammed is the result. Be satisfied with that."

"OK."

"Your name is Mr. Smith," he said. "Mine is Mr. Jones."

"Such stunning originality."

The Marylebone Plaza hotel was about three miles distant from Eaton Square geographically and in a different world economically. The Marylebone Plaza was frankly a bare-bones overnight stopping place for impecunious travelers, huge, impersonal, a shelter for the anonymous. I'd passed it fairly often but never been through its doors before, nor, it was clear, had Litsi. We made our way however across an expanse of hard gray mottled flooring, and took an elevator to the eleventh floor.

Upstairs the passages were narrow, though carpeted; the lighting economical. We peered at door numbers, found 1112, and knocked.

The door was opened to us by a swarthy-skinned man in a good suit with a white shirt, gold cuff links, and an impassive expression.

"Mr. Jones and Mr. Smith," Litsi said.

The man opened the door further and gestured to us to go in, and inside we found another man similarly dressed, except that he wore also a heavy gold ring inset with four diamonds arranged in a square.

"Mohammed," he said, extending the hand with the ring to be shaken. He nodded over our shoulders to his friend, who silently went out the door, closing it behind him.

Mohammed, somewhere between Litsi's age and mine, I judged, had dark hair, dark eyes, olive skin and a heavy dark mustache. The opulence of the ring was echoed in the leather suitcase lying on the bed and in his wristwatch, which looked like gold nuggets strung together round his wrist.

He was in good humor, and apologized for meeting us "where no one would know any of us."

"I am legitimately in the arms trade," he assured us. "I will tell you anything you want to know, as long as you do not say who told you."

He apologized again for the fact that the room was furnished with a single chair, and offered it to Litsi. I perched against a table, Mohammed sat on the bed. There were reddish curtains across the window, a brown patterned carpet on the floor, a striped cotton bedspread; all clean-looking and in good repair.

"I will leave in an hour," Mohammed said, consulting the nuggets. "You wish to ask about plastic guns. Please go ahead."

"Er . . ." Litsi said.

"Who makes them?" I asked.

Mohammed switched his dark gaze my way. "The best-known," he said straightforwardly, "are made by Glock of Austria. The Glock 17." He reached unhurriedly toward the suitcase and unclipped the locks. "I brought one to show you."

Beneath his educated English there was an accent I couldn't place. Arab, in some way, I thought. Definitely Mediterranean, not Italian, perhaps French.

"The Glock 17," he was saying, "is mostly plastic but has metal parts. Future guns of this sort can be made entirely from plastic. It's a matter of a suitable formula for the material."

From the suitcase he produced a neat square black box.

"This handgun is legitimately in my possession," he said.

"Despite the manner of our meeting, I am a reputable dealer."

We assured him that we hadn't thought otherwise.

He nodded in satisfaction and took the lid off the box. Inside, packed in a molded tray, like a toy, lay a black pistol, an ammunition clip, and eighteen golden bullets, flat caps uppermost, points invisible, arranged neatly in three horizontal rows of six.

Mohammed lifted the weapon out of the box.

"This pistol," he said, "has many advantages. It is light, it is cheaper and easier to make than all-metal guns, and also it is more accurate."

He let the information sink into our brains in true salesman fashion.

"It pulls apart." He showed us, snapping off the entire top of the pistol, revealing a metal rod lying within. "This is the metal barrel." He picked it out. "There is also a metal spring. The bullets also are metal. The butt and the ammunition clip are plastic. The pieces pop back together again very easily." He reassembled the pistol fast, closing its top into place with a snap. "Extremely easy, as you see. The clip holds nine bullets at a time. People who use this weapon, including some police forces, consider it a great advance, the forerunner of a whole new concept of handguns."

"Aren't they trying to ban it in America?" Litsi said.

"Yes." Mohammed shrugged. "Amendment 4194 to Title 18, forbidding the import, manufacture and sale of any such gun made after January 1, 1986. It is because the plastic is undetectable by X-ray scanners. They fear the guns will be carried through airports and into government buildings by terrorists."

"And won't they?" I said.

"Perhaps." He shrugged. "Approximately two million private citizens in America own handguns," he said. "They believe in the right to carry arms. This Glock pistol is the beginning of the future. It may result in the widespread development of plastic-detectors. And perhaps in the banning of all hand luggage on airplanes except small ladies' handbags and flat briefcases that can be searched by hand." He looked from me to Litsi. "Is terrorism your concern?"

"No," Litsi said. "Not directly."

Mohammed seemed relieved. "This gun wasn't invented as a terrorist weapon," he said. "It is seriously a good pistol, better all round."

"We understand that," I said. "How profitable is it?"

"To whom?"

"To the manufacturer."

"Ah." He cleared his throat. "It depends." He considered. "It costs less to make and is consequently cheaper in price than metal guns. The profit margin may not be so very different overall, but the gross profit of course depends on the number of items sold." He smiled cheerfully. "It's calculated that most of the two million people already owning guns in America, for instance, will want to upgrade to the new product. The new is better and more prestigious, and so on. Also their police forces would like to have them. Apart from there, the world is thirsty for guns for use—private Americans, you understand, own them mostly for historical reasons, for sport, for fantasy, for the feeling of personal power, not because they intend to kill people—but in many many places, killing is the purpose. Killing, security and defense. The market is wide open for really cheap good reliable new pistols. For a while at least, until the demand is filled, manufacturers could make big honest money fast."

Litsi and I listened to him with respect.

"What about dishonest money?" I asked.

He paused only momentarily. "It depends who we're talking about."

"We're still talking about the manufacturer," I said.

"Ah. A corporation?"

"A private company with one man in charge."

He produced a smile packed with worldly disillusion.

"Such a man can print his own millions."

"How, exactly?" I asked.

"The easiest way," he said, "is to ship the product in two parts." He pulled the plastic gun again into components. "Say you packed all the pieces into a box, like this, omitting only the barrel. A barrel, say, made of special plastic that won't melt or buckle from the heat caused by the friction of the bullet passing through."

He looked at us to see if we appreciated such simple matters, and seemingly reassured, went on. "The manufacturer exports the barrels separately. This, he says, ensures that if either shipment is diverted—which is a euphemism for stolen—in passage, the goods will be useless. Only when both shipments have reached their destination safely can the pistols be assembled. Right?"

"Right," we both said.

"The manufacturer does all the correct paperwork. Each shipment is exported accompanied by customs dockets, each shipment is what it purports to be, everything is legal. The next step depends on how badly the customer wants the guns."

"How do you mean?" Litsi said.

"Suppose," Mohammed answered, enjoying himself, "the customer's need is great and pressing. The manufacturer sends the guns without the barrels. The customer pays. The manufacturer sends the barrels. Good?"

We nodded.

"The manufacturer tells the customer he must pay the price on the invoices to the manufacturing company, but he must also pay a sum into a different bank account—number and country supplied—and when *that* payment is safely in the manufacturer's secret possession, then he will dispatch the barrels."

"Simple," I said.

"Of course. A widespread practice. The sort of thing that goes on the whole world over. Money up front, aboveboard settlement, offshore funds sub rosa."

"Kickbacks," I said.

"Of course. In many countries it is the accepted system. Trade cannot continue without it. A little commission, here and there . . ." He shrugged. "Your manufacturer with an all-plastic reliable cheaply made handgun could pass an adequate profit through his company's books and pocket a fortune for himself out of sight."

He reassembled the gun dexterously and held it out to me.

"Feel it," he said. "An all-plastic gun would be much lighter even than this."

I took the gun, looking at its matt black surface of purposeful shape, the metal rim of the barrel showing at the business end. It certainly was remarkably light to handle, even with metal parts. All-plastic, it could be a plaything for babies.

With an inward shiver I gave it to Litsi. It was the

second time in four days I'd been instructed in the use of handguns, and although I'd handled one before, I wasn't a good shot, nor ever likely to practice. Litsi weighed the gun thoughtfully in his palm and returned it to its owner.

"Are we talking of any manufacturer in particular?" Mohammed asked.

"About one who wants to be granted a license to manufacture and export plastic guns," I said, "but who hasn't been in the arms business before."

He raised his eyebrows. "In France?"

"Yes," Litsi said without surprise, and I realized that Mohammed must have known the inquiry had come to him through French channels, even if it hadn't been he who'd spoken to Litsi on the telephone.

Mohammed pursed his lips under the big mustache. "To get a license your manufacturer would have to be a person of particularly good standing. These licenses, you understand, are never thrown about like confetti. He must certainly have the capability, the factory, that is to say, also the prototype, also probably definite orders, but above all he must have the good name."

"You've been extremely helpful," Litsi said.

Mohammed radiated bonhomie.

"How would the manufacturer set about selling his guns? Would he advertise?" I said.

"Certainly. In firearms and trade magazines the world over. He might also engage an agent, such as myself." He smiled. "I work on commission. I am well known. People who want guns come to me and say, 'What will suit us best? How much is it? How soon can you get it?'" He spread his palms. "I'm a middleman. We are indispensable." He looked at his watch. "Anything else?"

I said on impulse, "If someone wanted a humane killer, could you supply it? A captive bolt?"

"Obsolete," he said promptly. "In England, made by Accles and Shelvoke in Birmingham. Do you mean those? Point 405 caliber, perhaps? One point two-five grain caps?"

"I daresay," I said. "I don't know."

"I don't deal in humane killers. They're too specialized. It wouldn't be worth your while to pay me to find you one. There are many around, all out of date. I would ask older veterinarians, they might be pleased to sell. You'd need a license to own one, of course." He paused. "To be frank, gentlemen, I find it most profitable to deal with customers to whom personal licenses are irrelevant."

"Is there anyone," I asked, "and please don't take this as an insult, because it's not meant that way, but is there anyone to whom you would refuse to sell guns?"

He took no offense. He said, "Only if I thought they couldn't or wouldn't pay. On moral grounds, no. I don't ask what they want them for. If I cared, I'd be in the wrong trade. I sell the hardware, I don't agonize over its use."

Both Litsi and I seemed to have run out of questions. Mohammed put the pistol back into its box, where it sat neatly above its prim little rows of bullets. He replaced the lid on the box and returned the whole to the suitcase.

"Never forget," he said, still smiling, "that attack and defense are as old as the human race. Once upon a time I would have been selling nicely sharpened spearhead flints."

"Mr. Mohammed," I said, "thank you very much."

He nodded affably. Litsi stood up and shook hands again with the diamond ring, as did I, and Mohammed said if we saw his friend loitering in the passage not to worry and not to speak to him, he would return to the room when we had gone.

We paid no attention to the friend waiting by the elevators and rode down without incident to the ground floor. It wasn't until we were in a taxi on the way back to Eaton Square that either of us spoke.

"He was justifying himself," Litsi said.

"Everyone does. It's healthy."

He turned his head. "How do you mean?"

"The alternative is guilty despair. Self-justification may be an illusion, but it keeps you from suicide."

"You could self-justify suicide."

I smiled at him sideways. "So you could."

"Nanterre," he said, "has a powerful urge to sharpen flints."

"Mm. Lighter, cheaper, razorlike flints."

"Bearing the de Brescou cachet."

"I had a powerful vision," I said, "of Roland shaking hands on a deal with Mohammed."

Litsi laughed. "We must save him from the justification."

"How did you get hold of Mohammed?" I asked.

"One of the useful things about being a prince," Litsi said, "is that if one seriously asks, one is seldom refused. Another is that one knows and has met a great many people in useful positions. I simply set a few wheels in motion, much as you did yesterday, incidentally, with Lord Vaughnley." He paused. "Why is a man you defeated so anxious to please you?"

"Well, in defeating him I also saved him. Maynard Allardeck was out to take over his newspaper by fair means and definitely foul, and I gave him the means of stopping him permanently, which was a copy of that film."

"I do see," Litsi said ironically, "that he owes you a favor or two."

"Also," I said, "the boy who gambled half his inheritance away under Maynard's influence was Hugh Vaughnley, Lord Vaughnley's son. By threatening to publish the film, Lord Vaughnley made Maynard give the inheritance back. The inheritance, actually, was shares in the *Towncrier* newspaper."

"A spot of poetic blackmail. Your idea?"

"Well, sort of."

He chuckled. "I suppose I should disapprove. It was surely against the law."

"The law doesn't always deliver justice. The victim mostly loses. Too often the law can only punish, it can't put things right."

"And you think righting the victims' wrongs is more important than anything else?"

"Where it's possible, the highest priority."

"And you'd break the law to do it?"

"It's too late at night for being tied into knots," I said, "and we're back at Eaton Square."

We went upstairs to the sitting room and, the princess and Beatrice having gone to bed, drank a brandy nightcap in relaxation. I liked Litsi more and more as a person, and wished him permanently on the other side of the globe; and looking at him looking at me, I wondered if he were possibly thinking the same thing.

"What are you doing tomorrow?" he said.

"Racing at Bradbury."

"Where's that?"

"Halfway to Devon."

"I don't know where you get the energy." He yawned. "I spent a gentle afternoon walking round Ascot racecourse, and I'm whacked."

Large and polished, he drank his brandy, and in time we unplugged the recording telephone, carried it down to the basement, and replugged it in the hallway there. Then we went up to the ground floor and paused for a moment outside Litsi's door.

"Goodnight," I said,

"Goodnight." He hesitated, and then held out his hand. I shook it. "Such a silly habit," he said with irony, "but what else can one do?" He gave me a sketchy wave and went into his room, and I continued on up to see if I were still to sleep among the bamboo shoots, which it seemed I was.

I dozed on top of the bedclothes for an hour or so and then went down, out, and round the back to get the car to fetch Danielle.

I thought, as I walked quietly into the dark, deserted alley, that it really was a perfect place for an ambush.

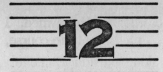

The alley was a cobbled cul-de-sac about twenty feet wide and a hundred yards long, with a wider place at the far end for turning, the backs of tall buildings closing it all in like a canyon. Its sides were lined with garage doors, the wide garages themselves running in under the backs of the buildings, and unlike many other mews where the garages had originally been built as housing for coaches and horses, Falmouth Mews, as it was called, had no residential entrances.

By day the mews was alive and busy, as a firm of motor mechanics occupied several of the garages, doing repairs for the surrounding neighborhood. At night, when they'd gone home, the place was a shadowy lane of big closed doors, lit only from the windows of the buildings above.

The garage where Thomas kept the Rolls was farther than halfway in. Next, beyond, was a garage belonging to the mechanics, which Thomas had persuaded them to rent temporarily to the princess, to accommodate Danielle's car (now recovered from the menders by Thomas). My Mercedes, unhoused, was parked along outside Danielle's garage doors, and other cars, here and there along the mews, were similarly placed. In a two-car family, one typically was in the generous-sized lockup, the second lengthways outside.

Around and behind these second cars there were a myriad of hiding places.

I ought to have brought a torch, I thought. Tomorrow I would buy one. The mews could shelter a host of monsters . . . and Beatrice knew what time I set off each night to Chiswick.

I walked down the center of the alley feeling my heart thud, yet I'd gone down there the night before without a tremor. The power of imagination, I thought wryly: and nothing rustled in the undergrowth, nothing pounced, the tiger wasn't around for the goat.

The car looked exactly as I'd left it, but I checked the wiring under the hood and under the dashboard before switching on the ignition. I checked there was no oil leaking from under the engine, and that all the tires were hard, and I tested the brakes with a sudden stop before turning out into the road.

Satisfied, I drove without trouble to Chiswick, collecting Danielle at two o'clock. She was tired from the long day and talked little, telling me only that they'd spent all evening on a story about snow and ice houses that she thought was a waste of time.

"What snow and ice houses?" I asked, more just to talk to her than from wanting to know.

"Sculptures for a competition. Some of the guys had

been out filming them in an exhibition. Like sandcastles, only made of snow and ice. Some of them were quite pretty and even had lights inside them. The guys said the place they were in was like filming in an igloo without a blanket. All good fun, I guess, but not world news."

She yawned and fell silent, and in a short while we were back in the mews: it was always a quick journey at night, with no traffic.

"You can't keep coming to pick me up," she said, as we walked round into Eaton Square.

"I like to."

"Litsi told me that the man in the hood was Henri Nanterre." She shivered. "I don't know if it makes it better or worse. Anyway, I'm not working Friday nights right now, or Saturdays or Sundays, of course. You can sleep, Friday night."

We let ourselves into the house with the new keys and said goodnight again on her landing. We never had slept in the same bed in that house, so there were no such memories or regrets to deal with, but I fiercely wished as I walked up one more flight that she would come up there with me: yet it had been no use suggesting it, because her goodnight kiss had again been a defense, not a promise, and had landed again any way but squarely.

Give her time. Time was an aching anxiety with no certainty ahead.

Breakfast, warmth and newspapers were to be found each day down in the morning room, whose door was across the hall from Litsi's. I was in there about nine on that Thursday morning, drinking orange juice and checking on the day's runners at Bradbury, when the intercom buzzed, and

Dawson's voice told me there was a call from Mr. Harlow.

I picked up the outside receiver fearfully.

"Wykeham?"

"Oh, Kit. Look, I thought I'd better tell you, but don't alarm the princess. We had a prowler last night."

"Are the horses all right? Kinley?"

"Yes, yes. Nothing much happened. The man with the dog said his dog was restless, as if someone was moving about. He says his dog was very alert and whining softly for a good half hour, and that they patrolled the courtyards twice. They didn't see anyone, though, and after a while the dog relaxed again. So what do you think?"

"I think it's a bloody good job you've got the dog."

"Yes, it's very worrying."

"What time was all this?"

"About midnight. I'd gone to bed, of course, and the guard didn't wake me, as nothing had happened. There's no sign that anyone was here."

"Just keep on with the patrols," I said, "and make sure you don't get the man that slept in the hay barn."

"No. I told them not to send him. They've all been very sharp, since that first night."

We discussed the two horses he was sending to Bradbury, neither of them the princess's. He sometimes sent his slowest horses to Bradbury in the belief that if they didn't win there, they wouldn't win anywhere, but he avoided it most of the time. It was a small country course, with a flat circuit of little more than a mile, easy to ride on if one stuck to the inside.

"Give Melissande a nice ride, now."

"Yes, Wykeham," I said. Melissande had been before my time. "Do you mean Pinkeye?"

"Well, of course." He cleared his throat. "How long are you staying in Eaton Square?"

"I don't know. I'll tell you, though, when I leave."

We disconnected and I put a slice of wholemeal bread in the toaster and thought about prowlers.

Litsi came in and poured himself some coffee. "I thought," he said conversationally, assembling a bowl of muesli and cream, "that I might go to the races today."

"To Bradbury?" I was surprised. "It's not like Ascot. It's the bare bones of the industry. Not much comfort."

"Are you saying you don't want to take me?"

"No. Just warning you."

He sat down at the table and watched me eat toast without butter or marmalade.

"Your diet's disgusting."

"I'm used to it."

He watched me swallow a pill with black coffee. "What are those for?" he asked.

"Vitamins."

He shook his head resignedly and dug into his own hopelessly fattening concoction, and Danielle came in looking fresh and clear-eyed in a baggy white sweater.

"Hi," she said to neither of us in particular. "I wondered if you'd be here. What are you doing today?"

"Going to the races," Litsi said.

"Are you?" She looked at him directly, in surprise. "With Kit?"

"Certainly, with Kit."

"Oh. Then . . . er . . . can I come?"

She looked from one of us to the other, undoubtedly seeing double pleasure.

"In half an hour," I said, smiling.

"Easy."

So all three of us went to Bradbury races, parting in the hall from the princess, who had come down to go through some secretarial work with Mrs. Jenkins and who looked wistfully at our outdoor clothes, and also from Beatrice, who had come down out of general nosiness.

Her sharp round gaze fastened on me. "Are you coming back?" she demanded.

"Yes, he is," the princess said smoothly. "And tomorrow we can all go to see my two runners at Sandown, isn't that nice?"

Beatrice looked not quite sure how the one followed on the other and, in the moment of uncertainty, Litsi, Danielle and I departed.

Bradbury racecourse, we found when we arrived, was undergoing an ambitious upgrading. There were notices everywhere apologizing for the inconvenience of heaps of builders' materials and machines. A whole new grandstand was going up inside scaffolding in the cheaper ring, and most of the top tier of the members' stand was being turned into a glassed-in viewing room with tables, chairs and refreshments. They had made provision up there also for a backward-facing viewing gallery, from which one could see the horses walk round in the parade ring.

There was a small model on a table outside the weighing room, showing what it would all be like when finished, and the racecourse executives were going around with pleased smiles accepting compliments.

Litsi and Danielle went off in search of a drink and a sandwich in the old unrefurbished bar under the emerging dream, and I, sliding into nylon tights, breeches and boots, tried not to think about that too much. I pulled on a thin vest, and my valet neatly tied the white stock around my neck. After that I put on the padded back-guard, which saved one's spine and kidneys from too much damage, and on top of that the first set of colors for the day. Crash helmet, goggles, whip, number cloth, weight cloth, saddle; I checked them all, weighed out, handed the necessary to Dusty to go and saddle up, put on an anorak because of the cold and went out to ride.

I wouldn't have minded, just once, having a day when I could stand on the stands and go racing with Danielle like anyone else. Eat a sandwich, have a drink, place a bet. I saw them smiling and waving to me as I rode onto the track, and I waved back, wanting to be right there beside them on the ground.

The horse I was riding won the race, which would surprise and please Wykeham but not make up for Col's losing the day before.

Besides Wykeham's two runners I'd been booked for three others. I rode one of those without results in the second race and put Pinkeye's red and blue striped colors on for the third, walking out in my warming anorak toward the parade ring to talk to the fussiest and most critical of all Wykeham's owners.

I didn't get as far as the parade ring. There was a cry high up, and a voice calling, "Help," and along with everyone else I twisted my head round to see what was happening.

There was a man hanging by one hand from the new viewing balcony high on the members' stand. A big man in a dark overcoat.

Litsi.

In absolute horror I watched him swing round until he

had two hands on the top of the balcony wall, but he was too big and heavy to pull himself up, and below him there was a fifty-foot drop direct to hard tarmac.

I sprinted over there, tore off my anorak and laid it on the ground directly under where Litsi hung.

"Take off your coat," I said to the nearest man. "Lay it on the ground."

"Someone must go up and help him," he said. "Someone will go."

"Take off your coat." I turned to a woman. "Take off your coat. Lay it on the ground. Quick, quick, lay coats on the ground."

She looked at me blindly. She was wearing a full-length expensive fur. She slid out of her coat and threw it on top of my anorak, and said fiercely to the man next to her, "Take off your coat, take off your coat."

I ran from person to person, "Take off your coat, quick, quick . . . Take off your coat."

A whole crowd had collected, staring upward, arrested on their drift back to the stands for the next race.

"Take off your coat," I could hear people saying. "Take off your coat."

Dear God, Litsi, I prayed, just hang on.

There were other people yelling to him, "Hang on, hang on," and one or two foolishly screaming, and it seemed to me there was a great deal of noise, although very many were silent.

A little boy with huge eyes unzipped his tiny blue anorak and pulled off his small patterned jersey and flung them onto the growing, spreading pile, and I heard him running about in the crowd, in his bright cotton T shirt, his high voice calling, "Quick, quick, take off your coats."

It was working. The coats came off in dozens and were thrown, were passed through the crowd, were chucked higgledy-piggledy to form a mattress, until the circle on the ground was wide enough to contain him if he fell, but could be thicker, thicker.

No one had reached Litsi from the balcony side: no strong arms clutching to haul him up.

Coats were flying like leaves. The word had spread to everyone in sight. "Take off your coat, take off your coat, quick . . . quick . . ."

When Litsi fell he looked like another flying overcoat, except that he came down fast, like a plummet. One second he was hanging there, the next he was down. He fell straight to begin with, then his heavy shoulders tipped his balance backward and he landed almost flat on his back.

He bounced heavily on the coats and rolled and slid off them and ended with his head on one coat and his body on the tarmac, sprawling on his side, limp as a rag.

I sprang to kneel beside him and saw immediately that although he was dazed, he was truly alive. Hands stretched to help him up, but he wasn't ready for that, and I said, "Don't move him. Let him move first. You have to be careful."

Everyone who went racing knew about spinal injuries and not moving jockeys until it was safe, and there I was, in my jockey's colors, to remind them. The hands were ready, but they didn't touch.

I looked up at that crowd, all in shirtsleeves, all shivering with cold, all saints. Some were in tears, particularly the woman who'd laid her mink on the line.

"Litsi," I said, looking down and seeing some sort of order return to his eyes. "Litsi, how are you doing?"

"I . . . Did I fall?" He moved a hand, and then his feet, just a little, and the crowd murmured with relief.

"Yes, you fell," I said. "Just stay there for a minute. Everything's fine."

Somebody above was calling down, "Is he all right?" and there, up on the balcony, were the two men who'd apparently gone up to save him.

The crowd shouted, "Yes," and started clapping, and in almost gala mood began collecting their coats from the pile. There must have been almost two hundred of them, I thought, watching. Anoraks, huskies, tweeds, raincoats, furs, suit jackets, sweaters, even a horse rug. It was taking much longer to disentangle the huge heap than it had to collect it.

The little boy with big eyes picked up his blue anorak and zipped it on over his jersey, staring at me. I hugged him. "What's your name?" I said.

"Matthew."

"You're a great guy."

"That's my daddy's coat," he said, "under the man's head."

"Ask him to leave it there just another minute."

Someone had run to fetch the first-aid men, who arrived with a stretcher.

"I'm all right," Litsi said weakly, but he was still winded and disorientated, and made no demur when they made preparations for transporting him.

Danielle was suddenly there beside him, her face white.

"Litsi," she was saying, "oh, God . . ." She looked at me. "I was waiting for him . . . someone said a man fell . . . is he all right?"

"He's going to be," I said. "He'll be fine."

"Oh . . ."

I put my arms round her. "It's all right. Really it is. Nothing seems to be hurting him, he's just had his breath knocked out."

She slowly disengaged herself and walked away beside the stretcher when they lifted it onto a rolling platform, a gurney.

"Are you his wife?" I heard a first-aid man say.

"No . . . a friend."

The little boy's father picked up his coat and shook my hand. The woman picked up her squashed mink, brushed dust off it and gave me a kiss. A Steward came out and said would I now please get on my horse and go down to the start, as the race would already be off late, and I looked at the racecourse clock and saw in amazement that it was barely fifteen minutes since I'd walked out of the weighing room.

All the horses, all the owners and trainers were still in the parade ring, as if time had stopped, but now the jockeys were mounting; death had been averted, life could thankfully go on.

I picked up my anorak. All the coats had been reclaimed, and it lay there alone on the tarmac, with my whip underneath. I looked up at the balcony, so far above, so deserted and unremarkable. Nothing suddenly seemed real, yet the questions hadn't even begun to be asked. Why had he been up there? How had he come to be clinging to life by his fingertips? In what way had he not been careful?

Litsi lay on a bed in the first-aid room until the races were over, but insisted then that he had entirely recovered and was ready to return to London.

He apologized to the racecourse executive for having been so foolish as to go up to the balcony to look at the new, much-vaunted view, and said that it was entirely his own clumsiness that had caused him to stumble over some builders' materials and lose his balance.

When asked for his name, he'd given a shortened version of his surname without the "prince" in front, and he hoped there wouldn't be too much public fuss over his stupidity.

He was sitting in the back of the car, telling us all this, Danielle sitting beside him, as we started toward London.

"How did you stumble?" I asked, glancing at him from time to time in the driving mirror. "Was there a lot of junk up there?"

"Planks and things." He sounded puzzled. "I don't really know how I stumbled. I stood on something that rocked, and I put a hand out to steady myself, and it went out into space, over the wall. It happened so fast . . . I just lost my footing."

"Did anyone push you?" I asked.

"Kit!" Danielle said, horrified, but it had to be considered, and Litsi, it seemed, had already done so.

"I've been lying there all afternoon," he said slowly, "trying to remember exactly how it happened. I didn't see anyone up there at all, I'm certain of that. I stood on something that rocked like a seesaw, and totally lost my balance. I wouldn't say I was pushed."

"Well," I said thoughtfully, "do you mind if we go back there? I should have gone up for a look when I'd finished racing."

"The racecourse people went up," Litsi said. "They came and told me that there was nothing particularly dangerous, but of course I shouldn't have gone."

"We'll go back," I said, and although Danielle protested that she'd be late for work, back we went.

Leaving Danielle and Litsi outside in the car, I walked through the gates and up the grandstand. As with most grandstands, it was a long haul to the top, up not-too-generous stairways, and one could see why, with a stream of people piling up that way to the main tier to watch the race, those going up to rescue Litsi from above had been a fair time on their journey.

The broad viewing steps of the main tier led right down to the ground and were openly accessible, on the side facing the racecourse, but the upper tier could be reached only by the stairways, of which there were two, one at each end.

I went up the stairway at the end nearest the weighing room, the stairway Litsi said he had used to reach the place where he'd overbalanced. Looking up at the back of the grandstand from the ground, that place was near the end of the balcony, on the left.

The stairway led first onto the upper steps of the main tier, and then continued upward, and I climbed to the top landing, where the refreshment room was in process of construction.

The whole area had been glassed in, leaving only the balcony open. The balcony ran along the back of the refreshment room, which had several glass doors, now closed, to lead eventually to the sandwiches. Inside the glass and without, there were copious piles of builders' materials, planks, drums of paint and ladders.

I went gingerly forward to the cold, open, windy balcony, toward the place where Litsi had overbalanced, and saw what had very likely happened. Planks lay side by side and several deep along all the short passage to the balcony, raising one, as one walked along them, higher than normal in proportion to the chest-high wall. When I was walking on the planks, the wall ahead seemed barely waist-high and Litsi was taller than I by three or four inches.

Whatever had rocked under Litsi's feet was no longer rocking, but several planks by the balcony wall itself were scattered like spillikins, not lying flat as in the passage. I picked my way among them, feeling them move when I pushed, and reached the spot where Litsi had fallen.

With my feet firmly on the floor, I looked over. One could see all the parade-ring area beautifully, with magnificent hills beyond. Very attractive, that balcony, and with one's feet on the floor, very safe.

I went along its whole length intending to go down by the stairway at the other end, nearest the car park, but found I couldn't: the stairs themselves were missing, being in the middle of reconstruction. I walked back to the end where I had come up, renegotiated the planks, and descended to ground level.

"Well?" Litsi asked, when I was back in the car. "What did you think?"

"Those planks looked pretty unsafe."

"Yes," he said ruefully, as I started the car and drove out of the racecourse gates. "I thought, after I'd overbalanced, and managed somehow to catch hold of the wall, that if I just hung on, someone would come and rescue me, but you know, my fingers just gave way. I didn't leave go consciously. When I was falling, I thought I would die . . . and I would have done . . . it's incredible that all those people took off their coats." He paused, "I wish I could thank them," he said.

"I couldn't think where you'd got to," Danielle reflected. "I was waiting for you on the stands, where we'd arranged to meet after I'd been to the ladies' room. I didn't imagine . . ."

"But," said Litsi, "I went up to that balcony because I was supposed to meet you up there, Danielle."

I stopped the car abruptly.

"Say that again," I said.

Litsi said it again. "I got this message that Danielle was waiting for me up on the balcony to look at the view."

"I didn't send any such message," Danielle said blankly. "I was waiting where we'd watched the race before, where we'd said we'd meet.."

"Who gave you the message?" I asked Litsi.

"Just a man."

"What did he look like?"

"Well . . . an ordinary man. Not very young. He had a *Sporting Life* in his hands, and a sort of form book, with his finger keeping the place, and binoculars."

"What sort of voice?"

"Just . . . ordinary."

I let the brakes off with a sigh and started off toward Chiswick. Litsi had walked straight into a booby trap that

186

had been meant either to frighten him or to kill him, and no one would have set it but Henri Nanterre. I hadn't seen Nanterre at the races, and neither Litsi nor Danielle knew him by sight.

If Nanterre had set the trap, he'd known where Litsi would be that day, and the only way he could have known was via Beatrice. I couldn't believe that she would have known what use would be made of her little tit-bit, and it occurred to me that I didn't want her to know, either. It was important that Beatrice should keep right on telling.

Litsi and Danielle were quiet in the back of the car, no doubt traveling along much the same mental track. They protested, though, when I asked them not to tell Beatrice about the fake message.

"But she's got to know," Danielle said vehemently. "Then she'll see she must *stop* it. She'll see how murderous that man is."

"I don't want her to stop it just yet," I said. "Not until Tuesday."

"Why ever not? Why Tuesday?"

"We'll do what Kit wants," Litsi said. "I'll tell Beatrice just what I told the racecourse people, that I went up to look at the view."

"She's dangerous," Danielle said.

"I don't see how we can catch Nanterre without her," I said. "So be a darling."

I wasn't sure whether it was the actual word that silenced her, but she made no more objections, and we traveled for a while without saying anything significant. Litsi's arms and shoulders were aching from the strain of having hung on to the wall so long, and he shifted uncomfortably from time to time, making small grunts.

I went back to thinking about the man who had delivered the misleading message, and asked Litsi if he was absolutely positive the man had used the word "Danielle."

"Positive," Litsi said without hesitation. "What he said to me first was, 'Do you know someone called Danielle?' When I said I did, he said she wanted me to go up the stairs to the balcony to look at the view. He pointed up there. So I went."

"OK," I said. "Then we'll take a spot of positive action."

Like almost everyone in the racing world, I had a telephone in my car, and I put a call through to the *Towncrier* and asked for the Sports Desk. I wasn't sure whether their racing correspondent, Bunty Ireland, would be in the office at that time, but it seemed he was. He hadn't been at Bradbury: he went mostly to major meetings and on other days wrote his column in the office.

"I want to pay for an advertisement," I told him, "but it has to be on the racing page and in a conspicuous place."

"Are you touting for rides?" he asked sardonically. "A Grand National mount? Have saddle, will travel, that sort of thing?"

"Yeah," I said. "Very funny." Bunty had an elephantine sense of humor but he was kind at heart. "Write this down word for word, and persuade the racing-page editor to print it in nice big noticeable letters."

"Fire away, then."

"Large reward offered to anyone who passed on a message from Danielle at Bradbury races on Thursday afternoon." I dictated it slowly and added the telephone number of the house in Eaton Square.

Bunty's mystification came clearly across the air waves. "You want the personal column for that," he said.

"No. The racing page. Did you get it straight?"

He read it over, word for word.

"Hey," he said, "if you were riding at Bradbury perhaps you can confirm this very odd story we've got about a guy falling from a balcony onto a pile of coats. Is someone having us on, or should we print it?"

"It happened," I said.

"Did you see it?"

"Yes," I said.

"Was the guy hurt?"

"No, not at all. Look, Bunty, get the story from someone else, will you? I'm in my car, and I want to get that ad in the *Sporting Life* and the *Racing Post*, before they go to press. And could you give me their numbers?"

"Sure, hold on."

I put the receiver down temporarily and passed my pen and notebook back to Danielle, and when Bunty returned with the numbers, repeated them aloud for her to write down.

"Hey, Kit," Bunty said, "give me a quote I can use about your chances on Abseil tomorrow."

"You know I can't, Bunty, Wykeham Harlow doesn't like it."

"Yeah, yeah. He's an uncooperative old bugger."

"Don't forget the ad," I said.

He promised to see to it, and I made the calls with the same request to the two sporting papers.

"Tomorrow and Saturday," I said to them. "In big black type on the front page."

"It'll cost you," they said.

"Send me the bill."

Danielle and Litsi listened to these conversations in silence, and when I'd finished, Litsi said doubtfully, "Do you expect any results?"

"You never know. You can't get any results if you don't try."

Danielle said, "Your motto for life."

"Not a bad one," Litsi said.

We dropped Danielle at the studio just on time and returned to Eaton Square. Litsi decided to say nothing at all about his narrow escape, and asked for my advice in the matter of strained muscles.

"A sauna and a massage," I said. "Failing that, a long hot soak and some aspirins. And John Grundy might give you a massage tomorrow morning."

He decided on the home cures and, reaching the house, disappeared into his rooms to deal with his woes in private. I continued up to the bamboo room, still uninvaded territory, where, in the evening routine, I telephoned to Wykeham and picked up my messages.

Wykeham said the owners of Pinkeye were irritated that the race had been delayed, and had complained to him that I'd been offhand with them afterward.

"But Pinkeye won," I said. I'd ridden the whole race automatically, like driving a well-known journey with a preoccupied mind and not remembering a yard of it on arrival. When I'd gone past the winning post I hadn't been able to remember much about the jumps.

"You know what they're like," Wykeham said. "Never satisfied, even when they win."

"Mm," I said. "Is the horse all right?"

All the horses were fine, Wykeham said, and Abseil (pronounced Absail) was jumping out of his skin and should trot up on the morrow.

"Great," I said. "Well, goodnight, Wykeham."

"Goodnight, Paul."

Normality, I thought with a smile, disconnecting, was definitely on its way back.

Dinner was a stilted affair of manufactured conversations, with Roland de Brescou sitting at the head of the table in his wheelchair, looking abstracted.

Beatrice spent some time complaining that Harrods was now impossible (*busloads* of tourists, Casilia) and that Fortnums was too crowded, and that her favorite fur shop had closed and vanished. Beatrice's day of shopping had included a visit to the hairdresser, with a consequent intensification of peach tint. Beatrice's pleasures, I saw, were a way of passing time that had no other purpose: a vista of smothering pointlessness, infinitely depressing. No wonder, I thought, that she complained, with all that void pursuing her.

She looked at me, no doubt feeling my gaze, and said with undisguisable sudden venom, "It's you that's standing in the way of progress. I know it is, don't deny it. Roland admitted it this morning. I'm sure he would have agreed to Henri's plans if it hadn't been for you. He admitted you're against it. You've influenced him. You're evil."

"Beatrice," the princess remonstrated, "he's our guest."

"I don't care," she said passionately, "he shouldn't be. It's he all the time who's standing in my way."

"In *your* way, Beatrice?" Roland asked.

Beatrice hesitated. "In my room," she said finally.

"It's true," I said without aggression, "that I'm against Monsieur de Brescou signing anything against his conscience."

"I'll get rid of you," she said.

"No, Beatrice, really, that's too much," the princess exclaimed. "Kit, please accept my apologies."

"It's all right," I assured her truthfully. "Perfectly all right. I do stand in Mrs. Bunt's way. In the matter of Monsieur acting against his conscience, I always will."

Litsi looked at me speculatively. I had made a very explicit and provocative declaration, and he seemed to be wondering if I was aware of it. I, on the other hand, was glad to have been presented with the opportunity, and I would repeat what I'd said, given the chance.

"You are after Danielle's money," Beatrice said furiously.

"You know she has none."

"After her inheritance from Roland."

The princess and Roland were looking poleaxed. No one, I guessed, had conducted such open warfare before at that polite dinner table.

"On the contrary," I said civilly. "If selling guns would make Monsieur richer, and if I were after Danielle's mythical inheritance, then I would be urging him to sign at once."

She stared at me, temporarily silenced. I kept my face entirely noncommittal, a habit learned from dealing with Maynard Allardeck, and behaved as if we had been having a normal conversation. "In general," I said pleasantly, "I would implacably oppose anyone trying to get their way by threats and harassment. Henri Nanterre has behaved like a thug, and while I'm here I'll try my hardest to ensure he fails in his objective."

Litsi opened his mouth, thought better of it, and said nothing. The speculation however disappeared from his forehead to be replaced by an unspecified anxiety.

"Well," Beatrice said, "well . . ."

I said mildly, as before, "It's really as well to make oneself perfectly clear, isn't it? As you have admirably done, Mrs. Bunt?"

We were eating Dover sole at the time. Beatrice decided there were a good many bones all of a sudden demanding her attention, and Litsi smoothly said that he had been invited to the opening of a new art gallery in Dover Street, on the following Wednesday, and would his Aunt Casilia care to go with him.

"Wednesday?" The princess looked from Litsi to me. "Where's the racing next Wednesday?"

"Folkestone," I said.

The princess accepted Litsi's invitation, because she didn't go to Folkestone normally, and he and she batted a few platitudes across the table to flatten out those Bunt-Fielding ripples. When we moved to the sitting room Litsi again helped make sure I was next to the telephone, but it remained silent all evening. No messages, threats or boasting from Nanterre. It was too much to hope for, I thought, that he had folded his tents and departed.

When Roland, the princess and Beatrice finally went to bed, Litsi, rising to his feet to follow them, said, "You elected yourself as goat, then?"

"I don't intend to get eaten," I said, smiling and standing also.

"Don't go up to any balconies."

"No," I said. "Sleep well."

I did the rounds of the house, but everything seemed safe, and in due time went to the car, to go to fetch Danielle.

The alley seemed just as spooky, and I took even more

precautions with the guts of the car, but again everything appeared safe, and I drove to Chiswick without incident.

Danielle looked pale and tired. "A hectic evening," she said. Her job as bureau coordinator involved deciding how individual news stories should be covered and dispatching camera crews accordingly. I'd been in the studio with her several times and seen her working, seen the mental energy and drive that went into making her the success she'd proved there. I'd seen her decisiveness and her inspirational sparkle, and knew that afterward they could die away fast into weary silence.

The silences between us, though, were no longer companionable spaces of deep accord, but almost embarrassments, as between strangers. We had been passionate weekend lovers through November, December and January, and in her the joy had evaporated from one week to the next.

I drove back to Eaton Square thinking how very much I loved her, how much I longed for her to be as she had been, and when I stopped the car in the mews I said impulsively, before she could get out, "Danielle, please . . . please . . . tell me what's wrong."

It was clumsily said and came straight from desperation, and I was disregarding the princess's advice; and as soon as I'd said it I wished I hadn't because the last thing on earth I wanted to hear her say was that she loved Litsi. I thought I might even be driving her into saying it, and in a panic I said, "Don't answer. It doesn't matter. Don't answer."

She turned her head and looked at me, and then looked away.

"It was wonderful, at the beginning, wasn't it?" she said. "It happened so fast. It was . . . magic."

I couldn't bear to listen. I unlatched the car door to start to get out.

"Wait," she said, "I must—now I've started."

"No," I said. "Don't."

"About a month ago," she said, all the repressed things pouring out in a jumble, "when you had that dreadful fall at Kempton and I saw you lying on a stretcher unconscious while they unloaded you from the ambulance . . . and it gave me diarrhea, I was so frightened you would die . . . and I was overwhelmed by how much danger there is in your life . . . and how much pain . . . and I seemed to see myself here in a strange country . . . with a commitment made for my whole life . . . not just enjoying a delicious unexpected romance but trapped forever into a life far from home, full of fear every day . . . and I didn't know it was so cold and wet here and I was brought up in California . . . and then Litsi came . . . and he knows so much . . . and it seemed so simple being with him going to safe things like exhibitions and not hearing my heart thud . . . I could hear the worry in your voice on the telephone and see it this week in your face, but I couldn't seem to tell you . . ." She paused very briefly. "I told Aunt Casilia. I asked her what to do."

I loosened my throat. "What did she say?" I said.

"She said no one could decide for me. I asked her if she thought I would get used to the idea of living forever in a foreign country, like she has, and also of facing the possibility you'd be killed or horrifically injured . . . and don't say it doesn't happen, there was a jockey killed last week . . . and I asked her if she thought I was stupid."

She swallowed. "She said that nothing would change you, that you are as you are, and I was to see you clearly.

She said the question wasn't whether I could face life here with you, but whether I could face life anywhere without you."

She paused again. "I told her how calm I felt with Litsi . . . She said Litsi was a nice man . . . She said in time I would see . . . understand . . . what I wanted most . . . She said time has a way of resolving things in one's mind . . . she said you would be patient, and she's right, you are, you are . . . But I can't go on like this forever, I know it's unfair. I went racing yesterday and today to see if I could go back . . . but I can't. I hardly watch the races. I blank out of my mind what you're doing . . . that you're there. I promised Aunt Casilia I'd go . . . and try . . . but I just talked to Litsi . . ." Her voice faded in silence, tired and unhappy.

"I love you very much," I said slowly. "Do you want me to give up my job?"

"Aunt Casilia said if I asked, and you did, and we married, it would be disastrous. We would be divorced within five years. She was very vehement. She said I must not ask it, it was totally unfair, I would be destroying you because I don't have your courage." She swallowed convulsively, tears filling her eyes.

I looked along the shadowy mews and thought of danger and fear, those old tamed friends. One couldn't teach anyone how to live with them: it had to come from inside. It got easier with practice, like everything else, but also it could vanish overnight. Nerve came and nerve went: there could be an overload of the capacity for endurance.

"Come on," I said, "it's getting cold." I paused. "Thank you for telling me."

"What . . . are you going to do?"

"Go indoors and sleep till morning."

"No . . ." she sobbed on a laugh. "About what I said."

"I'm going to wait," I said, "like Princess Casilia told me to."

"Told you!" Danielle exclaimed. "Did you tell her?"

"No, I didn't. She said it out of the blue in the parade ring at Ascot."

"Oh," Danielle said in a small voice. "It was on Tuesday, while you were in Devon, that I asked her."

We got out of the car and I locked the doors. What Danielle had said had been bad enough, but not as bad as an irrevocable declaration for Litsi. Until she took off the engagement ring she still wore, I would cling to some sort of hope.

We walked back side by side to the square, and said goodnight again briefly on the landing. I went on upstairs and lay on the bed and suffered a good deal, for which there was no aspirin.

When I went in to breakfast, both Litsi and Danielle were already in the morning room, he sitting at the table reading the *Sporting Life*, she leaning over his shoulder to do the same.

"Is it in?" I said.

"Is what in?" Litsi asked, intently reading.

"The advertisement," I said, "for the message-passer."

"Yes . . . it's in," Litsi said. "There's a picture of you in the paper."

I fetched some grapefruit juice, unexcited. There were photographs of me in newspapers quite often: result of the job.

"It says here," Litsi said, "that champion jockey Kit Fielding saved the life of a man at Bradbury by persuading the crowd to take off their coats . . ." He lowered the paper and stared at me. "You didn't say a word about it being your idea."

Danielle too was staring. "Why didn't you tell us?"

"An uprush of modesty," I said, drinking the juice.

Litsi laughed. "I won't thank you, then."

"No, don't."

Danielle said to me, "Do you want some toast?"

"Yes . . . please," I said.

She walked over to the sideboard, cut a slice of wholemeal bread and put it in the toaster. I watched her do it, and Litsi, I found, watched me. I met his eyes and couldn't tell what he was thinking, and wondered how much had been visible in my own face.

"How are the muscles?" I asked.

"Stiff."

I nodded. The toast popped up in the toaster and Danielle put the slice on a plate, brought it over and put it down in front of me.

"Thank you," I said.

"You're welcome." It was lightly said, but not a return to November. I ate the toast while it was still hot, and was grateful for small mercies.

"Are you busy again this afternoon?" Litsi asked.

"Five rides," I said. "Are you coming?"

"Aunt Casilia said we're all going."

"So she did." I reflected a little, remembering the morning conversation in the hall. "It might be a good idea," I said to Danielle, "if you could casually mention in front of Beatrice, but so as to make sure she hears, that you'll only be working on Monday next week."

She looked astonished. "But I'm not. I'm working a normal schedule."

"I want Beatrice to think Monday's your last night for coming home so late."

"Why?" Danielle asked. "I don't mean I won't do it, but why?"

Litsi was watching me steadily. "What else?" he said.

I said conversationally, "There's no harm in laying out a line with a few baited hooks. If the fish doesn't take the opportunity, nothing will have been lost."

"And if he does?"

"Net him."

"What sort of line and hooks?" Danielle asked.

"A time and place," I said, "for removing an immovable object."

She said to Litsi, "Do you know what he means?"

"I'm afraid I do," he said. "He told Beatrice last night that while he was here to prevent it, Roland would never sign a contract for arms. Kit is also the only one of us that Nanterre hasn't directly attacked in any way, although he has twice promised to do it. Kit's directing him to a time and place that we may be able to turn to our advantage. The time, I gather, is early Tuesday morning, when he leaves this house to fetch you from work."

"And the place?" Danielle said, her eyes wide.

Litsi glanced at me. "We all know the perfect place," he said.

After the briefest of pauses, she said flatly, "The alley."

I nodded. "When Thomas drives the princess and Beatrice to the races today, he'll say he's forgotten something essential that he has to fetch from the garage on the way. He's going to drive the Rolls right down the mews to the turning circle, to give Beatrice a full view of it, and on the

199

way back he'll stop by the garage but behind my Mercedes. He's going to say how deserted and dark the alley is at night. He's going to point out that the Mercedes is my car, and he's going to mention that I fetch you in it every night. If Beatrice does her stuff, there's just a chance Nanterre will come. And if he doesn't, as I said, nothing's lost."

"Will you be there," Danielle said, "in the alley?" She didn't wait for an answer. "Silly question," she said.

"I'll hire a chauffeur-driven car to go to Chiswick to bring you back," I said.

"Couldn't Thomas?"

"Thomas," I said, "says he wouldn't miss the show for anything. He and Sammy will both be there. I'm not walking into that alley on my own."

"I won't be able to work," Danielle said. "I don't think I'll go."

"Indeed you must," Litsi said. "Everything must look normal."

"But what if he comes?" she said. "What if you catch him, what then?"

"I'll make him an offer he can't resist," I said, and although they both wanted to know what it was, I thought I wouldn't tell them just yet.

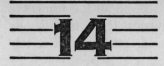

14

We all went to Sandown races, except of course for Roland, still in the care of Sammy.

The recording telephone was in Mrs. Jenkins' office, with instructions to everybody that if anyone telephoned about any messages from Danielle, every word was to be recorded, and the caller must be asked for a number or an address for us to get back to him.

"He may ask about a reward," I said to the wispy-waif secretary, and also to Dawson and to Sammy. "If he does, assure him he'll get one." And they all nodded and asked no questions.

Litsi, Danielle and I delayed leaving the house until after Thomas had driven away with the princess and Beatrice, who was complaining that she didn't like going to the races twice in one week. Thomas, closing her into the back seat, gave me a large wink before settling himself behind the wheel, and I thought how trusting all the princess's staff were, doing things whose purpose they didn't wholly understand, content only to be told that it was ultimately for the princess's sake.

There was no sign of the Rolls when we walked round to the mews, and I alarmed Litsi and Danielle greatly by checking my car again for traps. I borrowed the sliding mirror-on-wheels that the mechanics used for quick inspections of cars' undersides, but found no explosive sticky strangers, yet all the same I wouldn't let the other two get into the car before I'd started it, driven it a few yards, and braked fiercely to a halt.

"Do you do this every time you go out?" Litsi asked thoughtfully, as they eventually took their seats.

"Every time, just now."

"Why don't you park somewhere else?" Danielle asked reasonably.

"I did think of it," I said. "But it takes less time to check than find parking places."

"Apart from which," Litsi said, "you want Nanterre to know where you keep your car, if he doesn't know already."

"Mm."

"I wish this wasn't happening," Danielle said.

When we reached the racecourse they again went off to lunch and I to work. Litsi might have been lucky enough to dodge the publicity, but too many papers had spelled my name dead right, and so many strangers shook my hand that I found the whole afternoon embarrassing.

The one who was predictably upset by the general climate of approval was Maynard Allardeck, who seemed to be dogging my footsteps, presumably hoping to catch me in some infringement of the rules.

Although not one of the Stewards officially acting at that meeting, he was standing in the parade ring before every race, watching everything I did, and each time I returned I found him on the weighing-room steps, his eyes hostile and intent.

He was looking noble as usual, a pillar of society, a gentleman who wouldn't know an asset if it stripped in front of him. When I went out for the third of my rides, on the princess's runner Abseil, she at once remarked on Maynard's presence at a distance of no more than a few yards.

"Mr. Allardeck," she said, when I joined her, Litsi, Danielle and Beatrice in the parade ring, "is staring at you."

"Yes, I know."

"Who is Mr. Allardeck?" Beatrice demanded.

"Kit's sister's husband's father," Danielle answered succinctly, which left her aunt not much better informed.

"It's unnerving," Litsi said.

I nodded. "I think it's supposed to be. He's been doing it all afternoon."

"You don't, however, appear to be unnerved."

"Not so far." I turned to the princess. "I always meant to ask you what he said after Cascade won last week."

The princess made a small gesture of distress at the thought of her horse's fate, but said, "He insisted you'd flogged the horse unmercifully. Those were his words. If he'd been able to find a mark on Cascade . . ." She shrugged. "He wanted me to confirm you'd been excessively cruel."

"Thank you for not doing it."

She nodded, knowing I meant it.

"I'll be gentle on Abseil," I said.

"Not too gentle." She smiled. "I do like to win."

"He's still staring," Danielle said. "If looks could kill, you'd be in your grave."

The princess decided on a frontal approach, and as if spotting Maynard for the first time raised both gloved hands in greeting and said, "Ah, Mr. Allardeck, such a splendid day, isn't it?" walking three or four paces toward him to make talking easier.

He removed his hat and bowed to her, and said rather hoarsely for him that yes, it was. The princess said how nice it was to see the sun again after so much cloudy weather, and Maynard agreed. It was cold, of course, the princess said, but one had to expect it at this time of the year. Yes, Maynard said.

The princess glanced across to us all and said to Maynard, "I do enjoy Sandown, don't you? And my horses all seem to jump well here always, which is most pleasing."

This on-the-face-of-it-innocent remark produced in Maynard an intenser-than-ever stare in my direction—a look of black and dangerous poison.

"Why," Litsi said in my ear, puzzled, "did that make him so angry?"

"I can't tell you here," I said.

"Later, then."

"Perhaps."

The signal was given for jockeys to mount, and with a sweet smile the princess wished Maynard good fortune for the afternoon and came to say, before I went off to where Abseil waited, "Come back safely."

"Yes, Princess," I said.

Her eyes flicked momentarily in the direction of Danielle, and I suddenly understood her inner thought: come back safe because your young woman will be lost forever if you don't.

"Do your best," the princess said quietly, as if negating her first instruction, and I nodded and cantered Abseil to the start thinking that certainly I could ride round conscious chiefly of safety, and certainly to some extent I'd been doing it all week, but if I intended to do it forever I might as well retire at once. Caution and winning were incompatible. A too-careful jockey would lose his reputation, his owners, his career . . . and in my case anyway, his self-respect. The stark choice between Danielle and my job, unresolved all night, had sat on my shoulder already that afternoon through two undemanding hurdle races, and I had, in fact, been acutely aware of her being there on the stands in a way I hadn't been when I hadn't known of her turmoil of fears.

Abseil, a gray eight-year-old steeplechaser, was a fluid, agile jumper with reasonable speed and questionable stamina. Together we'd won a few races, but had more often finished second, third or fourth, because he could produce no acceleration in a crisis. His one advantage was his boldness over fences: if I restrained him in that we could trail in last.

Sandown racecourse, right-handed, undulating, with seven fences close together down the far side, was a track where good jumpers could excel. I particularly liked riding there, and it was a good place for Abseil, except that the uphill finish could find him out. To win there, he had to be flying in the lead coming round the last long bend, and jump the last three fences at his fastest speed. Then, if he faded on the hill, one might just hang on in front as far as the post.

Abseil himself was unmistakably keen to race, sending me signals of vigor and impatience. "Jumping out of his skin," Wykeham had said; and this one would be wound up tight because he wouldn't be running at the Cheltenham Festival, he wasn't quite in the top class.

The start of the two-mile, five-furlong 'chases was midway down the far side, with one's back to the water jump. There were eight runners that day, a pleasant-sized field, and Abseil was second favorite. We set off in a bunch at no great pace, because no one wanted to make the running, and I had no trouble at all being careful over the first three fences, also round the long bottom bend, over the three fences that would be the last three next time round, and uphill past the stands.

It was when we turned right-handed at the top of the hill to go out on the second circuit that the decision was immediately there, staring me in the face. To go at racing pace over the next fence with its downhill landing, graveyard of many a hope, or to check, rein back, jump it carefully, lose maybe four lengths . . .

Abseil wanted to go. I kicked him. We flew the fence, passing two horses in midair, landing on the downhill slope with precision and skimming speed, going round the bend into the back straight in second place.

The seven fences along there were so designed that if one met the first right, one met them all right, like traffic lights. The trick was to judge one's distance a good way back from the first, to make any adjustments early, so that when one's mount reached the fence he was in the right place for jumping without shortening or lengthening his stride. It was a skill learned young by all successful jockeys, becoming second nature. Abseil took a hint, shortened one stride, galloped happily on, and soared over the first of the seven fences with perfection.

The decision had been made almost unconsciously. I

couldn't do anything else. What I was, what I could do, lay there in front of me, and even for Danielle I couldn't deny it.

Abseil took the lead from the favorite at the second of the seven fences, and I sent him mental messages—"Go on there, go for it, pull the stops out, this is the way it is, and you're going to get your chance, I am as I am and I can't help it, this is living . . . get on and fly."

He flew the open ditch and then the water jump. He sailed over the last three fences on the far side. He was in front by a good thirty yards all the way round the last bend.

Three more fences.

He had his ears pricked, enjoying himself. Caution had long lost the battle, in his mind as in mine. He went over the first of them at full racing pace, and over the second, and over the last of all with me almost lying on his neck to keep up with him, weight forward, head near his head.

He tired very fast on the hill, as I'd feared he would. I had to keep him balanced, but I could feel him begin to flounder and waver and tell me he'd gone far enough.

"Come on, hang on to it, we've almost done it, just keep on, keep going, you old bugger, we're not losing it now, we're so near, so get on . . ."

I could hear the crowd yelling, which one usually couldn't. I could hear another horse coming behind me, hooves thudding. I could see him in my peripheral vision, the jockey's arms swinging high in the air as he scented Abseil flagging . . . and the winning post came just in time for me that time, not three strides too late.

Abseil was proud of himself, as he deserved to be. I patted his neck hugely and told him he was OK, he'd done a good job of work, he was a truly great fellow, and he trotted back toward the unsaddling enclosure with his ears still pricked and his fetlocks springy.

The princess was flushed and pleased in the way she always was after close races.

I slid to the ground, smiled at her, and began to unbuckle the girths.

"Is that," she said, without censure, "what you call being gentle?"

"I'd call it compulsion," I said.

Abseil was practically bowing to the crowd, knowing the applause had been his. I patted his neck again, thanking him. He tossed his gray head, turning it to look at me with both eyes, blowing down his nostrils, nodding again.

"They talk to you," the princess said.

"Some of them."

I looped the girths round my saddle, and turned to go in to weigh in, and found Maynard Allardeck standing directly in my path, much as Henri Nanterre had done at Newbury. Maynard's hatred came across loud and clear.

I stopped. I never liked speaking to him, because anything I said gave him offense. One of us was going to have to give way, and it was going to be me, because in any sort of confrontation between a Steward and a jockey, the jockey would lose.

"Why, Mr. Allardeck," said the princess, stepping to my side, "are you congratulating me? Wasn't that a delightful win?"

Maynard took off his hat and manfully said he was delighted she'd been lucky, especially as her jockey had come to the front far too soon and nearly thrown away the race on the run-in.

"Oh, but Mr. Allardeck," I heard her saying sweetly as I

sidestepped Maynard politely and headed for the weighing-room door, "if he hadn't opened up such a lead he couldn't have hung on to win."

She wasn't only a great lady, I thought gratefully, sitting on the scales, she actually understood what had been going on in a race, which many owners didn't.

Maynard troubled me, though, because it had looked very much as if he were trying to force me into jostling him, and I was going to have to be extremely careful pretty well forever to avoid physical contact. The film I'd made of him would destroy his credibility where it mattered, but it was an ultimate defense, not to be lightly used, as it shielded Bobby and Holly from any destructive consequences of Maynard's obsession, not just myself. If I used it, Maynard's life would be in tatters, but his full fury would be unleashed. He would have nothing more to lose, and we would all be in real peril.

Meanwhile, as always, there were more races to ride. I went twice more from start to finish without caution and, the gods being kind, also without hitting the turf. Maynard continued glaring and I continued being carefully civil, and somehow or other persevered unscathed to teatime.

I changed into street clothes and went up to the princess's box, and found Lord Vaughnley there with her and Litsi and Danielle: no sign of Beatrice.

"My dear chap," Lord Vaughnley said, his large bland face full of kindness, "I came to congratulate Princess Casilia. Well done, well done, my dear fellow, a nice tactical race."

"Thank you," I said mildly.

"And yesterday, too. That was splendid, absolutely first class."

"I didn't have any runners yesterday," the princess said, smiling.

"No, no, not a winner. Saving that fellow's life, don't you know, at Bradbury races."

"What fellow?" the princess asked.

"Some damn fool who went where he shouldn't and fell off a balcony. Didn't Kit tell you? No," he considered, "I suppose he wouldn't. Anyway, everyone has been talking about it all afternoon and it was in most of the papers."

"I didn't see the papers this morning," the princess said.

Lord Vaughnley obligingly gave her a full secondhand account of the proceedings that was accurate in essence. Litsi and Danielle looked studiously out of the windows and I wished I could eat the cream cakes, and eventually Lord Vaughnley ran out of superlatives.

"By the way," he said to me, picking up a large brown envelope that lay on the tea table, "this is for you. All we could find. Hope it will be of some help." He held the envelope toward me.

"Thank you very much," I said, taking it.

"Right," said Lord Vaughnley, beaming. "Thank you so much, dear Princess Casilia, for my tea. And again, congratulations." He went away in clouds of benevolence, leaving the princess wide-eyed.

"You were at Bradbury," the princess said to Danielle and Litsi. "Did you see all this?"

"No," Danielle said, "we didn't. We read about it this morning in the *Sporting Life*."

"Why didn't you tell me?"

"Kit didn't want a fuss."

The princess looked at me.

I said, shrugging, "That's true, I didn't. And I'd be

awfully grateful, Princess, if you didn't tell Mrs. Bunt."

She had no chance to ask me why not, as Beatrice reappeared as if on cue, coming into the box with a smug expression, which visibly deepened when she saw I was there. Watching me all the time she ate a cream cake with gusto, as if positively enjoying my hunger. I could more easily put up with that, I thought wryly, than with most other tribulations of that day.

The princess told Beatrice it was time to leave, the last race being long over, and shepherded her off to the Rolls. There was no chance of Litsi going with them, even if he wanted to, as Danielle clung firmly to his arm all the way to the car park. She didn't want to be alone with me after her explanations in the night, and I saw, as I suppose I'd known all day, that she couldn't have come at all without his support. Racing was again at Sandown the next day, and I began to think it would be less of a strain for everybody if she stayed away.

When we reached the car Litsi sat in the front at Danielle's insistence, with herself in the rear, and before starting the car I opened the large brown envelope Lord Vaughnley had brought.

Inside there was a small clipping from a newspaper, a larger piece from a color magazine, a black-and-white eight-by-ten photograph, and a compliments slip from Lord Vaughnley, asking me to return the pieces to the *Towncrier*, which now only had photocopies.

"What is it?" Litsi said.

I passed him the black-and-white photograph, which was of a prize-giving ceremony after a race, a group of people giving and receiving a trophy. Danielle looked over Litsi's shoulder and asked, "Who are those people?"

"The man receiving the pot is Henri Nanterre."

They both exclaimed, peering closer.

"The man at his side is the French racehorse trainer Villon, and at a guess, the racecourse is Longchamp. Look at the back, there might be some information."

Litsi turned the photograph over. "It just says 'After the Prix de la Cité, Villon, Nanterre, Duval.'"

"Duval is the jockey," I said.

"So that's what Nanterre looks like," Litsi said thoughtfully. "Once seen, easily remembered." He passed the photograph back to Danielle. "What other goodies do you have?"

"This piece is from an English magazine and seems to be a Derby preview from last year. Villon apparently had a runner, and the article says 'fresh from his triumph at Longchamp.' Nanterre's mentioned as one of his owners."

The newspaper clipping, also from an English paper, was no more helpful. Prudhomme, owned by French industrialist H. Nanterre, trained by Villon, had come to run at Newmarket and dropped dead of a heart attack on pulling up: end of story.

"Who took the photograph?" I asked, twisting round to see Danielle. "Does it say?"

"Copyright *Towncrier*," she said, reading the back.

I shrugged. "They must have gone over for some big race or other. The Arc, I daresay."

I took the photograph back and put all the bits into the envelope.

"He has a very strong face," Danielle said, meaning Nanterre.

"And a very strong voice."

"And we're no further forward," Litsi said.

I started the car and drove us to London, where we found that nothing of any interest had happened at all, with the result that Sammy was getting bored.

"Just by being here," I said, "you earn your bread."

"No one knows I'm here, man."

"They sure do," I said dryly. "Everything that happens in this house reaches the ears of the man you're guarding its owner against, so don't go to sleep."

"I'd never," he said, aggrieved.

"Good." I showed him the *Towncrier*'s photograph. "That man, there," I said, pointing. "If ever you see him, that's when you take care. He carries a gun, which may or may not have bullets in it, and he's full of all sorts of tricks."

He looked at the photograph long and thoughtfully. "I'll know him," he said.

I took Lord Vaughnley's offerings up to the bamboo room, telephoned Wykeham, picked up my messages, dealt with them: the usual routine. When I went down to the sitting room for a drink before dinner, Litsi, Danielle and the princess were discussing French Impressionist painters exhibiting in Paris around 1880.

Cézanne . . . Pissarro . . . Renoir . . . Degas . . . at least I'd heard of them. I went across to the drinks tray and picked up the scotch.

"Berthe Morisot was one of the best," Litsi said to the room in general. "Don't you think?"

"What did he paint?" I asked, opening the bottle.

"He was a she," Litsi said.

I grunted slightly and poured a trickle of whiskey. "She, then, what did she paint?"

"Young women, babies, studies in light."

I sat in an armchair and drank the scotch, looking at Litsi. At least he didn't patronize me, I thought.

"They're not all easy to see," he said. "Many are in private collections, some are in Paris, several are in the National Gallery of Art in Washington."

I was unlikely, he must have known, to chase them up.

"Delightful pictures," the princess said. "Luminous."

"And there was Mary Cassatt," Danielle said. "She was brilliant too." She turned to me. "She was American, but she was a student of Degas in Paris."

I would go with her to galleries, I thought, if that would please her. "One of these days," I said casually, "you can educate me."

She turned her head away almost as if she would cry, which hadn't in the least been my intention; and perhaps it was as well that Beatrice arrived for her "bloody."

Beatrice was suffering a severe sense-of-humor failure over Sammy, who had, it appeared, said, "Sorry, me old darlin', not used to slow traffic," while again cannoning into her on the stairs.

She saw the laugh on my face, which gravely displeased her, and Litsi smothered his in his drink. The princess, with twitching lips, assured her sister-in-law that she would ask Sammy to be more careful and Beatrice said it was all my fault for having brought him into the house. It entirely lightened and enlivened the evening, which passed more easily than some of the others: but there was still no one telephoning in response to the advertisements, and there was again no sound from Nanterre.

Early next morning, well before seven, Dawson woke me again with the intercom, saying there was a call for me from Wykeham Harlow.

I picked up the receiver, sleep forgotten.

"Wykeham?" I said.

"K–K–Kit." He was stuttering dreadfully. "C–c–come down here. C–come at once."

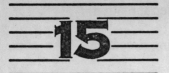

He put the receiver down immediately, without telling me what had happened, and when I instantly rang back there was no reply. With appalling foreboding I flung on some clothes, sprinted round to the car, did very cursory checks on it, and drove fast through the almost empty streets toward Sussex.

Wykeham had sounded near disintegration, shock and age trembling ominously in his voice. By the time I reached him, they had been joined by anger, which filled and shook him with impotent fire.

He was standing in the parking space with Robin Curtiss, the vet, when I drove in.

"What's happened?" I said, getting out of the car.

Robin made a helpless gesture with his hands and Wykeham said with fury, "C—come and look."

I followed him into the courtyard next to the one that

had held Cascade and Cotopaxi. Wykeham, shaky on his knees but straight-backed with emotion, went across to one of the closed doors and put his hand flat on it.

"In there," he said.

The box door was closed but not bolted. Not bolted, because the horse inside wasn't going to escape.

I pulled the doors open, the upper and the lower, and saw the body lying on the peat.

Bright chestnut, three white socks, white blaze.

It was Col.

Speechlessly I turned to Wykeham and Robin, feeling all of Wykeham's rage and a lot of private despair. Nanterre was too quick on his feet, and it wouldn't take much more for Roland de Brescou to crumble.

"It's the same as before," Robin said. "The bolt." He bent down, lifted the chestnut forelock, showed me the mark on the white blaze. "There's a lot of oil in the wound . . . the gun's been oiled since last time." He let go of the forelock and straightened. "The horse is stone cold. It was done early, I should say before midnight."

Col . . . gallant at Ascot, getting ready for Cheltenham, for the Gold Cup.

"Where was the patrol?" I said, at last finding my voice.

"He was here," Wykeham said. "In the stable, I mean, not in the courtyard."

"He's gone, I suppose."

"No, I told him to wait for you. He's in the kitchen."

"Col," I said, "is the only one . . . isn't he?"

Robin nodded. "Something to be thankful for."

Not much, I thought. Cotopaxi and Col had been two of the princess's three best horses, and it could be no coincidence that they'd been targeted.

"Kinley," I said to Wykeham. "You did check Kinley, didn't you?"

"Yes, straightaway. He's in the corner box still, in the next courtyard."

"The insurers aren't going to like this," Robin said, looking down at the dead horse. "With the first two, it might have been just bad luck that they were two good ones, but three . . ." He shrugged. "Not my problem, of course."

"How did he know where to find them?" I said, as much to myself as to Robin and Wykeham. "Is this Col's usual box?"

"Yes," Wykeham said. "I suppose now I'll have to change them all around, but it does disrupt the stable . . ."

"Abseil," I said, "is he all right?"

"Who?"

"Yesterday's winner."

Wykeham's doubts cleared. "Oh, yes, he's all right."

Abseil was as easy to recognize as the others, I thought. Not chestnut, not nearly black like Cascade, but gray, with a black mane and tail.

"Where is he?" I asked.

"In the last courtyard, near the house."

Although I was down at Wykeham's fairly often, it was always to do the schooling, for which we would drive up to the Downs, where I would ride relays of the horses over jumps, teaching them. I almost never rode the horses in or out of the yard, and although I knew where some of the horses lived, like Cotopaxi, I wasn't sure of them all.

I put a hand down to touch Col's foreleg, and felt its rigidity, its chill. The foreleg that had saved us from disaster at Ascot, that had borne all his weight.

"I'll have to tell the princess," Wykeham said unhappily. "Unless you would, Kit?"

"Yes, I'll tell her," I said. "At Sandown."

He nodded vaguely. "What are we running?" he said.

"Helikon for the princess, and three others."

"Dusty has the list, of course."

"Yeah," I said.

Wykeham took a long look again at the dead splendor on the peat.

"I'd kill the shit who did that," he said, "with his own damned bolt."

Robin sighed and closed the stable doors, saying he would arrange for the carcass to be collected, if Wykeham liked.

Wykeham silently nodded, and we all walked out of the courtyard and made our way to Wykeham's house, where Robin went off to telephone in the office. The dog-handler was still in the kitchen, restive but chastened, with his dog, a black Doberman, lying on the floor and yawning at his feet.

"Tell Kit Fielding what you told me," Wykeham said.

The dog-handler, in a navy-blue battle-dress uniform, was middle-aged and running to fat. His voice was defensively belligerent and his intelligence middling, and I wished I'd had the speedy Sammy here in his place. I sat at the table across from him and asked how he'd missed the visitor who had shot Col.

"I couldn't help it, could I?" he said. "Not with those bombs going off."

"What bombs?" I glanced at Wykeham, who'd clearly heard about the bombs before. "What bombs, for God's sake?"

The dog-handler had a mustache, which he groomed

frequently with a thumb and forefinger, working outward from the nose.

"Well, how was I to know they wasn't proper bombs?" he said. "They made enough noise."

"Just start," I said, "at the beginning. Start with when you came on duty. And, er . . . have you been here any other nights?"

"Yes," he said. "Monday to Friday, five nights."

"Right," I said. "Describe last night."

"I come on duty sevenish, when the head-lad's finished the feeding. I make a base here in the kitchen and do a recce every half hour. Standard procedure."

"How long do the recces take?"

"Fifteen minutes, maybe more. It's bitter cold these nights."

"And you go into all the courtyards?"

"Never miss a one," he said piously.

"And where else?"

"Look in the hay barn, tack room, feed shed, round the back where the tractor is, and the harrow, muck-heap, the lot."

"Go on, then," I said, "how many recces had you done when the bombs went off?"

He worked it out on his fingers. "Nine, say. The head-lad had been in for a quick look round last thing, like he does, and everything was quiet. So I comes back here for a bit of a warm, and goes out again half eleven, I should say. I start on the rounds, and there's this almighty bang and crashing round the back. So I went off there with Ranger . . ." He looked down at his dog. "Well, I would, wouldn't I? Stands to reason."

"Yes," I said. "Where exactly, round the back?"

"I couldn't see at first because there isn't much light round there, and there was this strong smell of burning, got right down your throat, and then another one went off not ten feet away. Nearly burst my eardrums."

"Where were the bombs?" I said again.

"The first one was round the back of the muck-heap. I found what was left of it with my torch, after."

"But you don't use your torch all the time?"

"You don't need to in the courtyards. Most of them have lights in."

"Mm. OK. Where was the second one?"

"Under the harrow."

Wykeham, like many trainers, used the harrow occasionally for raking his paddocks, keeping them in good shape.

"Did it blow up the harrow?" I said, frowning.

"No, see, they weren't that sort of bomb."

"What other sort is there?"

"It went off through the harrow with a huge shower of sparks. Golden sparks, all over. Little burning sparks. Some of them fell on me . . . They were fireworks. I found the empty boxes. They said 'bomb' on them, where they weren't burned."

"Where are they now?" I asked.

"Where they went off. I didn't touch them, except to kick them over to read what was on the side."

"So what was your dog doing all this time?"

The dog-handler looked disillusioned. "I had him on the leash. I always do, of course. He didn't like the bangs or the sparks or the smell. He's supposed to be trained to ignore gunshots, but he didn't like the fireworks. He was barking fit to bust, and trying to run off."

"He was trying to run in a different direction, but you stopped him?"

"That's right."

"Maybe he was trying to run after the man who shot the horse."

The dog-handler's mouth opened and snapped shut. He smoothed his mustache several times and grew noticeably more aggressive. "Ranger was barking at the bombs," he said.

I nodded. It was too late for it to matter.

"And I suppose," I said, "that you didn't hear any other bangs in the distance . . . you didn't hear the shot?"

"No, I didn't. My ears were ringing and Ranger was kicking up a racket."

"So what did you do next?"

"Nothing," he said. "I thought it was some of those lads who work here. Proper little monkeys. So I just went on with the patrols, regular like. There wasn't anything wrong . . . it didn't look like it, that's to say."

I turned to Wykeham, who had been gloomily listening. "Didn't *you* hear the fireworks?" I asked.

"No, I was asleep." He hesitated, then added, "I can't seem to sleep at all these days without sleeping pills. We'd had four quiet nights and I'd been awake most of those, so . . . last night I took a pill."

I sighed. If Wykeham had been awake, he would anyway have gone toward the commotion and nothing would have been different.

I said to the dog-handler, "You were here on Wednesday, when you had the prowler?"

"Yes, I was. Ranger was whining but I couldn't find anyone."

Nanterre, I thought, had come to the stable on Wednesday night, intending to kill, and had been thwarted by the dog's presence: and he'd come back two nights later with his diversions.

He must have been at Ascot, I supposed, and learned what Col looked like, but I hadn't seen him, as I hadn't seen him at Bradbury either: but among large crowds on racecourses, especially while I was busy, that wasn't extraordinary.

I looked down at Ranger, wondering about his responses.

"When people arrive here," I asked, "like I did a short while ago, how does Ranger behave?"

"He gets up and goes to the door and whines a bit. He's a quiet dog, mostly. Doesn't bark. That's why I knew it was the bombs he was barking at."

"Well, er, during your spells in the kitchen, what would you be doing?"

"Making a cuppa. Eating. Relieving myself. Reading. Watching the telly." He smoothed his mustache, not liking me or my questions. "I don't doze off, if that's what you mean."

It was what I meant, and obviously what he'd done, at some point or another. During four long quiet cold nights I supposed it was understandable, if not excusable.

"Over the weekend," I said to Wykeham, "we'll have double and treble patrols. Constant."

He nodded. "Have to."

"Have you told the police yet?"

"Not yet. Soon, though." He looked with disgust at the dog-handler. "They'll want to hear what you've said."

The dog-handler however stood up, announced it was an

hour after he should have left and if the police wanted him they could reach him through his firm. He, he said, was going to bed.

Wykeham morosely watched him go and said, "What the hell is going on, Kit? The princess knows who killed them all, and so do you. So tell me."

It wasn't fair, I thought, for him not to know, so I told him the outline: a man was trying to extract a signature from Roland de Brescou by attacking his family wherever he could.

"But that's . . . terrorism." Wykeham used the word at arm's length, as if its very existence affronted him.

"In a small way," I said.

"Small?" he exclaimed. "Do you call three dead great horses small?"

I didn't. It made me sick and angry to think of them. It was small on a world scale of terrorism, but rooted in the same wicked conviction that the path to attaining one's end lay in slaughtering the innocent.

I stirred. "Show me where all the princess's horses are," I suggested to Wykeham, and together we went out again into the cold air and made the rounds of the courtyards.

Cascade's and Cotopaxi's boxes were still empty, and no others of the princess's horses had been in the first courtyard. In the second had been only Col. In the one beyond that, Hillsborough and Bernina, with Kinley in the deep corner box there.

About a third of the stable's inmates were out at exercise on the Downs, and while we were leaving Kinley's yard, they came clattering back, filling the whole place with noise and movement, the lads dismounting and leading their horses into the boxes. Wykeham and I sorted our way round as the lads brushed down their charges, tidied the bedding, filled the buckets, brought hay to the racks, propped their saddles outside the boxes, bolted the doors and went off to their breakfasts.

I saw all the old friends in their quarters; among them North Face, Dhaulagiri, Icicle and Icefall, and young Helikon, the four-year-old hurdler going to Sandown that afternoon. Wykeham got half of their names right, waiting for me to prompt him on the others. He unerringly knew their careers, though, and their personalities; they were real to him in a way that needed no name tags. His secretary was adept at sorting out what he intended when he wrote down his lists of entries to races.

In the last courtyard we came to Abseil and opened the top half of his door. Abseil came toward the opening daylight and put his head out inquiringly. I rubbed his gray nose and upper lip with my hand and put my head next to his and breathed out gently like a reversed sniff into his nostril. He rubbed his nose a couple of times against my cheek and then lifted his head away, the greeting done. Wykeham paid no attention. Wykeham talked to horses that way himself, when they were that sort of horse. With some, one would never do it, one could get one's nose bitten off.

Wykeham gave Abseil a carrot from a deep pocket, and closed him back into his twilight.

Wykeham slapped his hand on the next box along. "That's Kinley's box usually. It's empty now. I don't like keeping him in that corner box, it's dark and boring for him."

"It won't be for much longer, I hope," I said, and suggested going round to see the "bombs."

Wykeham had seen them earlier, and pointed them out to me, and as expected they were the bottom parts of cardboard containers, each four inches square in shape, the top parts burned away. They were both the same, with gaudy red and yellow pictured flames still visible on the singed surfaces, and the words "golden bomb" in jazzy letters on the one under the harrow.

"We'd better leave them there for the police," I said.

Wykeham agreed, but he said fireworks would convince the police even more that it was the work of boys.

We went back into the house, where Wykeham telephoned the police and received a promise of attention, and I got through to Dawson, asking him to tell the princess I was down at Wykeham's and would go to Sandown from there.

Wykeham and I had breakfast and drove up to the Downs in his big-wheeled pickup to see the second lot exercise, and under the wide cold windy sky he surprised me by saying apropos of nothing special that he was thinking of taking another assistant. He'd had assistants in the past, I'd heard, who'd never lasted long, but there hadn't been one there in my time.

"Are you?" I said. "I thought you couldn't stand assistants."

"They never knew anything," he said. "But I'm getting old. It'll have to be someone the princess likes. Someone you get on with, too. So if you think of anyone, let me know. I don't know who's around so much these days."

"All right," I said, but with misgivings. Wykeham, for all his odd mental quirks, was irreplaceable. "You're not going to retire, are you?"

"No, I'm not. Never. I wouldn't mind dying up here, watching my horses." He laughed suddenly, in his eyes a flash of the vigor that had been there always not so long ago, when he'd been a titan. "I've had a great life, you know. One of the best."

"Stick around," I said.

He nodded. "Maybe next year," he said, "we'll win the Grand National."

Wykeham's four runners at Sandown were in the first three races and the fifth, and I didn't see the princess until she came down to the parade ring for Helikon's race, which was the third on the card.

Beatrice was with her, and also Litsi, and also Danielle, who after the faintest of greetings was busy blanking me out, it seemed, by looking carefully at the circling horses. The fact that she was there, that she was still trying, was something, I supposed.

"Good morning," the princess said, when I bowed to her. "Dawson said Wykeham telephoned early . . . again." There was a shade of apprehension in her face, which abruptly deepened at what she read in my own.

She walked a little away from her family, and I followed.

"*Again?*" she said, not wanting to believe it. "Which ones?"

"One," I said. "Col."

She absorbed the shock with a long blink.

"The same way . . . as before?" she said.

"Yes. With the bolt."

"My poor horse."

"I'm so sorry."

"I will not tell my husband," she said. "Please tell none of them, Kit."

"It will be in the newspapers tomorrow or on Monday," I said, "probably worse than before."

"Oh . . ." The prospect affected her almost as much as Col's death. "I will not add to the pressure on my husband," she said fiercely. "He cannot sign this wretched contract. He will die, you know, if he does. He will not survive the disgrace in his own mind. He will wish to die . . . as all these years, although his condition is such a trial to him, he has wished to live." She made a small gesture with her gloved hand. "He is . . . very dear to me, Kit."

I heard in my memory my grandmother saying, "I love the old bugger, Kit," of my pugnacious grandfather, an equal declaration of passion for a man not obviously lovable.

That the princess should have made it was astonishing, but not as impossible as before the advent of Nanterre. A great deal, I saw, had changed between us in the last eight days.

To save his honor, to save his life, to save their life together . . . My God, I thought, what a burden. She needed Superman, not me.

"Don't tell him about Col," she said again.

"No, I won't."

Her gaze rested on Beatrice.

"I won't tell other people," I said. "But it may not stay a secret on the racecourse. Dusty and the lads who came with Wykeham's horses all know, and they'll tell other lads. It'll spread, I'm afraid."

She nodded slightly, unhappily, and switched her attention from Beatrice to Helikon, who happened to be passing. She watched him for several seconds, turning her head after him as he went.

"What do you think of him?" she asked, her defense mechanism switching on smoothly. "What shall I expect?"

"He's still a bit hot-headed," I said, "but if I can settle him he should run well."

"But not another Kinley?" she suggested.

"Not so far."

"Do your best."

I said as usual that I would, and we rejoined the others as if all we'd been talking about was her hurdler.

"Have you noticed who's still staring?" Danielle said, and I answered that indeed I had, those eyes followed me everywhere.

"Doesn't it get on your nerves?" Danielle asked.

"What nerves?" Litsi said.

"Are you talking about Mr. Allardeck?" Beatrice demanded. "I can't think why you don't like him. He looks perfectly darling."

The perfectly darling man was projecting his implacable thoughts my way from a distance that signaled unmistakable invasion of psychological territory, and I thought uneasily again about the state of mind that was compelling him to do it. The evil eye, I thought: and no shield from it that I could see.

The time came to mount, and hot-headed Helikon and I went out onto the track. He was nervous as well as impetuous; not a joy to ride. I tried to get him to relax on the way to the start, but as usual it was like trying to relax a coil of barbed wire. The princess had bought him as a yearling and had great hopes for him, but although he jumped well enough, neither Wykeham nor I had been able to straighten out his kinks.

There were twenty or more runners, and Helikon and I

set off near the front because if he were bumped in the pack he'd be frightened into stopping; yet I also had to keep a tight hold, as he could take charge and decamp.

He went through the routine of head-tossing against the restraint, but I had him anchored and running fairly well, and by the third flight of hurdles I thought the worst was over, we could now settle a little and design a passable race.

It wasn't his day. At the fourth flight the horse nearest ahead put his foot through the obstacle and went down with a crash, slithering along the ground on his side. Helikon fell over him, going down fast, pitching me off: and I didn't actually see the subsequent course of events all that clearly, though it was a pile-up worthy of a fog on a highway. Five horses, I found afterward, hit the deck at that jump. One of them seemed to land smack on top of me; not frightfully good for one's health.

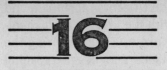

I lay on the grass, assessing things.

I was conscious and felt like a squashed beetle, but I hadn't broken my legs, which I always feared most.

One of the other jockeys from the melee squatted beside me and asked if I was all right, but I couldn't answer him on account of having no breath.

"He's winded," my colleague said to someone behind me, and I thought, "Just like Litsi at Bradbury, heigh ho." My colleague unbuckled my helmet and pushed it off, for which I couldn't thank him.

Breath came back, as it does. By the time the ambulance arrived along with a doctor in a car, I'd come to the welcome conclusion that nothing was broken at all and that it was time to stand up and get on with things. Standing, I felt hammered and sore in several places, but one had to accept that, and I reckoned I'd been lucky to get out of that sort of crash so lightly.

One of the other jockeys hadn't been so fortunate and was flat out, white and silent, with the first-aid men kneeling anxiously beside him. He woke up slightly during the ambulance ride back to the stands and began groaning intermittently, which alarmed his attendants, but at least showed signs of life.

When we reached the first-aid room and the ambulance's rear doors were opened, I climbed out first, and found the other jockey's wife waiting there, pregnant and pretty, screwed up with anxiety.

"Is Joe all right?" she said to me, and then saw him coming out on the stretcher, very far from all right. I saw the deep shock in her face, the quick pallor, the dry mouth . . . the agony.

That was what had happened to Danielle, I thought. That was much what she'd seen, and that was what she'd felt.

I put my arm round Joe's wife and held her close, and told her Joe would be fine, he would be fine, and neither of us knew if he would.

Joe was carried into the first-aid room, the door closing behind him, but presently the doctor came out with kindness and told Joe's wife they would be sending him to the hospital as soon as an outside ambulance could be brought.

"You can come in and sit with him, if you like," he said to her, and to me added, "You'd better come in too, hadn't you?"

I went in and he checked me over, and said, "What aren't you telling me?"

"Nothing."

"I know you," he said. "And everywhere I touch you, you stifle a wince."

"Ouch, then," I said.

"Where is ouch?"

"Ankle, mostly."

He pulled my boot off and I said "ouch" quite loudly but, as I'd believed, there were no cracked bits. He said to get some strapping and some rest, and added that I could ride on Monday, if I could walk and if I were mad enough.

He went back to tending Joe, and one of the nurses answered a knock on the door, coming back to tell me that I was wanted outside. I put my boot on again, ran my fingers through my hair and went out, to find Litsi and Danielle there, waiting.

Litsi had his arm round Danielle's shoulders, and Danielle looked as if this were the last place on earth she wanted to be.

I was aware of my disheveled state, of the limp I couldn't help, of the grass stains and the tear in my breeches down my left thigh.

Litsi took it all in, and I smiled at him slightly.

"The nitty gritty," I said.

"So I see." He looked thoughtful. "Aunt Casilia sent us to see how you were."

It had taken a great deal of courage, I thought, for Danielle to be there, to face what might have happened again as it had happened in January. I said to Litsi, but with my eyes on Danielle, "Please tell her I'm all right, I'll be riding on Monday."

"How can you ride?" Danielle said intensely.

"Sit in the saddle, put the feet in the stirrups, pick up the reins."

"Don't be damn stupid. How can you joke . . . and don't answer that. I know both the answers. Easily or with difficulty, whichever is funnier."

She suddenly couldn't help laughing, but it was partly

hysterical, and it was against Litsi's big shoulder she smothered her face.

"I'll come up to the box," I said to him, and he nodded, but before they could leave, the first-aid-room door opened and Joe's wife came out.

"Kit," she said with relief, seeing me still there. "I've got to go to the ladies' . . . my stomach's all churning up . . . they say I can go to the hospital with Joe but if they come for him while I'm not here they may take him without me . . . Will you wait here and tell them? Don't let him go without me."

"I'll see to it," I said.

She said "thanks" faintly and half ran in the direction of relief, and Danielle, her eyes stretched wide, said, "But that's . . . just like me. Is her husband hurt . . . badly?"

"It's too soon to tell, I think."

"How can she stand it?"

"I don't know," I said. "I really don't know. It's much simpler from Joe's side . . . and mine."

"I'll go and see if she needs help," Danielle said abruptly, and, leaving Litsi's shelter, set off after Joe's wife.

"Seriously," Litsi said, watching her go, "how can you joke?"

"Seriously? Seriously not about Joe, nor about his wife, but about myself, why not?"

"But . . . is it worth it?"

I said, "If you could paint as you'd like to, would you put up with a bit of discomfort?"

He smiled, his eyebrows rising. "Yes, I would."

"Much the same thing," I said. "Fulfillment."

We stood in a backwater of the racecourse, with the

stands and bustle out in the mainstream, gradually moving toward the next race. Dusty arrived at a rush, his eyes searching, suspicious.

"I've wrenched my ankle," I said. "You'll have to get Jamie for the fifth race, I know he's free. But I'm cleared for Monday. Is Helikon all right?"

He nodded briskly a couple of times and departed, wasting no words.

Litsi said, "It's a wonder you're not worse. It looked atrocious. Aunt Casilia was watching through binoculars, and she was very concerned until she saw you stand up. She said then that you accepted the risks and one had to expect these things from time to time."

"She's right," I said.

He, in the sober suiting of civilization, looked at the marks of the earth on the princess's colors, looked at my torn green-stained breeches, and at the leg I was putting no weight on.

"How do you face it, over and over again?" he said. He saw my lips twitch and added, "Easily or with difficulty, whichever is funnier."

I laughed. "I never expect it, for a start. It's always an unpleasant surprise."

"And now that it's happened, how do you deal with it?"

"Think about something else," I said. "Take a lot of aspirins and concentrate on getting back as soon as possible. I don't like other jockeys loose on my horses, like now. I want to be on them. When I've taught them and know them, they're mine."

"And you like winning."

"Yes, I like winning."

The hospital ambulance arrived only moments before

Danielle and Joe's wife returned, and Litsi, Danielle and I stood with Joe's wife while Joe was transferred. He was still half conscious, still groaning, looking gray. The ambulance men helped his wife into the interior in his wake, and we had a final view of her face, young and frightened, looking back at us, before they closed the doors and drove slowly away.

Litsi and Danielle looked at me, and I looked at them; and there was nothing to say, really.

Litsi put his arm again round Danielle's shoulders, and they turned and walked away; and I hobbled off and showered and changed my clothes after just another fall, in just a day in a working life.

When I went out of the weighing room to go to the princess's box, Maynard Allardeck stepped into my way. He was looking, as always, splendidly tailored, the total English gentleman from Lock's hat to hand-sewn shoes. He wore a silk striped tie and pigskin gloves, and his eyes were as near madness as I'd ever seen them.

I stopped, my spirits sinking.

Outside the weighing room, where we stood, there was a covered veranda with three wide steps leading down to the area used for unsaddling the first four in every race. There was a tarmac path across the grass there, giving access to the rest of the paddock.

The horses from the fifth race had been unsaddled and led away, and there was a scatter of people about, but not a crowd.

Maynard stood between me and the steps, and to avoid him I would have to edge sideways and round him.

"*Fielding*," he said with intensity; and he wasn't simply addressing me by name, he was using the word as a curse, in the way the Allardecks had used it for vengeful generations. He was cursing my ancestry and my existence, the feudal spite like bile in his mouth, the irrational side of his hatred for me well in command.

He overtopped me by about four inches and outweighed me by fifty pounds, but he was twenty years older and unfit. Without the complication of a sprained ankle I could have dodged him easily, but as it was, when I took a step sideways, so did he.

"Mr. Allardeck," I said neutrally. "Princess Casilia's expecting me."

He gave no sign of hearing, but when I took another sideways step he didn't move. Nor did he move when I went past him, but two steps further on, at the top of the steps, I received a violent shove between the shoulders.

Unbalanced, I fell stumbling down the three steps, landing in a sprawl on the tarmac path. I rolled, half expecting Maynard to jump down on me, but he was standing on the top step, staring, and as I watched, he turned away, took three paces and attached himself to a small group of similar-looking men.

A trainer I sometimes rode for, who happened to be near, put a hand under my elbow and helped me to my feet.

"He pushed you," he said incredulously. "I saw it. I can't believe it. That man stepped right behind you and pushed."

I stood on one leg and brushed off some of the debris from the path. "Thanks," I said.

"But he pushed you! Aren't you going to complain?"

"Who to?"

"But Kit . . ." He slowly took stock of the situation. "That's Maynard Allardeck."

"Yeah."

"But he can't go around attacking you. And you've hurt your leg."

"He didn't do that," I said. "That's from a fall in the third race."

"That was some mess." He looked at me doubtfully. "If you want to complain, I'll say what I saw."

I thanked him again and said I wouldn't bother, which he still found inexplicable. I glanced briefly at Maynard, who by then had his back to me as if unaware of my presence, and with perturbation set off again toward the princess's box.

The push itself had been a relatively small matter, but as Maynard was basically murderous, it had to be taken as a substitute killing, a relief explosion, a jet of steam to stop the top blowing off the volcano.

The film, I thought uneasily, would keep that volcano in check; and I supposed I could put up with the jets of steam if I thought of them as safety valves reducing his boiling pressure. I didn't want him uncontrollably erupting. I'd rather fall down more steps; but I would also be more careful where I walked.

The princess was out on the balcony when I reached her box, huddled into her furs, and alone.

I went out there to join her, and found her gazing blind-eyed over the racecourse, her thoughts obviously unwelcome.

"Princess," I said.

She turned her head, her eyes focusing on my face.

"Don't give up," I said.

"No." She stretched her neck and her backbone as if to disclaim any thought of it. "Is Helikon all right?" she asked.

"Dusty said so."

"Good." She sighed. "Have you any idea what's running next week? It's all a blank in my mind."

It was a fair blank in mine also. "Icefall goes on Thursday at Lingfield."

"How did Helikon fall?" she asked, and I told her that it wasn't her horse's fault, he'd been brought down.

"He was going well at the time," I said. "He's growing up and getting easier to settle. I'll school him next week one morning to get his confidence back."

She showed a glimmer of pleasure in an otherwise unpleasurable day. She didn't ask directly after my state of health, because she never did: she considered the results of falls to lie within the domain of my personal privacy into which she wouldn't intrude. It was an attitude stemming from her own habit of reticence, and far from minding it, I valued it. It was fussing I couldn't stand.

We went inside for some tea, joining Danielle, Litsi and Beatrice, and presently Lord Vaughnley appeared on one of his more or less regular visits to the princess's box.

His faint air of anxiety vanished when he saw me drinking there, and after a few minutes he managed to cut me off from the pack and steer me into a corner.

I thanked him for his packet of yesterday.

"What? Oh, yes, my dear chap, you're welcome. But that's not what I wanted to say to you, not at all. I'm afraid there's been a bit of a leak . . . it's all very awkward."

"What sort of leak?" I asked, puzzled.

"About the film you made of Maynard Allardeck."

I felt my spine shiver. I desperately needed that film to remain secret.

"I'm afraid," Lord Vaughnley said, "that Allardeck

knows you sent a copy of it to the Honours people in Downing Street. He knows he will never again be considered for a knighthood, because of your sending it." He smiled half anxiously but couldn't resist the journalistic summary: "Never Sir Maynard, never Lord Allardeck, thanks to Kit Fielding."

"How in hell's teeth did he find out?" I demanded.

"I don't know," Lord Vaughnley said uncomfortably. "Not from me, my dear fellow, I assure you. I've never told anyone. But sometimes there are whispers of these things. Someone in the civil service, don't you know."

I looked at him in dismay. "How long has he known?" I said.

"I think since sometime last week." He shook his head unhappily. "I heard about it this morning in a committee meeting of the charity of which Allardeck and I are both directors. He's chairman, of course. The civil service charity, you remember."

I remembered. It was through good works for the sick and needy dependents of civil servants that Maynard had tried hardest to climb to his knighthood.

"No one in the charity has seen the film, have they?" I asked urgently.

"No, no, my dear fellow. They've simply heard it exists. One of them apparently asked Allardeck if he knew anything about it."

Oh, God, I thought; how leaks could trickle through cracks.

"I thought you'd better know," Lord Vaughnley said. "And don't forget I've as strong an interest in that film as you have. If it's shown all over the place, we'll have lost our lever."

"Maynard will have lost his saintly reputation."

"He might operate without it."

"The only copies," I said, "are the ones I gave to you and to the Honours people, and the three I have in the bank. Unless you or the Honours people show them . . . I can't believe they will," I said explosively. "They were all so hush-hush."

"I thought I should warn you."

"I'm glad you did."

It explained so much, I thought, about Maynard's recent behavior. Considering how he must be seething with fury, just pushing me down the steps showed amazing restraint.

But then I did still have the film, and so far it hadn't been shown to a wider audience, and Maynard really wouldn't want it shown, however much he had lost through it already.

Lord Vaughnley apologized to the princess for monopolizing her jockey, and asked if I was still interested in more information regarding Nanterre.

"Yes, please," I said, and he nodded and said it was still flickering through computers, somewhere.

"Trouble?" Litsi asked at my elbow, when Lord Vaughnley had gone.

"Allardeck trouble, not Nanterre." I smiled lopsidedly. "The Fieldings have had Allardeck trouble for centuries. Nanterre's much more pressing."

We watched the last race, on my part without concentration, and in due course returned to the cars, Litsi and Danielle, deserting the Rolls, saying they were coming with me.

On the walk from the box to the car park, I stopped a few times to take the weight off my foot. No one made a remark, but when we arrived at my car Danielle said positively, "I'm driving. You can tell me the way."

"You don't need a left foot with automatic transmission," I pointed out.

"I'm driving," she said fiercely. "I've driven your car before." She had, on a similar occasion.

I sat in the passenger seat without more demur, and asked her to stop at a chemist's shop a short distance along the road.

"What do you need?" she said brusquely, pulling up. "I'll get it."

"Some strapping, and mineral water."

"Aspirin?"

"There's some here in the glove compartment."

She went with quick movements into the shop and returned with a paper bag, which she dumped on my lap.

"I'll tell you the scenario," she said to Litsi with a sort of suppressed violence as she restarted the car and set off toward London. "He'll strap his own ankle and sit with it surrounded by icepacks to reduce the swelling. He'll have hoof-shaped bruises that'll be black by tomorrow, and he'll ache all over. He won't want you to notice he can't put that foot on the ground without pain shooting up his leg. If you ask him how he feels he'll say 'with every nerve ending.' He doesn't like sympathy. Injuries embarrass him and he'll do his best to ignore them."

Litsi said, when she paused, "You must know him very well."

It silenced Danielle. She was driving with the same throttled anger, and took a while to relax.

I swallowed some aspirins with the mineral water and thought about what she'd said. And Litsi was right, I reflected: she did truly know me. She unfortunately sounded as if she wished she didn't.

"Kit, you never did tell me," Litsi said after a while, "why it annoyed Maynard Allardeck so much when the princess said her horses always jumped well at Sandown. Why on earth should that anger anyone?"

"Modesty forbids me to tell you," I said, smiling.

"Well, have a try."

"She was paying me a compliment that Maynard didn't want to hear."

"Do you mean it's because of your skill that her horses jump well?"

"Experience," I said. "Something like that."

"He's obsessed," Litsi said.

He was dangerous, I thought: and there was such a thing as contract killing, by persons unknown, which I didn't like the thought of very much. To remove the mind from scary concepts, I asked Danielle if she'd managed to tell Beatrice that Monday was her last evening stint.

Danielle, after a lengthy pause, said that no, she hadn't.

"I wish you would," I said, alarmed. "You said you would."

"I can't tell her . . . What if Nanterre turns up and shoots you?"

"He won't," I said. "But if we don't catch him . . ." I paused. "The princess told me today that if Roland signs the arms contract to save us all, he will literally die of shame. He wouldn't want to go on living. She's extremely worried that he'll give in. She loves him. She wants him alive. So we've got to stop Nanterre; and stop him soon."

Danielle didn't answer for two or three miles, and it was Litsi eventually who broke the silence.

"I'll tell Beatrice," he said firmly.

"No," Danielle protested.

"Last night," I said, "Nanterre killed another of the princess's horses. The princess doesn't want Roland to know. Or Beatrice, who would tell him."

They both exclaimed in distress.

"No wonder she's been so sad," Litsi said. "It wasn't just Helikon falling."

"Which horse?" Danielle asked.

"Col," I said. "The one I rode at Ascot."

"That didn't quite win?" Litsi asked.

"Yes," Danielle said, "her Gold Cup horse." She swallowed. "If Litsi tells Beatrice Monday's my last day, I won't deny it."

We spent another slightly claustrophobic evening in the house. Roland came down to dinner, and conversation was a trifle stilted owing to everyone having to remember what was not known and shouldn't be said.

Litsi managed to tell Beatrice positively but naturally that the last time I would be fetching Danielle at night would be Monday, as Danielle would no longer be working in the evenings, a piece of news that surprised the princess greatly.

Beatrice took in the information satisfactorily, with her eyes sliding my way, and one could almost see the cogs clicking as she added the hour to the place.

I wondered if she understood the nature of what I hoped she was going to arrange. She seemed to have no doubts or compunction about laying an ambush that would remove me from her path; but of course she didn't know about the attack on Litsi or about Col's death, which we couldn't tell her because either she would instantly apply breaking-point pressure to her brother by informing him, or she would suffer renewed pangs of remorse and not set up the ambush at all.

Beatrice was a real wild card, I thought, who could win us or lose us the game.

Nanterre again didn't telephone; and there had been no one all day asking about a Bradbury reward.

The advertisements had been prominent in the racing papers for two days, and noticeable in the *Towncrier*, but the message-bearer either hadn't seen them or hadn't thought answering worthwhile.

Well, I thought in disappointment, going a little painfully to bed, it had seemed a good idea at the time, as Eve no doubt told Adam after the apple.

Dawson buzzed through on the intercom before seven on Sunday morning. Phone call, he said.

Not again, I thought: Christ, not again.

I picked up the receiver with the most fearful foreboding, trying hard not to shake.

"Look here," a voice said, "this message from Danielle. I don't want any trouble, but is this reward business straight up?"

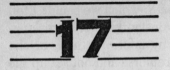

17

"**Y**es," I said, dry-mouthed, "it is."

"How much then?"

I took a deep breath, hardly believing, my heart thumping.

"Quite a lot," I said. "It depends how much you can tell me. I'd like to come and see you."

"Don't know about that," he said grudgingly.

"The reward would be bigger," I said. "And I'd bring it with me." Breathing was easier. My hands had stopped trembling.

"I don't want any trouble," he said.

"There won't be any. You tell me where you'll meet me, and I'll come."

"What's your name?" he demanded.

I hesitated fractionally. "Christmas," I said.

"Well, Mr. Christmas, I'm not meeting you for less than

a hundred quid." He was belligerent, suspicious and cautious, all in one.

"All right," I said slowly. "I agree."

"Up front, on the table," he said.

"Yes, all right."

"And if I tell you what you want to hear, you'll double it."

"If you tell me the truth, yes."

"Huh," he said sourly. "Right then. You're in London, aren't you? That's a London number."

"Yes."

"I'll meet you in Bradbury," he said. "In the town, not the racecourse. You get to Bradbury by twelve o'clock, I'll meet you in the pub there. The King's Head, halfway along the High Street."

"I'll be there," I said. "How will I know you?"

He thought, breathing heavily. "I'll take the *Sporting Life* with your ad in it."

"And . . . er . . . what's your name?" I asked.

He had the answer to that question all ready. "John Smith," he said promptly. "I'll see you, then, Mr. Christmas. OK?"

"OK," I said.

He disconnected and I lay back on the pillows feeling more apprehensive than delighted. The fish, I thought, hadn't sounded securely on the hook. He'd nibbled at the bait, but was full of reservations. I just hoped to hell he'd turn up where and when he'd said, and that he'd be the right man if he did.

His accent had been country English, not broad, just the normal local speech of Berkshire that I heard every day in Lambourn. He hadn't seemed overbright or cunning, and the amount he'd asked for, I thought, revealed a good deal about his income and his needs.

Large reward . . . When I hadn't objected to one hundred, he'd doubled it to two. But to him, two hundred equated large.

He was a gambler: Litsi had described him as having a sporting paper, a form book and binoculars. What was now certain was that he gambled small, a punter to whom a hundred was a substantial win. I supposed I should be glad he didn't think of a hundred as a basic stake: a large reward to someone like that might have been a thousand.

Thankfully I set about the business of getting up, which on the mornings after a crunch was always slow and twingy. The icepacks from bedtime had long melted, but the puffball my ankle had swollen to on the previous afternoon had definitely contracted. I took the strapping off, inspected the blackening bruising, and wrapped it up again snugly; and I could still get my shoe on, which was lucky.

In trousers, shirt and sweater I went down by elevator to the basement and nicked more ice cubes from the fridge, fastening them into plastic bags and wedging them down inside my sock. Dawson appeared in his dressing gown to see what was going on in his kitchen and merely raised his eyebrows much as he had the evening before, when I'd pinched every ice cube in the house.

"Did I do right," he asked, watching, "putting that phone call through to you?"

"You certainly did."

"He said it was to do with the advertisement: he said he was in a hurry as he was using a public telephone."

"Was he?" I pushed the trouser leg down over the loaded

sock, feeling the chill strike deep through the strapping.

"Yes," Dawson said. "I could hear the pips. Don't you give yourself frostbite, doing that?"

"Never have, yet."

Breakfast, he said a shade resignedly, would be ready in the morning room in half an hour, and I thanked him and spent the interval waking up Litsi, who said bleary-eyed that he was unaccustomed to life before ten on Sunday mornings.

"We've had a tug on the line," I explained, and told him about John Smith.

"Are you sure it isn't Nanterre setting a trap?" Litsi said, waking up thoroughly. "Don't forget, Nanterre could have seen that advertisement too. He could be reeling *you* in, not the other way round. I suppose you did think of that?"

"Yes, I did. But I think John Smith is genuine. If he'd been a trap he would've been different, more positive."

He frowned. "I'll come with you," he said.

I shook my head. "I'd like your company but Sammy has the day off because we're all here, and if we both go . . ."

"All right," he said. "But don't go onto balconies. How's your ankle? Or am I not supposed to ask?"

"Halfway to normal," I said. "Danielle exaggerates."

"Not so much." He rubbed a hand through his hair. "Have you enough cash for John Smith?"

"Yes, in my house. I'll go there on the way. I'll be back this afternoon, sometime."

"All being well," he said dryly.

I drove to Lambourn after a particularly thorough inspection of the car. It was still possible that John Smith was a trap, though on balance I didn't believe it. Nanterre couldn't have found an actor to convey the subtleties in John Smith's attitudes, nor could he himself possibly have imitated the voice. John Smith might be someone trying to snatch the reward without any goods to deliver; he might be a fraud, I thought, but not a deadly danger.

My house felt cold and empty. I opened all the letters that had accumulated there since Monday, took the ones that mattered, and dumped the junk into the dustbin along with several unread newspapers. I leafed through the present Sunday's papers and found two or three mentions, both as general news stories and as special paragraphs on the sports pages about Col being shot. All the stories recalled Cascade and Cotopaxi, but raised no great questions of *why*, and said *who* was still a complete mystery. I hadn't seen Beatrice reading any English newspaper since she'd arrived, and just hoped to hell she wouldn't start that morning.

I collected a few things to take with me: clean clothes, the cash, some writing paper, a pocket-sized tape recorder, spare cassettes and a few photographs sorted from a disorganized drawerful.

I also loaded into the car the video-recorder I'd used to make parts of the film indicting Maynard, and some spare tapes and batteries for that, but more on an "in case" basis than with any clear plans for their use: and I picked up from the kitchen, where I kept it, a small gadget I'd bought in New York that started cars from a distance. It worked by radio, transmitting to a receiver in the car that then switched on the ignition and activated the starter-motor. I liked gadgets, and that one was most useful in freezing weather, since one could start one's car from indoors and warm up the engine before plunging out into snowstorms oneself.

I checked my answering machine for messages and dealt with those, repacked my sock with new ice cubes and finally set off again to Bradbury, arriving in the small country town with ten minutes in hand.

The King's Head, I found, was a square smallish brick building, relatively modern and dedicated to beer. No old-world charm, no warming pans, oak beams, red lampshades, pewter mugs. The Bradbury Arms, across the road, looked plentifully supplied with everything.

I parked in the street and went into the King's Head public bar, finding a darts board, several benches, low tables, sisal matting and an understocked bar.

No customers.

I tried the saloon bar, genteelly furnished with glass-topped tables and moderately comfortable wooden arm-chairs, in one of which I sat while I waited.

A man appeared behind the bar there and asked what I'd like.

"Half of mild," I said.

He pulled it, and I paid.

I laid on the glass-topped table in front of me the large brown envelope that contained Lord Vaughnley's file photograph of Nanterre. The envelope currently bulged also with the tape recorder, four more photographs, two bundles of banknotes in small separate envelopes and some plain writing paper. All that I needed for John Smith was ready, but there was no sign of John Smith.

A few local people well known to the innkeeper came into the bar, ordering "the usual" and eyeing me, the stranger. None of them carried a newspaper. None of them, I noticed with surprise, was a woman.

I could hear the thud ... thud ... thud of someone playing darts in the public bar, so I picked up my envelope and my beer and walked back there to look.

There were three customers by that time; two playing darts and one sitting on the edge of a bench looking at his watch.

Beside him on the bench lay Saturday's *Sporting Life*, the bold-printed advertisement uppermost.

With a great sigh of relief I went over and sat down on the bench, leaving the newspaper between him and me.

"Mr. Smith?" I said.

He jumped nervously, even though he'd watched me walk across to join him.

He was perhaps in his fifties, wore a zip-fronted fawn jacket and had an air of habitual defeat. His hair, still black, was brushed in careful lines across a balding scalp, and the tip of his nose pointed straight downward, as if someone had punched it that way long ago.

"My name's Christmas," I said.

He looked at me carefully and frowned. "I know you, don't I?"

"Maybe," I said. "I brought your money. Would you like a drink?"

"I'll get it," he said. He stood up with alacrity to go over to the bar, and from that distance studied me doubtfully. I put a hand into the big envelope, switched on the tape recorder, and drew out the first of the packets of money, laying it on the table beside my glass.

He came back at length with a pint and drank a third of it thirstily.

"Why are you limping?" he said, putting the glass down watchfully.

"Twisted my ankle."

"You're that jockey," he said. "Kit Fielding."

I could feel alarm vibrating in him at the identification and pushed the money toward him, to anchor him, to prevent flight.

"A hundred," I said, "up front."

"It wasn't my fault," he said in a rush, half aggressively, on the defensive.

"No, I know that. Take the money."

He stretched out a big-knuckled hand, picked up the booty, checked it, and slotted it into an internal pocket.

"Tell me what happened," I said.

He wasn't ready, however. The unease, cause and effect, had to be dealt with first.

"Look, I don't want this going any further," he said nervously. "I've been in two minds . . . I saw this advertisement Friday . . . but, look, see, by right I shouldn't have been at the races. I'm telling you I was there, but I don't want it going no further."

"Mm," I said noncommittally.

"But, see, I could do with some untaxed dosh, who couldn't? So I thought, maybe if it was worth two hundred to you, I'd tell you."

"The rest's in here," I said, pointing to the brown envelope. "Just tell me what happened."

"Look, I was supposed to be at work. I made out I'd got flu. I wouldn't get fired if the bosses found out, just a dressing down, but I don't want the wife knowing, see what I mean? She thought I was at work. I went home my regular time. She'd bellyache something chronic if she knew. She's dead set against gambling, see what I mean?"

"And you," I said, "like your little flutter."

"Nothing wrong in that, is there?" he demanded.

"No," I said.

"The wife doesn't know I'm here," he said. "This isn't my local. I told her I had to come into Bradbury for a part for my motor. I'm draining the sump and I need a new filter. I'll have to keep quiet about meeting you, see? I had to ring you up this morning while I was out with the dog. So, see what I mean, I don't want this getting about."

I thought without guilt of my sharp-eared little recorder, but reflected that Mr. Smith's gusher would dry in a microsecond if he found it was there. He seemed, however, not the sort of man who would ever suspect its existence.

"I'm sure it won't get about, Mr. Smith," I said.

He jumped again slightly at the name.

"See, the name's not Smith, I expect you guessed. But well, if you don't know, I'm that much safer, see what I mean?"

"Yes," I said.

He drank most of the beer and wiped his mouth with a handkerchief: white with brown lines and checks round the edge. The two men playing darts finished their game and went out to the saloon bar, leaving us alone in our spartan surroundings.

"I'd been looking at the horses in the paddock," he said, "and I was going off toward the bookies when this character came up to me and offered me a fiver to deliver a message."

"A fiver," I said.

"Yeah . . . well, see what I mean, I said, 'Ten, and you're on.'" He sniffed. "He wasn't best pleased. He gave me a right filthy look, but in the end he coughed up. Ten smackers. It meant I'd be betting free on that race, see what I mean?"

"Yes," I said.

"So he says, this character, that all I'd got to do was walk over to a man he would point out, and tell him that Danielle wanted him to go up to the balcony to see the view."

"He said that precisely?"

"He made me repeat this twice. Then he gave me two fivers, pointed at a big man in a dark overcoat, very distinguished-looking, and when I turned round, he'd gone. Anyway, he paid me to pass on the message, so I did. I didn't think anything of it, see what I mean? I mean, there didn't seem any harm in it. I knew the balcony wasn't open, but if he wanted to go up there, so what, see what I mean?"

"I can see that," I said.

"I passed on the message, and the distinguished-looking gent thanked me, and I went on out to the bookies and put two fivers on Applejack."

Mr. Smith was a loser, I thought. I'd beaten Applejack into second place, on Pinkeye.

"You're not drinking," he observed, eyeing my still-full glass.

Beer was fattening. "You can have it," I said, "if you like."

He took the glass without ado and started on the contents.

"Look," he said. "You'd better tell me. Was it the man I gave the message to, who fell off the balcony?" His eyes were worried, almost pleading for any answer but the one he feared.

"I'm afraid so," I said.

"I thought it would be. I didn't see him fall, I was out front with the bookies, see what I mean? But later on, here and there, I heard people talking about coats and such. I didn't know what they were on about, though, until the next day, when it was all in the paper." He shook his head. "I couldn't say anything, though, could I, on account of being at the races when I'd said I wasn't."

"Difficult," I agreed.

"It wasn't my fault he fell off the balcony," he said aggrievedly. "So I thought, what was the point of telling anyone about the message. I'd keep my mouth shut. Maybe this Danielle pushed him, I thought. Maybe he was her husband and her lover got me to send him up there, so she could push him off. See what I mean?"

I stifled a smile and saw what he meant.

"I didn't want to be mixed up with the police, see? I mean, he wasn't killed, thanks to you, so no harm done, was there?"

"No," I said. "And he wasn't pushed. He overbalanced on some loose planks the builders had left there. He told me about it, explaining how he'd fallen."

"Oh." Mr. Anonymous Smith seemed both relieved and disappointed that he hadn't been involved in an attempted crime of passion. "I see."

"But," I said, "he was curious about the message. He thought he'd like to know who asked you to give it to him, so we decided to put that advertisement in the paper."

"Do you know him then?" he said, perplexed.

"I do now," I said.

"Ah." He nodded.

"The man who gave you the message," I said, casually, "do you remember what he looked like?"

I tried not to hold my breath. Mr. Smith, however, sensed that this was a crucial question and looked meaningfully at the envelope, his mind on the second installment.

"The second hundred's yours," I said, "if you can describe him."

"He wasn't English," he said, taking the plunge. "Strong sort of character, hard voice, big nose."

"Do you remember him clearly?" I asked, relaxing greatly inside. "Would you know him again?"

"I've been thinking about him since Thursday," he said simply. "I reckon I would."

Without making a big thing of it I pulled the five photographs out of the envelope: all eight-by-ten-black-and-white glossy pictures of people receiving trophies after races. In four of the groups the winning jockey was Fielding, but I'd had my back to the camera in two of them: the pictures were as fair a test as I'd been able to devise at short notice.

"Would you look at these photographs," I said, "and see if he's there?"

He brought out a pair of glasses and sat them on the flattened nose: an ineffectual man, not unhappy.

He took the photographs, and looked at them carefully, one by one. I'd put Nanterre's picture in fourth place of the five; and he glanced at it and passed on. He looked at the fifth and put them all down on the table, and I hoped he wouldn't guess at the extent of my disappointment.

"Well," he said judiciously, "yes, he's there."

I watched him breathlessly and waited. If he could truly recognize Nanterre, I would play any game he had in mind.

"Look," he said, as if scared by his own boldness. "You're Kit Fielding, right? You're not short of a bob or two. And that man who fell, he looked pretty well heeled. See what I mean? Make it two fifty, and I'll tell you which one he is."

I breathed deeply and pretended to be considering it with reluctance.

"All right," I said eventually. "Two fifty."

He flicked through the photographs and pointed unerringly to Nanterre.

"Him," he said.

"You've got your two fifty," I said. I gave him the second of the small envelopes. "There's a hundred in there." I fished out my wallet and sorted out fifty more. "Thanks," I said.

He nodded and put the money away carefully, as before.

"Mr. Smith," I said easily. "What would you do for another hundred?"

He stared at me through the glasses. "What do you mean?" Hopefully, on the whole.

I said, "If I write a sentence on a sheet of paper, will you sign your name to it? The name John Smith will do very well."

"What sentence?" he said, looking worried again.

"I'll write it," I said. "Then see if you will sign."

"For a hundred?"

"That's right."

I pulled a sheet of plain writing paper from the envelope, unclipped my pen and wrote,

At Bradbury races [I put the date] I gave a man a message to the effect that Danielle wanted him to go up to the viewing balcony. I identify the man who gave me that message as the man I have indicated in the photograph.

I handed it to Mr. Smith. He read it. He was unsure of the consequences of signing, but he was thinking of a hundred pounds.

"Sign it John Smith?" he said.

"Yes. With a flourish, like a proper signature."

I handed him my pen. With almost no further hesitation he did as I'd asked.

"Great," I said, taking the page and slipping it, with the photographs, back into the envelope. I took out my wallet again and gave him another hundred pounds, and saw him looking almost hungrily at the money he could see I still had.

"There's another hundred and fifty in there," I said, showing him. "It would round you up to five hundred altogether."

He liked the game increasingly. He said, "For that, what would you want?"

"To save me following you home," I said pleasantly, "I'd like you to write your real name and address down for me, on a separate sheet of paper."

I produced a clean sheet from the envelope. "You still have my pen," I reminded him. "Be a good fellow and write."

He looked as if I'd punched him in the brain.

"I came in on the bus," he said faintly.

"I can follow buses," I said.

He looked sick.

"I won't tell your wife you were at the races," I said.

"Not if you'll write down your name so I won't have to follow you."

"For a hundred and fifty?" he said weakly.

"Yes."

He wrote a name and address in capital letters:

A. V. HODGES,
44, CARLETON AVENUE,
WIDDERLAWN, NR. BRADBURY.

"What does the A. V. stand for?" I asked.

"Arnold Vincent," he said without guile.

"OK," I said. "Here's the rest of your money." I counted it out for him. "Don't lose it all at once."

He looked startled and then shamefacedly raised a laugh. "I can't go racing often, see what I mean? My wife knows how much money I've got."

"She doesn't now," I said cheerfully. "Thank you very much, Mr. Smith."

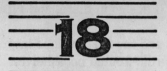

18

I had plenty of time and thought I might as well make sure. I dawdled invisibly around while John Smith bought his oil filter at a garage and caught his bus, and I followed the bus unobtrusively to Widderlawn.

John Smith descended and walked to Carleton Avenue where at number 44, a well-tended council semi-detached, he let himself in with a latchkey.

Satisfied on all counts, I drove back to London and found Litsi coming out of the library as I entered the hall.

"I saw you coming," he said lazily. The library windows looked out to the street. "I'm delighted you're back." He had been watching for me, I thought.

"It wasn't a trap," I said.

"So I see."

I smiled suddenly and he said, "A purring cat, if ever I saw one."

I nodded toward the library. "Let's go in there, and I'll tell you."

I carried the bag with clothes and the big envelope into the long paneled room with its grille-fronted bookshelves, its Persian rugs, its net and red velvet curtains. A nobly proportioned room, it was chiefly used for entertaining callers not intimate enough to be invited upstairs, and to me had the lifeless air of expensive waiting rooms.

Litsi looked down at my feet. "Are you *squelching*?" he asked disbelievingly.

"Mm." I put down the bag and the envelope and peeled off my left shoe, into which one of the icepacks had leaked.

To his discriminating horror I pulled the one intact bag out of my sock and emptied the contents onto a convenient potted plant. The second bag, having emptied itself, followed the first into the wastepaper basket. I pulled off my drenched sock, left it folded on top of my bag, and replaced my wet shoe.

"I suppose," Litsi said, "all that started out as mobile refrigeration."

"Quite right."

"I'd have kept a sprain warm," he said thoughtfully.

"Cold is quicker."

I took the envelope over to where a pair of armchairs stood, one on each side of a table with a lamp on it: switched on the lamp, sat in a chair. Litsi, following, took the other armchair. The library itself was perpetually dark, needing lights almost always, the gray afternoon on that day giving up the contest in the folds of cream net at the street end of the room.

"Mr. Smith," I said, "can speak for himself."

I put the small recorder on the table, rewound the cassette, and started it going. Litsi, the distinguished-looking gent, listened with wry fascination to the way he'd been set up, and toward the end his eyebrows started climbing, a sign with him that meant a degree of not understanding.

I showed him the paper John Smith had signed, and while he watched drew a circle with my pen round the head of Nanterre in the photograph.

"Mr. Smith did live where he wrote," I said. "I did follow him home, to make sure."

"But," Litsi said surprised, "if you followed him anyway, why did you give him the last hundred and fifty?"

"Oh . . . mm . . . it saved me having to discover his name from the neighbors." Litsi looked skeptical. "Well," I said, "he deserved it."

"What are you going to do with these things?" he asked, waving a hand.

"With a bit of luck," I said, "this." And I told him.

Grateful for the elevator, I went up three floors to the bamboo room to stow away my gear, to shower and change, to put on dry strapping and decide on no more ice.

The palatial room was beginning to feel like home, I thought. Beatrice seemed to have given up plans for active invasion, though leaving me in no doubt about the strength of her feelings; and as my affection for the room grew, so did my understanding of her pique.

She wasn't in the sitting room when I went down for the evening; only Danielle and the princess, with Litsi pouring their drinks.

I bowed slightly to the princess, as it was the first time I'd seen her that day, and kissed Danielle on the cheek.

"Where have you been?" she asked neutrally.

"Fishing."

"Did you catch anything?"

"Sharkbait," I said.

She looked me swiftly, laughingly, in the eyes, the old loving Danielle there and gone in a flash. I took the glass into which Litsi had poured a scant ounce of scotch and tried to stifle regret.

Beatrice walked into the room with round dazed eyes and stood vaguely in the center as if not sure what to do next. Litsi began to mix her drink the way she liked it: he'd have made a good king but an even better barman, I thought, liking him. Beatrice went across to the sofa where the princess was sitting and took the place beside her as if her knees had given way.

"There we are, Beatrice," Litsi said with good humor, setting the red drink down on the low table in front of her. "Dash of Worcestershire, twist of lemon."

Beatrice looked at the drink unseeingly.

"Casilia," she said, as if the words were hurting her throat. "I have been such a fool."

"My dear Beatrice . . ." the princess said.

Beatrice without warning started to cry, not silently but with "Ohs" of distress that were close to groans.

The princess looked uncomfortable, and it was Litsi who came to Beatrice's aid with a large white handkerchief and comforting noises.

"Tell us what's troubling you," he said, "and surely we can help you."

Beatrice wailed "Oh" again with her open mouth twisted into an agonized circle and pressed Litsi's handkerchief hard to her eyes.

"Do try to pull yourself together, Beatrice, dear," the princess said with a touch of astringency. "We can't help you until we know what's the matter."

Beatrice's faintly theatrical paroxysm abated, leaving a real distress showing. The overbid for sympathy might have misfired, but the need for it existed.

"I can't help it," she said, drying her eyes and blotting her mascara carefully, laying the folded edge of handkerchief flat over her lower eyelid and blinking her top lashes onto it, leaving tiny black streaks. No one in extremis, I thought, wiped their eyes so methodically.

"I've been such a fool," she said.

"In what way, dear?" asked the princess, giving the unmistakable impression that she already thought her sister-in-law a fool in most ways most of the time.

"I . . . I've been talking to Henri Nanterre," Beatrice said.

"When?" Litsi asked swiftly.

"Just now. Upstairs, in my room."

Both he and I looked at the recording telephone, which had remained silent. Neither Litsi nor I had lifted a receiver at the right time after all.

"You telephoned him?" Litsi said.

"Yes, of course." Beatrice began to recover such wits as she had. "Well, I mean . . ."

"What did he say," Litsi asked, not pursuing it, "that has so upset you?"

"I . . . I . . . He was so charming when he came to see me in Palm Beach, but I've been wrong, terribly wrong."

"What did he say just now?" Litsi asked again.

"He said"—she looked at him a shade wildly—"that he'd thought Roland would crack when you were nearly killed. He asked me why he hadn't. But I . . . I didn't know you'd been nearly killed. I said I hadn't heard anything about it, and I was sure Roland and Casilia hadn't, and he was furiously angry, *shouting* . . ." She shook her head. "I had to hold the telephone away from my ear . . . he was hurting me."

The princess was looking astounded and distressed.

"Litsi! What happened? You never said . . ."

"Henri boasted," Beatrice said miserably, "that he organized an accident for Litsi that would have brilliantly succeeded, except that this . . . this . . ." She didn't know what to call me, and contented herself in pointing. "*He* saved Litsi's life." Beatrice gulped. "I never thought . . . never ever . . . that he would do anything so *frightful*. That he would really *harm* anyone. And he said . . . he said . . . he thought Roland and Casilia wouldn't have wanted any more horses killed, and how had she reacted about her horse called Col? And when I told him I didn't know anything about it, he flew into a *rage*. He asked if Roland knew and I said I didn't know. He was shouting down the telephone . . . he was totally *furious*. He said he'd never thought that they would hold out so long. He said it was all taking too long and he would step up the pressure."

Beatrice's shock was deep.

"He said the jockey was always in his way, blocking him, bringing in guards and recording telephones; so he would get rid of the jockey first. Then after that, Danielle would lose her beauty—and then no one would stop Roland signing. He said," she added, her eyes round and dry again, "I was to tell Roland what he'd threatened. I was to say he had telephoned here and I'd happened to answer."

The princess, aghast but straight-backed, said, "I won't let you tell Roland anything, Beatrice."

"Henri put the telephone down," Beatrice said, "and I sat there thinking he didn't mean it, he couldn't possibly spoil Danielle's face. She's my niece as well as Roland's. I wouldn't want that, not for all the money in the world. I tried to make myself believe it was just a threat, but he did chase after her that evening, and he did kill the horses; he boasted of it . . . and I didn't want to believe he had tried to kill Litsi . . . to kill! . . . it wasn't possible . . . but he sounded so vicious . . . I wouldn't have believed he could be like that." She turned imploringly to the princess. "I may have been foolish, but I'm not *wicked*, Casilia."

I listened to the outpouring with profound disturbance. I didn't want her late-flowering remorse tangling the carefully laid lines. I would much have preferred her purposefulness to remain strong and intact.

"Did you ring him back?" I asked.

Beatrice didn't like talking to me, and didn't answer until Litsi asked her the same question.

"I did," she said passionately, asking for absolution, "but he'd already gone."

"Already?" Litsi asked.

Beatrice said in a much smaller voice, "He'd said I couldn't reach him again at that number. He wasn't there half the time in any event. I mean . . ."

"How many times have you talked to him?" Litsi asked mildly. "And at what time of day?"

Beatrice hesitated but answered, "Today and yesterday, at about six, and Thursday morning, and . . ." She tried to remember. "It must have been Wednesday evening at six, and Monday twice, after I'd found out . . ." Her voice trailed away, the admission, half out, suddenly alarming her.

"Found out what?" Litsi asked without censure.

She said unhappily, "The make and color of Danielle's car. He wanted to know. I had no idea," she suddenly wailed, "that he meant to attack her. I couldn't believe it, when he said on the telephone . . . when he told Litsi . . . saying that young women shouldn't drive alone at night. Danielle," she said beseechingly, turning to her, "I'd never cause harm to you, ever."

"But on Thursday you told him Danielle and I were going to Bradbury races," Litsi commented.

"Yes, but he *asked* me to tell him things like that," Beatrice said fiercely. "He wanted to know the least little thing, every time. He asked what was happening . . . he said as it was important to me for him to succeed, I should help him with details, any details, however tiny."

I said, in Litsi's unprovoking manner, "To what extent was it important to you, Mrs. Bunt?"

She was provoked all the same: glared at me and didn't answer.

Litsi rephrased the question, "Did Henri promise you perhaps a nice present if he succeeded?"

Beatrice looked uncertainly at the princess, whose gaze was on the hands on her lap, whose face was severe. No blandishments on earth would have induced her to spy comprehensively for her host's, her brother's, enemy, and she was trying hard, I imagined, not to show open disgust.

To Litsi, Beatrice said, self-excusingly, "I have the de Brescou trust fund, of course, but it's expensive to keep one's *position* in Palm Beach. My soirees, you know, just for fifty dear friends . . . nothing large . . . and my servants, just a married couple . . . are barely *enough,* and Henri said .. Henri promised . . ." She paused doubtfully.

"A million dollars?" Litsi suggested.

"No, no," she protested, "not so much. He said when the pistols were in production and when he'd made his first good arms deal, which would be in under a year, he thought, he would send a gift of two hundred and fifty thousand, and a hundred thousand each year afterward for three years. Not so very much, but it would have made a useful difference to me, you see."

A soiree for a hundred, I thought sardonically. A small rise in status among the comfortably rich. More than half a million dollars overall. One could see the difference with clarity.

"I didn't see any wrong in trying to persuade Roland," she said. "When I came over here I was certain I could do it, and have Henri's lovely money to spend afterward."

"Did he give you a written contract?" I asked.

"No, of course not," she said, forgetting she was speaking to me, "but he promised. He's a *gentleman.*"

Even she, once she'd said it, could see that although Nanterre was many things, from an aristocrat to an entrepreneur, a gentleman he was not.

"He promised," she reiterated.

Beatrice seemed to be feeling better about things, as if full confession excused the sin.

I was anxious to know how much information she'd passed on before the dawn of realization and the consequent change of heart: a lot of good plans had gone down the drain if she hadn't relayed what we'd wanted.

"Mrs. Bunt," I said diffidently, "if Henri Nanterre told

you he was going to get rid of the jockey, did he say how? Or perhaps when? Or where?"

"No, he didn't," she said promptly, looking at me with disfavor.

"But did you perhaps tell him where I'd be going, and when, in the way you told him about Danielle and Litsi?"

She simply stared at me.

Litsi, understanding what I wanted to know, said, "Beatrice, if you've told Nanterre where Kit might be vulnerable, you must tell us now, seriously you must."

She looked at him defensively. "It's because of him," she meant me, "that Roland hasn't agreed to Henri's plans. Roland told me so. So did *he*." She jerked her head in my direction. "He said it straight out at dinner . . . you heard him . . . that while he was here Roland wouldn't sign. He has so much power. You all do what he says. If he hadn't been here, Henri said, it would all have been settled on the very first day, even before I got here. Everything's *his* fault. It was *he* who drove Henri to do all those awful things. It's because of *him* that I probably won't get my money. So when Henri asked me if I could find out when and where the jockey would be alone . . . well . . . I said I would. I was glad to!"

"Aunt Beatrice!" Danielle exclaimed. "How could you?"

"He has my room," Beatrice said explosively. "*My room.*"

There was a small intense silence. Then I said mildly, "If you'd tell us what you told Henri Nanterre, then I wouldn't go there, wherever."

"You must tell us," the princess said vehemently. "If any harm comes to Kit because of you, Beatrice, you will never be received again either in this house or in the chateau."

Beatrice looked stunned by this direst of threats.

"Moreover," Litsi said in a tone loaded with strength, "you are not my sister, my sister-in-law or my aunt. I have no family feeling for you. You gave information that might have led to my death. If you've done the same regarding Kit, which it appears you have, and Nanterre succeeds in killing him, you'll be guilty of conspiracy to murder, and I shall inform the police to that effect."

Beatrice crumbled totally inside. It was all far more than she'd meant to involve herself in, and Litsi's threat sounded like the heavy tread of an unthinkable future of penal reckoning.

Beatrice said to Litsi with a touch of sullenness, "I told Henri where he keeps his car, while he's here. This evening I told Henri that he'll be fetching Danielle for the last time tomorrow, that he goes round to his car at one-thirty in the morning. Henri said that was excellent. But then he talked about you at Bradbury . . . and the horses dying . . and he started shouting, and I realized . . . how he'd used me." Her face crumpled as if she would cry again, but perhaps sensing a universal lack of sympathy, she smothered the impulse and looked from one to the other of us, searching for pity.

Litsi was looking quietly triumphant, much as I was feeling myself. The princess however was shocked and wide-eyed.

"That dark mews!" she said, horrified. "Kit, don't go down there."

"No," I assured her. "I'll park somewhere else." She relaxed, clearly satisfied by the simple solution, and Danielle looked at me broodingly, knowing I wouldn't.

I winked at her.

She almost laughed. "How can you?" she said. "How can you joke? Don't say it, don't say it . . . easily."

The princess and Beatrice looked mystified but paid not much attention.

"Are you absolutely certain," I said to Beatrice, "that you can't get in touch with Nanterre again?"

"Yes, I am," she said uncertainly, and looked nervously at Litsi. "But . . . but . . ."

"But what, Beatrice?"

"He's going to telephone here this evening. He wanted me to tell Roland about your accident and about Col being shot, and then he would find out if Roland was ready to sign . . . and if not . . ." She squirmed. "I couldn't let him hurt Danielle. I couldn't!"

Her eyes seemed to focus on her untouched drink. She stretched out a scarlet-nailed much-beringed hand and gave a good imitation of one fresh from the desert. The princess, hardly able to look at her sister-in-law, headed for the door, motioning with her hand for me to go with her.

I followed. She went into the dining room where dinner was laid and asked me to close the door, which I did.

She said, with intense worry, "Nothing has changed, has it, because of what Beatrice has told us?"

"No," I said, with a thankfulness she didn't hear.

"We can't go on and on. We can't risk Danielle's face. You can't risk that." The dilemma was dreadful, as Nanterre had meant.

"No," I said. "I can't risk that. But give me until Tuesday. Don't let Monsieur know of the threats until then. We have a plan. We have a lever, but we need a stronger one. We'll get rid of Nanterre," I promised, "if you'll give us that time."

"You and Litsi?"

"Yes."

"Litsi was the man who fell from the balcony," she said, wanting confirmation.

I nodded, and told her of the decoy message but not about finding the messenger.

"Dear heaven. Surely we must tell the police."

"Wait until Tuesday," I begged. "We will then, if we have to."

She agreed easily enough because police inquiries could lead to publicity; and I hoped for Arnold Vincent Hodges's sake that we wouldn't have to drop him into hot water with his wife.

I asked the princess if I could have ten minutes' private conversation with her husband that evening, and without more ado she whisked us both up in the elevator and arranged it on the spot, saying it was a convenient time as he would not be coming down to dinner.

She saw me in and left us, and I took the red leather armchair as indicated by Roland.

"How can I help you?" he said civilly, his head supported by the high-backed wheelchair. "More guards? I have met Sammy," he smiled faintly. "He's amusing."

"No, monsieur, not more guards. I wondered if I could go to see your lawyer, Gerald Greening, early tomorrow morning. Would you mind if I made an appointment?"

"Is this to do with Henri Nanterre?"

"Yes, monsieur."

"Could you say why you want Gerald?"

I explained. He said wearily that he saw no prospect of success, but that I needn't go to Gerald's office, Gerald would come to the house. The world, I saw in amusement, was divided between those who went to lawyers' offices and those to whom lawyers came.

Roland said that if I would look up Gerald's home number and get through to it, he would speak to Gerald himself, if he were in, and in a short time the appointment was made.

"He will come here on his way to his office," Roland said, handing me the receiver to replace. "Eight-thirty. Give him breakfast."

"Yes, monsieur."

He nodded a fraction. "Goodnight, Kit."

I went down to dinner, which took place in more silence than ever, and later, as he'd threatened, Nanterre telephoned.

When I heard his voice, I pressed the record button, but again not that for conference.

"I'll talk to anyone but you," he said.

"Then no one."

He shouted, "I want to talk to Casilia."

"No."

"I will talk to Roland."

"No."

"To Beatrice."

"No."

"You'll regret it," he yelled, and crashed down the receiver.

Litsi and I entertained Gerald Greening in the morning room, where he ate copiously of kippers followed by eggs and bacon, all furnished by Dawson, forewarned.

"Mm, mm," Greening grunted as we explained what we wanted. "Mm, no problem at all. Would you pass me the butter?"

He was rounded and jovial, patting his stomach. "Is there any toast?"

From his briefcase he produced a large pad of white paper upon which he made notes. "Yes, yes," he said busily, writing away. "I get the gist, absolutely. You want your intentions cast into foolproof legal language, is that right?"

We said it was.

"And you want this typed up properly this morning and furnished with seals?"

Yes please, we said. Two copies.

"No problem." He gave me his coffee cup absentmind-edly to take to the sideboard for a hot refill. "I can bring them back here by"—he consulted his watch—"say twelve noon. That all right?"

We said it would do.

He pursed his lips. "Can't manage it any faster. Have to draft it properly, get it typed without mistakes, all that sort of thing, checked, drive over from the City."

We understood.

"Marmalade?"

We passed it.

"Anything else?"

"Yes," Litsi said, fetching from a side table the buff French form that had been in the notary's briefcase, "some advise on this."

Gerald Greening said in surprise, "Surely the Frenchmen took that away with them when Monsieur de Brescou refused to sign?"

"This is a duplicate blank copy, not filled in," Litsi said. "We think the one Henri Nanterre wanted signed would have represented the first page of a whole bunch of docu-ments. Kit and I want this unused copy to form page one of our own bunch of documents." He passed it to Greening. "As you see, it's a general form of contract, with spaces for details, and in French, of course. It must be binding, or Henri Nanterre wouldn't have used it. I propose to write in French in the spaces provided, so that this and the accompanying document together constitute a binding contract under French law. I'd be grateful," he said in his most princely tone, "if you would advise me as to word-ing."

"In French?" Greening said apprehensively.

"In English . . . I'll translate."

They worked on it together until each was satisfied and Greening had embarked on round four of toast. I envied him not his bulk nor his appetite, but his freedom from restraint, and swallowed my characterless vitamins wishing they at least smelled of breakfast.

He left after the fifth slice, bearing away his notes and promising immediate action; and true to his word, he reappeared in his chauffeur-driven car at ten minutes to twelve. Litsi and I were both by then in the library watching the street, and we opened the front door to the bulky solicitor and took him into the office used by the elfin Mrs. Jenkins.

There we stapled to the front page of one of Greening's imposing-looking documents the original French form, and a photocopy of it to the other, each with the new wording typed in neatly, leaving large spaces for signing.

From there we rode up in the elevator to Roland de Brescou's private sitting room, where he and the princess and Danielle were all waiting.

Gerald Greening with vaguely theatrical flourishes presented the documents to each of them in turn, and to Litsi, asking them each to sign their names four times, once on each of the French forms; once at the end of each document.

Each document was sewn through with pink tape down the left-hand margin, as with wills, and each space for a signature at the end was provided with a round red seal.

Greening made everyone say aloud archaic words about signing, sealing and delivering, made them put a finger on each seal and witnessed each signature himself with precision. He required that I also witness each signature, which I did.

"I don't know how much of all this is strictly necessary," he said happily, "but Mr. Fielding wanted these documents unbreakable by any possible quibble of law, as he put it, so we have two witnesses, seals, declarations, everything. I do hope you all understand exactly what you've been signing as unless you should burn them or otherwise destroy them, these documents are irrevocable."

Everyone nodded, Roland de Brescou with sadness.

"That's splendid," Greening said expansively, and began looking around him and at his watch expectantly.

"And now, Gerald, some sherry?" the princess suggested with quiet amusement.

"Princess Casilia, what a splendid idea!" he said with imitation surprise. "A glass would be lovely."

I excused myself from the party on the grounds that I was riding in the two-thirty at Windsor and should have left fifteen minutes ago.

Litsi picked up the signed documents, returned them to the large envelope Gerald Greening had brought them in, and handed me the completed package.

"Don't forget to telephone," he said.

"No."

He hesitated. "Good luck," he said.

They all thought he meant with the races, which was perfectly proper.

The princess had no runners as she almost never went to Windsor races, having no box there. Beatrice was spending the day in the beauty parlor, renovating her self-esteem. Litsi was covering for Sammy, who was supposed to be resting. I hadn't expected Danielle to come with me on her own, but she followed me onto the landing from Roland's room and said, "If I come with you, can you get me to work by six-thirty?"

"With an hour to spare."

"Shall I come?"

"Yes," I said.

She nodded and went off past the princess's rooms to her own to fetch a coat, and we walked round to the mews in a reasonable replica of the old companionship. She watched me check the car and without comment waited some distance away while I started the engine and stamped on the brakes, and we talked about Gerald Greening on the way to Windsor, and about Beatrice at Palm Beach, and about her news bureau: safe subjects, but I was glad just to have her there at all.

She was wearing the fur-lined swinging green-gray showerproof jacket I'd given her for Christmas, also black trousers, a white high-necked sweater and a wide floral chintz headband holding back her cloud of dark hair. The consensus among other jockeys that she was a "knockout" had never found me disagreeing.

I drove fast to Windsor and we hurried from car park to weighing room, finding Dusty hovering about there looking pointedly at the clock.

"What about your ankle?" he said suspiciously. "You're still limping."

"Not when I'm riding," I said.

Dusty gave me a look as good as his name and scurried away, and Danielle said she would go buy a sandwich and coffee.

"Will you be all right by yourself?"

"Of course, or I wouldn't have come."

She'd made friends over the past months with the wife of a Lambourn trainer I often rode for, and with the wives of one or two of the other jockeys, but I knew the afternoons were lonely when she went racing without her aunt.

"I'm not riding in the fourth; we can watch that together," I said.

"Yes. Go in and change. You're late."

I'd taken the packet of documents into the racecourse rather than leave them in the car, and in the changing room gave them into the safekeeping of my valet. My valet's safekeeping would have shamed the vaults of the Bank of England and consisted of stowing things (like one's wallet) in the capacious front pocket of a black vinyl apron. The apron, I guessed, had evolved for that purpose: there were no lockers in the changing rooms, and one hung one's clothes on a peg.

It wasn't a demanding day from the riding point of view. I won the first of my races (the second on the card) by twenty lengths, which Dusty said was too far, and lost the next by the same distance, again to his disapproval. The next was the fourth race, which I spent on the stands with Danielle, having seen her also briefly on walks from the weighing room to parade ring. I told her the news of Joe, the jockey injured at Sandown, who was conscious and on the mend, and she said she'd had coffee with Betsy, the Lambourn trainer's wife. Everything was fine, she said, just fine.

It was the third day of March, blustery and cold, and the Cheltenham National Hunt Festival was all of a sudden as near as next week.

"Betsy says it's a shame about the Gold Cup," Danielle said. "She says you won't have a ride in it, now Col's dead."

"Not unless some poor bugger breaks his collarbone."

"Kit!"

"That's how it goes."

She looked as if she didn't need to be reminded, and I was sorry I had. I went out to the fifth race wondering if that day was some sort of test: if she were finding out for herself with finality whether or not she could permanently face what life with me entailed. I shivered slightly in the wind and thought the danger of losing her the worst one of all.

I finished third in the race, and when I returned to the unsaddling enclosure Danielle was standing there waiting, looking strained and pale and visibly trembling.

"What is it?" I said sharply, sliding down from the horse. "What's the matter?"

"He's here," she said with shock. "Henri Nanterre. I'm sure . . . it's him."

"Look," I said, "I've got to weigh in, just sit on the scales. I'll come straight back out. You just stand right outside the weighing-room door . . . don't move from there."

"No."

She went where I pointed, and I unsaddled the horse and made vaguely hopeful remarks to the mildly pleased owners. I passed the scales, gave my saddle, whip and helmet to my valet and went out to Danielle, who had stopped actually trembling but still looked upset.

"Where did you see him?" I asked.

"On the stands, during the race. He seemed to be edging toward me, coming up from below, coming sideways, saying 'excuse me' to people and looking at me now and then as if checking where I was."

"You're sure it was him?"

"He was just like the photograph. Like you've described him. I didn't realize to begin with . . . then I recognized him. I was"—she swallowed—"terrified. He sort of snaked round people, sliding like an eel."

"That's him," I said grimly.

"I slid away from him," Danielle said. "It was like panic. I couldn't move fast . . . so many people, all watching the race and annoyed with me. When I got off the stands the race was over . . . and I ran. What am I going to do? You're riding in the next race."

"Well, what you're going to do is dead boring, but you'll be safe." I smiled apologetically. "Go into the Ladies' and stay there. Find a chair there and wait. Tell the attendant you're sick, faint, tired, anything. Stay there until after the race, and I'll come and fetch you. Half an hour, not much more. I'll send someone in with a message . . . and don't come out for any message except mine. We'll need a password . . ."

"Christmas Day," she said.

"OK. Don't come out without the password, not even if you get a message saying I'm on my way to hospital, or something like that. I'll give my valet the password and tell him to fetch you if I can't . . . but I will," I said, seeing the extra fright in her expression. "I'll ride bloody carefully. Try not to let Nanterre see you going in there, but if he does . . ."

"Don't come out," she said. "Don't worry, I won't."

"Danielle . . ."

"Yes?"

"I do love you," I said.

She blinked, ducked her head, and went away fast. I thought Nanterre would have known I would be at Windsor races, he had only to look in the newspaper, and that I and anyone in the princess's family was vulnerable everywhere, not just in dark alleys.

I followed Danielle, keeping her in sight until her backview vanished into the one place Nanterre couldn't follow, and then hurried back to change colors and weigh out. I didn't see the Frenchman anywhere, which didn't mean he hadn't seen me. The highly public nature of my work on racecourses, however, I thought, might be acting in our favor: Nanterre couldn't easily attack me at the races because everywhere I went, people were watching. In parade rings, on horses, on the stands . . . wherever a jockey went in breeches and colors, heads turned to look. Anonymity took over at the racecourse exits.

I rode that last race at Windsor with extreme concentration, particularly as it was a steeplechase for novice jumpers, always an unpredictable event. My mount was trained not by Wykeham but by Betsy's husband, the Lambourn trainer, and it would be fair to say he got a good schooling run rather than a flat-out scramble.

Betsy's husband was satisfied with fourth place because the horse had jumped well, and I said, "Next time, he'll win," as one does, to please him and the owners.

I weighed in for fourth place, changed fast, collected my valuables from the valet and wrote a short note for Danielle.

"Christmas Day has dawned. Time to go."

It was Betsy, in the end, who took the note into the Ladies', coming out smiling with Danielle a minute later.

I sighed with relief: Danielle also, it seemed. Betsy shook her head over our childish games, and Danielle and I went out to the rapidly emptying car park.

"Did you see Nanterre?" Danielle asked.

"No. Nowhere."

"I'm sure it was him."

"Yes, so am I."

My car stood almost alone at the end of a line, its neighbors having departed. I stopped well before we reached it and brought the car-starter out of my pocket.

"But that," Danielle said in surprise, "is your toy for freezes."

"Mm," I said, and pressed its switch.

There was no explosion. The engine started sweetly, purring to life. We went on toward the car and I did the other checks anyway, but finding nothing wrong.

"What if it had blown up?" Danielle said.

"Better the car than us."

"Do you think he *would*?"

"I really don't know. I don't mind taking precautions that turn out to be unnecessary. It's 'if only' that would be embarrassing."

I drove out onto the highway and at the first intersection went off it and round and started back in the opposite direction.

"More avoidance of 'if only'?" Danielle said with irony.

"Do you want acid squirted in your face?"

"Not especially."

"Well, we don't know what sort of transport Nanterre's got. And one car can sit inconspicuously behind you for hours on a motorway. I'd not like him to jump us in those small streets at Chiswick."

When we reached the next intersection I reversed the process and Danielle studied the traffic out of the rear window.

"Nothing came all the way round after us," she said.

"Good."

"So can we relax?"

"The man who's coming to fetch you tonight is called Swallow," I said. "When the car comes for you, get those big men on the studio reception desk to ask him his name. If he doesn't say Swallow, check up with the car-hire firm." I slid my wallet out. "Their card's in there, in the front."

She took the card and passed the wallet back.

"What haven't you thought of?"

"I wish I knew."

Even with the wrong-direction detour, it was a short journey from Windsor to Chiswick, and we arrived in the streets leading to the studio a good hour before six-thirty.

"Do you want to go in early?" I asked.

"No . . . Park the car where we can sit and look at the river."

I found a spot where we could see brown water sliding slowly upstream, covering the mud-flats as the tide came in. There were seagulls flying against the wind, raucously calling, and a coxed four feathering their oars with curved fanatical backs.

"I have . . . er . . . something to tell you," Danielle said nervously.

"No," I said with pain.

"You don't know what it is."

"Today was a test," I said.

Danielle said slowly, "I forget sometimes that you can read minds."

"I can't. Not often. You know that."

"You just did."

"There are better days than today," I said hopelessly.

"And worse."

I nodded.

"Don't look so sad," she said. "I can't bear it."

"I'll give it up if you'll marry me," I said.

"Do you mean that?"

"Yes."

She didn't seem overjoyed. I'd lost, it seemed, on all counts.

"I . . . er . . ." she said faintly. "If you don't give it up, I'll marry you."

I thought I hadn't heard right.

"*What* did you say?" I demanded.

"I said . . ." She stopped. "Do you want to marry me or don't you?"

"That's a bloody silly question."

I leaned toward her and she to me, and we kissed like a homecoming.

I suggested transferring to the rear seat, which we did, but not for gymnastic lovemaking, partly because of daylight and frequent passersby, partly because of the unsatisfactoriness of the available space. We sat with our arms round each other, which after the past weeks I found unbelievable and boringly said so several times over.

"I didn't mean to do this," she said. "When I came back from the Lake District, I was going to find a way of saying it was all over, a mistake."

"What changed your mind?"

"I don't know . . . lots of things. Being with you so much . . . missing you yesterday. Odd things. Seeing how Litsi respects you . . . Betsy saying I was lucky . . . and Joe's wife . . She threw up, you know. Everything up. Everything down. She was sweating and cold . . . and pregnant . . . I asked her how she managed to live with the fear. She said if it was fear and Joe against no fear, no Joe, the choice was easy."

I held her close. I could feel her heart beating.

"Today I was wandering about, looking at things," she said. "Wondering if I wanted a life of racecourses and winter and perpetual anxiety. Watching you go out on those horses, with you not knowing . . . and not caring . . . if it's going to be your last half hour ever . . . and doing that five or six hundred times every year. I looked at the other jockeys on their way out to the parade ring, and they're all like you, perfectly calm, as if they're going to an office."

"Much better than an office."

"Yes, for you." She kissed me. "You can thank Aunt Casilia for shaming me into going racing again . . . but most of all, Joe's wife. I thought today clearly of what life would be like without you: no fear, no Kit . . . like she said . . . I guess I'll take the fear."

"And throw up."

"Everything up, everything down. She said it was like that for all of the wives, sometime or other. And a few husbands, I guess."

It was odd, I thought, how life could totally change from one minute to the next. The fog of wretchedness of the past month had vanished like ruptured cobwebs. I felt light-headedly, miraculously happy, more even than in the beginning. Perhaps one truly had to have lost and regained, to know that sort of joy.

"You won't change your mind, will you?" I said.

"No, I won't," she answered, and spent a fair time doing her best, in the restricted circumstances, to show me she meant it.

I saw her eventually into the studio and drove back

toward Eaton Square on euphoric autopilot, returning to earth in time to park carefully and methodically in the usual place in the mews.

I switched off the engine and sat looking vaguely at my hands, sat there for a while thinking of what might lie ahead. Then with a mental shiver I telephoned to the house, and got Litsi immediately, as if he'd been waiting.

"I'm in the alley," I said.

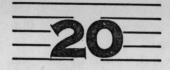

We didn't know how he would come, or when, or even *if*.

We'd shown him an opportunity and loaded him with a motive. Given him a time and place when he could remove an immovable obstruction: but whether he would accept the circuitous invitation, heaven alone knew.

Henri Nanterre . . . his very name sounded threatening.

I thought about his being at Windsor and making his way through the crowds on the stands, moving upward and sideways, approaching Danielle. I thought that until that afternoon he might not have reliably known what she looked like. He'd seen her in the dark the previous Monday, when he'd opened her tire valves and chased her, but it had been her car he had identified her by, not her face.

He'd probably have seen her with Litsi at Bradbury, but

maybe not from close to. He'd have known she was the young woman with Litsi because Beatrice had told him they were going together with me.

Nanterre might not have known that Danielle had gone to Windsor at all until he'd seen her with me several times in the paddock and on the stands during the fourth race. He couldn't have gone to Windsor with any advance plans, but what he'd meant to do if he'd reached Danielle was anyone's nightmare.

I was sitting with these thoughts not in my own car but on a foam cushion on the floor inside the garage where Danielle was keeping her little Ford. One of the garage doors was open about a hand's span, enough for me to see the Mercedes and a good deal of the mews, looking up toward the road entrance. A few people were coming home from work, opening their garages, shunting the cars in, closing and locking. A few were reversing the process, going out for the evening. The mechanics had long gone, all their garages silent. Several cars, like the Mercedes, were parked in the open, close to the sides, leaving a scant passage free in the center.

Dusk had turned to night, and local bustle died into the restless distant roar of London's traffic. I sat quietly with a few pre-positioned necessities to hand, like Perrier, smoked salmon and an apple, and rehearsed in my mind all sorts of eventualities, none of which happened.

Every half hour or so, I rose to my feet, stretched my spine, paced round Danielle's car, and sat down again. Nothing of much interest occurred in the mews, and the hands of my watch traveled like slugs; eight o'clock, nine o'clock, ten.

I thought of Danielle, and of what she'd said when I left her.

"For Aunt Casilia's sake I must hope that the rattlesnake turns up in the mews, but if you get yourself killed, I'll never forgive you."

"A thought for eternity," I said.

"You just make sure eternity is spent right here on earth, with me."

"Yes, ma'am," I said, and kissed her.

The rattlesnake, I thought, yawning as eleven o'clock passed, was taking his time. I normally went round to the mews at one-thirty so as to be at Chiswick before two, and I thought that if Nanterre was planning a direct physical attack of any sort he would be there well before that time, seeking a shadow to hide in. He hadn't been there before seven, because I'd searched every cranny before settling in the garage, and there were no entrances other than the way in from the street. If he'd sneaked in somehow since then without my seeing him, we were maybe in trouble.

At eleven-fifteen, I stretched my legs round Danielle's car and sat down again.

At eleven-seventeen, unaware, he came to the lure.

I'd been hoping against hope, longing for him to come, wanting to expect it . . . and yet, when he did, my skin crawled with animal fear as if the tiger were indeed stalking the goat.

He walked openly down the center of the mews as if he owned a car there, moving with his distinctive eel-like lope, fluid and smooth, not a march.

He was turning his head from side to side, looking at the silent parked cars, and even in the dim light filtering down from the high windows of the surrounding buildings, the shape of nose and jaw were unmistakable.

He came closer and closer; and he wasn't looking for a hiding place, I saw, but for my car.

For one appalling moment he looked straight at the partly opened door of the garage where I sat, but I was immobile in dark clothes in dark shadow, and I started breathing again when he appeared to see nothing to alarm him or frighten him away.

Nanterre was there, I thought exultantly; right there in front of my eyes, and all our planning had come to pass. Whatever should happen, I reckoned that that was a triumph.

Nanterre looked back the way he'd come, but nothing stirred behind him.

He came close to my car. He stopped beside it, about the length of a Rolls-Royce away, and he coolly fiddled about and opened the passenger's seat door with some sort of key as if he'd spent a lifetime thieving.

Well bloody well, I thought, and heard him unlatch the hood with the release knob inside the car. He raised the hood, propped it open with its strut, and leaned over the engine with a lighted torch as if working on a fault: anyone coming into the mews at that point would have paid no attention.

After a while, he switched off the torch and closed the hood gently, latching it by direct downward pressure of both palms, not by a more normal brisk slam. Finally he shut the open passenger door quietly; and as he turned away to leave, I saw he was smiling.

I wondered whether what he'd left by my engine was plastic, like his guns.

He'd walked several paces along the mews before I stood, slid out through the door and started after him, not wanting him to hear me too soon.

I waited until he was nearing a particular small white car parked on one side, and then I ran swiftly up behind him, quiet in rubber soles on the cobbles, and shone a torch of my own on the back of his neck.

"Henri Nanterre," I said.

He was struck for a long moment into slow motion, unable to move from shock. Then he was fumbling, tearing at the front of a bloused gabardine jacket, trying to free the pistol holstered beneath.

"Sammy," I yelled, and Sammy shot like a screaming cannonball out of the small white car, my voice and his whooping cries filling the quiet place with nerve-breaking noise.

Nanterre, his face rigid, pulled the pistol free. He swung it toward me, taking aim . . . and Sammy, true to his boast, kicked it straight out of his hand.

Nanterre ran, leaving the gun clattering to the ground.

Sammy and I ran after him, and from another, larger, parked car, both Thomas and Litsi, shouting manfully and shining bright torches, emerged to stand in his way.

Thomas and Litsi stopped him and Sammy and I caught hold of him, Sammy tying Nanterre's left wrist to Thomas's right with nylon cord and an intriguingly nice line in knots.

Not the most elegant of captures, I thought, but effective all the same; and for all the noise we'd made, no one came with curious questions to the fracas, no one in London would be so foolish. Dark alleys were dark alleys, and with noise, even worse.

We made Nanterre walk back toward the Mercedes. Thomas half dragging him, Sammy stepping behind him and kicking him encouragingly on the calves of the legs.

When we reached the pistol, Sammy picked it up, weighed it with surprise in his hand, and briefly whistled.

"Bullets?" I asked.

He slid out the clip and nodded. "Seven," he said. "Bright little darlin's."

He slapped the gun together again, looked around him, and dodged off sideways to hide it under a nearby car, knowing I didn't want to use it myself.

Nanterre was beginning to recover his usual browbeating manner and to bluster that what we were doing was against the law. He didn't specify which law, nor was he right. Citizens' arrests were perfectly legal.

Not knowing what to expect, we'd had to make the best plans we could to meet anything that might happen. I'd hired the small white car and the larger dark one, both with tinted windows, and Thomas and I had parked them that morning in spaces that we knew from mews-observation weren't going to obstruct anyone else: the larger car in the space nearest to the way in from the road, the white car halfway between there and the Mercedes.

Litsi, Thomas and Sammy had entered the cars after I'd searched the whole place and telephoned reassuringly again to Litsi, and they'd been prepared to wait until one-thirty and hope.

No one had known what Nanterre would do if he came to the mews. We'd decided that if he came in past Litsi and Thomas and hid himself before he reached the white car, Litsi and Thomas would set up a racket and shine torches to summon Sammy and me to their aid. And we'd reckoned that if he came in past Sammy, I would see him, and everyone would wait for my cue, which they had.

We'd all acknowledged that Nanterre, if he came to the area, might decide to sit in his car out in the street, waiting for me to walk round from the square, and that if he did that, or if he didn't come at all, we'd spent a long while preparing for a big anticlimax.

There had been the danger that even if he came, we could lose him, that he'd slip through our grasp and escape: and there had been the worse danger that we would panic him into shooting, and that one or more of us could be hurt. Yet when that moment had come, when he'd freed his gun and pointed it my way, the peril, long faced, had gone by so fast that it seemed suddenly nothing, not worth the consideration.

We had meant, if we captured Nanterre, to take him into the garage where I'd waited for him to come, but I did a fast rethink on the way down the alley, and stopped by my car.

The others paused inquiringly.

"Thomas," I said, "untie your wrist and attach Mr. Nanterre to the rear-view mirror beside the front passenger door."

Thomas, unquestioning, took a loop of cord off one of his fingers and pulled it, and all the knots round his wrist fell apart: Sammy's talents seemed endless. Thomas tied much more secure knots round the sturdy mirror assembly and Nanterre told us very loudly and continuously that we were making punishable mistakes.

"Shut up," I said equally loudly, without much effect.

"Let's gag him," Thomas said cheerfully. He produced a used handkerchief from his trousers pocket, at the sight of which Nanterre blessedly stopped talking.

"Gag him if someone comes into the mews," I said, and Thomas nodded.

"Was there enough light," I asked Litsi, Sammy and Thomas, "for you to see Mr. Nanterre lift up the bonnet of my car?"

They all said that they'd seen.

Nanterre's mouth fell soundlessly open, and for the first

time he seemed to realize he was in serious trouble.

"Mr. Nanterre," I said conversationally to the others, "is an amateur who has left his fingerprints all over my paintwork. It might be a good idea at this point to bring in the police."

The others looked impassive because they knew I didn't want to, but Nanterre suddenly tugged frantically at Sammy's securely tied knots.

"There's an alternative," I said.

Nanterre, still struggling under Sammy's interested gaze, said, "What alternative?" furiously.

"Tell us why you came here tonight, and what you put in my car."

"*Tell you* . . ."

"Yes. Tell us."

He was a stupid man, essentially. He said violently, "Beatrice must have warned you. That cow. She got frightened and told you." He glared at me with concentration. "All that stood between me and my *millions* was Roland's signature and you . . . you . . . everywhere, in my way."

"So you decided on a little bomb, and pouf, no obstructions?"

"You made me," he shouted. "You drove me . . . If you were dead, he would sign."

I let a moment go by, then I said, "We talked to the man who gave your message to Prince Litsi at Bradbury. He picked you out from a photograph. We have his signed statement."

Nanterre said viciously, "I saw your advertisement. If Prince Litsi had died, no one would have known of the message."

"Did you mean him to die?"

"Live, die, I didn't care. To frighten him, yes. To get Roland de Brescou to sign." He tried ineffectually still to unravel his bonds. "Let me go."

I went instead into the garage where I'd waited and came out again with the big envelope of signed documents.

"Stop struggling," I said to Nanterre, "and listen carefully."

He paid little attention.

"Listen," I said, "or I fetch the police."

He said sullenly then that he was listening.

"The price of your freedom," I said, "is that you put your signature to these contracts."

"What are they?" he said furiously, looking at their impressive appearance. "What contracts?"

"They change the name of the de Brescou et Nanterre construction company to the Gascony construction company, and they constitute an agreement between the two equal owners to turn the private company into a public company, and for each owner to put his entire holding up for public sale."

He was angrily and bitterly astounded.

"The company is *mine* . . . I manage it . . . I will *never* agree!"

"You'll have to," I said prosaically.

I produced the small tape recorder from the pocket of my jacket, pressed the rewind button slightly, and started it playing.

Nanterre's voice came out clearly, "Live, die, I didn't care. To frighten him, yes. To get de Brescou to sign."

I switched off. Nanterre, incredibly, was silent, remembering, perhaps, the other incriminating things he had said.

"We have the evidence of the messenger at Bradbury," I said. "We have your voice on this tape. We have your bomb, I suspect, in my car. You'll sign the contract, you know."

"There's no bomb in your car," he said furiously.

"Perhaps a firework?" I said.

He looked at me blankly.

"Someone's coming into the mews," Thomas said urgently, producing the handkerchief. "What do we do?" A car had driven in, coming home to its garage.

"If you yell," I said to Nanterre with menace, "the police will be here in five minutes and you'll regret it. They're not kind to people who plant bombs in cars."

The incoming car drove toward us and stopped just before reaching Sammy's white hiding place. The people got out, opened their garage, drove in, closed the doors, and looked our way dubiously.

"Goodnight," I called out, full of cheer.

"Goodnight," they replied, reassured, and walked away to the street.

"Right," I said, relaxing, "time to sign."

"I will not sell the company. *I will not.*"

I said patiently, "You have no alternative except going to prison for attempting to murder both Prince Litsi and myself."

He still refused to face facts: and perhaps he felt as outraged at being coerced to sign against his will as Roland had done.

I brought the car-starting gadget out of my pocket and explained what it was.

Nanterre at last began to shake, and Litsi, Sammy and Thomas backed away from the car in freshly awakened genuine alarm, as if really realizing for the first time what was in there, under the bonnet.

"It'll be lonely for you," I said to Nanterre. "We'll walk to the end of the mews, leaving you here. Prince Litsi and the other two will go away. When they're safely back in the house in Eaton Square, I'll press the switch that starts my engine."

Litsi, Sammy and Thomas had already retreated a good way along the mews.

"You'll die by your own bomb," I said, and put into my voice and manner every shred of force and conviction I could summon. "Goodbye," I said.

I turned away. Walked several steps. Wondered if he would be too scared to call my bluff; wondered if anyone would have the nerve to risk it.

"Come back," he yelled. There was real fear in the rising voice. Real deadly fear.

Without any pity, I stopped and turned.

"Come back . ."

I went back. There was sweat in great drops on his forehead, running down. He was struggling frantically still with the knots, but also trembling too much to succeed.

"I want to make guns," he said feverishly. "I'd make millions. I'd have *power*. The de Brescous are rich, the Nanterres never were. I want to be rich by world standards, to have power. I'll give you a million pounds . . . more . . . if . . . you get Roland to sign . . . to make guns."

"No," I said flatly, and turned away again, showing him the starter.

"All right, all right . . ." He gave in completely, finally almost sobbing. "Put that thing down . . . put it down."

I called up the mews, "Litsi."

The other three stopped and came slowly back.

"Mr. Nanterre will sign," I said.

"Put that thing down," Nanterre said again faintly, all the bullying megatones gone. "Put it down."

I put the starter back in my pocket, which still frightened him.

"It can't go off by itself, can it?" Litsi asked, not with nervousness, but out of caution.

I shook my head. "The switch needs firm pressure."

I showed Nanterre the contracts more closely and saw the flicker of fury in his eyes when he saw the first page of each was the same sort of form he'd demanded that Roland should sign.

"We need your signature four times," I said. "On each front page, and on each attached document. When you sign the attached documents, put your forefinger on the red seal beside your name. The three of us who are not in any way involved in the de Brescou et Nanterre business will sign under your name as witnesses."

I put my pen into his shaking right hand and rested the first of the documents on top of my car.

Nanterre signed the French form. I turned to the last page of the longer contract and pointed to the space allotted to him. He signed again, and he put his finger on the seal.

With enormous internal relief, I produced the second set for a repeat performance. In silence, with sweat dripping off his cheeks, he signed appropriately again.

I put my name under his in all four places, followed each time by Thomas and Sammy.

"That's fine," I said, when all were completed. "Monsieur de Brescou's lawyers will put the contracts into operation at once. One of these two contracts will be sent to you or your lawyers in France."

I put the documents back into their envelope and handed it to Litsi, who put it inside his coat, hugging it to his chest.

"Let me go," Nanterre said, almost whispering.

"We'll untie you from the mirror so that you can remove what you put in my car," I said. "After that, you can go."

He shuddered, but it seemed not very difficult for him, in the end, to unfix the tampered-with wiring and remove what looked like, in size and shape, a bag of sugar. It was the detonator sticking out of it that he treated with delicate respect, unclipping and separating, and stowing the pieces away in several pockets. "Now let me go," he said, wiping sweat away from his face with the backs of his hands.

I said, "Remember, we'll always have the Bradbury messenger's affidavit and the tape recording of your voice. And we all heard what you said. Stay away from the de Brescous, cause no more trouble."

He gave me a sick, furious and defeated glare. Sammy didn't try to undo his handiwork but cut the nylon cord off Nanterre's wrist with a pair of scissors.

"Start the car," Litsi said, "to show him you weren't fooling."

"Come away from it," I said.

We walked twenty paces up the mews, Nanterre among us, and I took out the starter and pressed the switch.

The engine fired safely, strong, smooth and powerful.

I looked directly at Nanterre, at the convinced droop of his mouth, at the unwilling acceptance that his campaign was lost. He gave us all a last comprehensive, unashamed, unrepentant stare, and with Thomas and Sammy stepping aside to let him pass, he walked away along the mews, that nose, that jaw, still strong, but the shoulders sagging.

We watched him in silence until he reached the end of the mews and turned into the street, not looking back.

Then Sammy let out a poltergeist "Youweee" yell of uncomplicated victory, and went with jumping feet to fetch the pistol from where he'd hidden it.

He presented it to me with a flourish, laying it flat onto my hands.

"Spoils of war," he said, grinning.

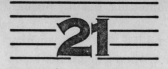

21

Litsi and I drank brandy in the sitting room to celebrate, having thanked Thomas and Sammy copiously for their support; and we telephoned to Danielle to tell her we weren't lying in puddles of blood.

"Thank goodness," she said. "I haven't been able to think what I'm doing."

"I suppose what we did was thoroughly immoral," Litsi commented, after I'd put down the receiver.

"Absolutely," I agreed equably. "We did exactly what Nanterre intended to do: extorted a signature under threat."

"We took the law into our own hands, I suppose."

"Justice," I said, "in our own hands."

"And like you said," he said, smiling, "there's a difference."

"He's free, unpunished and rich," I said, "and in a way

that's not justice. But he didn't, and can't, destroy Roland. It was a fair enough bargain."

I waited up for Danielle after Litsi had gone yawning downstairs, and went to meet her when I heard her come in. She walked straight into my arms, smiling.

"I didn't think you'd go to bed without me," she said.

"As seldom as possible for the rest of my life."

We went quietly up to the bamboo room and, mindful of Beatrice next door, quietly to bed and quietly to love. Intensity, I thought, drowning in sensations, hadn't any direct link to noise and could be exquisite in whispers; and if we were more inhibited than earlier in what we said, the silent rediscovery of each other grew into an increased dimension of passion.

We slept, embracing, and woke again before morning, hungry again after deep satisfaction.

"You love me more," she said, murmuring in my ear.

"I loved you always."

"Not like this."

We slept again, languorously, and before seven she showered in my bathroom, put on yesterday's clothes and went decorously down to her own room. Aunt Casilia, she said with composure, would expect her niece to make a pretense at least of having slept in her own bed.

"Would she mind that you didn't?"

"Pretty much the reverse, I would think."

Litsi and I were already drinking coffee in the morning room when Danielle reappeared, dressed by then in fresh blues and greens. She fetched juice and cereal and made me some toast, and Litsi watched us both with speculation and finally enlightenment.

"Congratulations," he said to me dryly.

"The wedding," Danielle said collectedly, "will take place."

"So I gathered," he said.

He and I, a while later, went up to see Roland de Brescou, to give him and the princess the completed contracts.

"I was sure," Roland said weakly, "that Nanterre wouldn't agree to dissolve the company. Without it, he can't possibly make guns, can he?"

"If ever he does," I said, "your name won't be linked with it."

Gascony, the name we'd given to the new public company, was the ancient name of the province in France where the Chateau de Brescou stood. Roland had been both pleased and saddened by the choice.

"How did you persuade him, Kit?" the princess asked, looking disbelievingly at the Nanterre signatures.

"Um, tied him in knots."

She gave me a brief glance. "Then I'd better not ask."

"He's unhurt and unmarked."

"And the police?" Roland asked.

"No police," I said. "We had to promise no police to get him to sign."

"A bargain's a bargain." Litsi nodded. "We have to let him go free."

The princess and her husband understood all about keeping one's word, and when I left Roland's room she followed me down to the sitting room, leaving Litsi behind.

"No thanks are enough. How *can* we thank you?" she asked with frustration.

"You don't need to. And . . . um . . . Danielle and I will marry in June."

"I'm very pleased indeed," she said with evident pleasure, and kissed me warmly on one cheek and then the other. I thought of the times I'd wanted to hug her; and one day perhaps I would do it, though not on a racecourse.

"I'm so sorry about your horses," I said.

"Yes . . . When you next talk to Wykeham, ask him to start looking about for replacements. We can't expect another Cotopaxi, but next year, perhaps, a runner anyway in the Grand National. And don't forget, next week at Cheltenham, we still have Kinley."

"The Triumph Hurdle," I said.

I went to Folkestone races by train later that morning with a light heart but without Danielle, who had an appointment with the dentist.

I rode four races and won two, and felt fit, well, bursting with health and for the first time in weeks, carefree. It was a tremendous feeling, while it lasted.

Bunty Ireland, the *Towncrier*'s racing correspondent, gave me a large envelope from Lord Vaughnley: "Hot off the computers," Bunty said. The envelope again felt as if it contained very little, but I thanked him for it, and reflecting that I thankfully didn't need the contents anymore, I took it unopened with me back to London.

Dinner that evening was practically festive, although Danielle wasn't there, having driven herself to work in her Ford.

"I thought yesterday was her last night for working," Beatrice said, unsuspiciously.

"They changed the schedules again," I explained.

"Oh, how irritating."

Beatrice had decided to return to Palm Beach the next day. Her darling dogs would be missing her, she said. The princess had apparently told her that Nanterre's case was lost, which had subdued her querulousness amazingly.

I'd grown used to her ways: to her pale-orange hair and round eyes, her knuckleduster rings and her Florida clothes. Life would be quite dull without the old bag; and moreover, once she had gone, I would soon have to leave also. How long, I wondered, would Litsi be staying . . .

Roland came down to dinner and offered champagne, raising his half-full glass to Litsi and to me in a toast. Beatrice scowled a little but blossomed like a sunflower when Roland said that perhaps, with all the extra capital generated by the sale of the business, he might consider increasing her trust fund. Too forgiving, I thought, yet without her we would very likely not have prevailed.

Roland, the princess and Beatrice retired fairly early, leaving Litsi and me passing the time in the sitting room. Quite late I remembered Lord Vaughnley's envelope, which I'd put down on a side table on my return.

Litsi incuriously watched me open it and draw out the contents: one glossy black-and-white photograph, as before, and one short clipping from a newspaper column. Also a brief compliments slip from the *Towncrier*: "Regret nothing more re Nanterre."

The picture showed Nanterre in evening dress surrounded by other people similarly clad, on the deck of a yacht. I handed it to Litsi and read the accompanying clipping.

"Arms dealer Ahmed Fuad's fiftieth birthday bash, held on his yacht *Felissima* in Monte Carlo harbor on Friday evening drew guests from as far as California, Peru and Darwin, Australia. With no expense spared, Fuad fed caviar and foie gras to jet-setting friends from his hobby worlds of backgammon, night clubs and horseracing."

Litsi passed back the photograph and I gave him the clipping.

"That's what Nanterre wanted," I said. "To be the host on a yacht in the Mediterranean, dressed in a white dinner jacket, dispensing rich goodies, enjoying the adulation and the flattery. That's what he wanted . . . those multi-millions, and that power."

I turned the photograph over, reading the flimsy information strip stuck to the back: a list of names, and the date.

"That's odd," I said blankly.

"What is?"

"That party was held last Friday night."

"What of it? Nanterre must have jetted out there and back, like the others."

"On Friday night, Col was shot."

Litsi stared at me.

"Nanterre couldn't have done it," I said. "He was in Monte Carlo."

"But he said he did. He boasted of it to Beatrice."

I frowned. "Yes, he did."

"He must have got someone else to do it," Litsi said.

I shook my head. "He did everything himself. Threatened the princess, chased Danielle, set the trap for you, came to put the bomb in my car. He didn't trust any of that to anyone else. He knows about horses, he wanted to see his own filly shot. He would have shot Col . . . but he didn't."

"He confessed to all the horses," Litsi insisted.

"Yes, but suppose he read about them in the papers . . . read that their deaths were mysterious and no one knew who had killed them . . . He wanted ways to frighten

Roland and the princess. Suppose he *said* he'd killed them, when he hadn't?"

"But in that case," Litsi said blankly, "who did? Who would want to kill her best horses, if not Nanterre?"

I rose slowly to my feet, feeling almost faint.

"What's the matter?" Litsi said, alarmed. "You've gone as white as snow."

"He killed," I said with a mouth stickily dry, "the horse I might have won the Grand National on. The horse on which I might have won the Gold Cup."

"Kit . . ." Litsi said.

"There's only one person," I said with difficulty, "who hates me enough to do that. Who couldn't bear to see me win those races . . . who would take away the prizes I hold dearest, because I took away his prize."

I felt breathless and dizzy.

"Sit down," Litsi said, alarmed.

"Kinley," I said.

I went jerkily to the telephone and got through to Wykeham.

"I was just going to bed," he complained.

"Did you stop the dog patrols?" I demanded.

"Yes, of course. You told me this morning there was no more need for them."

"I think I was wrong. I can't risk that I was wrong. I'm coming down to your stables now, tonight, and we'll get the dog patrols back again, stronger than ever, for tomorrow and every day until Cheltenham, and probably beyond."

"I don't understand," he said.

"Have you taken your sleeping pill?" I asked.

"No, not yet."

"Don't do it until I get down to you, will you? And where's Kinley tonight?"

"Back in his own box, of course. You said the danger was past."

"We'll move him back into the corner box when I get down to you."

"Kit, no, not in the middle of the night."

"You want to keep him safe," I said; and there was no arguing with that.

We disconnected and Litsi said slowly, "Do you mean Maynard Allardeck?"

"Yes, I do. He found out, about two weeks ago, that he'll never get a knighthood because I sent the film I made of him to the Honours department. He's wanted that knighthood since he was a child, when he told my grandfather that one day the Fieldings would have to bow down to him, because he'd be a lord. He knows horses better than Nanterre. He was brought up in his father's racing stable and was his assistant trainer for years. He saw Cascade and Cotopaxi at Newbury, and they were distinctive horses . . . and Col at Ascot . . . unmistakable."

I went to the door.

"I'll telephone in the morning," I said.

"I'll come with you," he said.

I shook my head. "You'd be up all night."

"Get going," he said. "You saved my family's honor. Let me pay some of their debt."

I was grateful, indeed, for the company. We went round again to the dark mews where Litsi said, if I had the car-starter in my pocket, we might as well be sure: but Nanterre and his bombs hadn't returned, and the Mercedes fired obligingly from a fifty-yard distance.

I drove toward Sussex, telephoning to Danielle on the way to tell her where and why we were going. She had no trouble believing anything bad of Maynard Allardeck, saying he'd looked perfectly crazy at Ascot and Sandown, glaring at me continuously in the way he had.

"*Curdling* with hate," she said. "You could feel it like shock waves."

"We'll be back for breakfast," I said, smiling. "Sleep well." And I could hear her laughing as she disconnected.

I told Litsi on the way about the firework bombs that had been used to decoy the dog-handler away from Col's courtyard, and said, "You know, in the alley, when Nanterre said he hadn't put a bomb in my car, I asked him if it was a firework. He looked totally blank. I didn't think much of it then, but now I realize he simply didn't know what I was talking about. He didn't know about the fireworks at Wykeham's because they didn't get into the papers."

Litsi made a "Huh" sort of noise of appreciation and assent, and we came companionably in time into Wykeham's village.

"What are you going to do here?" Litsi said.

I shrugged. "Walk round the stables." I explained about the many little courtyards. "It's not an easy place to patrol."

"You do seriously think Allardeck will risk trying to kill another of Aunt Casilia's horses?"

"Yes. Kinley, particularly, her brilliant hurdler. I don't seriously suppose he'll try tonight rather than tomorrow or thereafter, but I'm not taking chances." I paused. "However am I going to apologize to Princess Casilia . . . to repay . . ."

"What do you mean?"

"Cascade and Cotopaxi and Col died because of the Fielding and Allardeck feud. Because of me."

"She won't think of it that way."

"It's the truth." I turned into Wykeham's driveway. "I won't let Kinley die."

I stopped the car in the parking space, and we stepped out into the silence of midnight under a clear sky sparkling with diamondlike stars. The heights and depths of the universe: enough to humble the sweaty strivings of earth.

I took a deep breath of its peace . . . and heard in the quiet distance the dull unmistakable thudding explosion of a bolt.

Dear God, I thought, *we're too late*.

I ran. I knew where. To the last courtyard, the one nearest to Wykeham's house. Ran with the furies at my heels, my heart sick, my mind a jumble of rage and fear and dreadful regrets.

I could have driven faster . . . I could have started sooner . . . I could have opened Lord Vaughnley's envelope hours before . . . Kinley was dead, and I'd killed him.

I ran into the courtyard, and for all my speed, events on the other side of it moved faster.

As I watched, as I ran, I saw Wykeham struggle to his feet from where he'd been lying on the path outside the doors of the boxes.

Two of the box doors were open, the boxes in shadow, lit only by the light outside in the courtyard. In one box, I could see a horse lying on its side, its legs still jerking in convulsive death throes. Into the other went Wykeham.

While I was still yards away, I saw him pick up something that had been lying inside the box on the brick windowsill. I saw his back going deeper into the box, his feet silent on the peat.

I ran.

I saw another man in the box, taller, grabbing a horse by its head-collar.

I saw Wykeham put the thing he held against the second man's head. I saw the tiny flash, heard the awful bang . . .

When I reached the door there was a dead man on the peat, a live horse tossing his head and snorting in fright, a smell of burning powder and Wykeham standing, looking down, with the humane killer in his hands.

The live horse was Kinley . . . but I felt no relief.

"Wykeham!" I said.

He turned his head, looked at me vaguely.

"He shot my horses," he said.

"Yes."

"I killed him. I said I would . . . and I have."

I looked down at the dead man, at the beautiful suit and the hand-sewn shoes.

He was lying half on his face, and he had a nylon stocking pulled over his head as a mask, with a hole in it behind his right ear.

Litsi ran into the courtyard calling breathlessly, asking what had happened. I turned toward him in the box doorway, obstructing his view of what was inside.

"Litsi," I said, "go and telephone the police. Use the telephone in the car. Press O and you'll get the operator. Ask for the police. Tell them a man has been killed here in an accident."

"*A man!*" he exclaimed. "Not a horse?"

"Both, but tell them a man."

"Yes," he said unhappily. "Right."

He went back the way he'd come and I turned toward Wykeham, who was wide-eyed now, and beginning to tremble.

"It wasn't an accident," he said, with pride somewhere in the carriage of his head, in the tone of his voice. "I killed him."

"Wykeham," I said urgently, "listen. Are you listening?"

"Yes."

"Where do you want to spend your last years, in prison or out on the Downs with your horses?"

He stared.

"Are you listening?"

"Yes."

"There'll be an inquest," I said. "And this was an *accident*. Are you listening?"

He nodded.

"You came out to see if all was well in the yard before you went to bed."

"Yes, I did."

"You'd had three horses killed in the last ten days. The police haven't been able to discover who did it. You knew I was coming down to help patrol the yards tonight, but you were naturally worried."

"Yes."

"You came into this courtyard, and you saw and heard someone shoot one of your horses."

"Yes, I did."

"Is it Abseil?" I longed for him to say no, but he said "Yes."

Abseil . . . racing at breakneck speed over the last three fences at Sandown, clinging to victory right to the post.

I said, "You ran across to try to stop the intruder doing

any more damage. You tried to pull the humane killer out of his hands."

"Yes."

"He was younger and stronger and taller than you. He knocked you down with the humane killer. You fell on the path, momentarily stunned."

"How do you know?" Wykeham asked, bewildered.

"The marks of the end of the barrel are all down your cheek. It's been bleeding. Don't touch it," I said, as he began to raise a hand to feel. "He knocked you down and went into the second box to kill a second horse."

"Yes, to kill Kinley."

"Listen . . . He had the humane killer in his hand."

Wykeham began to shake his head, and then stopped.

I said, "The man was going to shoot your horse. You grabbed at the gun to stop him. You were trying to take it away from him . . . he was trying to pull it back from your grasp. He was succeeding with a jerk, but you still had your hands on the gun, and in the struggle, when he jerked the gun toward him, the thick end of the barrel hit his head, and the jerk also caused your grasp somehow to pull the trigger."

He stared.

"You did *not* mean to kill him; are you listening, Wykeham? You meant to stop him shooting your horse."

"K–Kit . . ." he said, finally stuttering.

"What are you going to tell the police?"

"I . . . t–tried to s–stop him shooting . . ." He swallowed. "He j–jerked the gun . . . against his head . . . It w–went off."

He was still holding the gun by its rough wooden butt.

"Throw it down on the peat," I said.

He did so, and we both looked at it: a heavy, ugly, clumsy instrument of death.

On the windowsill there were several small bright golden caps full of gunpowder. One cocked the gun, fed in the cap, pulled the trigger: the gunpowder exploded and shot out the bolt.

Litsi came back, saying the police would be coming, and it was he who switched the light on, revealing every detail of the scene.

I bent down and took a closer look at Maynard's head. There was oil on the nylon stocking where the bolt had gone through, and I remembered Robin Curtiss saying the bolt had been oiled before Col . . . Robin would remember. There would be no doubt that Maynard had killed all four horses.

"Do you know who it is?" I said to Wykeham, straightening up.

He half knew, half couldn't believe it.

"Allardeck?" he said, unconvinced.

"Allardeck."

Wykeham bent down to pull off the stocking mask.

"Don't do that," I said sharply. "Don't touch it. Anyone can see he came here trying not to be recognized . . . to kill horses. No one out for an evening stroll goes around in a nylon mask carrying a humane killer."

"Did he kill Kinley?" Litsi asked anxiously.

"No, this is Kinley. He killed Abseil."

Litsi looked stricken. "Poor Aunt Casilia. She said how brilliantly you'd won on Abseil. Why kill that one, who couldn't possibly win the Grand National?" He looked down at Maynard, understanding. "Allardeck couldn't bear you being brilliant, not on anything."

The feud was dead, I thought. Finally over. The long obsession had died with Maynard, and he had been dead before he hit the peat, like Cascade and Cotopaxi, Abseil and Col.

A fitting end, I thought.

Litsi said he had told the police he would meet them in the parking place to show them where to come, and presently he went off there.

Wykeham spent a long while looking at Kinley, who was now standing quietly, no longer disturbed, and then less time looking at Maynard.

"I'm glad I killed him," he said fiercely.

"Yes, I know."

"Mind you win the Triumph Hurdle."

I thought of the schooling sessions I'd done with that horse, teaching him distances up on the Downs with Wykeham watching, shaping the glorious natural talent into accomplished experience.

I would do my best, I said.

He smiled. "Thank you, Kit," he said. "Thank you for everything."

The police came with Litsi: two of them, highly official, taking notes, talking of summoning medical officers and photographers.

They took Wykeham through what had happened.

"I came out . . . found the intruder . . . he shot my horse." Wykeham's voice shook. "I fought with him . . . he knocked me down . . . he was going to shoot this horse also . . . I got to my feet . . "

He paused.

"Yes, sir?" the policemen said, not unsympathetically.

They saw, standing before them on the peat inside the

box, standing beside a dead intruder with the intruder's deadly weapon shining with menace in the light, they saw an old thin man with disheveled white hair, with the dark freckles of age on his ancient forehead, with the pistol marks of dried blood on his cheek.

They saw, as the coroner would see, and the lawyers, and the press, the shaking deteriorating exterior, not the titan who still lived inside.

Wykeham looked at Kinley; at the future, at the horse that could fly on the Downs, tail streaming, jumping like an angel to his destiny.

He looked at the policemen, and his eyes seemed full of sky.

"It was an accident," he said.

The End

A QUESTION OF PRINCIPLE

BY

JEFFREY ASHFORD

Published by special arrangement with St. Martin's Press, Inc.

CHAPTER 1

The dining-room, which led directly off the kitchen, was small and the low, beamed ceiling and the wide, open fireplace made it seem even smaller still. There really was no room for the Elizabethan court cupboard, but this had come from Anne's home and she kept it because of the memories it held.

The four of them sat around the reproduction refectory table, Anne nearest the kitchen door. Elham brushed his lips with a serviette. 'That was a truly delicious piece of pork,' he said in his deep, fruity voice.

'Yes, wasn't it?' echoed Penelope. She turned to her sister. 'I just don't know how you learned to cook so well.'

'Necessity,' replied Anne, a touch of light irony in her voice.

'But Mother never taught us a thing. I mean, I simply wouldn't know where to begin.' 'Simply' was verbally underlined. She seldom spoke without underlining one word or another.

Rickmore had drunk enough not to guard his tongue as carefully as Anne would have had him do. 'If the need ever arises, no doubt you'll manage very successfully.'

'I don't think she needs to worry,' said Elham pompously.

An oblique reference, wondered Rickmore, amused, to the fact that Terence Elham was a man with credit while Dennis Rickmore was a man of credit—mortgage, overdraft, strained relations with the credit card firm . . .

'Let's clear the table, Dennis,' said Anne, 'and bring the sweet in.'

He looked briefly at her. There was a warning gleam in

her eyes. Don't start sniping at them. She was right, of course, but it was a pity not to pull the legs of two people who were so self-satisfied that they seldom realized their legs were being pulled. He stood, saw that Elham's glass was empty and picked up the bottle of wine. He went round the table to top up Penelope's glass.

She put her hand over the rim. 'Not for me, thanks. I'm on cloud nine already.'

More affectation? She seemed totally unaffected by what she'd drunk. Or were the effects merely well camouflaged? Anne had told him that Penelope was drinking heavily nowadays and always had a couple of vodkas before going out to a party in case the hospitality was poor. She claimed that vodka wasn't really alcoholic, not like gin or whisky. She had the useful ability of being able to believe whatever it suited her to believe.

'Come on back to earth,' said Anne.

He refilled Elham's glass.

'The Spaniards,' said Elham, 'seem to be improving the quality of their wine these days.'

'They are. You ought to try all the different Riojas one can buy now.'

'I most certainly will.'

He most certainly wouldn't, thought Rickmore. He emptied the bottle into his own glass after Anne had shaken her head to show she didn't want any more. It wasn't smart to drink Spanish wine; French, of course, German provided it didn't contain too much anti-freeze, and Californian if one were slightly eccentric. He raised his own glass and drank. Bad manners to drink standing up. It was fun confirming their opinion of him .. . He checked his thoughts, vaguely astonished to discover that they were becoming slightly incoherent. He carried the now empty bottle and the meat dish through to the kitchen.

The kitchen, part of the outshut, was very small and there

was little working surface; what there was, was now crowded with the bowls, dishes and utensils, used in the cooking and preparation of the meal. He stood in the centre, his head only an inch beneath the ceiling. 'Where . . . where shall I put the meat dish?'

Anne, her dark blue eyes expressing amusement, murmured: 'You, sir, are half sloshed!'

'Absolute nonsense.'

'Repeat after me, I've sipped solely a sustaining sufficiency, certainly insufficient to succour a social solecism.'

'Like hell!'

'Probably very wise of you.' She moved a mixing bowl and then took the meat dish from him and put it down.

'You wrong me.' Even when completely sober, he occasionally mispronounced his R's.

'I doubt it.'

'Very well. I will prove I can speak in many tongues. I see . . . I saw sea shells . . .'

'If I were you, love, I'd look some other time, when the sea's not quite so choppy . . . The pud's in the fridge, along with cream. Are you up to whipping that?'

'Any more cheek and I'll show you exactly what I am up to whipping.' He went across to the refrigerator and, very carefully, brought out four individual bowls of chocolate orange mousse, putting each one on top in turn. 'Where's the . . . the cream?'

'In front of your nose.'

He lifted out the carton, shut the refrigerator door—a little more enthusiastically than he'd intended—moved over to the food mixer.

'Dennis, you know that's not working.'

He remembered.

'Use the beater.'

He poured the cream into a plastic bowl and whisked it, bothered for most of the time by the bowl's tendency to crab sideways. When the cream held a point, he tapped the whisk to clear it, then began to walk over to the doorway.

'Are you thinking of serving the cream in that bowl?'

He looked down and was immediately amused by the thought of his sister-in-law's and brother-in-law's expressions at the sight of whipped cream being served in a kitchen bowl . . . He corrected his thoughts. Terence was a man of precision. So it was sister-in-law and sister-in-law's husband . . .

'For heaven's sake, wake up. Here, give it to me.'

He handed her the bowl. 'I'll get the white wine.'

'Don't you think . . .' She stopped. They didn't drink wine very often and it seemed a pity to suggest he left the third bottle unopened merely because he'd obviously had enough. Since the pre-dinner drinks, some of the lines had disappeared from his face and his manner had become light and ironic, reminding her of when they'd first known each other and the world had been all sunshine . . . She sighed as she opened the cupboard to the right of the sink and brought out the small silver dish, another legacy from her parents' home. Normally, other people's prosperity was no cross to bear, but when those other people were close relations who made a point of underlining their prosperity . . . There was laughter from the dining-room. Had Dennis been misguided enough to tell them about the judge who stuttered? If so, Terence's laughter had been very false. For him, the law was not a subject about which one joked . . .

'Not your chocolate orange mousse?' said Penelope, as Anne walked through the doorway, carrying a tray with the four glass bowls and the cream on it. 'Didn't I say before we left home, Terence, that we'd have the most perfect meal?'

'You most certainly did.'

'Much nicer than if we'd gone to the Gordons' . . .' She stopped abruptly.

'What's this?' asked Rickmore. 'It sounds to me, Penny, as if you had a second invitation for tonight.'

'Well, we . . .' She looked at her husband.

'As a matter of fact, we did,' said Elham, now at his most urbane. 'But since we didn't receive it until after yours, and since we'd no doubts about which one we'd rather accept, we naturally refused the Gordons.'

'We're flattered.' Even Rickmore accepted that this was a moment to keep quiet, but the wine was too lively for him to do so. 'And very highly honoured!' Never let it be forgotten that Sir Francis was a high court judge and therefore an invitation from him was to be regarded in the light of a royal command. So could Terence, a man who knew the value of every relationship (but the price of none), have willingly turned down this invitation? Surely not. Penelope must have persuaded him that they could not go back on their prior acceptance. Although every bit as much of a snob as he, she did make a point of honouring family ties . . .

Penelope, aware that there was a danger of something being said that could not easily be laughed off, changed the conversation and talked about a cocktail party to which she and Elham had recently been. Her remarks were amusing and only slightly catty.

Think what you like about her, Rickmore decided, as he poured out the white wine, you had to admit that her social skills were second to none.

The sitting-room was on the far side of the massive central chimney about which the house had been built. Like all the other rooms in the house, it was heavily beamed and the central one was deep so that anyone with any height had to duck to pass under it unscathed. Roughly square, the room had a single small window and was naturally rather dark. A modern fireplace had been built within the very wide inglenook one and although from any æsthetic point of view this should have been ripped out, since it gave out so much more heat than the original would have done, it had been left. As Anne had once said, it was much easier to be an æsthete when one was well off.

Rickmore got up from one of the armchairs, crossed to the fire and threw on a couple of split logs; there was a rush of flame which caused a patch of soot to sparkle briefly as it caught fire. He turned. 'How about the other half?'

'No more for me,' said Penelope. 'One more drop of alcohol and I'll be seeing quadruple.'

'You'll be seeing what?' Elham, who'd begun to slump in the armchair, jerked himself upright. 'What did you say, Penelope?'

'I said I can't possibly drink any more or I'll be seeing quadruple.'

'Nonsense. Do think before you speak.'

'But you're always saying that thinking is dangerous for me.'

'You're talking ridiculously.'

She was hurt by his bad-tempered words.

Rickmore said: 'You'll join me in another brandy, won't you, Terence, even if the girls have chickened out?'

'But we brought it as a present for you,' protested Penelope, 'not for us to drink.'

'A present shared is a pleasure doubled.'

'What a marvellous sentiment. I just can't think how you can be so clever as to think up something like that.'

Anne said drily: 'He adapts the original.'

Rickmore made a face at her. 'Can't you leave any illusions in other people's minds?'

'Don't you mean delusions?'

He laughed, went over to the small mother-of-pearl inlaid table and picked up the bottle of Martell VSOP the Elhams had brought. 'You didn't get the chance to answer me, Terence. Will you have another snifter?'

'Snifter?' replied Elham. 'It's a long time since I've heard that expression.'

'I'm firmly rooted in the past.' He collected Elham's glass, poured into it a very generous measure, returned it. He collected his own glass and helped himself equally liberally. When he sat, he did so much more heavily than he'd intended and a little cognac slopped over the edge of the glass. He licked his hand. 'As my mother always taught me, waste not, want not.'

Elham sententiously thought it was a pity that Rickmore's mother hadn't also taught him that a gentleman did not lick his hand in public.

It was a clear night and the sky was alive with stars; the rising moon was beginning to cast vague shadows. In the distance, a vixen began to cry, in reality calling for a mate, but sounding as if in agonized torment; much nearer, a roosting pigeon was disturbed and the clap of its wings carried far.

Penelope passed through the outside doorway of the porch, then turned. 'It's become very much colder,' she said, from within the comfort of her full-length silver fox coat. 'Don't stand there with the door open, go on back into the warmth.'

'You're right, it is colder,' said Anne, 'so I think I will.'

Penelope stepped forward to embrace her sister and kissed her on both cheeks. 'It's been an absolutely perfect evening. I haven't enjoyed one so much in years and years.'

'Good.' Anne freed herself.

'Good night, Anne,' said Elham. 'The meal was truly delicious.' From their first meeting, he had correctly judged that, in direct contrast to her sister, she eschewed all affectation and he never made the mistake of showing her more than genuine respect. This respect occasionally made him wonder why she'd married Rickmore. With her attractive looks and warm personality, her reasonable and logical approach to everything, and her determination, she surely could have found a husband with a much sounder financial background.

Anne said one last good night and then closed the outside door of the porch; since it was glass, light continued to spill out on to the brick path to help them until they came within range of the outside light on the corner of the house.

Elham's dark green Jaguar was parked outside the garage —a World War Two army hut which was beginning to look as if it dated back to World War One. The Jaguar was an XJ-S, breathed upon and customized by Steerson; the V12 engine had been developed to produce 340 bhp, the suspension had been modified to accept this extra power, and the interior was even more luxurious than was that of the standard model. It was impossible to mistake the fact that this was a rich man's car.

'How's it going?' asked Rickmore.

'As smooth as silk,' replied Elham, with deep satisfaction.

'From what I've read, the engine is built like a Swiss jeweller's watch.'

'I wouldn't know how it's built; only how it goes.' He went to pull out the keys from his pocket and was surprised to discover how clumsy his fingers had suddenly become.

'She does use rather a lot of petrol, though?'

He shrugged his shoulders. He couldn't be expected to concern himself about that; if a man had to worry about the fuel consumption, he had no business buying the car. He finally managed to bring out the keys and went to insert one in the lock of the door; somehow he missed and the point of the key briefly scraped along the paintwork. He swore, conscious he was making a bit of a fool of himself. He tried again and this time the key went home. He turned it and the four doors unlocked. He pulled open the door and

Penelope, after kissing Rickmore on both cheeks, climbed in and sat.

Elham went round to the driver's door. 'Thanks again, Dennis.'

'It's been a pleasure.'

But for whom? he wondered as he settled behind the wheel. He started the engine and then blipped it, unable to resist the satisfaction of showing how much power lay under his command. Then he engaged Drive, released the handbrake, and accelerated.

The drive, perhaps more accurately described as a slightly upmarket yard, ended at wooden gates which were always left open; in the headlights, the broken bottom crosspiece of one of them was obvious. Rundown, like so much about the place, he thought. As they turned left on to the road, there was a muted squeal from the tyres. He was vaguely surprised to discover that they'd been travelling that quickly.

The slightly undulating road ended at a T-junction. He turned right, came to a halt at crossroads fifty yards further on. On their right was a pub. Rickmore had said that occasionally he went in there and had a drink. A typically pointless exercise since only the local yokels would use it— but his brother-in-law had no grasp of priorities.

The road was clear and he accelerated, fiercely enough momentarily to pin them back in their seats.

'Don't drive so fast,' she said petulantly.

'You call that fast?' He laughed. When he'd been young . . . He corrected his thoughts, which had been about to indulge in fantasy. When he'd been young, he hadn't owned a Jaguar and burned up the roads. He hadn't even owned a clapped-out Mini. He could still remember the scorn of a girl he'd met at a bottle party when he'd confessed to being carless. She'd turned down a suggestion of another meeting. That, surely, had been some time during his pupillage, when every penny had had to be made to do the work of four . . .

'For God's sake, Terence, slow down and keep to your side of the road.'

'Stop fussing,' he snapped. It was generally supposed by their friends that she couldn't be as vacuous as she appeared and that therefore it was all a pose. But the pose was that she couldn't. But she was beautiful and when he saw the envy and desire in other men's eyes, he was content, except . . .

'Do look what you're doing.' Her voice was now shrill.

He steered for the nearside as he stamped on the brakes. The car skidded very slightly on the damp road, but then corrected itself without any action on his part; indeed, he didn't even become aware that they had begun to skid until it was all over.

Despite his braking, they still entered the left-hand corner too fast, especially remembering that there was a sharper right-hander a hundred yards further on. He was considering the need to brake again—and to return to the left-hand side of the road—when from a rough copse on their right a man ran out. Elham swung the wheel to the left, but the off-side wing hit the man and sent him flying, a Catherine wheel of arms and legs.

CHAPTER 2

Elham braked as he looked up at the rear-view mirror. The soft moonlight was just strong enough for him to be able to make out the dark bundle in the middle of the road. He tried to assure himself that it was moving.

'What are you doing?' she demanded shrilly. 'You fool, don't stop.'

'But . . .'

She gripped his shoulder and shook it, careless of what effect this had on his driving. 'For God's sake, keep going.'

'He may be hurt,' he mumbled.

'Someone else can cope.'

The car had slowed to little more than a walking pace. He half-turned and looked at her as he desperately tried to force his mind into focus. 'But I daren't just drive on. The law . . .'

Her voice rose still higher. 'Can't you understand? If you report it, they'll breathalyse you.'

He realized that she was right. It wouldn't matter that the accident had not been his fault, that the man had run into the car rather than that the car had hit him. They would insist on checking his blood/alcohol level and they'd find it was over the limit. From that moment on, it would prove impossible to maintain that the collision had been unavoidable because insobriety raised a presumption of guilt which was almost impossible to rebut . . . So if he stopped now, he must inevitably end up by being charged . . .

The Bar was jealous of its reputation and demanded that those who practised at it were beyond criticism. To be found guilty of any criminal offence was likely to lead to disbarment; to be found guilty of a serious one inevitably did. So disaster lay ahead. And this at a time when he had applied for Silk and his future seemed set to attain heights which thirty years ago had appeared unrealistic daydreams . . .

His mind was trained to cut through confusion and to recognize essentials and now, despite the acohol, despite the shock and panic, he understood that disaster need not lie ahead if only he could conceal his part in the accident. Could he?

Hit-and-run cases presented the police with difficult investigations and their clear-up rate was not high. Usually, they only solved them when someone was able to give an initial indication of the vehicle's identity—only then could they call in experts to make the necessary positive identification. This initial indication normally came from one of three sources—an eyewitness (who might be the victim), the sighting of a vehicle damaged in a manner consistent with the accident, or as a consequence of a report from the garage called upon to repair such damage (ironically, requested in an attempt to conceal it). Here, there had been no eyewitness other than the victim. He had run out from the copse so carelessly that it was impossible to believe he could have taken any notice of the approaching car through the glare of the headlights. After the impact, shock must surely have prevented accurate observation? So if he drove on now, the odds were heavily against the victim being able to give the police any useful evidence. And once back at Popham House, he could check the damage the car had suffered and decide what steps needed to be taken to conceal it . . .

Although this was never a busy road, there was bound to be another vehicle along fairly soon, so the injured man would not be long without help . . .

He accelerated. They rounded the right-hander and drew level with the cricket pitch, fenced off from the sheep which grazed the outfield during the winter. Ahead of them, another vehicle approached, its headlights picking out the pollard willows which lined the stream which separated the road from the field. He realized that if he'd hesitated even a few more seconds, he'd have been unable to escape disaster and he felt sick at the thought.

'I do believe that Terence is getting even more pompous,' Rickmore said, as he used a pair of tongs to lift a partly burned log to one side of the fireplace.

'What lies behind that observation—sour grapes?' asked Anne.

He put the tongs back on the stand, picked up the fireguard and set it in front of the fireplace. As he stood upright, he said: 'You really think that?'

She regarded him for several seconds, then answered as she ran her fingers through her thick curly black hair which refused to be constrained or styled and had filled her with despair until she had learned to leave it to grow as it demanded. 'Not in the sense that you envy him his possessions. But maybe yes in the sense that you envy him the security that those possessions give him.'

'I suppose I have to admit I'd like to be able to forget the more mundane problems of life, such as how can we afford to live next week.'

'We always manage.'

'But I can't buy you all the new clothes you need . . .'

'If you're thinking of that silver fox, forget it.'

'The what?'

'Wasn't it Penny's new coat which made you say that?'

'I didn't realize it was new—I thought it was the old one.'

She laughed as she came forward and rested her forearms on his shoulders and linked her fingers behind his head. 'If she knew that you never realized she was wearing a brand new silver fox coat, she'd be spitting six-inch nails.'

'I'm just dead unobservant and ignorant.'

'When it comes to fur coats, undoubtedly.' She kissed him. 'That's one of your attractions.'

'Then you're prepared to admit I do have some?'

She kissed him again, then released him and stepped back. 'You know what I think of fishing for compliments?'

'The bait's never right?'

'The fish you catch are rotten . . . Come on, instead of talking nonsense, let's go to bed.'

'Right,' he said with enthusiasm.

'You've had too much to drink to think along those lines; aren't you remembering your Shakespeare?'

'At this time of night? Anyway, didn't he also say that he always hath a way?'

She knew a warm happiness that she was married to a man who could talk stupidities instead of stocks and shares and futures. She yawned. 'I thought that pud I made was quite nice.'

'So now who's fishing?'

'All right, I am. So you can damn well tell me what you thought of my chocolate orange mousse.'

'Lumpy.'

She whirled round, picked up a cushion from the settee, and hurled it at him. He ducked and the cushion swept across the top of a small occasional table, sending objects flying. 'Damn!' she exclaimed.

'No doubt you expect me to apologize for ducking?'

'Of course.' She went over and knelt, to discover exactly what, if any, damage she'd caused. The chased silver snuff-box was undented. 'That's all right, thank goodness ... I do wonder what's happened to Uncle Paul? It's strange to have a blood relative who took off from home and hasn't been seen or heard from since.'

'One day he'll turn up, looking for his favourite niece because he wants to leave her all those vulgar oil wells he owns back in Texas.'

'When I was young, I used to have that kind of daydream. But when I mentioned it to Mother, she said that Paul would only reappear if he were broke.' She returned the snuffbox to the table. 'He gave me this two days before he disappeared. I often wonder why he did.'

'Perhaps he thought he was about to snuff it.'

'God, your sense of humour doesn't improve! ... What's this? Blast!'

'Now what's the matter?'

In answer, she held up a blue spectacle case.

'Are they Terence's?'

'Can't be anyone else's, can they? And he's bound to need them tomorrow, so he'll have to come back now and fetch them. Ring him up, will you, while I finish tidying up?'

He went through to the hall—like the kitchen, originally part of the outshut—and across to the corner cupboard by the doorway into the kitchen. He lifted the receiver off the telephone and dialled. The call was unanswered. 'They can't be back yet.'

She stood in the doorway of the sitting-room and looked at her watch. 'It's nearly twenty minutes since they left here. They must be back by now if they went straight there.'

'They're not likely to have done anything else at this time of night—Terence reckons that a late night leads straight along the path of unrighteousness.'

She thought for a moment, her features slightly blurred by the combination of light and shadow which softened them and added a touch of beauty to a face which normally held too much character to be termed beautiful. 'Try again.'

He dialled and there was still no answer.

'D'you think something's happened to them on the way back?'

'Very unlikely. The devil always looks after his own.'

'But they couldn't possibly take more than a quarter of an hour . . . I think I'd better drive over to see if they're all right and to return the glasses.'

'Why can't we just leave it . . .'

'Because we can't.'

'They would, if the roles were reversed.' He sighed. 'I know, they aren't.'

'That's not very fair.'

'Facts often aren't.'

'Now who's being pompous?'

'The final insult! OK, OK, I'll drive his spectacles back so that in the morning he can appear in court with his usual brilliance.'

'Are you sure you're up to driving?'

'I'm as sober as a judge.'

'Then heaven help justice ... Darling, please go carefully.'

'On tiptoe, fairy-like ... On second thoughts, not a very safe expression in this gay day and age.'

'Don't worry, you'll never be mistaken for one of them.' She returned to the sitting-room, brought back the spectacle case which she handed to him. 'Don't stay on for a nightcap, or anything.'

'Not a dram shall pass my lips. And as far as the anything is concerned, Penelope has never bewitched me while Circe weaves.'

'Idiot! Sometimes I think you're certifiable.'

'But charming.'

'God, you don't dislike yourself!'

'What cause have I ever had to? ... I'll be back in a rush.'

'Just go and return at a sober pace.'

'Is our old banger capable of any other?'

He left the hall and went through the small porch to the outside. He was about to shut the porch door, when she called out: 'What about a coat?'

'Don't need one,' he replied, forgetting how cold it had become.

He walked along the brick path, round the corner of the house. He was, he thought as he opened the wooden gate, a very lucky man to be married to Anne. Life would be perfect if only he could earn a bit more money ... It was funny how life usually made certain there was an if. Take Elham. He had success, money, and a very beautiful wife. Yet it had become clear in only the last few days that his life might hold an if. The previous Tuesday, over a drink in the Reckton squash club, Hugo Beeston had over-casually mentioned seeing Elham in a restaurant just off the Fulham Road, lunching with a sculptor who'd created a hullabaloo with her work. Beeston, a born gossip, had obviously been fishing for information as to whether the relationship was possibly more than a casual one. He'd gone away empty-handed. But could Elham be having an affair with a sculptor who was, apparently, noted for depicting the male member in unusual guises? It was a delightful thought . . .

He reached the garage, opened the right-hand set of doors and clipped them back. He didn't bother to switch on the light, but edged his way between the workbench and the Escort to the driving door. He settled behind the wheel, turned the key, and the engine churned over but did not fire. He tried again, with the same result. He remembered how the Jaguar had fired immediately and how the exhausts had burbled with the tenor of a running brook which might, at whim, be transformed into a raging torrent. When Anne had said that perhaps he envied Elham his sense of security, but not his material possessions, she'd forgotten that cus-tomized XJ-S.

The Escort's engine finally fired; the engine ran lumpily. Only recently, the garage had said that he couldn't expect much from a car which had been right round the clock once and seemed to be heading for its second century. He needed a new car. They hadn't added where he was to find the money to buy this new car.

He backed out, turned, drove on to the road and turned left to go down to the T-junction. Seven minutes later he approached the left-hand corner just before the cricket field to find that traffic cones had been set up on the road, together with a police notice to slow. Round the bend were parked two cars. Clearly, there had been an accident. He slowed down to a crawl, suddenly very conscious of the fact that he had drunk more than enough to be driving.

A policeman in uniform, reflector tabs on his sleeves and a reflective lollipop in his right hand, waved him on, his quick movements suggesting impatience. Probably, Rickmore thought, some of the passers-by had tried to rubberneck. He dropped down to second gear, hugged the left-hand verge, and drove past the policeman. He was aware of a group of people, but could not make out what they were doing. He reached the right-hander and passed a policeman who was ready to slow traffic coming in the opposite direction. By the time he was through the corner, all signs of the accident were gone from the rear-view mirror.

The road, turning this way and that for no obvious reason —the course of the rolling English drunkard?—crossed the tributary of the Wort and then climbed up over the railway line and into the village of Ailsham, a haphazard collection of centuries-old cottages, a few ugly modern council houses, a general store, and a pub. Beyond the village the road forked and he turned left.

Popham House lay a mile outside the village. Originally a typical farmhouse, probably built for a yeoman farmer of some consequence, with high-pitched roof, peg tiles, bricks made from clay dug nearby, and beams cut out from locally felled oaks, it had been enlarged and modernized by previous owners. Since they had had considerable taste and sympathy for period, the result had not been noticeably incongruous or anachronistic. Lacking such constraining influences, the Elhams had, when in turn they'd decided to have the enlarged house enlarged, demanded size and luxury irrespective of any other standards. Popham House was now the home of wealthy people who wanted others to admire and envy.

The large, fussily designed wrought-iron gates were open. So they had returned, thought Rickmore. Then why hadn't they closed them? Was Elham tighter than he'd seemed?

He drove through the gateway and into the macadamed drive. To the left was a three-car garage. The Jaguar was parked outside and Penelope and Elham were standing by it. Elham had a torch in his hand and this was switched on even though the outside lights on the garage were also on. As the Escort came to a stop, Rickmore was momentarily struck by the expression on their faces; it looked like fear, but since this must be an absurd flight of fancy, he dismissed the idea.

He opened the door, climbed out, and approached them. 'We tried to phone, but there wasn't any answer.'

They said nothing, but continued to stare at him. 'Is something wrong?' he asked.

'No,' Elham mumbled.

'You forgot your specs and we reckoned that as you'd need them tomorrow, I'd better run them over.'

'What . . . what's that?'

'Your spectacles—I've brought them.' He held out the case.

Elham took it and then there was a silence, which Rickmore finally broke. 'I'll be getting back home, then.'

Penelope made an effort to behave normally. 'Thank you so very much for bringing them. It's wonderfully kind of you.'

Despite their previous denial, Rickmore thought, they were behaving as if something were very wrong. But obviously they didn't want to discuss what that something was. He began to turn away when a brief fleck of light drew his attention to the offside wing of the Jaguar. He saw that there was a slight dent in it. Then his gaze moved down and, thanks to the angle at which he stood, he could just see that the offside light pod was smashed. Obviously Elham, his judgement affected by drink, had bumped into something as he drove in. No wonder the atmosphere was strained! And ten to one Penelope, whose second name was not discretion, had not had the sense to keep her opinions to herself . . .

Rickmore returned to the Escort and left.

Anne was in bed, the duvet drawn up half over her head as she often liked it—squirrelling warm, she called it. 'Was he grateful?' she asked sleepily.

'I wouldn't know.'

'What d'you mean?'

'When I arrived, both of them were still outside, standing around the Jag and staring down at a dent in one wing and a smashed headlamp.' He chuckled. 'For once, Terence's driving obviously wasn't up to genius standard.'

'Why's that so amusing? You have a mean sense of humour.'

'Like as not,' he replied complacently.

CHAPTER 3

Detective-Sergeant Ridley read through the brief typewritten report. At 11.17 the previous night, a man driving from Reckton to his home in Ackley Cross had come across a body lying in the road just past Ailsham cricket ground. He'd telephoned for help from the nearest house and the ambulance had arrived at 11.39, a couple of minutes after the first patrol car. The victim had suffered a hit-and-run accident. He had been taken to the Latimer General Hospital in Reckton, where his condition had been diagnosed as serious; he had a broken arm and two crushed ribs, but his main injury was a fractured skull and internal cranial bleeding. No prognosis had yet been given. Patrol car Tango Bravo Seven had gone to the hospital and PC Fielding had tried to identify the victim, but without success.

At the conclusion of the report was the usual compressed

description. Name, unknown; sex, male; colour, white; nationality, unknown; occupation, unknown; age, between 20 and 30; height, about 5ft 11ins; weight, about 160 lbs; build, medium; complexion, fair, freckles on cheeks; hair, brown, straight, bottle-brush style; eyes, small iris, light brown; eyebrows, arched, thin; nose, straight, very narrow saddle; face, long, clean-shaven; chin, square, dimpled; lips, thick, upturned corners; mouth, large; ears, large, close to head; forehead, slightly receding; distinguishing marks, tattoo 'BA' on right forearm; clothes (all without makers' tabs), black wool sweater, green shirt, navy blue jeans, vest, pants, socks, woollen gloves, plimsolls; jewellery, gold ring, plain, left middle finger; habits, heavy smoker, no sign of drugs. No papers. Prints taken and sent on.

He dropped the single sheet of paper on to the desk, yawned, ran the fingers of his right hand through his wavy brown hair. He lit a cigarette, looked at his watch. Five minutes to reporting to the DI.

Elham entered the first-class carriage and settled in the only vacant corner seat. ''Morning,' said Templeton, from immediately opposite. He nodded in reply. Templeton resumed reading his newspaper. Their conversation seldom went beyond this briefest of greetings. The train started and quickly gathered speed and soon they were rattling over the complicated system of points by the large marshalling yard which was used by passenger trains. Beyond this, the countryside stretched out, bare and dedraggled from the recent heavy rain.

Normally, Elham opened *The Times* at the law reports, studied these and agreed or disagreed with the decisions reached; then he spent the rest of the hour's journey learning what new mess the politicians had led the country into. Today, however, he left the newspaper unopened and stared out of the window. As the telegraph poles flicked by and the carriage rocked steadily, without any audible rhythmic accompaniment since here the line was continuously welded, he suffered a growing sense of resentment which, for the moment, even subdued his fears. There had been no need for Penelope to become so aggressively—and contemptuously?—commanding. He'd been shocked, of course, but he had not lost his wits. Why had she treated him like a child and spelled everything out? He'd appreciated the situation just as well as she. Given a little more time, he'd have done all that it was necessary to do. He'd always worn the trousers in their household and he'd no intention of handing them over now . . . This morning, when he'd said he was feeling too rotten to go to chambers, she could have shown sympathy instead of sarcastically asking if he really wanted people to wonder why he hadn't gone to work on the morning following the accident . . .

The train flashed through a small station so quickly that it was quite impossible to read the name; he didn't have to read it to know where it was because he'd been born four miles away—in a small, dingy semi-detached, one of a row of ten, inhabited by women who walked around in public in carpet slippers with curlers in their hair and men who sat down to meals in their braces. People born in such streets usually only left them in their coffins. But he'd had the drive and ambition to claw his way up and out into a different world and that was something Penelope shouldn't ever forget . . .

When he'd first met her, she'd had a circle of admirers, how large a circle and how admiring he'd been careful never to determine. But by then he'd discovered self-confidence —some might have described it as arrogance—and he had decided to marry her even though he was considerably older than she and totally lacking in the feckless, to-hell-with-tomorrow attitude towards life that her other male friends had possessed and which, in their stupidity, they'd considered one of the charms of their gilded circle. His self-confidence had been well founded. He'd had something to offer which none of them had: a glittering future . . .

Such reminiscences, with their underlying theme of self-approval, had the effect of lessening his resentment. And as it lessened, so his fears returned. What were the police doing at that moment? Searching the road and the grass verge for anything that would help lead to the identification of the hit-and-run car? The fleck of paint which could be matched with the paint from the suspect car (every car manufacturer cooperated with the police and sent in samples of the paints they used; the exact composition of the layers of anti-rust, undercoat, and topcoat, could identify the model); the sliver of glass from the headlamp which could be matched with the remaining glass; the tyre impression which could some-times be nearly as damning as a fingerprint; the pellet of mud, knocked off from the underside of the wheel-arch, which possessed peculiar characteristics and so identified an area where the car had been? . . . Certainly the police would have already circularized all garages and repair shops, asking to be informed if any car were brought in with damage that was consistent with its having hit a body . . . He'd explained all this the previous night, after the third whisky, when the horror of what had happened had gripped his lungs until he'd had difficulty in breathing. He'd said that running away hadn't solved anything because there was that dent in the offside wing of the Jaguar, together with the broken glass of the headlamp pod, and they didn't dare leave them as they were for fear of their being seen by a patrolling constable, and they didn't dare try to have them repaired because if they did then a report would be made to the police . . . He could still 'hear' the scorn with which she'd said that he was supposed to be the one with the brains, so hadn't he realized that the safest place in which to hide something was in full view? So all he had to do was drive the Jaguar into the corner of the garage, making certain that he caused enough further damage to erase all previous signs . . . He'd stared at her, slack-jawed, wondering how in the hell she, of all people, could have come up with the solution? And an answer had come to him. She had realized that the whole of her way of life was at stake and so she was fighting to preserve it with all the ferocity and ingenuity of a mother defending her young . . .

It was drizzling when they arrived at Cannon Street. He took a taxi to chambers and when he paid the fare and added to this his precisely calculated tip, the driver showed his contempt for such parsimony.

Haldane Buildings had originally been a large Edwardian block with four floors. During the war it had suffered some bomb damage which had left the top floor untenantable and as soon as possible after the war the block had been demolished and in its place a more elegant building, in Georgian style, had been erected, with much better use being made of the available space so that now there were six floors.

He climbed three flights of stairs, beginning to puff as he started on the third one. At the head was a small landing, on either side of which was a set of chambers. He turned left. The outer door was pinned back, displaying on its upper half a list of members; the names of those who were practising being in bold letters, while those who were merely associated with chambers were in light lettering. His name headed the list; occasionally, he spent a few seconds recalling the times when it had been at the bottom of the list of his first chambers. He opened the inner door and went in.

There was a passageway off which led five rooms, a cloakroom, and the clerks' room. A murmur of conversation came through the doorway of the clerks' room. He walked on, although normally he stopped to say good morning, a routine that started his working day.

He entered his room. Until he'd decided to apply for Silk, he'd always had a pupil who'd shared the room with him; since a Silk was not allowed to have a pupil, he'd not replaced the last one when that self-opinionated young man had reached the end of the year; now he had the room to himself—the only member of chambers to do so.

He hung his umbrella and hat on the mahogany stand, added his overcoat. He crossed to the desk and looked down at the several briefs, then walked past the shelves of books to the single large sash window. He stared out at the small square which consisted of grass and four small flowerbeds surrounded by a gravel path. Had the police found anything of significance? Was there anything they could find . . . ?

His thoughts were interrupted by a quick knock on the door. Arnold, the chief clerk, entered. He closed the door, carefully so that it made no noise, walked with his strange, almost mincing gait up to the desk, coughed once, and said: 'Good morning, sir.' His first greeting was always formal. After that, it would be 'Mr Elham'.

It struck Elham—with complete inconsequentiality— that he'd never before realized quite how ungainly Arnold was; as if head, arms, body, and legs, had not originally been meant for each other.

'Not a very nice morning. And the forecast is that the rain will become quite heavy.'

Elham returned to his desk, pulled out the chair, and slumped down on it. He was conscious that Arnold was looking at him with concern. 'I had a bit of a thick night, Tom.'

'Then there's no need to worry. You're not in court today.'

'I'm not?'

'I did mention it last thing last night. Wicks and Chamfers has been moved to Monday. Of course, that meant I had to do something about Stevens and Stevens, so I rang Mr Baldwin and explained and asked if it would be all right if

Mr Young took the brief. After a bit, he agreed.' Arnold sucked in his thick lower lip, then let it go with a plopping sound; a frequent mannerism of his when he was pleased with himself. 'I did suggest at the time that the brief wasn't really marked high enough.'

For once, Elham was uninterested in the markings on his briefs. Let the police gain even a hint that it might have been the Jaguar . . . But there'd been no eyewitnesses and now the original damage was completely masked . . .

'Are you all right, Mr Elham?'

Arnold, looking like a dehydrated dugong, was peering down at him with an expression of concern. 'Of course I'm all right,' he snapped.

'A very thick night!' Very occasionally, Arnold permitted himself a touch of familiarity; it was as out of character as a Stradivarius playing rock. Penelope often referred to him as Uriah Heep, but this nickname was inappropriate since however unctuous his manner, however ungainly his appearance, his sense of loyalty to Elham was unbounded.

The phone rang and Elham picked up the receiver. The caller said that he was passing on unofficial word that Elham's application to be granted Silk had been accepted. Congratulations and that was going to cost a couple of glasses of champagne at their next meeting.

Elham replaced the receiver and stared at the nearest brief on his desk. It was marked £500, of which Arnold would receive ten per cent. As a fashionable and successful Silk, briefs marked £5000 would be far from unusual. He said: 'I'll be taking Silk.'

'Congratulations, Mr Elham. Indeed, many, many congratulations. Not that I ever had the slightest doubt. It was merely a question of choosing the right time.' He was filled with excited pleasure and pride.

CHAPTER 4

The PC parked by the side of the road, stepped out and slammed the door shut. He looked at the oblong house and correctly judged that it had once been two primitive, semi-detached cottages which had been converted into one reasonably comfortable home. There were still two front doors, but no path across the lawn to either of them. He went along the cinder path to the back door. This was half glass and through it he could see a woman standing by a solid fuel cooker. He knocked and she walked across and opened the door. 'Mrs Daley?'

'That's right.' In contrast to his Kentish acent, she had a much harder, sharper London one.

'I'd be glad of a word with Mr Daley, if he's around.'

'He ain't. He's at work.'

'Where would that be?'

'At Mill Farm.'

'Which is where?'

She told him how to drive there, then her manner became slightly easier. 'I suppose it's on account of last night.'

'It is.'

'It real shook him.'

'It would.'

'Coming round the corner and seeing someone lying in the road . . . How is the poor man?'

'The last heard, he was still not conscious and they don't really know yet how badly injured he is.'

'And it was someone in a car what hit him and didn't stop?'

'That's right.'

'D'you know what I'd do to people like that?'

'No, missus, I don't, but I do know what I would
... Thanks a lot, then, sorry to have disturbed your
work.'

'I hopes you find the driver.'

'We will.'

He turned away and walked back to his car, hardly aware
of the distant view of farmland and woods. He'd been born
in the country, but was happy to live in a town. In winter,
the countryside was either knee deep in mud and muck or
frozen solid.

Mill Farm—there was no stream and no sign that there
had ever been a windmill—was on the right-hand side of
the road; a square, red brick house, uncompromisingly
functional, lay close to the road and leading past it was a
concrete drive which ended at a range of farm buildings
which dated from the same time as the house. Three wings
jutted out from the long, central building and the dairy was
in the near end of the middle one of these. Inside, a man
was cleaning down the sides of a large stainless steel bulk
milk tank. The emptying valve was open and the waste
water was gushing out on to the concrete floor; the PC had
to step carefully to avoid getting his shoes soaked. 'Mr
Daley?'

Daley nodded. A tall, thin man with a face tanned by sun
and wind, he spoke sparingly and moved with the slow,
regular action of someone who'd spent all his working life
with animals.

'I'd like a word if you've the time?'

He nodded again. He looped the hose over the side of the
tank so that the jet continued to play into it, went over to a
tap and turned this off. He moved across to a control panel,
opened a couple of valves and switched on a pump to
circulate cleaning fluid around the milk lines.

'D'you smoke?' asked the PC, producing a pack of cigarettes.

'Not in here I don't.'

The PC grinned. 'Sorry.'

'It's not me, it's the boss . . . D'you feel like a coffee?'

'I wouldn't say no to a cuppa.'

Daley led the way out of the dairy and round to the far wing and a small side room in which were a couple of wooden chairs, a butane gas-ring, and an old, deep stone sink above which was a tap. On the far side of the sink was a stained and battered table on which were a kettle, a jar of instant coffee, a jug of milk, a packet of sugar, a couple of teaspoons, and four earthenware mugs. He filled the kettle, lit the gas-ring, and put the kettle on this.

The PC sat, somewhat gingerly since the chair looked less stout than in fact it was, then said: 'It was you who found the injured man near the cricket field at Ailsham?'

'It were.'

'So maybe you can help us trace out the car which knocked him down?' He again brought out the pack of cigarettes from his pocket and this time Daley accepted one without demur. 'As I understand it, you came round the corner by the cricket field and there was the man in the road?'

'That's how it was.'

'And a bit before you reached the corner, you met a car going in the opposite direction?'

'Yes.' The kettle began to steam and Daley turned off the gas. 'How d'you like it—strong?'

'Not too strong, but then neither too weak. A bit like a Piccadilly whore.'

Daley did not smile. He spooned instant coffee into two of the mugs, lifted up the kettle, and poured in water. 'There's the milk and sugar. Ain't no call to worry how much milk you use.'

'You can always pump yourself up some more?' The PC stood, went over, helped himself to three spoonfuls of sugar and a generous measure of milk. He returned to his chair.

'This other car—d'you think the driver of that had seen the man in the road?'

'Can't think of no way he didn't.'

'How was the car being driven?'

'Fast.'

'What d'you mean by that?'

'What I says.'

The PC smiled. 'Would you like to give an estimate of its speed?'

'No, I wouldn't.'

'Was it going straight or weaving about a bit?'

Daley shrugged his shoulders. 'No saying. Never dipped his bloody lights so all I was worried about was seeing where I was going.'

'How many headlights did it have?'

'One.'

'One?'

'That's what I said, ain't it?'

'Which side was this?'

'Nearside.'

The preliminary findings were that the man had been hit by a car driving in the direction of Ailsham, well over on the wrong side of the road—the offside light would have taken the force of the blow. There had been a doctor who'd travelled with the ambulance and he'd judged that the accident had taken place within a short time—say a quarter of an hour—of his examination, so the accident had occurred very shortly before Daley had reached the scene. While the driver of this other car with only the nearside lights working might have been someone unwilling to become involved, it was, on present evidence, more reasonable to assume he was the hit-and-run driver. 'Can you suggest what kind of car it was?'

Daley spoke scornfully. 'I said, he never dipped. Blinded me, even if they was yellow.'

The PC didn't say that this was fresh evidence. The French always had yellow lights. If this had been a French car, the chances of identifying it became very slim unless the driver was caught at the port of embarkation with a smashed headlight and a dented wing (forensic evidence suggested the car must have suffered obvious, but not heavy, damage). 'You got no impression at all of what sort of car it was?'

Daley showed himself to be a stubborn man. 'Didn't you hear—I was blinded?'

'Sure. But even under those conditions one can still sometimes gain some sort of overall impression of a car. Have a go. Was it big or small?'

Daley drank, drew on his cigarette, then said, with some reluctance: 'Big.'

'What kind of big? Something like a Land-Rover?'

'No. It were one of them smooth jobs.'

It took a little time to determine that in this context smooth meant curved and sporty.

'A bit like a Ferrari, for instance?'

'What's that?'

'You must know what a Ferrari looks like.'

'Well, I bloody don't.'

Such ignorance was, in the eyes of a car enthusiast like the PC, quite heretical. There was something about having much to do with cows which addled a man's brains. He asked a few more questions, but it had become obvious that there was nothing more to be learned.

Rickmore crossed over to the window of his office and stared out. On the far side of the street, two boys were playing marbles under the bare branches of a large horse-chestnut tree. The course of their game eluded him since it bore no resemblance to any of the variations he had known in his youth. He turned, a shade too energetically, and winced.

The aspirins he'd taken after breakfast—a breakfast restricted to coffee—were having little effect and his head still thumped at about 9 on the Richter scale. It was damnably unfair that he should suffer so much since he hadn't been drunk, he'd merely drunk too much. When he'd complained to Anne, she'd shown a callous lack of sympathy. Alcohol always reacted badly on him, so why drink as much as he had?

He returned to his chair and carefully sat. He read what he'd written ten minutes earlier, scrumpled up the sheet of paper and threw it at the wastepaper basket. It dropped outside. It was just one of those mornings. He picked up his ballpoint pen, squared up a fresh sheet of paper, and thought. He thought that his headache was becoming worse and his stomach was revolting. The telephone rang and the assistant sales manager, overseas, asked him if he'd heard from Julot in Paris. He said he hadn't and as he replaced the telephone, he thought that that was hardly surprising. Selling refrigerators to Eskimos was a simple task compared to selling English perfumes to Parisians . . .

An old friend had said not long ago that all right, the job wasn't the best paid in the country, but who was he to complain when his life was spent in the company of glorious, glamorous, half-naked women? Impossible to make Mike understand that as PRO he was seldom, if ever, in the company of the frolicsome ladies who appeared in the firm's advertisements.

How to say something fresh about the firm's products? How to fill up the monthly newsletter with little snippets of information that would attract the attention of the press and so lead to a mention of those products in the newspapers? How to persuade the glossy magazines to add to their list of acknowledgements, perfumes by Teerson Products. Teerson Products sounded more like the manufacturers of pot scourers than seductive perfumes for exotic women. A suggestion he'd made soon after joining the firm had been that they change the name of the brand products to something more suited to the image they wanted to capture. The suggestion had been received with frosty disapproval. Mr Teerson was very, very proud of his name and wanted it heralded far and wide. A chemist by training, he'd discovered a way of making personable perfumes using wholly synthetic and cheap materials; the discovery had made him rich. Rich men paid poor men to glorify them, not to extinguish them under pseudonyms. Realizing that here was a verity which might repeatedly prevent him doing his job as effectively as he'd want to do it, he'd considered resigning and looking for a position where his ability would not be stifled by pride. But the recession had begun to bite hard and jobs had not been as easy to find as before and he simply hadn't been prepared to take the risk of finding himself unemployed for months on end . . . And to look on the cheerful side, the job was not demanding—one learned to overcome, or ignore, the frustration—and it did leave him time and energy for his writing . . .

He often wished he'd as much confidence in himself as an author as Anne had. Then he wouldn't ask himself if her confidence rested on loyalty rather than critical honesty. The public had received his one published book with a notable lack of acquisitive enthusiasm and his royalty returns had looked rather like a census of Jews living in Mecca —but his editor was always encouraging him and had stated with apparent honest authority that one day his books would become a critical and popular success . . . It was a strange fact that the only time Elham had treated him without the slightest condescension had been when he'd offered him one of the six free copies of his book. It did seem that somewhere within Elham's breast there lurked a faint respect for things other than financial success and social standings . . . He smiled. Since the book had, indirectly, questioned the integrity of success and the merit of wealth, Elham must have found the book very distasteful. Or perhaps he'd never bothered actually to read it. Certainly Penelope wouldn't have done. She never read anything but her horoscope and probably that occasionally taxed her intelligence . . .

He checked the time. Ten minutes to coffee. Two hours and ten minutes to lunch. Five hours and ten minutes to packing-up. And the end of another day devoted to furthering the future of Mr Teerson, private egotist, public philanthropist, and staunch defender of free enterprise's right to exploit its workers.

CHAPTER 5

Elham put the last of the accompanying documents down by the side of the twenty pages of instructions. At stake in this action was the contingent liability arising from alleged malfeasance under a contract in which the terms were ambiguous. Both sides had a case and one of the points of law at issue was highly arcane. Normally, it would have been just the kind of brief to please him. To begin with it was highly marked, and beyond that he was a born lawyer, enjoying the subtleties of shades of meaning and seeing nothing odd in spending endless time pondering the true significance of a single sentence. But today this case merely irritated him to the point where he wondered why the two parties couldn't summon up sufficient common sense to resolve their own difficulties. Today his mind repeatedly returned to that moment when the man had run out into the road, to be sent flying by the Jaguar . . . If only they'd left Oak Tree Cottage five minutes earlier or later. If only he'd driven a little slower or a little quicker . . .

How far had the police now got in their investigations?

Whatever happened, they couldn't possibly trace the car. Could they? There'd been no one else on the road, the victim could have seen nothing ... Those whose work brought them close to the police knew that, often through no fault of their own, far from the highly successful crime detection force many believed them, they were frequently all at sixes and sevens. When there was no direct evidence of identity, it was probably true to say that they didn't solve four out of five hit-and-run cases. But that still left the one that was solved ...

Years ago, soon after he'd been called, he'd defended a man from a good background who'd been accused of swindling the firm for whom he'd worked. During the course of one of the interviews, the man had said: 'I've discovered something. The worst thing is the fear, not the fact.' At the time, he'd not fully understood what the man had meant, but now he did.

He looked at the telephone. There must be someone he could speak to to discover what progress the police were making ... Only a fool drew attention to himself by asking such questions ... But he'd soon go bloody mad from the stress ...

The question suddenly formed in his mind: Why didn't he see Lucy? However mentally tired he might be, she fed fresh life into him. Surely, then, she could also banish his fears? Never mind for once that it was the middle of the day. (He'd never been to her place during the day, only at night. Buried within his subconscious was the belief that daylight adultery was sordid.)

He collected his hat and overcoat and put these on, picked up his umbrella. He looked at the briefcase, but left it. He walked down the corridor to the clerks' room. Allwyn, one of the younger members of chambers, was talking to Betty Greer, Arnold's assistant. ''Morning T. E. I hear from the grapevine you're taking Silk. Congratulations.'

He muttered a few appropriate words.

'Don't forget, I never mind being led. Especially astray.'

Elham ignored that weak attempt at humour. He said to Betty: 'Where's Tom?'

Betty, fast approaching middle age, plumpish, level-headed, reliable and efficient, if slow, replied: 'He had to go across to the courts a moment ago; he'll be back soon.'

'When he does, tell him I've gone out and won't be returning until some time in the late afternoon.' He nodded at Allwyn, left. He wondered if Betty and Allwyn were now trying to guess what had caused him to act so out of character? If so, Allwyn would doubtless hint at something salacious, little realizing how right he was . . .

He walked along the road, past Middle Temple Hall, to Fleet Street. He stood on the edge of the pavement and hailed every approaching taxi; the fourth one was free and it stopped. 'Twenty-two, Cuthbertson Road,' he said, as he opened the back door.

'Is that at the back of Harrods, Guv?'

'That's right.' He settled on the back seat. In ten days' time, he thought, it would be a year since he'd first met Lucy at a cocktail party, given by acquaintances rather than friends, to which he'd not wanted to go, but had because Penelope had insisted they did. It was ironic that Penelope's insistence had been fuelled by the possibility that some rather important people would be present—they'd never turned up. There was even more, and harsher, irony in the fact that Penelope was so beautiful and desirable that at that party no man under the age of senility had looked at her without desire, yet she was totally uninterested in sex. At first, after their marriage, he'd put this down to shyness —even in a permissive age, perhaps not every woman permitted. But then, unwillingly, he'd been forced to understand that she just was not interested in the physical act of love because she gained no pleasure from it. She'd never actively rejected him. She didn't refuse his demands while inventing headaches, she simply never responded and nothing he had ever said or done had altered that fact. Finally accepting that that was the situation, he'd tried to come to terms with it logically. He gained physical pleasure from her body, so why should it matter to him that she gained none from his? The loss was hers, not his. But while the law might cherish logic, emotions did not. The more she denied him her passion, the more he longed for it, at the cost of his own pleasure . . .

At the cocktail party—composed, as he'd previously guessed, of people right outside his milieu and of little consequence to him—he'd been cornered by a man who had been castigating the latest negotiating platform of the printing unions with boring fluency when Lucy had come up and said that his wife wasn't feeling too well and she wanted to go home. 'Not again, for God's sake!' the man had exclaimed bitterly. After he'd left, Lucy had said: 'I do so hate that kind of comment. It leaves one vainly wondering whether she's tight, pregnant, or just a hypochondriac.'

'Don't you know?' he'd said, surprised that he responded to her uncalled-for comments instead of ignoring them.

'How on earth could I when I've only just met the woman?'

'Then wouldn't it have been better . . .' He stopped, realizing—just in time—that now it was he who was in danger of ignoring a basic rule of social conversation.

She'd grinned, a mischievous, challenging grin. 'Wouldn't it have been better if I'd minded my own business? Of course. But then think how much more boring . . . Are you Lloyd's, lawyer, or layabout in the Foreign Office?'

'Why should I be any of those?'

'The mould's unmistakable.'

'I've no idea what you mean.'

'Then there's no point in my explaining, because you'd never understand.'

That night, as he and Penelope had prepared for bed—separate beds—she'd said: 'Who was that extraordinary women you were talking to for such a long time? The one dressed so outrageously in stretch pants.'

For some reason, which he'd not then attempted to analyse, he'd answered with defensive brevity. 'God only knows! I was stuck with her when she came across with a message for someone I'd been talking to before.'

'Oh!' Penelope had ceased to be interested in the woman whose social tastes were so obviously lacking.

Lucy had haunted his mind. She'd appear without warning when he was shaving, when Penelope asked him what he thought of her new frock, when he started to read the law reports in the train, when Arnold spoke about the latest brief to come in to chambers. Since he tried to hide himself from himself as well as from other people, it had been quite some time before he'd accepted the fact that she was haunting his mind because he was convinced, even on so short an acquaintance, that in her the fires of passion didn't just burn, they raged. Once this acceptance was made, her images became lascivious.

He'd managed to hold the haunting images in check for a time, then they had become too febrile to be contained any longer. One Thursday he'd set out to identify the small, sparkling, outrageous woman whose eyes had suggested, whose mouth had demanded, whose body had promised. He'd telephoned the host of the party, spent several minutes discussing matters of no consequence, then had casually introduced the one that had come to concern him so deeply.

'You mean it was Lucy you were talking to?'

'That's right.'

'I wish I'd known that. I'd have listened in.'

'Why?' he'd asked, with pompous stiffness.

'Because I can't imagine a more disparate duo and it would have been amusing to hear you misunderstanding each other. Did she shatter your remaining faith in femininity?'

'As a matter of fact, I did find her rather forthright.'

'What you mean is, plain bloody rude. Her trouble is, she's fruity.'

For some reason, impossible to recall, he had accepted this as a slang word, not met before, for lesbians. He'd known a sharp, and clearly illogical, sense of loss. 'Is she? I must say, she didn't strike me as one, but you just can't tell these days, can you?'

'She didn't strike you as one what?'

'Lesbian.'

'Lucy? She'd die of laughing if you told her that. What ever gave you such a crazy idea?'

'You said she was fruity.'

Another bellow of laughter. 'I've always said that you lawyers know less about the world you live in than a newborn babe . . . As fruity as a nut cake. Nutty. As mad as they come.'

'She's rather unusual?'

'My God, you've only got to see some of her sculptures to know that. Why d'you think one of the Sunday papers keeps referring to her as an up-and-coming sculptress?' An even louder bellow of laughter, the reason for which Elham only discovered later. 'So why all the interest? Thinking of joining her lists?'

'Good God, no!'

'It makes a lovely thought. From what I hear, in five minutes flat—' a pause, for that to be appreciated—'she'd have a misogynist renouncing his faith.'

For a time, he'd struggled with himself. He was a sober, decent, respectable husband; sober, decent, respectable husbands did not betray their marriages, even in modern times . . . It was, of course, true that Penelope refused him her passion—but many men were refused not only passion but body as well, and yet they continued to honour their marriages . . .

Now that it had been confirmed that by repute she was every bit as passionate as he'd imagined, the mental images became too painful to be borne. He'd telephoned her on the Friday. 'My name is Terence Elham. I don't suppose you'll remember me . . .'

'Then you lack supposition. Ever since that ghastly cocktail party, I've been wondering if you really can be as starchy as you appear.'

He'd taken a taxi to her flat and as he'd climbed out on to the pavement, he'd become aware of the fact that he was clammy from sweat. He'd almost returned into the taxi . . .

She'd been wearing a loose pair of overalls and—it seemed to him—little else, since the day was warm. The gently outlined flesh beneath the overalls, changing shape as she moved, had excited him to the point where his breath became short . . .

She'd led the way through to her studio because, she'd said, she'd a spot of work to finish before she showered and changed and they went out to dinner. She'd suggested they had a drink right away and had asked him to pour her a Campari and whatever he wanted for himself. Several bottles and half a dozen glasses had been on a tray on a table against the far wall. Next to that table had been a second and much larger one and on this had been a few of her sculptures. He'd examined them with an interest which initially turned to puzzlement, then to consternation, when he realized he was looking at the male member, in virile state, cast in the form of Cleopatra's Needle, the Eiffel Tower, the Post Office Tower, Nelson's Column, the Empire State Building, and the Leaning Tower of Pisa.

'Wonderful!'

Slack-jawed, he'd turned and stared at her.

'I bet myself you'd react exactly as you have. I am going to enjoy getting to know you very, very much.'

For dinner, she'd chosen a nearby restaurant, dimly-lit and smoochy, on the grounds that it would be as different as possible from the places to which he normally went. It was. Afterwards they'd walked to her flat arm-in-arm—something he hadn't done in years—and the smile on her face had been tantalizing, promising, and triumphant . . .

The taxi came to a stop. He climbed out and paid, adding an exact tip. He went up the stone stairs to the front doorway, recessed under a portico, and pressed the top button on the answerport. Lucy's voice came through the speaker loud and clear.

'I've got to see you.'

'Terry?' From the first day, she'd used the diminutive because he'd told her that no one else did. 'What the hell's up?'

'I . . . I need you.'

There was a buzz as the door catch was released. He went inside and climbed the stairs to the third floor. She was standing in the doorway and he saw she was wearing the same overalls as she had on his first visit. She stared at him, her expression intense. 'You really do need me?'

'Yes,' he said hoarsely.

She put her arms round him and pressed him to herself. 'Shall I tell you something, my lovely lawyer? Those are the sweetest words you could say to me.'

CHAPTER 6

Ridley left his office and went along the passage to the lift, found it was up at the top floor, and decided to go down the stairs. These brought him to the outside door on the north side of the building. The wind had become stronger and colder and it made him wish he'd had the sense to bring his mackintosh; for a moment he thought about returning to get it, but decided it wasn't worth the bother.

He walked briskly up Bank Street, turned left into High Street and the pedestrian precinct, and continued along this to the laundry. The redhead behind the counter greeted him with a smile. ''Afternoon. Getting chilly, isn't it? Bart says he thinks we're in for snow.'

'Tell him from me that he's a miserable old b.'

'Don't you like snow?'

'Well, do you?'

'If there's enough of it. Then the roads get blocked and I can't come in to work.'

'It's all right for some! If I had a six-foot drift all round my house, the boss would just expect me to grab a shovel and start digging . . . Have you got my jacket?'

'Where's the ticket?'

'Sorry and all that, love, but I forgot to bring it from home.'

'Then you're out of luck.'

'Sports jacket, a kind of a check in green and grey, with black stripes in all directions.'

'Suppose I tell you we've fifty jackets like that?'

'I wouldn't believe you.'

'Men!'

'Where would you be without 'em?'

'Happier.' She sighed. 'All right, I'll see what I can do.'

'That's my girl.'

'Yeah. Just so long as I do what you want.'

'Is that an offer?'

'Didn't you once tell me you was married?'

'She's generous.'

'I'm not.' She left and went through swing doors, careful to move her hips with grace.

He remained by the counter and stared out through the glass door. Still nothing on the hit-and-run victim, despite reference to the local and national missing persons' lists . . . Odd that so far no one had come forward to report a husband, son, or lodger missing. The man had been in good physical shape, so he hadn't been living rough—someone must know he hadn't returned to his home, even if that someone was only an inquisitive neighbour. Another odd thing, there'd been no means of identification on him; most people carried around with them personal papers of one sort or another. And where had he been going at that time of night on foot (there'd been no parked car nearby) . . .

The redhead pushed open one of the swing doors and returned into the shop, in her right hand a flimsy wire hanger on which hung a sports jacket. 'This is the only one like you described.'

'Thought you'd got fifty? That's mine, all right; straight from Savile Row. You're a marvellous girl.'

'I know.' Expertly, she extracted the hanger, folded the coat, and wrapped it in brown paper. 'That's four quid.'

'Christ! Started cleaning 'em in champagne?' He paid her and left.

Lucy gently ran the tips of her fingers down Elham's chest. 'Now tell me what the matter is.'

'Nothing.'

'Don't be silly. When you said you needed me, I thought you were just extra horny. But you needed to screw me because you're in some sort of trouble and it's a way of getting some relief.'

He hated it when she spoke so crudely.

'Come on, tell me what's biting you—apart from me . . . Nothing's ever so bad as it seems when you keep it to yourself.' She leaned over and gently nibbled his right breast.

'Last night . . .' He stopped.

'What about it?'

'We went to dinner with my brother-in-law.'

'I don't suppose that was enough to knock you sideways, so what went wrong there?'

'I was driving back afterwards and . . . and there was an accident.'

'Your wife was hurt?'

'It wasn't like that, it was . . .' He stopped once more, then spoke quickly. 'I was driving very slowly and carefully, I swear I was. But suddenly this man ran out from some trees, straight in front of the car. There wasn't anything I could do. You've got to understand, there wasn't anything at all I could do because there wasn't the time. It all happened too quickly.'

'You hit him?'

'Only a little,' he answered, quite unaware of the absurdity of his words.

'Was he badly hurt?'

'Not really.'

'Surely no one can begin to blame you, if you didn't even have time to brake?'

'I swear I didn't.'

'Love, you mustn't torture yourself like this, if there was nothing you could do.'

'There wasn't.'

'Well, then . . . Sometimes things happen which there's just no way of avoiding. And if this man wasn't seriously hurt, you've no need to go on worrying about him.' She kissed him, full-mouthed, hungrily. 'Are you going to remember that now?'

He wanted to tell her the full story so that she could agree he'd done the only sensible thing and that it would have been absurd for him to risk the destruction of his career, but he couldn't be certain that he'd still hold her sympathy; she had some odd ideas . . .

She nibbled his ear. 'Are you going to remember that now?'

'Yes.'

'Then maybe you'll screw me because you want to, not to help you forget last night?'

Emmery was twenty and ambitious. And he possessed the instinct which told him a story was stronger than the facts so far in evidence suggested which was the hallmark of a good journalist.

He said, over the phone: 'Then you've still no idea who he is?'

'That's right.'

'He doesn't fit anyone on the missing list?'

'No.'

He asked a few more questions, to which he received unsatisfactory answers, rang off. He didn't think the police were deliberately playing it close to their chests—they really had no idea who the injured man was. But who, other than a drop-out, could go missing without someone trying to trace him?

He told the news editor that he'd a lead which looked promising, OK to follow it up? The editor agreed. Emmery left the square, dirt-stained building, crossed to the much-used Nova, climbed in, started the engine, and drove out on to the road.

It was an eighteen-mile drive to Reckton, through gently rolling, well farmed countryside with the North Downs as a backdrop. At the large roundabout immediately outside the town, he took the second exit.

Thirty years before, Reckton had been a market town, unremarkable, but possessing a quiet, rather sleepy charm. Then the railway line to London had been electrified, bringing the town within the commuter belt, and the planners had been let loose, their brief to modernize and enlarge in order to cope with the projected increase in population. With unerring instinct, they'd destroyed all that was worth preserving and preserved all that should have been destroyed. Now, the town was without a soul.

They'd changed the course of the ring road since he'd last used it and he missed the turning he wanted. He found there was no right turn at the next junction so had to take the one after that and, swearing freely, finished up in an area he did not know. Inevitably, the first person he asked for directions was a stranger, but the second was not and she directed him to the hospital.

He spoke to a sister who answered his questions as briefly and generally as possible. The patient was still in a coma, in intensive care. He had suffered chest and arm injuries, but these were relatively minor; far more serious had been the blow to his skull which had fractured it and caused internal bleeding and possibly further injury, the extent of which could not yet be determined. It was impossible to give any sort of prognosis. No one had visited him.

Emmery returned to the Nova. It was odd, he thought, to be lying in hospital, in a coma, unidentified—it made of him a no-man. Which suggested the heading, The Abominable No-man . . .

He drummed on the wheel with his fingers. He'd discovered nothing solid that would build a story. At best, unknown man lying in a coma after hit-and-run accident might make for a small filler in next Tuesday's *Gazette*. But, now that he was here, it seemed a pity to return to Etchinstone without following up his hunch a bit further . . . Surely it was worth questioning the man who'd discovered the victim?

Daley was milking. Five at a time, the Friesians came into alternate sides of the herringbone milking parlour where they were fed automatically while he clamped on the clusters.

'I wonder if you've time for a word?' shouted Emmery, as he stood on the steps leading down to the pit.

Daley looked briefly up at him. 'Does it look like I've nothing to do?' He removed the cluster from the end cow on the right-hand side, glanced along the row of bags (which, from the pit, was almost all he could see of the cows), pulled down on a lever which opened a gate and allowed the cows to make their way out of the standings and the parlour. He closed that gate, opened the far one, pulled on a rope which slid back the door into the collecting yard. Cows came through and he shut the door behind the fifth one, then the gate. He sponged down the bags. A cow urinated and the hot liquid splashed down on the concrete and rebounded. Emmery hurriedly retreated and Daley showed his sarcastic amusement.

'I'm from the *Gazette*,' Emmery said, once satisfied he was safe.

Daley dropped the cloth back into the bucket of disinfectant. It took all sorts to make a world.

'You found the injured man after the accident, didn't you?'

He picked up the first of the clusters from its hook, arranged the cups over his hand in a star pattern with the rubber tubes twisted to block the vacuum, placed the cluster under the first cow's bag, in turn untwisted each cup and slipped it over a teat.

'It was you who found the injured man, wasn't it?'

He nodded.

'It must have been a bit of a shock?'

He moved down to the second cow.

'And you also saw the car that hit him?'

'I saw a car; that's all.'

'But the police think . . .'

'What they think is their business; it ain't mine.'

Emmery smiled; he rather liked awkward characters.

'They say that you said one of the car's headlights wasn't working, so since the man could only just have been knocked over, it like as not was that car. What make was it?'

'How would I know?'

'I thought you told the police?'

'Then you thought wrong.'

'What did you actually tell 'em, then?'

'Same as I'll tell you now, before you clear out of here and leave me to do me work. It was a big, smooth car and it was going fast.'

'You can't make a guess at what kind it was?'

'No. And the police can say it were a Ferrari from now until Christmas and it won't make no bloody difference.'

'Then it probably was a Ferrari?'

'I said I don't know.'

Emmery left, glad to escape the dangers of urinating cows. He walked through the dairy to his car. A Ferrari was a rich man's car . . . Unknown victim seriously injured by wealthy hit-and-run driver . . . That could make a story. And if it was angled adroitly, one or more of the London papers might pick it up, with financial advantage to himself.

They were watching a nature programme on BBC1 when the telephone rang. 'I'll get it,' Rickmore said. Anne loved films about birds, but he'd seen so many recently that they were beginning to bore him. He went out into the hall and crossed to the corner cupboard on which the telephone stood.

Penelope said: 'Dennis, I just had to ring and say how very much we both enjoyed last night. It was such fun to be with just the two of you.'

Was that an oblique way of saying that a dinner-party should always be composed of at least two couples other than the hosts? 'It was fun seeing you,' he replied.

'Anne's a wonderful cook; that mousse was simply the nicest I've ever eaten. You're a very lucky man.'

'And perhaps she's a lucky woman?'

'As I've always said, you're the perfect husband.'

Even Penelope ought to have choked on that piece of hypocrisy, he thought. 'Sounds to me as if we'd start favourites for the Dunmow flitch.'

'I'm sure you would.'

He was convinced she hadn't understood the reference. It occurred to him that she sounded even falser and more brittle than usual. 'How's Terence?'

'He's all right. Why shouldn't he be?'

'No reason, except I thought maybe he's still suffering from the remains of a hangover.'

'Don't be ridiculous. He had nothing of the sort.'

Even if he had been slightly tactless in his words, it seemed odd that she should have responded so sharply. He tried to pour a little verbal oil. 'If he was lucky, I wasn't. I spent most of the morning wondering whether to cut my throat to end the agony.'

'Terence did not have too much to drink last night.'

'Lucky man.'

'He was perfectly sober when we left you.'

'Couldn't have been more so.' He managed to keep the irony from his voice.

There was a brief pause. 'Will you tell Anne how much we enjoyed ourselves?'

'I will.'

'Goodbye.'

He'd never before known her to end a telephone conversation so abruptly. Usually, there were protestations of regret at having to ring off and promises to meet again just as soon as the so-crowded social calendar permitted . . .

He returned to the sitting-room. The nature film was finished and the credits were showing.

'Turn off, sweet,' she said.

'Let's just see what's on next . . .'

'It's that awful series where people get beaten up every five minutes. I can't stand so much violence.'

He switched off the television set.

'Who was that on the phone?'

'Your sister, making her bread-and-butter call.'

'How is she?'

'Same as ever, except not quite.'

'A very intelligent answer!'

He went over and rumpled her hair and she grabbed his hand and dragged it down, then pressed it once in a silent message of love before releasing it. 'What's wrong with Penny?'

'Nothing definite, but her manner was a bit odd.'

'I thought that as far as you're concerned, it always is?'

'Maybe I should have said, odder than usual. When I asked her how his lordship was because he might have had a touch too much vino last night, she took considerable um.'

'For goodness sake, what d'you expect? You really are quite hopeless.'

'If she'd said that about me to you, would you have become really huffy?'

'Of course not, but I'm not Penny.'

'For which the gods be thanked.' He crossed to his chair. 'Come to think of it, they were both a bit odd when I returned his glasses last night.'

'If you want my opinion, in the state you were in everyone and everything was odd. I should never have let you drive. There could so easily have been another terrible accident.'

He stared at the wood fire, flames dancing high. 'Have you heard any more about that?'

'No, but then I've only been to the local shops.'

'Usually, that's the source of all news.'

'Gossip, not news.'

He yawned. 'How about making tracks for bed? ... Rejoice! Tomorrow's Friday, the last working day of the week.'

'Do you really hate the job all that much?'

'I suppose not. After all, it's no more unnecessary and vapid than most and as far as I know the firm's products haven't ever actually killed anyone.'

'But you wish you were at home, writing?'

'That's the masochistic streak in me.'

'Don't be so stupid, and stop denigrating your own work. One day, you'll be famous.'

'But for what?'

CHAPTER 7

The laboratory assistant stared at the ancient Olympia typewriter with dislike. His training assured him that it was ridiculous to credit a piece of machinery with a diabolical sense of humour, but this machine had one. Why else should it type Y every time he meant to strike T?

He pulled out the form from the roller, scrumpled it up, and threw it into the wastepaper basket. He threaded in a fresh form and started typing once more. Reference number, source of exhibit, remitting police officer, date of receipt, date of examination, name of examiner . . . So far, only one typing error and that easily covered up since an n could be turned into a reasonable h. He resumed typing. Description of exhibit, results of examinations . . . One very small sliver of glass recovered from sweater, sample too small for comparison tests but consistent with glass from a vehicle's headlamp; quantity of dirt, pulverized and forced into jeans, probably by impact, containing traces of brick dust and very fine sawdust—type of wood . . .

He reached the end of the report, gratified by the fact that in all he'd made only three unimportant errors. He signed with a flourish, then noted that the time recorded was 110P hours. He swore, as he changed the P into a 0 with a pen. That bloody typewriter!

The Detective-Inspector was a man who suffered constant frustration because he tried to have almost every case which came in fully investigated, even though he knew that there was neither the manpower nor the time available to do this. The trouble was, MacMahon had joined the CID in an era of much less lawlessness when it had been possible to deal efficiently with all but the very minor crimes and he'd never been able to come to terms with a time when even a burglary might be left to a uniform PC.

He scratched the top of his head, then tried to smooth the remaining hair to hide his baldness. 'How's the Pierce job going?'

Ridley answered: 'John's got that in hand, but so far he's not had any breaks.' Had he ever been asked, he'd have said that the DI was soft to work himself so hard; there were no medals for growing ulcers. Not that Ridley viewed his work with a cynical detachment. But he did divide it into crime against property and against the person; the one was a fact of life, the other an obscenity. No one could work harder than he in a case involving the mugging of an old woman or the raping of a young one, and had he had his way those guilty would have been punished with physical violence so that they could taste the pain, the terror, the humiliation, of what they had inflicted.

'John?' The DI looked up. 'Doesn't the case call for someone a bit sharper?'

'Maybe. But do we pull that someone off something else?'

One of the two telephones rang and the DI picked up the receiver. He listened, muttered a few words, replaced the receiver. 'The victim of the hit-and-run at Ailsham—he's just died without ever regaining consciousness.'

'Poor sod!'

'Not heard from Dabs yet?'

'Not a word. But we'll be near the bottom of their priority list on that job.'

'And there are no other leads as to the man's identity?'

'None.'

'It's strange he's not been reported missing.' MacMahon fiddled with a pencil. 'And nothing leading to the car?'

'You've got my report mentioning the yellow headlights? And the one which arrived from the lab this morning?'

The DI indicated the uneven pile of papers in front of himself. 'None of that takes us very far.'

'Doesn't take us any bloody where.' Ridley's tone was hard. The driver of the car hadn't given a damn about his victim; all he'd been interested in was saving his own skin. The car could well have been large and expensive, in which case the driver was a wealthy man. If there was one type of person Ridley scorned more than a coward, it was a rich coward.

Lucy's father had been a creative potter of a somewhat anarchical turn of mind and before her marriage her mother, daughter of a shopkeeper, had happily worked in a bank. It was, so Lucy claimed, this dichotomy of parental characteristics which left her a walking encyclopædia of contradictions.

She believed she was entitled to say and do whatever she wanted; but there were some things that she would never say and some she would never do. She believed that social conventions were ridiculous and so deliberately flouted them; but there were one or two she always observed and there was no logic in the distinctions. She went out of her way to shock; but would never shock if to do so might cause hurt. She was a pacifist and very CND, but she was extremely patriotic. She despised wealth, but liked the things that money bought. She demanded that each person be independent, yet allowed no exception to the rule that every individual on earth owed a love and a duty to every other.

She started breakfast at half past one, not because it was now everybody else's lunch-time, but because she had enjoyed a couple of joints the previous night and they always made her sleep like the dead. The simile bothered her. What was death? Would she know she was dead? If so, part of her mind must have lived on and therefore she could not be dead; if not, how could death have any meaning to the person it most concerned? . . . Such thoughts troubled her deeply and depressed her and it was then that she created her priapic sculptures. After all, one couldn't get any further away from death than the start of life. And ever since that first *succès de scandale* such sculptures had sold well, which meant she could spend and spend and prove to herself that she was alive . . .

She buttered a piece of toast, cut a large section of Edam and put this on the toast, reached across the debris-laden table for the jar of Hero black cherry jam. She claimed it was her Welsh ancestors who gave her her liking for jam with cheese. As far as she knew, she didn't have any Welsh ancestors.

As she ate, she skimmed through the *Guardian*. As a person of unimpeachable liberal outlook, she would have countenanced no other daily paper. On Sunday, however, she had the *Sunday Telegraph*. On Sundays, she was a reactionary.

Wars, threats of wars, politicians behaving like children, children behaving like politicians . . . And a brief report on a road accident near the village of Ailsham on Wednesday night in which an as yet unidentified man had been knocked down and seriously injured by a hit-and-run driver. Nothing was spelled out, yet everything was there for those who could read between the lines. The driver was wealthy, the victim was poor. The driver had been drunk, the victim hadn't had a chance. The driver had fled, careless of the fact that medical attention might be essential to save the victim's life . . .

Elham had told her that he'd been in an accident on Wednesday night, near Ailsham. But he'd said he'd been driving very carefully, it had not been his fault, and the man had not been seriously injured; his silence had implied that he'd naturally stopped and done what he could to help. All lies. He'd been drunk, the accident had been wholly his fault, and he'd abandoned the severely injured victim without a second's thought. He'd lied to gain her sympathy and she'd given it, whereas had she known the truth . . . A woman of sharp, occasionally overpowering emotions, she knew the anger and contempt which swept away all rational thought. Without giving herself time to consider her actions, she went across to the desk, picked up the telephone receiver, dialled 999, and when the operator asked her which emergency service she wanted, replied 'Police' in a tone which turned the word into one of moral violence.

CHAPTER 8

MacMahon drove into the courtyard at the back of the concrete and glass divisional HQ and parked in a free space. Before climbing out of the car, he raised the collar of his overcoat to try to ward off the north wind which had started blowing. He saw Ridley approach, obviously wanting to speak to him, and he gloomily decided that this meant more trouble.

'I'm glad I've caught you, sir.'

MacMahon was intrigued by that 'sir'. Most of the young-sters eschewed such a form of respect these days; instead, being television fans, they called him 'guv'nor'. But at their first meeting of the day, Ridley usually called him 'sir'. He would have liked to know why. He doubted it was a sign of respect. 'Don't tell me what the trouble is, let me guess. The mayor's been shot, the chairman of the county council has been found chasing little girls, and the police committee has named me fascist pig.'

Ridley didn't smile. 'We've had a call from London to tell us that a woman, who refused to identify herself, has been in touch to say that if the police want to know who was driving the hit-and-run car at Ailsham, they need to talk to Terence Elham.'

MacMahon walked towards the building, hurrying be-cause the wind was giving his balding head a bad time. 'Elham . . . The name rings a bell, but for the moment, I'm damned if I can remember why.'

'I've asked around. He's a fairly prominent barrister.'

'Hell!' said MacMahon, just before he opened the door to go inside. The building was well heated and as they came to a stop by the lift, he lowered the collar of his coat. 'My old sergeant used to say that if you had the chance to choose between the Devil and a lawyer, settle for the Devil every time . . . What more d'you know?' He pressed the call button.

'Apart from the fact that he lives in Ailsham, nothing.'

The lift arrived and they took it to the fifth floor, walked along the corridor to the DI's room. MacMahon hung up his overcoat, then went round the desk and sat. 'Tim might be able to fill the picture in a bit.' He looked up a number, dialled it, spoke briefly. He thanked the other, replaced the receiver. 'Elham's a prominent junior barrister who's expected to take Silk very soon. A good all-rounder, hot on contract, well known at the criminal bar. He's rated as tough and clever and never hesitates to knock the police when he's defending.'

'One of them! Then it'll be a positive pleasure to land him.'

MacMahon leaned back in his chair. 'Maybe. But just remember that when you're dealing with a man with his background, if you've got any sense you'll go carefully.'

Typical! thought Ridley, with sudden anger. Just because the man didn't come from the slums, he had to be treated with kid gloves. Hadn't the DI realized the world had moved on? If it was Elham who'd knocked the man down and had then run, he deserved . . .

'His kind defend themselves with very heavy guns,' said MacMahon quietly. 'I'm trying to protect you, not him.' He saw that he was not believed. He sighed. Some people never learned, except the hard way. He hated violence and the waves of suffering it generated, just as much as Ridley, but he had learned long ago that meeting it with any kind of further violence was seldom satisfactory. He looked at his watch. 'The odds are, Elham's up in London. Tomorrow's Saturday, so he'll be at home all day.'

'I'll drive there . . .'

'We'll drive there,' MacMahon corrected.

Saturday was overcast. The clouds were dirt-coloured and they threatened rain or sleet; the increasing north wind suggested that sleet was the more likely.

In the room he used as a study—it had originally been the housekeeper's bedroom—Elham looked through the window and saw Juana, shopping basket in her left hand, come through the gateway into the drive and walk towards the back door, passing out of sight as she drew abreast of the small greenhouse. They'd been fortunate to find the Carvajals, he thought, with the complacency of someone who believed he was entitled to good fortune. Juana was an excellent cook and Miguel a reasonable gardener and neither believed in wasting time. Originally, he remembered, he'd been slightly reluctant to employ them because they might have left Chile for political reasons and he'd had no desire to support a couple of reds, but at no time since then had either of them ever shown the slightest sign of political awareness. And perhaps, his thoughts continued, considering how difficult it had become to find any servants, let alone good ones, a few left-wing sympathies—as opposed to activity—were not all that important.

He looked away from the window and down at the nearest brief on his desk. It was from Marsden & Slingfolds. Craig, the senior partner, had asked Arnold whether Mr Elham was thinking of taking Silk. Arnold's reply had been evasive and thus, in effect, an answer. Craig had then said good, there'd be quite a bit of work for Mr Elham, QC . . . To take or not to take Silk was a question which usually caused much heartburning. That one was a busy junior was no guarantee that one would become a busy Silk, since the junior was the all-rounder, the Silk the specialist. Further, Silks, to all intents and purposes, never appeared in court on their own, but always had juniors. This meant two sets of fees, with the Silk's noticeably higher than the junior's. So Silks were only briefed in major cases or where the client was wealthy, and therefore the amount of work potentially available was far less than when they'd been juniors; successful Silks made far more money than successful juniors, unsuccessful ones, far less. Many had discovered the bitter truth of this, but always too late. That ambition dug its own pit became very clear when one saw an underemployed Silk earning far less than he had, yet prevented from reverting to being a junior . . .

His thoughts changed course. It wasn't too fanciful to compare himself now with a man who'd awoken from a terrifying nightmare thankfully to find himself surrounded by the familiar, safe world. There'd been a short article in one of the papers about the hit-and-run case and this had named the car as a Ferrari. If that was what the authorities believed, then he could stop worrying . . .

He heard the front doorbell chime. Stephanie? Penelope said she might be calling. If so, he'd stay right where he was. Stephanie was loud-voiced; she was horsey and, like so many horsey people, had the manners of a groom; she was often downright rude to him. If she had not been so closely connected with one of the county families, Penelope and he would have had nothing to do with her.

He heard footsteps approach just before Penelope came into the room. 'Terence, two detectives have called and want to have a word with you.'

The icy waves of shock swept over him.

She closed the door and came up to the desk. 'For heaven's sake, pull yourself together.'

'But . . . but . . .'

'They'll be questioning everyone. But if they see you as you're looking right now, they won't need to question anyone else.'

'Why have they come here?'

'Why not? It's the biggest house in the village. They're bound to start with us.'

Were they?

'Just answer their questions. Don't volunteer anything.'

With a sense of bitter irony, he identified that as the advice he had given to many of his clients.

'And act as if you've absolutely nothing to worry about.'

He was again surprised to discover how sharp and cool she was, qualities with which, before the accident, he would never have credited her. In the face of such determination, he forced himself to subdue and overcome his fears . . . They could ask all the questions they liked, but he'd taken steps to make certain that no one could ever prove the truth . . .

Both men came to their feet as he entered the sitting-room. MacMahon was dressed in an old, badly cut, heavily creased suit; he had a round face, pleasantly featured, which looked drawn, as if from long-term fatigue. A typically hardworking, but not over-intelligent middle-aged detective-inspector. The detective-sergeant was much younger and clearly far less tolerant and far more self-opinionated. Elham spoke carefully, not hurrying his words; he was satisfied that he sounded confident. 'I understand from my wife that you'd like a word with me? Do sit down. And may we offer you something to drink? Or, if it's too early, some coffee?'

'That's very kind of you,' replied MacMahon, as he sat, 'but we had a cup before we left.'

Elham walked over to the fireplace, turned to face the room, and joined his hands together behind his back. By taking that pose, he was reminding them that he was the master of the house, successful, and wealthy. 'I'm a busy man, so perhaps you'd tell me quickly how I can help?'

'That's easily answered, Mr Elham. We're looking for someone who can tell us something about that hit-and-run on Wednesday night . . . I don't know whether you've heard, but the victim has unfortunately died.'

'Has he?' He was very conscious of the fact that his tone had changed.

'So we are dealing with a very serious case. Is there any way you can help us in identifying the driver of the car concerned?'

Penelope was looking at him with an expression he had no difficulty in reading. The death of the man altered nothing; keep calm. 'No, I'm afraid I can't. If I had been able to, I'd have been in touch with you before now.'

'Yes, of course.' MacMahon spoke so easily as to sound almost deferential. 'And you haven't heard any rumours?'

'I do not listen to rumours.'

'You don't? I suppose that's fair enough. Although just once in a while we find that a rumour does have some truth in it.'

'Really?'

MacMahon smiled. 'You remain unconvinced.'

'I do. And I am quite unable to suggest who might have been driving the Ferrari.'

'Ferrari?'

'That is the make of car the paper mentioned.'

'Oh, that! A typical load of cod's. Right now, we've no idea what make it was, except that it was a sporty model.'

'What does that mean?'

'Some kind of sports saloon; or maybe even an exotic.'

'Then it might have been a Ferrari?'

'Indeed. But, as I said, we've nothing as yet to suggest a make . . . That seems to be that, then.'

Ridley, sounding annoyed, said: 'What about—'

MacMahon interrupted. 'But I suppose we'd better just ask you the same question we're asking everyone else. Where were you on Wednesday night?'

'Has that any relevancy?'

'Only to this extent, that if you were out and returned here roughly about the time of the accident, you might have seen something that could help us. Were you out that night?'

'Yes.'

'Do you mind saying where?'

'We dined with my sister-in-law and her husband.'

'Where do they live?'

'Yew Cross.'

'So they're almost in the next village . . . It's like my brother-in-law. And, frankly, I never know whether that's a good thing or a bad one.' He smiled briefly. 'Have you any idea what the time was when you got back here?'

'No, not really.'

'We left there just after ten-thirty,' said Penelope firmly.

'Which road would you have returned on?'

'The usual one.'

'I'm sorry, Mrs Elham, but I'm afraid I don't know which is your usual road,' MacMahon said good-humouredly.

'Three Oaks crossroads and then direct to here.'

'Would that take you past the cricket field?'

'Yes.'

'About what time d'you think you'd have passed there?'

She shrugged her shoulders. 'Sometime between twenty and a quarter to.'

'In other words, a little before the accident. Did you by any chance see anyone walking along the road near the cricket ground?'

Elham answered. 'There were no pedestrians.'

'Did you observe any car which, in the broadest sense, could be termed sporty?'

'We met only one car that I can remember, at the cross-roads, it was an ordinary saloon.'

'Then now that finally is everything and we don't have to bother you any longer.' MacMahon stood. 'Thanks very much for your help.'

'I've hardly been able to help,' said Elham, a shade more forcefully than he'd intended.

'Maybe not directly, but indirectly, yes. We now know for certain that just before a quarter to eleven there was no sign of the victim walking along the road, or of a sporty car . . . Which does jog my memory. Just for the records, what kind of car do you run?'

'A Jaguar and my wife has a Volvo.'

MacMahon came forward and held out his hand. 'Good-bye.'

Elham led the way out of the sitting-room and across the

hall to the front door, which he opened. MacMahon smiled as he stepped past, Ridley merely nodded, his expression surly.

Elham closed the door and turned, to see Penelope standing in the doorway of the sitting-room. He went to speak, but checked the words because he couldn't be certain where Juana was. He hurried towards his wife. He needed to know whether he'd sounded convincing.

As he drew out on to the road, MacMahon turned right instead of left, which he would have done to return to Reckton. 'Well?'

Ridley did not try to hide his resentment. 'You went soft on him.'

'Did I?'

'You didn't follow up the fact that he was on the road just before the accident, you didn't ask him about the dinner-party and how much he'd drunk, you didn't—'

'Steve, are you too young to have heard the expression, "Softlee, softlee, catchee monkee"?'

'I've heard it, yes, but what's that to do with some poor sod getting knocked down by a car that didn't stop?'

'He's our man, isn't he?'

'That stuck out a bloody mile. Which is why I can't understand why you didn't squeeze him.'

'And immediately cause him to shut up tight, since with his experience in court he knows that the police's best friend is the accused's tongue. As of now, we've nothing that can be called proof—you know that as well as I do—so we need to keep him talking. And by letting him think he was clever and we were dumb and awed, we had him talking without ever realizing he was. How many cars were there in the garage?'

'Two.'

'A Volvo and a Metro, which probably belongs to staff.

Since both he and his wife are at home, where's the Jaguar? At a garage, being repaired?'

'We've asked to be notified about any repairs consistent with the accident and no reports have come through.'

'Quite. But take this scenario. He turns up at his usual garage and spins them a yarn of how his car got crunched. They know him as a pillar of the establishment. They'll believe him and it won't cross their minds that it could be his car we're interested in.'

'All that because he's Mister Bloody Elham?'

'Because it's an automatic reaction with ninety-nine people out of a hundred to believe that those who've really made it in life are like Cæsar's wife.'

'Who was probably a right old bag.'

Ridley, MacMahon thought, had this fatal blind spot which was fuelled by jealousy. Sooner or later, it could get him into trouble; probably, it would deny him the promotion that he deserved. 'When we get back, check the local garages for his Jag. In the meantime, we'll pay a call on the brother-in-law. I'm banking on the fact that Elham was too satisfied he pulled the wool right over our eyes to think of warning him to keep a tight mouth.'

Yew Cross consisted of several old cottages, three modern bungalows, and a pub; they were grouped around cross-roads. MacMahon braked to a halt in front of the entrance to the saloon bar of the Black Swan. 'Nip in and find out the brother-in-law's name and where he lives.'

Ridley's sense of humour took its first airing of the day. 'That requires a pint of best bitter.'

'Half a pint and you're paying.'

Ridley went inside, returned in just under five minutes. He settled in the front passenger seat. 'The woman behind the bar's not a bad bit of crackling; not bad at all. Wearing one of those dresses that make you want to drop a quid on the floor and watch her pick it up.'

'In between assessing her cleavage, did you find time to ask questions?'

'His name's Rickmore, he lives in the first house on the right down that lane, there, and he's an author.'

'We shouldn't treat him as untrustworthy just because of that.'

CHAPTER 9

Rickmore stared through one of the hall windows and convinced himself that the garden was far too sodden for him to be able to dig it, despite the fact that the day was dry. He heard a car door slam, thought it was Anne returning from the shopping, then heard a second door slam and knew it almost certainly wasn't her. He went through to the porch and after a moment two men, neither of whom he'd seen before, came round the corner of the house.

He opened the porch door as they came to a stop. 'Mr Rickmore? My name's Detective-Inspector MacMahon and this is Detective-Sergeant Ridley. Could we have a word with you?'

'Of course. Come on in.'

They entered and he pulled open the panelled door into the sitting-room, but MacMahon did not immediately move forward. 'A lovely old house, Mr Rickmore.' He stared up at the sloping ceiling which made the hall triangular in shape.

'I like it, when I can remember the ceilings are so low . . . And talking about that, keep your heads down as you go through and do mind the central beam; that's the most deadly of all.'

They settled in the sitting-room.

'I don't know whether you've yet heard,' said MacMahon

in his slow, friendly voice, 'but the man who was injured in the hit-and-run at Ailsham on Wednesday evening has died?'

'No, I hadn't. The poor devil.'

'His death obviously makes the case even more serious than it was. In fact, to put it bluntly, we'd really like to get our hands on the driver who just cleared off.'

'Yes, of course.' Rickmore's voice made it clear that he hoped they succeeded.

'So now we're trying to draw up a list of those who were on the road just before and just after the accident; that way, we may find someone who saw a car which could be the one we're looking for, while equally we'll be able to eliminate others. We've just had a word with Mr Elham and he told us he was here on Wednesday night.'

'That's right; he and his wife.'

'And he was in his Jaguar, which is . . . What model did he say it was, Steve?' MacMahon turned to Ridley, who looked uncertain.

'An XJ-S,' said Rickmore.

'Of course! A beautiful job. One needs to be a first-class driver to get the best out of that sort of machinery. Presumably, your brother-in-law's a very good driver?'

'He'll certainly agree with the assessment.'

'But you'd rather not add yours. What do they say? You can question my daughter's parentage, but not my driving skill . . . And Mr Elham also told us that when they left here, he was driving?'

'Yes, he was.'

'Neither Mr Elham nor his wife could be quite certain what the time was when they left. We need as accurate a time as possible when it comes to plotting out the cars we've had reported, so is there any chance that you can give us a sharper time than they could?'

'I don't think I can . . . Although, hang on, I've just

remembered. I went out and saw them off, then returned into the house and my wife remarked that it was just after eleven.'

'How long d'you reckon the drive back would take?'

'Quarter of an hour, give or take.'

'So he'd have arrived at his place at a quarter past eleven?'

'That's about it . . . You're trying to identify all the cars that were on the road near the time of the accident?

'That's right.'

'Then you need to include mine. I drove over to Popham House.'

'Do you mean, after Mr and Mrs Elham had left here?'

'We found he'd left his glasses behind. We knew he'd need them the next day so tried to ring to tell him, but there wasn't any answer so I drove over.'

'What sort of time are we talking about now?'

'It must have been well after half eleven when I left here.'

'What was happening at the scene of the accident?'

'The ambulance was just pulling away.'

'That'll enable us to fix the time exactly . . . Presumably, you found Mr Elham when you reached Popham House?'

'Yes. They were outside the garage.'

'Having just arrived back?'

'I don't really know.'

'Was the Jaguar inside the garage?'

'No, it was still outside.'

'Then you can confirm that as far as you could see, it was quite undamaged?'

Rickmore hesitated. 'No, I can't.'

'Why not?'

'They'd recently bumped into something.'

'You mean, the car was damaged?'

'Slightly, yes. There was a bit of a dent in the offside wing and the light was smashed.'

'I imagine you asked what had happened?'

'I reckoned that that wouldn't have been at all popular. I don't want to make too much of this, but Terence is always very proud of his possessions and if anything of his gets damaged or refuses to work, he feels as if . . . Well, this probably sounds ridiculous, but I'm sure he feels as if he's being deliberately mocked. Can you understand what I'm trying to get at?'

'Indeed. Lots of people are like that. Steve, here, positively believes a car hates him when it won't start!'

Ridley's expression was sour.

MacMahon stood. 'Many thanks, Mr Rickmore. 'You've been a great help.'

Rickmore saw them out of the house, then shut the outside porch door and returned inside. He thought about what had been said and the impression grew that right at the end, when he'd been expressing his thanks, MacMahon had been trying to hide some emotion; a sense of triumph? But why, when he'd learned nothing pertinent to his investigations? Unless, that was . . .

'Softlee, softlee, caughtee monkee,' said MacMahon with satisfaction, as he drove on to the road and turned left.

'What a slice of luck!' said Ridley.

'Luck?'

'Sorry, masterly interrogation . . . With Elham's brother-in-law testifying against him, even the stupidest jury will have to convict.'

MacMahon changed into top. 'He obviously couldn't see the significance of the questions . . . Like I said earlier, with people in Elham's position there's an automatic and instinctive assumption which it takes a hell of a lot to destroy. But if Rickmore's as intelligent as I judge him to be, by now he'll have had to realize where our questions were leading. So will he stick with what he's told us, or will he change his tune because Elham's his brother-in-law? The answer to that will, to a large extent, depend on how they get on with each other. After meeting the two of 'em, I'd say they've very little in common.'

'They can't be too different or they wouldn't have been having dinner together.'

'Doesn't follow. Like as not, it'll have been the sisters who arranged things. The brothers-in-law just did as they were told.'

'You're being pretty cynical. For once,' Ridley added.

'My wife has a sister. Doesn't yours?'

'She's an only.'

'That you should be so lucky!'

They reached the T-junction, turned right, and came to the crossroads, where they stopped. There was no traffic coming in the opposite direction and MacMahon drove on. He enjoyed a certain sense of complacent satisfaction. Thanks to an anonymous telephone call and then to a brother-in-law too innocent and too conditioned to realize what was really happening until it was too late, Elham was now fingered for the hit-and-run. Provided nothing blew up in their faces, they ought not to have much trouble in finding the evidence to prove his guilt.

Anne, a shopping basket in her right hand, entered the house. Rickmore took the basket from her. 'Thanks, that's heavy,' she said. 'Tinned peaches were on offer and I bought three because you like them so. Incidentally, I met old Mrs Peacock in Sainsbury's and she asked how your writing was going. She seems to think you're a cross between Dickens and Zola.'

'Then obviously she hasn't read my book.'

'You'll be buried in Poets' Corner yet.'

'A consolation too delayed to be enjoyed.'

'You sound as if the world's all grey.' She walked into the kitchen. 'Have a drink and cheer up. You and Terence didn't drink us dry, did you?'

'Not quite.'

'Love, is something wrong? When I left, you were all chirpy, now you're acting like a man who's just discovered a large bill.'

He put the shopping basket down on the nearest working surface. 'While you've been out, a couple of detectives called. They're questioning people in order to try to draw up a list of who was on the road on Wednesday night at around the time of that fatal accident so that they can eliminate cars which couldn't have had anything to do with it. At least, that's what they claimed.'

'Why d'you say that?'

'I'm certain now that the real reason was solely to question me about Terence.'

'If so, why get uptight about it? He must have gone past the accident spot not long before it happened. You'll have been able to corroborate his times.'

'It was more than that.'

'More?'

'They wanted to know if I'd say anything to confirm their suspicions.'

'Suspicions about what?'

'That it was Terence who was involved.'

'My God! That's a horrible thing to say. All right, you don't like him, but really . . .'

'Whether I like or dislike him has nothing to do with it,' he said harshly.

'Yes, it has. If you didn't dislike him, you couldn't begin to think so nastily.'

'He'd had too much to drink . . .'

'And so had you, but you drove there and back and didn't knock anyone down. Thousands of men are so bloody stupid that they drink too much and then drive, but they don't knock people down.'

He said quietly: 'Do you remember what I told you when I got back? That Terence must have hit something because one wing was dented and the light was bust?'

'Well?'

'I went outside with them when they left here; the car was undamaged.'

'Oh my God! But . . . but if he'd run into someone, he'd have stopped and called for help.'

'Realizing that if he did so he'd inevitably be breathalyzed. That he'd be found to be over the limit and so he'd be accused of drunken driving, or worse; worse, as it's turned out.'

'You've got to be wrong.'

'I hope so,' he answered, without conviction.

'What do we do?'

'First tell Terence what's happened. I'll phone him now.' He left the kitchen, stood by the corner cupboard, lifted the receiver, dialled the number. There was no answer. 'They're out.'

'It's Saturday, isn't it? I've just remembered, Penny told me they were going to friends for lunch. At least, I think she did.' She was speaking disjointedly, her mind not on what she was saying.

'Then I'll try again later on.'

'Dennis, it's impossible. Terence and Penny couldn't just drive on after something like that, knowing what that could mean to the injured man . . . Oh, God, I really need that drink,' she said, in little more than a whisper.

CHAPTER 10

Titchbourne's Garage lay on the boundary of the smaller of Reckton's railway station's car parks. Originally a small, family-run business, it had been taken over twelve years previously and a four-storey administration and spares building had been erected to the right of the repair sheds. The garage held Rover, Jaguar, and Vauxhall agencies. In the forecourt, to the right of the pumps, were a number of secondhand cars for sale and amongst these there was sometimes a replica D-Type Jaguar, built by a small local specialist.

Ridley, glad to get out of the wind which had started blowing a couple of hours before and which felt as if it was coming straight in from the Arctic, went into the main shed and asked for the foreman. He was directed over to a Rover Vitesse whose bonnet was raised and into whose engine compartment two men in overalls were peering. 'If you can't get it to work, send it over to Stradley's,' he said, naming one of the three rival garages in town.

The foreman straightened up. 'What's it this time? On the bum for a rotor arm for that wreck of yours?'

'Are you offering me one?'

'Do I look that stupid?'

'No comment. How about having a chat in your office?'

'Come on, then. And maybe we can find a cup of coffee.'

They threaded their way past numerous cars being serviced and repaired, and reached a small office, built out from the wall of the shed. An electric fire was on and the interior was warm and muggy. The foreman went over to the desk and searched through a number of forms, found the one he wanted and put it by the telephone. 'I've got to ring up the owner of that Vitesse to say she can't have it back today. She'll scream. Bloody old bitch.' Two steps took him across from the desk to a small gas-ring set up on bricks, on which stood a kettle. He checked there was enough water in the kettle, lit the gas. 'So what brings you snooping about the place?' He went round the desk and gratefully slumped down on the chair behind it.

Ridley picked up a couple of loose-leaf service manuals from a second chair, put these on the floor and sat. 'Is Terence Elham one of your customers?'

'Yeah.'

'Have you got his car in for repair now?'

'Can't say off-hand.'

'Will you check?'

'When the coffee's inside me.'

The kettle boiled. The foreman reluctantly stood, went over and made two mugs of instant coffee; from the bottom drawer of the desk he brought out a half-pint bottle of milk, a jar of sugar, and a teaspoon which looked as if from time to time it was used to repair cars. 'Help yourself to what you want.'

Five minutes later he wiped his mouth with the back of his hand, belched, returned the milk and sugar to the bottom drawer, wiped the spoon on the leg of his overalls and dropped it in the drawer which he pushed shut with his foot. He reached across his desk for a thick loose-leaf file. After checking through several pages, he said: 'Elham's Jag is in for repairs.'

'What's the trouble?'

'A smashed-up offside front; wing, bonnet, wheel, radiator, suspension . . .'

'Any idea how it happened?'

'According to his wife, when they got back at night and he was driving into the garage, they ran onto some black ice. Went straight into the wall.'

'Did you collect the car?'

'With that sort of damage, d'you think it drove itself in?'

'So was it still where it had crashed when it was collected?'

'That's right; hard up against the garage wall.'

'Shit!'

'Watch the language. I've got cultured ears.'

'Have you done the repairs?'

'Can't say off-hand, but I doubt they'll have got much further than stripping down. There's a lot of work there.'

'What will have happened to the damaged bits?'

'They'll have been thrown out at the back, ready for the scrap merchant; he's maybe already collected 'em.'

'Can we find out if he has?'

The foreman closed the file with a snap. 'So what's all this in aid of?'

'Routine inquiries.'

'And my second name's Getty . . . There was a nasty hit-and-run at Ailsham recently, wasn't there?'

'It's dangerous to draw conclusions.'

'So it could have been him!' He whistled. 'A bloke in his position, eh?' He stood. 'Isn't he something to do with the law?'

'A barrister.'

'Doesn't say much for being a barrister.'

'From where I stand, there never has been.'

They left the office and went through the first shed to a yard which was littered with empty oil drums, cardboard cartons, parts of cars, and a wreck which looked as if the light van had fallen over a hundred-foot cliff. The foreman checked briefly, then said, as he kicked a badly crumpled green panel: 'All the bits and pieces are still here. You were born lucky.'

'And handsome to boot. Put 'em on one side, will you? I'll see they're collected p.d.q. . . . Can we go and have a look at the car?'

The front end of the Jaguar was on stands and two mechanics were fitting a new shock absorber. Ridley walked round to look at the nearside light pod. 'Yellow bulbs!'

'He swears blind they give a much better light. I told him they didn't and it was just a gimmick of the Frogs, but he wouldn't listen. Knows it all, that one does.'

'He doesn't know the half of it yet.'

Back at divisional HQ, MacMahon, grey-faced, obviously tired, was in his office. Ridley told him what he'd discovered.

'So he was smart enough to realize that the only way of concealing the first and incriminating damage was to overlay it with further and far more extensive damage.' MacMahon plucked at a couple of hairs on the side of his chin which his electric razor constantly missed. 'What's happening about the damaged bits?'

'I've already sent a couple of lads along to pick 'em up. I've alerted the lab and they've promised to take their fingers out. If there are any incriminating traces, they'll find 'em.'

'It'll all depend on how good a job he made of the second crash . . . Let's be pessimistic. The lab boys can't come up with anything definite enough for the court. Then Rickmore's evidence is going to be crucial.' He let go of his hairs. 'What's he going to do now he knows it's his brother-in-law's skin at risk?'

Rickmore braked to a halt in front of the garage at Popham House and the headlights of the Escort picked out the damaged brickwork. 'I wonder when that happened?' Anne said.

He ignored the question. 'D'you think we're doing the right thing, coming here now?'

'Yes, I do.'

He sighed. 'I hope you're right . . . I'm not looking forward to it.'

'You don't imagine I'm jumping with joy, do you.'

He switched off the lights and then the engine. They left the car and walked across, past the small greenhouse, to the back door. She rang the bell three times, opened the door; Elham disliked their entering by the back, but she refused to go all the way round to the front just to satisfy his social pretensions.

They passed through the deep-freeze and laundry room and entered the kitchen, which was empty but in which all the lights were on. 'Is anyone at home?' she called out. The door from the kitchen into the hall was open and they could just hear the louder notes of a Duke Ellington record. She called again and this time was answered.

They went into the blue room. The smaller of the two sitting-rooms, it possessed charm—which the larger one did not—despite the over-use of the colour which was Penelope's favourite.

Penelope was welcoming. 'What fun having you both drop in like this! I was getting so bored with my own company. Dennis, turn the record down, will you, and then you must pour us some drinks.'

She'd managed to sound as if she really were glad to see them, he thought, as he went over to the stacked disc-player and slid the volume control to its minimum setting.

'There are all the usual drinks in the cupboard, or bubbly in the fridge. Let's have that?'

He said: 'Penny, we've come to have a word with Terence. I think we ought to do that before we drink.'

'But he's upstairs, working; he never does anything else these days . . . I tell you what. We'll open one bottle and finish that before you call him down. Then he'll have to open a second one.'

'It is very important.'

'Oh, very well. I'll go and tell him to come down and be sociable. I said only the other day that when he's a Silk, I'm not having him spend all his time at home working . . .

Oh!' She touched her cheek in a quick gesture of dismay. 'I wasn't supposed to breathe a word of that to anyone. For goodness sake, do remember to forget it . . . That's rather a mix-up, isn't it?'

'Yes,' he answered.

'Penny, for God's sake, get Terence,' said Anne.

She showed both astonishment and fear and they realized that she had been trying to delay what she knew, or guessed, was going to be a painful meeting. 'All right,' she said stiffly. She stood, left.

He looked round the room. It spoke of success. The French print curtains, the Shiraz and Daghestan carpets, the authenticated Raffaelli and Dawson, the unauthenticated Modigliani, the eighteenth-century display cabinet with its lovely collection of early Staffordshire pottery, the silver, some of which was reputed to have come from the Tsar's Winter Palace . . .

Elham, followed by Penelope, entered. He said, ''Evening,' then crossed to stand in front of the fire, in the pose which came so easily to him. 'Penelope seems to think there's some sort of trouble you want to talk about?' He spoke pugnaciously, as if ready to contradict everything that was said.

'I had a couple of detectives along this morning asking questions about Wednesday evening.' Rickmore could not have missed the effect his words had had. The last, slender hope that his suspicions might, after all, be wrong, was gone.

'What questions?'

'What the time was when you left us Wednesday evening?'

'What did you answer?'

'I said that it was around eleven.'

'That's ridiculous,' snapped Penelope. 'It was only just gone ten-thirty.'

He shook his head.

'I know it was ten-thirty.'

He looked at Elham and saw that Elham's pugnacity had been replaced by fear. 'They explained why they were interested—they were trying to identify all the cars on the road before and after the accident so that they could clear all those which definitely didn't have anything to do with it. To help them, I told them I'd driven over here later on.'

'What did they say to that?' asked Elham.

'They wanted me to confirm that your Jaguar was undamaged.'

'Which you did?'

'I could hardly do that, could I? The offside wing was dented and the light pod was smashed.'

'You told them that?'

'Yes.'

'How could you?' shouted Penelope.

Rickmore didn't answer.

'Did they ask you what you meant by "dented"?' asked Elham.

'No.'

'Then you didn't explain that the whole wing was wrecked and the wheel was buckled?'

Rickmore said tightly: 'The wing was only dented and the wheel was undamaged.'

'We'd skidded on black ice and went into the corner of the garage. Both the wing and the wheel were completely wrecked.'

'The corner of the garage was undamaged.'

'Go and look at it now and see for yourself.'

'I know that when I came here Wednesday night, the corner of the garage was untouched.'

'And I'm telling you, it wasn't.'

There was a silence, which became more painful for each of them the longer it lasted. Rickmore finally broke it. 'Terence, was it the Jaguar which hit that man?'

'No,' replied Elham violently.

'Then why does it matter quite so much to you exactly when the garage was damaged?'

'Because if the police believe you're telling the facts, they may start beginning to suspect me of having been the driver.'

'If you're innocent, you'll soon clear yourself.'

'For God's sake, how can you be so stupid? Don't you know that acquittal and innocence are two different things.'

'That's one hell of a thing for someone like you to say.'

'D'you think innocence has a shining ring of truth about it that can't be missed? D'you believe that old saw; Witnesses may lie, but circumstances cannot? Are you so naive that you accept that the police are more interested in a man's innocence than their own clear-up rate?'

'But you're saying . . .'

'I'm saying that if you persist in telling the police what you've just said here, they're going to suspect me; and once that happens, every piece of evidence that is turned up will be carefully angled towards confirming my guilt.'

'You do realize something, don't you? The man who was knocked down has died. Doesn't that mean something to you?'

'I had nothing to do with his death.'

'When you left our place, you weren't in a fit state to drive.'

'No? I'd had no more to drink than you, yet you drove over here. Were you in a fit state to drive?'

'I . . . If I'd knocked someone down, I'd have stopped to do what I could for the poor devil.'

'Are you so certain?'

'What d'you mean?'

'Would you be seized by quite so much righteousness if it weren't someone else who was involved, it was you?'

'The principle's the same.'

'Principles are never the same for oneself.'

'That's an extraordinary thing for you to say.'

'It's an extraordinary fact that you liberals can never . . .' He stopped. He ran the back of his hand across his forehead. 'This is quite ridiculous. We're arguing and becoming quite heated, yet there's nothing to argue about . . . I am not trying to say the police would ever deliberately set out to inculpate a man they know to be innocent. What I am pointing out is that they're human, grossly overworked, and unfortunately judged by results. So if the evidence in a case appears to point to one conclusion, they're sometimes over-ready to accept that conclusion and do not exert themselves to find out if it might, after all, be incorrect.

'You can see what that means here. They're searching for a car that was near the cricket ground at the relevant time and which bears signs of damage compatible with an impact with the victim. The moment they find such a car, they'll tend to concentrate on that one to the exclusion of all others . . . Because of what you've already told them, they're bound to think it could be my car they're looking for. So they'll have checked with all the garages and will have found that the Jaguar is being repaired in Titchbourne's. They'll have examined the damage and inevitably have come to the conclusion that it is far greater than would have been sustained in the accident. But because, by now, they'll have come to the conclusion it could have been my car, they're going to claim I deliberately crashed my car into the garage after the accident in order to hide the signs of damage resulting from it. So if you insist, wrongly, in maintaining that when you were here the Jaguar was only lightly damaged and the garage wall was untouched, their false accusations are going to appear to be corroborated.'

Rickmore said very slowly: 'The wing was only dented, the wheel was not buckled, the garage was untouched.'

'You filthy swine!' Penelope shouted.

'I . . . I have to tell the truth.'

'Hypocrite.'

He flushed. 'I do happen to believe that justice means justice for everyone . . .'

'Justice? You don't give a damn for justice.'

'Penny . . .' began Elham.

'If you won't tell him, I will.' She faced Rickmore, her expression ugly with hatred. 'All you're interested in is in getting your own back on Terence.'

'Doing what, for God's sake?'

'Getting your own back because he's a success and you're a failure. The police didn't come to you, you deliberately went to them and tried to implicate Terence with your filthy lies.'

Anne stood. 'I think we'd better leave.'

'Then go.'

Elham gestured with his hands, looked at Rickmore, then at his wife. He turned away, shoulders, slumped.

Anne and Rickmore left the sitting-room and went through the hall, the kitchen, and deep-freeze room to the yard. They climbed into the Escort and, for once, the engine started at the first turn of the key.

He drove slowly, his thoughts jumbled and painful. All his thinking life, he'd accepted that for a country to have freedom, it must have justice. Justice depended on just laws and people who observed their duty to obey them. Each time such a duty was dishonoured, justice suffered and therefore freedom was imperilled . . . But could Elham be right? Was there for every individual a line which drew the boundary between duty and self-preservation? Could he, hand on heart, honestly affirm that in Elham's position he would have done his duty at no matter what cost to himself?

Anne said: 'It was Terence who hit the man, wasn't it?'

'Yes.'

'Oh God!' She put her forearm on the back of his seat so

that she could touch his neck, needing the comfort of physical contact. 'What's going to happen?'

He shook his head. He knew only one thing. He would do his duty, which was to tell the truth, no matter what this cost in emotional terms.

CHAPTER 11

Monday was dry and fine, with only good weather clouds; but for the temperature, it might have been the beginning of spring.

Rickmore stared at the cuttings from the French agent which had arrived from Paris by the morning's post. Each cutting contained a reference to Teerson's Products and was presumed to have appeared in response to the newsletters which Rickmore sent out; as such, the cuttings were held to provide an indication of how effective his newsletters were and it was his job to translate the relevant passages into English so that they could be read by the directors. Had he, as he'd claimed when he'd applied for the position of PRO, been fluent in French it would not have been a difficult task; as it was, it was one that invariably taxed his ingenuity and patience. But he'd learned to work on the principle that if the references were never less than complimentary, no one would ever bother to check the translations.

The intercom buzzed and he pressed down the appropriate switch. 'Yes, Daphne?' He shared his secretary with Advertising. She was dumpy, yet dressed as if she had the figure of a model. Parkes had once asured him that she was a girl with potential. Since then, he'd always considered Parkes rather odd, even for someone in Advertising.

'There are two gentlemen who'd like to see you, Mr Rickmore. They're detectives.'

'OK, send them in.' That would start the rumour mills turning, he thought.

MacMahon and Ridley were shown into the room by Daphne, who was wearing a pleated skirt in a bright tartan which added inches to her already generous waist. She tried to stay to learn at least a little of what was going on, but he thanked her in a way that left her no option but to go.

MacMahon, he thought, wasn't looking fit, Ridley appeared aggressive. They shook hands with careful formality, then he set two chairs in front of the desk.

'I'm sorry to bother you during working hours,' said MacMahon.

'As far as I'm concerned, don't apologize.'

MacMahon smiled. 'Even so, we won't keep you for long . . . When we had a word with you before, you mentioned that on Wednesday night Mr Elham and his wife had dinner with you and that he left his spectacles at your place. You tried to ring him to say so, but couldn't get through, so you drove them over. Have I got that right?'

'Yes, you have.'

'Will you tell us again, as exactly as you can, what happened when you arrived?'

He described the events, his voice hard because there was no way now of avoiding the knowledge of what might be the consequences of his words.

'I'd like to get a mental picture of this dent in the wing. How deep would you say it was?'

'I don't think I can make a reliable estimate.'

'Why not?'

'One needs some sort of yardstick and I didn't have one.'

'Fair enough. Then how would you describe it in general terms?'

'Not very large and not very deep.'

'You place it on the turn of the wing, some way back from the lights. And the bonnet was untouched?'

'That's right.'

'This was night-time, but the outside lights of the garage were switched on. Do they give a reasonable light?'

'A good one.'

'Then if the wing had been buckled and torn, instead of being merely dented, and the bonnet had been crumpled, you'd have noticed the fact.'

'Yes.'

'Did you look at the offside wheel?'

'Not specifically, no.'

'You can't say if it was badly buckled?'

'Not directly. But if it had been, I'd have thought I'd have noticed it.'

'Was the corner of the garage in any way damaged?'

'No.'

'You are quite certain about that?'

'Positive.'

'Then that, I think, is all we need to know for the moment.' MacMahon stood. 'I'd like to thank you for being so frank. It can't have been very easy for you.'

'It hasn't been.'

'I hope it'll help if I tell you that you've done the right thing.'

After they'd left, Rickmore resumed his seat. MacMahon said he'd done the right thing. But had he? Could consequences be ignored? Yes, he decided; they could and must be when justice demanded that.

An hour and a half later, Ridley walked into MacMahon's office. 'You're looking rotten,' he said, as he came to a stop in front of the desk.

'Just tired.'

'Are you quite sure? Wouldn't it be an idea if . . .'

'I am quite sure.' MacMahon pulled himself upright.

'If you say so . . . I've had a bloke from the lab on the

phone. Damage to the various bits is consistent with running fairly hard into a brick wall. They've recovered traces of brick dust and want to know if we'd like 'em to run comparison tests with samples taken from the wall?'

'Not much point to that. It's Elham who claims to have rammed the wall.'

'That's what I reckoned . . . One interesting bit of news. At one point of the offside wing, the force of the impact split and folded the metal back on itself, forming a pocket that was never in direct contact with the wall. The lab's managed to raise an impression on the paintwork inside this and they say that in their opinion the impression was formed by an article of clothing of woollen texture.'

'The sweater the victim was wearing?' said MacMahon, his voice suddenly sharp.

'They're testing. But the chap I spoke to warned me that the impression was blurred and, because of the deformation of the metal, distorted. He said the odds were against their being able to make a unique comparison.'

MacMahon began to tap on the desk. 'Then at best it'll be no more than corroborative evidence and a good defence lawyer could probably turn it inside out.'

'If it's on its own, maybe. But if it's in there with other evidence, the jury will get the right idea.'

'Provided there's some central, unshakable fact on which to hang all this.'

'Rickmore's evidence, surely?'

MacMahon stopped tapping. 'What about the sliver of glass—did the lab mention that?'

'Similar to the control glass, but the crime sample was too small for any definite comparison.'

'I suppose if we'd given them half the headlamp glass, they'd have shouted for the other half before they'd commit themselves . . . Every time defence counsel makes an expert witness look like a wally, the lab boys expend a bit more energy on defending their backs and a bit less on doing their job . . . We've not yet checked out the dirt forced into the victim's clothes, have we?'

'There's not been time.'

'There never is. Find out if there've been any repairs carried out recently on the house or garage; if there have been, get samples of the brick and wood. And find out if the Elhams employ full-time staff. If they do . . .'

'They will. Too bloody lazy to do the work themselves.'

MacMahon leaned back in his chair. 'I've said it before and I'm about to say it again. If you go on carrying around that chip on your shoulder, sooner or later you'll end up in right royal trouble.'

'What chip?'

'Your resentment of anybody who has more than you.'

Ridley's expression became sullen.

'No one ever will invent a society where there aren't have-nots as well as haves.'

'So the haves aren't complaining.'

MacMahon sighed. Ridley would never understand. 'If any staff were around on Wednesday night, find out what they heard or saw. And try to discover if we're ever going to be told whether the dead man's dabs are on file. It's four days now since we requested a search.'

'I got on to 'em earlier and was given a lecture. The present computer is so slow that it can take up to ten days to go through its database of three hundred and fifty thousand prints. But some genius is working on a new computer that'll cut the time down to one day.'

'Always jam tomorrow,' said McMahon.

Juana opened the door and Ridley introduced himself. He then explained what he wanted, speaking very simply because he'd never overcome the teachings of his mother that all foreigners were stupid. Juana was worried, since neither the señor nor the señora was in the house to guide her as to what to do, but Ridley could be charming when bothered to take the trouble and soon she had forgotten her worries and she asked him into the kitchen for a cup of tea.

While he was eating a second wholemeal biscuit, a man came into the kitchen and was introduced by Juana as her husband, who worked in the garden. That, thought Ridley, was fairly obvious; Cavajals had brought part of it in with him.

'Have you had any repairs done recently?' he asked.

Cavajals looked at his wife, who spoke more English than he did. 'You wish to know the garage?' she asked.

He shook his head. 'No, not just for the moment. Have any repairs been done, to a window or a door maybe? Has anything been made or altered?'

'There is the . . .' She came to a stop.

'The what?'

'I do not know how is called.'

'Is it part of the house?'

She shook her head. 'It is . . .' She stopped again. Then she said, very impatient at being unable to express herself clearly: 'Please to come with me.'

He followed her out to the yard and the garden immediately beyond this and she showed him a cold-frame, newly put together by her husband—if he understood her correctly —from a kit supplied by a local firm. Her husband had had to alter one corner. Her husband was a very clever man with a hammer, saw, or screwdriver . . . Yes, he had had to do a bit of sawing. And because it had been cold and the Jaguar had been out, he had done it inside the garage . . .

The floor of the garage was concreted and in one place it had cracked; in this crack—which, she said, was about where her husband had worked—was a sprinkling of saw-dust. He used an old and battered tablespoon, found on a workbench, to lift out the sawdust and drop it into a plastic bag she brought him.

They returned to the kitchen. Cavajals had left and the coffee in their mugs was cold. Ridley said he didn't mind cold coffee, but she emptied both their mugs and switched on the electric kettle.

He asked her about Wednesday night once she'd made fresh coffee and was seated at the kitchen table. She explained that they'd been in their house which was beyond and behind the garage.

'What was the time when you went to bed?'

As usual, they'd gone to bed early. Because he didn't understand the television, her husband only watched sport and if she tried to watch anything else he became annoyed, so they seldom stayed up at night.

'Did you hear the Elhams return?'

'They come back, yes.'

'Have you any idea what that time was?'

She shrugged her shoulders.

'Was it soon after you'd gone to bed?'

'Not soon. Miguel is asleep. I could not be sleepy and I read.'

'Have a guess what the time was.'

She was silent for so long that he thought she wasn't going to answer, then she said: 'I think it was a good time after eleven.'

'Did another car arrive after them?'

'I stop the reading and turn the light off. Then it come.'

'Was it here for long?'

'Not long. And after it go, there is a crash. I think something bad is happened. But there is no more noise.'

'Can you describe what kind of a noise it was?'

'I think was the señor to hit the garage.'

'And this was definitely after the other car had left?'

'Please?'

He repeated the question and she confirmed that the crash had been after and not before.

They were, Ridley thought with deep satisfaction, gradually tightening the noose around Elham's cowardly neck; soon, they'd pull it tight.

CHAPTER 12

Rickmore left the garage and walked towards the garden gate. Even on a winter's day, Oak Tree Cottage was attractive. Not because the proportions were good—they weren't; the cottage was unreservedly boxy—but because three centuries had made it as much part of the countryside as the large and majestic oak whose upper branches could be seen to the right and beyond. He sometimes wondered who'd been the original occupants and what kind of a life they'd led. A thought which other authors had exploited . . .

As he opened the gate, he noted that one of the upright slats was still loose and needed nailing back; he assured himself that he'd do that at the first opportunity, knowing that he'd put it off for as long as he possibly could. For him, nails bent and hammers missed. Anne had described his carpentry as Mack Sennett comedy.

Anne entered the hall from the sitting-room and he kissed her.

'Well! It's some time now since you've been romantic on your return from work. Have you had a rise?' She studied his face and her tone changed. 'No, it's not like that at all, is it?'

He hung his lined mackintosh on one of the hooks on the wall to the right of the porch door. 'The two detectives called at the office. I confirmed all I'd told them before, so now I'm left wondering if I'm a rotten bastard.'

'Do you think you are?'

'More to the point, do you?'

Her gaze never left him, her high-boned face expressing conviction, but also sadness. 'Not if you truly believe you had to do what you've done.'

'He is your brother-in-law.'

'Does that alter the principle?'

'Of course not. But it must affect the light in which other people will see my actions.'

'You're worried by what people will think?'

'I don't give a damn about them if I know I've done the right thing.'

'Have you?'

He managed a wry smile. 'Hasn't that brought us round in a circle?'

'What is it, Dennis? D'you want me to agree that you had to do it?'

He was worried by her tone, but tried not to show that. 'I suppose I would like confirmation that my motives for telling the truth are as pure and high-minded as I've been assuring myself.'

'And not as mean and contemptible as Penny suggested?'

'Ouch!'

She stepped forward and kissed him again. 'Listen, my love. If the whole world said that your motives were utterly sordid and despicable, and you assured me they weren't, I'd know the whole world was wrong. You're an idealist and if that sometimes means you're difficult to live with, I don't care. I wouldn't change you for anyone.'

He hugged her. 'I'm a very lucky man.'

'Quite right.'

'No false modesty?'

'None whatsoever.' After a moment, she disengaged herself. 'I'll make some coffee.'

He followed her to the doorway of the kitchen, leaned

against the side. He watched her fill the coffee machine with water and not for the first time wondered how two sisters could be so different in character.

Ridley was late and he hurried up to his room, which was smaller than MacMahon's but which he did have to himself —something that rarely happened in the older stations. He checked the desk top, but there was no ironic message asking him if he'd be good enough to go to the DI's room if and when he had a moment to spare. So MacMahon wouldn't know he'd been late . . . The telephone rang and the caller was Mrs MacMahon. Her husband had been unwell during the night, the doctor had seen him and had called for an ambulance, and he was now in hospital; the hospital doctors seemed to think he might have suffered a slight heart attack. So he would not be in to work for a while. She didn't say so, but she was obviously worried sick that perhaps he never would be back.

Ridley used the internal telephone to tell the divisional superintendent that the DI was ill, then the outside one to give the same message to the detective chief superintendent at county HQ. He was informed that a relief DI would be sent down as soon as possible, but because the Force was so short staffed at the moment, this might take time; until then, he was acting DI.

He went through to the DI's room, ostensibly to find out if any of the morning's mail needed urgent attention, in reality to see how the room fitted him. It fitted him like a glove.

The laboratory assistant telephoned at four fifty-six on Wednesday. By then, Ridley, while no less confident of his own abilities, was prepared to admit that the job of detective-inspector was a more difficult one than he'd supposed. Especially when the detective-constables couldn't—or wouldn't—carry out their orders exactly as he wanted them carried out.

The assistant said: 'Both the control and crime samples of sawdust were softwood, treated against rotting with some fungicide. As you'll know with sawdust, there's seldom much hope of a positive identification and the best we can do here is to say that the samples are similar. There's no chance of specifically identifying the fungicide used.'

'Is that all?'

'What more do you want?'

He wanted a positive identification, but obviously was not going to get one. He thanked the woman and rang off. Every time, it was the same. The two samples were similar, but not uniquely so. They'd still not one single piece of unshakable evidence to complement Rickmore's testimony . . . That left only one way of going about things. Pressure Elham until he admitted his guilt. MacMahon had steadfastly denied that this was the way, but he'd joined the Force in the days when a policeman metaphorically doffed his helmet to the gentry. All that gibberish about softlee, softlee, catchee monkee. A smokescreen, to try to obscure the fact that he could not shake himself free of his instinctive deference . . .

Ridley looked at his wristwatch. When would the old bastard get back from London? Certainly by eight. So hit him then, at the end of his working day, when he'd be too tired to be fully alert mentally. Force him to admit that it had been his car which had slammed into the as-yet unidentified man . . .

Elham had hired a Granada, since the Jaguar would not be ready until the following day. He turned into his drive and saw, with sharp annoyance, that a dirt-stained car was blocking his way into the garage.

Penelope met him in the hall. 'The police are here,' she

said in a low voice. He experienced immediate tension and fear. 'Pull yourself together,' she said fiercely.

He briefly wondered how he could have been married to her for years, yet never have realized that when necessary she could be as hard as nails.

'If you don't tell them anything, they can't prove anything.'

Had she no idea how the police worked; how they uncovered one small piece of evidence here, one small piece there, then stitched them all together to prove the accused's guilt?

'They tried to question me. I told them their suspicions were disgusting and libellous.'

Slanderous, he automatically thought. Into his mind there came the image of the man suddenly appearing in the car's headlights . . . A few seconds only, but which now threatened the whole of his future life . . .

'Show some backbone.'

He'd said the same thing, more elegantly phrased, to men he'd defended and whose servile attitudes had virtually been admissions of guilt. He was learning it was not so easy when one was the accused . . .

She dug her fingers into his arm, so tightly that even through the thick, good quality cloth and the sleeve of his shirt, the grip was almost painful. 'Make them believe you.'

He went into the blue sitting-room. Ridley briefly introduced Detective-Constable Cricks. Elham wondered where MacMahon was and wished he'd come instead of Cricks; MacMahon had been pleasant and understanding.

'I want to go over a few points again,' said Ridley, his manner openly antagonistic. 'On Wednesday evening, you left your brother-in-law's house at around eleven o'clock . . .'

'At around ten-thirty,' he corrected.

'Mr Rickmore says that it quite definitely was eleven.'

'He is mistaken.'

'Your maid agrees that you returned some time after eleven.'

'Juana? I fear she's not a good time-keeper, as we soon discovered after she started working for us.' He was surprised how easily confident he managed to sound; just the right amount of casual indifference as to how his answers were received; a man of consequence, naturally willing to assist the police, but certainly not to be browbeaten . . .

Penelope confirmed what her husband had said, in a way that sharply exacerbated Ridley's resentment, since she sounded condescending. Because of this, he made the mistake of claiming too much. He said that the forensic laboratory had definitely concluded that the imprinted pattern on the damaged wing from the Jaguar had been made by the dead man's sweater . . .

Elham, knowing that the detective-sergeant could not be telling the truth—had he been, he'd have come to arrest, not question—understood that the other had thought to panic him into an admission. The knowledge gave him confidence. He asked what proof there was that the impression had not been implanted at some time after the car had been taken to the garage—could the police prove constant reference? What gave the so-called impression its unique quality . . .'

Angrily, Ridley introduced the sliver of glass. This had been identified as coming from the headlamp of the Jaguar. This time, Elham asked only one question. Was the laboratory prepared to say that it had come from the headlamp of the Jaguar and could not possibly have come from any other car? When Ridley did not answer, he ostentatiously shrugged his shoulders as he would have done if addressing a jury.

Ridley spoke with even greater antagonism. What about the sawdust found in the victim's clothing? Had it been proved beyond question, Elham asked quietly, that the sawdust was similar in every respect, uniquely similar in every respect, to the sawdust found in the garage? Ridley said that the car Daley had seen had had yellow lights. So, remarked Elham, did every French car on the roads. But perhaps there had been something about those yellow lights which positively identified them as British, not French?

When Ridley left, his expression was bitter.

As they heard the car leave, Penelope said: 'You were really marvellous!' Her surprise was less flattering than her words.

He went out to the drinks cupboard and poured himself a whisky and her a Campari. He noticed that his hands were shaking. He was like an actor who'd suffered stage fright right up to the moment of appearance, yet had acted superbly as the adrenalin flowed, then suffered badly from reaction the moment the curtain dropped.

He returned to the sitting-room and handed her a glass.

'You completely silenced the insolent man!'

As he stared at her, he noticed several small and wholly immaterial things, as often happened in a moment of mental stress. She was using a different shade of lipstick and was wearing the ear-rings he'd given her the previous Christmas; there were lines about her mouth that hadn't been there before; her dress was tight and her breasts were well outlined, breasts which should have summoned passion . . .

'Terence, have you been struck dumb?'

'No.'

'Then why don't you say something? Why are you still looking so miserable?'

'You obviously don't understand.'

'I understand you sent that man packing, with his tail between his legs.'

He sat down on the nearest chair, drank. 'I'm worried because they've found out so much.'

'They've discovered nothing of importance. Every time he tried to claim they had, you showed he was lying.'

'It's true I could knock each piece of evidence independently. But when they're all put together, they're good enough to strengthen the central evidence. And when that's strengthened, it in turn strengthens them.' He finished the whisky, stood, saw she had not yet touched her drink, left the room and refilled his glass. When he returned, he stood in front of the fire instead of sitting. 'Take the imprint they've found on the wing. Obviously, it's not good enough to prove that a specific sweater must have made it. But it fits in with the central evidence which says that it was my car which hit the man; one moves on from there to the fact that if it was my car, it's probably the dead man's sweater which made it. And if there's other evidence which fits in in the same way, then before long all these pieces of evidence cease to be separate but become part of the pattern. In other words, they corroborate the central evidence—Dennis's.'

'He can't do it to you,' she said fiercely.

'Perhaps, after what you said to him the other night, it's become more of a pleasure than a duty.'

'I was terribly upset.'

'But will he allow for that.'

'My God, he is my brother-in-law, isn't he?'

'And also a man of principles.'

'What's that to do with it? He can't do it to us. You've got to talk to him and make him understand.'

'Since when has any liberal ever understood the nature of the world he lives in?'

CHAPTER 13

Seated in his office, Rickmore knew a painful embarrassment. Elham seemed to have lost all sense of self-respect.

'Can't you realize what it would mean to Penelope and
me?'

'Yes, of course, but . . .'

'If you tell the court exactly the same as you've told the
police, I'm bound to be found guilty. At worst, I'll be jailed,
at best I'll receive a suspended sentence; either way, I'll be
disbarred.'

'We've been through all this before . . .'

'I'll be out of work and unqualified to do anything else.
For God's sake, think what it would mean to Penelope, even
if you've never bothered to consider what it would mean to
me.'

'Not considered it? I've not thought about much else . . .
All I'm doing is telling the truth.'

'And you think it's right to do that no matter what
happens to the family?'

'But the truth . . .'

'Do you hate me that much?'

'For God's sake, I don't hate you at all.'

Elham leaned forward until he was sitting on the edge of
the chair. 'Suppose I admitted it was the Jaguar, but I swore
by everything I hold sacred that I had absolutely no chance
of avoiding him; that even if I hadn't had a single drink all
night, it wouldn't have made the slightest difference? What
then?'

'How could that alter the need to tell the truth?'

'You'd still think it right to see me ruined over something
over which I'd no control?'

'You should have stopped the car after it happened.'

'There was an oncoming car and that reached the man within seconds.'

'You didn't know at the time whether seconds might have made the difference between life and death.'

Elham said, not realizing that he had virtually abandoned the fiction that his last few questions had been hypothetical: 'What gives you the right to set yourself up as the judge?'

'I'm not.'

'Do you imagine that there's another man in the whole country who'd betray his own family like this?'

Rickmore said desperately: 'I don't know; I just don't bloody know what any other man would do in this God-awful situation. I only know what I've got to do.'

'Got to?'

'Yes.'

Elham stood. He stared down at Rickmore, his expresion strained. 'If . . . if I offered you ten thousand pounds?'

Rickmore tried to keep his contemptuous anger under control. 'If the offer was made to get me to change my evidence, I'd tell you just what to do with it.'

Elham's shoulders slumped. He turned, went over to the door, then suddenly swung round. His voice was shrill. 'Every man has his price. I just wonder what yours is?'

Because of the time of day, the train arrived at Charing Cross and not Cannon Street. Elham left the first-class carriage and walked along the platform to the ticket barrier. He showed his season ticket and went through. He felt as if part of him was standing aside and observing, with clinical detachment, his ever-quickening advance towards disaster.

He looked up at the large overhead clock. Half past eleven. He should have been in court, but earlier he'd telephoned Arnold and told him to see if Trent could take the watching brief. He suddenly knew an overwhelming pity for himself. Why? Why had it happened to him?

Lucy, he suddenly thought. She couldn't offer him escape, but she could give him temporary forgetfulness. He turned and went through one of the exits to the pavement and the taxi-rank.

The taxi went through Admiralty Arch and down The Mall. His thoughts raced ahead. Because of all that had happened, it was days since he'd phoned her, let alone seen her. She must have become worried. So she'd be even more passionate than usual and in the white heat of that passion, he'd be able to forget . . . Defining what he'd forget made him remember it. He stared through the glass partition, silently urging the driver to greater speed.

The taxi arrived at Cuthbertson Road and drew up outside No. 22. He paid, crossed to the steps, climbed these, pressed the bell for the top flat. The speaker crackled into life and a man said: 'Who is it?'

Stupidly, he checked that he had pressed the button for the top floor.

'Who is it, then?'

He knew that she employed male models (better never to wonder, remembering those sculptures, what pose she required) and decided the speaker must be one. 'Is Lucy there?'

'Yeah. So now who are you?'

'Terence.'

As he waited, he wondered how old the model was.

'She says she's busy.'

'But I must see her.'

There was a long silence. He pressed the bell again. This time, Lucy answered him. 'Terry, go away. I can't see you.'

'I'm in trouble; terrible trouble. I need you desperately.'

The man spoke again. 'Look, Terry-boy, the lady doesn't want to know you any more. Got it?'

He stood there for over a minute, absurdly waiting for her to tell him that it had all been a silly mistake and to come straight up . . . Finally, he turned and went down the steps, feeling sick and old. It did not occur to him that it had been shame which had made her refuse to meet him.

Betty returned to the clerks' room and sat behind her desk, but did not immediately resume work on the Statement of Claim. 'It was Mr Elham who came in just now. He looks really terrible.'

Arnold stared at her over the tops of the half-moon glasses he wore when his eyes were tired. 'What exactly do you mean?'

'I think he must be ill. Either that or something terrible has happened.'

He wondered if she was being stupid.

'You know, if you come to think about it, he's not been his usual self for days.'

There was some truth in that.

'D'you think he's worried about taking Silk?'

'Of course not,' he replied sharply.

'Then maybe it's something which has happened at home. I mean, with a wife like his, anything . . .'

'Shall we leave his private life private? Suppose you get on with the work.'

'All right, all right.' She liked him, but that didn't stop her finding him, at times, a pompous old fool. She wound a sheet of paper into the typewriter and typed in the name of counsel, the case, and the name of instructing solicitors. She looked across at Arnold and saw that his high, greasy forehead was creased, as it always was when he was worried. He could huff and puff as much as he liked, but Mr Elham's wife was a bitch . . .

Arnold tried to concentrate on the fees' book he was bringing up to date, but his mind kept returning to what she'd just said. Was Mr Elham either ill or desperately worried over something?

After a while, he left and went along to Elham's room and with even greater disquiet saw that Elham was not working but was slumped back in his chair, staring into space, his expression that of a man under intolerable pressure. 'Mr Trent appeared for your clients; everything went smoothly.' Elham turned and looked directly at him and he was shocked by the expression now in the other's eyes. He blurted out: 'Is something wrong?' Then he added: 'Is there anything I can do?'

Arnold, at the age of four days, was named Thomas Arnold as he had been found on St Thomas's day in Arnold Street. Since the small wooden box had been left at one of the rear entrances of the Clarence Hertchwitz Memorial Hospital, he should, perhaps, have considered himself lucky.

The orphanage in which he'd spent his early life had been well run, but his years there had been filled with dull despair. His nature was of the kind that needed a deep, lasting, and particular relationship if it were to be fulfilled and this he failed to find; the staff were too busy, and trained to be too egalitarian, to give more to him than to the others in their care, and because he was shy and solitary he failed to strike up any deep friendships with his peers.

He'd almost married when he was twenty-two. But a fortnight before the wedding, the woman, seven years older in time, seventy years older in experience, had met a merchant seaman from Glasgow who'd offered her Nirvana and, despite all her experience, she'd gone off with him. The humiliation of this had hurt deeply, although he eventually realized that in fact she would have made him very unhappy. He never contemplated marriage again and very seldom went out with women, even though he was not a homosexual; he usually felt uncomfortable in their presence.

His first job, gained through the influence of one of the governors of the orphanage, had been as an old-fashioned office boy in chambers which had been headed by a QC who'd been as successful as he was objectionable. The QC had died suddenly, the head clerk had retired, and he'd been promoted to assistant clerk. Several years later the building had been redeveloped and the chambers had split up; he'd found work in another set, almost at the same time as Elham joined them as a pupil.

As he was given more responsibility, so he discovered that not only did he enjoy the work, he was very good at it. Solicitors liked him, probably because he treated them with considerable respect and their egos were always finely tuned when dealing with the senior branch of the law; barristers liked him because they found they could trust his judgement; his judgement was good because he had a natural flair for bargaining which seldom let him down and he could tell how high he could demand a brief be marked before instructing solicitors rebelled. At the same time, he also developed an instinct which suggested how successful any barrister was likely to be.

He'd soon judged that the highest posts in the judiciary were not beyond Elham's reach. So he'd carefully hitched himself to Elham's star. And strangely, although this had been a material decision—as Elham's status grew, so would his—he'd found that relationship for which he'd been searching all his life. He didn't know what Elham felt about that, but he didn't care. It was sufficient for him that he could be a part of his life and climb the ladder in his shadow.

So he'd been shocked and frightened when Elham told him all that had happened; so shocked and frightened that for the rest of the day he'd been unable to do any work and Betty had fussed, believing him to be sickening for the 'flu.

He left chambers sharp on five—a unique event—and caught the tube to Clapham. A ten-minute walk brought him to the house in which he'd lodged for the past seven years. He let himself in, called a greeting to the landlady in the kitchen, and went up the stairs to his two rooms. He settled in the armchair in the sitting-room and stared at the blank screen of the large television set he'd bought himself the previous year . . . Desperately, he tried to think clearly. Because he was totally unconcerned with the morality of Elham's actions, the question was not whether he should try to help, but how. How, in God's name, to save Elham from being ruined by his brother-in-law? Because he'd never met Rickmore, he had to imagine him in a villainous guise in order to hate him the more. If only he could be knocked down and killed in another road accident before he gave his evidence in court! Would it be any good travelling down to Reckton and seeing Rickmore and pleading with him not to testify? But Elham had said that Rickmore was motivated by a sense of duty and therefore it was impossible to talk sense with him. Then how to silence the prosecution's main witness? Or reduce the value of his testimony to the point where it was no longer strong enough to support the circumstantial evidence . . .

Frustration squeezed his mind. He longed to sacrifice himself, yet could not discover how. He stood and crossed the room to the small cupboard beyond the television set and brought out a bottle of whisky and a glass. It was his invariable custom to have one whisky before his supper. Tonight, he had three. And because he was unaccustomed to so much alcohol, his mind began to wander, to twist and turn . . . And suddenly he realized that there was one way in which the value of Rickmore's evidence could be fatally weakened . . .

He paced the floor, the alcohol no longer confusing his thoughts but seemingly sharpening and polishing them. Two years back, a brief had come into chambers from solicitors working for a trust which helped people in need.

The scent of charity had kept the markings low and so the brief had gone to Vernay. The trial had not been a long one and Vernay had been extraordinarily lucky with one of the main prosecution witnesses, but the accused, Dean, had believed he owed his freedom to brilliance rather than luck (a common mistake with those who, to their complete astonishment, were acquitted). Dean had come up to them outside the courtroom (Elham had not been in court that day, so Arnold had been free to accompany Vernay to see how he was shaping) and had said: 'If ever I can do either of you gents a good turn, just ask. That's all, just ask and I'll come running.' Later, Vernay had said that they must remember the offer in case either of them wanted to go in for burglary. At the time, Arnold had disapproved of such levity. Now he remembered the words in a very different light . . .

CHAPTER 14

The phone rang and Ridley picked up the receiver. 'DI,' he said, no longer aware that he had promoted himself.

'It's Dabs here. We've an identification for you, reference seventeen six stroke nine.'

That was the hit-and-run victim. So MacMahon had been right when he'd surmised that the victim had been engaged in some criminal activity. Ridley picked up a ballpoint pen. 'Shoot.'

'Richard Tamworth. One conviction, for indecent assault.'

'A sex merchant!'

'His last known address is twenty-six, Updyke Road, Evenham. But that's pretty old, so it may not be worth much.'

'You'll send us a copy of his file?'

'Of course.'

'By the way, he's died.'

'Then I'll transfer him to the gone and unlamented section.'

After replacing the receiver, Ridley stared down at the sheet of paper on which he'd written the name and address. It was now possible to postulate two facts. That Tamworth's disappearance hadn't been reported because whoever knew he'd disappeared also knew the possible reason for his disappearance and was too ashamed, or scared, to draw attention to it. That the reason for his sudden and fatal appearance on a section of road where there were no homes nearby had been that he'd committed an offence of a sexual nature and had been fleeing pursuit... Yet against this last was the fact that there'd been no report of any such incident on the Wednesday night...

Behind the desk was a large-scale map of the county, with the divisional boundaries marked in red. He found Ailsham cricket ground and the double bend in the road just south of it. Where could Tamworth have come from? Somewhere where there were potential victims. The countryside was populated, but except in the villages the houses were fairly well apart. That could appeal to a sex criminal, since he was less likely to be disturbed and caught; on the other hand, it meant far fewer potential victims from which to choose and a much greater risk of being noted. Ridley visually examined the surrounding countryside, searching for somewhere that would have attracted a sex criminal... Hacksley House. Once a rich man's mansion, now a geriatric hospital. Nurses worked in hospitals and nurses' hostels were frequently targets. A long shot, but not impossibly so...

He drove the four miles to Hacksley House and parked against the raised flowerbed in the centre of the turning circle immediately in front of the portico. He climbed out of the car and looked up at the large Queen Anne mansion. Once, just one man had owned all that, together with the park which stretched right round it; dozens of servants had catered to his every whim. Ridley knew a brief satisfaction at the thought that the man and his descendants had been dispossessed.

The matron had an office on the ground floor, to the rear of the house. She was a tall, firmly proportioned woman, quiet in manner, with a face which expressed both strength and compassion. She showed no surprise when he explained what he was looking for and he was pretty certain that after a working lifetime in nursing there was little that could surprise her.

Her voice was well pitched and brisk. 'There were no official reports of any incident on that Wednesday night.'

'There weren't.' He was disappointed, but not surprised.

'However, there was something . . . At what time was the road accident?'

'Soon after eleven; say just short of a quarter past.'

'And how long would you imagine it would take a man to get from here to the point at which the accident took place?'

'In the dark . . . Having to find gates . . . Twenty minutes, or maybe a bit more. But that's pure guesswork.'

'If we accept that figure, we're back to roughly five to eleven. And if my memory's correct, that's about the time when Nurse Trott, who was off duty and in her bedroom, caused a commotion by screaming.'

'Because she'd been attacked? But you said there was no incident that night?'

'She screamed because she had a nightmare which frightened her very badly.'

'Then I'm sorry, but I just don't see the relevance of this.'

'Mr Ridley, that is the explanation which Nurse Trott

gave. It was not given directly to me, which from her point of view is perhaps as well. It is my experience that while young children may wake up screaming because of nightmares, adults do not.'

'Then you think . . . ?'

'The circumstances were such that I was not called upon to decide what really happened.' She saw that he was about to speak. 'Nor do I wish to give my opinion now. There are rules which govern not only the working lives of our nurses, but also their off-duty lives. While I demand adherence to the former, I am, I hope, sufficiently realistic to realize that the latter are mostly out-of-date.' She smiled briefly. 'The world is a very different place from when they were drawn up. Yet as matron, it is my duty to see that while they exist, any official breach of them is dealt with.'

'You're saying . . .' He stopped, uncertain how to put the question tactfully.

'I'm saying that a blind eye is an advantage to people other than admirals.'

'Then it would be best if I had a word with Nurse Trott on my own?'

'Probably essential.' Again that quick smile.

'Can you tell me what kind of a person she is?'

'Intelligent, quick-witted, attractive, and something of an iconoclast, which at her age is right and proper.'

'Would you also say she's . . . well, sexy?'

'I feel you are better qualified to answer that than I.' She reached across to the intercom, but did not immediately press down on the switch on which her forefinger rested. 'I think I'll ask her to see you in the almoner's waiting-room. That can fairly be called neutral territory.'

The waiting-room was a lot more cheerful than he had expected. The walls were painted in two shades of green, there were four comfortable chairs and a settee, on the low, glass-topped table were a number of up-to-date magazines of general interest, and the four framed prints on the walls were of attractive, colourful country scenes.

Nurse Trott was an extremely attractive blonde with an artless manner which at one and the same time made a man both protective and hopeful. She was also very wary. She expressed surprise and excitement at meeting a real detective and even more surprise when it turned out that the detective was interested in the night she had screamed. She began to explain just how frightening that nightmare had been . . .

'You're sure it wasn't something else which made you scream?'

'Of course not.' She was very wide-eyed.

'The matron was saying that young kids wake up screaming from nightmares, but she'd never known an adult to do so.'

'She said that?'

'Yes.'

'Oh! . . . Well, she's wrong. I did.'

'You remember I'm investigating the hit-and-run case and one of my jobs is to trace out what the dead man was doing before the accident?'

'Of course I remember you telling me that. Which is why I don't see how I can possibly help.'

'By telling me if you screamed because you were threatened or attacked by a man?'

'If anything like that had happened, I'd have reported it.'

'Unless the circumstances were such that you didn't dare report them.'

'I don't know what you mean.'

'Miss Trott, the matron is quite a woman.'

'She can be an old battle-axe.'

'She probably has to be, with you lot to keep an eye on.' She giggled.

'She's convinced you were breaking the rules that night.'

'Of course I wasn't.'

'But she hasn't been called upon officially to decide whether you were so she's prepared to play at being Nelson.'

'To play at what?'

'To put the telescope to the blind eye.'

She nibbled at her lower lip.

'I'll lay it straight down the line. All I'm interested in is what really happened; how it affects anyone here doesn't concern me. And matron's not asking me to pass on to her what you say to me. But if you don't tell me what I've got to know, I'll have to start asking around and then things can't remain all nice and private and pretty soon matron's going to have to take official note of what's going on. And that means, no more blind eye.'

She looked at him for a while, then made up her mind. She spoke with great earnestness, conveying the fact that she was sharing her deepest secrets with him because she recognized a soul-mate. Everyone was agreed that the rules governing the conduct of nurses who lived in were positively Victorian—just imagine, no visitors allowed except in public rooms and all visitors to be off the premises by seven at night. It positively cramped a girl's style. Especially if the boyfriend hadn't anywhere to take her when they wanted to be alone. So it was accepted practice to smuggle a friend into the nurses' wing; dinner was the best time for getting him in because authority was busy eating, between two and five in the morning the safest time for him to leave. It was, of course, almost impossible to keep a visit secret from one's friends and neighbours, but it was absolutely essential to keep it from the sister in charge of the nurses' wing and the cleaning women. A week ago on Wednesday, she'd smuggled Bill in. Bill was . . . someone special. And this was the last quarter of the twentieth century and only the dodos believed that there was still one law for the man and another for the

woman. And what harm did it do if it was a deep relationship, based on love . . .

'You were in bed together?'

She found that rather too direct and blushed.

The lucky bastard, he thought. 'So what happened to
make you scream?'

She became even more embarrassed, rather upsetting the
image of a daughter of liberation. It seemed that their love
had blossomed, almost to the point of fruition, when she'd
looked by chance at the window and had seen a truly horrific
face staring at her . . . She'd screamed from shock—and,
perhaps, also from a sense of outraged modesty. Whereupon,
she'd found herself faced with the necessity of explaining what had frightened her, without disclosing Bill's
presence . . .

'Where did he disappear to?' Ridley asked, more from
curiosity than because it was of any importance.

'The cupboard. It's rather small and he was terribly
uncomfortable.'

And, perhaps only temporarily, frustrated. 'You didn't
tell anyone you'd seen this face?'

'I couldn't, could I?'

He wondered if she'd ever stopped to realize what the
tragic consequences could have been of remaining silent.
'From what you've said, the curtains weren't drawn. Yet
you and Bill . . .' Tactfully, he did not finish.

'I don't like being closed in and my bedroom's on the first
floor so I never draw them. I didn't think anyone could ever
look in.'

Nobody had told her about ladders. 'How would you
describe this face?'

Her description was poor which, considering the circumstances, was not really to be wondered at, but it did convince
him that the man's face had been concealed by some kind
of a mask.

There was little more she could add and he thanked her for her help and promised her, on his honour as a gentleman, that he'd tell no one else at the hospital what she'd just told him.

He left the building and stood on the lawn outside the nurses' wing and worked out in which direction Ailsham cricket ground lay. Then he returned to the car, opened the boot, and changed into a pair of wellingtons. He walked across the park and went through a gateway, across a lane, and over a metal five-bar gate into a fifteen-acre field that was down to permanent pasture, but too sodden even to carry sheep. The man's route lay almost directly to the opposite corner. He searched the thorn hedge on either side for a distance of fifty feet, then crossed the field and searched there. There was a break in the hedge which had been stopped with a hurdle that now lay on its side. He went through, into another and larger field, down to winter wheat. He thought he could make out footprints which crossed the field. He went round the edge to a thin belt of trees beyond and near a clump of brambles he found a woollen ski mask. The pattern picked out eyes, nose, and mouth, in different colours from the background. He imagined what it must have been like to be making love and to look up suddenly to see that at the window and he wondered if the experience had left Nurse Trott with a neurosis.

On his return to the station, Ridley collected the OC file and carried this through to the DI's room. He read through the summary of cases from all over the country, stretching back over the past year, which had been reported and investigated without success, but not closed, for whatever reason. At the end of forty minutes, he had picked out three rapes, one attempted rape, and one sexual assault, each of which had been carried out by a man who had been described as having a face from a horror film.

CHAPTER 15

On Monday evening, a blustery, rain-threatening evening, Arnold was too preoccupied with his problems to realize what a strange figure he cut in the district. There was no mistaking his clerkiness, just as there was no mistaking the fact that in this part of Lewisham at times the writ of the law might not run very far. Several times in his walk from the bus stop he was eyed speculatively, but his very indifference to what lay about him provided a protection. He reached his destination and spoke to a slatternly woman who said that bloody Fred was down in the bloody pub where he was every bloody evening, spending the money she bloody needed.

The pub, on a corner site, was wedge-shaped. Dean was in the larger of the bars, drinking heavily. He was a small, foxy man who might have looked less untrustworthy if he had cut off his Zapata moustache. It really was astonishing that, two years before, the jury had found him not guilty.

'I can't say I do remember you,' said Dean uneasily.

'We met in court.'

'Never been in no court.'

'When Mr Vernay got you off that charge of housebreaking in Reading.'

'Yeah? . . . Well, maybe now I do remember a bit.'

'I'd like a little chat, if you've time?' He looked at the bar. 'What will you have?'

'If you're asking, it's a large brandy and ginger.'

Arnold bought the drinks and Dean suggested they went over to an empty table close to the outside door. They sat and Dean drank quickly, reckoning that if he had to cut and run for it, he might as well leave an empty glass behind.

'D'you remember what you said to Mr Vernay and me after the trial was over?'

'Can't say as I do.'

'That if ever you could do either of us a favour, we only needed to ask.'

'I said that?' Dean was astonished and disbelieving.

'I've come to ask you to do me a favour now.'

Dean's manner became very much more confident. 'There's favours and favours.' He fiddled with his glass to remind the other that it needed refilling.

Arnold, who hadn't yet touched his whisky, took the glass over to the bar. As the barmaid refilled it, he noticed how grubby her frock was. It completed the picture of slatternly failure and small-time villainy in which he found himself; he would have entered hell and supped with the Devil to help Elham.

He returned to the table. Dean drank, then said: 'So what's it all about?'

'I want you to do a job.'

'Jesus!' Dean was shocked by such stupidity. He looked round, but the table nearest to them was unoccupied and the couple at the one beyond were in a clinch and even the Last Trump might not have disturbed them. 'Are you round the twist, talking like that?' he demanded in a fierce whisper. 'And I don't have nothing to do with that sort of thing.' Then he realized that Arnold would have seen his list of previous convictions and he amended his denial. 'Leastwise, not since I got off when I hadn't done the job.'

'But you'd had plenty of experience before then?'

'That ain't nothing to do with you. I've done me bird. Look, mister, I'm finishing this drink and then I'm clearing off. And don't never come near me again.'

Arnold had not supposed that Dean would help him merely from a sense of gratitude. 'I'm willing to pay.'

'For what?'

'Carrying out a burglary.'

Dean was scared. Scared that this was all a trick, lining him up for the Norwich job which had gone badly wrong and left him only one small step ahead of the law. He hastily stood, picked up his glass and emptied it. 'You try and follow me and I'll do you rotten.' It was a ridiculous threat; he did not have the bearing of a man who would ever use physical violence.

Arnold produced an envelope. Certain it was hidden from everyone but Dean, he opened it and riffled through the corners of the twenty-pound notes. A man of simple tastes, he had for years saved a large proportion of his income and he had several thousand pounds in a building society account. He was prepared to spend everything.

Dean stared at the money and he started to think. The coppers wouldn't ever use someone in Arnold's position.. And Arnold was dead serious. Only a right fool turned his back on easy money . . .

The Jaguar turned into the drive of Oak Tree Cottage and came to a smooth halt. Elham climbed out, switched on the torch, and went round the bonnet to open the front passenger door, but Penelope had forestalled him and was already standing on the drive.

'Don't forget,' she said.

'I won't.'

'Don't let him be all nauseatingly hypocritical.'

He wondered whether she still underestimated the strength of Rickmore's convictions or whether her words were merely a sign of how desperately nervous she was.

They walked towards the gate into the garden, buffeted by the gusty wind. The beam of the torch picked out a puddle. 'Mind that, dear.'

'Why can't he get the drive properly surfaced. It's like a slum.'

Had she ever allowed herself to understand what a slum was really like? Almost certainly not. She lived in a world where money put an impenetrable barrier between herself and slums. But if they failed tonight, that barrier would come crashing down . . . How to find the words that would convince Rickmore . . .

He opened the gate and they passed through. She complained about the unevenness of the brick path and said that if she didn't break an ankle, she'd be lucky. He liked this path, which wasn't really uneven, because it was so in character with the house. He'd always gone along with her desire for the new and the smart, but he knew a respect for the past which she lacked.

When they reached the small porch, he shone the torch on the bellpush, pressed it. They could look through the nearest hall window and they saw Rickmore step out of the sitting-room. He was wearing a polo-neck sweater and a pair of creased grey flannels. Elham imagined his wife's thoughts. Dressed like a tramp, as usual. He wondered, surprising himself by doing so, whether she'd ever dressed for comfort rather than effect? But perhaps she couldn't face the world without protection.

The porch light was switched on. When he identified them, Rickmore could not conceal his astonishment. He greeted them and now amazement had been replaced by reserve. Guessing the object of the visit, thought Elham, but not the content. They went inside.

'We hadn't seen you for such ages,' said Penelope in her most social voice, 'so I said we simply must pop in and find out how you both were. Aren't you going to kiss me hullo?' The ugliness of their last meeting might never have been.

Rickmore kissed her on the right cheek.

'Both, continental style.'

He kissed her on the left cheek.

'How's the new book coming along?'

'I'm afraid I've been neglecting it recently.'

She failed, or appeared to fail, to see any connection between recent times and the hit-and-run case. 'We went to a cocktail party the other evening and when I mentioned to our host that you were my brother-in-law, he was very much more impressed than when I told him Terence was taking Silk. So you see, you're famous.'

'And so a fool?'

'What do you mean?'

'"As yet a child, nor yet a fool to fame . . ."'

She was confused, yet determined not to appear to be. 'Sometimes, Dennis, you really do say the most amusing things.'

Anne came out of the sitting-room. 'I thought I recognized the voices.'

'It's such ages since we last saw you both.' Penelope came forward and embraced her sister, careless that there was no response; some of the jewels on her fingers sparkled as she moved under the overhead light.

'Come on in here where it's a sight warmer than in the hall,' said Anne, as soon as she had disengaged herself.

In the sitting-room, Penelope, who frequently complained of feeling cold, sat in the armchair nearer the fire. Elham hesitated, then said: 'D'you mind if I stand for a bit? Been sitting all day.' He took up his accustomed position with his back to the fire.

'What will you drink?' Rickmore asked. 'There's sherry, red Vermouth, or Scotch.'

Penelope chose Vermouth, Elham Scotch.

Conversation, while Rickmore moved around with glasses, was brittle; they were four people who were trying to ignore what had been said the last time they met, because that was the civilized way to behave, yet were unable actually to forget.

Elham drank quickly, put his glass down on an occasional

table. He coughed. 'We've just learned something very important.' He paused, but when there was no comment, he added: 'The police have identified the dead man.'

'Who was he?' asked Rickmore.

'His name was Tamworth. He had one conviction for indecent assault. Beyond that, the police are satisfied that he has been responsible for three rapes, one attempted rape, and one sexual assault, although he was not charged with any of these because of lack of evidence.'

There was a silence, broken only by a hiss as part of a log suddenly began to flame.

Elham leaned forward with his shoulders slightly hunched, an attitude he often adopted in court. 'You do realize what that means, don't you?'

'I don't know, not yet. It takes a bit of thinking about.'

'It's obvious,' said Penelope.

'Is it?'

She ignored the worried look her husband gave her. 'He was a filthy pervert. God knows how many women he molested.'

'Almost certainly many more than reported having been raped or assaulted,' said Elham.

'He deserved to die,' said Penelope viciously.

Rickmore said slowly: 'Deserved?'

'That's right.'

'I can't accept that.'

'Why? Because you're a typical man? You think there's no such thing as rape, it's always initially encouraged by the woman who then panics and tries to stop? But it's often not like that and it wasn't this time.' She turned. 'Just tell him, Terence.'

'I know the details of two of the cases,' said Elham. 'In each, the woman was grabbed as she was walking along a street at night, threatened with a knife to her throat, made to walk to somewhere dark where she was forced to strip and then subjected to the most obscene assaults.'

'How ghastly,' murmured Anne.

There was another silence. Penelope broke it. 'He deserved to die,' she said, even more pugnaciously than before.

Rickmore said: 'He obviously was a vile menace. But when you say "deserved to die", where's your authority?' As always, when he became excited or earnest, his slight speech impediment became more noticeable.

Anne, worried by the impression her husband was now giving, said: 'Dennis, all Penny is saying is that that kind of a man is so great a menace that he's better dead than alive. Surely not even you can argue against that?'

'I can start by asking, better from whose point of view?'

'For goodness sake!' snapped Penelope. 'From the point of view of all the women he'd have raped if he'd gone on living. Or are you now so liberal that you think they don't matter at all?'

'It's not a case of being liberal, or anything like that, it's not setting myself up as God. I don't know what motivated him. Suppose he was subjected to overwhelming desires, so overwhelming that he was totally unable to resist them; that morality and self-will simply had no meaning for him?'

'You've not begun to understand. He's better dead because now he can't rape any more women.'

Rickmore spoke quietly to Elham. 'You did say he had one conviction, but in all the other cases there was not enough evidence to charge him?'

'That's right.'

'Then he may well have had nothing to do with them?'

'The police are satisfied he did.'

'Maybe. But thankfully we live in a country where police certainty isn't enough to convict. I repeat, he may not have comitted any of those other offences. In which case, all he'd ever been guilty of was one indecent assault. A man can commit one such act, be caught, and be so shocked by his conviction that he never does such a thing again. Then surely no one can say he deserves to die?'

'Dennis,' said Anne angrily, 'you're being very stupid.'

'Because I refuse to give way to emotion?'

'Because you're arguing just for the sake of arguing.'

'That's unfair and untrue.'

'Dennis,' said Elham, 'the police aren't as blindly biased as you obviously think. They've traced out Tamworth's movements on the night he died. He went to Hacksley House, the geriatric hospital, and used a ladder to get up to one of the nurses' rooms. She saw a hideous face at the window and screamed, which alarmed Tamworth, who fled. In a copse half way between the hospital and the cricket ground, they found a ski-mask, which the nurse identified as having been worn by the man at the window; it also fits the description given by two of the women previously assaulted. His build matches the description of one woman's assailant and she stated that the fingers of the man were noticeably short and stubby and the nails looked disgusting because they were constantly being bitten and so had re-treated part of the way down the fingers—Tamworth's fingers were very short and stubby and his nails had re-treated from constant biting . . . There can be no reasonable doubt that he was guilty of several sexual assaults.'

'Then I'll accept that he was.'

'You're satisfied?' demanded Penelope.

'Satisfied that he was probably a rapist, yes; I've just said so.'

'And if he hadn't died, he'd have continued to commit rape and sexual assaults?' asked Elham.

'I suppose that has to follow.'

'Then he was better off dead,' snapped Penelope.

Rickmore's expression hardened, but he said nothing.

Elham picked up his glass and drained it, replaced the

glass on the table. 'You'll have realized why I've told you this?'

'I imagine so.'

'Without renewing the argument about whether he deserved to die, it's clear that by his death an unknown number of women are saved the most revolting of experiences. Those women would certainly regard his death as an act of providence.'

'That's taking things too far . . .'

'It is not,' cut in Anne fiercely.

Rickmore looked at her. He had lost all her understanding and sympathy.

'I wasn't negligent in hitting him,' said Elham. 'He ran straight out into the path of the car because he was panicking, fearing pursuers were immediately behind him. I had absolutely no chance of avoiding him. It is true that I did not stop. If I had, I'd have been breathalysed and probably would have been found to be over the limit. In those circumstances, it's inevitable that it would have been held that the accident was to a large extent due to my intoxication and there would have been nothing I could have said that would have refuted that presumption. Yet it would have been totally wrong. I could not have missed hitting him if I had not had a drop of liquor for the previous week.

'You said I should have stopped; that it could have been a situation where his life depended on how soon aid could be summoned. But the alarm was given by the other driver very soon after I could have given it, so very little time was lost. In fact, time was not of the essence. Nothing would have changed for Tamworth if I had stopped.

'You have told the police certain facts which identify me as the driver. If you confirm that evidence, I'll be charged, probably with causing death by reckless driving, and will be found guilty. I will be imprisoned or given a suspended sentence. My career will be finished and my life ruined. Can you now, in the light of what I've told you, bear that responsibility?'

'You're claiming . . .'

'I am claiming nothing. I am asking you to understand that the law does not always serve justice; to recognize that in some cases the law can be as merciless as the criminal.'

'And you're also putting forward the proposition that a crime can be excused if the victim deserved to be the victim. That can't possibly be right. Crime is crime and the nature of the victim is irrelevant.'

'Are you still going to tell the police?' demanded Penelope shrilly.

'I . . . I don't know.'

'You swine!'

'Penny . . .' began Elham.

'Haven't you the courage to say it to his face? Well, I have. All he wants to do is to see you in prison and me reduced to rags. He's always been so jealous of us that he couldn't even be polite.'

'I am not, and never have been, jealous of either of you,' Rickmore said angrily. 'And if you won't believe me, ask Anne.'

Anne looked away, unable to confirm his words.

They were in their bedroom, but had not yet begun to undress. 'Why won't you understand?' demanded Rickmore.

'Because I can't begin to see how you can believe it's more important to honour the law than to help Penny and Terence.'

'You've got to forget what kind of a man Tamworth was.'

'Forget? How can I forget? For God's sake, climb down from that ivory perch. Penny was absolutely right. He deserved to die. And if I'd been driving, I'd feel I'd served justice, not betrayed it. And don't start talking about principles. Just tell me why it's so important to ruin your own relations.'

'You really do think it's jealousy?'

'I . . . I just don't know what to think. I can't understand how you can go on and on and on as you are.'

'Because the law is our only defence against anarchy and if we betray it . . .'

'For Christ's sake, stop pontificating; just think on this. If that man hadn't been killed, I could have been his next victim. So what would you have felt about your wonderful justice if you'd come home to find me raped?'

He knew what he would have felt.

CHAPTER 16

Because it was impossible to live for long at a high level of emotional conflict, it was implicitly agreed that the subject should be dropped until Rickmore wanted to return to it. And because he'd been forced to accept that there was no way of escaping both Scylla and Charybdis—he would either have to betray his principles or destroy Elham's happiness and career in circumstances which appeared to make a mockery of his principles—throughout Tuesday he was careful never to broach the subject, even obliquely. But from time to time he'd seen Anne look at him with quick puzzlement and he'd known that she was trying to understand how he could find the decision so difficult a one to make.

On Wednesday morning, he went downstairs to the kitchen where she was cooking breakfast and he made an attempt to break the feeling of restraint between them. 'Eggs and bacon? What about our cholesterol levels?'

She responded to his lighter mood. 'Worry about yours,

not mine. I'm sticking to one piece of toast and an apple. But I decided you were beginning to look pinched around the face and it was time to fill you up a bit. And since we normally have so little fried food, I can't believe this one indulgence will clog your arteries.'

'You know the trouble with one indulgence? It breeds a second.'

'Try using some will-power.'

'In the olfactory face of eggs and bacon?'

'Instead of talking nonsense, see if the coffee's made. It should be, but I haven't heard the machine belch yet.'

He lifted the aluminium lid and coffee, which had been surging up the central spout, splattered him. 'There's a law which states that one always checks at the most dangerous moment.'

'Did it reach your coat?'

'No, only the back of my hand.'

'That's all right, then.'

'Even if I'm severely burned?'

'If you'd been even lightly burned, you'd now be shouting for an ambulance.' She turned away from the stove and kissed him lightly. Then she turned back and used the bottom of the slice to surge hot fat over the yolks of the two eggs. 'I've buttered a piece of toast and it's on the plate—push it over, will you?'

He passed it to her and she began to dish. 'You've got a clean handkerchief to go to work with, haven't you?'

'No.'

She placed the two rashers of bacon to the side of the toast, lifted up the eggs and placed them on the toast. She handed him the plate. 'Go and eat. You're a bit behind time.'

'Not to worry, my hours are flexible.'

'Do Teerson Products know that?'

He carried the plate through to the dining-room and sat

at the table. She appeared in the doorway. 'Did you say a moment ago you did have a clean handkerchief?'

'I said I didn't.'

'That's odd.'

'Why?' But she'd returned into the kitchen and didn't answer him. He cut the yolks of the eggs and let them run over the toast, then started eating.

She came into the dining-room, a mug of coffee in each hand. She passed him one, put one in front of her place setting, then returned to the kitchen for a tray on which were toast, butter, an apple, and a jar of marmalade. She began to quarter and peel the apple.

'You didn't say what was odd about the clean handkerchief I haven't got?' he said.

She ate a piece of apple. 'You know yesterday you needed one for work and there weren't any respectable ones in your cupboard? I knew there was one of the new ones in the load of laundry I'd put on the ironing-board.' She ate another piece of apple. 'But when I went into the spare room this morning, I couldn't find it, so I naturally thought you must have taken it . . . Are you sure you didn't?'

'Quite sure.'

'Then where on earth's it got to?'

'Search me. And I hasten to add that that won't solve the puzzle.'

'Then where is it?'

'A good question.'

'But no answer?'

'Not this early in the morning . . . By the way, the bacon's rather salty.'

'Is it? I'm sorry. I bought it in one of the supermarkets in Reckton and their bacon's never as good as the stuff the local shop sells, but it's a lot cheaper.'

'Champagne tastes, beer income, that's me.'

'Who's any different? . . . And come to that, now I think

about it, the pile of washing was different.'

'Being of a fairly logical mind, I fail to follow you. Or to put it another way, I don't know what the hell you're talking about.'

'I've a funny habit which probably means I'm suffering from some deep and quite unmentionable repression that whenever I move a pile of freshly laundered clothes, I always make certain I put it down exactly square to whatever I put it on. Yesterday I unwrapped the parcel—we had to have the washing done at the laundry because our machine was on the blink—and I put the pile down on the ironing-board, meaning to take it upstairs later, but I forgot. This morning, it was slightly caterwise to the board. Did you move it?'

'Why should I?'

'Looking for a clean handkerchief.'

'Remember something? I haven't got one.'

'Yes, I know . . .'

He ate the last piece of egg and toast, put the plate on one side. 'Shove the toast over, will you?' Then he noticed her expression. 'Is something wrong?'

'I . . . I'm not certain. I suppose really I'm being very silly'

'That sounds unlikely.'

'The thing is, I'm wondering if something funny has been going on.'

'In what way?'

'The handkerchief missing, the pile of washing that's been moved, and . . . Dennis, I woke up in the middle of the night and there just didn't seem to be any reason why. And then I thought I heard a noise in the kitchen.'

'What kind of a noise?'

'I don't know, really. A kind of clink, as if something had touched something else.'

'A mouse charging around in clogs?'

'When I didn't hear anything more, I decided it must

have been a mouse—without the clogs. But now . . . You don't think we had someone in the house last night, do you?'

He was startled by the suggestion. 'Presumably the front door was locked when you came down this morning?'

'Yes. And when I opened up, everything was as it should be.'

'Then it had to be a mouse you heard, or the house turning over in its sleep; and for once you did not line up the washing with geometric certainty on the ironing-board, and my one new clean handkerchief has been lost at the laundry and I'll have to go on using an old one with holes in it. People will say my wife neglects me.'

'And you'll agree?'

'Enthusiastically.'

Looking now at Reginald Gilles—pronounced Gil-lays—it was difficult to imagine his winning the 220 yards and quarter-mile for his college because the years had crinkled his flesh and his wife's death had seared his mind. But that did not mean that he was ready to accept the loss of many of his sporting trophies with equanimity.

'The damned scoundrel's taken all the best ones,' he said furiously.

The detective-constable decided he looked exactly like an old bantam cock.

'They're irreplaceable.'

The DC stared at the glass-fronted showcase.

'You've got to get them back for me.'

'We'll do our best.' By now, they had probably been hammered flat and melted down.

'How could anyone stoop to taking something so obviously personal?'

Poor old bastard, thought the DC; never come to terms with the modern world. Perhaps he thought that villains still had scruples.

'And what's more, the damned man helped himself to a drink!'

The DC had to work hard not to smile at that. But he'd been told to treat the old boy with respect. He'd been chairman of the magistrates for a number of years and could almost certainly still raise a stink if he felt the police were treating him with indifference or condescension. 'As far as you know, sir, is anything more missing?'

'I haven't checked. When I came in here and saw me trophies had gone . . .' He stopped abruptly. It was difficult to explain, but a little more of his life had just been taken from him.

'Do you have a safe?'

'Yes, but there's not much in it. Gave all my wife's jewellery to my daughter-in-law. But I don't think she really likes any of it. Bit old-fashioned, I suppose, but it's been in the family for quite a time. As I said to my son, if Erica doesn't want to wear it, keep it and pass it on to your daughter. It's comforting to see something go down the generations.'

It was comforting to have some jewellery for oneself, never mind the next generation; they could look after themselves. The old boy must have been well-heeled. Probably still was, only one wouldn't think so, looking at the way he dressed and the state of repair and decoration of the house. 'Would you check now and see if the safe was forced? And then make certain nothing else is missing?'

'The cups and medals are insured, of course, but it's the sentimental value that matters.'

You keep the sentiment, I'll take the insurance payout, the DC thought as Gilles walked out of the room, his leg movements laboured from arthritis. The DC went over to the nearest of the three windows. One pane had been smashed and then the intruder had reached in and unlatched the window. A crude method of entry into a house in which only one man, hard of hearing, lived. A draught of cold, damp air came through the broken window as he looked out. Stretching away from the outside wall was a flowerbed in need of weeding, and he saw a clear footprint in the soft earth. Chummy was not only crude, but careless. He moved out of the draught and visually examined the room. Furniture had a look of class about it, but the upholstery was faded and in places tattered; the huge carpet must have cost a bomb when it was new, but that was a long time ago; pictures, with display lights, for which he wouldn't have bid a quid, but which might well be worth a lot more than he'd ever see; a carved wooden overmantel which incorporated a mirror that reflected the central chandelier—shades of high life; a mobile cocktail cabinet with a split top that opened out to form two shelves at the same time as a shelf of bottles and glasses rose up to that level . . . He went over and examined it. On the right-hand leaf was a bottle of Haig and a glass. Gilles had said that he hadn't used that glass, so Chummy had. There might just be prints on it; there were still one or two villains who were so thick they didn't know about fingerprints. And if Gilles had to be bullshitted into believing his peasant-sized robbery was receiving the full attention of the police, taking the glass for testing would be a good move . . .

He returned to the show cabinet. The ornamental key had been in the lock, so there'd been no problem about opening the door. Because of the key's design, there'd not be any decipherable prints on it . . .

Gilles returned. 'Found the safe, but he didn't open it.'

'Would you show me where it is, sir?'

They went along one corridor, wood-panelled and dark, turned into another that was even darker, and then almost immediately entered a small room furnished with only a table, a chair, and two paintings. One of the paintings was on hinges and it had been swung back to reveal a safe.

The safe's make was Mackay and the DC knew that the firm had ceased production fifty years or more before; even then, they'd been known more for their fire-resistant qualities than their security. A clever twirler would have cracked it in one minute flat. That it hadn't been forced confirmed that the intruder was useless. Some young punk on hard drugs who needed to buy his next fix and didn't care what risks he took. 'I'll have that checked for dabs, sir, so maybe you'll leave opening it until I say?'

'Of course.'

'Have you any valuables anywhere else in the house that need checking?'

'I don't think so. My wife and I gave my son a great many things when he married. It seemed to us that that was the sensible thing to do, because when one gets old . . .'

The DC blocked. He didn't want to know about old age.

They returned to the drawing-room and the DC had one last look round, and this was when he found the candy-striped handkerchief on the floor behind the sofa. He picked it up. 'Is this yours, sir?'

'No. I never use anything but white.'

The handkerchief had been recently laundered and there was a mark on one corner. It began to look as if Chummy was not only crude and careless, but stupid as well.

CHAPTER 17

Macey, specialists in dry-cleaning delicate fabrics as well as general cleaners, was owned and run by a husband and wife. The wife, a small bustling woman, seldom quite still, said to the CID aide: 'Let's see the handkerchief and I'll tell you.'

He produced a plastic bag, extracted a candy-striped handkerchief, and handed it over.

She examined it very briefly. 'Yes, that's our mark.'

'Can you say who it belongs to?'

'Certainly, once I've checked the records.'

She turned round and opened the middle drawer of a metal filing cabinet, flicked through the cards inside, then came to a stop. 'The name's Mrs Rickmore.'

'How d'you spell that?'

She told him.

'Are there any initials?'

'D.P.'

'What about an address?'

'I haven't one. We don't deliver any more, so there's no call for them.'

He read through what he'd written a second time. He'd been working with CID for only two weeks and was still obsessively conscientious.

Ridley, sitting behind the desk in the DI's room, said: 'Did you say Rickmore?'

'That's right, skipper,' said the CID aide.

That was quite a coincidence. 'D'you get any initials or an address?'

'Initials are D.P. The laundry didn't have an address.'

'I just wonder . . . Right, that's it for the moment. You can get back on to the Swift job.'

The aide left. Ridley searched in the desk for a local telephone directory, found it, and checked the initials of the Rickmore who lived in Oak Tree Cottage, Yew Cross. D.P. So how in the hell had Rickmore's handkerchief appeared in a house that had been burgled?

Lineport, twelve miles from Reckton, had had a flourishing fishing trade until, starting some thirty years previously, spiralling costs had rendered the small inshore boats un-economic. There had never been any quays or docks; the fishing-boats had been winched up the gently sloping pebble beach, their keels protected by a wide metal band known as the Lineport guard. Now, the winch had rusted into immobility and few people remembered what the Lineport guard was.

The town had narrow, twisting streets and a population older than the national average; doctors were reluctant to practise there because so much of the work was geriatric. Sensibly, successive councils had tried to retain the atmos-phere and there had been very little development. The largest of the four antique shops was in a Georgian house which had once been owned by a wealthy man who'd seduced his maid and then murdered her when it appeared she was pregnant. He had been tried, found guilty, and hanged. The antique shop specialized in silver, but it also sold miniature scaffolds that were made from the wood of the original scaffold and these had always proved to be very popular. Luckily, despite the large numbers which had been sold over the years, there still seemed to be no lack of the original wood from which to make them.

On Saturday, a man entered and offered to sell a large and handsome silver-gilt cup. The owner of the shop exam-ined this and then asked what had happened to the plinth? The question disturbed the man, who muttered something to the effect that he didn't know whether he did want to sell the cup after all. He returned it to the holdall and hurried out.

The owner called his wife down into the shop and asked her to look after things while he went along to the police. He walked the short distance to the station and spoke to the detective-sergeant.

'Hullo, Mr Chapman, not seen you for quite a time. How are things—going all right? . . . Let's sit down over there and then you can say what's up.' The DS led the way over to a table and chairs. They sat.

Chapman was a precise man, inclined to speak pedantically. 'A little earlier, immediately before I came here, in fact, a man came into my emporium and asked if I was interested in buying a silver-gilt cup. It would be very difficult to explain precisely why, but from the beginning I was rather suspicious of his *bona fides*.'

'You've got a nose for these things, haven't you?'

'It's certainly big enough!' Chapman might be pedantic, but he had a sense of humour. 'The cup had been set on a plinth, but he did not produce this. When I asked him where it was, he became nervous, said he was not certain after all if he did wish to sell the cup, took it back, and left.'

'Went out in a hurry?'

'That is how I would describe his mode of departure.'

'What kind of a bloke was he?'

'He had a moustache, which I must say struck me as looking false, but I'm wondering now whether that impression was perhaps due to my original suspicions. Otherwise he was ordinary, neither short nor tall, with the kind of face which is sometimes said, I believe, to melt into a crowd. Much of his face was obscured by a cap with a large peak.'

'Anything else at all about him that struck you?'

'Yes, there was. He had a very slight speech defect. Once or twice he had trouble in pronouncing his R's.'

'How about this cup he tried to sell you—can you describe it?'

'It was about eight inches tall, six in diameter, and shaped in the style which is known in the trade—erroneously, in my view—as Portland. It was silver-gilt, hallmarked in London in nineteen twenty-one. It bore an inscription, "Two hundred and twenty yards".'

The DS looked down at his notes. 'Your description's got

me wondering . . . Hang on, I shan't be long.' He left and was gone for a little over two minutes. When he returned, he had a sheet of paper in his hand. 'There was a robbery last Wednesday and a load of sporting trophies was pinched. The owner's given a list and this is it—as a matter of fact, you'd have had a copy before the day's out. What d'you think?' He passed the paper across.

Chapman read carefully and slowly, then looked up. 'It is very probable that the item listed as number six is the cup I was shown.'

'I thought it might be. And since there was a whole load of tiny shields listing winners' names, including Mr Gilles's three times, on the plinth, it would explain why you weren't offered that as well . . . I think we'll need a stronger description of this man.'

'I'm afraid I'm not very good at that sort of thing.'

'You're not doing yourself justice. Look how much you've given me already!' The DS was very good at persuading witnesses to tell far more than they'd realized they'd known.

Ridley put the receiver down. He leaned back in the chair and, with unfocused gaze, stared at the window. There was little doubt that the cup which had been offered for sale to Chapman in Lineport was one of those which had been stolen from Gilles. (All doubt would soon be resolved; Gilles had a photograph of himself receiving that cup and this photograph was going to be shown to Chapman.) At Gilles's house, a handkerchief belonging to D. P. Rickmore had been found. The aide who'd taken the handkerchief to be identified had forgotten to ask the cleaners whether they had more than one D. P. Rickmore on their books, but it was a small omission, soon put right—and what were the odds against? Chapman's description of the man who'd come into the antique shop had not been good generally;

specifically, however, it had been promising. The man spoke with a very slight speech impediment.

Ridley picked up a pencil and fiddled with it. The investigating DC had pointed out that the burglary had been carried out by someone with little skill or experience. To offer that silver cup for sale only a dozen miles from where it had been stolen suggested either stupidity or no knowledge whatsoever of how the police worked. Rickmore spoke with a slight speech defect . . . But it strained credulity to imagine that he would suddenly take up burglary unless so desperately strapped financially that he was faced by disaster. Although he obviously wasn't wealthy, equally, he showed no signs of poverty . . . There was something here which Ridley couldn't grasp, perhaps because the conclusion to which the facts pointed was contrary to common sense. For the first time since he'd moved into the DI's room, he felt unequal to the job and wished there were someone he could go to for advice and instruction. He swore. It was not a feeling he liked.

Rickmore finished washing down the Escort and squeezed out the leather. Considering the mileage the car had done, it was a reasonable runner, but only an optimist could think it had many more miles left to go. Was he the only PRO in the country who did not have a company car? What was it like to be so well off that one could walk into a showroom and order the car of one's choice? What was life like when money—or rather, the lack of it—ceased to be central to everything one did or considered doing? Which brought him back to Elham.

He picked up the bucket, carried it across to the spile fence, and threw the dirty water into the small orchard which lay between the road and the garden. He left the bucket and leather to dry in the near corner of the garage.

He walked round the house and entered the porch where

he changed out of wellingtons into shoes. Anne was in the kitchen, cooking. 'Are you doing anything?' she asked.

'I have been and I'm about to.'

'Good. Will you chop an onion up for me? They make me cry so.'

'Why not use those goggles you were given?'

'They steam up.'

'Be difficult!'

'You know they hardly ever affect you.'

'If I have tears, prepare to shed them now.' He picked an onion out of the vegetable rack, carried it across to a working surface, reached across for the board she'd been using, and brought down a steel knife from the magnetized strip. 'I've been thinking.' He sliced off the two ends, began to peel away the skin. 'About Terence.'

'Oh!' She looked at him, then quickly away. It was the first time the subject had been broached since the night Elham had told them that the dead man had been identified.

'I can't do it.'

'What can't you do?' she asked tightly.

'Be directly responsible for ruining him, the circumstances being what they are.'

'Thank God for that.'

He finished peeling the onion, cut it longitudinally several times. 'I couldn't face the knowledge that I'd wrecked his whole life. I'm right in principle—but I've learned something you knew from the beginning. Principles can be right, but the observing of them wrong.' He cut the onion at right angles to the previous cuts.

'When are you going to tell him?'

'I'll phone . . .'

'No. It's something you've got to do face to face.'

'I was afraid you'd say that.'

'Will it help if I come and hold your hand?'

'Squeeze it hard.'

'To try to stop you thinking?'

'You know me too well for my own comfort.'

She carried the casserole dish with the mince in it over to where he stood and used a wooden spoon to sweep the diced onion on to the mince. Then she kissed him. 'And love what I know.'

The suggestion didn't come from either of them, and it was without a word being spoken that Anne and Rickmore left the parked car and walked round to the front door of Popham House, instead of the back.

Penelope opened the door and her astonishment was complete. She stared at them, the surprise slowly giving way to tension.

'May we come in?' asked Anne.

She moved to one side and they entered.

'Is Terence in?'

She nodded.

Rickmore said: 'I want to tell him something.'

They went through to the blue sitting-room. Elham had identified their voices and he now stood, not in front of the fire, but by the armchair in which he invariably sat. On the table by his side was a cut-glass tumbler half filled with whisky and soda.

'Dennis wants to talk to you,' said Penelope unnecessarily.

'Well?' Elham tried to give the impression of defiance; an impression denied by his expression.

Rickmore said: 'I'm going to tell the police that after all I can't be certain about the state of the car or the garage.'

Elham reached for the glass and picked it up with a hand that shook. Penelope began to cry silently, tears welling out of her eyes and coursing down her cheeks.

CHAPTER 18

Ridley braked the CID Metro to a halt, switched off the engine, and climbed out. The wind had freshened and he zipped up the front of his parka before crossing the pavement and opening the front gate of No. 64.

The front garden, even at this time of the year, was tidy. MacMahon, he recalled, was a keen gardener who spent much of his spare time cutting this, planting that, digging here, weeding there. Since he lived in a police house and when he retired would have to leave it, Ridley considered all that work a stupid waste of time and effort. But then, it was totally short-sighted to live in a police house and these days a policeman with any sense invested in a place of his own. But in every respect, MacMahon was of the old school.

Ridley rang the front-door bell and Mrs MacMahon opened the door. She was a large, rather coarsely featured woman who had never been physically very attractive, even when young, but who was possessed of an unmistakably warm nature. 'Hullo, Steve.'

''Morning, Mrs MacMahon. Sorry to bother you like this on a Sunday, but I was wondering if it would be all right to have a bit of a chat with the boss?'

'According to the doctor you shouldn't, that's for sure, not if it's business. But I reckon it'll do more good than harm. A bear with a sore head would be better company than he's been since he got back from hospital. Never could stand being idle.'

'How is he?'

'He seems a lot better, but it's going to be a bit more time before we're certain. Seems they still can't tell whether he did have a slight heart attack and they've got to make more tests. Beats me—I thought you'd either had had one or you hadn't . . . But come on in, instead of standing out there in the cold.'

He stepped into the hall.

'He's in the front room. Tell him I'm making you some coffee and warming a cup of milk for him—and whatever he says, he's not getting coffee.'

He went into the sitting-room. MacMahon was on the settee, his legs up. 'Saw it was you through the window. How are things?'

'Not too bad. But more to the point, how are you?'

'Bloody fed up and bored. There's nothing wrong with me and the doctors are a bunch of old women . . . I expect Elsie's already told you that I'm impossible to live with?'

Ridley grinned.

'Sit down; there's no extra charge for a chair.'

He sat on a large, well-upholstered armchair which showed signs of wear. The MacMahons preferred comfort to style. 'The missus said to tell you that she's making me coffee and warming you up a cup of milk.'

MacMahon swore, but without much conviction.

Ridley said, with uncharacteristic diffidence: 'I've come looking for a bit of advice.'

'Let's hear the problem.'

'Old Gilles's place was done on Wednesday night.'

'Reginald Gilles, the man who used to do a lot of running and was chairman of the local bench for God knows how many years?'

'That's the bloke.'

MacMahon chuckled. 'I'll bet he had something to say about things.'

'He did! . . . It was only a small job and really only warranted someone from the uniform branch, but seeing it was him, I sent Alan.'

'Good thinking.'

'Alan says Chummy was a real beginner—stepped on to a flowerbed and left a good print, smashed a window to get in, nicked a load of silver cups that can't be worth all that much, but left a safe with quite a bit of cash in it. The safe was a Mackay and I reckon I could do it with a screwdriver. He helped himself to a drink and dropped a handkerchief with a laundry mark on it.

'Come yesterday, he—or a mate—was in one of the antique shops in Lineport trying to sell a large silver-gilt cup, missing its plinth, and with "Two hundred and twenty yards" engraved on it. Chapman, the owner, was suspicious and the man cleared off. The cup did come from Gilles's place.'

'Was Chapman able to give a reasonable description?'

'Not really. Could have been anyone, wearing a false moustache and a cap. But he did pick out one useful fact. The bloke had a slight speech defect and occasionally couldn't pronounce his R's properly.'

MacMahon saw that Ridley was looking at him intently, as if expecting some reaction. 'That's not much use on its own, is it?' he asked, worried that perhaps his brain wasn't working as quickly and clearly as it should.

'Suppose I add that we've identified the laundry mark and it's D. P. Rickmore's?'

'God's teeth!' exclaimed MacMahon, who sometimes used such ancient expletives when his surprise was too great for mere four-letter words.

'It all fits,' said Ridley exasperatedly, 'but who the bloody hell's ever going to believe that a bloke like Rickmore has suddenly taken up breaking and entering?'

'He could need money desperately?'

'Could he? He's not rolling in it, sure, but who is, except for a few lucky bastards? We both saw his place. He's not getting ready to queue at the soup kitchen.'

'No, he isn't.'

'Then who's going to believe it was him?'

'That depends on how strong the evidence becomes. If you know Chummy had a drink, presumably a glass was left around?'

'Glass and bottle. I've sent 'em both off for dabs.'

'What about comparison dabs from Rickmore?'

'One of the things I want to know is, do you think I should go for them yet?'

MacMahon thought for a moment. 'Probably not; at least, not openly. This has to be treated very, very carefully. After all, we wouldn't want . . .' He came to a sudden stop.

'What?'

There was no answer.

Ridley waited. MacMahon had the habit of disappearing into a brown study, which could be infuriating; but he'd come here to learn if any such brown study could bear fruit.

The door opened and Mrs MacMahon, carrying a tray, entered. Ridley stood and took the tray from her. 'Thanks, Steve. Just wait a moment while I clear a table.' She briefly studied her husband, worried that it might after all have been a mistake to allow Ridley to discuss work with him, but judged from his expression that it had not. She removed some newspapers from a small table. 'Put the tray down here and help yourself. There's milk and sugar and some biscuits.'

'Can I do your cup?'

'Will you? A little milk, but no sugar, thanks.'

'And what about me?' demanded MacMahon.

'No sugar and a whole cupful of milk,' she answered.

'That muck's only fit for calves and babies.'

She laughed and said that she'd rather look after a crèche full of babies than him.

Some fifteen minutes later she collected up the dirty cups, saucers and plates, put them on the tray, and left.

'What wouldn't I give for a double Scotch,' said Mac-Mahon longingly.

'Have you been knocked off that as well?' asked Ridley.

'Been knocked off everything that makes life worth living . . . Look, Steve, let's discuss motive. There's always a motive, except when you're dealing with freaks like psychopaths. Was the motive here financial?'

'What else?'

'You don't think it might have been to create a lever?'

'I don't get it,' said Ridley bluntly.

'Remember the circumstances. Elham, too much alcohol aboard to risk a breath test, runs away after the accident. Unexpectedly, Rickmore turns up at Popham House, sees the damage to the Jaguar and notices that the garage isn't damaged.

'We interview Rickmore and he gives evidence which provides a peg on which all the circumstantial evidence can be hung and which will nail Elham. Elham's a very smart lawyer who can appreciate the value in court of evidence better than we can. He sees clearly that if Rickmore can't be persuaded to change his evidence, he—that is, Elham—is for the chopper. So Rickmore's value as a witness for the prosecution has to be undermined to the point where no jury will believe him. What quicker way of doing that than making him appear to be a criminal?'

'Elham wouldn't do anything like that.'

'Why not? Because of his position? But it's precisely because of his position that he would. Think of all he stands to lose if he's found guilty of a serious crime.'

'But . . .'

'You're the one who's always sneering at the rich; are you sure you aren't now investing him with a sense of justice, honour, and fair-mindedness just because he *is* rich? He was willing to knock a man down and not stop, wasn't he?'

'That's different.'

'Is it?'

To his angry embarrassment, Ridley realized that Mac-Mahon was right—he had been instinctively supposing Elham incapable of deliberately entrapping another person in order to save himself.

'If you're thinking it could be different because they're related by marriage, just ask yourself, when did that ever stop two people disliking each other? Rickmore's never held back on the evidence. On the contrary, he volunteered the news of his drive over to Popham House without any prompting from us and we'd not have learned about it but for him. He's obviously no fool, so we must assume he realized the significance of what he was saying. He's not starving, but financially he's not in the same league as Elham. It can get on a man's wick to have a brother-in-law who goes out of his way to show how much better off he is. He may well have shown his jealousy, which will have exacerbated the ill-feeling between them. And can you imagine Elham's thoughts when he learned that it was Rickmore who'd fingered him? My guess is, he'd laugh all the way to the nearest bottle of champagne if Rickmore's nailed for something he didn't do.'

'I still can't see Elham setting it up. He hasn't enough balls.'

'Suppose you stood to lose everything you have and are faced with a future of poverty instead of luxury . . . Wouldn't your balls grow?'

'Maybe.'

'And remember one thing more. We first homed in on Elham through a tip-off. Who was the anonymous caller?'

'All we know is, a woman.'

'Prompted by Rickmore? Do you imagine that Elham hasn't worked that out?'

'You've got one hell of a mind! You've turned them into a couple of right royal bastards.'

'If I've learned one thing in the Force, it's that everyone can be a right royal bastard, given tight enough circumstances.'

'They're going to find that . . .'

'Steve, I said at the beginning that this was a case to be taken carefully. I'm telling you now, it's a powder keg. Whatever you do, remember Agag.'

'Where's he come into it?'

MacMahon smiled briefly.

'Are you going to ring now?' asked Anne.

Rickmore looked across at her. 'I wasn't, no.'

'You can't put it off for ever.'

'Not when you're around.' He stood, put a log on the fire.

'Get it over and done with. And remember, it's the right thing to do.'

'Is it?'

'You're not thinking of going back on what you said?'

'No. I'm just trying to convince myself that there really are times when circumstances change wrong into right.'

'Yes, there are.'

'Ever the pragmatist?'

'It makes life more liveable.'

He crossed the carpet and kissed her.

'You're lucky you married me, Dennis Rickmore.'

'You're always claiming that. Don't you think it would be more becoming to leave me to say it?'

'Haven't you realized yet that in the wrong hands you'd have developed into an impossible prig?'

'Thanks very much.'

'But as it is . . .'

'Finish and put me out of my agony.'

'You're one of the nicest men in the world.'

'I can resist everything except praise.' He kissed her a second time.

'Then what about temptation?'

'Let's find out.'

She smiled. 'Go and make the phone call and stop trying to lead me astray.'

He went into the hall and across to the telephone. This was his Rubicon; the moment when he betrayed his principles. Quickly, as if delay might make him renege, he checked the number and then dialled it, asked to speak to Detective-Inspector MacMahon.

'I'm afraid he's away ill.'

'I'm sorry to hear that,' he said automatically. 'Is Detective-Sergeant Ridley around?'

'I'll put you through to CID.'

'Duty DC speaking. Can I help you?'

'Will you give a message to Mr Ridley, please? My name's Rickmore. Will you say that I'm afraid I've realized I've made a mistake and my evidence regarding the damage to the Jaguar and the garage is wrong.'

The DC repeated the message.

Rickmore returned to the sitting-room.

'That was very brief,' Anne said.

'MacMahon's away so I left the message for the detective-sergeant.'

'Thankfully? . . . Look, my love, stop questioning and criticizing yourself. You've done the right thing, the only thing.'

He wished he could be half as certain as she was.

CHAPTER 19

Ridley read the message and swore. Rickmore was going back on his evidence. And without that, the case was a non-starter. The lever had worked. Elham was proving once

again that money and power were what really mattered in
life; if you possessed them, you could kick the rest of the
world in the goolies; if you possessed them, you could distort
and cheat justice . . .

But, he thought, maybe this time it would turn out to be
not quite so straightforward as the bastard imagined. He'd
gone to considerable trouble to set up that lever to force
Rickmore to recant or, if he wouldn't, to destroy his value
as a witness. Might he not have gone a little too far? Clever
men were sometimes too clever for their own health . . . By
God, he'd get Elham yet! Or if he couldn't, he'd make
Rickmore curse the day he'd recanted.

It was the first time that Rickmore had entered the divisional
HQ, situated at the back of the parish church and in such
hideous architectural conflict with it. He was conscious that
he was breathing quickly and sweating. Like visiting the
dentist, he thought.

There was a counter at one end of the front room and this
was manned by a sergeant and a PC. He spoke to the PC.

'Detective-Sergeant Ridley? I'll tell him you're here, Mr
Rickmore. If you'll just sit over there until I can find
him.'

At the opposite end to the counter were padded wall seats,
a few rather spartan chairs, and two tables on which were
several magazines, some with direct connection with the
police force, and several pamphlets aimed at helping and
advising the general public.

He was reading—and hardly taking in—a pamphlet de-
tailing some of the measures a householder could take to
protect his home when he heard someone approaching and
he looked up to see Ridley.

''Morning, Mr Rickmore. Nice of you to come along.'

He had expected resentment, but Ridley had sounded
pleasant.

'I've found an interview room that's free, so let's go along there.'

They left and went down a corridor to the second of three rooms off to the right. It was small, with a single window high up which was barred; the only furniture was a table and six chairs.

'Not the Ritz,' said Ridley, 'but it's quiet . . . Now, about this message—I thought it would be best if you came along and explained things personally.' He produced a pack of cigarettes. 'D'you use these?'

'No, thanks.'

'I wish I could say the same.' He tapped out a cigarette, but before he had time to light it there was a knock on the door and a PC looked in. 'D'you want a cuppa, skipper?'

Ridley turned to Rickmore: 'Which do you drink, tea or coffee?'

'I prefer coffee.'

He said to the PC. 'Two coffees. And get 'em from the canteen, not that flaming machine that can't tell the difference.'

The PC withdrew and shut the door.

Ridley had brought a folder with him and he now opened this and read the top sheet of paper. 'Your message said that you'd made a mistake over your evidence concerning the damage to the Jaguar and the garage. Would you like to be specific?'

Elham had advised him very carefully what to say. He was not to admit to making too direct a mistake; rather, he was to blame the surrounding circumstances. That way, his change of testimony would be very difficult to challenge in court, should he still be called for the prosecution and named a hostile witness. He took a deep breath. 'This last Saturday night my wife and I had dinner at Popham House. We arrived after dark and parked directly in front of the garage because I knew my brother-in-law wouldn't be going out.'

'Just one moment. As I remember it, that's a fairly large garage, so opposite which part of it were you?'

'Well over to the right. We left the car and were moving towards the house when my wife suddenly remembered that we'd forgotten to pick up a magazine we'd brought over for my sister-in-law, so I started back and then happened to glance at the front end of my car and I was convinced there was a dent in the bonnet which hadn't been there before. Yet when I checked, there wasn't anything and I realized it had been a trick of light.'

'When you say light, does that mean that the outside lights of the garage were switched on?'

'Two were, but a third one wasn't working. It was obviously the mixture of shadow and light which had given the impression of a dent.'

'But I seem to remember you saying originally that all three outside lights were working on the night the accident took place?'

'I'm certain I didn't say one way or the other. In fact, one wasn't, just as it wasn't on Saturday. Terence says it's got one of those irritating faults where sometimes it works and sometimes it doesn't. And every time he decides to call in an electrician, it starts behaving itself again.'

The PC returned, carrying a tray on which were two mugs, a teaspoon, and a bowl of sugar. He put the tray in front of Ridley, then left. Ridley pushed the tray to the middle of the table. 'Help yourself.' After Rickmore had taken one mug, Ridley spooned sugar into the second one and then drank. 'Today, it doesn't taste of either tea or coffee.'

Rickmore smiled.

'At least it's hot . . . Getting back to the accident. Originally, you said the offside light was smashed.'

'I said it wasn't working.'

'Both Mr MacMahon and I heard you say that it was smashed.'

'Whatever you heard, that's not what I was trying to say. After all, I didn't go round the bonnet, so there's no way I could have known how it was.'

'Then how did you know the light wasn't working?'

'The headlights were switched on; the offside one wouldn't come on.'

'Why were they switched on if the car was parked?'

'Terence was trying to see if he could get the offside one to work. Personally, I think that that was being rather unrealistically optimistic. He's about as good an electrician as I am mechanic.'

'Do you know if the light failed on the journey back?'

'It went just before they reached our place before dinner.'

'But you told us that when the car left your house, it was unmarked and undamaged.'

'It was. A malfunctioning light isn't damage; that connotes some structural fault.'

'Somewhat pedantic, surely?' said Ridley, not as lightly as he'd intended.

'I'm sorry. Anne says I'm becoming more and more pedantic; one of the penalties of growing older.'

'Or of trying to explain away the difference between what you are saying now and what you said originally?'

'That's nonsense. I haven't changed a thing.'

'Tell me, don't you think it strange how many lights failed that night?'

'Sod's Law. Things never go wrong singly. That's why, if I break something I hurry to break two matches as well.'

Ridley shut the folder. 'Do you realize the full import of what you've just told me?'

'In what way?'

'Your evidence was central to proving your brother-in-law

was driving the car which hit and killed Tamworth. Now, you're denying all you said before.'

'I'm denying nothing that doesn't need to be denied because of the facts.'

'Facts?'

'Yes.'

'Not very pedantic when it comes to the truth?'

Rickmore didn't bother to answer.

'How much did Mr Elham drink at your house that Wednesday night?'

'As far as I can remember, the same as I did. Which was one drink before the meal and a couple of glasses of wine with it.'

'That seems considerably less than your previous estimate.'

'I talked it over with my wife and she has a much better memory than I.'

'So if I asked her, she'd say the same?'

'Yes.'

'As, no doubt, would Mr Elham?'

'I can't answer for him.'

'I expect you can,' said Ridley, no longer bothering to sound pleasant.

Rickmore waited, then said: 'Is there anything more I can tell you?'

'A hell of a lot. But I'm certain you won't.'

'Then I think I ought to get back to work.' Rickmore stood.

'It's a funny thing,' said Ridley, 'how your type always thinks that you've a divine right to escape consequences ... It must come as a hell of a shock when you discover you haven't.'

As Rickmore went down the passage and into the front room, he wondered uneasily why at the very end there had been an abrupt change of tone in the detective-sergeant's voice—almost as if he'd remembered he'd reason to gloat. He left the building to find that the clouds had lifted and there was some weak sunshine.

Back in the interview room, Ridley used his handkerchief to pick up the mug from which Rickmore had drunk and pack it in a cardboard box, carefully wedging it in place with pieces of foam. He carried the box up to the DI's office. A couple of minutes later, the PC who'd brought the coffee into the interview room, entered. 'Got him as he was leaving, skipper.'

'Let's see it.' The PC handed him a Polaroid snap. Rickmore was three-parts full face on to the camera. It was a good, clear snap.

Unusually, but as previously arranged, Rickmore returned home for lunch. When Anne met him in the hall, she studied his face. 'How did it go?'

'Not nearly as bad as I'd feared.'

'Thank goodness for that . . . Tell me exactly what happened.'

'Over a drink. It may not be the weekend, but I need a strong one.'

'Then have two. The meal's Cumberland hotpot, so it won't spoil.'

He poured out a gin and tonic and a sherry and they settled in the sitting-room. 'Ridley didn't start shouting, or anything like that. In fact, right until the end he seemed to be taking it all in his stride. Then he did show his teeth; said that my sort thought we'd a divine right to escape consequences.'

'If only he'd known a bit more.'

'"Whose conscience with injustice is corrupted."'

She shrugged her shoulders impatiently. 'Did he believe you?'

'Not for one second. Terence said he wouldn't. But apparently they're so used to witnesses going back on their evidence that they learn to treat it as one of the hazards of the profession. My job wasn't to convince him, it was to convince him that I'd be able to convince a jury I was telling the truth.'

'And you think you did that?'

'I'm pretty sure I did.'

'Thank God!'

'I'll drink to that.'

Because Lineport was in a different division, Ridley had first to telephone the local DI and ask permission to carry out the inquiries; on arrival, he had to report to the DI.

'The Guv'nor's been called out,' said the detective-sergeant, 'but he said it's OK to carry on. I've detailed a bloke to go with you.'

'There's no need for anyone.'

He laughed.

The PC who accompanied Ridley was young and quiet and Ridley gained the impression that perhaps he wasn't very smart. That suited him. 'All I'm aiming to do is see whether Chapman can identify from a photo the man who tried to sell him the cup,' he said as they walked briskly up the side road that led into the High Street.

The PC nodded.

'D'you know Chapman?'

'Can't say I do, skipper.'

'So you wouldn't know how quick on the ball he is?'

'No, I wouldn't.'

'Well, we'll sure as hell soon find out, as the young lady said when her boyfriend discovered the rubber was torn.'

The PC hardly smiled.

They entered the antique shop and Ridley introduced himself to Chapman and explained the reason for this visit.

'You want me to recognize him from a photo? I'm afraid

that's going to be difficult. You see, because of that cap he was wearing . . . I believe it has a name, but I don't know what it is.'

'Baseball cap?'

'Perhaps,' he answered doubtfully. 'Certainly, it didn't look very English . . . Anyway, the brim which was very large was pulled right down and the man's moustache was rather large, so much of his face was obscured.'

'But you were able to see his eyes, nose, ears, and chin?'

'I still don't think I'll be able to identify him from a photograph.'

'Have a look at this, will you?' Ridley handed him the Polaroid photograph of Rickmore.

Chapman studied the photograph briefly, then said: 'Just a minute.' He went through to the room behind the counter, returned with a pair of gold-rimmed glasses. He examined the photograph again. 'I can't see any real resemblance.'

'Then I'll just touch things up a bit. Let's have the photo a moment.' Ridley used a pencil to sketch in a baseball cap and a thick moustache. 'Now have another look.'

Chapman studied the photograph a second time. After a while he looked at Ridley over the tops of his spectacles. 'You think this was the man?'

'Let's just say, it's not impossible.'

He held the photograph a little closer. 'It does make quite a difference with the cap and the moustache.'

'Things like that can change a face completely for people who aren't trained observers and who don't know which points to look for. Ears are something which can't be changed. Would you say his ears—' Ridley indicated the photograph—'are similar to those of the man with the cup?'

'They could be.'

'And perhaps the chin's similar?'

'I think it is.'

'And the width of the face at cheekbone level?'

'That's certainly the same.'

'From the sound of things, then he might well . . .' Ridley let his voice die away.

'He might well be the same man. But I still can't be absolutely certain.'

'Never mind. You're saying the next best thing which is that if the man in the photo had a moustache and was wearing a baseball cap, he could very easily have been the man who tried to sell you the cup . . . Thanks very much, Mr Chapman, you've been of great assistance.'

Ridley led the way out of the shop, paused until the traffic eased, then crossed the road and walked briskly along the pavement.

'You were pushing hard, weren't you?' said the PC. 'Out to land Chummy, are you?'

The PC wasn't quite as thick as he'd first judged, thought Ridley. But that didn't really matter. Chapman was the kind of self-opinionated, fussy little man who, now that the seed had been well planted, would swear blind that there was a strong similarity between the two faces.

Because it had been a straight comparison and not a search for which Ridley had called, the fingerprint section were able to report on Tuesday afternoon. Some of the prints on the glass were the same as those on the mug; there were no prints on the bottle.

As Ridley replaced the receiver, he said aloud: 'I've got one of you, you bastards.'

CHAPTER 20

Rickmore was on his feet when he heard the car turn into the drive and he crossed to the window of the sitting-room and parted the curtains. Headlights swept round and then settled on the garage doors, just before being switched off.

'Can you see who it is?' asked Anne. She was knitting a sweater with a complex pattern and the various colours were, temporarily, in something of a cat's-cradle.

'No. Are you expecting someone?'

'Not that I know of.'

He left the sitting-room, switched on the hall and porch lights. He went into the porch and opened the outside door. The light drizzle had stopped, but the wind was damp, suggesting there was more rain to come; not a night for tramps or bald ducks, as his father would have said. He heard the squeal of the garden gate's hinges, then a few seconds later, Ridley came into view.

Ridley came to a stop. ''Evening.' There was no missing his cockiness. 'Got time for a bit of a chat, have you?'

'You'd better come in.' Once Ridley was in the hall, he offered to hang up the sergeant's short overcoat.

'That's very kind of you.' Now there was mockery as well as cockiness.

After hanging up the overcoat, Rickmore said: 'I'll just tell my wife what's happening and then we can go into the dining-room.' He went into the sitting-room and carefully closed the door behind him. 'It's the detective-sergeant. He wants a word. We can go into the dining-room . . .'

'No,' she said. He was trying to shield her from whatever trouble this visit was bringing and she was determined not to be shielded. 'Bring him in here—it's so much warmer.'

He hesitated, then finally nodded. He called Ridley into the room. Ridley said good-evening to Anne with exaggerated politeness. He sat on the settee, faced the fire, and remarked on how much heat it was giving out—he wished the fire in his house was half as good. It became obvious that he was savouring every minute of the run-in to whatever had brought him here.

Rickmore brought an end to the social chit-chat. He said, speaking tightly: 'You wanted a word about something?'

'That's right. About whether you feel like changing the evidence you gave at the station yesterday.'

'No, I don't.'

'You are quite certain?'

'I told you precisely what happened and there's nothing to change. And with regard to thinking I saw a dent in our car, my wife will confirm it all.'

'I'm sure she will. She'll confirm anything to help her brother-in-law escape conviction for running a man down and injuring him so badly that he later died, when he was too tight to know what he was doing.'

'What the devil do you mean?' Rickmore tried to sound indignant, rather than scared.

'I mean that we're not the simple fools you take us for. We know that originally you told us the truth, but now you're lying as hard as you can go.'

'You've no right to come into our house and talk like that,' said Anne fiercely.

'No right? No right when I'm faced by people who are supposed to be law-abiding and an example to the proles like me and I find 'em desperately trying to help one of their own kind escape the consequences of his drunken driving and cowardice?'

Anne spoke to Rickmore. 'You'd better telephone Mr Archer and ask him to drive over here right away.'

'Would that be Mr Archer, the solicitor?' asked Ridley. 'By all means telephone him and tell him to come here. That is, if you don't mind seeing your husband end up in prison.'

'What do you mean by that?'

'Exactly what I said.'

'He's done nothing.'

'Come off it, missus. He's lied his head off.'

'Sergeant,' said Rickmore angrily, 'I don't know what the hell you think you're at, but I do know you're not coming into my house and insulting my wife. Get out. And tomorrow I'll make an official complaint about your behaviour.'

'Sure. Maybe it'll make you feel good. Only perhaps I ought to tell you that complaints from someone about to be indicted for burglary don't cut much ice.'

'Indicted for burglary—are you crazy?'

'D'you know a man called Reginald Gilles? Ever been to his house?'

'And if I have?'

'It was burgled last Wednesday by someone who ought to have been wearing L-plates. Left a footprint in a flowerbed as clear as crystal, broke a pane of glass to force a window, nicked some cups and medals the old boy had won at running, but couldn't open a safe that only called for a bent hatpin. Then on Saturday he tried to sell one of the stolen cups to an antique shop in Lineport. The evidence says it was you who did that job.'

'That's utterly absurd.'

'Is it? Item. What size shoe d'you wear?'

'What's it matter what size?'

'Scared of answering?'

'Ten and a half,' snapped Anne.

Ridley smiled. 'Item. Chummy left a handkerchief with a laundry mark behind. That mark is yours.'

'It can't be . . .' began Rickmore.

'It is. Item. The intruder poured himself a drink to calm his nerves. Your fingerprints are on the glass.'

'They can't possibly have been mine.'

'Then the impossible's happened. Item. When you left the police station, a photograph of you was taken. After a moustache and a baseball cap were shaded in, the owner of the antique shop identified the person in the photo as the man who'd tried to sell him the stolen cup.'

'I haven't been in an antique shop in Lineport in the last couple of years.'

Anne said sharply. 'When was the burglary at Mr Gilles's house?'

'Last Wednesday.'

'I meant, at what time?'

'There's no saying. He went to bed around ten and got up at eight. So it was somewhere between those times.'

'On Wednesday, my husband was here all night.'

'So who's going to alibi him?'

'I am.'

'It's funny, but a wife's alibi never kind of rings very true.'

'He was here all night . . . Damnit, can't you see how ridiculous it is to claim my husband committed a burglary? People like him don't do that sort of thing.'

'If you were to ask me, I'd say that these days there's no knowing who'll do what. After all, there are people like him who drink too much, drive, knock someone over, and haven't the courage to stop and see how badly the victim's injured and if there's anything can be done for him.'

'That . . . that's different.'

'To whom? The victim?'

'You're trying to say Dennis has done something which is totally absurd. How can you begin to believe he'd commit a burglary in the house of someone we know?'

'Meaning he would in the house of someone you didn't know?'

'That's deliberately twisting what I said.' She forced herself to speak more calmly. 'Why would he ever do such a thing?'

'Ask him, not me.'

'You're determined not to understand . . .' She stopped, swung round to face her husband and stared at him for several seconds before she said: 'When was it that I woke up during the night and thought I heard someone downstairs?'

'God knows,' he muttered.

'Wasn't it . . . I know! It was the day I'd been to see Ruth and that was last Wednesday.' Her voice quickened. 'And it was on the Thursday that I couldn't find the handkerchief. You remember, I asked you about it.' She turned back to Ridley. 'What kind of handkerchief was it that was found in the house?'

'It was striped, in three colours; grey, chocolate, and light green.'

'That's the one that went missing! Then I did hear someone that night! And he stole the handkerchief and a glass with Dennis's fingerprints on it and left them at Reggie's house. He was trying deliberately to inculpate Dennis . . . You must see that that's what happened.'

'Must I?'

Rickmore said: 'You're obviously not surprised.'

Ridley did not answer.

'You know very well that I couldn't have carried out that burglary, whatever the evidence suggested. So why try and make out you believe I did?'

Ridley spoke contemptuously. 'You still can't read the score, can you? Not up in the art of self-survival; always had someone ready to come to the rescue . . . Your brother-in-law's a smart lawyer so it didn't take him any time at all to realize that if you persisted in standing by your original evidence, there was sufficient additional circumstantial evidence to nail him; that meant the end of his lifestyle. Equally, he could judge that if you could be persuaded to go back on your evidence, the circumstantial evidence on its own wouldn't be strong enough for him to be charged. So he did everything he could to persuade you to go back on what you'd told us. The trouble was, though, that you were so jealous of him, you wouldn't . . .'

'That's not true,' Anne cried sharply.

Ridley shrugged his shoulders. 'He reckoned your husband was and that's what counted.'

'It was a matter of principle. There are still people who have principles.'

'Sure. Just so long as they don't become inconvenient.'

'You don't know much about people, do you?'

'Mrs Rickmore, after you've been a copper for as long as I have, you know too much about people ever to believe in any of 'em again . . .' He turned to Rickmore. 'Since he wasn't getting anywhere asking, your brother-in-law set about saving himself in the only way left open to him—to destroy your value as a witness. That's why he found someone to set you up for a burglary.'

'He'd never have done such a thing,' said Anne.

'He'd have done anything to anybody to save his own skin.'

'Oh God, you've got a filthy mind!'

'Maybe. But I'll tell you one thing. I respect the law, not treat it with contempt.'

'My husband respects it just as much; maybe more.'

Ridley smiled. 'You could have fooled me, missus . . . Neither of you knew about the burglary before I told you, so Elham hasn't put the screws on you. Why go to all the trouble of fixing the burglary if not to use it? Obviously, because in the event he didn't need to. Why? Because after he'd set things rolling, the dead man was identified as a rapist and suddenly your principles weren't important enough. Like I said, people only hold principles until they become inconvenient.'

Rickmore bitterly acknowledged that in the present context, this was true.

'You decided to agree to go back on your evidence. So now there's no firm case against your brother-in-law, unless . . .'

'Unless what?'

'You decide to tell the truth after all.'

'I've told you the truth.'

'You told me a pack of bloody lies.'

'I swear it was the truth.'

Ridley said with pleasure: 'Still not understood? Not realized that when he set out to fix you for burglary, your brother-in-law did a good job; too good a job. If all the evidence is presented, you're going to go on trial and you're going to be found guilty.'

'That can't happen now,' said Anne.

'Why not?'

'You've admitted you don't believe Dennis had anything to do with it.'

'What I believe is immaterial; it's the evidence that counts. It always is.'

'But you know that he's innocent.'

'Strange how things work out, isn't it? You were ready to see someone guilty be found innocent, but now you're screaming because someone innocent may be found guilty.' He paused, then added: 'I hope you noticed I said "may be", not "is going to be".'

'What are you getting at now?' demanded Rickmore.

'Tell the truth about your brother-in-law and you won't be put on trial for burglary.'

'You're trying to blackmail me.'

'Blackmail, hell. I'm offering you a choice.'

'You're no better than the crooks you're meant to catch,' said Anne.

Ridley's anger finally overflowed. 'Me? All I want is to see justice done. But you lot—you want to bury justice. So who is it who's no bloody better than the villains?'

CHAPTER 21

Rickmore braked the Escort to a halt outside the garage of Popham House. Anne put her hand on his left arm. 'Don't lose your temper.'

'Do you know what I'd like to do . . .'

'Yes. But don't.'

'He doesn't give one solitary damn for anyone but himself. He'd see me jailed and our lives ruined, if that meant he could escape the consequences of his own drunkenness. He hasn't the guts to face . . .'

'I know all that, but I also know that if you lose your temper, as you can do when you're really worked up, you won't accomplish anything.'

A man who abhorred violence, no matter what the cause, he would have inflicted violence on Elham without a second's thought because, by his actions, Elham was threatening Anne.

She said quietly: 'If Terence knows the police have told us the facts, I'm sure he'll admit the truth. He can't have thought it would get to the point where you might actually be charged with burglary; all he was trying to do was destroy your potential value as a prosecution witness in the eyes of the police.'

'You'd have found an excuse for Judas Iscariot.' He climbed out of the car.

She joined him and linked her arm with his. 'Remember, count ten before you say anything.'

'I'll need a goddamn calculator.'

Penelope was in the kitchen and she greeted them with warmth, twice saying how nice it was to see them again so soon; but she could not hide her apprehension in the face of Rickmore's grimness.

'Is Terence back?' he asked.

'Not yet; he phoned to say he'd be catching the later train.' She looked up at the wall clock. 'But he shouldn't be long now. Let's go through and have a drink. And you will stay to supper, won't you?'

'No.'

'But you must; honestly, there's masses of food because I ordered a sirloin and the butcher must have thought we were entertaining an army. Terence so dislikes cold meat and if you don't eat with us, I don't know what I'll do with it all.'

'We can't stay.'

She nibbled her lower lip and looked at her sister, but merely gained confirmation that something was very, very wrong. 'I . . . Let's go through.'

They had been in the blue sitting-room less than ten minutes when they heard a car door slam. 'I'll go and tell him you're here.' Penelope hurried out.

A couple of minutes later, Elham, in black coat and striped trousers, entered the sitting-room, closely followed by Penelope. ''Evening, Anne; 'Evening, Dennis.' His manner was watchful, but not fearful, as was his wife's. 'Either of you ready for a refill while I get a drink for myself.'

'No, thanks,' answered Rickmore curtly.

'I'd like another vodka and tonic,' said Penelope hurriedly.

He took her glass and left. When he returned, and after handing her one glass, he moved to his favoured position in front of the fire.

'We had the detective-sergeant round at our place again,' said Rickmore.

'What did he want?'

'To tell me that you had done your damnedest to destroy

my value as a witness if I refused to change my original evidence; to tell me that you'd been a bit too clever before we learned the dead man was a rapist, and now the evidence against me is so strong that if I don't change my story back to what it was, I'll be on a charge of burglary and he'll personally guarantee that I'm found guilty.'

'God Almighty!'

'Don't bother to try to sound surprised and outraged . . .'

'You surely don't think that there's any truth in all that?'

'I'd say there's quite a bit.'

'You really believe I'd deliberately let you be falsely accused of a crime?'

'If it got you off a charge.'

'I promise you I had nothing to do with this. I know absolutely nothing about it . . . Did the detective-sergeant detail the evidence?'

'You don't remember what it was? The handkerchief, the glass with my prints on it, the attempt to sell the cup stolen from Reggie Gilles.'

'What cup was stolen from Reggie? What d'you mean by the handkerchief and the glass?'

'Forget the innocent act. Who else is going to bother to try to destroy my character? Who else stands to gain if it is destroyed? No one.'

'Tell me all the facts.'

'You bloody well know them better than I do.'

'I know nothing.'

He didn't want to believe Elham, yet the other's quiet sincerity, following a bewildered amazement that surely would have been difficult to simulate, began to undermine his certainty.

'What exactly did the detective say?'

Rickmore stared at him, still unwilling to admit his accusations might be unfounded, and it was Anne who answered.

Elham listened, saying nothing until she'd finished. 'You

definitely heard someone in the house that night?'

'No. If I'd been certain, I'd have woken Dennis. There was just this noise which wasn't repeated.'

'Did you miss a glass as well as a handkerchief?'

She shrugged her shoulders. 'I can't say how many glasses of each kind we should have; not to the nearest one. You know how it goes—some are smashed and get replaced, some don't—one just doesn't keep count of everyday drinking glasses.'

'Did the detective-sergeant indicate how strong an identification the owner of the antique shop made and how he made it?'

'As far as I can remember, he told us he'd got a photo of Dennis and when a cap and a moustache were shaded in, the owner identified the photo as being of the man who'd tried to sell him the cup.'

'Did he say anything to suggest that the owner was offered several photos of different people to choose from and he picked out this one?'

'I don't think so.' She looked at Rickmore and he shook his head.

Elham drained his glass, put it down on the table, began to pace the floor, passing between his wife and Anne. After a while, he came to a stop and faced Rickmore. 'I swear I did not have anything at all to do with this burglary—that was clearly designed to destroy your credibility as a witness.'

'Who else would have fixed it?'

'Precisely. When the only possible motive uniquely concerns myself . . . It could only have been one person.'

Elham entered chambers and stood in the doorway of the clerks' room. Arnold was on the phone, Betty was typing. ''Morning, Mr Elham,' she said.

''Morning. Tell Tom I want a word with him as soon as he's finished.'

She showed her surprise at so unnecessary an instruction —Arnold always reported in the morning.

In his room, Elham crossed to the window and looked down at the small square. He had no doubts, but until the facts had been confirmed he could not begin to try to find a way out of the seemingly hopeless position in which he and Rickmore now found themselves. If things remained as they were, he would go free, but Rickmore would be charged with burglary and probably be found guilty. He could not and would not let that happen. But the alternative was for him to tell the truth about the accident and then he himself would be on a criminal charge. He dare not let that happen . . .

Arnold entered the room. 'Good morning, sir.'

Arnold was looking old, Elham thought, yet he was not quite sixty. But then he'd probably never looked young. 'Sit down.' He walked over to his desk.

Arnold moved one of the chairs and set it in front of the desk.

Elham said: 'You fixed for someone to fake evidence which would inculpate my brother-in-law on a charge of burglary.'

There was a long silence.

'Didn't you?'

'I had to,' Arnold replied, pleading for understanding. 'I had to try to make certain that if he went into court, the jury wouldn't believe him.'

'Who planted the evidence?'

'A man called Dean. Two years ago, Mr Vernay defended him and got him off, against the evidence. He was so pleased that he said if either of us ever needed help, we had only to ask.'

'You told him what to do?'

'Yes. I tried very hard to work out how best to arrange things.'

'And succeeded a damned sight too well.'

'How d'you mean?'

'Mr Rickmore, when he learned the dead man was a rapist, decided to change his evidence . . .'

'To . . . to change it?'

'In my favour. But now the evidence you had planted is strong enough to have Mr Rickmore found guilty, despite the inherent unlikelihood of someone in his position turning to burglary.'

Arnold was uninterested in Rickmore's problems.

'So now either he tells the truth and I end up in court, or he doesn't and he ends up in court.'

'You?'

'Yes.'

'You can't . . .'

'I can't keep quiet and see him jailed.'

Arnold struggled to understand this sudden development, one he had entirely failed to foresee. He stared with anguish at Elham. 'I didn't . . . I didn't realize . . . I'll go to the police and tell them what I've done.'

'Then you'll have to explain about the car accident as well as the burglary, since your confession can only carry validity if your motive's fully explained.'

'But . . . but . . .'

'And do you think that anyone, in the light of all the facts as others will see them, will ever believe you acted entirely on your own initiative? The net result of your going to the police would just be a further charge of attempting to pervert the course of justice.'

'Then what am I to do?'

'God knows! But if you get any bright ideas, tell me what they are before you do anything . . . That's all.'

Arnold stared beseechingly at Elham, then stood and shuffled out of the room.

Elham returned to the window and once more stared

down at the square. A man, red bag in his hand, was just passing out of sight through the archway at the far end. Tewksbury-Smith, thought Elham, identifying him by the very characteristic way in which he walked with his head thrown back. A contemporary, whose career his own had closely parallelled, even to the fact that he was taking Silk at the same time . . . Or would have been, had the rapist not suddenly run out on to the road in a scene that was replayed again and again in his tortured mind . . . Again and again. Again and again. Had he discovered a way of escape?

CHAPTER 22

The rain, driven by a north-east wind, beat against the window of the sitting-room of Oak Tree Cottage. Intermittently, there was the teeth-twitching sound of an unpruned rose trail scratching at the glass.

They heard neither the rain nor the rose trail; only Elham as he explained the situation.

'That's how things stand,' he said finally. He took a handkerchief from his pocket and lightly wiped his mouth.

Rickmore was silent for a while, then he said: 'If your chief clerk confesses to the police what really happened, I'll be in the clear?'

'You would be, if he were believed.'

'Why shouldn't he be?'

'Because Dean, the man who carried out the burglary, will naturally deny everything and then Arnold's evidence will be uncorroborated. In those circumstances, he'll only be believed if his motive is obviously strong enough to make it likely he's telling the truth.'

'In other words, if he says he did it in order to incriminate me so that my evidence against you wouldn't be believed?'

'Yes.'

'Which makes it obvious that it was your car which ran down the rapist?'

'Yes.'

'Then what you're really saying is that one of us will be prosecuted?'

'On the face of things.' He paused, then said, very hurriedly: 'But so that there's no room for doubt, if one of us is to be prosecuted, I will make quite certain that it is not you.'

'I don't understand,' said Anne. 'One moment you say it has to be one or other of you, the next you say "if" it is.'

'A criminal case is usually concerned very much more with the evidence than the law, as opposed, for instance, to a complicated company case. The laws of evidence—which among other things lay down what is and what is not admissible—are very arcane and even to us lawyers not always certain. Added to this is the fact that the evidence often does not carry in the minds of the jurors the weight it should and would in an ordered and trained mind. That's why there'll often be a situation where the police are properly satisfied a man committed a crime, but the case never appears in court. Bitter experience has shown them that it's certain either some vital piece of evidence will be held to be inadmissible, or the jury, with their untrained, emotional, and frequently illogical minds, will incorrectly interpret the evidence in the accused's favour. Because of this, I think . . .' He stopped.

'You think what?'

'I think the value of the evidence against you can be undermined.'

'How?'

'By making certain it would be incorrectly interpreted in your favour.'

'That's impossible. When the detective listed it all, he almost had me believing I must have done it.'

'Difficult, not impossible.' He was plainly nervous and uncertain and there was a suggestion of humility in his manner. 'There is one way in which both of us can escape prosecution. But it would mean your taking a risk.'

'Both of us escape?'

'If it's certain the DPP would decide it would be stupid to bring a charge of burglary against you because no jury would ever find you guilty, the police won't be able to blackmail you into telling the truth about the night of the accident.'

'How much of a risk?' demanded Anne.

'Probably very little. Obviously, though, something can always go wrong.'

'What are you asking Dennis to do?'

Elham did not immediately answer her. He faced Rickmore and spoke quickly. 'I know we've never got on too well together. And so maybe you'd rather not risk anything. If so, I've told you, I'll tell the police the truth about the accident. But if you could do this . . .' He came to a stop. He was unwilling to plead any further, not because of pride, but because he did not want to seem to be using emotional pressure to persuade.

Anne looked at Rickmore and it was that look, more than anything Elham had said, which decided him. 'I'll give it a go.'

Rickmore had read many personal accounts of going into battle and he had often wondered how he would feel in the moments immediately before an action began. Now he thought he knew. Sick with fear.

He hid the bicycle in a clump of brambles and then listened for any sounds which might suggest that he had been spotted. He discovered that the night had a thousand tongues. A sound to the right convinced him all was over before it had begun; but the sound was repeated and he now identified it as some small animal, frantically scuttling away. Seconds later, a more distant sound made him freeze, but that turned out to be a bulling cow, declaring her passion. He shifted his weight and a twig snapped, sounding to his straining ears like a rifle shot . . .

He moved forward and almost tripped as a bramble trail caught his right foot. When he regained his balance, he could feel the sweat under his armpits. He'd been crazy to agree to this nightmare. He hadn't been under any obligation. Dammit, he didn't even like Elham. Elham had shown himself to be a coward and a traitor, ready to betray the law he served . . . Rickmore's right hand, which he'd been holding out in front of him, banged into the bole of a tree and he exclaimed aloud from the shock, not the very brief pain. Christ! he thought, a fool hits not the same tree that a wise man sees.

He briefly shone the torch ahead of him, the bowl carefully masked with tape to narrow the beam. Immediately to his right was the tree he'd just encountered, five feet further on was a hedge, beautifully cut and laid. So he'd reached the edge of the rough land and ahead was the field which led up to the garden of Heskthorne House.

Elham had said that the Moffats were on holiday in France. He hoped to God that was right. He'd only met Moffat once, but that had been sufficient to convince him that he was a man who'd pull both triggers of a twelve-bore before he asked what the intruder wanted.

He clambered over the hedge, snagging his trousers on one of the uprights around which the laid branches were woven. He moved forward into the field and there was a snort from his right and the sounds of several animals moving. Cows. He remembered the friend of Anne's whose herd of Ayrshires had suddenly and for no discernible reason attacked her, inflicting serious injuries. His mind had become a forcing ground for catastrophes.

The field was not large and he soon reached the tall yew hedge which surrounded the garden. A hundred yards to the right was a wooden gate, and looking over this he could see the black bulk of the house, just discernible against the clear, star-studded sky. There was a light on upstairs. Elham had said that there would be. The Moffats used time-switches in different parts of the house to give the impression of active habitation. But what if this light had not been activated by a time-switch, but by someone brought in to house-sit . . . ?

He pulled on a pair of gloves, opened the gate, and passed through. A grass verge ran the length of the kitchen garden and ended at a gravel path; just before the path, he carefully left a firm footprint in the rich loam. Then he crossed the path as carefully as he could, yet still making so much noise that he doubted whether an elephant could have made more.

To the right of the kitchen door was a window, some four feet above the ground. He picked up a stone and, praying that it was true that the kitchen lay outside the alarm system, threw it through the glass. The explosion of noise terrified him, but after it was over there was nothing to suggest it had alarmed anyone. He knocked away a couple of dangerous slivers of glass, then reached in and pushed the catch up so that the window could be opened inwards. He climbed over the sill. And as he stood in the kitchen, the unwelcome thought came to him of how ironic it was that he, a man who had always believed in the law, should now be committing burglary . . .

Elham had described the alarm system, explaining that Moffat had asked him what kind to install and he had suggested the same make and type as was in Popham House.

The kitchen was large and equipped with every conceivable piece of electrical equipment, including an extremely large refrigerator of American make. Immediately to the left of this was a built-in cupboard and in the cupboard was a wooden box which contained two switches, two pilot lights, one red, one green, and ten numbered buttons like those found on a simple pocket calculator. To de-activate the alarm system, which sounded not only in the house but also in the nearest police station, it was necessary to punch in a six-figure code before pushing one switch up and the other down. Get the code wrong and within minutes a police car would arrive . . . Moffat, a man with a very poor memory, had—so Elham swore—chosen the numbers of his birthday. Rickmore punched out one four one ten one seven. The green light went out, the red one came on. He pressed one switch up, the other down, reversing the positions in which they had been.

Mouth dry, heart thumping, he crossed to the far door and opened this. The alarm stayed silent. He stepped into the passage.

Moffat had been an administrator in the Colonial Service —which explained his aggressive manner—and when in West Africa he'd made a small but good collection of carved wooden masks which now hung on the walls of the sitting-room; Rickmore picked off the two smallest ones and put them on a chair. At the far end of the room, to the left of the fireplace, was a cupboard and on the shelves of this was a wide selection of bottles and glasses. He chose a bottle of Glenfiddich and put it on an unusually shaped table, carved out of a single piece of heavily grained wood. He brought from his coat pocket a glass which had been protected with bubbled plastic wrapping. He unwrapped the glass and placed it by the bottle, returned the wrapping to his pocket, poured just enough whisky into the glass to make it appear it had been used.

The library was traditional in style, with two alcoves. The safe was in one of the alcoves, concealed by panelling which matched that around the rest of the room. He left the concealing wooden door open. Finally, he dropped a handkerchief near the beautifully inlaid partner's desk.

After collecting up the two wooden masks, he returned to the kitchen. He crossed to the alarm control box and reversed the positions of the switches; the red light went out and the green one came on.

He went over to the door leading into the passageway he'd just come down, took a very deep breath, and opened the door. Immediately, the alarm sounded.

He left the house, assuring himself that more haste meant less speed, but nevertheless moving far more quickly than conditions—but not the thought of the approaching police car—warranted.

The gates of Popham House were shut, but not locked, and he opened the right-hand one and wheeled the bike through. Keeping within the cover of the garage—to obviate the very slight risk that one of the Cavajals was awake and looking out of a window—he returned the bike to the small lumber room at the back of the garage.

Elham, his face puffy from tension, met him in the kitchen. 'Well?' he demanded hoarsely.

'I've grown a wonderful crop of ulcers, but there was no alarm until the end.'

'Thank God!'

'Where's Anne?'

'I tried to persuade her to go to bed, but she wouldn't. She's fallen asleep on the settee.'

'Then I'll wake her up and inform her that she won't have to visit me in jail in the morning . . . But first, I could use a whisky in the biggest glass you've got.'

Elham's need was no less.

CHAPTER 23

DC Wrybot—his surname was a constant source of childish ribaldy in the CID general room—entered the DI's room. ''Morning, skipper.'

'If you insist,' muttered Ridley, who had had a heavy night with his wife and two other married couples.

'I thought you'd want to know that there was a break-in at Polhurst last night.'

'So why get excited?'

'The property belongs to Moffat, who they say is some sort of bigwig on the county council.'

Ridley swore. 'And I suppose now he's yelling blue murder and wants the whole bloody Force switched to his case?'

'Probably would if he knew about it, but he's on holiday in France somewhere. The lucky sod.'

'Was much nicked?'

'There's been no word through on that yet.'

'Find out.'

'But I am busy . . .'

'Do as you're told without bloody arguing.'

Pardon me for living, thought Wrybot, as he left.

County HQ rang to ask why hadn't they received the weekly T254 forms? Ridley replied that he'd posted them the previous evening, as he stared at them by the side of the blotter. After the call was over, he began to fill them in. He no longer wondered why MacMahon had always looked harassed. He'd been working for less than five minutes when the telephone rang again. He swore, but it kept on ringing.

'Midge here, skipper,' said Wrybot. 'I'm phoning from Heskthorne House. According to the daily, all that was nicked was two wooden masks that were hanging on the wall. Bloody ugly things if they were anything like the ones that are left. Anyway, that's all she can tell us about and it doesn't look as if we'll know any more until the owners get back. Chummy found the safe, with the family jewels inside —so the daily says—but he didn't do anything about it. And that's odd, really, since a sectional jemmy would have opened it up as easy as you like.'

A thought began to form in Ridley's mind, but then Wrybot spoke again and the thought failed to coalesce.

'He was either cool or bloody nervous. Helped himself to a whisky; Glenfiddich, no less!' Wrybot chuckled. 'Cool or nervous, he was careless. They found a hankie near the desk in the library and the daily swears it's nothing to do with her and wasn't there the last time she did that room.'

Ridley suddenly realized what that half-formed thought a moment ago had been signposting. 'Is there a laundry mark?'

'As a matter of fact, yeah, there is. I was just about to say . . .'

'Is it R one four four?'

'Jeez . . . How the hell d'you know that?'

'Because I'm bloody psychic, that's how. And I'll tell you something else. Somewhere outside, there's a nice clear footprint of Chummy.'

'If you know it all, skipper, why bother to send me out?'

'Because now you're going to search the place so hard that if a single grain of dust fell off Chummy, you'll find it. I'll send a couple of lads along to help.'

'All this for a job where only a couple of wooden masks have been nicked . . . Skipper, you wouldn't be thinking of standing for the council, would you?'

'Stop trying to be bloody smart . . . And get the bottle of whisky and the glass off to Dabs.'

'Will do . . . By the way, I was due to collect a couple of

witnesses' statements this morning from over Delsham way. What shall I do about them?'

'Forget 'em.'

'The pleasure's all mine.'

After he'd replaced the receiver, Ridley balled his fist and slammed it down on the desk in a display of impotent anger. This was one move he had not foreseen.

The fingerprint laboratory rang on Wednesday morning. The whisky bottle and glass had been checked for prints and comparison tests had been made. Several prints, from two different persons, were on the bottle; none of them had been made by the named person. The glass had been wiped clean at some recent time and there had been only one set of prints on it; these had been made by the named person.

Ridley turned off the road and into the yard of Oak Tree Cottage, where he parked. He and Wrybot climbed out.

'Neat little place,' said Wrybot, as they began walking. 'Give me half a chance and I'll be living in somewhere like this.' When there was no comment, he looked sideways at the detective-sergeant. Sour, he thought; like the girlfriend's quince jelly.

Ridley opened the gate and led the way round the brick path to the porch. He was about to ring the bell when Anne stepped into the porch and opened the outside door. 'I'd like a word with your husband,' he said curtly. 'I tried to ring him at the office, but they said he was ill.'

'That's right.'

'Not too ill, I imagine, to answer a few questions?'

'I can find out.' She showed them into the sitting-room, carefully reminding them both to duck their heads as they went in and to beware of the central beam once inside. She then offered them coffee, but Rickmore bad-temperedly refused.

'Then do sit down while I go and see how my husband's feeling now.' She left, closing the door behind herself.

Wrybot looked up at the beams. 'I really go for these, skipper.'

'Yeah?'

'It's a bit of history, like.'

'Never could stand the subject.'

Wrybot briefly wondered what was bugging the DS so hard, then let his mind wander. He was on holiday with his girlfriend, enjoying most of the pleasures that life had to offer, when footsteps overhead jerked his mind back to reality. Very soon afterwards, Anne returned with Rickmore who, Wrybot decided, did not look particularly ill.

'Sorry to be a bit of time,' said Rickmore, 'but I was lying down . . . My wife says you've refused coffee. Would you prefer a drink?'

'No, thanks,' replied Ridley, angered by their courtesy. 'We're investigating a burglary which took place on Monday. A house at Polhurst belonging to Sir Rupert Moffat was broken into. Do you know him?'

'We've met him and his wife once, but I think that's all.'

'Did you meet them at their house?'

'No, we've never been there. It was at a home belonging to mutual friends.'

'The intruder smashed a window to get in and then neutralized the alarm system. The method of entry was crude, but the alarm system is sophisticated and to deactivate it one has to punch in six figures on a control board. Obviously, the possible combinations are far too many for anyone to punch in the right one by chance. So the intruder had to know the correct code. This all says something, doesn't it?'

'I'm afraid I don't follow.'

'It says that the intruder didn't know much about housebreaking, but he did know a lot about the Moffats.'

'That sounds logical.'

'He found the safe, but didn't do anything about it. Yet any half-competent peterman with a sectional jemmy would have ripped it open inside five minutes. So he doesn't know much about safe-cracking either. Is this all beginning to sound rather familiar?'

'Should it?'

'He helped himself to a whisky and left the bottle and glass out, making it obvious. He dropped a handkerchief, which happened to have a laundry mark. He planted a footprint in the kitchen garden ... Now has the penny dropped?'

'It sounds a bit like that other burglary.'

'Exactly similar. And just to make certain we weren't so dumb we didn't get the message, there were fingerprints on the glass.'

'Presumably that makes things easier for you?'

'The laundry mark was yours and the prints were yours.'

'Impossible.'

'Why won't you understand something? I'm not as thick as you'd bloody like me to be. I know that you broke into Heskthorne House, not to nick whatever was going, but to leave those clues.'

'When they appear to inculpate me? I'd have to be mad to do that.'

'Or trying to save both your brother-in-law's and your own skins.'

'How in the wide world do you bring him into it?'

'How d'you bloody think? ... Understand something. I'm going to prove it was you. Not with the clues you wanted us to find, but with the ones you don't even know about. No one ever goes anywhere, or does anything, without leaving traces; I'll find 'em, if it takes me a bloody month of Sundays.'

'You hate my husband,' said Anne.

About to reply that he'd cause to, Ridley realized just in time that to do so would be both stupid and dangerous.

'You're twisting everything he says.'

'I've stated facts, nothing more.'

'The fact is,' said Rickmore, 'if a glass with my prints on it and a handkerchief with our laundry mark appeared in a house that's been burgled, someone is obviously trying to inculpate me.'

'That was true the first time, but not now. You've deliberately pointed the finger at yourself in the belief that it will never be accepted that anyone in his right senses would deliberately incriminate himself twice.'

'When was this burglary?'

'You know that just as well as me. You re-activated the alarm when you'd finished, to make certain that the police had a time. No doubt you're now going to offer an alibi?'

'I can't answer that until I know the time.'

'A quarter to one on Tuesday morning.' Ridley's voice became thick with sarcasm. 'Presumably you're now going to tell me that your wife will vouch for the fact that you were in this house at that time?'

'No, she won't do that.'

The answer completely surprised him. It was several seconds before he said: 'You don't have an alibi?'

'I do. But not one based on this house. That night, we had dinner at my brother-in-law's and stayed on very late.'

Ridley's confidence returned. 'You're hoping his evidence will carry a bit more weight than your wife's?'

'I imagine so, since his wife was there as well. That makes three people who can vouch that I'm telling the truth.'

'You're so goddamn naïve ... They've all as much motive to lie as you have. They couldn't alibi Father Christmas.'

'Are you suggesting that not even the evidence of all three of them is sufficient?'

'I'm suggesting exactly that.'

'Then who would satisfy you? St Peter?'

'No need to bother him. Just give me someone who's even half-way independent.'

'How about Arnold?'

'Who?'

'Mr Elham's chief clerk. There was some problem that needed thrashing out, so Arnold came down and stayed at Popham House on Monday night. He and Mr Elham left us after dinner and went up to the study; they didn't come down until considerably later. Then, when we said we ought to go, my brother-in-law said he'd hardly had a chance to have a word with us and he persuaded us to stay on. I don't know what the time was when we left, except it was after one.'

Ridley knew a growing bitter frustration.

CHAPTER 24

A DC from the Metropolitan police telephoned Ridley on Friday. 'Reference your request to question Thomas Arnold. I'm just back from having a word with him. He states categorically that Rickmore and his wife were at Popham House all evening and didn't leave there until sometime after one on Tuesday morning.'

'The bastard's got to be lying.'

There was a short pause, then the DC said: 'He was pretty confident.'

'I don't care how confident, he was bloody lying.' Ridley forced himself to calm down. 'What's he like; how would he make out in a witness-box?'

'He's a funny old boy—all dust and antique. But I reckon if you matched him against a mule, you'd soon hear the mule shout uncle.'

Ridley swore.

*

Mrs MacMahon opened the front door of her house. She smiled. 'Hullo, Steve, nice to see you again. Come to have a word with Jim?'

'If he's up to it?'

'He's much better, especially since they say now that he did have a heart attack, but it was so minor that if he leads a sensible life he won't know any more about it. Of course, being him, he started talking about returning to work immediately, but I soon put a stop to that . . . But come on in instead of standing there and listening to me going on and on. The thing is, it's such a weight off my mind that half the time I feel as if I'd had a fix.' She laughed. 'Jim says I'm acting as giddy as when he first met me. Too much extra weight for anything like that, I told him.'

MacMahon was in the greenhouse in the back garden. 'I'm getting ready for Spring,' he said, pointing to a propagator. He studied Ridley. 'You're beginning to look like a man with responsibilities.'

'Frustrations.'

'The two go together, like corruption and politicians. And the best way of coping with 'em is to have a beer—and a fag, if the wife's not around to see me.'

They went into the kitchen, where MacMahon picked up two cans of beer, and then on through to the sitting-room. He handed Ridley a can. 'You don't mind managing without a glass, I hope? I'm doing the washing-up these days, so I keep it down as far as possible.' He sat, pulled the tab off the can, and drank. 'OK, so what's got you more frustrated than a eunuch in a harem?'

Ridley told him.

'You know something?' said MacMahon. 'You've largely got yourself to blame.'

'What the hell for?'

'For things being as they are now. Remember me saying softlee, softlee?'

'Not that again?'

'You pushed 'em too hard, too quickly. You squeezed 'em into a corner so that they had to do something dramatic if they were to do anything. If you'd moved slowly, maybe appearing a little soft as if you'd not understood what had been going on, they'd have assumed they were safe and their guards would have been down and then, like as not, you'd have been able to dig up something really incriminating that would have nailed Elham.'

Ridley said heatedly: 'You say I've made a balls-up. But it doesn't matter how smart they've been, I'll show 'em I'm smarter. I'll get 'em.'

MacMahon looked quizzically at him, then stood and went over to the low bookshelf which was filled with book-club volumes. He brought out the first three volumes to reveal a pack of cigarettes. He offered this, then helped himself to one, replaced the pack and the books, and returned to his chair after accepting a light from Ridley. 'How?'

'How what?'

'How are you going to get them? How are you going to persuade a jury that any man in his right mind is going to lay a trail that points directly at himself?'

'By setting out the facts.'

MacMahon shook his head.

'Why not?'

'Can you prove Elham was driving the car which ran down Tamworth so long as Rickmore sticks to his present evidence?'

'No.'

'Then you're left with charging Rickmore. At his trial, evidence concerning Elham's hit-and-run is inadmissible. And if you can't show that that's the thread which binds together the hit-and-run case, the burglary at Gilles's place which appeared to have been committed by Rickmore but wasn't, and the burglary at Heskthorne House that was committed by him, you can't begin to offer a logical explanation of why Rickmore should deliberately incriminate himself.'

'It's bloody obvious.'

'To you and me, but not to any jury. And something else. You're faced with an alibi—four people prepared to swear that at the time of the burglary, Rickmore was in Popham House.'

'Four people all with a motive for seeing Rickmore gets off.'

'What are their motives?'

'Rickmore's wife is trying to protect him, Elham wants to save him in case he decides to tell the truth about the hit-and-run case, and Elham's wife is naturally backing up her husband.'

'And Arnold?' MacMahon tapped ash from the cigarette into the palm of his other hand. 'Who's not a relative by blood or marriage so that there's no obvious link to make him lie.'

'He works for Elham.'

'Not strong enough.'

'Well, it's obvious, isn't it? He helped rig the first burglary.'

'How do you go about proving that, which you must do to break the image of him as an independent witness?'

'By showing what . . .' He stopped.

'By showing what was his motive for helping Elham? But such evidence would be inadmissible in a trial of Rickmore for burglary.'

'All right, then,' said Ridley violently, 'add in the first burglary. Between them . . .'

'Put the two together and the proposition that Rickmore's twice left behind the same incriminating evidence becomes patently absurd . . . And, as a matter of interest, would you like to have it brought out in court that you've held back evidence?'

'I've done what?'

'Is it in the official records that the prints on the mug were Rickmore's and they matched the prints on the glasses found at the two burglaries?'

'I . . . Maybe I . . .'

'Maybe you've held that information back, hoping to use it to pressure Rickmore into telling the truth?'

There was a long silence. MacMahon drank some beer. As he put the can down, there was a sound from outside the room and he quickly held the cigarette ready to throw into the fireplace in an attempt to hide from his wife the fact that he had been smoking. But a moment later they heard her go up the stairs and he relaxed. 'There's something else you need to consider. How'd you feel in the witness-box, faced by a counsel determined and delighted to prove how inefficiently you've handled the case?'

'Come off it,' said Ridley angrily.

'Handled inefficiently because you've allowed yourself to be blinded by your dislike of the people involved.'

'What are you getting at?'

'Rickmore's wife spoke of hearing someone in their house on the Wednesday night, the suggestion being that an intruder stole the handkerchief and a glass bearing Rickmore's prints, to plant in Gilles's house. Did you have the other prints on the glass checked to see if they were Mrs Rickmore's?'

'No.'

'Did you check whether the glass matched others in the burgled house, or, alternatively, those in Oak Tree Cottage?'

'No.'

'Remember the bottle? There weren't any prints of Rickmore's on it. Why not? He wasn't wearing gloves when he handled the glass. Presumably, you wouldn't try to suggest that he wore gloves to pick up the bottle, but took them off to pick up the glass?'

'For Christ's sake, which side are you batting for?'

'Although you sound as if you'd have trouble understanding right now, yours. I don't want to see you ruin your career.'

'But you don't mind seeing them get off scot free?'

'They won't.'

'If they never appear in court, they goddamn will.'

MacMahon shook his head. He drank and emptied the can, drew on the cigarette and then leaned over to stub it out in the ashtray that Ridley was using. 'They're not villains, they're just ordinary people who got caught up in a situation where cowardice, stupidity, fear and a mistaken sense of loyalty, drove them to breaking the law. They're people whose entire lives would be shattered by being found guilty of a crime. So from now on they'll be living in fear that one day some extra piece of evidence will come to light that will be enough to shoot one or both of them into court. And on top of that, it's an odd thing, but in my experience people who commit crimes almost always suffer some kind of a loss, never mind what the state does to them. I sometimes think it must be an outside force which makes certain all of us pay a penalty for our misdeeds.'

To Ridley's bitter anger, there was now added contempt for such Holy-Joe philosophy.

It was February 18th. In the main bedroom of Popham House, Penelope drew her dress up over her shoulders, hung it on a hanger, put it in one of the built-in cupboards. Elham, already in bed, watched her and experienced a growing desire. She took off her lace-edged petticoat and dropped this into the Ali-Baba basket by the side of her dressing-table; she never wore underwear more than once. She reached up behind her back and unclipped her brassière, removed it, put it in the hamper. She had pert breasts, with prominent nipples and generous areolæ. He imagined his fingers caressing her nipples and his mouth dried. She slid off her pants and put those in the basket, bent down to pick up the lid which she put in place. Obviously aware of the intensity with which he was regarding her, she walked over to her bed, unzipped the bag in the shape of an elephant, and brought out her frothy and very expensive nightdress.

'Leave that and come over here,' he said thickly.

'No. It's been a heavy day and I'm tired.' She slipped on the nightdress and climbed into bed.

By her actions and the way in which she had spoken, he understood something which should have been clear to him before. Until the accident, he had always been proud of her, not least because she aroused envy in other men, but he had condescendingly assumed his superiority; this superiority had made him the dominant partner. She had accepted her subservience. But after the accident, he had shown himself to be weak and she had proved herself to be strong. His dominion had been destroyed, just as she had ceased to be subservient. And because she had grown strong at his expense, she was now going to deny him her body as well as her passion in revenge for the past.

He stared up at the ceiling and in his mind saw Lucy, naked, passionate, and he knew an impotent desire so strong that it was pain.

Anne said: 'Do I dare risk offering you a penny for them?'

Rickmore jerked his mind back to the present and looked across the sitting-room at her.

'Or are your thoughts too interesting to be traded for sordid money?'

He smiled.

'You'd rather not tell me?'

'I don't remember what I was thinking.'

'You're a very poor liar. Your ears give you away because they wiggle.'

'Rubbish!'

'Was she blonde or brunette?'

'A redhead, with a body to make the Venus de Milo go on a crash diet.'

'No hands? What a pity. Cuts out so much of the fun . . . In fact, it wasn't a woman, was it? You were looking sad, not lustful. What's the trouble?' Her tone was no longer light and bantering; now it was soft and comforting. 'Were you mourning your lost principles?'

He looked at her with uneasy surprise.

She stood, crossed to his chair, kissed him. 'It's not a total disaster, you know. One good result is, it makes you more at one with the rest of us.'

'"Damn your principles! Stick to your party."?'

'Perhaps . . . Come on, love, let's move and go to bed.' She kissed him again.

He stood and reached out for the fire-guard to put in front of the fire which had burned low. He wondered how long it would be before he could stick to his party without any regrets.

The End

THE CAPE MURDERS

BY

DOLORES WEEKS

Published by special arrangement with Dodd, Mead & Co.

For Allen

**With Special Thanks to
Zola Helen Ross**

One

Dr. Scott Eason was on the deck of his summer cabin, soaking up the morning sun and trying hard not to think about the surgical practice he'd walked away from in Seattle, when Al Turner burst in, his bony chest rising and falling in great gulps. Al was a retired professor of ancient history and in pretty good shape for a man in his mid-seventies, but right now he looked like an out-of-breath scarecrow.

"Come . . . quick . . . Scottie. S-somebody shot Owen . . . Went . . . worth."

It was, of course, exactly the sort of thing Scott was trying to avoid. The trouble was, Al looked desperate. Scott squeezed into his tennis shoes and slipped on a shirt. "Did you run all the way?"

Al nodded, not wasting his breath on an answer.

"Dumb thing to do!" The old man could easily have a coronary running in the heat, and a dozen Owen Wentworths weren't worth one Al Turner.

Scott snatched the key to the Jeep from the kitchen table and started for the door. The large black and white sheep dog that had been lying beside him on the deck rose to follow. "Not this time, Dandy."

It was a little under a mile, over dirt and rock roads, to Owen's cabin. There were strict rules on the island about driving speeds in the dust season. Scott broke them all. "How bad is it?" he asked as they bumped along, stirring up a thick cloud behind them.

Al set his thin lips in a grimace and shook his head. "Don't know," he said, getting his wind back slowly. "Millie ran out of Owen's place . . . said to get you quick. You know Millie—takes a lot to unnerve her."

It was a strong indication of trouble, Scott agreed, and he pressed his foot harder on the accelerator. Scott could think of a dozen people in Seattle who might enjoy inflicting bodily harm on the high-living attorney, but this wasn't Seattle. This was a quiet summer community on Cape San Juan.

Owen's house stood in a small stand of wind-shorn firs, isolated from its nearest neighbor by a hundred feet of sand, grass, and brush. It was a flat-topped rambler, fair in size for the Cape, with a wide deck that hung over the rocks, the beach ten feet below. Large picture windows and skylight bubbles everywhere made it look like a plastic box.

Scott and the professor piled out of the Jeep and raced toward the house. Millie Rogers poked her gray head from around the breezeway.

"In there," she said in a high-pitched quivering voice as she pointed to the door. She was ghostly pale and shivering, even though the temperature was already in the seventies. Millie was the day woman from Friday Harbor who cleaned for most of the summer people on the Cape. She'd been widowed for ten years, raised her teenage daughter herself, and was what Scott thought of as levelheaded. The front door was standing wide open. Scott and Al walked through ahead of her.

The inside reeked of whiskey and tobacco, not an uncommon condition for Owen's place. They found the attorney in the living room, lying in the middle of the big ivory area carpet, his blood spilled all over it.

Al drew in his breath. "Oh, my God!"

Owen was a big man, inclined to overweight and tall, at least three inches taller than Scott, who stood right at six feet. Owen had been good-looking once, but in the last few years dissipation had brought on heavy jowls and puffiness under the eyes. At forty-four, he looked sixty.

2

Right now, Owen, dressed in a brightly flowered sports shirt and jeans, lay out flat on his back, his big head resting on the carpet and his long legs stretched over the carpet fringe onto the oak-planked floor. His mouth was open, and he was staring straight up into one of his skylights. The sun shone down on his stomach. It was ripped open so he looked like one of the rabbits run over on the Cape road. In the ten years Scott had been in surgical practice, he'd developed a necessary objectivity about death and violence, but as he looked at Owen with a hole in his abdomen the size of a baseball, he thought he'd never really get used to it. "Oh, hell!" He sighed.

He pressed a finger to the attorney's neck. No pulse. He pulled back on the eyelid. No corneal reflex. He'd been dead for some time.

Scott shook his head at the professor. "A job for the coroner, I'm afraid."

The old man didn't say a word. He held on to a chair, his small blue eyes glazed over. He looked as if he might be sick.

"Better sit down, Al."

The professor folded up into the chair. "Shotgun?"

Scott nodded. "The only thing I know of that could drive a hole like that. Did anyone call the police?"

"I did," Millie said, picking her way around the potted palm tree, keeping her distance from Owen. She'd come from town that morning to clean for Owen after his party of the night before. "I found him just like that." She tossed her head in Owen's general direction, not looking at him. "Didn't feel I should leave till you came. Must've lost my head. It was the sight of all that blood, and those eyes, staring at nothing. I called Leroy. That was twenty minutes ago. Can't imagine what's keeping him. He was only coming from Friday Harbor. Doesn't take that long, the way *he* drives. I would've cleaned up this mess, but Leroy said I wasn't to touch a thing." She stared at the room sorrowfully.

Scott laid an arm around the slender shoulders and gave her a squeeze. "You did fine, Millie." He signaled the professor with his eyes, but the old man wasn't looking too good himself and didn't pick up on it. "Al, why don't you take Millie outside to get some air."

"Be happy to," Al said, and, taking Millie by the arm, steered her to the door.

Alone, Scott surveyed the rooms in which Owen had breathed his last. The house said much about the attorney—contemporary, almost everything white, the walls, sectional sofa and chairs, the rug. Even the tables were of glass and blond wood. The only exceptions were the African artifacts displayed throughout the rooms. Owen had been into African art in a big way—carved figures into ebony and ivory, wood ritual objects, masks and headpieces—but his obsession clearly had been death masks. A row of them hung down the hall like inverted clown faces in blacks, whites, and browns. He used to boast he paid a half-million dollars for his collection, surprising because he'd always been such a sharp operator, and African art was a high-risk business.

The house wasn't designed for privacy. Someone standing in the middle of the living room could see directly into the master suite and study. Rumor had it Owen wandered in the nude, giving passing boaters an eyeful, and there were ugly stories about his overnight guests and perversions.

Scott strolled down the marble-tiled hall and looked into the bedroom. Everything in place. Beds not slept in. The kitchen was a different story. Three empty fifths of Gordon's gin, two large empty bottles of Seagram's, and a half-empty bottle of Ballentyne's stood on the counter that divided the kitchen from the living area. The ice buckets were full of water, and a tray of leftover shrimp and crabs' legs were starting to smell up the dining room. The ashtrays spilled cigarette butts onto the floor, and unwashed highball glasses were putting rings on the tables.

Al returned and stood tentatively in the entryway. "I left Millie on the beach. She'll be all right. Sea air was just what she needed."

They heard the siren first, then tires braking on gravel. A car door slammed. Al grinned. "Big Buck has arrived."

Leroy Freeman walked in with his usual air of self-importance. The Colt .38 was strapped to his side and the Stetson firmly planted on his head. He took one look at Owen. "Dead?"

Scott nodded. "I'd say four or five hours."

"I better call Frank."

Leroy strode into the kitchen, barked orders over the phone to the mortician in Friday Harbor. "It's going to run in the eighties today, so get a move on." It was the only indication the sheriff was upset. He studied Owen a moment, then glanced out the window. "Tide's changing." He removed his hat and mopped the brown strands of hair that matted around his temples, exposing a thin line of pale skin on his otherwise darkly tanned face. "Hot in here." He dropped the hat on the sofa and faced Scott. "Shotgun!"

Scott nodded. "Fired at close range. Pushed pieces of his pants into the abdominal cavity."

"Anything else?"

"Struck an artery, ruptured the spleen. Died in five, ten minutes."

"Painful?"

"Damn."

Leroy walked around the room, took in the mess. "Quite a party. You one of the guests?"

"No."

Leroy turned to the professor.

"Don't look at me," Al snapped. "I was *not* a friend of Owen Wentworth."

"Where's Millie?"

"Outside."

"Call her in, would you?"

Scott and Al exchanged glances.

"Don't you want to cover him up first, Sheriff?" Al said.

"Oh, hell." Leroy stalked down the hall to the bedroom

wing and started opening doors. He rummaged through the linen closet until he found a sheet, pulled it out, and draped it over the body so only Owen's sandaled feet stuck out the end. "Now, do you suppose we can get Millie in here?"

Millie's eyes went right to the spot. She relaxed when she saw the sheet. Yes, she said, she had a key to the house. Had keys to most of the houses on the Cape, since very often she cleaned after the summer people left for the mainland. As a general rule, she liked to air the places between cleanings. "Houses closed up get musty. A little sea breeze does wonders for sweetening the air. Owen's was the worst for bad air. Cigar smoke. Enough to make a person sick. Real bad this morning. My sinuses started acting up soon as I opened the door. Don't know how I'll ever get the blood off that rug. Never could keep it clean. Always getting liquor spilled on it. Whole house is like that. A mess after one of his weekends."

"He entertained a lot?"

A smile tugged at Millie's lips. "Long as I been cleaning for the man—going on six years next month—it's been one party after another."

"Ever been to one of these parties?"

"Sometimes I served if he was having a sit-down dinner."

"And last night?"

"That was one of his drinking affairs."

"Who came?"

"I wouldn't know. I never went to those."

"Not any of them?"

"No."

"What about the dinner parties?"

"I never thought it my business to keep a list."

Leroy tried pinning her down, but Millie had a code, and no amount of persuading swayed her.

"So all of the Cape and half the island could've been on his guest list?" Leroy said in an irritated voice.

"It's possible."

Leroy threw Millie a disgusted look and went back to

questioning the professor. Al repeated what he'd told Scott. He was on his usual morning stroll, returning from American Camp, about nine-thirty, when he ran into Millie on the road. She told him to get the doctor, that Owen had been shot. He didn't stop to ask questions. He just rushed right over to get Scott.

Leroy whipped out a notepad from his back pocket and began writing. "You passed the house twice?"

"That's right."

"What time was it on your first pass?"

Al thought a moment. "Eight, or thereabouts."

"Takes you that long to walk from American Camp?"

"I stopped at the digs."

"Did you see anything different when you were walking?"

"Mmm. Saw the big bald eagle circle over the lighthouse. A small doe sprang out of that grove of Norwegian pine on Chapman's drive."

Leroy sighed impatiently. "*Hear* anything?"

"Heard the gill-netters going back from Eagle Cove. Sherman's roosters were crowing. Heard the jets taking off from McCord."

"Hear anything like a shot?"

"No, but I don't think I would with the noise of the big diesels. And those jets sound like a bolt of thunder sometimes. Hard to hear anything over that."

Leroy wrote it all down. "Anybody touch anything here?"

"No."

Leroy paused in front of one of the death masks. It was particularly hideous, with a ropelike braid that dangled along the pointed jaw to the chin. Perversely, it brought to Scott's mind a hanging.

"Tell me, Doc, what the hell are these things?"

Scott smiled. "African art. Mid–seventeenth century, I think. Some of them represent religious rituals, fertility rites, ceremonial stuff. That one is a death mask."

"Expensive?"

"Very."

7

He shook his head in bewilderment, and Scott felt an instant bond with Leroy.

"How well did you know Wentworth, Doc?"

"About like everyone on the Cape. None of us *really* knew him."

"Why's that? From the looks of things here, he was a very friendly fellow."

"Outwardly, he was affable enough."

"What in hell does *that* mean?"

The professor sniffed impatiently. "What Scottie's trying to tell you is the man was one of those hail-and-well-met boys, who, given half a chance, would pick your pockets and start on your mother-in-law's gold inlays."

"Do you speak from personal knowledge, Professor Turner?" Leroy asked.

"I do not."

"That include you, Doc?"

"No."

Leroy had a tendency to repeat himself. He went over their stories again. "And this morning while you were sunbathing, Doctor, did *you* hear or see anything?"

"No, but I'm quite a distance. I don't think I would."

"Sound carries on the water, particularly a gunshot."

Certainly Scott's neighbors had complained often enough about the music that blared from Owen's stereo on clear nights. Scott didn't say anything.

"What about his next-door neighbors?"

"Fred and Lorene Chapman. They're off the island right now."

"How do you know that?"

"They're friends of mine. I saw them off last Friday."

"How can I get hold of them?"

"You could call Fred at his office in Seattle. He's with Price and Sloan, stockbrokers. I don't think he can help much. He and his wife weren't friendly with Owen."

"Who was?"

Al answered. "A few people around here would go anywhere for a free drink, but Owen was not well loved."

Leroy said he'd check out Fred's cottage for a break-in, just in case this was a simple burglary, although nothing in the condition of the house lent itself to this theory. Scott and Al left.

Al was quiet on the drive back. The sun burned bright overhead. Along the sandy shoulders of the road the pine trees were parched gray, almost black, like the death masks, like Owen's face. Scott knew he ought to feel remorse, but couldn't.

As if reading his mind, the professor said, "Only the good die young. Owen must've been a lot older than I thought."

"Did you know he was throwing a party last night?"

"Didn't even know he was on the island. He usually doesn't roll in until Friday night. This is Thursday, remember?"

"Didn't see him yesterday on your walk?"

"No, but that's not unusual. He always slept till noon."

Scott pulled up in front of the professor's cabin. "I didn't know you walked as far as American Camp every day, Al."

"Anything wrong with that?" The old man's testiness was a sure sign he was still upset.

"No. You have more energy than I, that's all."

"That's nothing to be proud of. Here you are—big strapping fellow—only thirty-five."

"Thirty-seven."

The old man sniffed and said nothing.

"How about dinner?"

The suggestion warmed him up, and he nodded agreement. "But you'll have to come here. I'm not sticking my big toe out tonight."

Scott nodded agreeably. "I'll bring the steaks. How's seven suit you?"

"Suits me fine."

When Scott wheeled the Jeep onto his drive, the sheriff was waiting. Leroy stepped out of the patrol car, wearing a catty expression, and Scott guessed he'd discovered something about Owen's murder. He was holding a small piece of glossy paper,

9

worn on the edges. He handed it to Scott. "I think this belongs to you."

Scott looked at the photograph of a woman's face, and a lump settled painfully in his throat. It was Toni, raven hair, flashing brown eyes, as beautiful and vibrant as the day they'd married. Scott felt the force of Leroy's gaze. He hoped the moisture starting at the corners of his eyes didn't show. "Where?" he said, fighting to keep his voice even. "Where did you get this?"

"Didn't I tell you? I found it in Owen Wentworth's wallet."

Two

The thought of Toni and Owen brought an ache to Scott's chest. He couldn't believe it. Yet, looking back over the last year, it fit in many ways—her drinking, running up to their cabin by herself when she professed to hate the island, swings in her moods, not her normal pattern at all. And there'd been someone. He'd known that.

Leroy's voice came from a great distance. "Any reason your wife's picture would turn up in Owen's wallet?"

Scott shook his head in bewilderment. "We were separated before . . . before—" Scott cleared his throat and tried again. "Before her death," he finished softly.

Leroy kicked at a rock. "I heard about the accident. I don't like asking this, Doc, but was there anything between her and Wentworth?"

Scott shook his head at Leroy and thought to himself, But I don't know. I don't really know.

"Did your wife go to Wentworth's parties?"

"We went to a few, years ago."

"Why did you stop?"

"I've never been much for that kind of thing."

"What about your wife?"

"She didn't mind them."

"You ever do business with Wentworth?"

"No."

"Why not?"

"I have my own attorney in Seattle."

Leroy looked off at the water and then down at his shoelaces. "How long ago was the accident?"

"Six months next Sunday." And they'd lost the baby eight months before that. He'd never forget the despairing look in her eyes when they told her she couldn't have another.

Leroy's voice broke in again. "You say you were separated. When was that?"

"A month before the accident." Scott stirred. "Leroy, I don't see the point in all of this."

Leroy removed his hat and mopped his head. His big face was sympathetic. "Sorry, Doc, it's my job to ask questions. Doesn't mean I have to like it." He started for his car. "Say, on those African masks. Did you notice one was missing?"

Puzzled, Scott shook his head. "No, can't say I did."

"Gone, all right. Left a mark on the bedroom wall. Oh, I checked out the neighbors' house. Everything looks okay." He paused by his car door. "Maybe I can get you to fill me in on those African artifacts one of these days."

"Be glad to do what I can," Scott said, sighing, "but my wife was the authority on the subject."

Long after Leroy left, Scott stood on the deck staring blankly at the water, thinking of Toni and trying to imagine her with Owen. Six years living with someone, you'd think you'd know those things, which only showed how far apart they'd actually been. Toni had lived in her own private world of high fashions, New York buying trips, shows, meetings. She found island life too slow. That first time he'd brought her to the Cape, she spent the entire weekend studying the winter lines for the store and never set foot on the beach. When he asked her to sail in the *Picaroon*, a terrified look came over her face, and she shook her head fiercely.

"I hate the water," she said.

No wonder. She couldn't swim a stroke.

A gull landed on the long piece of driftwood below the rocks. Scott grabbed the binoculars from the kitchen table and found a spot on the south corner of the deck where the sun beat down the strongest. He stretched out on the webbed chaise, one of a pair of bright yellow folding lounges Toni had bought for his birthday two years before. For a moment he imagined her snuggled up beside him, her toe poking against the calf of his leg. He reached out to touch her, and his hand fell on Dandy's long fur. Scott jerked up, and sweat trickled down the back of his neck. The gull flew off the log, soared overhead, and landed on the kelp.

There had to be a reasonable explanation for Toni's picture in Owen's wallet, one that didn't leave this taste of bitterness. Toni and Owen. Like the way she'd died, there was something very wrong about it.

Then it struck him. Does Leroy think I killed Owen? Leroy could be maddeningly noncommunicative at times, but he was no fool. Still, someone murdered Owen. Leroy couldn't rule out anyone. Fortunately for Fred and Lorene, they'd picked this week to go off island. If they'd been there last night they might have heard those shots, might have stumbled over Owen's killer.

Scott considered calling Fred with the bad news—or good, depending on how one looked at it—and quickly rejected the idea. They'd find out soon enough, and to be honest about it, he had no desire to do anything that might hasten their return to the island. It had only been a week since they'd left, a week without Lorene's intrusions. Scott had been there to see them off.

"C'mon, Lorene," Fred had said. "It's two-thirty, and I need to be in that meeting at four."

"It takes an hour and a half to get to Shishole," Scott said in disbelief.

Fred grinned and held up one finger.

"One hour? You must be running on jet fuel."

"He always travels like that," Lorene said, laughing as she trudged up behind them, a strand of ash-blond hair in the way of one eye. Lorene was a big-boned woman, but she was puffing under the strain of the load she was carrying. Fred, slightly built and two inches shorter than his wife, took her physical capacities for granted.

Scott relieved Lorene of the pile, loaded it into the Bayliner, and helped undo the lines. He waved at the two of them as they backed out of the slip. Lorene was talking all the way.

"Call Cynthia."

Scott pretended not to hear. Lorene had been pushing Cynthia Woods at him for weeks, and though Scott had nothing against Lorene's friend, liked her, actually, he resented being matched up.

"I mean it, Scottie. She's expecting you to call."

Fred played the innocent. "You have the keys to the Mercedes. Go ahead and use it."

"No, thanks."

"We'll be back as soon as I get things squared away," Fred said and added something else that died in the roar of his big outboard.

The small boat took off like one of the jet foils and planed across the water at high speed. An hour to Seattle? Scott shook his head. For a sane man, at least two. He'd cautioned Fred about it once. "Those waters can get damn rough."

"Yeah," Fred said with the lopsided grin, "but I move quick."

"What if your engine conks out? Do you have an auxiliary?"

"Nope," Fred replied breezily, appraising his nineteen-foot Bayliner with obvious pride. "If the engine goes, I've had it."

Lorene laughed at Scott's frown. "That's just Fred, Scottie. You should know that."

How wonderful it must be to hold such an easygoing outlook on life.

The water clicked peacefully across the rocks. From behind the driftwood below the deck, there was a flapping of giant wings as a great bald eagle took off from a log. In flight he caught an air current and slowly circled the swirling waters in front of the deck.

Scott regarded this corner of the islands as a world apart, one that he needed right now. Yet few of his friends understood. Certainly not his partner, Ralph Nelson. When Scott told Ralph he was quitting practice to move full-time to the island, Ralph typically leaped to his own conclusions.

"I don't like to speak ill of the dead, but Toni was never right for you. Look on the positive side. You've no children, no alimony. You'll meet someone else." Twice divorced, Ralph had views that reflected his own outlook on marriage. "You're no Greek god, but you have that rugged look some women fancy."

He wasn't a pretty man, wouldn't have liked it much if he were. An average face, he supposed. He ran his hands through his hair. Hair and eyebrows bleached from the sun, a bit too much, perhaps. He was healthy-looking, anyway.

"At least blonds don't show gray," Ralph said.

"I'm not gray, Ralph."

"The point is you're too old to go running around barefoot like a beach bum."

"That's not the idea." Scott tried to explain Toni wasn't the reason he was quitting. He and Ralph had been over it a thousand times, how medicine had become a computerized paper factory where the patient-doctor relationship was losing to HMOs, rules, and malpractice suits. Everyone questioned. No one trusted. The patient had lost the right to choose. The doctor had lost his independence of judgment. No, he'd had his fill. Without Toni to consider, the decision had been easy.

"How are you going to get along without an income? Had you thought about that?"

"I may go back to commercial fishing. That's how I paid my way through med school."

Ralph smiled. "You'll be back by the end of the summer, when you've worked this out of your system."

Ralph never had been a good listener.

Scott set the binoculars on the deck, stretched out under the sun, and closed his eyes. Toni was dead, so was Owen, and life went on.

He woke to Dandy's wet nose nuzzling his feet. A slight breeze had started up, and he wondered how long he'd slept. Out on the water a new procession of small boats strained against the powerful current. The flood tide was well under way. The passage, which had been as calm as a stagnant pool earlier, now turned and foamed like a river after the spring thaw.

Eventually, the boat traffic thinned, and there was only the small blue silhouettes of the giant tankers in the distance, heading east to Anacortes to unload the oil from Alaska's north slopes.

Laughter trailed up from the beach. The cocktail hour had begun for his neighbors. Someone shouted, "Bring the steaks," and there was more laughter. All at once, Scott felt an urge, a deep longing to be part of it. From the rock ledge between their properties, Paul Martin waved. Scott waved back, and the feeling passed. He was the third man now, and conversation had a discouraging way of ending up in a discussion of Toni or his views on medicine, all of which required painful explanation. Maybe Ralph was right. He was a natural-born recluse.

The shadows on the water lengthened and the pass turned into a pond again as the flood tide was complete. On the strait a hazy mist began to settle over Partridge Point, and Scott wondered if it were going to bring in the fog. From the distance he heard the deep chugging of a diesel. Three masts appeared over Goose Island's hump. Scott perked up. "Gotta be a big one."

He stationed himself on the corner of the deck so as to spot her as she rounded the island. In a few seconds the rest of her came into view. A staysail schooner, gaff-rigged, fore and aft, with a flying forsail. He held his binoculars on her. Beautiful! Didn't see many like her anymore. Eighty feet, if she were an inch.

The sails were up and hanging limp as she moved under power. Her long sheer cabin hugged the decks. An aftercabin sat gracefully behind the wheelhouse, and two dinghies hung from her davits behind the mizzenmast. Quite a contrast to his own little sloop. This ship could stack three or four *Picaroons* alongside and still have room to spare. He tried to make out her name, but there was nothing on her forward gunwale, no name, no numbers. She flew Canadian colors. Had to be a ship of registry. Funny he hadn't seen her before. He held the glasses on her, admired the sleekness of lines as she motored into the channel. Something else different. The gaff-rigging. Always gave them the look of a pirate ship.

A camp following of gulls and terns, mostly terns, trailed

16

the ship. Smaller in size and swifter than the gulls, the grayish seabirds put on a spectacular show. Squeals of *kik-kik-kik* filled the air as they flew straight up, tucked neatly, and plunged straight down, zipping into the water like bullets.

Another flicker of light, steel flashing. Movement on the afterdeck. Three men worked around the jigger halyards. Scott ran the glasses on them. One was tall and wore a yellow slicker. Another was short, built like an ape with long arms. He wore a stocking knit cap and a heavy sweater. The third was tall, bone-skinny, lightly dressed in jeans and bare to the waist. The movements of these men, strained and jerky, contrasted sharply with the graceful sweep of the birds.

The terns worked the water near the kelp bed. One by one they struck the water like bright-silver knives. On the schooner's stern an arm went up, and metal glistened, almost like one of the terns. A splash off the starboard kicked up a fountain of spray. Water spurted and died in a circular puddle of foam.

The helmsman was forward of the mizzenmast, nearly hidden by a half-dozen cylinders of deck cargo. Aft of the cabin, two crewmen, one short with long arms, the other wiry and tall, secured the lines around the cleats. No yellow slicker was visible. Scott ran the glasses over the ship, looking for the third man. No sign of him. No reason to be alarmed, yet Scott was uneasy about the missing deckhand.

The ship fell behind the jetty, and only the topsails stuck out over the small rise of land. Scott trained the glasses on the schooner's aftertrail, tracked the clean white wake all the way back to Goose Island. Nothing. Still, he couldn't shake the feeling someone or something had gone over the side and been swallowed up in the sea. Stupid, no good reason, probably, but he wanted another look. It was fairly common this time of the evening for the northbound sailing ships to drop the hook in Griffin Bay just outside Fish Creek, behind the Cape.

He raced the Jeep on the winding road to Fish Creek, but when he reached the small opening overlooking Griffin Bay, the strange ship was nowhere in sight. He counted four sloops and a ketch anchored near the fish-buyer's barge and a half-dozen cruisers, lying outside the creek.

Scott was confident he'd spot the tall masts headed north up San Juan Channel, but the fog, now moving quietly into the bay, had already covered the passage all the way north to Lopez Head. Scott stared up the slot into nothingness and shook his head in disgust. It was that kind of day, everything inside out and imagination set to run wild.

Had he been thinking about Owen lying there in a pool of his own blood, the face masked in death, or was it Toni? He was doing it again. When he thought he'd seen a man fall off the stern of that ship, he was really only seeing Toni in her big yellow Mercedes, crashing through the barriers, flying off the end of the ferry landing pitched forward and falling, sinking deep, drowning in the cold waters of the sound.

Three

Scott always looked forward to his evenings with the professor. The old man lived by himself with Chips, a small gray terrier, and a cat, a long-haired, rather frightening creature called Archimedes. Al's wife had passed on years before. Except for a granddaughter who visited on occasion, this was all the family the old man had left.

He was bundled up in a coat sweater over a flannel shirt, stoking up the fire in the stone fireplace when Scott and Dandy arrived. It must have been eighty in the room. "C'mon in, Scottie. Just thought I'd get the chill out of the night air."

In shirtsleeves himself, Scott smiled and set his parcels on the kitchen drain. "Here are the steaks. Thought we could throw them on the barbecue."

The old man nodded. "I'll toss some lettuce in a bowl. Sit yourself down, and I'll fix us a drink."

Glad to see his friend in a lighter mood, Scott dropped into a chair. Dandy had already found a cool spot by the window next to Chips. The more aloof cat sat on a table near the hearth, cleaning itself. Scott settled back with a sigh.

The place was bachelor simple: a sofa; soft, bulging cushions, the kind to sink in; and a scuffed green leather chair Scott had long coveted. For Scott, who'd been living in the Seattle town house with Louis XV chairs and Grecian sofas, it was the ultimate in comfort and sensibility. The whole room was like that. A desk held the professor's beat-up old Underwood. Books jammed an entire wall; some were stacked around the floor, as well. "Been meaning to get some more shelves for those," Al said, dismissing the mess as unimportant.

The professor worked at the sink, chipping ice cubes out of the tray with a knife. He poured from a bottle of Gordon's, added a splash of tonic, and stirred with the knife. "Saw Leroy over at your place. Anything new?"

Scott took the glass from his hand and swirled the cubes. "Apparently one of the African masks was missing from the bedroom."

"He raced over here to tell you that?"

"That, and to thank me, I guess."

"Leroy? Thank you? Look out! He's after something."

Scott sipped the tonic and said nothing.

"He doesn't think they killed Owen over a jungle mask, I hope."

"Those masks are worth a lot, Al."

"Pure nonsense. They wouldn't have left the rest of the junk."

Scott conceded the point. With thousands of dollars of statues and artifacts lying around for the taking, why would a thief bother with only one mask? "At least we can rule out the people on the Cape. We're pretty much a live-and-let-live bunch. No nuts. No psychopaths."

Al laughed.

"Don't you agree?"

Al brandished his drink like a pointer at a chalkboard. "People on this Cape are exactly the same as people everywhere—same problems, same frustrations, same passions."

Scott grinned back at him. "You don't think one of our neighbors walked into Owen's living room, unloaded two barrels into his chest, and, casual as you please, strolled back home."

"There are more people around here than you might expect who won't shed a tear at Owen's passing."

"How about a for instance?"

"Henry Mason."

Scott couldn't picture the Cape's only multimillionaire

tightening his arthritic fingers on the trigger of a shotgun. "What possible reason?"

"Owen borrowed money from Henry and managed to write a loophole in the contract so he didn't have to pay back a cent."

Scott laughed. "I underestimated Owen. I thought ol' Henry had his first nickel."

"That's what I mean. Henry isn't the sort to allow a four-flusher like Owen to get the better of him. And Henry's not alone. You talk to Vic recently?"

"Three or four days ago," Scott said guardedly.

"Did he tell you about the West Coast fish deal?"

"He said they'd gone under, and he hoped to get better prices from the new fish-buyer."

The crinkles around Al's eyes deepened. "Did he tell you Owen talked him into investing in West Coast just before they filed for Chapter Eleven?"

"Owen sucked Vic into that?"

Al nodded. "Vic lost a bundle."

Vic Larson was the owner of a string of purse seiners, and in his time had made a small fortune fishing. The trouble now, the fishermen had come upon bad times with the restrictions placed on their fishing rights by the government, and their seasons were shorter and leaner. Scott counted Vic among his closest friends, and the idea he'd suffered a financial setback at the hands of Owen upset him. "Vic's not your man, Al."

"How about Bob Delaney? Owen cheated him out of a big real estate commission. From what I hear, Delaney was so hopping mad, he threatened to kill Owen."

Scott shook his head on the idea. Delaney bordered on being the town drunk. "It takes a certain kind of nerve to empty a twelve-gauge into a man, Al. Delaney doesn't have it."

Al played a Beethoven sonata on his stereo, and, after dinner, with the fire hissing and snapping in the grate, they retreated to the living room. Al poured coffee, a wonderful brew he boiled in an open pot, and complained about the aging process that robbed a man of the joys of life.

Scott's gaze fell on his friend's telescope, which sat by the windows, aimed at Cattle Pass. "Did you catch the schooner that went through this afternoon?"

"Mmm. The *Pilgrim*. Beautiful job."

"You've seen her before?"

Al nodded. "Charter ship. Last summer the Sea Scouts had her. This year it's the experimental lab. They use her to test the quality of the water, or some such nonsense."

"Kind of an expensive job for that." This touched off a lengthy sermon from Al on university waste. Satisfied the old man had seen nothing, Scott said, "How's the book coming?"

Al grunted disinterest, but from the typewritten pages scattered across his desk, it appeared he'd been working diligently on his history of the islands.

"Must be fun researching the misadventures of renegades and smugglers," Scott said. "Islands have quite a past."

"Do you imagine it's changed?"

Scott laughed. "You're not going to tell me they're still hijacking ships and that sort of skulduggery."

"Shows how much you know. If you've been reading the papers, there's been a half-dozen ships pirated in these islands in the last year alone. Forced a couple off their cruiser at gunpoint up near Campbell River. Took them two days to flag a passing ship."

"At least no one was hurt."

"That'll be next." From this typically gloomy view, Al launched into stories about the early San Juan settlers who'd come around the Horn. From this he branched into ancient Greece. Although Scott had heard much of it before, he was fully absorbed.

"You're quite a storyteller, Al. Why don't you go back to teaching? Guest lecture, something like that?"

"All those department heads climbing on top of each other to get to the top of the monkey tree? Don't want any part of it." That ended the conversation.

"How long you been up here on the Cape, Al?"

"Going on twelve years."

"Do you ever miss, uh, being away from things?"

"Spit it out, for heaven's sake. No, I don't mind being alone, if that's what you're getting at." He walked over to the fire and poked at a log. "Course, I have Chips and Archimedes. They're good company. And these darn fool people around here are always popping in, never know when to leave a person alone. And there's Erin." He doffed his pipe stem at a picture on the top of his desk of a fair-haired girl with blue eyes, even, white teeth, and a smile that suggested a happy outlook.

All Scott could remember about Al's granddaughter from previous summers was a pleasant, long-legged teenager who asked too many questions and was fascinated by the fishing boats. He hadn't seen her at all in the last few years when his own life had been too complicated for him to spend much time on the island. So he more or less missed a part of her growing up. "I imagine Erin's in college now."

Al grinned. "Where you been? She's been out of college nearly five years. She's a decorator. Tells people how to doll up their homes." He chuckled. "She's got her eye on my place, calls it a challenge. I tell her hands off."

Scott groaned. "Don't let her touch a thing, Al. Your place is perfect."

It was late when Scott finally asked what had been on his mind all evening. "When Toni came up those last times, was she alone?"

"She had a guest or two. Lorene dropped by, and the Martins. I ran into her on the beach a few times myself."

"How did she seem to you?"

"Preoccupied."

Scott remembered her moods of silence. "Those parties of Owen's—did you ever hear of her going?"

Al grabbed the poker stick and dug at a log that had flamed up, shoved it to the back of the firebox. "All hearsay, you understand, but someone did mention he'd seen her there, talking to that bird who works at the experimental lab, the dark-haired slicker. You know who I mean?"

"Preston Fields."

"That's the one."

It was like going the wrong direction on a one-way street. Scott knew Fields, never liked him. He thought Toni had felt the same. "What do you know about him, Al?"

"Oceanographer, biologist, hotshot. Got his Ph.D. before he was thirty. A Rhodes scholar. Comes from wealth. Arrogant, self-impressed, and sneaky. I think that about covers it." Al smiled.

But Scott couldn't laugh, for he felt the same way about the man, and the idea of Toni taking up with Preston depressed him.

Al read his thoughts. "I said she was *seen* there with him. Doesn't have to mean she came with him."

Scott nodded and decided if Al knew more, he didn't want to know.

Four

Friday Harbor was the usual summer mess, boats and tourists everywhere, as Scott and Dandy pulled in. Cars, campers, vans, bicycles, and mopeds clogged the three blocks of the main street, and in the harbor, cruisers and sailboats filled up the docks behind the breakwater and overflowed to anchorage across half the bay.

Al had a meeting of his historical society, and in a weak moment, Scott volunteered to pick Erin up from the noon ferry, an offer he already regretted. "C'mon, Dandy," Scott said, piling out of the Jeep, "let's get this over with."

He had no trouble picking Erin out of the crowd of foot passengers milling around the ferry hut. She was the tall, healthy-looking young woman with shoulder-length blond hair holding on to a two-suiter and a backpack. Up close, she was as he remembered, no more freckles across the bridge of her nose, but soft features, inquisitive eyes, and a brilliant smile. The gentle curves and a certain matureness in her direct gaze were new.

She squeezed in beside Dandy in the front seat of the Jeep, and they started out. Their conversation quickly turned to her profession, and he made the mistake of expressing his views that the decorators he'd known had been more concerned with putting their artistic stamp on a house than with the people who had to live in it. It was an opinion formed because of Toni, of course, and unfair, but Erin took it well.

"It's not quite like you think," she said. "You have to study your clients and work to achieve a mood they want." It was, she said, a combination of psychology and crossword puzzles. "You have to start with what's given and go from there." She talked about trade-offs and getting to know the people you're working for and architectural limits and the use of space, and Scott soon realized there was more to it than he'd thought.

In a fenced stretch along the road, a small herd of goats was at work pulling up the tall grass. Beyond the field, yellowed pastures layered the hillside all the way to the tide pools of Griffin Bay.

"I suppose," Scott said, still not completely convinced, "that you prefer the kind of job where someone gives you the key to the house and a checkbook and tells you to do whatever you like."

The wind from the open window blew the fine golden strands of hair into her eyes. She brushed them back. "There's no challenge in that, not to have to please anyone, no wish lists."

"Wish lists?"

"A family heirloom or an exotic teapot, a painting or a special color." She flashed the smile again, a very nice smile. "The idea is to bring all those personal desires together into a harmonious whole so you get the home the people wanted all along."

How, he wondered, could she have managed it with two who disagreed as much as he and Toni had? There hadn't been a comfortable chair in the place, and rooms so orderly even the copy of his surgery journal on a desktop looked out of place.

"You might not believe it," she said in a spirited voice that bordered on defense, "but I'm actually pretty damn good at what I do."

He liked her self-confidence, imagined she was, indeed, good at what she did. He also imagined she could manipulate a man with her smile and soft voice. Make certain it's not you she manipulates, he warned himself. He drove over a hill and fell in behind a long line of cyclers, pedaling earnestly toward American Camp. An irrigated field on the hill glistened emerald green against the straw slopes around it. Griffin Bay opened up again across the yellowed thickets of grass.

The road curved through the woods by American Camp, and the fields turned into stands of newly planted pine, spruce, and firs. Erin breathed deeply of the air. "Wild berries and pine needles. I used to dream about those marvelous smells. I spent entire summers here before college, after the accident."

Scott remembered when she lost her parents. He hadn't known Al at the time, but Al told him about it later, the fiery crash on the mountain road. At first Erin and Al had clung to each other like nesting swallows. Then, gradually, they'd come out of it, but the bond between them remained. Thinking of Erin's loss, Scott felt a sudden bond with her himself. "You were very young to lose your parents."

She shrugged. "I was fifteen, but I was lucky. I had Grandpa."

Somehow the notion of Al playing mother and father to a girl in her delicate growing years didn't fit. Still, Scott could see his friend had done a remarkably good job. She had survived with a fatalistic acceptance that did Al credit. "You didn't stay on the island for school?"

"No. Grandpa sent me to boarding school in Canada, but I stayed close to home for college. Grandpa's getting on, you know."

"Mmm," Scott said, suddenly feeling old.

The road dipped and rolled. The grass slopes of Mount Finlayson had turned into a parched bog, tinder dry. Fire warnings had been out for days. Erin's eyes followed the movements of a hawk who appeared to be suspended over the swirling blue eddies of the strait. Below them a white surf was running, and across the wide expanse of shimmering water, the Olympic Mountains stood in a misty outline against a sun-hazed sky.

The road wound around Finlayson and opened up a view of the lighthouse and the string of small islands that clustered across Cattle Pass. A wind had started up, and big rollers put a spray over Deadman's Island that Scott guessed rose over fifty feet in the air. It was a smashing sight, and never failed to restore him. Erin leaned out the window to get a better look. A flock of gulls flew by, squealing like a crowd of frightened puppies.

Erin released a deep sigh. "If I came here a million times, I'd never get over the feeling. It's such a joy to see, just to know it's there."

In that moment she closed the age gap, and in this state of rapport, they drove the next half-mile, hypnotized into silence by the sight of the whirling waters and the tiny islands that strung out from the toe of Lopez. At the bend in the road where the grass had grown over the sandy trail to the lighthouse, they passed the blockhouse, freshly painted. Here, in the Second World War, sailors had protected the coast with a giant radar net and used the concrete building as a radar station and pillbox. Now it lay empty, with holes for windows and doors, a place for the tourists to crawl through.

The road dipped one more time, and out of a grove of leafy ash and madronas, Owen's skylighted roof pitched above the trees. Erin had heard about Owen. "Isn't it awful, knowing someone was killed here in this breathtaking spot? Gives you a terrible feeling, not just that a killer is loose, but the whole idea of someone violating this beautiful place. I hate that especially. Do you know what I mean?"

He knew exactly. Evil had touched the Cape, and it didn't belong there.

Erin was on the island for her vacation, and Al made such a point of Scott's coming to her "homecoming dinner" that he couldn't refuse. It was amusing to see her influence on the old man. Al wasn't what Scott called a moody person. Still, living alone he could go for days communicating in monosyllables. Tonight, he was in exceptional humor and talkative as a jay.

Erin was in the kitchen preparing dessert when he dropped one of his little bombs. He'd run into Leroy's deputy in town. "They found the missing death mask. According to Harold, some bird sold it to an antique dealer in Victoria."

Erin walked back into the room carrying a large bowl of strawberries. "Did I hear you say something about Owen's African art collection?"

Al came up in his chair. "What do you know about it?"

"Didn't I tell you? I saw some of his collection last summer."

Al sucked in his breath and looked like he might explode. "You went to one of Owen's parties?"

"I didn't say that, Grandpa. What do you take me for?"

"A girl with a nose for other people's business," Al said, a little less excited.

"I was walking back from the lighthouse," Erin explained, "and Owen came out for his morning jog. He stopped me, said he'd heard I was an interior decorator and asked if I knew anything about African artifacts. Of course, I'd done some work for clients. Anyway, there was nothing suggestive about it. He merely wanted my professional opinion."

"And Owen's stuff? Is it very valuable?" Scott said.

Erin nodded. "Besides the fact that the wood is highly perishable in the tropics, the trible customs discouraged preservation of ritual masks, so those that come through a few centuries, like Owen's, are rare and dearly priced. As for the terra-cotta head, it probably dates back to two or three hundred B.C."

Impressed by her knowledge, Scott said, "I read recently that some art dealers were making a killing selling fake Dali prints for thousands of dollars."

Erin nodded. "You can imagine the problem in African art with centuries of artifacts to deal with. But Owen's were of high quality, the material old, the color good. I'd say whoever picked them knew what he was doing."

"You don't think it was Owen?"

Erin shook her head. "When he showed me the ivory piece he didn't even know what century it came from. I suggested he consult the museum curator in Seattle if he wanted to be absolutely certain, but he didn't like that idea at all. I wouldn't be surprised if the terra-cotta head was worth a quarter of a million."

Scott whistled. "A quarter of a million bucks sitting on a table in a summerhouse."

"It figgers," Al said. "Owen was an operator and a cheat, but an intellect he was not."

Erin laughed. "That's nothing. The chain he wore around his neck was a museum piece."

Scott exchanged glances with Al. "Damn," Scott said. "How could I have forgotten those bilious gold sticks hanging down his bare chest like a Tahitian witch doctor? Better call the sheriff, Al. He'll want to know about that."

Erin looked puzzled.

"It wasn't on him when we found the body," Al explained.

Leroy responded with uncharacteristic swiftness. He rumbled up the drive, strode through Al's door, wearing the Stetson and the .38, and there was an uncommon look of urgency on his face. He saw Erin and removed the hat, brushed life back into the thin matted brown hair, and shifted from one foot to the other while Al explained about Erin and the necklace.

"How valuable is it?" Leroy asked Erin.

"Taking a guess . . . twenty-five thousand. To be sure, you'd have to ask an authority, which I'm really not."

Leroy pulled at an earlobe. "Do you know such a person?"

"The museum curator in Seattle, for one. I also know a collector, a client of mine, who's made it his hobby. Brice Randall, the Seattle developer. You may have heard of him."

Small damn world, Scott thought. Who hadn't heard of Randall, the contractor who'd built shopping malls and office complexes all over the Northwest? Scott knew him from Toni's store parties, met him first at the opening of one of Randall's malls. He wasn't a physically big man, but he had a forceful personality. Meeting him was like being hit by a strong wind. He was quick, always knew just the right thing to say.

"I decorated his offices in the Pacific building a year ago," Erin told Leroy. "We designed a whole room around pieces he picked up in auctions."

Leroy whipped out his notepad and began writing on it. He looked up once and saw Scott's frown. "You ever see Owen wearing the necklace?"

Scott nodded unhappily. "Yes, I've seen it on him, and, no, it wasn't on him when I examined him, and yes, it only now occurred to me."

Leroy shrugged. "You can't think of everything."

Al, who'd been strangely quiet through all this, said, "Your deputy tells me you found the missing African mask."

Leroy frowned. "Harold talks too much."

Al bit down on his pipe irritably.

Leroy had investigated the guests at Owen's party, most of whom were now living out of the state. None of the ladies held any regret at Owen's passing.

This evoked a sympathetic "Poor man!" from Erin.

"Ummmph," Al said, meaning Owen deserved whatever he got.

"But he wasn't lucky at marriage, was he? A man without friends."

His eyes on Erin, Leroy left them with a warning. "Better not talk it around, this business of Owen and the necklace."

Al drew up like a rooster. "Leroy, are you telling my granddaughter she's in danger because she saw Owen's collection of African art?"

Leroy turned his serious gaze on the old man. "I'm saying when you're dealing with a deranged killer, it pays to be careful. The fewer people who know what you know, the better."

Five

After Leroy left, Scott started across the road to his house in the dark. Forgot his yard lights. The Martins' lights were out, too. He glanced at his watch. Two-thirty. Tonight he knew he'd sleep, sleep without the gremlins of Toni and Owen, and the promise of it filled him with a peace he hadn't known in weeks.

Off Goose Island the moon spun a white trail across the kelp bed. From the Cattlepoint rocks the lighthouse lamp flickered on and off, and another answered. There was an occasional cry from a wayward gull, and then silence. Stars overhead blinked back mutely, and not an engine rumbled anywhere. It was one of those peaceful nights on the Cape when even the tide slipped in quietly.

Dandy spotted it first, the long shadow darting across the grass by the corner of the house. With a low growl, he left the road at a gallop, headed toward the rocks below the deck.

It's hard to prepare oneself for combat on such a night, and it was pure reflex that sent Scott running across the road behind Dandy. The memory of Leroy's warnings brought a shout from his lips. "Hey, what's going on here?" His voice shattered the silence like the Cape's fire horn, and a sorry second thought followed. Probably the Martins' tabby, Sam, getting another lick off Dandy's dish.

Fresh scuffling sounds, definitely not the soft scampering of a cat. Someone was coming out of his house. Another shadow limped off the deck, Dandy in rumbling pursuit.

"C'mon, Charlie," someone shouted, "let's get the hell outta here."

"Watch out for the fuckin' dog. . . ."

Scott raced to the deck and whistled to Dandy, but the dog was already thundering across the hard turf, charging over the logs and rocks on the heels of the intruders. Scott reached the mound above the beach, close enough to hear their grunting exertions. The light was too poor to make out faces but he had had time to consider the very real possibility that men who break into other people's homes quite likely also carry guns. He stepped lightly across the grass and whistled again for the dog, but received only Dandy's bark in answer.

If they'd run to the beach, Scott reasoned, they must have a way of escape by water, but if he ran after them he'd be an easy target. Scott knew every inch of the beach, knew where the driftwood piled up in a long chain, sticking out like giant toothpicks, and where the mammoth first-growth fir, stripped of its bark and slippery as a seal's skin, lay like a teeter-totter over the top. Nestled in between the stumps and logs that had been cast there by earlier storms was a pebbled stretch of beach, sometimes turned to sand by a high tide. In this spot he and Toni had basked together in the sun, made love in the shelter of the driftwood. Here the rocks formed a small cove with a tide pool in its center. There was a sand strip between the jetties where a small boat could slip into shore, and, if tied to a rock in a gentle sea, like tonight, could sit on the mud bottom, free of trouble.

Close to the bank, footsteps crunched across the hard sand. Dandy lunged through the dark at two figures scrambling for the logs. Barking fiercely, Dandy forced them up against the big fir where they stood on the poles underneath and began fending the dog off with kicks and karate chops.

"Hold him off. I'll get the line." The shorter of the two, the one called Charlie, left the protection of the tree and loped across the beach, stumbled over a rock, regained his footing, and hobbled to the mushy sand at the water's edge where a small boat sat tied to the rocks. There he began unsnarling the boat's line, which appeared to be fouled in a heavy patch of seaweed.

The stick-shaped man by the tree dropped to a squat,

groped around between the logs. "Get back, you bastard, or I'll fix you good." His hand rested on a thick piece of driftwood. He raised the hunk of wood at the dog like a club, and brought it down with savage force. It struck a large rock and splintered, missing Dandy, but not, Scott figured, by much.

"Dandy," Scott shouted, starting to panic. "Dandy!"

Normally Dandy would have come at this command, and normally he would have been content to chase the intruders off as he would the neighbor's cat, with a good deal of barking and growling. But this man had lashed back so viciously that the dog sensed he was a threat and turned mean. He went after the man with the club, snarling and snapping, not actually biting but keeping him pinned against the tree.

"Shit, stand still, you bastard." The man with the club raised it, swung, missed, swung again.

Scott leaned over the bank. "Knock it off!"

Neither the man nor Dandy paid the least attention. How, Scott wondered fearfully, was he to get Dandy safely out of there without taking on these men himself? As he stood over them weighing his options, he saw the man's hand slide inside his jacket. The unmistakable sound of a .38 chamber slamming into place chilled the air.

"I'll fix the son of a bitch."

Too late for help. Too late for argument. Scott leaped over the rock embankment to the beach, landed on his feet, and knew in the splash of cool air from the water that he'd done the dumbest thing possible. On the bank the two men were merely vandals in flight, but here, down on the sand, they were fury locked in a small room. The fear for Dandy had prompted him to do what all reason warned against. Scott's throat muscles constricted. The words when they came out sounded like they were coming out of frozen lips. "Shoot that dog and you'll be sorry. I promise you."

The head turned, and Scott saw black, tightly curled hair, a face blotted out by darkness, and the nose of the automatic, trained on his chest. The man holding it laughed. It wasn't a pleasant laugh. It wasn't a pleasant feeling, staring down the barrel of a loaded automatic in the hands of a man intent on using it. "You want it first?"

From the water's edge, "Charlie" paused in his work. "Jerry, you stupid bastard, put it away!"

"If he doesn't get this fuckin' dog off me, I'll put them both away for good."

"*Dandy, come!*" The dog knew the voice of serious command. He returned to Scott's side, panting. His whole body quivered.

Scott faced them both now—Charlie, the short scruffy one struggling to unsnarl the line that was hung up in the kelp, and his partner, the one called Jerry, who still held the automatic, still, apparently, undecided what he would do with it. In the dark their faces were blurs, but their hate charged across the beach like a broken high-power line.

"That's right!" Jerry said. No mistaking the madness in that voice. "Keep that mutt off me, or I'll blow his brains all over the beach."

Scott took a firm hold on Dandy's collar. Close by, the man near the boat managed to undo the lines, and, in one swift motion, was in the boat, working to get it started. He turned the key, choked it. The engine sputtered, quit. He snapped the key another time with the same result. He tried it again and again.

"Hurry it up, will you?"

"It's not getting gas. Oh, shit—dammit to hell."

The obscenities showered from the cockpit as Charlie hand-pumped fuel through the hose. There would, Scott thought, be no better opportunity to move, to see what they'd taken from the house. He took a step toward them. The stringy shadow shot up in front of him.

"That's far enough."

"Now look," Scott said, trying reason, "what do you want here?"

Laughter, cruel and wild, pealed out of the shadows.

Scott advanced another step. It was a mistake.

The automatic came up. "Fuck off!"

The gun, the words hurled with the unchecked anger of the insane, worked at Dandy's instincts to protect. The dog pulled free. Everything exploded at once. Dandy dove, and the gun went off, cracked across the water like an engine backfiring on a quiet street. Jerry went down, and the gun spit loose, sailed across the sand. Dandy landed on top, snarling, biting, and this time, Scott feared, tearing flesh. Scott raced in, got a handhold on Dandy's fur, and with his free hand grabbed the collar, pulled with all his might. Dandy's teeth let go their hold, and Scott dragged him off. Jerry had crawled behind the log, curled up in a ball, protecting his face with his arms.

"You son of a bitch. I'll get you." Spitting out mouthfuls of sand and kelp, he crawled out from under the log and scratched at the ground. He was after the gun, dropped somewhere in the piles of rock, mud, and seaweed. He was near crazy, digging and clawing. Finally his fingers curled around the only weapon he could find. He struggled to his feet, getting his breath in stuttering heaves, and started toward Scott, clutching the club, arms upraised, out of control.

Charlie thumped around the bow of their boat, waving a wrench and yelling at his companion, "Don't, you damn fool." Dandy broke loose. Scott saw the club going up, coming down. He moved. It wasn't quite far enough. The club missed his head, struck his shoulder, a stinging, staggering blow. He reeled back, pain radiating all the way up his neck and down his arm to his fingertips, jarred from his chest to his toes. He fell into mud, fighting to keep his equilibrium. The beach started to spin. Above him, through half-open eyes, Scott saw the club go up one more time.

Teeth bared, Dandy sprang from the pebbled patch of beach, a hundred pounds of solid, straining muscles, aimed, on target. But this time Jerry was ready. He didn't miss. The club slammed into the dog's side. Dandy flew across the sand and landed with a thud, his whimpering cry dying in the back reaches of the bank.

In a dazed state, Scott saw the boat float free in the tide

pool, then the burst of horsepower as the engine caught hold, sputtered, and throttled into a roar. It was a Whaler, a fast boat, revved up, ready to go. Anger choked up in Scott's throat. Fighting waves of dizziness, he staggered to his feet, stumbled after them.

"Get in," he heard the driver shout to his companion.

Club still in hand, Jerry half-somersaulted over the bow into the boat. Scott grabbed the bow plate. It was round and smooth, hard to grip, but he held on. If he'd stopped to think, he would have known it was a futile gesture against two hundred horses of powerful outboard. But he was past thinking.

The club rose like a heavy hunk of steel, and he heard the sharp intake of breath—his own—and the laugh of this man who so enjoyed inflicting pain. Until now Scott had been moving at half speed, impeded by the burning in his shoulder and the wooziness. But when it came to protecting his hands, he had good reflexes. The club dropped. Scott unzipped his fingers. Plastic cracked. Scott fell facedown into mud and seaweed with the sickening crunch of splintering fiberglass grinding in his ears, and the knowledge that crept into his consciousness that, had the club struck its target, it wouldn't have been the plastic parapet crushed and pulverized, but the bones in his fingers, the surgeon's hands crippled.

Lying in the sand, Scott watched the driver of the Whaler back it up, turn, nose into a wave, and shove the stick forward. The small boat, bow up, lifted off its sandy slip, bounced over its own wake, and, spinning a silver tail, planed across an otherwise quiet sea on a reckless course up San Juan Channel. The engine rumbled into the distance and left the Cape in silence.

Scott dragged himself to the slippery log, his heart heavy with remorse. He scanned the rocks where he'd last heard Dandy's pitiful yelp. Nothing. It was all his fault. If he'd only held on to the dog, not provoked the fury of the intruders. Nothing those two could have taken from the house was worth a hair of Dandy's head. With dread, he called the dog's name. A wave splashed across the pebbles and fell softly back.

"Where are you, boy?" he called as he inched across the sand, testing the ground with his toes, afraid of what he might find. He found nothing. He started for the house to get a flashlight.

At first it sounded only like the tide coming in.

"Dandy?"

This time there was a faint scuffling sound to raise his hopes. It came out of the logjam at the foot of the rocks just below the deck. He called again.

The answering whimper gave fresh life to Scott's sore limbs. He ran to the logs, fearful and hoping at the same time. The whimper turned into a sharp bark, and Scott's spirits soared. He ran his hand through the gaps in the pile and touched the soft tufts of fur. A warm tongue ran over his hand, and Scott wanted to cry out in relief. Dandy was wedged between two logs, squirming frantically to get out, and from all appearances, still in one piece.

The logs were big and firmly set and hard to budge, and Scott wondered how the dog had been trapped there. The only thing Scott could imagine was that, when struck, he had landed on the pile, slipped on the slick surface of the wet wood, and slid between the poles, causing the top ones to settle in around him.

"Don't worry, boy, I'll have you out in a minute."

Using his good shoulder, Scott got under the top log and managed to work it up and to the side. Still not enough. He needed to move the one underneath, but this was cedar, water-soaked, and heavy. If he dislodged the wrong pole, it might bring the pile down on top of the dog. Scott took a deep breath and went at it again. But he needed leverage, not brawn. He stumbled across the beach until he found a pole, just the right size. He placed it under the cedar log and pressed down. The log inched up.

"Come on, boy, help."

Dandy needed no encouragement. He wiggled, shoved, clawed, and finally burst free. The pole snapped up and spit out, and the logs tumbled back into place. Exhausted, Scott fell to the sand. He was close to weeping. He wrapped his arms around the dog's neck. Never had that thick bundle of hair felt so good.

Dandy licked his face and whined and pranced around like a puppy, answering Scott's fears about broken limbs and injured inner organs. With the heavy padding of fur and fat, he'd been stunned, nothing more.

"We're tougher than we think, ol' boy."

Bruised muscles and injured pride—they were much better off than they might have been. No bullets had flown, Scott thought gratefully, and he and Dandy were still alive and on their feet. "C'mon," Scott said, "let's see what they did to the house."

Six

The house was a mess. Sofa cushions, coats, and jackets all over the floor, linings ripped, kindling from the wood box splintering the rug. In the kitchen, cupboards stood empty. On the floor broken pieces of china lay buried in a sea of sugar and flour beside drawers, turned upside down, with silverware and fishing tackle spilling out.

The den was the worst, books thrown around and medical papers ripped out of files. Scott retrieved a red leather-bound copy of Shakespeare's *Sonnets* and let out a soft "Damn!" It had been a gift from Toni on their anniversary. It looked like a bird with a broken wing.

Anger turned to gloom as Scott waded through the rooms. They'd ransacked his bureau drawers, stripped the bed, and tossed sheets, blankets, socks, shirts, slacks, underwear, and towels into one big pile. The bathroom reeked of after-shave. A broken bottle of it leaked onto the tile. Clearly, Charlie and Jerry had been intent on doing as much mischief as possible. Strangely, a bottle of Demerol prescribed for Toni when she had root-canal work done lay unopened on the floor.

Apparently, he'd interrupted the two before they'd finished in the living room. His surprise arrival had spared the loss of his ship models, the oil seascape that hung over the hearth, his stereo, and his shortwave. Even more amazing, not one bottle of wine had been dislodged from its rack over the kitchen pass-through.

It was too early to be certain, but upon first look there appeared, in fact, to be nothing missing, which made no sense. If they weren't thieves, who were these men, and what had they been after? They were too old to be vandals. Could the break-in be tied in with Owen? If so, had it anything to do with Toni?

He went back to the bedroom, dug through the underwear and the socks, and found the few remnants of Toni he'd saved— her evening bag, the photograph album, her Sunday missal. Sighing heavily, Scott telephoned the sheriff.

Leroy didn't sound cheered by the news of another problem on the Cape. "Just took my shoes off."

"I don't think I'm missing anything," Scott said, "so there's nothing urgent about it."

"Umm. They got away clean?"

"At those speeds they could be in Canada by now."

"All right," Leroy said, "I'll stop out in the morning and see if we can lift some prints. Try not to touch anything."

Scott didn't remember the .38 until he put down the phone. There seemed to be no point in calling the sheriff again, but he knew the gun might be a means of identifying the two, and it was somewhere on that beach. With another half hour to high tide, there was the chance of losing it to an outgoing wave.

Scott dug out the big flashlight and, every muscle protesting, trudged wearily back to the beach. Dandy limped loyally behind him. Scott shone the torch in all the likely and unlikely places, into the crevices between the rocks, around the fir near where the thug had stood, poked it into the hollowed-out ends of logs, under stacks of driftwood. He shoveled seaweed with his foot. Dandy helped, digging and pawing the sand. They uncovered nothing. Scott finally concluded the gun was either tucked between the logs or buried in a tide pool. In either case, there was no way he'd find it in the dark. He gave up and, thoroughly exhausted, returned to the house, hopeful he'd uncover it in the morning at low tide.

He swept the broken dishes into one big pile in the center of the kitchen. The rest, he decided, could wait until morning. He threw sheets on the bed and, totally drained from his efforts, fell onto it.

Lights from across the water blinked on and off into his

room. After his struggle on the beach it was inevitable that his mind go back in time, seeing it all as though it had happened minutes ago. Fred at the door, his face as gray as the early-hour fog that brought him.

"Toni's dead, Scottie."

Scott could still see her lying lifeless under the pathologist's thin cloth, palid and puffed up from the salt water, looking defenseless. Toni, who'd always been in control of everything. He remembered thinking he ought to cover her with his coat, and the police sergeant saying, "You'll want this, I imagine." It was Toni's black evening bag. The policeman had spilled its water-soaked contents out on the table—her lip gloss, compact, comb, keys, wallet, and the small appointment book she took with her everywhere. There was no living relative, only Scott, to receive it. Scott had stared at it bleakly. Not much to show for thirty-five years of life.

"C'mon, Scottie," Fred said, "you can't do anything here."

The house had a deep-winter chill when he returned to it that night, damp and emptier than the day she'd left, and he couldn't stand to stay in it. For hours he drifted down mist-blotted streets, staring blindly at the hazy outlines of unlit homes, unable to get the sight of her from his mind.

It was something like that now, except for the first time since that cold November night, other thoughts raced through his head as he lay staring into the darkness: Owen and the marine biologist Preston Fields, Owen and the fishermen, Owen and Toni, and then, strangely, like a warm wind coming after a blizzard, Erin and the way she looked when she said, ". . . the idea of someone violating this beautiful place . . . I hate that. . . ."

He finally fell into a fitful sleep, interrupted by questions too disturbing to chase away. Why had Toni gone to Owen's parties? Why had she driven through the barricade? Toni, whose only real fear in life was of the water? What happened at the store opening to drive her off that way? The coroner called it an accident and, privately, said suicide, but Scott knew Toni and could accept neither theory. In the predawn darkness, the glow from the lighthouse flickered on and off. If he found the reasons for Owen's death, would he also discover the truth about Toni? As the sun poked over Mount Baker, Scott drifted off to sleep.

He woke abruptly again with the ringing of the phone. It was Fred, calling from Seattle, and he sounded excited. "Scottie, where you been? I tried to reach you for hours last night. What's going on up there, anyway? The papers say someone shot Owen. Do they know who?"

Scott raised himself to one elbow and mumbled into the receiver. "Oh, hi, Fred." Fred went right on talking.

"Why didn't you call me? That's right next door, you know."

"Don't know who did it or why," Scott said through a yawn, and told Fred what he knew.

"Good God, I wonder if they've checked our house. Who's handling it, anyway?"

"Leroy. And don't worry, he checked your place first thing. Nothing was touched. You know I would've told you had it been otherwise."

Sounding slightly mollified, Fred said, "It sounds like we've got a maniac running loose up there."

Scott yawned again. "If that's the case, if it's not the work of a thief, your house is perfectly safe."

"Yeah," Fred said, not laughing and not sounding reassured either. Finally he said, "See you in a day or so. Oh, Lorene says she'll work something out with Cynthia."

Scott groaned. "I don't want her to work something out with Cynthia."

Fred laughed. "If you expect me to intervene for you, ol' buddy, forget it."

Scott set the phone down with an annoyed sigh. It was a good five minutes before he realized he hadn't told Fred about his own break-in. Unintentional or Freudian, it was just as well. It would have sent Fred chasing back on the next ferry.

Scott showered and dressed, ignoring an ache in his head that he wasn't sure was a result of no sleep or the blow on the shoulder. He shoveled debris aside so he could feed Dandy, and marveled at how heartily the dog ate, showing no ill effects from the encounter on the beach.

Scott was picking up broken dishes when Leroy's wagon rolled into the drive. Leroy walked in carrying a valise. There'd been more calls last night, and he was clearly in a bad mood.

"Hope you didn't touch anything. I can't get prints if you mucked it up with your own."

Scott led him to the kitchen and pointed to the cupboards. "The handles, the drawer pulls, the counters—all untouched."

"Arrogant doctors," Leroy mumbled. He started rattling around the kitchen, shaking charcoal powder on the countertops and blowing it all over the place. He proceeded from there to the living room and started on the big circular coffee table.

"My God," Scott protested, "you're destroying my house."

Leroy shrugged. "You want to find those two or not?"

"I'm not sure," Scott said as some of the powder settled on the rug.

"Mmm, got something here. 'Course, could be yours." He blew on the powder, and the imprint of three fingers appeared. He laid a plastic tape over this and lifted it off. He repeated this process several times on the fireplace hearth and the tables. "I'm going to need your prints, too."

"Okay." Scott sighed. "But in the kitchen, please."

Scott submitted to the fingerprinting, and Leroy finally packed up his equipment, took a half-dozen prints with him that he thought might be "possibles," and started for the door. Then Scott remembered about the gun. Leroy's disposition did not improve at the news.

"Why in hell didn't you tell me that last night?"

"I forgot. Anyway, what would you have done? Come out here and crawled through the slime and rocks in the pitch dark? I did that, and came up with sore knees and an aching back for my trouble."

"Okay," Leroy said in a tone of resignation, "let's get it done."

They worked their way across the beach from one log pile to

another, poked into all the places Scott had looked before and in some he'd missed. They raked and scooped up wet sand and dipped into the spots where water still collected from the outgoing tide. They found seaweed, an empty beer can, wet rocks, and barnacles, but no .38.

After an hour of this, Leroy shook his head. "You sure this bird didn't pick it up again?"

Scott thought about being knocked flat and, for those several spinning seconds, not seeing or hearing clearly. Could either of them have retrieved the gun while he lay there, dazed? "I suppose it's possible."

Beside his patrol car, Leroy expressed the view that it was, after all, only a break-in. Nothing had been stolen and no one seriously hurt. "Keep it to yourself, though. If the people 'round here get an idea there's a crime spree going, the next thing you know we'll have the whole Cape armed to the teeth and shooting every time a dog barks."

The sheriff wasn't five minutes out of the drive when Scott was forced to break his word. Al appeared at the door, took one look into the kitchen, and blanched visibly. "God almighty, somebody broke in."

There was hardly any way to hide it, so Scott told him the whole story, including Leroy's desire to keep it quiet.

"Won't say a word," Al stuttered. "We got something awfully wrong going on here, Scottie, something awfully wrong."

"And I don't think we need worry Erin with it, do you?"

Al nodded dumbly and dropped down onto a kitchen chair. He looked at the pile of broken dishes and then at the powder covering the counters, and shook his head. "This is a mess. You better call Millie."

"I'm not calling anyone, Al. Leroy wants to keep it quiet, remember?"

"Oh, sure." He didn't say anything for another minute. Then, "These two men, did you ever see them before?"

"Can't be sure. Too dark to see their faces clearly."

"And you think they still have the gun?"

"That's the sheriff's idea, not mine. I figure if they'd picked it up again, they would've used it."

"Then it's still out there somewhere?"

"If it is, it's out to sea by now. We scoured that beach."

Al looked like he had when they'd found Owen—pale and deeply worried. "What do you think it all means?"

"Not sure. I can't find anything missing. They even passed up a five-dollar bill on my dresser. Still, it's clear they were looking for something."

"Do—do you suppose they're the ones who killed Owen, that they were looking for something at Owen's place, and he caught them at it, and they shot him? Maybe they didn't find what they were after and so they came here, and . . ."

But what could Scott have in common with Owen? Toni? Was it something to do with Toni?

Al shook his head. "Doesn't make sense, does it? No connection between you and Owen. Besides, we know the killers took the mask and the necklace. Maybe they're part of a burglary ring."

"Then why didn't they steal anything here?"

Al waved his arm in the direction of the kitchen. "How would you know?"

None of the explanations fit, and Al returned to his original theories, that someone on the Cape had killed Owen, which left no explanation for the break-in, but relieved Al's mind. The two were looking for drugs. Everyone knew doctors kept drugs lying around.

Scott hadn't the heart to tell the old man the only drugs in the house were Toni's Demerol capsules, and that the burglars had left those right in the middle of the bathroom floor.

Seven

Bothered by Al's observations about Vic Larson and the West Coast fish-buyers, Scott decided to pay a visit to Fish Creek. It was so out of character for Vic to fall for one of Owen's questionable business investments that Scott had to believe Vic's finances were far worse than he'd realized.

Behind all the fishermen's financial woes was the State Fishing Commission closures. These posed a special hardship for owners of the big purse seiners, like Vic, whose ships represented investments in the millions. Compounding the problem was the federal court ruling on an old Indian treaty that allotted half the salmon catch to the Indians. In effect, this meant the Indians had three times as many days as fishermen like Vic to make their catch. It was a situation bound to cause trouble. Scott hoped eventually the hatcheries would improve the runs and alleviate the problem, but Vic saw only ruin at the end of the road.

"It'll be the Japanese and the Russians getting all the fish," he predicted gloomily. "This country will go begging."

It wasn't a prospect Scott liked to think about.

Fish Creek sat in the backwash of Griffin Bay, exposed to the north but protected from the worst of the south winds by Mount Finlayson and the sand dunes that stretched from the toe of the tiny inlet to Cattle Pass. The midmorning sun was beginning to heat things up as Scott and Dandy drove up in the Jeep. The *Picaroon's* single mast poked invitingly over the gates to the south dock. No wind for sail today. It was going to be a scorcher. The air already smelled of dead fish. One of the gill-netters had dumped a load of hake that was piled up on the rocks waiting for the next tide to wash it out.

In the creek, a sprinkling of pleasure cruisers and sailboats lay peacefully at anchor, and the long string of gill-netters and purse seiners were still rafted together along the north finger dock. Not a whisper of wind disturbed the water, and on the fishing boats there was a tomblike quiet that reminded Scott of Sunday morning after the fishermen's usual Saturday-night brawls. But this was still Saturday, and there was a disturbing cheerlessness about it.

Scott expected to see some of the Cape residents whose homes fronted on the creek complaining about last night's noise, but there was no one in sight. There'd been a move afoot on the Cape to get the fishermen out of the creek, a move Scott had fought, in spite of his reluctance to get involved in Cape affairs. There was no denying the fishermen were foul-mouthed and noisy at times, but Scott had crewed with them and knew firsthand what a hard life they lived, made harder by the current problems. They were entitled to blow off a little steam.

Scott climbed out of the Jeep and started across the gravel road toward the docks, Dandy running ahead of him. Even from the road the *Nellie J* was an imposing ship. All wood, the big purse seiner measured a hundred feet or better, and her skiff, made of steel and powered by a big diesel inboard, was a good six feet longer than the *Picaroon*.

Scott reached the rock that stuck up over the ramp and spotted Vic's deeply tanned face coming out of the *Nellie J*'s doghouse. Vic wasn't tall, but he was muscular, with shoulders so straight you could almost see him on a parade ground drilling his old platoon, a marine sergeant's cap set forward on a closely shaved head, his lips set in a determined line.

This morning he had the night's growth of stubble on his cheeks, and the black hair on his chest glistened wet as though he'd just stepped out of the shower. He lit a cigarette and blew a small cloud of smoke into the windless air. He stood there, hunched over the port rail, and stared across the bay. Scott knew the feeling of standing alone on the deck, the water slapping gently against the hull. It wasn't a moment to interrupt.

He walked softly toward the ramp. As he grew closer he observed the droop to Vic's shoulders. Concerned, he started down the ramp onto the fishermen's pier, which was separated by another gate from the Cape's own pleasure-boat dock. "Morning!"

Vic looked up, raised a brawny tattooed arm in greeting. "Oh . . . hi, Doc. You heard they shut us down again?"

Scott nodded, and saw, as he'd feared, Vic's face had misery written all over it.

"Yeah, they treat us like yo-yos—give us a day, take it back. Piss on all of them. C'mon aboard. We'll break out a six-pack and shoot the shit."

Scott swung a leg over the *Nellie J*'s rail. Dandy was already bouncing all over the stern deck, his shoulder clearly back to normal. His tail banged against the metal inside rails, sending a rattle across the peaceful cove like the clap of kettledrums. "Easy, Dandy!" Dandy skidded to rest under the skiff.

Georgie Ross, Vic's skiffman, stumbled out of the cabin. His red beard bristled like a broom, and, from the swelling under his half-closed eyelids, Scott guessed young Georgie had most definitely partied late. Georgie carried a large plastic sack that, from the lumpy bulges, looked to be full of empty beer cans. Georgie spotted Dandy and dropped the bag. It hit the deck with a clunk. "Hey, Dandy!"

Dandy squirreled out from under the skiff and bounded like a horse over the fish locker. He and Georgie went down, black fur and red hair rolling around with boots and paws like colliding linemen on a football field. They went on with the game until Dandy had mopped Georgie's whiskered cheeks wet.

Vic grinned at their antics; he had a soft spot for both the boy and the dog. "C'mon, Georgie, you'll wake the neighbors."

The words came too late. The racket woke up the other boats. Facing the *Nellie J*'s bow on the *Mollie O*, Davey Olson cracked the hatch open, stuck his unshaved face out, and squinted at the sun. His sandy hair was uncombed, and his unsmiling face showed no trace of his usual breezy disposition.

"Morning," Scott said cheerfully. "Big party last night?"

Davey lit a cigarette. "More like a fuckin' wake."

"Sorry about the shutdown," Scott said.

Davey had no interest in conversation and looked off at the water, much as Vic had a few moments earlier, smoking and staring glumly into space. Slowly, the other fishermen began to show signs of life, not with the usual shouting and kidding around, but with a lot of bitching and long faces. Everyone was taking the shutdown hard, which only pointed more clearly to their mounting financial troubles. It was, Scott thought, catching some of the mood himself, not a fair world.

Further evidence the men were getting beat down was the lack of care they were taking with their boats. Even on the *Nellie J* there were bottles, boots, fishing tackle, cans, and plastic buckets cluttering up the deck, and the whole ship looked in need of a hosing down. Normally, Vic ran one of the sharpest boats around, and, for all that, Vic, Davey, and the others were also happy men by nature. Scott found it depressing.

Vic leaned over the port rail to lower a crab pot into the water.

"Where's the rest of your crew, Vic?"

"They took off."

"Don't see the *Olga* anywhere."

"She's up on the block."

"You're selling her?" This was a new revelation and something of a surprise, since Vic had a deep attachment to the boat.

Vic shrugged. "Who needs two boats?"

Scott knew there was another reason. In the good years, Vic ran three boats—the *Nellie J*, named after his first wife, the *Olga C*, named after his second, and the *Brunhilde*, which, following the last divorce, he'd named after his since-departed German shepherd. Vic's son Mark had skippered the *Brunhilde*, but when Mark returned to college at the end of the season, Vic sold the ship because, as he told Scott, two boats were enough. Now, apparently, one was to be enough.

As was their usual routine, Georgie started the lift that unrolled the net from the reel and spilled it over the boom. They let it roll until yards of loose pieces of net drifted onto the dock. Here it would dry while they repaired the tears from their last catch. As Vic said, he wanted it ready when the "fuckin' bureaucrats" decided to let them out again.

"I'll help," Scott said.

"There's some waders in the cabin."

Scott fetched the waders and pulled them on over his jeans, and they all went at it, rolling out the net while water sloshed under their boots. For the next hour they worked tying string to broken sections of mesh and spreading the coarse fabric out on the deck to dry. Doing something, even this monotonous task, gave one a sense of purpose.

Vic's spirits picked up. He became chatty, teasing Georgie and showing more than a bystander's interest in Owen's murder. "I heard you got called in on it, Doc."

Scott nodded. "Too late, though. He'd been dead a couple hours. Had a hole in his middle the size of a baseball."

"Gawd." Georgie whistled.

"Had to get pretty damn close to do that kind of damage, even with a shotgun," Vic observed as he cinched up a loose end of mesh. "I remember a lieutenant in Korea, took an M16 in the chest. Split him open like a can of spaghetti. Poor bastard didn't know what hit him."

Georgie stopped working, removed the waders, and dangled his bare feet over the stern. "Wouldn't you think Owen would've beat it out of there? I mean, hey, if somebody pointed a double-gauge at me, I'd split so fast all they'd see of me would be my butt."

Interested in Georgie's observations, Scott said, "As a matter of fact, he didn't look like he'd run a step. Must've froze. Fear will do that."

Vic disagreed. "Didn't expect to get shot."

"You think it was someone he knew and trusted?"

"Why not? Everybody who knew him hated his guts."

"Add to that, his house is impossible to see from the road."

"Not from the water," Georgie said, catching Vic's frown.

"We see those flaky friends of his flitting 'round there, boozing it up every weekend."

"You were out that day, weren't you, Vic?" Scott said.

"Wasn't anywhere near the place."

After a time they quit work to sit on the deck in the shade of the skiff. The conversation worked its way back to Owen. Georgie, who'd given much thought to the murder, had his own suspicions.

"Do you have anyone particular in mind?"

Georgie folded up his long legs Indian-style and leaned forward confidentially. "I'd take a hard look at Bob Delaney."

Scott was surprised at the second mention of the real estate man.

"Or that wired-up wife of his."

"Marilyn?"

"Yeah, the foxy blonde who whips in and out of here in the Tollycraft."

Scott had a mental picture of Marilyn Delaney aiming her Tolly at Griffin Bay and shooting out of the creek like a rocket on a sled. The commission had warned her more than once about breaking the five-knot speed limit for the creek. Scott also remembered Toni had never liked Marilyn, and that Al thought her sadly lacking in gray cells. To this point, Scott disagreed. Marilyn was bright enough, but was the type who thought empty-headedness won male approval.

"'Course, she's not the only dame jets outta here, but you can tell when it's her 'cause she's always talking. Voices carry real good on the water, and you can hear her all the way to Seal Rock, going on about those parties of Owen's."

"Anything in particular about them?"

"Well, the drinking, and the wheeling and dealing . . . lotta that, and stocks, condo deals, and the like."

"Were Delaney's involved?"

"Up to their necks. According to Marilyn, Wentworth screwed them real good on one deal."

"Which one was that?"

Georgie shrugged, apparently bored with details. "I dunno. She was talking to the mousy-looking lady who runs a Bayliner. I think she said something about a land deal in Gold River, or maybe it was Campbell River." He thought a moment. "Anyways, somewhere on Vancouver Island."

In all of what Georgie said, nothing incriminated Delaney any more than the other victims of Owen's sharp dealings. It proved what Scott already knew—that Owen had been a cheat—and left Scott with the same gnawing questions. Why had Toni had anything to do with a man like Owen? And, for that matter, why had Vic invested in West Coast?

They went back to mending the nets. Without a breeze of any kind, the creek soon heated up like an oven. Scott took off the waders and stripped to his shorts. Dandy crawled under the skiff, rolled over on his back, and fell asleep, snoring loudly. The sun put a glare on the water, so Scott had to squint. The masts of a big ketch flashed white as it started out of Griffin Bay in front of the sun. It was under power and fell in behind a line of pleasure cruisers heading north up San Juan Channel.

After a while they stopped working and sat around, drinking beer, while Vic told stories about his Alaska runs, about ships colliding and disappearing in the fog. "You never saw anything like it. The *Anna Marie* went right off my radar, never saw her again."

"Were you running heavy seas?"

Something of a mystic in many ways, Vic rolled his brown eyes and talked about mysterious forces. "No storms. Nothin' like that. Mark said it had to do with magnetic pulls. Carl said there were big undertows on the Inside Passage. All I know is we never saw her again, not a trace, and all hands were lost."

Scott had heard the story a number of times, each time told with a different twist, and whether true or a figment of Vic's imagination, Scott had never been sure.

"I hear you picked up a nice load of sockeye in the trap this week." The trap was a deep tidal pool about four hundred yards off South Beach where the experienced fishermen often found good runs of salmon. It was a relatively small spot, which the older men, like Vic, considered their private reserve. Too late, Scott caught the eye signals from Georgie, whose face screwed up as though he'd bit into a lemon.

Curses rolled off Vic's lips. It was an incident involving Vic's boat and the Indians. The *Nellie J* had started her set off South Beach, and one of the Indian boats, a bow picker, moved in and crowded her. Vic's face darkened. "Laid his net right into the pocket just as Georgie started the swing. I fixed him. I cranked the wheel, turned into his net, and the son of a bitch crossed his own net beating it out of there."

"They left hoppin' mad," Georgie agreed. "We nearly ran over them. Almost lost our own net in the bargain."

"They won't be back," Vic said, ignoring the disapproval in Georgie's voice. "If they come 'round again, I'll blow their fuckin' canoe right out of the water."

"But you got a good price for the sockeye?" The question, intended to defuse his friend's anger, only stoked the fire.

"Hell no! The new buyer's stealing us blind."

Georgie explained: "This is the same bunch that put West Coast on the skids. Outbid them until West Coast ran outta dough and chased all the small buyers out."

It was familiar enough. The new buyer was now all there was, and the fishermen had to take whatever price was offered. No wonder Vic had put money into West Coast. It was a move of desperation. What else might a desperate man do?

Eight

The following day, Scott decided to get the engine on the *Picaroon* in top working condition. He'd promised Erin a sail, and weather reports forecast moderate winds. He was bent over the engine well, changing the oil on the Grey, when he heard the sound of heels on the dock. It was Marilyn Delaney, decked out in snow-white slacks, a bright red sun top, and open-toed sandals. She clicked right over, leaned over the well, and smiled tobacco and perfume all over him.

"Scott," she said. "Thought it was you. Lorene said you were on the island. Where you been hiding yourself?"

Scott wiped grease off his hands with a rag and looked up into canary-blond hair and an evenly tanned face. "A looker," Georgie called her. She was that, by any standards.

He smiled up at her. "Where you off to?"

"I'm meeting Bob at Roche. He's taking some clients out for a spin."

"How *is* Bob?"

She lifted her arms in disgust. "All wrapped up in real estate. Sales, sales, sales! We're running these people over to Sidney for lunch today, the mainland tomorrow. Bob uses the boat for business so he can take it off his taxes, which is all right if you don't mind who you associate with. For my part, I like to pick my friends, if you know what I mean."

Georgie hadn't exaggerated about Marilyn. "Wired," Georgie said.

"Next week it's Campbell River again, and that's how it goes.

Hard to catch ourselves coming and going. Never see anyone on the Cape anymore." Except Owen. She'd seen him the night he died. "Terrible, wasn't it?" She hugged her long brown arms. "I shiver thinking about it. Getting so a person isn't safe anywhere."

"Hard to think of a killer among one's neighbors," Scott said.

It wasn't what she had in mind. "You don't honestly think someone on our Cape shot Owen? It was the motorcyclists, I'm just sure of it, the way they tear around the lighthouse, all doped up. Bob says they'd do anything for money to buy their drugs. You heard they stole one of Owen's African masks? Owen told me once how much they cost. Would you believe we could buy a brand-new thirty-foot Tolly for the price of just one of those creepy things? I told Owen he should keep them under lock and key. He'd be alive today if he had. Makes you sick, doesn't it?"

She continued talking long after her mind ran out of thoughts, then, looking at her watch, said, "Damn! Bob will be chewing nails." With a little toss of her head, she started for the twenty-six-foot Tollycraft tied to the outside slip.

"Won't take you long in that job," Scott said, looking at the inboard-outboard that powered her. "What have you there? Couple hundred horses?"

She smiled. "Three hundred. Marvelous, isn't it? Bob says I get carried away when I get behind the wheel, but I love going fast, letting the spray hit my face. Gives me a feeling of power, you know what I mean?"

Scott laughed. "I'm a sailor, remember?"

"You don't know what you're missing. When you want to try it, let me know. It's exhilarating, I can tell you."

She climbed the ladder to her flying bridge and turned on the big engine. With surprising skill, she backed the boat out of its slip, paused briefly to wave, then, as Georgie had described, rocketed out of the creek, her hair blowing like straw in the wind. The Tolly kicked up a wake that would have swamped a tug.

Scott was just finishing with the Grey when Erin arrived. "A perfect day," she said, breathing deeply of the air.

"Fair wind," he agreed.

A ripple started across the creek. The forecasts called for freshening late in the afternoon, but it was still only eleven, which gave them plenty of time for a good run before any problems might develop.

They started out with a gentle wind at their backs, bright sun, and no cloud cover. Scott set a course up San Juan Channel to Upright Head, and the jib billowed out like a plumped-up pillow, leading the way. The only sound was the soft rush of water against the hull and the rustle of Dacron filling in the wind. Two seagulls on a log floated past. Erin saluted them. They looked back, uninterested.

"You won't feel we're going fast with the wind behind us, but we're actually running close to four knots, which isn't bad," Scott said.

Erin's only previous experience had been with the little C-Larks on the lake. This was totally different.

He steered toward Shaw Island. They spoke infrequently, and Erin seemed not the least uncomfortable with the silence. She was content to watch, learn by observing, and do, without asking pointless questions. She was a good sailor and good company.

Beyond Turn Rock, the wind shifted. There was a little bite to it now. It stung the cheeks and moistened the eyes. Erin took the helm and quickly had the *Picaroon* heeled so water spilled lightly over the gunwales and trickled along the decks. A flotilla of pleasure cruisers coming from Upright Head overtook them, rumbled past, stirring big rolls of water that broke over the *Picaroon's* bow. Water gushed and tumbled into a cascade of spray that traveled the length of the deck and showered them both. It ran off Scott's jacket and puddled up in the cockpit, where Erin stood in a pool of water. Erin pushed dripping strands of pale hair back from her face and put on a jacket. They headed into Friday Harbor, and a small ketch moved up swiftly behind them.

"Should I fall off the wind?"

"Keep your course. He'll pass on our starboard."

She watched the ketch doubtfully. It was a race. The boy piloting the ketch was enjoying the contest, running a little recklessly with sails trimmed taut, gaining on them, crowding. Another string of cruisers increased the chop, and the *Picaroon* bobbed and pitched. The ketch moved up, ran so close they heard her sails whipping and snapping in the wind. She closed the gap to a whisker. Erin's eyes fastened on the threadlike path of water that separated the two boats.

"Should we come about?"

"Just hold her steady."

The ketch had more square footage of sail, which gave her the edge. A fresh burst of wind drove her forward. In one quick surge, she winged by, jib trimmed to the wind, sails working in concert, passed with only the flash of a whitecap and the whipping of sails between them. Her skipper waved a victory salute, and Scott was so close he could have counted every button on his shirt. Erin waved back, her face flushed with energy. "She handles beautifully, Scott."

It was just past noon when they drew near the breakwater in Friday Harbor. They handed down the sails and motored in. Friday was its usual mangle of boaters and tourists. They tied up at the guest float and hiked to the top of the hill and a small café that overlooked the customs dock. It was a particularly pleasant spot, and the restaurant quickly filled with more boaters.

"Grandpa says you're up for the whole summer," Erin said conversationally.

"Didn't he tell you I've more or less moved to the islands permanently?"

She seemed surprised. "You left your practice?"

"Yes."

"What a shame. Everyone says you're such a wonderful surgeon."

He sipped a glass of Chardonnay and waited for the next assault, the one Al constantly harped on, about his training and the rest of it. It never came. She started talking about the sail.

At the patio's edge, the flag on the pole snapped like a

starched shirt on a line. More boats coming in. None going out. The waitress brought coffee and dessert, and Erin talked about Victoria, Vancouver Island's largest city, "a little bit of old England," and only an hour's run by fast boat from the Cape.

"Funny about the African mask turning up in Victoria," she said. And then, "Did I tell you Leroy called yesterday? He wanted to see if we had overlooked anything. Oh, that reminds me. I ran into a friend of yours yesterday. Preston Fields."

The second time Fields had come up in the past few days. "How do you happen to know Pres?"

"I met him when he stopped in to see Grandpa."

"I didn't know he and Al were friends."

"I don't think they are. Preston wanted Grandpa to serve on the committee to save the whales. Actually, what Preston wanted was the use of Grandpa's name, to give the group prestige."

"Did Al join?"

"No. He wants the whales to have the protection of law and all that. He says it's that he doesn't trust Preston."

"And you, what do you think of Preston?" His mind was on Toni at Owen's party with the marine biologist, and the sarcasm slipped into his voice.

She picked it up. "He's intelligent, sensitive. Did you know he organized an athletic workshop for the high school kids on the island?"

No, he hadn't known. Scott attacked the rest of his pie.

They finished lunch and headed out of the harbor in gusting winds, with sails up and Scott at the helm. A cloud speared the southern sky, and the water took on broad patches of gray. The wind blew the spray against his face, and he tasted salt. Ought to have warned him. Suddenly there were no boats coming or going through the passageways. Only the wind kicked up the chop. Coming around Brown Island, Scott's windometer registered twenty knots. No problem, but a look at the fast-disappearing sun told him the wind might build. He looked at his watch. Only one-thirty. Should he go back to Friday or run it out?

Unaware of his concern, Erin began talking about how she'd

always wanted to sail in a good wind with a skipper who knew his stuff, or something equally silly. The wind let out a howl and blew his jacket full. Across the bay the waters churned up. They were only an hour's run to the creek, and Scott had, after all, sailed in much heavier winds. It wasn't particularly enjoyable, and required concentration and hard work. But he'd done it many times, usually alone. "We'll run for it," he said.

He studied the peaks of the waves as the rolls tumbled and toppled into foam. They were breaking at a height of three to four feet. He could handle it. But in the distance the waves appeared to rise and fall more sharply. Could get rougher as they started into more open waters.

Erin sensed his indecision. "Should we have left earlier?"

"No problem. A bit more wind than we had coming up. We'll reef down, give less sail to the wind. Makes for a smoother ride, even if it takes us a few minutes longer. I think it would be a good idea to slip on the life jackets, though."

Erin went below to retrieve them, handed Scott one, and put hers on. Over the heavy outer clothing the jacket made for a lot of bulk, and she made a joke about it as she struggled to make it fit. The wind whistled through the open hatch.

Scott considered taking the inside passage around Turn Island, but decided against it. Maneuvering the shoal pass in bad weather could be difficult under sail. He ran the main down until it looked like a crib-size sheet, and steered a course the long way around Turn. The *Picaroon* quickly settled in. The action was mostly up and down, not too uncomfortable. But when they rounded the buoy off Turn Rock, everything changed. The boat started to roll. With the water moving in so many different directions it was hard to keep her pointed. Big whirling rollers lifted her up out of the water and dropped her back. She swayed and heaved. It was miserably uncomfortable now, with the waves striking from all sides. Erin had to hold on to the cockpit rail to keep from falling.

"Always get a rip in here," Scott said, trying to reassure her.

The windometer edged over thirty knots, and the increased noise made hearing difficult. He had to shout to be heard. "We've been overpowered. We'll go on the reach, let out the main, take some of the pressure off."

It meant a change of direction. If she was frightened of changing direction in these heavy seas, she gave no sign of it. She understood about turning from her experience in the C-Larks. She knew about letting the bow swing into the wind, allowing the jib to flutter free while the boat took its new heading. There was only one potential problem.

"We need enough momentum to swing the hull around," Scott explained. "The cross chop tends to slow our forward motion, which means we have to cinch the jib down quickly so we don't lose the wind and wallow in the waves." He didn't add that if they lost their forward progress in these swirling seas, they could go over too far. Boats sometimes heeled far enough to capsize when coming about in a storm, and it was this possibility he was thinking about as he prepared to start their turn. "Ready to come about?"

She nodded, and watched for his signal.

"Hard alee!" He cranked the wheel. The *Picaroon* started to turn. The jib fluttered loose as Erin let go the sheets that held the boat. Waves piled up on all sides. Water smashed into the bow, let loose over the cabin, and spilled into the well. Erin worked frantically to secure the lines. Scott helped her winch in. The *Picaroon* started over on her side, leaned so far her gunwales brushed the cresting waves. She gained speed, started back up, and stretched out in her new direction. Scott eased the main sheet to unleash the boom, and played out the big sail. She bulged like a parachute. The rocking motion subsided. The boat gained speed, started back up, and stretched out on her new tack.

"Well done!" Scott said.

But across the cockpit, Erin, her eyes on the water behind them, did not look pleased. Scott soon saw the cause, a small Whaler coming out of the passage by Turn Island, tracking a bumpy path toward the channel.

"Who would be crazy enough to take a runabout out in this?" she asked.

"Don't worry. He'll head back as soon as he sees what it's like out here."

The weather worsened. Their jackets blew puffy sleeves, and the water splashed their faces so much that seeing was a problem. Gale-force winds are defined as thirty-five knots or more, and, according to Scott's instruments, some of these gusts were blowing in excess of forty. These were the kind of winds that demasted ships, the kind of winds that could pick a small boat out of the chop, flip her upside down, and throw her back, head-down into the sea. Scott looked back, strained to see through the gushing stream that flew through the rigging. Twisting and turning, the Whaler cleared the pass and pressed on. Must be kids, Scott decided.

The opposing forces of the incoming tides formed cavernous foaming eddies, and the *Picaroon* began to pitch, climbing up one wave, crashing down another. The boat caught one on her side and rolled. It was more uncomfortable than dangerous, but it took all Scott's attention to keep her head up, and he started to think about bringing the main down farther. Motoring without his sail would be worse, he decided. The *Picaroon* had been converted from a lifeboat hull, and hadn't much ballast. She'd roll even more without the sail to stabilize her. There was uncertainty in Erin's face.

"It's always the worst out here in the open," Scott shouted. "Won't be long. We're moving well."

Erin nodded. By now she knew the dangers that still faced them. Scott fixed a bearing on Seal Rock across Griffin Bay. A few more minutes to the creek.

"Scott, the little boat, it's still coming."

The Whaler was fighting its way toward them, two people aboard. It slammed over the whirlpools, motor in and out of the waves, planed and dipped, spouting water over her bow like one of the killer whales, and, like the whales, came up for air and kept going.

The long cloud that had started like a sword across the horizon lengthened. All at once the entire sky was filled with it. The Whaler continued to beat a choppy and determined path directly behind them.

"Are they racing us? They couldn't be that stupid, could they?" Erin asked.

"If they aren't careful, they'll get themselves broached." And fall overboard, and, Scott thought irritably, we'll have to risk our necks pulling them out. Who were these fools who'd come out in gale-force winds in a small outboard? Then he remembered that he was a fool who'd come out in it, too.

The Whaler gained on them. A hundred yards off Pear Point, Erin made an observation. The two men aboard the Whaler, the ones called Charlie and Jerry, were the same two who'd come into the café on Friday. They'd ordered a beer, she said, and started to leave without paying, and the waitress had called them back. The incident had gone by Scott completely.

It had been an insane idea until now. Scott hadn't seen their faces that night. Now, as he strained to see across the short fetch of water, he still couldn't make them out clearly, but he remembered the heavy shoulders on Charlie, the driver, and the long arms of his companion, arms that swung a club like a baseball bat. It couldn't possibly be coincidence.

All that separated the Whaler from them now was the unpredictable breaking of the waves, which impeded the Whaler's forward motion. Who were these men? What was their purpose out here in the nearly empty seas? Scott already had an answer. It was crazy, dangerous; but these weren't careful men. They'd taken the sheltered passage out of Friday, hoped, staying close to shore, to catch the *Picaroon*, unprotected, alone, force her into a broach, capsize her, and return safely to Friday the same way they came. To be capsized wasn't necessarily the worst of it. Going over with sails furled, chances are air would be trapped under the boat, and she wouldn't sink right away. But these waters were cold, less than forty degrees even in the heat of summer. When a plane crashed in the sound sometime back,

Scott remembered, people had died of hypothermia in less than fifteen minutes. What a stupid mess he'd gotten them into.

He weighed his alternatives. He could lift the main and get their speed up and quite possibly be demasted or risk tearing the sails to shreds, or he could wait for the Whaler to play a game of chicken in which the *Picaroon* would veer to avoid being cut in two and be broached. There appeared no choice at all.

The *Picaroon* dropped into a trough. Water flooded the cockpit. It was an effort just to hold on to the wheel against the power of the wind and the sea. For the first time, fear showed itself on Erin's face.

"They're going to hit us."

Scott shook his head. That wasn't the idea. Even if they rammed the *Picaroon* and managed to drive a hole big enough to sink her, the impact would most likely upend the Whaler as well. It was a matter of angles and forces of the waves. Maybe these two could do it, get out unscathed, but Scott doubted it very much.

"You think they're playing a game?" Erin's voice edged up.

He didn't tell her what he actually thought, that they wanted to force the *Picaroon* to turn abruptly, which would send the boat over in six-foot swells, then, if need be, put a line on her and finish the job. The *Picaroon* couldn't outrun the Whaler even in this chop, even if they ran with full sail, which was, at this point, unthinkable. If he came about too swiftly he would most likely accomplish what they were after, anyway, and possibly get struck midships in the bargain. Whoever these two were, they knew ships and were familiar with these waters.

Erin had a desperate look in her eyes as she held on to the cockpit rail, her hair blowing wildly in the wind. There was no time left in the test of wills. The pilot of the Whaler took a bounce and opened her up. In speed, the *Picaroon* was no match for the double-hulled speedboat. Scott remembered thinking, *We'll go over, be thrown into the sea, left to drown.* An eight-foot roller broke over their stern. The Whaler hurtled over it. Scott had no time to prepare Erin. He pulled in the main. "Ready to jibe!" He was counting on her experience with those C-Larks.

Erin flew across the cockpit to the lines.

"Jibe!" A turn *away* from the wind, not into it, to gather speed, not lose it, a racing turn, with danger of demasting in heavy winds.

The Whaler's bow nosed up. The *Picaroon* swung 'round. Scott watched the mast with a tight chest as he thought: Have to warn Erin to stay away from the main, find the high place, hang on. The sloop pulled and twisted, gaining speed. Another roller crashed over the bow. The *Picaroon* nosed up, aimed at the Whaler's belly.

The pilot of the Whaler had a look of panic as he laid on the wheel. For one breathless count of five he spun, around and around in a dizzy circle. Erin's scream died on the wind as the Whaler skipped loose and pounded over the waves, up and down and sideways, out of control. It flew across the reef, ran up the pumice-scarred beach at Pear Point, and, scraping and cracking, piled up on the rocks.

Nine

"I don't believe it," Erin said in a voice close to breaking. "They made it!"

The two crawled out of the Whaler, and, on hands and feet like crabs, scrambled across the beach. Too damn easy, Scott thought. If they'd been tossed into the ice-cold sound and left to drown, it would have been no more than they deserved.

No time for a second look. The wind had increased. It whiffled and moaned through the rigging, rattled around the cabin, and blew in Scott's face, bringing with it fresh spurts of frothing spray. The waves twisted around them wildly, slamming against the sides of the hull and throwing water over the decks and into the well faster than the scuppers could handle it. Below decks the pots that had fallen off the stove banged against the toeboards, a mild annoyance in the midst of their other troubles, but a reminder they weren't out of danger yet. Ahead was Griffin Bay, but between the bay and the creek were three miles of open, thundering sea.

"If only the wind would let up," Erin said dispiritedly, pushing back thick strands of wet hair that blew into her eyes and dripped water on her cheeks.

Scott pointed to Mount Finlayson's hump rising over the Cape and tried to force lightness into his voice. "We'll be protected once we get inside the lee of the land. We'll have to come about once more, but then it's a straight shot to the creek."

She smiled feebly. Clearly the clash with the Whaler had weakened her nerve. He knew what she was thinking: another turn into the wind, another chance at being broached. They hadn't much choice.

"Ready?"

She nodded and waited, hand poised on the cleat.

Scott turned into the flurry of two crossing waves. It was like riding a chute. Water piled up all around. The bow went up, and the whole deck slid out from under them. Water rushed over the side onto the decks in a flood, and they started to roll like a canoe. The ballast wasn't heavy enough to counter the forces of wind and sea, and she started over. The boat creaked and groaned and kept right on going. If the main touches the water, Scott thought with a sickening sense of helplessness, we've had it.

He thought about the *Anna Marie* coming down from Alaska on the Inside Passage, running alongside Vic when she was pulled into the undertow. Scott stared into the giant ring of swirling waters and felt the *Picaroon* continue to slip. He could feel his heart pound. He was breathing in spurts, his air choked off by the realization they might be sucked into a black hole a hundred fathoms deep.

Erin braced her feet against the bulkhead, her eyes fixed on the mast. "We're going over!"

Her faint voice, like a whisper over the wind, trumpeted in Scott's ears. "No, we're not!"

He eased the line, played it out until she started to luff and whip free in the wind. Another roller hammered the bow, and it looked as though they'd be swamped in a final tug-of-war between the crossworking breakers, dragged under like the *Anna Marie*, "disappearing without a trace."

"No, dammit," Scott said again, this time to himself. He let the sails go completely free. Dacron flapped violently in the wind, and he feared the sails might rip right up their seams.

Almost in response to his voice, with the pressure off the mast, the *Picaroon* stopped her horizontal descent. She wavered a moment, undecided, and then, water sloshing the decks, inched back up. The struggle to remain upright turned into an up-and-down action as the *Picaroon* ploughed around in the enormous whirls of water.

Scott and Erin hauled the main in until it resembled a shrunken pillowslip, and he started up the Grey. Under power and sail, the *Picaroon* resumed a pitching and yawing course straight for the creek. The waves continued to build in front of them. They started down, dropped four feet into a hole, scaled back up. There were more of these, heart-stopping drops, breath-holding climbs. Scott had to catch them head-on, had to roll gently with the chop, there being no margin for miscalculation. Not much farther to go, almost out of the cross chop. All he had to do was keep her headed. A plunging wave curled and broke into foam over the bow. They shot across the crest of the next swell. They were closing in on the shore's shelf. The jetty rose to their port.

Scott shouted encouragement. "We're almost in the lee of the point."

Another wave spilled over the bow, and water trickled down the deck. Another followed, putting up only a fine spray. Definitely easing. Ahead was Fish Creek and Mount Finlayson acting like a giant breaker on the wind. The creek opened up its protective arms in front of them, and the *Picaroon* settled to a gentle rock. The rollers turned into slop, and Scott steered a course past Seal Rock, into the creek, bounced over a wavelet, and turned past the gill-netters rafted along the north dock. He wanted to send up a cheer, but there was no one aboard the fishing boats to hear. He turned easily into the slip, and with Erin secured the boat to her cleats.

Scott let out a long, gratifying sigh and grinned across the cockpit. He hugged Erin, and she hugged him back in joyful relief. "You were great," he said. "Just great."

There was concern on Al's face as they walked through the doorway, the wind ushering them in with a howl. "Been watching those waves for the past half hour. Pretty wild out there."

Erin kissed his cheek and began to jabber as people do after a release of great tension. "No need to worry. Scott can manage anything." She heaped praise on him, saying nothing about the obvious, that he'd used abominably bad judgment getting them in the fix in the first place.

"You should have seen your granddaughter," Scott said. "Hauled those sails like a pro." He reached for the telephone, then paused to breathe in the aroma of brandy from the glass Al handed him. "Isn't this your Christmas stuff?"

The old man shrugged, and his thin face lit up in a smile. "You're both back safe and sound."

Scott called Leroy. He was out, according to the dispatcher. This was urgent, Scott explained. She said she'd try to find him, and rang off.

Erin settled in front of the fire and began drying her hair. The phone rang.

It was Leroy, and he was at Roche Harbor, on the other side of the island, a good thirty-minute drive from Friday Harbor. Scott poured out the story. Could Leroy send his deputies right over to Pear Point? "Better check out the airport and the ferry landing, too. You might want to call ahead to Anacortes. They might've caught the three-thirty ferry."

Leroy groaned on the other end, and Scott figured he resented the advice. "Sorry," Scott said, "but they've had a good head start. I thought you'd want to get right on it."

"Wouldn't do any good. Can't touch them without a warrant or a positive ID."

"I'll come right in."

"Not necessary."

"If we don't do something, they'll be gone."

"Relax, Doc. I'll call you as soon as I turn up something."

Scott put the phone down with a dissatisfied sigh and faced the questioning faces of Erin and Al.

Al frowned. "Apparently you had more of an afternoon than I thought."

"What's all this about a break-in?" Erin said with accusing eyes for both of them. Al explained, and Erin looked at Scott, bewildered. "But what were they after?"

"I haven't a clue."

"You didn't tell me you'd seen them before."

"But I never really *saw* them. Not their faces, anyway."

"Then how do you know it's the same two?"

"They move the same, the boat's the same." They were familiar in other ways, but he wasn't sure why.

Outside, the wind let out a quick burst that rattled the windows. Al checked the firepit for a downdraft, but the flames rose steadily up the stack.

"You think those men killed Owen, right?" Erin said. "And now they're after you."

"Doesn't add up," Al said. "If they'd wanted to kill Scottie, they would have shot him on the beach when they had the chance."

"But they were after him today. I was there. And I think they'll try again."

Scott shook his head in disagreement. "I think the sheriff has it right there. It was undoubtedly an idea they dreamed up on the spur of the moment. When it didn't work, they took off. The only question is what they were after when they broke into my house."

Erin wasn't persuaded. "If it's tied into Owen, as you both seem to think, why would they be after anything at your house?"

Looking a little less upset, Al said, "Maybe it has something to do with Scott examining Owen."

Erin thought that over and rejected it.

They were still puzzling it when Leroy called again. "No trace of them," he said. "But we found the Whaler piled up on the beach at Pear Point, just like you said." According to Leroy, it belonged to one of the university people at the experimental lab who'd reported it stolen three days before. "Thanks for putting us on to it, Doc. 'Course, it's a total washout. Cracks in the glass, and the motor's bent all to hell." They would, he said, keep looking for the two men. "It's a little like picking needles out of haystacks until we get a better description."

"I told you we'd come in."

"No hurry. Tomorrow morning will do. We've covered every

corner of town. Let's face it, they aren't going to show their faces on the streets tonight." Clearly, he didn't see a tie-in to Owen, and catching them wasn't among his highest priorities. "This island might surprise you. We get break-ins all the time, and it's damn seldom we find the ones who did it."

"But they didn't take anything."

"They probably wanted to shake you up a little, get even for the fight on the beach. We see it all the time."

Scott agreed to see the sheriff in the morning, then put the phone down in disgust. Erin was certain Leroy had misunderstood. "He understood, all right. The way he sees it, we're still among the living, and the *Picaroon* is none the worse for wear." Scott shrugged. "For anyone who wasn't there it sounds far-fetched suggesting they tried to kill us."

By the window, Al had been silent. "I see they gave the fishermen a night out." He pointed to the procession of gill-netters bouncing through Cattle Pass.

"What a tough way to make a living," Erin said. "Going out in this awful stuff."

Scott nodded. Vic wouldn't be out tonight. The purse seiners had the daytime run, but the smaller boats, the gill-netters, would be out there, working their nets with a wall of water coming at them.

Scott's gaze fixed on Davey Olson's bow picker, the *Mollie O*, as she took the passage in front of Goose Island at full throttle, skillfully avoiding the rock outcropping hidden by the high tide. The *Mollie O* was small, her cabin aft, her reel midships, a planing boat with plenty of speed. That's what Davey counted on to keep him out of trouble. Of course, for him, as for all the boats, there were always those nights when the motor would go, and they'd sit it out, rocking around in a black pit until another gill-netter might happen by to give a tow, and both boats would be out their catch for the night. Scott had always admired the fishermen their toughness, their peculiar mix of fatalism and mulish will.

"They go out in everything," he said.

Ten

The sky, like the water, was dark and unfriendly as Scott and Dandy walked against the bracing chill of the wind across the road to his cabin. Late, and getting to be a habit, Scott thought pleasantly. It had been a day full to the limit. Caught in a gale, nearly run down, almost broached, and, strangely, looking back on it, he'd enjoyed himself more than he had in months.

He switched on the lights in the living room, and Dandy went for his dish and the remains of his morning kibble. The dog's crunching and the wind rushing through the eaves were the only sounds in the house. Scott snapped on his shortwave and dropped into the big chair. One of his favorite pastimes on the lonely nights was to listen to the fishermen chattering on their radios. Sometimes the calls were important, a boat in trouble, a net hooked by another boat that could wipe out an entire season's profits. Mostly, however, the calls were just talk to fill a long night.

The voice from the marine weather station in Victoria droned monotonously: ". . . high pressure ridge building on the coast . . . Cape Mudge, gale- to storm-force southerlies . . . Strait of Juan de Fuca, gale-force winds, gusting to forty knots . . ."

Scott switched channels. The voices of the fishermen bleated in and out, about as usual.

"Got a full load, Ray. I'm heading into Friday."

"Lucky son of a bitch."

Another voice: "Whatcha pickin' up, Todd?"

"Nothing but fuckin' green-eyes. They're tearing hell outta my nets."

The talk went on. Finally Scott looked at the clock. Time to close up shop. He reached to turn off the set. It was exactly five minutes after one. Davey Olson's baritone voice broke into the channel, sounding like a second tenor. "This is the *Mollie O* calling the Coast Guard. Come in, Coast Guard." Davey repeated the call and, receiving no reply, repeated again, this time frantically, "Where the hell are you, Coast Guard?"

Scott started for the phone, and a voice, slow and calm, answered Davey. "This is the Coast Guard cutter 00539. What's the trouble, *Mollie O?*"

"I picked up a body in my net. White male, I think. What in hell do I do with it?"

"What's your location?"

It was off South Beach. Scott grabbed his car keys and his jacket and started out the door, Dandy on his heels. The Coast Guard was still talking. "Keep your heading, *Mollie O*. We should pick you up in twenty minutes."

The wind buffeted the Jeep so much that the vehicle swung across the center stripe as Scott took the curve by the lighthouse at a good clip. The sky was black, but over the water the bouncing lights from the gill-netters blinked like stars. Beyond the sand dunes the road straightened, and he laid a heavier foot on the accelerator. Dandy lost his balance and slid into Scott's lap. Scott eased up on the pedal.

He was thinking about that body in Davey's net and the two men and remembering why they'd been familiar. Had the *Mollie O* dragged up a victim from a skirmish on the decks of the *Pilgrim* four nights ago? Were the men on the Whaler the same ones who'd worked the lines on the schooner's afterdeck? Had those two clubbed a man to death in the fog that night, or was it only Scott's nightmare revisited?

Scott braked the Jeep against a stack of driftwood, and, fighting violent gusts of wind, he and Dandy started climbing over the logs that littered the path to the water's edge. Big waves lifted logs out of their sand and rock beds and rolled them back into the sea.

They'd be transferring the body to the Coast Guard cutter not far from here. Big plunging breakers thundered over the beach, sending off a phosphorescent glow that lit up the sand.

The wind was sharp. Scott turned up his jacket collar and plodded closer to the stretch of sea where the fishing boats were at work. He picked a spot where the sand and rocks converged and stood there, listening for the rumble of diesels over the howling wind. All across the water in front of South Beach the gill-netters stretched out end to end, bobbing like corks. Somewhere among them was the *Mollie O*, waiting, half her net dragging against the tide and the chop, with a crab-picked body snarled in the other half.

Out over the strait, like a well-choreographed ballet, the little boats forged a path between their nets for the Coast Guard to slip through. Flashing signals lit up the center of their ring, and these, Scott guessed, came from the *Mollie O's* lamps.

Time passed slowly on the darkened beach. The roar of wind and tide blotted out the voices that he could have heard on a calm night, the cursing and bitching at the delay that was costing the men a set, at the frustration of Davey and his crew as they cut up their net, separating fish and seaweed to unload their unwanted cargo.

Strong floods lit up the channel around Cattle Point, signaling the arrival of the Coast Guard. Scott imagined he heard the cheers of relief from all the boats, the loudest aboard the *Mollie O*. The cutter steamed through the path provided by the gill-netters, and the transfer began. It would be no fun on a night like this, with the water pounding their hulls, boats tossing and banging against each other, scraping paint and jarring nerves. From the beach, Scott waited. After what seemed hours, but in actuality was less than thirty minutes, the cutter started to back up and swing out as it headed for Friday Harbor.

Scott started for the Jeep, anxious now to see what Davey had dragged up from the bottom of the trap.

In Friday Harbor a crowd collected around the customs dock as Scott parked the Jeep. For a town already reeling from one murder, Scott imagined this latest would have everyone stirred up. The docks were well lit from the Coast Guard floods, so it looked like a Seahawk game on a Saturday night in the Dome. "You stay here, boy," Scott told Dandy, and he walked down the ramp toward the lights.

The sheriff's staff was doing its level best to deal with the latest crisis, but it was much more than they were used to, considering a normal day's log consisted of complaints about barking dogs and domestic arguments. Leroy's deputy, Harold Cane, stood beside the sheriff's patrol car, blocking entrance to the dock. He grinned when he saw Scott.

"Leroy will be glad to see you. One of the gill-netters dragged up a corpse."

"Where's Leroy?"

Harold jerked his head in the direction of the Coast Guard cutter. "They got a big flap going out there. They pulled this guy up in the strait, so Leroy says the Coast Guard should have him. The Coast Guard says since they fished him out near South Beach, he belongs to us."

Apparently Leroy lost the argument. Scott found him, head bent in thought beside the draped body. "Harold said you had a problem."

"Talk about Murphy's Law," he said. "Old Doc Miles is out on a case on the west side, Frank's on the mainland—hours before he gets back—and I have to ID this bird, check him against missing persons in Canada." He outlined the tasks that were his, which, by Scott's calculations, would take him the rest of the night and then some. "Oh, hell," he said finally, lifting his big hands in disgust. "Sorry, Doc, didn't mean to unload on you."

Since it was unlike the big man to "unload" on anybody, Scott guessed he was tired to the point of exhaustion, and, considering the events of recent days, understandably. The sheriff and his small staff were being strained to the limit.

"How can I help?" Scott said.

"I know the water changes the rate of deterioration, but could you give me a ballpark guess on when this guy died?"

"Let's have a look."

Leroy drew a deep sigh. "It's not a pretty one." He lifted the tarp.

Scott drew in his breath. It wasn't a pretty one. The carnivorous creatures of the sea had worked him over badly enough to make identification a serious problem. It wasn't that, however, that brought the sharp pull at Scott's chest. The dead man was wearing a torn and seaweed-crusted, but still clearly yellow, slicker, exactly like the one on the man who'd disappeared from the stern of the *Pilgrim*.

He was tall, well built, white male, late thirties. Beyond that, however, all Scott could tell with certainty was that he had chestnut hair. Scott tried to put a time on tissue decay that had been partially slowed by the cold salt water. He tried to spot injury marks. This, too, was difficult with so much tissue missing. The head, or what remained of it, was bloated and like pulp, nothing to tell from it without extensive examination. He unfastened the torn pieces of jacket. No wounds on the upper torso. He probed as much as he thought he should without making the coroner's work more difficult. It all fit, but he couldn't be sure.

"Seen enough?" Leroy said.

Scott nodded, and Leroy quickly threw the cover back.

"How long do you think he's been in the water?" Leroy continued.

"Four days, I should think."

"Between four and six, or two and four?"

It was time to tell Leroy what he'd seen that night. "If my hunch is right, he's been in the water exactly four days."

Leroy looked puzzled. "Run that by me again."

"It might sound a little wild."

"Doc, nothing could sound wild to me tonight."

Scott told him about the *Pilgrim* and the three men on the afterdeck and finished with, "I didn't actually see them throw him over, but it looked like someone had gone in, so I followed the ship out of sight. Never saw the man in the yellow slicker again."

Leroy stared quietly at his shoelaces.

Scott had no idea if Leroy thought the story plausible or off the wall. "Well?" Scott said, beginning to get an uncomfortable feeling it was the latter.

"He could've gone below, couldn't he?"

Off the wall it was. "Until tonight, that's what I thought," Scott said. "But at the time I didn't think so, and after the run-ins with those two—"

Leroy groaned. C'mon, Doc, you're not going to tell me it was the two clowns from the Whaler."

He was, of course, going to say exactly that. "I told you it would sound crazy."

Leroy removed his hat and wiped his brow. "No—didn't mean that. It's just—well, hell, half the people on this island have yellow weather gear, and you say yourself from the distance you couldn't see their faces." Leroy sighed. "Not that seeing *his* face would do any good. So what about the time?"

"I still say three or four days. No way you can be sure without a thorough examination." Yes, Scott thought vengefully, leave it to the coroner. If he says the man died of a skull fracture, then maybe Leroy will be ready to listen. "If you're sending out notices to Canada, I'd list it as three to six. That should cover you pretty well."

Leroy nodded satisfaction. On the cause of death, he was content with accidental drowning.

"There again, you'll have to wait," Scott cautioned. "There's always the possibility of heart arrest, seizure, a blow to the head."

Leroy grinned. "Okay, Doc. Anything else?"

Scott confessed he'd found nothing definite, nothing to confirm his suspicions, and, certainly, injuries were to be expected in a fall, not to mention the bumping around the body received being pulled out by the fishermen. Any bruises or contusions would be hardly conclusive at this point.

"It's probably the wrong time to ask," Scott said, "but how are you coming on your other investigations?"

"Did I tell you we found shotgun shells in the old radar station? Looks like they match up with the ones that killed Owen."

"Odd, to shoot a man and leave the evidence only a few hundred yards away."

Leroy stuck his hands in his pockets and stared absently at the blanketed body on the deck. "Guess they had no reason to hurry."

"Unless they came by boat and left the same way. Maybe someone interrupted them, and they ducked into the radar station and waited until it was safe and then left in their boat." Scott was thinking of the Whaler.

"No evidence of a boat."

"It was a high tide that night."

Leroy smiled knowingly. The Whaler had been stolen after the murder, he pointed out.

"Look," Scott said, "I admit I didn't see them clearly, but there are other ways of identifying people."

"Such as?"

"Body build, physical aberrations."

"Did they have any?"

"The one who ran the boat, the one called Charlie, had a congenital hip problem, walked with a slight limp."

"What about the chase out there in the channel? Did you get a good look at them then?"

"I was busy, but Erin did. She saw them when they came into the restaurant, too. I'll bring her in tomorrow. You can ask her. The two from the Whaler are the same two from the break-in, I'm sure of that."

Scott slept fitfully, and not just because of Leroy's doubts.

The gill-netter traffic was particularly heavy, and the noise of the diesels, combined with those brilliant flashes off Iceberg Point, like someone shining a flashlight in his room all night, made sleep difficult.

At first he thought the blinking lights came from the Iceberg beacon, but he soon observed they ran in tandem and were much brighter, sometimes like the blips on a sonar screen, sometimes like lightning bolts that stopped for a while and then struck again when you were sure they wouldn't.

He didn't remember sleep when it came, only remembered the dream, the one where Toni walked down the beach, her long black hair unfettered and flowing free. Only this time clownlike faces without eyes floated around her. He called to her, and she began to run. Suddenly, from behind the rocks two men appeared and pounded down the pebbled tide flats after her. Scott chased them, but as he raced over the sand his feet began to sink into the pools of mud. The harder he ran the deeper he sank, until he couldn't move at all, could only watch helplessly while the two men picked Toni up and tossed her over the rocks like a rejected fish into the rolling sea.

Scott woke wringing wet. He ran his hand over the sheets, confirmed he was in bed, alone, and Toni was gone. Shivering, he snapped on the bedlight and squinted at the clock. Three! Too early to get up, but the prospect of another dream was more than he could face.

It was quiet in the room except for Dandy's heavy breathing and the rippling of water running over the rocks below the deck. The wind had subsided considerably, so only a gentle breeze blew through the screen, and even the lights from Lopez had stopped sending their unwelcome signals through his window. Scott swung his feet over the side of the bed and forced himself up. He padded into the bathroom, turned on the tap, and splashed cold water on his face.

He walked barefoot to the study, scanned the bookshelves, and selected an intriguing title, a book Fred had given him for Christmas, *How to Profit in Stocks and Bonds*. He'd given

serious consideration to stock trading as an alternative to medicine and had accumulated several books on the subject, but so far
hadn't been able to concentrate on any of them.

"This one's a sure winner," Fred promised.

He took the book back to bed with him. Dandy stirred,
looked up, saw Scott in bed, and promptly went back to sleep.
Scott finally found his own antidote for insomnia. He read only a
few moments before he, too, fell asleep, this time without
dreams.

Eleven

Erin and Al had heard about the body at South Beach.

"It's on all the morning news," Al said. "Some darn fool out there in a little boat. See it all the time. They got no respect for these waters, don't have the foggiest idea what they're doing."

Reminded of yesterday's stupidity, Scott abandoned any thought of telling them about the *Pilgrim*, and he and Erin set out for the sheriff's office.

Erin had a sharp memory for detail. She described the driver of the Whaler as a man of about thirty-six, not very tall, round face, tendency to overweight, ruddy complexion, and wispy sand-colored hair.

"Wispy?"

"Not much of it."

A limp? On this point she wasn't certain. She had noticed a tattoo on his right forearm. One of those symbols like the marines wear.

This evoked a lifted eyebrow from Leroy.

She described the second man as in his early twenties, tough, all bone and muscle, mostly bone, "mean eyes," black hair, permed.

Leroy screwed up his face. "Permed?"

"I may be wrong, but it didn't look like natural curl to me."

Leroy wrote it all down, but Scott thought it was more to please Erin, that he had already closed the book on those two. As for Owen, the only real lead so far, he said, was turning up the mask in Victoria. "So I think I'll call this expert of yours, this Brice Randall."

"What about the museum curator?" Scott said.

"She's out of town for a whole month. Not as many experts on that stuff as you might think."

Back on the street, Erin didn't appear to share Scott's feelings that Leroy had little interest in finding the two men. As they strolled down Spring Street she was still trying to recall little things about the two. When they reached the corner, she wondered if Scott was in a hurry. She wanted to check out the yarn shop.

He left her at the shop and headed out on the road to the university's experimental lab on the north shore of the harbor.

The long wooded drive into the five-hundred-acre facility opened up around the central building that housed the tanks. Here the biochemists and fisheries people studied marine plant and invertebrate sea life. Below the main research building were the docks that harbored the university vessels. A float plane was tied up to the inside dock, and beyond it were a couple of runabouts. The rest of the piers were empty. On the hillside overlooking the docks was the staff housing for faculty, visiting scientists, and the students who rotated through the center as part of their classwork.

Scott parked the Jeep and strolled over to the main building. He found Preston in the lab, wearing heavy-rimmed reading glasses as he examined a tank full of sea anemones. In the year since he'd last seen him, Preston hadn't changed. He still could have passed for thirty, though he was Scott's age. He was about six feet, sparely built, with a well-shaped face and thick, carefully groomed dark brown hair. He was good-looking and knew it, intelligent and knew that, too. He came from a wealthy Long Island family and had been eastern school trained. Scott had first met him when he was in graduate school at the university. The women had pursued him in those days, but as far as Scott knew he'd remained a bachelor.

Preston was wearing designer jeans and an expensive soft-collared shirt. He had the kind of face that seldom showed surprise. When he saw Scott he rose from his chair and rationed a half-smile. "Scott, been a while." He still spoke with the accent of the eastern well-off. He reached out slowly to accept Scott's outstretched hand.

Preston had heard about Owen. He leaned against a fish tank and stared off through the big windows at the harbor. He hadn't seen the attorney in months, he said, "but Owen was a man who made enemies without effort." He had no new ideas on the murder. His work kept him out of touch and tied down.

"You here for the summer?"

Preston nodded. "I'm senior resident. Corny is on sabbatical in Australia, so that leaves me." His sigh suggested the responsibility placed an unwanted burden on him. Since Scott knew taking Dean Cornwell's place, even for the summer, was bound to boost Preston's standings, he found the marine biologist's attitude amusing.

"You're next in line for top dog, then?"

Preston acknowledged this was "probably" true, sounding as though the whole prospect bored him immensely.

"Your work must cut into your social life."

Preston showed the first trace of a real smile. "Until recently it's been almost nonexistent, but I'm working on it."

"You missed Owen's last party. I thought you and Owen were such pals."

Scott said it in a teasing voice, but Preston had never had a sense of humor. His smile vanished. "Owen was a crude, disgusting man who took advantage of everyone he ever met. He was no friend of mine."

It was a strong indictment from a man who seldom ventured a strong opinion. Scott also remembered Preston had gone to the parties in the old days, that he, like most of the people on the Cape, used to regard Owen as a generous host and took it as a high honor to be on his guest list. Preston had his guard up now. Scott felt the force of those intense eyes, watching and waiting, waiting for the one question that had stood between them these many months. The question formed on the edge of Scott's tongue about Toni, his mind already dreading the answer. "I—ah—was looking over your docks. Where are all the big ships?" It wasn't the question Scott intended, the one he still couldn't bring himself to ask.

"We're running only the small ones around here this summer."

"What about the *Pilgrim?*"

Preston followed the path of the big *Kaleetan* ferry that was docking in the harbor. "We chartered her for the summer. She's in Campbell River at the moment."

"Kind of unusual to use a schooner in your research, isn't it?"

"It's experimental this year. Our big ships were delayed in Panama, and the people who own the *Pilgrim* came along with an offer we couldn't refuse."

"A popular decision with the students, I imagine."

"We had no trouble getting volunteers," Preston agreed with another faint smile.

"So the students crew?"

Preston turned cagy. "Officially, no."

"Has the ship been in Canada long?"

"Quite some time, yes."

Scott traced a pattern on the glass tank with his finger. "That's funny. I thought I saw her run through here last week."

The dark eyes flickered. "Yes, that's right. They ran down for a few days and left again."

Preston seemed reluctant to discuss the operation of the *Pilgrim* except on the sketchiest of terms, and Scott finally gave up. He didn't want to arouse Preston's curiosity. He asked about the lab and people they both knew and tried to make it appear this had been a social call. He must have succeeded, because Preston began looking at his watch, a clear sign he was losing interest and wanted to return to his work. Scott finally left him with his question still unanswered. Preston returned to the sea anemones and didn't look up as Scott let himself out the door.

Erin made her purchases at the yarn shop, and Scott suggested lunch at Roche Harbor on the other side of the island. Built on the site of an old lime quarry, the resort maintained an historic hotel that once was a Hudson's Bay trading post and a restaurant that overlooked the bay. A white-steepled church sat on the hill, and a short distance away were the tennis courts and the swimming pool. Mostly, it was a haven for boaters. The cruisers and sailors stacked in, side by side, across a long dock in front of the restaurant, and beyond the docks, more boats sat at anchor, their masts and counting towers stretching across half the bay. Scott found a carefree atmosphere here that was less in evidence in Friday Harbor where the townspeople took themselves more seriously.

Roche basked a brilliant blue in the summer sun, not a wind ripple in the entire bay. Scott and Erin sipped clear white Chablis from tall goblets and watched the boats come and go. A group of pleasure cruisers started in around Henry Island, coming past Center Reef on the long way from Speiden Channel. A few smaller boats ran the closer passage around Davison Head on Pearl's east corner, which prompted Erin's observation.

"Why didn't all the boats take the shortcut?"

"There's a treacherous rock outcropping out there that surfaces only at slack tide. I've seen a dozen props twisted out of shape on that little shortcut."

Erin's gaze shifted to the long passage. A tall ship, sixty or seventy feet, had turned around the jetty and was motoring toward customs.

"Beautiful. Looks a little like the *Pilgrim*."

"Except the *Pilgrim*'s a schooner. This one's a yawl."

She nodded. "That slanted topsail reminds me of buccaneers. I remember thinking that when the *Pilgrim* went through Cattle Pass last summer. By the way," she said, "is it much of a sail to Victoria?"

"Not long with a stiff wind." He emphasized the "stiff," and they both broke up laughing. People at nearby tables began to stare.

"Sorry." Erin stifled another giggle. "Wasn't funny yesterday, though, was it?"

She was, he thought, the sort of girl who would always laugh a lot.

"Do you think Leroy will ever find Owen's killer?"

"Hard to say. Leroy does a good job, but in many ways his hands are tied. His jurisdiction is the islands. Sooner or later everything goes off the islands—killers, thieves, and their booty. That makes Leroy far more dependent on the police in other areas than most law-enforcement people."

She looked into her wineglass. "As you say, the sheriff can't very well go off island to chase these people, and the authorities in other areas have their own priorities, probably don't give a hoot about San Juan Island. That's an idea, isn't it? I mean, there's nothing to stop you and me, and it could be fun to poke around ourselves."

"What had you in mind?" he said warily.

She traced a circle on the table mat with her fork. "The antique shop in Victoria."

"Do you know where it is?"

"No, but there can't be too many antique shops in downtown Victoria, and we could ask."

Scott laughed. It wasn't likely Leroy would tell. He was digesting her proposal when she pointed to the finger docks directly below them. "The yawl is tying up."

"Would you like to walk along the docks and get a closer look?"

"Oh, yes, let's do."

They were admiring the tall ship when Scott felt manicured fingernails wrap around his wrist like Archimedes' claws. "Scott!" It was Marilyn Delaney in bright red shorts, smiling at him. "Bob, see who's here!"

From the flying bridge of the shiny white Tollycraft, Bob Delaney appeared, holding the ever-present highball glass. He was wearing a brightly flowered Hawaiian shirt and Bermuda shorts, which didn't quite cover the knobby knees or fully hide a stomach that was beginning to press the limits of its belt. He hadn't changed much since the last time Scott had seen him a year ago. His brown hair under the captain's hat looked a little thinner, but he had the same fleshy face, nicely tanned, with a few more lines. Sunglasses covered his eyes. As always, his smile flashed automatically, the tool of the salesman who took his work wherever he went.

He climbed down from his boat, still holding the highball. Marilyn tugged Scott the remaining few feet, and Bob stuck out his free hand. Scott gripped it. It was wet, cold, and soft to the touch. He smelled strongly of bourbon and after-shave.

"Hi. C'mon aboard. I'll fix you a drink."

"Bob," Marilyn said, "I promised Scott a run in the boat."

"Sure—good idea."

"No—no," Scott protested, reaching behind him for Erin. "We were really just going."

Marilyn's hands moved faster to reclaim his arm than Scott could move away from them. Erin watched in amusement. "Erin," Scott said, "I think you remember Marilyn and Bob Delaney. Al Turner's granddaughter, Erin."

"Nice to see you again," Erin said, still smiling.

"Where you been hiding?" Bob said, taking her hand and steering her toward the boat.

The Delaney cabin was surprisingly roomy for a twenty-six-foot boat, well furnished with stove, refrigerator, sink, table, and cushioned benches. The walls were bare except for a picture of Bob getting a Rotary award for community service. On the bulkhead over the sink was a small Apple computer that, Scott guessed, housed Bob's real estate listings and other sales data. A nice layout. Bob must do pretty well at sales, Scott thought.

Erin said they'd sailed yesterday.

"I hope you didn't get caught in the squall," Marilyn said. "That stuff scared the skinny out of me. Bob looked at the barometer, and it was blowing thirty-five knots, and he said to hell with it, let's stay put. We tied up here and bounced like tops all night. Didn't sleep a wink."

"Wind's no problem for a sailboat," Scott said, and Erin bit back another attack of the giggles.

With the dark glasses removed, Bob's pale-brown eyes were watery and vague as they tried to focus on Scott's face. "Bourbon or vodka?"

"Bourbon with water, thanks."

"Same," Erin said.

Bob performed his bartending chores like a man happy with his work and delivered the drinks to Scott and Erin.

"You didn't fix me one," Marilyn said, none too sweetly.

Dutifully, Bob took her glass, poured in a large portion of vodka, added tomato juice, returned it to her, and sat down, looking like a man with a problem.

"How's the real estate business?" The way he brightened to the question, Scott guessed business wasn't the problem.

"I closed a big condo deal yesterday."

"How's raw land doing?"

"Great. If you're interested, got some real nice buys." In a voice starting to slur, Bob described an assortment of parcels, estimating prices so liberally that Scott imagined they came more out of the Seagram's bottle than the computer that sat over his head.

Bob finished his drink and rolled the ice cubes around the glass, touched one with his tongue, and let it slide back to the bottom. "Another?"

"No, thanks."

"What kin' of property you lookin' for?" Bob said, returning to the sink.

"Acreage."

"Ah—hobby farm. Tax dodge, huh?"

Marilyn, who was adept in the wifely practice of following two conversations at the same time, burst in. "Tell him about Canada. Bob's got some great buys on Vancouver Island, horse ranches, mining properties."

Bob's flaccid face twitched. "Marilyn, butt out."

She didn't take the suggestion well, and Erin glanced uncomfortably across at Scott while husband and wife glared at each other. Marilyn lightened up first. "C'mon," she said to Erin, "let's you and I sit on the deck and let them talk business."

Erin looked relieved as she followed Marilyn out of the cabin.

"Canada, is it?" Scott said to Bob. "I've been interested in property on Vancouver Island for years."

Bob was now having great difficulty focusing. "If you like, I can show you pieces 'round Nanaimo that'll knock your eyes out."

"I was thinking more about Campbell River."

Bob's fingers lost their grip on the glass, and ice and bourbon spilled all over the carpet. Scott reached for the paper towel and started mopping up. Bob watched, saying nothing. "There." Scott sponged the last drop. "I think I've got it all."

Bob shook his head as though he were just coming out of a trance. "Campbell River? Why ya' want anything up there? Your resale won't be worth shit."

"I've always liked the wilderness," Scott said truthfully, handing Delaney the empty glass.

Delaney gripped the table for support. "Tell you, Doc, my memory's fuzzy today. How 'bout if I look up the listings and give you a call?"

Erin was quiet on the drive home. It was the Delaneys, Scott thought darkly, spoiling a perfect afternoon. Scott turned onto Valley Road, where the foliage opened up from the densely forested parkland onto fields, farmhouses, and mud ponds. "The Delaneys are a trial," he said apologetically, "particularly when they're drinking."

"Marilyn's very friendly. Bob travels a lot. I imagine she drinks because she gets lonesome. Did you know Marilyn has been very worried about you?"

She might have said, "Did you know your house is on fire?" Scott looked at her in surprise, and the Jeep lurched toward the center stripe. He drew back into their lane. "Where did she come up with that?"

"I assumed she was talking about . . . about your wife's death," Erin said in a small voice.

He resented being the subject of Marilyn's gossipy tongue. "Her husband's got it right," he said in a terse voice. "Marilyn talks too much." He gripped the wheel tighter and took the curve a little faster than he'd intended.

"Is it hard to talk about her? About your wife, I mean?"

"Why should it be?"

She sighed. "I'm sorry. I shouldn't have brought it up."

"No reason to be sorry. What else did good old Marilyn have to say?"

"Not much."

"Don't stop now. It sounds like you two had a jolly good gabfest at my expense." Once the words were out, childish, angry, there was no way to reclaim them.

"If you really want to know," she said with an anger to match his own, "Marilyn thought Toni was beautiful and spoiled and the kind who didn't care about anyone's feelings except her own. Satisfied?"

The words stung, but he'd heard them before. Ralph had said it often enough, and Lorene, and they'd lost their capacity to shock. Erin's anger started to soften his own. "Satisfied," he said meekly.

She was quiet until they turned onto the Cape road. As they rounded the bend by American Camp and started through the grove of pine trees, she finally spoke. "You're right," she said, looking down at her hands, "it wasn't any of my business."

Twelve

Fred and Lorene were back on the island and turning everything upside down as usual. Scott felt his answering voice go flat on the phone. "Hi, Fred. Good to have you back."

If Fred noticed Scott's lack of enthusiasm, he gave no sign of it. Business was fine, he boasted. He'd taken a spread in wheat that had paid off handsomely, but he quickly added that making money wasn't everything. Scott stopped a laugh.

"We want you to be a fourth for bridge tonight," he said when he finally got the preliminaries out of the way.

"You know I hate bridge, Fred."

"C'mon, Scottie, Lorene asked Cynthia. She's counting on you to fill out the table. You can't let her down."

"I'm not interested in getting anything on with Cynthia, Fred." If the truth were known, Scott thought, Cynthia probably felt the same way.

"Come over for a cup of coffee, and let's talk."

"Fred, you haven't heard a word I've said."

On the outside, Fred and Lorene's house was like the other ramblers on the Cape—cedar siding stained in sand tones, large windows. Inside, it was expensively furnished, generally in good taste, but always cluttered. Lorene, who'd had everything done for her as a child of wealthy parents, had never learned to keep house. Thanks to Millie, who came in once a week, there was no dust and the floors were clean, but the tables and chairs were always piled high with magazines, Fred's business papers, and pamphlets from Lorene's community projects. Their golf clubs nearly always stood in a corner of the entry hall, probably deposited there weeks earlier, since Fred and Lorene were only sporadic golfers. Generally, the place always looked in need of a good shoveling out.

Fred didn't seem to mind Lorene's lapses in the housekeeping department, for had he cared enough to say anything, Lorene would have moved heaven and earth to change her ways. Pleasing Fred had always been her life's passion. "She smothers poor Fred," Toni had said. If that were the case, Fred was a man who liked being smothered.

In spite of the clutter, it was a warm house, lots of light pouring in from the big windows, particularly in the kitchen, which was most often where they gathered whenever Scott stopped. They sat around the big round table and drank from mugs, and there was nothing here that would have given away that Lorene had grown up a spoiled little rich girl, or that Fred, who'd grown up poor, was now making money hand over fist.

It was Lorene's tendency to get involved with other people's problems that Scott was having trouble with. Lorene had all kinds of other projects, from Campfire Girls and Blood Bank to the Home for Unwed Mothers and the University Drug Abuse Counseling Center. She'd not had children—Fred's decision, according to Cynthia—and had never worked for a salary, not wanted to, according to Lorene herself. So projects it was, and right now, matching Scott with Cynthia Woods was high among these.

Fred waved Scott in with a grin. Lorene was in the kitchen at work over the sink. She was dressed in her usual tight blue jeans, which did little to hide the extra pounds she always complained about, and a pale blue smock. The sink overflowed with pots and bowls. She looked distracted, a normal condition, and happy to see Scott, which instantly made him feel guilty. He stepped over a box of unpacked clothes and weaved a path to her side.

"Scottie!" Her wet fingers dug into his shoulders as she

hugged him. Her green eyes shone brighter than usual. She planted a kiss on his cheek.

"You're looking good," Scott said, easing himself from her arms.

Fred dropped into a chair at the table. "Lorene, fix us some coffee."

Scott looked for a chair that wasn't piled high with papers, and not seeing one, moved a stack of magazines to the floor and sat next to Fred. Dandy found his favorite corner by the refrigerator, which quickly proved a judicious choice, because Lorene had saved him a piece of steak from their dinner. Dandy accepted the gratuity with a friendly wag of his tail, and Lorene placed a kettle of water on the burner.

She was on a new kick about her coffee, grinding it herself and using a different method of brewing. She busied herself with this while Fred insisted on hearing every grisly detail of Owen's murder. Lorene paused now and again to moan or gasp as Scott described the murder scene. The fact that it had occurred only a few feet from their front door clearly had jolted them both.

It was on Scott's lips to tell Fred about his own break-in, but remembering his promise to Leroy and not anxious to upset them further, he told Fred only Al's theories about the murder and about the missing death mask. "Al doesn't think one mask is motive for murder."

"Why? I thought those clown faces were worth a fortune."

"They are, or at least I think they are. Here I see Al's point. Why leave most of them there?"

"Maybe the killer was scared off." Fred leaned back in his chair and rested his short legs on a stack of newspapers. "Hey, Scottie, 'member when a bunch of the guys lifted the bones out of old Worthington's anthro lab and strung them up in the living room of the Kappa house?"

Lorene's laugh sounded like a shriek as she recalled the incident.

"As my memory serves me, they blamed it on the med students."

Fred laughed. "Too bad you missed all the fun, ol' buddy."

Scott smiled at the memory of Fred constantly in the middle of every fraternity prank, and a feeling of affection for his friend swept over him.

Lorene took some sweet rolls out of the freezer and set them in the oven, nodding occasional interest in the conversation. Fred went back to dissecting Owen's murder, with questions about the position of the body and the nature of the wound. Scott couldn't remember his friend ever taking so much interest in anatomy.

On the stove the coffeepot threatened to boil over. Lorene removed it from the burner and began pushing down frantically on a knob at the top of the glass. A strong aroma of fresh-brewed coffee floated across the room.

"I can't wait for you to try this, Scottie," she said. "It's Swiss, or maybe it's French. Anyway, you plunge the coffee through the water and then you put a glob of cream on top, and it comes out positively yummy." She rolled her eyes. "I discovered it when I was in Geneva."

Scott glanced at Fred to see if he still smarted at mention of Lorene's solo trip to Europe, a decision of Lorene's that at the time had caused a family crisis. But Fred was screwing up his nose over the coffee.

Lorene's parents had died shortly before that; first her mother, of cancer, and then her father, of a coronary. So Lorene had been anxious to get away. According to Fred, she was tired of vacations on the island and wanted to travel abroad. Fred didn't feel he could leave his business, and Lorene surprised everyone by going anyway. Scott had always thought there was more to it than that, but for whatever reasons, Lorene had gone and from all accounts enjoyed six grand weeks on the Continent.

She'd been different when she returned, a little distant at first. But after Toni died, she and Fred were both so concerned for Scott that she was soon like her old self again. Scott often wondered if, in a grim way, Toni's death had strengthened the bond between Fred and Lorene. Anyway, their crisis had ended.

Right now there was a crisis over the coffee.

Fred moaned. "Not that stuff again."

"Fred, be quiet. Let Scott judge for himself." She took three mugs from a stand on the sink and poured.

With some apprehension, Scott sipped. It was the bitterest stuff he'd ever drunk. "Very nice," he lied, swallowing hard.

Fred looked at him and started laughing. "Liar. My God, Lorene, this tastes worse than the last pot."

Unfazed, Lorene said, "Try the cream, Scottie. I like it, Fred, so get used to it."

Scott laughed at Fred's unhappy face.

"All very fine for you," Fred grumbled, "but I'm stuck with it, and me with an ulcer."

"When did you develop an ulcer?"

"Don't pay any attention to him," Lorene said. "He's just playing on your sympathy. He doesn't have an ulcer."

"I have a nervous stomach," Fred insisted.

Scott smiled. "You're smoking too much."

"Traitor!" Fred stared glumly at his cup.

Lorene went back to the rolls, and Fred poured an extra-large portion of cream into his cup and started talking about Owen again. "That's all that was missing? An African face mask?"

Scott followed Fred's example with the cream. Definitely an improvement. "Unless you count Owen's necklace."

Fred stoppped stirring his coffee. "What necklace was that?"

"You remember, the thing with the spikes? You said it reminded you of a voodoo chain you'd seen when you and Lorene cruised the Caribbean."

Fred nodded. "Yeah, I remember."

"The point is, he wore it all the time, but it wasn't on him when we found him. And according to Erin, it's very valuable."

Lorene looked up from her work at the sink. "Erin?"

"Al Turner's granddaughter, you know the blond kid who used to run around the Cape barefoot?"

Lorene had been beating sugar and water in a small bowl.

She stopped, and with lifted eyebrows said, "She's not a kid, Scottie."

Scott raised his shoulders uncomfortably. "Yes, well, anyway, she's a decorator and knows a little bit about African art. She claims this necklace could be worth a lot, like twenty grand or more."

Fred perked up. "Owen was full of surprises. What happened to it?"

"I suppose the killer snatched it."

Fred sipped thoughtfully from his mug. "So they did take more."

Lorene had no interest in the stolen necklace. "You been seeing much of this girl, Scott?"

Outside, a flurry of seagulls was fighting and screaming over a run of candlefish. "No . . . not much."

"Lorene," Fred said, "mind your own business."

Scott smiled gratefully at his friend. "Say, Fred, what do you know about land in Canada? I ran into the Delaneys, and Bob, well, actually, Marilyn said there were some pretty hot buys up in the Campbell River area. You've a business head; what do you know about that?"

Fred's even face opened up in a grin. "I'm a commodity trader."

"What's the difference, trading in land or commodities?"

Fred sighed tolerantly. "A heap big difference, ol' buddy. Hey, there are a few tricks in my business. You medical men don't have a corner on tough."

Fred was joking, but there was enough behind it to make Scott realize his friend was still sensitive about not finishing college. Scott had been tactless. "Start educating me," he said, smiling sheepishly.

"Scott," Lorene said with the hysterical pitch to her voice she'd acquired recently, "you wouldn't really buy anything on the advice of the Delaneys!"

"Lorene's got a point there."

"No!" Scott shook his head emphatically for Lorene's benefit. "Absolutely no!"

Scott avoided the subject of Cynthia, but Lorene didn't forget. Scott finally took the hardheaded approach. "I'm sorry, Lorene, but I have other plans for this evening."

"All right," Lorene said with a heavy sigh, "but you must come with us to Henry Mason's party next Saturday. Promise?"

"What party?" Scott said.

"You haven't opened your mail," Lorene accused.

He confessed he hadn't looked at it for a day or two. Never anything in it except bills and solicitations, anyway.

"Everyone on the Cape is invited," Lorene said in an excited voice. Henry's celebrating the completion of Santana."

"Santana?"

"That's what he's called his new house. Wonderful, isn't it? He named it after the warm winds that sweep across Southern California from Mexico. His last wife was Spanish, you know. 'Course, the winds on the Cape are hardly what you'd call warm, but the idea's nice. You *must* go, Scottie. Not to would be, well, rude."

Fred looked at Scott and lifted his shoulders in amused silence.

Only when Scott started back in the Jeep did it occur to him this would be the first time everyone on the Cape would be together since Owen's murder, and among Henry's guests would be several who'd been there that fateful night. Then he wondered if Erin would be going, too.

Thirteen

Fish Creek was quiet at early morning. The fishermen were beached again, and the boats swung empty at their slips. Dandy raced ahead of Scott down the pier to the *Nellie J*, barked, and drew no response.

The decks were wet with the morning dew and slick underfoot. Scott stepped lightly. Squealing protests, a gull flew off the piling and found another spot at the opposite end of the docks. Scott leaned on the *Nellie J*'s rail and shouted, "Anybody aboard?"

Shortly, Vic, droopy-eyed, stuck his head out of the cabin. The strong smells of beer and whiskey came with him, mixing poorly with the nets, which reeked of dead fish. Vic was hitting the bottle heavier these days.

He grinned when he saw Scott. "Thought it was one of those goddamned Caper's come to bitch about last night."

Scott laughed. "No, just me."

Scott climbed over the rail behind Dandy, who was dancing around the doghouse in search of Georgie. But Georgie, according to Vic, was in town with the rest of the crew, "screwin' off." Vic's mood was improved some over their last meeting, however, and Scott guessed the reason.

"Good catch?"

"Not bad."

"Getting any more time out?"

"Two, three days next week maybe."

They sat on the wet deck, backs against the fish locker, breathing in the fumes of fish, and Vic listened thoughtfully while Scott described what he thought he'd seen that night on the *Pilgrim*, tying it to the incidents with the two men. When Scott finished, Vic grunted, "How about a beer?" He ducked into the cabin and returned with two cans.

"I know it all sounds crazy," Scott said, fearing Vic would agree, "but it was just so real at the time."

Vic uncapped his beer, and foam sprayed his bare arms and spouted in a stream that puddled up on the deck. Dandy licked it dry. "Not crazy at all. Happens more than you might care to think." Vic drank from the can, and froth dribbled down his chin. He wiped it with the back of his hand and released a satisfied sigh. "Reminds me when I was skiffman on a seiner in Alaska. We had a hand who was always mouthing off. Everyone hated his guts. One night we hit seventy-knot winds, lashed everything down, rolled all night and the next. When the wind blew itself out we couldn't find the bastard anywhere. We searched the ship, patrolled the waters. Not a trace." Vic's eyes darkened. "Sure as I'm sitting here, someone pitched him over the side. Couldn't prove it, but everybody knew. It's the same thing in battle. The guy that gives everyone a hard time draws first fire. Who checks to see if the bullets hit his back or his chest? Had a shavetail lieutenant went out that way."

"You think this could be the same sort of deal?"

Vic scratched his head. "One thing different. Up north you're far from everything. Hard to check up. In Korea everyone was getting shot up, so who was keeping count? But to pitch someone overboard right in the middle of Cattle Pass strikes me as pretty dumb. You'd think they'd at least wait until they're in open waters. If you're thinking of trying to convince Leroy, I'd say forget it."

Vic didn't mean it as a rejection, but Scott was disappointed nonetheless.

Vic finished off the beer and went below, returning with

99

another. Scott drank from his first. It was warm, and settled poorly on his empty stomach. He set it down beside him on the deck. "Do you happen to know who owns the *Pilgrim*, Vic?"

"A Canadian outfit, I think."

"I suppose it's a matter of record with the Canadian Coast Guard."

Vic laughed. "When you want to know something like that, you don't ask the fuckin' Coast Guard. You ask another fisherman. I'll check around."

"While you're doing that, maybe you can find out who's been blinking their floods off Iceberg the past few nights. Damn things are keeping me awake."

Instantly serious, Vic came up with his standard answer to all unexplained trouble. "Fuckin' Indians."

"Don't think so. First I thought it was the lighthouse lamp, but it blinks out of sync, goes on for several minutes, on and off, and then quits."

"Sounds like the navy signal ships."

This struck a thought buried somewhere.

Boots shuffled on the ramp, and Vic raised his head. "Hey, here's the man who'd know. Why don't you ask Billy?"

Billy Leroux, black hair, tall, rod-slender, stepped lightly down the steeply sloped ramp and flashed the familiar white smile. "Hi, Vic, Doc." Then, looking at the green-quilted rocks on the beach, "Tide's out. Should be good fishing."

"Billy, you're full of shit," Vic said.

Billy's laugh was high-pitched and happy. Billy was a local half-breed who ran a gill-netter, the *Billy Jean*, which, since the court ruling, was officially considered an Indian boat. He and Vic had been friends long before the treaty, but this didn't stop Vic from being bitter when Billy went out and Vic had to sit ashore. Billy rested his lean brown arms on Vic's rail and, still grinning, said, "Ask Billy what?"

"Why are those Indian boats signaling each other all night long? They're keeping the Doc here awake."

Billy blinked bewilderment, and Scott explained about the lights.

Billy looked at Vic, his black eyes amused. "You think the Indians are sending smoke signals with their floods? Don't be dumb, Vic. Hey, even the Indians have radios." Billy had no explanation for the flashing lights, but he had seen the *Pilgrim* the day of the fog. "She nearly ran me down. We were heading outta Shaw."

"How do you know it was the *Pilgrim*?" Vic said sourly.

"Hey, I know that boat. My boys went out on her with the Sea Scouts. Don't know the turkey who's running her this year, but he's not long on brains. It was so foggy in the strait you couldn't see your feet, and this guy barrels through there like he's running the Indianapolis Five Hundred."

"Did you see where they went?"

"Not sure, but I'd have punched him out if I'd caught up with him." Two of Billy's crew started down the ramp carrying Thermos bottles and duffel bags. They nodded silent greetings to Vic and Scott and climbed aboard Billy's boat. "That's my signal to go," Billy said.

While Vic watched glumly, Billy backed up his gill-netter and, waving, took off out of the creek, stirring a giant white trail behind him. Scott laid a hand on his friend's shoulder. "I know what you're thinking, Vic, but remember, it's not Billy's fault."

"Not mine either," Vic said unhappily.

By late afternoon the fog moved into Cattle Pass with the same swiftness as on the night of the *Pilgrim* encounter, covering the rocks and the water like a milky blanket, heavy, cool, and damp. The gray outside world quickly permeated Scott's rooms. Scott looked at the dishes piled up in the sink and decided dinner could wait. He opened a box of crackers, fed some to the dog, munched one himself. He poured a glass of sherry, put on a Mozart wind concerto, and settled down in the big leather chair with the book on stock-trading techniques. Dandy curled up on the floor at his feet, and Scott read. In less than twenty minutes, he was asleep.

Dandy's barking played faintly on his subconscious before he jumped awake, aware someone was ringing the bell. He opened the door, and there was Erin, smiling back at him. Blinking away sleep, he tucked his shirt in, brushed his hair with his hand, and felt as awkward as he had on his first date.

"I wonder if I could borrow a cup of sugar," she said.

Fully awake, he threw the door open wide and waved her in. "A whole pound, if you like."

She burst out laughing. "It's not true, about the sugar. I saw you were alone, and Grandpa and I hoped you'd join us for dinner. Grandpa's tired of just me underfoot, and wishes you'd come."

She selected her borrowings—a bottle of sauterne and a cube of butter—and he and Dandy followed her out the door like spaniels after a duck.

Dinner was veal tenderloin, new potatoes, and greens, and Scott was certain no meal had ever tasted better. He and Al ate shamefully huge portions while Erin talked and picked at her food. She was excited; he could see that from the sparkle in her eyes. She had news, she said, about the African death masks. "I talked to Brice Randall on the phone this afternoon, and guess what?"

Scott shook his head unenthusiastically.

"It's the most amazing coincidence. He saw Owen's collection only three weeks ago at one of Owen's parties. Fact is, he wanted to buy some of the pieces, but Owen wouldn't sell. He said they're definitely of high quality."

"So is he coming to take another look?"

"He can't get away just now, but I talked to the sheriff, and he says if Brice says they're authentic, that's good enough for him. He says they can appraise them anytime."

Scott was surprised at Leroy.

It was quickly clear Erin had something else on her mind. Far from forgetting about going to Victoria to look for the antique

102

shop where Owen's killer had unloaded the stolen face mask, she was now more firmly fixed on the idea.

"How about it, Al?" Scott said, winking knowingly at the old man. "Give Erin a chance to do a little shopping."

"That's not the idea at all," Erin said huffily, starting to clear the table.

Scott spent the next ten minutes apologizing, while Al smiled and stoked up his pipe.

Fourteen

They left Al slumped contentedly over his typewriter. In happy spirits, they caught the midmorning ferry to Sidney and drove the twenty-minute distance into downtown Victoria.

The *Princess Marguerite* from Seattle was just docking in the Inner Harbor to deliver its daily mass of visitors as Scott parked the Jeep. Luxury yachts and sailboats of the clipper class stood at rest in the sun. Everything else around the stone breakwater was in motion—tourists walking briskly down Government Street, the London double-decker buses rumbling back and forth, and the Tally-ho horse carriages clopping past the Empress Hotel, whose steeply pitched slate roofs and ivy-covered brick and stone columnades among green lawns and hanging flower baskets had stood over the harbor since the turn of the century.

In the bustling lobby of the Empress, they plotted their next move.

"All we know for certain," Erin said, "is that the mask turned up in an antique shop in downtown Victoria. We have no name and no address. That could make it tough."

Scott grinned. "I have complete confidence in you."

"Go ahead and laugh, but I do have a plan."

The plan amounted to walking through downtown Victoria, stopping in all the antique shops until they came upon the right one. According to Erin, very few antique shops dealt in African artifacts. She'd been surprised, she said, at the mask turning up at one in the first place. "Most of the good stuff comes out of auctions, and most of those are held in New York, London, or Paris."

They started their hunt on Government Street, intent on working their way north and west, and back to the hotel. Erin walked evenly at Scott's side, her eyes on every shop, passing up woolens and yarns with regretful glances. When she spotted a little shop in Trounce Alley with a display of women's accessories, he insisted they go in.

Erin admired a counter layered with a cheerful assortment of silk scarves. "Pick one," he said.

"I shouldn't."

He selected one on the top with geometric patterns in blazing reds and brilliant blues and held it against her face. "Matches your eyes."

"Didn't you know I'm a summer?"

Scott went blank. "Something out of the decorator's lexicon, right?"

She laughed. "Everyone has a group of colors that best suits their coloring." She studied his face. "Fair hair, blue eyes. You're a spring," she decided. "Your best colors are beige, browns, blues."

"So what colors are yours?"

"Pinks, pastels."

"Mmm. So, we'll find one more to your suiting." He reached for another of the silk squares.

She stopped him. "Don't you dare. I want this one." She held the silk to her face and rubbed it against her skin and laughed. "I've always loved bright colors."

"If I live to be a hundred," he said, shaking his head at her logic. He made the purchase, and they left the shop in high spirits. "To business," he said. She took his arm, and in this determined manner, they proceeded onto the side streets of downtown Victoria.

She found her first prospect in a cloistered little place off

Pandora Street that specialized in Eskimo sculpture. Scott pointed to a window full of stone and whalebone carvings and expressed the view that it appeared slightly afield of African art.

"Yes," Erin said, "but the point is they deal in artifacts, not just old china and chairs. Trust me."

He bowed to her superior knowledge, and they went in. The proprietor was a gaunt-looking woman in her mid-thirties. She had coal-black hair, pale skin, and dark, distant eyes. Erin started to explain her interest in African artifacts. The woman didn't wait for her to finish.

"You can find Indian artifacts here in Victoria, but I can't imagine where you would find any of African derivation. We deal exclusively in the works of the Eskimos." There was a definite condescension in her manner.

Erin left with her defensive shoulders up. "That woman acted like we were total amateurs."

"In my case, it's quite true," Scott said.

They walked through alleys and small shopping malls, and finally they found one in another out-of-the-way corner, which Erin pronounced "authentic."

To Scott it looked more like a small art gallery with dusty old prints and a few cracked pots, but Erin said it was typical of the antique business, and she entered with high hopes. The shopkeeper was an older man—gray hair, gray face, gray eyes, three-piece gray suit, and a manner like the winter fog on the Cape. Scott was more than content to leave him wholly to Erin.

"I'm an interior decorator," Erin began.

Scott traced a finger over a dusty old globe, spun it lightly into orbit. The proprietor shot him a dark look, and Scott stopped the globe's spin and stuck his hands in his pockets.

"I'm on the lookout for a particular piece of African art," Erin continued.

"We deal in English articles."

"This is a face mask."

The gray head moved back and forth. "No, definitely not."

Scott began to wonder how antique dealers made a living.

They started up Yates, continued shop by shop, each dustier than the last, with much the same result. Erin looked at her tourist folder. "I think Fort Street looks like our last best hope."

Fort Street had several galleries and antique dealers. They went to three whose shops were situated very nearly next door to each other, and not one of them knew the first thing about African art. They walked a long block to reach the fourth shop on Erin's dwindling list. It was a little shop that had dirt-clouded windows and smelled suspiciously of rotting wood. A woman of middle age gave them their first real prospect.

"African art? Yes, I believe there was someone around here a few days ago. As I told him, I don't know much about it myself, but I know a dealer who just might."

It was two blocks away, and next door to a yarn shop. "The Stewart McDonald Gallery, Antiques, Gifts, and Tea Rooms. If this isn't it"—Erin held crossed fingers in the air—"I don't know."

Scott gave her an encouraging hug, and, in a mood of resignation, they walked into the tidy little shop. Agnes McDonald, widow of Stewart, was a nice old lady with pale, soft-tissued cheeks, alert brown eyes, and neatly curled gray hair. Erin explained the reason for their visit.

"An African death mask, did you say?"

"A funeral ceremonial, I suppose, would be more accurate. Eighteenth century, I think. As my friend described it, it was a long grotesque face, charcoal, deeply oiled with white across the eyes."

The old lady nodded her head, and Erin squeezed Scott's arm in excitement.

"But I had it only a day, you see. It's gone now."

Erin put on a creditable show of disappointment.

"I'm so sorry," Mrs. McDonald said sympathetically. "You knew, of course, it was only a copy?"

"A copy!" Scott blurted the words in unison with Erin. The surprise this time was genuine.

Erin quickly explained she had her heart set on an original, and Mrs. McDonald accepted this with a shake of her unsuspicious head.

"It was an RCMP matter," the old lady said, and she told them about the solidly built man with the tattooed arm and salty manner who'd brought it in. "He wasn't the sort one associates with collectors. He knew nothing about African artifacts, which naturally aroused my curiosity. In our work we hear about people selling stolen goods. I have to say that for a criminal, he was a gentleman. He swore when I told him what it was worth, but he apologized and didn't put up an argument. Unusual, I think. If you're hoping to get fifty thousand dollars and must settle for a hundred, I imagine some men might become violent over less."

"What happened to the mask?"

"The RCMP impounded it. It's in the States by now." Her milk-white cheeks crinkled in a smile. "It was peculiar from the start. Victoria isn't the place for trading African artifacts. I only deal in an occasional piece because my late husband and I spent some time in Africa. The dealers here are afraid of it."

Erin nodded understanding. "Too much money involved and too easy to be cheated. Only an experienced eye would know if it's from the Gold Coast or the bush, or if it's middle Bennin period or nineteenth century, or if it's been restored or is in its natural state."

The old lady smiled at Erin appreciatively. "Quite so. You have such an interest, I wonder if you would like to see something my husband found on our last trip. It's not for sale, mind, but quite unusual." She slipped into the back of the shop and returned with her prize, a small statuette of a native African bearing a sword. It was a highly polished piece, and at first glance looked to be carved of stone. It turned out to be ebony, crude in its detail but with simple lines, definite style, and, in a curious sort of way, beautiful.

"This is an ancestral statue," she explained. "To the man who carved it, this figurine holds his ancestral spirit." She repeated its history, and Scott began to see African artifacts in a new light. These weren't the ostentatious trappings of an Owen Wentworth, grotesque and gaudy. They were highly individualistic cultural links with the tribes of West Africa and the Congo, with a people and a history about which the Western world still had much to learn. Scott thought of Al's stories of mysterious ruins and ties to the ancients and wished he'd tried harder to persuade him to come today. Then he thought about Owen and his collection. It didn't fit.

"It's beautiful," Erin said with meaning. "If ever you decide to sell it, I'm certain I have a buyer."

They sailed back on the ferry through quiet, moonlit seas. "Think of all the progress we've made," Erin said, pleased with their day's work. "We discovered the mask is a fake."

"Which Leroy undoubtedly already knows and is why he was so anxious to consult an expert."

"Why do you suppose he didn't tell us?"

"Did we confide this trip to him?"

"I see your point. Anyway, now we know something is wrong. I saw those masks of Owen's not more than four months ago, and Brice saw them just a few weeks ago."

"So?"

"Either this mask isn't from Owen's collection or someone switched one of the masks."

"Just one?"

She nodded thoughtfully. "They might have switched more than the one, mightn't they?"

"And what about the man who came into Mrs. McDonald's shop?"

"Charlie, from the Whaler, although I wouldn't have described him as a gentleman. Of course, Mrs. McDonald is such an old dear, she'd not say an unkind word about anyone."

It was after midnight when they arrived back at the Cape. In the soft light of the doorway, her face was still flushed with excitement. "Thank you for the scarf, the wonderful day," she said, giving him a sisterly hug. Her hair brushed his lips, and he got the heady scent of her perfume. "Good night," she whispered and went in. He left with thoughts that were far from fraternal.

Dandy led Scott back to the house in the dark. From his living-room window Scott tracked the waters rising below the deck. Off across the pass, beyond Deadman's Island, the lights still flashed. Dark recesses in the rocks brightened with every flash. He fell hypnotically into its pattern, a long streak followed by a short one, on and off.

Fifteen

Scott woke with Leroy's warnings echoing on his brain. The mask turning out to be a fake underscored the danger, for it pointed to a frustrated killer.

Scott let Dandy out for his early-morning run and stepped barefoot onto the deck behind him. Below the deck where the sun bounced off the water, a seal swam nearly undetected through the thick, brown seaweed, turned, and stared back at Scott through hollow eyes. Until yesterday and Mrs. McDonald's shop, it had all begun to make sense. Now, like a fogged-up window, Scott got a glimmer, but not enough to make a clear pattern. Was it that or was it like putting off telling a patient grim pathological findings? Maybe he didn't want to see where this trail led?

The seal ducked under a patch of kelp in search of the morning offerings of the sea shelf. Dandy sprang back onto the deck, shook the water off his fur, and led the way to the kitchen. "Hungry, boy? Me, too." Scott opened the refrigerator and his hopes died; the dreaded task of grocery shopping could no longer be put off. "We'll stop by Al's and see if he needs anything, and then off we go."

Al shook his head. "Thanks, don't need a thing."

Erin strolled out of the kitchen, greeted Scott with a smile, and talked about their "wonderful day." She then began to write down the items they needed from the store. Scott grinned at the old man, and Al grunted something about "know-it-alls" and reached for his pipe.

"Did Erin tell you about the African mask?"

"Always knew Owen was a phony," Al said. "By the way, I ran into Millie in town yesterday."

Scott said the first thing that came to his head. "Did she know anything about the necklace?"

"I asked her that. Might as well have asked about snow on the moon. She was so upset about her daughter, Prissie, she couldn't talk about anything else."

"What about Prissie?"

"She's missing again."

Erin stopped writing. "You didn't tell me that."

Al shrugged his spiny shoulders. "She ran off. Not the first time. The girl's a perpetual runaway. Didn't want to tell Millie, but it's plain as the nose on my face her daughter has taken up with those potheads on Cady Mountain. Probably up there right now, living in tents and blowing pot."

Erin said, "Isn't anyone doing anything about it?"

"Sure. Leroy's looking, for all the good it'll do. He'll round them up, get her to a counselor. Never accomplishes anything."

Scott had heard about the drug parties on the mountain, which no one on the island seemed able to stop, partly because of the mobility of the kids involved and partly because of a general tendency of the islanders to look the other way. No one wanted to think their kids would get into drugs. In truth, a good number of the drug users were off-islanders.

Al lit his pipe. "I been trying to tell you both, this island is no different than anywhere else. It's all sick."

Erin suggested they get a group of people together and hunt for Prissie. "You can't just write her off. You have to try."

Scott knew the old man felt as badly about the girl as anyone, but his natural pessimism prevented him from raising false hopes. "C'mon, Erin," he said less gruffly, "you can't take on the world's problems. Let the sheriff do his job."

Scott left for town thinking he would add Leroy's office to his stops. There had to be something they could do about poor Prissie.

Friday Harbor was such a small town that Scott never walked down the main street without running into someone he knew. In town, as on the island, people fell into two categories, the full-timers and the summer people, and Scott now felt so much a part of the island's permanent part that he could spot the off-islanders every time.

When he saw the slightly built man in pinstripes coming out of the sheriff's office, he was instantly curious. There was something familiar—and yet different. The line mustache, the dark, almost black hair flecked with silver at the temples, the lean face that had impatience indelibly etched in it. That face didn't belong on the island. It belonged in Seattle, in the boardrooms of the high rises, at the champagne parties.

Scott caught up to him in front of the hardware store. It was Brice Randall all right, and up close, Scott realized what had been different. This wasn't the immaculately groomed, self-assured giant of industry facing him with watery eyes, hair unbrushed, wearing a Bond Street suit that looked like it had gone through a night in the back seat of a car. "Brice Randall, I'll be damned," Scott said.

Brice stared back uneasily. "Scott. What a surprise."

Clearly it was. Besides his nervous manner, his hand lacked a firmness of grip, Scott remembered, and it wasn't hard to see that Brice wasn't at all happy running into Scott. "Been a long time."

"Uh—yes, has, hasn't it? Uh—see you're vacationing. Good idea. Take a little breather from the practice." He glanced at his watch and started to back away, in a hurry to get somewhere.

"What brings you to San Juan Island?"

"Oh . . . sheriff wanted my opinion about Owen Wentworth's art collection."

"What did you think of it?"

Brice shifted uneasily. "Nice. Too valuable to keep in a

summerhouse unprotected. No wonder one of them got lifted." Brice took another step in the direction of the harbor.

"Then Leroy didn't tell you?"

Brice stopped in his tracks. "Tell me what?"

"That the stolen mask was a copy?"

His mouth dropped open. "They recovered it. No . . . I guess he forgot to tell me that."

"Did you talk to Erin?"

Brice drew in his breath. "Damn! Knew there was something. You'll be seeing her, won't you? Could you tell her I'll call first chance I get?"

"Why don't you call her right now? She's home."

He took two more steps to the curb. "Can't . . . plane waiting. Nice talking to you, Scott . . . sorry I have to run. Let's get together for coffee sometime . . . been too long." He forgot to wave as he walked briskly toward the marina and the waiting plane.

The whole meeting took less than five minutes and left Scott with questions that had been on the tip of his tongue unanswered, questions about Toni and Owen and that last party at the store, the last one for Toni ever. Maybe that's why Brice had been in such a rush.

Scott had never known Brice well. He was Toni's associate, not Scott's. At the store parties Scott had avoided him whenever possible, didn't like the way he used a handshake and a smile to get what he wanted. From the stories Scott had heard, he could be ruthless when it served his needs. Not a crude manipulator, like Owen, but with the same lack of concern for whose toes he crushed.

"He makes it go," Toni argued, obviously admiring the man.

"Smooth," she'd said. Not today. Scott smiled. Wonderful how the island dropped a man down to size.

Leroy was clearly displeased Scott had run into Brice, and Scott guessed it was because now Leroy had to explain more than he'd intended. Leroy tipped back in his swivel chair and looked up at Scott. "They're all authentic."

"I thought Randall had already vouched for that."

Leroy grinned sheepishly and told him about discovering the mask in Victoria was a fake. Scott decided not to mention that he already knew.

About Prissie, predictably, Leroy had done it all: searched Cady Mountain, the usual hangouts, posted notices in town, interrogated the usual crowd. "They don't talk, these kids. Have a peculiar code of their own. Last time she ran off she moved in with a bunch out near English Camp. Don't worry. We'll find her." On the matter of the man dragged up off South Beach, Leroy still knew nothing. Scott left him poring over a stack of reports, a troubled man fighting a giant wave.

Scott purchased his groceries, stopped by the hardware store and picked up a few more dishes to replace the broken ones, rejoined Dandy in the Jeep, and headed back to the Cape. A breeze started up off the strait and cooled the air. Just when he thought he'd worked it out, along came a new piece that didn't fit. Scott altered course and headed for Fish Creek.

The Commission had given the fishermen another day out, and aboard the *Nellie J* Vic and his crew were fitting out for the morning. Vic was bent over the engine wall, cussing and fuming, and most of the crew were working on the nets, trying to stay out of his way.

"Son of a bitch," Vic muttered, banging at the iron block with his big wrench.

"What's the matter?" Scott asked.

"The timing on these fuckin' injectors is shitty. Could quit on us right in the middle of a set."

"Probably needs to be reset in the shop." Jonesy, the pole man, spoke the obvious.

"Tell me what I don't know," Vic snapped. He tightened a lug, dropped the wrench to the deck, swearing, and climbed out of the well. "We'll have to run with them as they are."

"They sound fine to me," Georgie said cheerfully.

Vic glared at him. "What the hell do you know?"

Georgie shrugged and joined the others who were rewinding the spool.

As Scott had hoped, Vic had news about the ownership of the *Pilgrim*. "I talked to a gill-netter I know who operates out of Nainamo. He says the *Pilgrim* got bought up by a big conglomerate called Camstar, that they're buying up everything in sight."

"When did they buy the *Pilgrim*?"

"End of season three years ago."

"Is it a Canadian company?"

"He didn't know for sure, but said they were big shots. Multinationals is my guess, don't belong to any country. Gets them around the taxes." Vic grinned. "Tell you, Doc, I wish I could get so fuckin' smart."

"Your friend said they were buying up other properties?"

"Yeah—real estate, small businesses, fishing boats." The frown returned. "Bet they picked *them* up dirt cheap."

As a natural progression, Vic started in on the problems of the Canadian fishermen, which, apparently, were much the same as those for the Americans. Then Georgie bounced over with a report from one of the gill-netters that the sockeye run was in, and Vic cheered up like a newly lit candle. "Hey, Doc, wanna go out with us?"

Scott started to say yes, remembered Henry's party, and regretfully declined.

Vic laughed. "Next time maybe." Scott started for the Jeep, and Vic called after him, "By the way, Doc, on those blinking lights. Billy says to tell you it's definitely not the Indians."

Scott delivered Erin's groceries and the unwelcome news about Brice's visit.

"But he told me he couldn't possibly get away," she said with an unhappy face.

"That was before Leroy found out the mask was a fake, I imagine."

Al looked up from his typewriter. "Well? What did the big man say?"

"They're for real. I imagine Owen either got taken on one or he filled out his bedroom with a phony to make the walls come out even." Scott grinned, but Erin continued to look glum. "Better be going," Scott said, starting for the door.

"Wait, I haven't paid you for the groceries." She started counting out bills. "Comes to ten dollars and nine cents. I'm short a penny."

"I'll trust you." They were standing in the doorway, and he remembered about Henry's housewarming. Thinking it would cheer her, he invited her to go.

"I'm sorry, Scott. I already promised Preston."

If it had been anyone but Preston Fields. This wasn't totally true. He'd looked forward to taking her to the party. He'd turned Vic down for fishing, and now he had to go to Henry's party and endure Cynthia and Lorene. He couldn't very well not go or Erin would think she was the cause, and as foolish as it was, his pride wouldn't permit that.

Sixteen

Preston rumbled into Al's drive in his red Porsche. He stepped out, brushed off a pale-blue sports jacket, adjusted his tie, and sauntered confidently up to the door. After a moment, the door opened, and he went in. Scott waited by the window until he came out again, squiring Erin. She was dressed in a stunning green dress, low-cut. Her fair hair flowed evenly over the suntanned shoulders. To say she was a knockout would have been understating it. They were both laughing and looked like one of the television commercials for the beautiful people, Preston's dark head bent over hers. Preston held the door of the little car while Erin stepped in like she'd done it many times before. Preston got in the driver's side, and they drove off.

Disgusted, Scott left the window. He rummaged through his closet until he found his best gray jacket. It matched the charcoal slacks, he decided, but needed a press. He shook it, with little results. Sighing deeply, he selected a tie of bright blue and finished dressing. "I won't be late," he promised Dandy, walking slowly across the road to pick up Al. At eight o'clock the sun was still setting over the creek.

Al wore his familiar tweed jacket, but his deference to the occasion wouldn't go as far as a tie. He had on one of those western rings with a shoelace looped through it, and, in spite of himself, looked very sprightly.

Scott greeted the old man sourly. "I guess it's just you and me."

Al grunted an answer that said he hadn't approved Erin's

choice himself. We're like two crusty old bachelors, Scott thought unhappily as they trudged up the road the short distance to Henry's housewarming.

It was coming on dusk, and the air still smelled of wild strawberries and dried pine needles. Cars stuck out along the narrow gravel road all the way north and around to the creek.

"Looks like he asked every nitwit on the island," Al complained as they turned into Henry's drive and the loud brass sounds of the Island Jazz Band.

Henry's four acres stood on a windy point. Shaded by huge spruce and pine, it was constantly in the shadows on the roadside, and on the waterside looked out under a single fir to a sweeping view south to Goose Island and north up San Juan Channel. From deeper in the woods where Henry kept the kennel for his hunting dogs, one of his black Labs started to howl in tune to the shrill blasts of the trumpets. The wailing continued for a moment, followed by a sharp yelp, and then silence.

"They may be good duck hunters," Al said with a smile, "but they sure kick up a racket."

"They seemed to have stopped quickly enough."

"Roger saw to it."

Henry's hired man saw to everything.

Bright lanterns lit up the drive, tunneling a path through pines and madronas, at the end of which rose a series of gables and interconnecting roofs of burnt-red tile. White stucco and massive hand-carved oak doors framed the entry. Henry stood in the open doorway, immaculately dressed in a hand-tailored gray suit, white shirt, and bright red tie, looking prosperous and much younger than his eighty-two years. His appearance was in remarkable contrast to the way he normally looked walking the beach in the torn flannel shirt, baggy old suit-pant castoffs, zipper half down.

Henry Mason was a self-made millionaire who had, according to the stories, built his empire on hard work, shrewd manipulations, thrift, and distrust. He made his poke in Alaska, some said by unsavory means, and went into the loan business.

"He plays by the rules," Fred, who knew about such things, told Scott. "He picks companies where the book value is high enough to cover him, and he's a damn good judge of horseflesh. I can't remember anyone ever defaulting on old Henry." Fred grinned. "One wouldn't dare."

"You mean Henry's a loan shark?"

Fred laughed again. "If you ask him, he's just saving capital-starved small businesses when no one else will loan them a dime."

Henry had married and divorced three times. He'd sired no children from those marriages, and now, alone except for his hired man, Roger, he lived the life of a semirecluse. When he built Santana, curiosity ran high. The man who'd spent his life counting every nickel was now spending it like there was no tomorrow. Skilled workmen from Seattle ferried on and off the island, laying marble and wood floors, setting sunken tubs and select fir beams.

"I wonder," Scott said, looking around at the custom-made Spanish windows, "how the old boy bore up under all those cost overruns."

"Poorly," Al chuckled.

At the moment, Henry appeared to be holding up remarkably. "Doctor, glad you could come." His bony fingers gripped Scott's hand firmly. "Al tells me you were called in on Owen last week."

"Yes, that's right."

The eagle eyes flickered interest. "I ran into Brice Randall in town. He tells me one of Owen's artifacts was missing. How much do you imagine it was worth?"

"Don't know," Scott said, feeling Al's curious gaze.

The indifferent look Scott so often saw in the craggy face settled in again, and shortly Henry left to greet another guest.

"Mmmpf," Al muttered. "Was there some secret about the mask being a fake?"

"I was thinking of Erin and what Leroy said about keeping quiet what we know."

"Umm—see what you mean," Al said.

Al led the way through the entry hall into the dining room.

He remarked that the large turnout wasn't out of character for Henry. "What fun in having all that money if you can't flaunt it now and again?"

Like a heavy shadow, a big man in his fifties, dark-complexioned with sharply contrasting white hair shaved so short his brown scalp glistened under it, moved around them into the great hall. It was Roger.

"Man gives me the shivers," Al said. "Always slithering in and out. Henry's watchdog. Frankly, I'd sooner keep a Doberman."

There was a jam around the marble fountain at the far end of the room where pink champagne spouted in bubbling streams from the alabaster mouth of a child in a toga. In the room's center, the caterers had spread a lavish table, flown in from Seattle, oysters on the half-shell, tiny puff pastries filled with a smoked salmon mousse, crab legs, giant shrimp, slices of turkey and ham, and an endless assortment of salads, rolls, tarts, and pastries.

Al brightened at the sight of it. "This is more like it." He took an empty plate off the server and began busily filling it up.

Through the great hall to the terrace where the jazz combo played, Scott caught a glimpse of Erin. She and Preston were weaving and bending to the music and looking very pleased with each other. Scott wandered back to the fountain. The first person he brushed arms with was Millie. She was carrying a tray of dirty glasses to the kitchen. Scott stopped her to ask about Prissie.

Leroy had found her, she said. "She's home. That's the main thing. I guess the rest will take a little time." She forced a smile, but behind it there was pain and a disturbing hint of something Scott had not observed in Millie before. Millie wasn't a vindictive person, but clearly she bore a grudge against whoever had brought this trouble on her daughter.

The crowd around the fountain thickened. On the fringe of it, sipping a highball and leaning against the built-in server that filled up the west wall, was Fred, all by himself. "Don't worry," he said, reading Scott's mind, "they'll be back. They've just gone to the powder room. Ah, here they come now."

From the long hall, Cynthia and Lorene were squeezing

their way into the dining room. Lorene's mousy hair had more order to it than usual, puffed up and well lacquered. A rare trip to the local hairdresser, Scott guessed. Lorene looked determined. Cynthia, long, willowy, the auburn hair short and trimly brushed in soft waves, looked as she always looked—bored. Cynthia was attractive, but the vitality was definitely missing.

Cynthia was one of Lorene's oldest friends. They'd gone through private prep schools together and then to Vassar. Lorene left Vassar after her first year and transferred to the University of Washington where she met Fred. Cynthia stayed, graduated with a major in foreign languages, went on to graduate school in Georgetown, and married a member of the diplomatic corps. The marriage ended after two years. Cynthia returned to Seattle and moved casually from job to job with long periods of living the life of the idle rich, part of the time in her Seattle condo and part in the family house on the Cape. She'd been Lorene's pet project ever since.

"Here they are," Fred announced cheerfully as Lorene and Cynthia elbowed their way to Fred and Scott.

"Scottie," Lorene said in a scolding voice, "why didn't you call?"

Cynthia's smile lit up her face with a surprising release of energy. "Scott, nice to see you."

"How's the summer going?" Her answering laugh had new sparkle to it, usually pale cheeks bloomed with color, and, on second look, there was something different about Cynthia.

"I've been off the island," she said. "Just flew in for the weekend to catch old Henry's bash. Couldn't miss that."

"She's taken a job," Lorene said, as though she were describing a case of the measles.

"Good for you," Scott approved.

Cynthia flashed another smile. "I've opened my own travel agency. Seemed a shame to let all my experience go for naught. I work long hours, and I'm up to my eyes in clients, computers, and airline schedules. But do you know, Scottie, I love it. Can't wait to get back."

This was definitely a new Cynthia, and Scott had to start readjusting all his favorite clichés for the woman who'd always reminded him of the last leaf on the oak in winter. The transformation was heartening.

Lorene, however, wasn't at all pleased. She was like a possessive mother, reluctant to give up a daughter to an unwanted son-in-law. "That means you won't be here for the Windsure," Lorene said with a pout. "You know, we always go to Victoria for the races, and Scott's racing the *Picaroon* again this year."

Scott looked at Lorene in amazement.

"Are you, Scottie?" Cynthia asked.

"I haven't actually decided."

Feeling she was losing her cause, Lorene decided to retreat. "Talk to her, Scottie. Tell her she has to stay."

Fred shrugged and allowed Lorene to lead him away.

Cynthia laughed after them. "Don't mind Lorene. If she isn't directing someone's life, she just isn't happy."

"I know," Scott said with feeling.

"Still, it's good to see her firing again. I was worried about her last year."

"Oh, the trip to Switzerland?"

Cynthia nodded. "Her world fell apart all at once, losing her parents and the family fortune petering out."

This was something new.

"You didn't know about the bad investments? Swindle is really a better name for it. Come to think of it, I probably shouldn't be mentioning it. I don't think Fred knows the extent of the damage even now. Lorene's trust went under, too."

Scott felt a twinge of guilt, for he'd been going through the throes of the breakup at the time, and most likely Fred and Lorene had spared him their own problems. A wave of penitent forgiveness came over him. "Yes," he said. "Good to see her doing well." The sad moment passed. "Now, tell me about this budding business of yours."

It was all the encouragement she needed. She was more animated than he'd ever seen her, talking about travel snafus, tours, customers who wanted individual service. It was quickly clear that Cynthia, who'd always been directionless, had at last discovered what she wanted from life. Scott was frankly envious.

Al walked into the conversation. He'd always wanted to visit Europe and the Greek Isles, he said. That he'd never done so surprised Scott, who'd always thought him well traveled. Scott left the two of them huddled around the server in a lively discussion about tombs, cathedrals, and ruins.

Scott had never been comfortable with Toni's store parties. A most singular-minded group, store executives. As a consequence, he'd learned the solo art of circulating, which amounted to hanging on to the periphery of conversations, nodding owlishly, smiling appropriately, and moving on.

When Scott rejoined Cynthia and Al, Fred and Lorene were back. The room was densely packed, and someone bumped arms with Cynthia and spilled a few drops of champagne on her dress. Scott suggested a tour of the house would be safer.

The second part of Santana was as Scott had envisioned— sculptures and murals on white walls, but no trinkets or memorabilia, nothing personal. Here he missed Erin's insights, wondered what she thought of the strange mix of stone, marble, and concrete.

Fred admired the swimming pool, an inside-outside job with a sliding roof, now closed, and doors that opened onto the terrace. He stood on the pool's tiled edge, flexed his arms, and poised for a racing dive, just as he had in their college days when he'd been captain of the swim team. The smells of salt vapor and chlorine were almost overpowering, and the women started to look a little wilted.

Lorene complained that the steam was taking the curl out of her hair, and they left.

On the upper terrace the band played a lively rendition of "Sugar Blues," and several couples danced on the smooth stone tiles. In the far corner a bar had been set up, and two barmaids in black tights and silky bare-backed tops worked feverishly to keep up with the orders.

Fred and Lorene took to the dance floor and went at it, as they did everything, with a good deal of energy, swinging shoulders and hips. Scott looked at Cynthia, feeling an uncomfortable sensation in the pit of his stomach. "Want to try?"

Cynthia laughed. "I'm content to watch, if you are."

"A drink, then?" he asked.

"Seven-Up. Got an early day tomorrow."

Scott shouldered his way to the bar, ordered the drinks, returned with them, and found Cynthia enjoying the view from the terrace. The water was all in darkness, and the moon was settling over the Pass.

It had been hot in the dining room, but out here a breeze rustled off the water and cooled things down pleasantly. Just below, in the glow of the lower terrace lights, two people shared the moon. No mistaking the golden hair or the slim bronzed shoulders. It was Erin with Preston. A memory flashed painfully. Scott looked quickly away.

"What a lovely spot," Cynthia said, sitting down on the stone bench beside a big tree.

He settled down beside her. "Oh, yes—nice."

"How has it been going for you, Scottie?"

"Fine."

She sensed the change in him. "Do you still miss her terribly?"

It was so far from his thoughts and so unlike her to speak of Toni, it surprised him. Yet when he thought of it, from Cynthia, who'd known him through the difficult times, the question seemed natural and caused him none of the old distress. "I don't know if it's that. I'd like to understand."

"And you don't?"

"Not entirely."

Cynthia nodded, and for a moment he had the feeling she wanted to say something but didn't quite know how. The look went away, and she said, "I had a feeling you were different, that you weren't suffering anymore."

Suddenly he realized how it must have been for her, putting

up with his moods, not peppering him with questions. "And you, my dear Cyn, are different, too." The warmth and openness, misery shared, not held in. Yes, she was different.

She grasped his hand and held it. "We are a pair, aren't we? I've managed to get my life back together. God knows, it took long enough. Anyway, I know what it is to flounder, to need something and not have it." She looked away, and her color deepened. "I want you to know if you ever need a shoulder to cry on, I'm always available."

He knew what she was offering. They were alike in many ways, private and often lonely people. He kissed her softly on the cheek. "I appreciate that, Cyn. I do."

She laughed shyly. "You have always been a true friend."

He was afraid it wasn't true. He thought back to the times he'd worked so assiduously to avoid Lorene's arrangements. But apparently Cynthia hadn't known, or if she had, she'd understood, and there'd always been the mutual respect. If he came away from the evening with nothing else, this understanding between two old friends was worth it all.

On the dance floor the couples were still swinging to the music of the Island Jazz, but something new had been added. "Don't look now," Scott said, "but isn't that Marilyn Delaney dancing with Fred?"

Cynthia nodded, not smiling. "And if you could see Lorene's face."

Such a dark look! Scott guessed the reason. Marilyn, who'd had a great deal too much to drink, was draped around Fred, and they were shuffling around the floor to the fast tempo of the drums and putting on quite a show. The crowd from the bar began collecting near the dance floor to watch. Prominent among them was Bob Delaney, who, for a change, appeared sober and, like Lorene, was none too happy. Fred threw Marilyn into a spin, retrieved her before she fell. Marilyn's laughter trilled across the room.

Scott figured Fred could handle the situation, but Cynthia was worried, and breathed a sigh of relief when the number ended and Fred returned Marilyn to her husband.

"Don't worry about Fred. He enjoys being the life of the party."

"It's not Fred I'm worried about."

Scott followed the direction of Cynthia's gaze to Lorene, who was still glowering at Fred. Fred beat a dutiful path back to her side.

Scott chuckled. "She'll get over it."

But Bob showed no signs of getting over it. He grabbed Marilyn by the wrist and pulled her to the doorway. "You need air."

"I don't," she protested, slipping from his grasp and almost falling again.

He got another hold on her. They scuffled, and everyone pretended not to notice as Bob half led and half dragged his wife toward the hall. "You're going home!" he said, the veins pulsating in his temples.

Lorene thought it terrible how some people couldn't hold their liquor. Al said Marilyn had been talking wild all evening about blinking lights and fishing boats and all sorts of nonsense. "Did the right thing taking her home."

"Mmm," Fred said.

From the shadows of the giant fir, Henry's man Roger watched and said nothing.

Shortly, Cynthia said she had to go—a late flight, morning appointments.

"I'll drive you to the airport," Scott offered.

Cynthia smiled and shook her head. "Lorene's taking me after she drops Fred off. Women talk, you know. But don't forget, Scottie, the standing invitation."

Beside him, Al lifted a curious eyebrow, and Scott waved good-bye to Cynthia.

Seventeen

The happy mood of Henry's turned to tragedy before the coming of the morning tide. It was shortly after two, and the party was still going strong. During music breaks from Santana, from his bed Scott heard occasional bursts of laughter pealing down the beach.

Scott lay there, between snatches of semiconsciousness, dimly aware of the brass sounds from the Island Jazz trumpeting sweetly across the water. The music ended abruptly with a clarinet note and the jangled empty noises of trumpets and reeds being blown clean for packing back into their cases. Laughter and talk drifted louder from the beach, the unmistakable sign that Henry's party was finally breaking up.

From the driftwood, a crane squawked noisily and with rustling of heavy wings, took flight. A distant wail followed, not a living sound. Scott felt displaced, as though he were somewhere else. His immediate sense was of standing in the OR at the hospital while they wheeled in a victim of an accident on the freeway. The operating-room lights blazed. He was gowned, waiting for anesthesia to confirm the patient was under.

The wail turned to a shriek, and Dandy started to howl. Coming fully awake, Scott shot up and padded barefoot to the window. Across Cattle Pass the lights blinked steadily. From the road, an engine rumbled, and tires scraped over gravel and thudded to a stop. Dandy's howl turned to a sharp bark, and Scott realized someone was pounding on the door. It was Leroy's deputy, Harold, and from his face Scott knew right away there was big trouble.

"There's been another shooting. Can you come quick?"

For one long petrifying second, Scott knew fear. "Who?" he said, his voice breaking above a whisper.

Harold looked like he was going to be sick. "Marilyn Delaney—another shotgun blast. Leroy says she's dead."

"I'll just get some clothes on."

They drove the short distance to the Delaney cottage at full speed and with the blue lights flashing. Outside the rustic cedar cabin, Pauline and Craig Deekins and Jerry Butler, who'd been part of the Delaney party earlier, hovered under the dim lights of the lamppost. Anxiety was written all over their faces.

"How is she?" Craig asked in a husky voice, his eyes resembling the hollow rings of an owl in the semidarkness.

"We—we only just heard," Pauline whispered. "Someone said she was dead."

Across the road a dog barked. This was followed by the echoing yelps from Henry's hunting hounds several hundred yards away.

Scott followed Harold through the front door directly into the living room, and there she was, dressed in a short sheer nightgown, a gaping wound in her chest. Marilyn had always been well filled out, but she was much thinner and smaller in death. She lay crumpled on her back on the carpet, much as Owen had lain only a few days earlier. The room smelled strongly of bourbon, and it all worked to give Scott an overpowering feeling of déjà vu, the nasty hole that had blown her breast and neck open, the bulging eyes that stared sightless at the ceiling. Harold took one look and shot for the door.

"Where's Bob?"

Leroy pointed to the kitchen where Bob sat slumped over the table, his head buried in his arms, an untouched tumbler of bourbon in front of him. Another of Leroy's men stood guard over him, but there was no need. Bob wasn't going anywhere. He didn't even look up.

"Shotgun again."

Leroy nodded.

"Who reported it?"

Leroy pointed at Bob. "He called a few minutes ago. Said he'd gone for a walk and when he returned he found her that way."

"Then he didn't hear the shot?"

"So he says."

"I doubt anyone could have over the noise of the Island Jazz."

"Except Bob." Leroy's mouth was set grimly.

"You don't think *Bob* did it?"

Leroy didn't answer. "I wonder, could you fix a time of death?"

"It was after eleven. That's when Marilyn left the party."

"Leaves a lot of time in between."

Scott touched Marilyn's arm. It was cool and firm. "An hour is my guess."

Leroy glanced into the kitchen. Bob hadn't moved. Leroy lowered his voice to a whisper. "You saw her at the party at eleven?"

"Yes, and so did everyone else," Scott whispered back.

"I understand she had too much to drink."

The smell of liquor in the room was something of a giveaway. Scott nodded.

"How long did the party last?"

"It just broke up a few minutes ago."

Leroy rubbed his chin thoughtfully. "She left pretty early. Did she pass out, have to be carried home? Something like that?"

"She was walking when I last saw her."

"Any arguments?"

Scott shrugged. "Not really." He repeated the scene between Marilyn and Bob.

"Did he shove her around?"

"No—nothing like that. She was a little unsteady on her

feet, and I imagine he wanted to get her out of there before she passed out. That's all there was to it."

Leroy wrote on his notepad.

"Where's the coroner?"

"He's on his way."

Harold, still ghostly pale, stuck his head in the door. "Lotta people collecting here. What should I do about them?"

"Anyone know anything?"

"They say not."

"Unless you find someone who knows anything, tell them to go on home."

"What about Kenny?"

"What about him?"

"He says he has a deadline."

With public image a concern for Leroy at this point, the reporter from the local paper was a little harder to put off. Leroy sighed heavily. "Okay, tell him to wait a minute."

Harold nodded and backed out.

Around the rooms all else appeared normal. It was a small cabin with a living room that opened into the kitchen, a single bedroom, and bath. The Delaneys had been renting it summers for the past three years from the owners, who were from off-island and using the place for a tax write-off. It was designed for two people, which was no problem for the Delaneys, who had only one grown son from Bob's previous marriage.

Bright watercolors hung on the walls, and white tie-back curtains, crisp and neat, framed the big windows, giving the room a cheerful look. Erin would approve. Scott looked across at Leroy, suddenly feeling very tired.

"Well, Doc?"

Dutifully, Scott bent over Marilyn's body again, studied for a moment the way one leg was bent under the other. From here, his eyes traced a slow pattern to the chest and neck.

"What is it?" Leroy said. "Something crazy. I can see it in your face."

"See this little red mark on her throat, like a bruise, above the wound?"

Leroy dropped to his knees and inspected the barely visible spot.

"Now look at the wound itself."

Leroy concentrated on the hole in her chest. "Uh-huh."

"There's not enough blood. It's not red and oozing like it ought to be. I don't know what the coroner will say, but my guess is she was strangled to death."

"Killed twice?"

"In a manner of speaking."

Leroy wiped sweat from his forehead with his sleeve. "What do you think was used?"

"A silk stocking, something like that."

"Take someone strong?"

"Not in Marilyn's condition."

Noise from the kitchen distracted them. Bob was weeping. He looked up for a moment, his face ash-white and full of pain. Scott knew the look. He'd seen it in his own mirror not many months ago. Yet, as things stood, it didn't look at all good for Bob Delaney.

Frank Gilly, funeral director and *pro tem* coroner for the island, arrived in his usual breathless state. He saw Marilyn and shook his head. "Needs an autopsy. Better get her to Mt. Vernon. Can't do much here."

"I don't think you need me anymore," Scott said.

Leroy looked up, distracted. "Thanks for coming, Doc. Oh, when you go out, would you tell Kenny to come on in?"

Scott stepped out into the cool dampness of the predawn morning and sucked in a giant breath of air, inhaled the sweet smells of dew-soaked fir needles, and felt much better. He delivered his message to Kenny, who rushed past and banged into the house. Scott reminded himself that Kenny probably hadn't known Marilyn. To him, she was just a story, and on the small island newspaper, perhaps the biggest story of Kenny's career. How could he be expected to care? The Seattle reporters would be next. May as well get used to it.

In spite of Harold, a much larger crowd now gathered on the road outside the cottage. The presence of the coroner's wagon told them all they needed to know, but they stayed anyway, as though expecting more. Some were still dressed in their party clothes; a few were in pajamas and robes.

The front door of the cottage opened, and Bob stepped out, followed by the deputy. Bob's face and eyes were red and swollen, and his mouth grimly shut. He walked by them, not looking or talking, even to his friends. He piled into the patrol car, and the door shut on his grieving face. The chatter grew, the predictable speculations about how Marilyn died. Bob was an easy answer, one most probably accepted. But there were doubts, the doubts raised by the specter of Owen.

When Owen died everyone had been shocked, but not particularly sorry. Even from those who'd attended his parties one received no feeling of remorse about Owen. It was as if his death were somehow earned, a result of the way he lived. Marilyn was quite different. Who could find a reason for it? She drank too much, talked too much, and raced her cars and the boat too fast, but she wasn't the sort of person who generated hate, who aroused the kind of malice that provokes murder. If her husband hadn't killed her, that meant a deranged and dangerous killer was loose, a killer who might strike again, and Scott knew it was this idea that was bringing fear to them all.

The door opened again, and Frank wheeled out Marilyn's draped body. There was a low moan across the grass. Leroy banged out behind and stood guard by his patrol wagon while they shoved the stretcher into Frank's van. Leroy turned to Scott. "I'm leaving one of my deputies to watch the place." Then he climbed into his wagon and stuck his head out the window. "Go on home," he told the crowd. "You're no help here."

The revolving lights on both vehicles flashed through the big branches of the firs, a depressing reminder of what had called them to this peaceful spot. Everyone moved back slowly; a few already drifted down the road to their homes, heads bowed in depressed silence. Scott started to follow, and a dark form walked uncertainly toward him.

"Scottie, that you?"

"Fred?"

"Yeah. My God, what's going on? Lorene came back from the airport and said she saw the sheriff's wagon go by flashing his lights. I sent her to bed and decided to run up and see what was going on. Ran into Henry's man, Roger. He said Marilyn had been shot, just like Owen. Is it true?"

Scott nodded. "Afraid it is."

Fred sagged against a tree, shaking his head. "Only a couple of hours ago we were dancing, and she was having a helluva time. Oh, shit! We got a madman running loose around here, do you know that?"

"Yes," Scott said grimly, "and I hope Leroy gets a handle on it soon."

Fred drew in his breath sharply. "You think he'll kill again?"

"Seems a strong possibility, don't you think?"

Fred's face froze, and Scott imagined he was thinking of Lorene, alone. "I'll talk to you later," he said, starting for home at a trot.

The lights were on in Al's house. Al was still in his pajamas. Erin had thrown a robe over her nightgown. She wore no makeup, but she was wide awake and clearly apprehensive.

"Siren woke us," Al said. "Then Henry called, all shook up. He said he'd heard somebody shot Marilyn Delaney." Al studied Scott's face. "I can see it's all true."

Scott nodded glumly. "She's dead."

"Oh, no," Erin said. "We'd so hoped . . . poor Marilyn." She sank into Al's big chair, looking lost in it. How vulnerable she was, Scott thought.

He touched her hand. "How about some coffee?"

Erin made the coffee and they sat, staring into the mugs,

and tried to puzzle out the strange circumstances of Marilyn's death.

Erin thought Bob cared too much for his wife to have done it.

"What's that got to do with it?" Al sniffed. "You'd be surprised what goes on in families. I heard a statistic the other day about the number of husbands and wives who get into rows that end in a shooting. Marilyn probably mouthed off, and Bob let her have it, simple as that."

"That doesn't explain Owen's death, and Marilyn was killed the same way."

"Not quite." Scott told them about the strangling.

Erin paled, and Al stuck his pipe tightly between his teeth.

"You do think the murders are connected?" Erin said.

"I'm afraid I do."

They fell silent.

"We have to do something," Erin said, breaking the silence.

"Do what?" Al snapped.

"I don't know, but we can't just sit around while some mad person goes after us, one by one."

"You're overdramatizing it," Al said in a voice that lacked conviction.

"Am I? Two dead, three, if you count the person found off South Beach, and Prissie's missing."

Scott smiled. Good news on that, at least. "The sheriff found her. I talked to Millie at the party. She's home, and she's all right." He didn't think the lie would harm anyone. Prissie was a long way from all right.

Erin looked much relieved. "But you haven't said anything about the killings. Don't you agree this person is crazed?"

"I think 'crazed' is the wrong word."

"Don't you think strangling someone and then shooting them with a shotgun is crazed?"

"Panicked, maybe. No, there's a pattern here that is entirely too rational to be put off to mere madness. Do you see?"

"I suppose, but isn't there anything we can do?"

"Yes—I think there is."

They both perked up.

"It would mean going off the island."

Erin brightened. "Where?"

"Campbell River."

The smile spread across her face. "Why did I know you were going to say that?"

"When do we start?" Al asked, appearing to read Scott's fears.

"How about catching the noon ferry today?"

"I'll call Paul, have him look in on the animals," Al said.

"We might be staying a couple of days," Scott told Erin. "You'll want to take some warm clothes. It can get cold up there, and we'll be going for a boat ride."

Eighteen

A warm south wind blew off Cape Mudge at the passage to Campbell River, stirring up a wild sea. It was hot and dusty as Scott drew up in front of Discovery Inn. The inn stood on the quay overlooking the breakwater. Only a few paces away a small car ferry ran the twenty-minute hop to Quadra, the largest island in the Discovery Island chain. It was from Quadra Scott hoped to set out in the morning.

Now, at midday, he wanted to spend the afternoon following a hunch. The problem at the moment was Al. The long drive from Sidney had proved an ordeal after a night with little sleep, and he was clearly out of sorts. He piled out of the Jeep, looking tired and complaining of a backache.

They checked into the inn, and over lunch Scott suggested Al see what he could learn from the local library while Scott and Erin covered the real estate offices. It was a move designed more to take the pressure off him than out of any hope they'd find anything.

"We can meet back here for dinner and compare notes. How does that suit you, Al?"

The professor, who'd logged more hours in reference rooms than most had in classrooms, pounced on the idea. "Can't see what you hope to learn from a bunch of real estate agents."

"Probably nothing. All I know is Delaney got a good case of the shakes every time Marilyn mentioned Campbell River. I have to wonder why."

Campbell River, a hundred miles north of Victoria, sat at the northwestern end of the Strait of Georgia not far from Kelsey Bay, the jumping-off place for the Inside Passage to Alaska. Unlike in Victoria, one saw few men in three-piece suits in Campbell River. This was the home of the Tyee salmon, the land of hobnailed boots, wind slickers, and heavy Cowichan sweaters.

Scott had sailed here in his college days, poked around the hundreds of tiny islands that shaped the narrow waterways in this northern chain, and remembered unpredictable storms, fierce tidal rips, dense forests, and rocky beaches. He found himself excited at the prospect of probing again the tiny coves, arms, and inlets. Tomorrow they would do that when they began their search for the *Pilgrim*. Vic said she'd been spotted around Read and Cortes, so that's where they'd look. It might all be for nothing, but Scott didn't mind.

"Where do we begin our sleuthing?" Erin asked.

"We start by walking."

"I hate to ring a sour note, but isn't it a little hard when we don't know what we're looking for?"

"We're looking for something bizarre."

"I should have guessed."

With that, they set out.

The real estate offices hummed with their Apples and IBMs. The salespeople were friendly and looked to their computer screens for listings such as Scott described. The computers spit out ranchettes, river lots, and farms, all pretty normal stuff. Scott looked at maps and pictures of view property and forested acreage, and in none of it did he see anything out of the way or connected to American real estate interests. After a half-dozen realtors, it began to appear Al had been right about the futility of this task.

After walking for most of two hours, they found themselves back on the quay. Erin looked longingly across the parking lot at the hotel. Scott gave her hand an encouraging squeeze. "Shall we just try that little office there by the marina and then call it a day?"

The windows of the Donald Miller Real Estate Agency were almost totally obscured by pictures of houses and waterfront properties. Inside was little different. In contrast to the computer-run offices they'd been in, it lacked any kind of filing system whatsoever. Plot plans, pictures, and real estate listings, printed and mimeographed, were piled atop the desk, tables, and chairs, so there wasn't a clear space anywhere. On the walls were a series of dusty-framed aerial shots of the islands and a giant map of the region. The only concession to the computer age here was a small copying machine that sat half hidden by the papers.

Miller, a slight-boned man with bright red cheeks, rose from behind the manila folders, shifted papers around until he'd cleared two chairs, and invited them to sit down. It became quickly clear why he didn't need the computers. He kept his listings firmly filed in his head.

He hummed happily as he thumbed through his folders. "Yes—yes, we have some nice pieces. Might be just what you're looking for. Yes, here it is." He pulled one folder from the stack. "A lovely one. A hundred acres on the river. Only twelve miles inland." He slipped an aerial photograph of a large tract of land with a dense stand of firs and a wide stretch of river from the file and laid it in front of them.

"Interesting," Scott said. "How much?"

Here Miller turned cagy. "You may have heard real estate is depressed in this area. This parcel would normally sell for four or five hundred thousand, but with the American dollar difference and the market being down, I think you might pick it up for half that. Can't guarantee it, but I think the owners would entertain a reasonable offer."

"Do you have anything closer to Gold River?"

Miller's smile wavered. "You won't do as well in that direction."

Scott's interest picked up. "Why? I thought the mines were shut down."

"Not entirely." Miller doodled with his pencil on the notepad in front of him. "There's been some American interest over there. Upped the prices."

Beside Scott, Erin drew in her breath softly.

"Oddest thing, I haven't the least idea what's causing it. I imagine it's speculation with future mining in mind, but I must say there's more potential for new deposits in the river piece I've showed you."

"*Very* odd," Erin said, with a meaningful glance at Scott.

"Where is this property?"

Miller walked over to the map on the wall and traced a line with his finger. "South and just a little east of Gold River."

"And you've had a number of sales there?"

"I haven't, no. This is an exclusive run by a large combine. I believe it's what you call a REIT."

"A Real Estate Investment Trust?"

"Yes. This company calls itself Stark, or something of the sort. I know of one section they've sold and resold three times in the past twelve months, and each time the price doubled, and the same company carried the paper for all of it. Much of it, of course, is stock sales." He shrugged. "At least, so I've heard."

"Sounds like they struck gold," Erin said.

"Not according to our local geologists. No, it's my opinion they've done an overly creative selling job."

"A fraud?"

Miller smiled. "Those wouldn't be my words, but I think you have the idea. I like to warn Americans, but in most cases the sales occur from the States' side, and the people never see the property."

"That's the whole idea of a REIT, isn't it?" Erin said. "To place trust in a company that knows where good buys can be found?"

"Yes, but here the prices are much too high. The worst part for us, it artificially raises land values in that area."

Scott promised to call Miller back, and they left the realtor's office. On the street, Erin puzzled over their findings. "I can feel we're getting close, but what does it all mean?"

They slipped into the marina and arranged for a twenty-two-foot Whaler Revenge that had a roomy cockpit with pedestal chairs for the pilot and the passenger and storage under the bow. Erin lifted an eyebrow at the price, but Scott pointed out they knew firsthand it was a fast boat and maneuverable, and with the two-hundred-horsepower Mercury outboard engine, just what they needed if they were going to cover a long distance in a hurry. He paid the deposit, and they left.

It was four when Scott left Erin at her room with plans to meet in the lounge for drinks at six. Just enough time to do what he had to do.

In the town hall the clerk kept all the records of sales and transfers of title, but couldn't help without a code number to feed into the computer. The clerk asked if he had thought of checking with title insurance.

Scott went directly to the offices of the title insurance company. "I am considering purchasing a large tract, and I'd like to be certain the title is clear," Scott told the man in charge.

The man looked back, bewildered. "That is why you buy title insurance."

"True, but I represent a consortium, you see, and my people like to be sure they're dealing with a reputable company."

The agent poked a pencil at his chin. "I don't see how I can help."

"Can you tell me if you've handled sales for a company called Camstar?"

"I don't recall that name."

"They could go by another—Stark, something like that."

He thought a moment. "You wouldn't by chance mean Star Limited?"

"I think that is just what I mean," Scott said, with effort not sounding too excited.

"You don't need to worry about them. They're part of a conglomerate based in Ottawa, heavily capitalized."

"Would any of their properties be recorded in the town records?"

"Ask the town clerk to show you the Gold River additions M-6705. Star has been a prime mover of that property."

"I'd heard the mines were mostly out of production now."

"That isn't actually mine property." He winked knowingly. "Tax credits. Not good for much else."

In the town hall, Scott struck a silver lode of his own. It

turned up on the computer names, dates, sales, and Owen, listed as the company's officer of record. It confirmed Delaney's connection to Owen, but left unexplained what they were doing with the property and how they were selling it at such big markups. Had they struck gold, as Erin had suggested? If so, why the resales? And who was successor to Owen?

Nothing in it refuted Scott's original hunch. Still, he needed at least one or two more pieces of information to complete the puzzle. One thing was grimly clear. The mere mention of this connection brought poor Marilyn a ghastly death, and now both he and Erin undoubtedly knew as much as she.

Vacationers filled up the cocktail lounge where Scott waited for Al and Erin. They arrived with Erin, looking fresh and unaware of danger in any form. He vowed to keep it that way. He also decided he wouldn't tell them about the trip to the town hall, which could only increase their exposure to risk.

"Incredible library they have here," Al said.

"Find anything?"

"Didn't have enough time." Al had decided he didn't want to run the boat trip around Quadra in the morning.

"We know the *Pilgrim's* running in these waters, Al," Scott argued. "It's not a complete waste."

"What do you hope to learn if you find her?"

"How she operates. If she is what she claims to be, a researcher for the experimental lab."

"And if she isn't, what then? You could find a peck of trouble."

Scott laughed. "They're just students, Al. Anyway, we don't plan on getting that close."

"And if you don't find her?"

"We'll have a nice run in the islands. Doesn't that tempt you?"

"Not one little bit."

Nineteen

The Whaler cut a clean path across the channel toward Cape Mudge and the southern tip of Quadra Island. From Campbell River there were two passages to the north. One went through the swift waters of Seymour Narrows, where the peaks of Ripple Rock, since blasted out, had once made this a graveyard for ships. The other, around Cape Mudge with its exposure to strong southerly winds, went through the channels and arms that filled the waterways all the way north to Johnstone Strait. Scott took this heading and within ten minutes closed in on Cape Mudge and the Indian carvings. Grim faces carved into the granite boulders stuck out along the tidal flats, the curious remains of the early Indians.

"Like the African masks," Erin said.

"Petroglyphs. Date back to prehistoric times. Spirit beings to ward off storms and marauding tribes."

"Somber."

As they rounded the point, a dragon's head with the sharp fangs of a wolf protruded ominously from the tide flat. Erin shivered, and for a moment Scott had a second thought about their quest. He turned into the ice-blue waters of Sutil Channel. A peaceful flock of gulls flew over, and the feeling passed.

He raced toward Read, where he hoped they might find the *Pilgrim*. It had been years since he'd cruised these islands, but he remembered the rocks and swift current and logs that broke free of their booms from nearby logging operations. He reminded himself to keep an eye out for deadheads, those half-submerged logs so deadly to props and hulls.

Erin caught the idea and gave up the comfort of the cushioned chair to stand beside him. She gripped the cockpit rail and scanned the water ahead. "I'll be lookout."

Off to the north, a needle-shaped cloud marred the blue sky, and Scott had another memory of the squalls that came up with some frequency in these waters. In a way this was one of the fascinating parts of the northern islands. Storms rolled in off the strait without warning. The north part of the chain—Sonora, Stuart, and Thurlow—was, in fact, much like a rainbelt, with overcast weather a good part of the time, undoubtedly one reason these islands remained the most uninhabited of them all. The Whaler scooted past Quadra's small marina at Rebecca Spit, where a flotilla of pleasure boats sat tied to the floats. From here on marinas and gas docks would fall few and far between, and they'd have to check their fuel carefully.

"We'll try Read first," he said.

Read Island hung directly west of Quadra and meandered north. Despite its proximity to Quadra and a history of early exploration and settlement, few families lived here, and abandoned homesteads scattered along its backwood roads. There were good anchorages around the island, most still in their natural state of seclusion and tranquility. Expecting to find the big schooner in one isolated anchorage among hundreds was a little like trying to find one tree in a forest. But Scott counted heavily on Vic's information, and, according to Vic, the *Pilgrim* had been sighted several times around Read and Cortes. This might mean they had a regular run between the two islands, and this narrowed the field of search considerably.

They ran the open waters for only a few minutes before they reached the coves and pockets along Read's southern banks. Scott eased the throttle, and they started through what first appeared to be a narrow passageway. Oyster catchers and terns fluttered into the air in a thick cloud of black and gray. The water rippled all the way across the shallow inlet. The low-pitched *kee-er* of a single gull cried out in protest.

"A lagoon!" Erin said.

It was a tidal backwash, overgrown with trees and ferns that dropped between large boulders right to the water's edge. Scott lowered their speed again, and they cut a slow trail through the still waters. Running close to shore they could reach out and touch the twisted boughs of firs and elms with their fingers.

From the lagoon, they broke out into the open again and came upon a trio of cabin cruisers traveling together. They ran alongside the small boats, all churning up white foaming tails. A cluster of tiny islands stretched out ahead of them. The cruisers angled off on a southeasterly heading toward Cortes. Erin waved and received answering waves, and their fellow wanderers quickly put distance between them. Scott continued north.

"We'll swing into Evans Bay. We can gas up at Government dock and go on. There's a little inlet up there; might be a nice stop for lunch."

Erin nodded contentment with the plan, and in this pleasant fashion they cruised on, most of the time at trolling speed, pausing to drop into an intriguing cove here and there and not giving much thought to their intended purpose.

There were only a few boats at Evans Bay, and they had no waiting time at the gas dock. The Whaler took twenty gallons, which meant the big Mercury engine had used half a tank. By Scott's calculations they had four hours' running time to find the *Pilgrim* before they would need to fill up again.

It was eleven-thirty when they found the place Scott had in mind for lunch, a small nook behind Frederic Point, completely walled in on all sides by grassy banks and trees, with a generous stretch of sand beach. They stuffed their gear into the backpack and dropped over the side into ankle-high water. They waded ashore, slipping and stumbling barefoot over the slime-green pebbles. The water was surprisingly warm. Like many of the protected coves in summer, the sun had baked in here, so there was a greenhouse effect on the water and plants.

"I wish I'd brought my swimsuit," Erin said.

"Swim as you are," Scott suggested. "I won't mind."

Erin laughed at the idea and found a sandy mound in front of a clump of driftwood that she quickly declared an ideal spot for their picnic. Scott secured the bowline to a rock and Erin laid out the beach towel.

She apportioned the contents of the lunch and Scott opened a bottle of wine, and they dug their bare toes into the warm sand and spent the next half hour conjecturing about the *Pilgrim*. Scott still thought it too much ship for students. Erin argued it was a wonderful training experience for them. Maybe that was the idea.

After lunch they took up their course again along the shoal passageway into Evans Bay. It was Scott's intention to run up the arm beyond Bird Cove, and if they didn't sight the *Pilgrim* in short order to run across to Cortes, where they could refuel and return to Campbell River. It wasn't much of a plan, but with what he knew about the anchorages in this area, it was the best he could come up with.

"How close are we to Bird Cove?"

"Not far."

Across to the north the needle-shaped cloud had ballooned into a whale.

"Anything wrong?"

"No. We could get a change in weather. Might have to cut it short. Might have to give up Cortes altogether."

Scott increased their speed and pondered the shorelines with new doubts. It was like running through an eight-foot-high maze of hedgerows, impossible to see the opening to one cove until you were fully upon it, each arm hiding the next. He glanced at the gas gauge and knew they had time and fuel to check only a few.

Bird Cove was a small, shallow anchorage. Scott shook his head. "Not enough draught for her here."

It was as he'd thought. If she were here at all, she'd undoubtedly gone up one of the long arms. But which, the one that veered west or the one that turned east, miles deep and wild? The shadows lengthened on the water, and all across Sutil Channel to Cortes the sea turned from sapphire-blue to a dark turquoise, sending definite signals of a coming turn in the weather.

Scott chose the east arm, thinking it the most protected and the most likely to have deep enough waters for a ship of the *Pilgrim's* size. The inlet had a number of bends and turns, and in most there was no sign anyone living had ever set foot on her before. There weren't even traces of logging trails or abandoned pastures, nothing except trees, moss, and rocks.

"Gives you a strange feeling," Erin said, and he wondered if the thought had hit her, too, that coming upon the *Pilgrim* in such a remote place might not be such a good idea after all.

Until now it had been a warm run, the only wind coming from their own movement through the quiet waters. All at once a small breeze sent a quiver over the water, and with it, cooler air. There wasn't much time left for their exploring. "Just a couple more turns. She twists in here."

They came upon it almost by accident. It looked like a long jetty, but when they turned into it, they found a deep cove with thick stands of firs, spruce, pine, and oak growing from the water's bank, backed by a steep rise of land, also densely covered with trees. Scott throttled down. They coasted around another bend, and there she was, looking like an oversize dolphin in a backyard swimming pool: the long cutter bow, the three tall masts, sails fastened to her rails, the Maple Leaf hanging limp from her mizzen gaff, lying at anchor, peaceful as a child at sleep. It was the *Pilgrim*.

"Fantastic," Erin murmured.

He had only half expected to find her, and at least thought to come upon her from a distance, just in case those two were on board. Stumbling on her this way, up so close they could see the scuff marks on her rails and the rust stains on her canvas, and no place to run without being seen, concerns ran through his head. Marilyn's murder led him to believe the two men called Charlie and Jerry were either still hiding somewhere on San Juan Island or headed for parts unknown, but what if his hunch they were tied in with the *Pilgrim* was right and they'd sought refuge here?

It was a stupid time for such thoughts. His instincts told him he'd better cut and run. But they'd come a long way, and there was no good reason for such fears. They couldn't observe the big ship from afar as he'd planned, but if they took reasonable precautions, they could avert a confrontation. They drifted quietly back into the cove, slipped around the schooner from her stern. Nothing moved, and Scott began to breathe more normally. "Hello, there!"

There was only the sound of a wavelet from the Whaler's wake slapping gently against the sides of the ship. "Anyone aboard?" Still no answer.

Scott tried to think how they would operate. Go out in skiffs to gather samples, with faculty or without. Scott brought the Whaler alongside and tied a line on her starboard cleat. A rope ladder hung over the gunwale as though it had been recently used, and there was only one skiff on her decks.

"Looks like they've gone ashore," Scott said. "I'll have a quick peek. Give a whistle if you see anything."

Erin nodded. "Don't be long." The quiver in her voice said she shared his concerns.

He killed the engine and left her with her eyes firmly fixed on the shore. "I'll be right back."

The cabin door was open, which indicated either trust in the remoteness of their anchorage or that the residents would soon be back. Opting to suspect the former, Scott leaned over the well. "Hello, there!" Above him, the boom creaked as it shifted, stirred by the Whaler's wake. All clear. Scott started down the gangway, confirmed almost immediately that no one was aboard, and instantly felt better. It was a roomy cabin with bunks forward and aft, and a galley and lounge in the center. The smell of morning bacon was trapped in with the musty odor of wet wood. Wet wood was not uncommon in old boats, and pointed suspiciously to a diagnosis of dry rot.

The cabin looked well lived in, with jeans, dirty sweats, underwear, towels, books, and other assorted gear sprinkled around the cushioned benches. There was a stack of unwashed dishes in the sink and several empty beer cans on the center table. A fly buzzed around an open jar of peanut butter on the drain.

The counter extended for several feet along the port bulkhead, holding a neat collection of specimen bottles, mostly filled with dirty water and an assortment of seaweed, and pieces of equipment one might expect to find in a marine studies lab. Not elaborate, but giving every indication this operation was what Preston said it was. Forward, the storage bulkheads offered more evidence of student involvement, with hand calculators, swim trunks, scuba gear, more books, and backpacks. Nothing out of the ordinary here.

Scott was halfway up the gangway when he heard Erin's whistle. He grabbed the top rail, took the rest of the ladder up in one swing. He stepped out onto the deck to the distant putter of a small outboard. He flew across the deck, dropped into the Whaler. Erin undid the lines, and, without exchanging a word, they hand-guided the Whaler along the gunwales of the schooner. Scott pointed to the shore, where the branches of elms and alder brushed the water's surface. They shoved off the *Pilgrim's* sternpost. The Whaler coasted the twenty or so feet to shore, and they fell under the cover of the trees just as the skiff appeared from the bed to the north with the returning students. There were three boys and two girls, and they were talking and laughing and, fortunately, showing little interest in anything around them.

Should he pull alongside, ask his questions,, and then beat it out of there before the weather turned and the students grew overly curious? There was one problem with that. Five students, by Preston's own admission inexperienced in sail, were not by themselves enough to handle the massive gaff-rigged gear on the *Pilgrim.* Somewhere, there had to be a captain and crew. Scott's hand hesitated on the starter.

It began as a distant buzz. Scott tensed up automatically. "Listen."

Erin was already looking up. The buzz turned into an ear-shattering roar. A float plane dropped from the rise of land to the north. The long wings almost brushed the tops of the trees in its swift descent. The pontoons touched the water, skied down the arm, and coasted to a stop alongside the *Pilgrim*. There was no reason for him to feel this uneasiness. No sense to the cramping in his gut. He'd seen nothing suspicious on the ship, nothing to tie it to the murders. The cabin door opened, and they stepped down onto the pontoon, one tall and blade-thin, Jerry, the other built like a small gorilla, Charlie, their pilot, who could have been the helmsman on the *Pilgrim* for all Scott knew. It was one of those improbabilities, the worst fears come true.

Erin gasped. "Scott, it's those two from the Whaler!"

There was no question. These were the same men who'd shot at him and Dandy on the beach, chased him and Erin in Griffin Bay, the same two who'd struck the man on the deck of the *Pilgrim* that night and thrown him into a watery grave. What an inopportune way to prove he'd been right. He and Erin were alone with two killers in the middle of nowhere, barely hidden by the lacy arms of the trees, a good five hundred yards' distance from the safety of open seas and no way out except the way they came in, past the big ship and the three men.

Scott started to sweat. If they left now they would most certainly be seen. There was, of course, the very real prospect they'd already been spotted from the air. Their one chance, it seemed to Scott, was to get out quickly before the men had time to think.

Scott pressed the starter and nosed the Whaler out of the trees. *Easy. Act normal. They don't know who we are. Not yet!* Erin gripped the cockpit rail so tight her knuckles blanched white. She didn't say a word. They started around the *Pilgrim* by the stern. He didn't need to tell her to keep out of sight. She was as aware as he that if the man recognized them, they would strike swiftly.

Scott eased by the *Pilgrim*'s blind side. Perhaps they wouldn't notice. Maybe Charlie and Jerry would think it normal for a runabout to wander into an anchorage miles from nowhere and hide behind the trees. Perhaps they wouldn't be alarmed by the presence of strangers in their hideaway, wouldn't expect them to speak or at least show their faces.

They made it to the opening, and Erin pronounced the bad news. "They're getting back into the plane."

"Hang on!" Scott shoved the stick fully forward. The Whaler's bow shot up like a bird in flight, and they vaulted out into the open bay. "We'll hit for Government dock." It was his second mistake.

The plane's engine did another job on their ears as it poised for takeoff.

"Maybe they're just flying out again."

It was a good thought. The plane didn't take off at all. By running, Scott had only confirmed to himself the paranoid fears of the two. The plane cruised behind the Whaler. Capable of speeds upward of sixty-five knots, Scott guessed, it was a virtual certainty the plane could overtake the Whaler, whose maximum speed was closer to forty. The clouds to the north extended, and ahead the water stirred restlessly. He couldn't keep the Whaler at even these speeds in choppy seas. The plane, with her big pontoons, on the other hand, would have much less trouble handling the chop, and if the ride grew too bumpy, could always lift off and fly above it.

Scott abandoned the straight course and took a southwest heading. They would have a better chance, he reasoned, if they hugged the shore. Wings, after all, weren't made to navigate through tree branches. The plane was faster, but the Whaler more maneuverable.

"There are rocks in here," Erin warned.

"We've not much more than a foot of draught, and the tide's up. We should manage it." He didn't want to tell her that, rocks or no, they had no choice.

Behind them, great gushers of water spurted up from under the plane's pontoons, bearing in on them fast. Scott began a zigzagging course across the channel. The pilot made an adjustment and followed.

"He's going to head us off."

Certainly he had the speed for it. Scott took a starboard turn and circled back toward the east shore. Across the small fetch of water, the plane corrected, slowed, and stopped. Scott turned on the wheel and circled again, but the plane, with its wide spread of wings, blocked the entrance to the bay. "He's waiting for us."

A soft breeze put little wavelets over the water. It was still clear sky to the southwest, but the clouds had extended overhead. The wind couldn't have come at a worse time. Right now they needed speed, and they weren't likely to get it if the seas turned to chop. Maybe, he thought hopefully, we can outrun the weather, pass up Evans Bay, and head straight for Quadra, hope the fuel holds out. But getting into open waters remained a problem, since the plane sat squarely in their path.

Providence offered a helping hand. Erin observed it first. The plane was dead in the water. On the pontoon, the pilot had the engine cowling off. Engine trouble. There would never be a better chance. Scott opened her up. The Whaler hurtled forward, picked up speed, scalded past the silver wings, close enough to read her numbers, close enough, he feared, for Charlie and Jerry to confirm what they must already have guessed, close enough to feel their rage, to sense the frustration. Scott saw it first as a flash of light from the cabin door—an arm lifted, taking aim. The report from the gun resounded like a thunderclap across the narrow bay.

"They're shooting at us!"

"Get down on the floor!"

Erin dropped to her knees as bullets spit into the wind around them. One struck the cockpit windshield and shattered the glass.

"Scott!"

"I'm all right. Stay down!" His knees felt like jelly as he held tight to the wheel. Boulders and swift currents marked the passages here, but he knew his chances of maneuvering the tricky passageways was better than escaping a bullet from determined killers. He twisted back and forth crazily. More blasts sounded behind them, but the marksmanship of the gunman, impaired by the bounce of the boat, was fortunately poor. Only a few more minutes and they would be out of range; only a few more zigging turns and they would reach the protection of Bird Cove. Only a few more pounding seconds and his heart would start beating normally again.

The bends in the shore would put them out of range, or so Scott hoped. He zipped into the trees at full speed. Rock outcroppings rose dangerously from the shoreline, but Scott gave no thought to the prop or the boat's fiberglass bottom, for here, he felt certain, the plane couldn't follow, and he much preferred a torn-up hull or a bent prop to a hole in his head.

Erin came up off the floor to brave a look. "I don't see them. Maybe they've given up."

He wished he could believe it. For the moment they were out of firing range, but the pilot could get their plane in the air again at any time. With this in mind, Scott cut along the beach, continuing to dodge the rocks and limbs of trees. Still no sign of the plane. It was time to take another chance.

"Where now?" Erin asked.

"We head for home."

"Do you think they'll follow?"

He imagined they would try. Across the open waters between Read and Quadra, a seagull hovered suspended in the air by the force of freshening winds, and he had new concerns. The waves were piling up with surprising strength, and the gray look that had threatened to the north had spread over the south as well. Added to this, the gas gauge, which had been gyrating undependably around the quarter-full mark, now pointed to empty. He had the five gallons in reserve, but was it enough to take them to Rebecca Spit? One thing he was learning about the Mercury: that big engine had an insatiable thirst. They were a mile out in open seas when it produced the first telltale sputters. Erin's face read alarm.

"We're out of gas."

"I'll switch over to the reserve tank."

He flicked off the engine and repositioned the spare tank.

He had time to think as they rolled around in the chop, engine dead, while he attached the hose to the reserve tank and hand-primed gas into the new line. Why had those two returned to the *Pilgrim*? Was the *Pilgrim* a cover, and, if so, what did this say about Preston Fields?

Scott tried the engine. The *Mercury* coughed. He tried again. It sputtered and shook. Nothing. He returned to the engine well, went through it all another time, squeezed the hose, tried to feed fuel through. The waves threw them around, and Erin looked a little sick. "I'll try now. Should work."

He turned on the starter. The *Mercury* sputtered, stopped; they continued to bounce. He turned it on a second time. It choked, gasped, stuttered into a rumble, and they started out once more, Erin looking sickly pale but much relieved.

Their best hope of making it on the reserve was to head straight for Quadra. The problem was weather. The waves were turning wild, forcing him to cut his speed. With the wind also came cold. In her light jacket, Erin shivered. "Let's button her up. At least we can keep the wind out."

Erin worked quietly beside him, snapping the plastic covers into place. Zipped up, the plastic shut out the wind, as he'd said, but they quickly saw a new problem. The plastic reduced their visibility so severely that Scott couldn't judge the water's twists and turns, slowing them all the more.

"Better to see," Erin decided.

They knocked down again. The changeovers took time, and each howl of the wind brought renewed fears the plane would return. Someone had once said boating was a continual trade-off. The Whaler, for example, was the right boat for calm seas, and got places in a hurry. Coming up in the Whaler, they'd made good time. Now, in the cresting waves, they could only inch along; the shoreline passed so slowly, at times it appeared they were standing still. For these seas, a sailboat was what he needed. As the weather worsened, Scott wished fervently he had the *Picaroon* under his feet.

"I think I see the Spit."

He saw nothing but another rise of land. He didn't want to tell Erin, but by his calculations they were a good ten miles from the marina. What ran through his mind now were alternatives. He could take a heading to Read's west side so that if the storm raged out of control, he could run the Whaler up on the beach. There were problems with that, too. If he spent too much time off his heading they could run out of gas. This he feared most at this point. Hard to spot a small boat tossing helplessly in whirling seas. Should he go for the beach or try for Rebecca Spit?

"I'm sure I see it," Erin shouted.

He saw, too. A ten-minute run. At these speeds, twenty? Hug the shore or cut into the open and fight the cross chop? Forget the plane. Erin had her eyes on the water directly ahead.

"Rock!"

A large boulder burst out of the trough, just off their bow. Scott held his breath and spun the wheel, caught a roll. More rocks erupted off their side. He spun again. The Whaler nosed up out of the water, lifted above the swirling waves, spinning dizzily, and fell back, bow down, stern up. The engine faltered, and Erin groaned. Scott let go the wheel. The Whaler dropped back, reeling into the swell. They bounced over another wave, ballast gone, the engine doing a good imitation of a dying drum. His neck and shoulders ached from straining to see. Erin's eyes riveted on the auxiliary tank.

"We're out of gas," she said.

"No." Not yet, they weren't. "She stalled when we came out of the water."

Scott had been so busy at the wheel that he hadn't heard the sound of the giant engine or seen the pontoons settling over them like a dark rain cloud ready to burst. There was no time to worry about their dwindling supply of fuel or the forces of the wind. Ahead was Rebecca Spit, where there were people and telephones. Hovering over them was the float plane carrying the two men who had killed at least one person, possibly three. And he and Erin were the only ones around to tell.

Off their port, a roller threw its spume thirty feet into the air, and overhead silver wings dipped and lifted, the rumble of the plane's giant engine muffled by the wind. Scott cranked the wheel into the chop. Only a few yards now, the long sandy strip of land rose in front of them. The plane banked. Scott slid toward the dock, and the plane carrying Charlie and Jerry turned and headed north.

Twenty

Out of gas and floundering, the Whaler caught a rush of wind, blew against the dock, and thumped into the hands of a stranger. "I've got her!" It was a deep, wheezing voice. A giant of a man stood on the float and held off the bow, preventing another collision with the dock.

Scott and Erin jumped onto the float beside him, and the three tied the boat to the cleats so she still bobbed restlessly in the chop, but without scraping.

"There, that's a proper job," the big man wheezed. His name was George Storey, and he was the owner of the marina. He had thick reddish-gray hair and a full beard, stood between six and seven feet, and to Scott was as welcome as Santa Claus to a child at Christmas. "Rough going," the big man said, tossing his head at the big breakers slamming against the floats.

Scott nodded, and then, because it was uppermost in his mind, said, "Is there a phone we could use?"

"Just up the hill."

Besides running the gas dock and the moorage, Storey and his wife rented rooms from their home that sat high above the marina overlooking the strait. "Americans, are you?" he said as he led Erin and Scott up a steep path to the house, pausing often to get his breath and running words together when he talked. "We're used to the squalls. They always take strangers by surprise."

"Do they last long?" Erin asked.

"Not unless it's the beginning of a weather change. Can hang on for days. Even the ferry shuts down when the gales come up."

Erin took this news with a look of total rejection, which didn't go unnoticed by the big man. "Don't worry," he said with a bearded grin. "Looks like this one will blow out by morning." He stopped at a small rise to catch his breath. "There's a silver lining to this," he wheezed. "My wife's a very good cook."

Erin smiled, but Scott knew she was thinking about Al and that they were already overdue in Campbell River.

The Storey house was a modified Cape Cod, shingle-sided and weathered a pale gray, which tended to confirm what Storey said about the storms that struck this corner of the island on a regular basis. The Storeys were a congenial couple who had mastered the act of making their guests feel at home. Martha Storey was a dimply, cheerful, middle-aged woman with a plump figure and snappy dark eyes, and from the aromas that floated out of her kitchen, all her husband promised in the culinary department. She also enjoyed fussing over people, which her husband attributed to the fact that she'd looked after four daughters, all married and gone now, and couldn't get out of the habit.

"Poor things," she said, taking one look at Scott and Erin. "Never mind, a wash-up and a hot cup of tea will set you right."

Scott placed his first call to the RCMP in Campbell River. The officer took it all down: the description of the plane, the numbers, which Scott remembered after some mind-jogging from Erin, the location of the *Pilgrim*, and Leroy's private line in Friday Harbor. The officer wasn't particularly optimistic about finding Charlie and Jerry. A small plane could fly across borders faster than customs could track them, he said, and it was his guess these two would get as far from Campbell River as possible. He promised to do his best.

Erin accepted the judgment of the RCMP happily. "That means they won't be back."

"They're out to save their own skins now," Scott agreed.

Scott called next to alert Leroy, but reached Harold instead, who promised to deliver the message. Erin placed a call to Al. Professor Turner was out, the hotel operator told her. Erin left a message, and Scott promised they'd try again later. Thoroughly cheered, they put themselves in Martha Storey's hands.

She served them hot tea and biscuits fresh out of the oven, a delicious little raisin cake that dripped with melted butter, fresh strawberry jam—homemade—and a small glob of whipped cream. Scott put three away without a trace of conscience while they got acquainted with the Storeys.

Outside, the sky continued to darken, and Erin grew anxious about Al. "Isn't there a chance we can get back today?"

George walked over to the barometer that hung beside the kitchen clock, studied it a moment, and returned shaking his head. "You won't want to take that little boat around the Cape today. Only last month a big trawler went down in winds just like this."

"We have two lovely rooms," Martha said. "You can stay the night and get a fresh start in the morning."

Al must have been waiting by the phone. Erin barely got a word in. Scott could hear him from across the room. "Rebecca Spit? Where the devil is that? I expected you back an hour ago."

Erin took some time trying to placate him, and Scott finally took over. "Sorry, Al, we ran into some weather."

The old man sniffed irritably. "I can see that. I told you, didn't I?"

"You did, and you were right."

When Scott finished explaining about the risks of running in the storm, Al's voice softened. "Stay put till it clears."

As George had predicted, the weather worsened. With the wind still wailing outside, they dined with the Storeys. After dinner, Erin and Martha sat on the big plumped-up living-room sofa and exchanged recipes and decorating ideas, a conversation that drew an amused smile from George, who rested his big frame in a leather reclining chair. Scott stood by the window watching the giant rollers breaking over the rocks, wondering if it would quit by morning. In the fireplace, wood cracked and spit as the wind sucked the flames up the stack.

"Martha tells me you're a surgeon," George said. Erin had let that information out of the bag.

"Yes," Scott said.

"Tired of it, are you?"

"Does it show that much?"

"Most people vacation to get a break from what they do. They're usually busting to go back after a week or two, especially industrious fellows like yourself."

"Don't you ever tire of what you do?"

"Haven't been at it that long. I was a floor man—knees gave out, and lungs. The doc said clean air, and we came here. That was seven years ago."

"And you still like it?"

"Once in a while you get unpleasant guests, and you think about chucking it. But most people are nice, and it's good fun."

The rooming arrangements were puritan. Scott's room was down and across the hall from Erin. At her door, Scott looked into her sleepy face, so pale in the shadowed hall, and felt guilty. "Sorry about the day."

"Why?" she said, stopping a yawn.

"Getting you into another mess."

"It was a wonderful day," she said, smiling.

As George had promised, the morning restored summer to the Spit. The water was like a duck pond, and the heat of the sun sent a layer of steam off the docks. They filled the Whaler's gas tanks, Scott paid the modest bill for the lodging, and they parted with the Storeys with much laughing and promises to return.

Waiting at the marina in Campbell River, Al looked happy to see them. Scott arbitrated with the manager of the marina over the damages to the windshield and the extra day, finally settling on a price slightly greater than Scott thought it worth, and they left, everyone talking at once.

"How did you get that hole in the glass?" Al asked suspiciously as they walked across the Quay.

Erin told Al about the chase, never quite getting around to the shooting, which only aroused the old man's suspicions the more. She soft-pedaled it about the plane having engine trouble and what the police had said, but Al saw through it and didn't like it. "Scottie, from here on out, let Leroy handle it!"

It was quickly apparent on the drive back to Sidney that Al had learned something from his library prowlings but was going to pick his own good time to tell it. Erin knew the signs, too: the silent smile; the slow stoking of his pipe; the meaningless chatter about the weather, the scenery, and the cost of the rooms, which he thought exorbitant. It was all designed to drive them crazy, and Erin endured it for most of an hour before she said, "Come on, Grandpa, let's hear it."

"I was in the library most of the day yesterday." He chuckled. "You wouldn't believe it, Scottie. Wonderful collection. First editions, antiquities, modern material, all well researched, nicely collated."

Erin started to laugh. "C'mon, Grandpa, you've had your fun. Tell us. You know you're dying to."

"I did pick up one bit of information I thought curious. Don't know that it matters now that we're turning this all over to Leroy, but I asked about the history of Canadian industry. Recent history, of course. They had some fascinating pamphlets about people who had their start in Campbell River and went on to achieve fame and fortune, like the well-known educator and conservationist Roderick Haig-Brown."

"I remember that name," Erin said. "We saw some of his books in Victoria."

"Yes, you would. He was a chancellor of the University of Victoria. Anyway, he comes from Campbell River. And guess who else comes from these parts? Brice Randall."

It was like hearing a voice from a dream. Butterflies started floating around Scott's stomach. Erin looked a little sick.

"Grandpa, what are you trying to say?"

"Not trying to say anything, except isn't it a great big coincidence that the big-shot developer from Seattle got his start in land development in Campbell River?"

Twenty-One

In the morning a light rain pitted the gentle waters of Cattle Pass and put a chill on the summer air. A front coming off the Pacific would continue to bring unstable weather to the region, the forecasters said. Scott made his call to Perth, Australia.

"No," his party concluded after five minutes of questions and intermittent pauses, "I don't know anything about it." The voice on the other end was definite and aroused, and later, Scott knew, there'd be more questions, accusations. Scott didn't relish causing trouble, even for someone he'd never liked, but there came a point when there was no choice, and he'd already passed it.

His first stop was only a few hundred yards down the road where the big house on the point was immersed in the heavy cloud layer that had settled over the Cape. Henry Mason, bundled up in an old army surplus jacket, was exercising the black Labs in the woods behind the house. The murders had intensified his basically untrusting nature. "What about Brice Randall?" he said, considering Scott suspiciously across the kennel yard.

"Is he solvent?"

"He has an A-1 credit rating from Dun and Bradstreet," Henry said, amused by the question. "And he has friends at City Hall. Cuts his risk, if you see what I mean." Randall had done very well, Henry said. Had only one flaw. "He likes the ladies."

This wasn't at all the kind of information Scott wanted to hear.

From Henry's, Scott drove directly to the sheriff's office. Harold looked up from Leroy's desk and cheerfully delivered his news. They'd identified the man hauled up in the fishermen's nets as a treasury agent. On this news, Scott dropped into a chair.

"Yeah, Leroy flew to Seattle an hour ago to meet with the federal boys. It's their case now. Too bad you missed all the fun, Doc. We ran all over your beach yesterday, looking for that .38. Found it, too. And guess what. The FBI came up with a positive ID on those two who broke into your place. One of them is wanted for killing a bank clerk in Boston."

Scott felt a sick pitch in his stomach, remembering how close he and Erin had come to being one of his victims. "Does Leroy think they're the ones who murdered Owen and Marilyn?"

"Not much doubt of it."

Scott's pulse raced as he left Harold and headed for the university experimental lab. He found Preston Fields slumped over his desk, the picture of dejection. In the few days since their last meeting, his boyish look had disappeared. Preston had aged ten years. "The *Pilgrim?*" he repeated dully, looking back at Scott through the heavy-rimmed glasses. "I don't understand."

"Cut the games, Pres. You're covering for men who killed a treasury agent, and I talked to the dean. The university did not authorize the use of the *Pilgrim* for research. You did!"

Preston jerked back as though he'd been struck. "You called Corny? In Australia?" His face twitched in anger. "For your information, I just talked to my students. They're in Campbell River, flying back here this afternoon, and, for the record, it wasn't my idea."

"Whose, then?"

"I'm not at liberty to say."

Scott stared at him in disbelief. "With four people dead?"

A dark flush rose from under Preston's collar. "What do you mean four?"

"Had you forgotten Toni?" It was, of course, only a hunch.

The muscles around Preston's mouth twitched again. "That was an accident. Wasn't it?"

Scott shook his head. "C'mon, Pres, give!"

Preston sighed unhappily and finally began to tell his story. It all started in the spring, he said, when some of the people in town complained that students from his lab were pushing narcotics on the local kids. Preston looked into it and found a few pot smokers, but no evidence of hard drugs.

Not long after, a man walked into his office who said he was a treasury agent, gave his name as Don Smith. He was working undercover on a drug ring operating in the islands and said university students might be involved. He said they'd discovered drugs in the storage barrels used by the lab on their research ships and suspected students or staff of bringing it in from Central America.

"I imagine you were pretty upset."

Preston looked up through angry eyes. "I was pissed! To think of anyone jeopardizing this important work—for profit, for drug running."

"What did you do?"

"What could I do? I appealed to Smith, told him about our grants and what we're trying to do here. He said he only wanted the ones who'd engineered the whole business, that he'd keep us out of the news if I'd cooperate."

"And you agreed?"

"Didn't think I had a choice. Anyway, a few weeks before that I'd received a letter from an outfit called Camstar, who said they owned this schooner and were looking for a tax write-off. They'd studied our program and were particularly impressed by our work on the moon snails. They offered the use of the *Pilgrim* and a crew. I don't know how, but Smith knew all about that offer. I was going to reject it. With all the liability problems, it sounded hare-brained to me. That's when Smith showed up and asked me to accept and put him on board as a visiting professor, which I did."

"Did Smith communicate with you during the time he was on the ship?"

"After about a week, he called, said he was making progress.

He didn't believe any of the students on the *Pilgrim* were involved, but there could be involvement from here."

"Did he call again?"

Preston nodded glumly. "He stopped in about two weeks ago, said he was getting close, that he expected a big shipment, and I got the idea that would be the end of it."

"When?"

"Before the end of the month, I think." He shook his head. "Don't hold me to it."

"In the name of heaven, weren't you even curious?"

"No!" Preston grew defiant. "And I'll tell you something else. I wish I'd never allowed myself to be talked into it in the first place. What good has it done me? I allowed our students to go out with known felons. I didn't know, but do you think the dean will believe that? And no one's proved to me any of our people were in on it, anyway."

"Okay, Pres, Smith said the end of the month. This is the twenty-eighth. When is the big research ship due back from Panama?"

"Sometime today."

"And you told no one about Smith?"

Preston shook his head wearily. "I only learned about his death this morning. Heard it on the news. I've been sitting here ever since, wondering what in hell to do."

"Call Leroy. What else?"

With a defeated droop to his shoulders, Preston nodded. They'd never been friends, but at this moment, watching Preston's neat, orderly world split apart, Scott couldn't help feeling sorry for him.

"About Toni, Scott. I only know what I read in the papers, that it was an accident or a suicide."

Strangely, this time Scott felt no pain at the words. "Neither one. She had enough Valium in her system to put down a horse. She was allergic to Valium. She would never have taken it voluntarily."

"Sorry," Preston said softly. "So sorry. But why did you think

I would know anything about it? There was never anything between Toni and me."

Getting an uneasy sensation in the pit of his stomach, Scott walked to the window and looked across the harbor at the boats swinging in the wind. "You were seen with her at Owen's parties."

"I saw her at Owen's once or twice, but she never came with me. Why don't you ask the man who brought her?"

Scott felt a tingling in his neck that started down his spine. He turned and searched Preston's bewildered face. "Who?" he asked, steeling himself for the answer. "Who should I ask?"

"But I thought you knew, Fred! Why don't you ask Fred?"

It was a long drive back to the Cape in the rain. Water flooded the windshield, and through the glass the whole world was a thick gray mist. Toni and Fred! It had been there in front of him all the time. Fred, charming, affable, attractive, a man who seldom had a serious thought, and Toni, who loved a good time. The wind kicked up off the strait and blew the rain harder against the glass, totally blotting out the trees and the road. Dandy stirred restlessly beside him, and Scott reduced his speed to a crawl.

His wife and his best friend, the two couples, both childless, always together, the knowing glances, all overlooked. So many little things now clear. Lorene and her trip abroad. What was it Cynthia had said, that Lorene had gone off the deep end for a while? Fred so distraught when he brought the news of Toni's death. Scott shook his head to dislodge the suspicions and stared bleakly at the rain-pelted road.

A squall ripped up the waters of Cattle Pass as Scott turned into his drive. Dandy raced for the door. Scott trudged dispiritedly behind. "We'll get a fire going," he said, shivering. But he knew it wasn't the rain or the sharp wind blowing off the strait that chilled him down to his toes.

There was something. Owen? What was Fred doing at Owen's parties? He'd always professed to detest Owen and his soirees. And Toni's picture in Owen's wallet. No sense to it. Had

166

Lorene known? The presumption was she had. Scott shook his head sadly, thinking of the pain it had brought to them all. A blast of wind threw a sheet of spray against the big living-room windows. Water rolled down the outer glass and dripped off the sill onto the deck. The memories came in painful flashes, not productive, best forgotten. Scott gave up plans to go by Fish Creek and talk to Vic. The questions he'd wanted to ask his friend seemed suddenly unimportant. Even the murders were blotted out by the pain of knowing he'd lived for months or years with a delusion about his wife and his best friend.

"Forget Toni," Ralph had said, "she's not right for you, never was." Could it be his partner had known, too? Maybe everyone had known but him.

The phone's ring jarred like an unwanted visitor. It was Leroy, returned from Seattle. "Where you been, Doc? Been trying to reach you for two days." Before Scott could answer, he said, "Guess I have you to thank for that half-witted professor finally coming forward. Can you believe a well-educated man could be so stupid?"

Scott only half listened while Leroy told him about Preston and the *Pilgrim* and the drug ring. The treasury people would make an arrest within hours, Leroy said.

"Mmm," Scott said, unable to get excited at the news.

"Say, is something wrong with you? You sound all washed out."

"No," Scott lied. "Tired, that's all." He wished Leroy well, and when he put the phone down remembered he hadn't asked who was behind the whole operation. Then, as he started sorting it out, he began the painful process of answering his own question.

He couldn't accept the idea that Charlie and Jerry had gone on an aimless killing spree. There had to be a reason for each killing. Easy to understand the treasury agent. Smith had found them out, and they'd struck him senseless, thrown him overboard to protect their own skins. But why Owen? He was a key man in the drug scheme, on the same side. And why Marilyn? She'd talked out of turn, but how could they have known, unless someone told them? Who? Bob? If his grief over his wife's death wasn't real, he was a hell of an actor. Who else knew of Marilyn's rantings? Almost everyone at the party, as well as Vic, Georgie, and the fishermen.

Another question that had bothered him from the start. Why break into Scott's house, tear everything upside down, and take nothing? He sat with that a minute; then it stirred, a notion buried deep. He dug it out of the bedroom bureau drawer—Toni's evening bag. This time he searched its insides. Comb, lip gloss, wallet, key, everything except the one item Charlie and Jerry had broken into his house to find. Toni's appointment book was gone, and there was only one other person who'd known of its existence.

Scott shook his head, in rejection or denial he wasn't sure which. He was, he decided, looking at it from the wrong side, needed a clinical view. Read the symptoms before making the diagnosis. He thought about obsessions, about a look in an unguarded moment, about emotional imbalance, and about the unstable mind driven too far. Sadly, it began to make sense. With dread, Scott made the calls to Seattle, asked the questions that only confirmed what he'd begun to suspect. He shoved a log on the fire and watched unhappily as it exploded up the stack.

He was considering the alarming drift of his findings and wondering what he should do when Dandy alerted him to a visitor at their front door. It was Al. He was wearing the old yellow rain slicker with the big floppy hat, and the water spilled off the brim like the runoff from an overfull gutter as he stood in the darkened doorway.

"Come on in, Al. Get that wet stuff off and pull up a seat by the fire."

Al shook his head and didn't budge, and Scott saw he was upset. "Where's Erin?"

"I hoped she was here."

"No. Has she been gone?"

"Couple hours. Left after dinner."

She'd probably got hung up in town. Scott pulled the old boy over the threshold and shut the door on a rush of wind. "If she drove into town, she'll be a while. Hard to see a thing on that road in this weather, believe me. I crawled back myself. Don't worry. She's a good driver. She'll be along soon."

"She didn't go to town."

Scott got an uneasy feeling. "Where did she go?"

"It was all that stuff about Brice Randall." He shook his head in disgust, and water from the rain jacket splashed onto the floor. "Sorry. I told you I was wet."

"Never mind that. Where the hell *did* she go?"

"She said she was going to check on Owen's artifacts."

"You mean she went to Owen's?" Scott's voice lifted. "You let her go alone to Owen's?"

"I didn't let her do a darned thing," Al said morosely. "She called Millie to see if Millie could let her in, so she could take a quick look. Satisfy herself, she said."

"So she met Millie at Owen's?" Scott sighed with inner relief. "Come on, we'll go over and roust her. Millie's quite a talker when she gets started."

Al shook his head. "She didn't meet Millie. That's what I've been trying to tell you. Millie was busy, suggested Erin ask one of the neighbors to let her in. You know how everyone around this Cape has a key to his neighbor's in case of fire when they're off the island?"

"So who had a key to Owen's?" Scott asked, feeling a tightening in his chest.

"Fred and Lorene. Erin said she was going to stop by their place, but that was two hours ago. I called Fred; got no answer. Called Owen's, and the phone's been disconnected. Guess I should walk over there." Al stopped talking and looked at Scott. "Something's wrong."

Scott was already at the phone dialing the familiar numbers. He let it ring a dozen times before he finally replaced the receiver and looked into Al's anxious face. "Al," he said, working to keep the fear out of his voice, "Erin's probably gone over to Owen's with

Fred, and Fred's as big a gossip as Millie. Why don't you take Dandy, run along home, and fix a drink. I'll fetch Erin and join you in a few minutes."

Relief poured into the old man's face.

Scott waited only until Al and Dandy were out the door and then rushed back to the phone, placed the hurried call to Leroy, told him what he knew—or thought he knew—finished in a rush of words, and rang off, leaving the sheriff to fill in the rest. Leroy could handle the drug shipment. More important to Scott was Erin. He'd failed Toni. He wouldn't fail Erin.

Twenty-Two

The Jeep lurched as the heavy truck wheels struck the potholes on Beach Lane. Erin is all right, Scott told himself over and over. She won't be harmed, not if she doesn't say anything about the *Pilgrim* or the land deals in Campbell River, and there's no reason she would. The masks! Would she feel she had to explain about Owen's artifacts? Would she tell what she'd undoubtedly guessed, that they were all fakes, substituted for the ones Randall had purchased from Owen for cash?

A normal person wouldn't kill for so little. But this wasn't a normal person. This was a deranged and highly dangerous paranoid schizophrenic who'd already killed twice and wouldn't hesitate to kill again. Such a person would quickly assume Erin knew it all—the elaborate scheme for laundering drug money, the network of pleasure and fishing boats, of university ships used to smuggle drugs into the islands, and the identity of the one who'd put it all together, the unlikely person with the cunning and the obsessed determination of the mad.

Scott jammed his foot on the accelerator, and the Jeep bounced onto the Cape road. If only he'd taken the trouble to pursue the thing with Randall. If only he'd wrung the truth out of Preston long ago. If only he'd known about Fred and Toni, recognized those early signs of something wrong, he might have prevented four murders. And Erin—it was like the night they found Toni, the nightmare all over again.

Owen's roof rose out of the rain-soaked scrub trees. Scott took the turn into the drive on two wheels and braked the Jeep.

He ran to the door, saw that it was ajar, and burst in, calling Erin's name. Silence greeted him. As on the morning they found Owen, even the wind's howl had no chance against the double-paned glass that insulated the rooms.

The room looked much as it had the morning they'd found Owen lying in the pool of his own blood, except the ugly patch of red no longer stained the living-room carpet, and the trays of cigarette ashes and clam dips were gone. The place was immaculate, undoubtedly from Millie's earnest efforts. Even the sofa was restored to a milk white, and the curved sections returned to their places around the spot where Owen had fallen. The smell of death, shut in by the thick doors and windows, a house closed up in the summer heat, remained. Scott stared painfully at the walls. The gaping ebony faces, the long-jawed pieces of petrified wood that held the grim secrets of the life-and-death struggle that had taken place here, laughed back.

Scott started through the rooms, fearful of what he might find, more fearful of not knowing. Kitchen—empty. Halls—still. Utility—washer, dryer, closets—all empty. Bedrooms—spotless. Then he saw it on the dressing-room floor, shockingly brilliant against the white marble floor tiles, the small cloth of silk with the geometric swirls of bright blues and reds. Scott picked it up, held it in his hand, and breathed in the scent of Erin's perfume—the scarf he'd bought for her that day in Victoria. "I'm a summer, didn't you know?" she had said with the teasing laugh. "But I love bright colors." Scott's spirits soared as he clutched the certain evidence Erin had been here, and, just as swiftly, sank. She'd been here, all right, but clearly she was gone now, and her fate was more uncertain than before. There was only one other place to look.

He ran out the door and sprinted over the sandy hump, stumbled in the dark through the grove of Scotch pine, and splashed across the water-soaked dirt path. Out of breath and thoroughly drenched, he landed at Fred's back porch. The door was unlocked. He rushed in, took two sloshing steps into the kitchen, and stared into the surprised face of his best friend. "Fred, what the hell you doing here?"

Recovering, Fred said, "I live here, remember?" Then, "My God, Scottie, you're raining all over the floor."

Scott still wasn't absolutely sure, still didn't want to believe. "Don't you ever answer your phone?"

Fred laughed. "Oh, that. Sorry, Scottie. I thought it was the office. Meant to take the phone off the hook."

Typical, Fred's way of not facing things.

"What's up, ol' buddy? You don't look too happy."

"Where's Lorene and Erin?"

"They went out for a while. Anything wrong?"

"Where did they go?"

"Umm. I think they said they were stopping at Owen's. Something about the masks."

"They're not there."

"Umm. Probably went to town. Lorene said something earlier about needing a few things at the store." Fred's eyes flickered. "There *is* something wrong. What is it?"

Scott shook his head. All seemingly normal. Was it possible Fred didn't know? He looked into the open, friendly face and wondered why he'd never guessed about Toni. Nothing could stay hidden on that face. It was simply that he hadn't been looking. Suddenly, without good reason, Scott felt a surge of sympathy for his friend, and then new fear.

"Fred, does Lorene ever take the Bayliner out by herself?"

"All the time. Didn't you know? She handles the thing better than I do. 'Course, she's a bit reckless. Goes out at the oddest times." He sighed deeply. "I suppose she feels the need to get away." He shook his head, and an inexplicable sadness came over his face. Scott thought how truly blind he'd been to his friend's needs. "Why do I get a feeling you're trying to tell me something?"

"I'm worried about Erin, Fred. Do you think they might have gone out in the boat?"

Fred glanced out the window at the rollers crashing against the rocks below his deck. "In this stuff? My God, I hope not."

"I think I'll just swing by the creek," Scott said.

Fred got a look in his eyes. He pulled his jacket off the hall peg and started behind Scott. "I think I'll go with you."

Vic and Georgie popped out of the doghouse when Scott and Fred reached the creek. "Yeah, I saw them." Vic shoved an arm into the sleeves of his rain slicker. "Thought it damn weird, going for a joyride in this slop."

"Which way they headed?"

"South, I think." Vic studied Scott's face. "Something wrong, huh?"

"I have to catch them, Vic."

Beside Scott, Fred dripped rain and grew anxious. "What the hell is this all about, Scottie?"

"I'm not sure. You better stay here."

"The hell I will. What's going on? Let's have it."

Scott took a deep breath and through the blinding rain faced the dark, worried eyes. "I think Lorene's involved in a drug-smuggling operation." Scott stopped, couldn't tell him the rest.

Fred's mouth gaped. A lightning bolt couldn't have jolted him more. "You can't be serious."

"Wish I weren't." There was no time—no time to go into it now.

Vic had the picture. "Davey's bow picker is the fastest thing around."

There were few surprises among the fishermen, who all along had known more about the whole business than they'd let on, about Lorene and her night runs, about the lights off Iceberg. While Fred watched, angry, bewildered, Davey revved up the big diesel.

"About time someone did something," Davey said. "Get aboard."

Scott climbed over the side. Fred leaped after him. "I'm going, and when I prove you wrong, you'll eat shit." The rainwater slid down his cheeks like tears. "I thought you were my friend."

It was like having a knife twisted inside him. Scott wished he was wrong, that he'd read all the signs incorrectly, that Lorene hadn't committed the terrible crimes in order to protect what she thought needed protecting, to save all she cared about in the world—her husband.

Georgie undid the lines on the *Mollie O* and boarded. "You might need an extra hand."

The *Mollie O* was an open boat, a small cabin aft and the spool and the wheel forward, mostly built for speed. From the deck of the *Nellie J*, Vic cupped his hands around his mouth and yelled, "We'll follow. Keep your channels open."

Scott waited by the rail and wished they'd get started.

Davey backed the *Mollie O* out of the slip, and, driving into sheets of rain, headed out. "Where to?"

"Around the lighthouse, out there with the blinking lights."

"Iceberg?"

No, not if he was right. If it were as Scott feared, she'd be going north. "Up Haro."

They shot out of the creek. Fred stared glumly over the rail. He was beginning to get an inkling of what was going on, and growing more fearful by the minute. "You can't think Lorene had anything to do with these murders." His voice pleaded for support.

Scott couldn't bring himself to answer.

"You nuts, Scottie? Lorene wouldn't hurt a fly."

"What about Toni, Fred?"

Fred's face was a mix of horror and guilt. "Toni was an accident." But his voice held less conviction than before.

Davey took the turn out of the creek and caught a roller. The *Mollie O* lurched. The wind howled so loudly Scott had to shout to be heard. "The Lorene we know wouldn't. This is a different Lorene—hasn't been herself in months. Swings of mood. Obsessed . . ."

Spray splashed over the rails. Fred's lips trembled. No words came out.

"Something threatened her, and like a circuit breaker overloaded, she blew. Happens that way sometimes."

"She worries about things," Fred blurted. "Who doesn't?"

"And the trip to Switzerland? I talked to your doctor, Fred. It's more than that, and you know it."

"Fuckin' doctors. All stick together." Fred said something more that Scott missed. Then, "How did you know about Switzerland?"

"Cynthia."

"Don't know what Cynthia told you . . . wasn't anything like that. Lorene had a case of nerves. I'm not the easiest person to live with, you know. She'd been upset, losing her parents. But she's okay now. You're wrong. You'll see." Fred took a blast of wind and sea in the face. He licked the salt off his lips and slumped against the rail, looking miserably unsure.

Scott could find no words to comfort him. All he could think of was Erin alone with madness and nowhere to run.

At the helm, Davey was having his own problems trying to get full speed out of his boat. "Wish I could open her up. Too much chop."

Scott nodded grimly and told himself for the hundredth time that it was not too late. They have a head start, but Lorene won't do anything until she gets well out in the strait and probably not until she meets whoever it is she's racing to meet. On a clear summer day Lorene's Bayliner could outrun most boats. But not tonight, not with the wind gusting and blowing rain in their faces so much that a reef or the unpredictable dips in the waves couldn't be seen. She'd have to slow down, too.

They thumped over a big roller, and Scott hung on to the rail to keep from being swept over the side. He looked quickly for Fred, saw he was clutching the metal sides of the reel, his eyes fixed on the water. Davey's bow picker wasn't as fast as the Bayliner, but it had the durability of a tug and handled better in heavy seas. On this, Scott pinned his hopes.

Around Seal Rock, the waves rolled in from the north, building to six-foot peaks. They went through rocking, putting spray across the decks, but never losing forward momentum. Past the point they ran into a cross chop. The *Mollie O* pitched, but only slightly. It would be a problem for the lighter Bayliner. This prompted a new fear. Scott prayed Lorene was as skilled at handling the small boat as Fred said she was.

Davey took the shortcut between Goose Island and the kelp bed, and drove into the rain and wind coming around the lighthouse. It was like the inside of a mine shaft. The rain fell so hard they couldn't see two feet in front of their bow. But Davey knew every rock and sandbar in the passage. He surged through with his throttle close to wide open. With rain blowing in his eyes, Scott looked for Fred. He saw only a dim outline against the spool.

Vic's voice shouted over the radio. "This is the *Nellie J* calling the *Mollie O*. Come in, *Mollie*."

Davey unhooked the mouthpiece from the radio hanging from his doghouse bulkhead. "This is the *Mollie O*. Go ahead, Vic."

"I'm just rounding the point. Where are you?"

"West of the lighthouse, coming up on the trap. It's black as pitch out here. Can't even see the lights of Victoria."

"Run your floods. Billy's fishing near there. He says he saw the Bayliner shoot past about ten minutes ago with two people aboard."

Scott's spirits lifted. Erin was alive.

"Billie said he isn't doing worth shit with the fishing so he's going to reel in and follow you. You might tell the doc, Billy says he knows all about those blinking lights."

Scott was moved at Billy's sacrifice of a night's fishing.

"Hey," Davey said, "Billy's got two kids. He knows the score."

Fred dropped into a sitting position by the reel and buried his head in his hands. Water ran over his open collar and down his neck. The boat pitched. Fred rolled with it and didn't look up.

Two minutes later they spotted Billy's net. The lights on the gill-netter flickered faintly in the darkness, almost like the lights off Iceberg, signals from those fishing boats involved in an operation more profitable than fishing. Who these fishermen were Scott didn't want to know. He preferred to leave it to Leroy and the treasury men, for he feared there might be among them old friends, men he'd once liked and admired, men who'd worked damn hard for their living; embittered men, recruited by Owen and his cohorts. Scott couldn't condone what they'd done, but he knew the despair that had led them to resort to such desperate acts.

A wave broke over the bow. Its spray illuminated the deck. In the shimmering fountains of water, Scott imagined Erin's blue eyes filled with terror. He pulled his jacket collar tighter around him and shoved his hands in his pockets.

Vic's voice cut in, in a three-way hookup with Billy. "I talked to Leroy. He says there's a big bust going down, somewhere near Davison Head in Speiden Channel."

"Any trouble?" Davey asked.

"Might be. He said we ought to leave it to the professionals." Billy laughed. "What did you tell him?"

"I told him to blow it out his . . ." The wind and Billy's laughter blotted out the rest.

Davey approached Mitchell Bay and eased up on the throttle. "Do we head outside Henry Island or go through Mosquito?"

There was no way to be sure, but it stood to reason Lorene would take the safer, shorter run through Roche. "Mosquito."

Davey nodded and throttled up, started through the narrow passage between Henry Island and Hanbury Point.

"This gets shoal in here," Scott warned.

There was no need to worry. Davey knew the waterways in the islands as well as Scott knew the veins and arteries through which human life flowed.

Inside the protection of Henry Island the wind died, and in the distance, Scott imagined he heard the sound of another boat. Davey heard, too. He cut his engine, and they bounced through the slop. At first there was only the noise of the water splashing against the sides of the *Mollie O.* Then it broke through, the distant rumble of an engine, falling and rising as it worked through the chop. The lamps from the Roche docks and the lights of a dozen ships bouncing at anchor blinked brightly across the harbor. A veiled specter moved laboriously between them. The Bayliner! Scott's pulse raced. "She's going out Davison Head."

Fred was on his feet now, fearful, uncertain. "I hope—" He barely breathed the words. "I hope she remembers about Channel Rock."

The rock, hidden at high tide, had deceived a number of cruisers, destroyed their props and hulls. Covered by water and darkness, the treacherous reef waited to claim another. "She'll veer off, take the starboard side," Scott said, praying he was right.

The Bayliner gave no ground.

"She knows we're on her trail. She's running without lights."

Did she know, or was she in too much of a hurry to keep an appointment with the two who'd been the legmen for this poisonous operation from the beginning? Was she planning on turning Erin over to those two, let them do her dirty work as they had with the treasury agent and Owen? It had been easy, Scott imagined, for her to kill Toni, whom she'd hated, and not too difficult to kill poor Marilyn in her drunken state. But Erin— Erin would be another matter.

"My God," Fred cried out, "she's going right over it."

She went at full throttle. There is nothing so sickening as the sound of wood scraping against rock, of a ship's hull being crushed by a solid mass of stone, unless it is the sound of plastic ripping under the cutting blades of a reef, pulverizing and punching apart. The engine faltered, and a woman screamed. Davey edged closer to the dark shadows of the unlit boat. Scott threw off his shoes and poised on the bow, straining to see. Davey switched on the big pole lights, and the bright flash lit up the water, swept the sea around them, and finally fell on the small boat that lay tipped on its side, water flooding into the hole in its hull. Beside it a form fought to stay afloat.

Georgie tossed the lifeline. For one chilling moment they watched while it sailed over the waves and landed short of its mark, bounced back in the rolling seas.

Fred hit the water first. He dove into a rising wave. Fred, who'd captained the swim team in college. Taking strong arm-over-arm strokes, he reached the Bayliner just ahead of Scott. One person hung on to the prop; one woman choked for breath, looking done in from the effort. She clutched the long shank of steel. Fred got his arm around her, pulled her free, and the Bayliner lurched a notch closer to capsizing.

Scott reached Fred's side, afraid to see who'd been spared, but hoping. Fred turned, one arm holding his survivor. The floods from the *Mollie O* shone on the pale face. It was Erin, confused but conscious. Scott let out a prayerful sigh of thanks. Fred released his limp charge into Scott's waiting arms and then turned wordlessly, drew a deep breath, and dropped into a wall of whitecapped surf in search of Lorene.

Scott pulled Erin close, held her against his chest as the swell lifted them up and dropped them back down. He held her while they both choked on mouthfuls of salt water, blinded by the frothy spray that blew into their faces from the gusting winds. He'd been so overjoyed to find her alive that he'd ignored the problem of getting her back safely in these seas. Water smashed against them with the force of dinghies colliding, filled up their clothes, weighing them down, sucking them under. Erin offered no resistance. *Have to hold on,* Scott told himself.

On the *Mollie O*, Georgie and Davey were both throwing lines. The ring bobbled in front of Scott and danced out of reach. Waves piled up. New fears came over him as he held Erin with one arm and paddled with the other, kicking desperately to keep their heads above water, only half succeeding. A big roller fell over them, filled the space between them. Erin started to slip. Scott got his hand on her waist, pulled her in. She didn't move. His heart stopped. Then he felt her breast rise. She was alive, but barely. He had to get her on board the *Mollie O*, get her warm, for hypothermia came swiftly in these waters. He worked his way toward the *Mollie O*. It was pitch-dark, and the pleasure boats were too far away to be of any use, but Davey had moved the *Mollie O* closer and waited with lines, shouting encouragement.

It wasn't an easy maneuver, trying to lift someone up over the slippery sides of a boat from the water, with waves pounding on all sides. Scott tried to grab the line, but with Erin in his arms it was impossible. Georgie leaned over and, half hanging by his toes, tried to reach her, with no success. Davey joined in the effort and failed. Scott's legs were like two gas tanks, full and too heavy to lift. He kicked. Nothing happened. He kicked again, and his chest sent stabbing pains to his limbs. He tried once more, and slowly, painfully, boosted her up. Georgie was waiting, and this time caught hold. "Got her," he said, and Scott knew Erin was safe.

Georgie and Davey pulled her up over the side and encased her in blankets. From below, both arms free, Scott treaded water and began to shed clothes. He stripped down to his shorts and felt a welcome freedom of movement and the bite of ice-cold water on his bare legs and arms.

"Come on, Doc," Davey shouted, dangling the line over the side for Scott to grab hold.

Scott waved him off. "Have to help Fred." Erin's cry of protest whimpered in the wind. Slowly, Scott started back to the sinking Bayliner.

The pants and jacket had acted like an anchor. Now at least he had only to fight the thrashing action of the seas. It was enough. Davey worked the wheel, and backed the *Mollie O* within a few feet of the reef. The trouble was holding her there. With the action of the waves and the tide, the boat tended to bounce shoreward. It was only a short swim to the Bayliner, maybe no more than thirty feet. In the water, it looked like a mile. Scott plunged ahead. He went down with a roller, trying not to fight, working to make headway. Another roll. He drifted back to where he started.

Finally, he resorted to a breaststroke that succeeded in getting him through the waves. By the time he reached the reef, the Bayliner listed badly to starboard, and there was no sign of either Fred or Lorene. The cold hadn't bothered him that much before. Maybe the jacket had held in his body heat. Now he began to shiver. He yelled Fred's name. A useless effort. He paid for it with a mouthful of salt water.

Scott managed to reach the Bayliner. He took a deep breath and got under her sinking side. He saw only murky water and the shadow of the cabin hanging dangerously over his head. Davey must have seen the problem. From the boat, the big strobe lights started dancing over the Bayliner, swinging back and forth, lighting up one section and then another. Scott rose to the surface and treaded water, waiting. Finally, the roving spots from Davey's bow picker picked up movement. It was only a splash. Scott started toward it. Fred burst out of a wave, opened his mouth, sucked in air, and went down again. There was total desperation in the act. Scott tucked his knees to his chin and dove after him, down where even Davey's floods couldn't penetrate the darkness—underneath the Bayliner.

Scott used his fingers to feel his way along the broken hull, ran them blindly along the slippery wood, over barnacles, grass, more barnacles, hand over hand. Then he felt something unlike any of the properties of the boat or the sea. He touched hair, bumped shoulders. Arms moved. It was Fred, pulling and tugging desperately against the cruiser's ridgepole. Lorene was trapped under her boat. She'd been down a long time—too long—and Fred couldn't budge her loose. If he continued to try, they would both drown.

With hand signals to Fred, Scott laid his shoulder to the hull. Fred did the same, and they both pushed. Nothing moved. They tried again. Still nothing. Lorene was caught between the reef and the splintered hull, and there was no way two men could dislodge the ten tons of water and hull that held her captive.

Fred wasn't going to give up. Scott's chest constricted like a tied-off blood vessel; his lungs were near bursting. He had to have air. In one push he shot up, broke the surface, and choked for breath, throat and chest burning. A second later, Fred followed, took another deep gasping breath, and prepared to go down again. Fred was weakening, his breath coming in uneven jerks. In that dangerous condition he would have gone. He would have gone and maybe drowned, but forces beyond his control made further attempts irrelevant. A large wave struck, and the Bayliner rolled off the rock and sank. While Scott and Fred watched, Lorene's lifeless body floated to the surface.

Twenty-Three

There was nothing they could do for Lorene. Scott kneeled on the wet deck, his bare knees digging painfully into the slippery wood as he tried mouth-to-mouth resuscitation, more to satisfy Fred than out of hope he could breathe life back into Lorene's flaccid body. She'd been lost minutes ago, died, he guessed, when she'd struck her head on the bottom of her boat.

"I'm sorry, Fred," Scott said.

Fred stared blankly at the slender white fingers protruding from under the piece of tarp they draped over her and said nothing.

Vic and Billy arrived and rafted alongside. Vic cracked out some blankets from his cabin and handed one to Scott. Scott hadn't even thought about the cold or how ridiculous he looked in his shorts and the wet sports shirt that clung to him like plastic wrap. Vic looked at Fred, still standing over Lorene, getting rained on and dripping water, and stuck one of the blankets in his hands. "Better put this over you."

Fred didn't move. Scott unfolded the blanket and threw it around Fred's shoulders, and they left him to his lonely vigil.

Scott found Erin hiding under the tentlike protection of a Poncho. She was on the bow of the *Nellie J*, leaning against the rail, staring into water. When she turned her face to look up at him, her eyes filled with tears. "I couldn't stop her, Scott. I didn't know what to do. I—I just jumped."

"A good thing you did."

Underneath all the rain gear she wore an old pair of

184

Georgie's sweats. She looked so small and defenseless. He kissed her, a long dizzying kiss, and the blanket slipped to the deck. The wind whipped at his bare legs, and he started to shiver.

Erin stood back and considered his condition with a concerned frown. "Scott, you're going to freeze to death."

He gathered the blanket up and wrapped himself in it again. "I'm—I'm fine." The shivers turned violent, and he began to shake all over.

Georgie walked over, curious. "I've seen scuba divers do that, shake for hours that way. It's going in without a wet suit. Kills them every time."

Billy took one look at Scott, climbed across to his own ship, and returned a minute later holding a pile of clothes. "Get out of those wet things before you make me dizzy."

"Better get some for Fred," Scott stuttered, accepting the clothes gratefully.

Changed into Billy's jeans and Vic's old fish-net sweater, Scott was a long way from warm, but the shakes stopped. Feeling better, he sought Fred. His friend was still on the bow of the *Mollie O*, standing over Lorene, the blanket resting loosely on his shoulders. He still held the clothes Billy had brought, but had made no attempt to do anything with them.

"Getting pneumonia won't help anything."

Fred looked up and slowly began to peel off his pants and shorts. Suddenly he found his voice. "You knew . . . about Toni?"

"Yes." No point in telling him he'd only known for a few hours.

Fred pulled on the dry trousers. They were too long, but Fred didn't notice. "Sorry, Scottie. Don't know how it started. Never meant to go so far."

"It's in the past, Fred." So much in the past there seemed little to forgive.

"My—my fault." Fred slipped on a shirt and began rolling up the pants legs. "Poor Lorene, we—we should've had children. Would've helped. She wanted to. It was me that didn't." His lips trembled, and as if the memory were too much, stopped talking.

Scott guessed he was going back in time, thinking of those twists in his wife's behavior pattern, warnings he'd chosen to ignore, just as he'd always avoided anything unpleasant. Scott imagined he was asking himself what he might have done to stop a lonely and desperate woman from taking a wrong turn, a turn none of them had seen. Perhaps, sadly, one no one could have prevented. In an obtuse way, I'm as much to blame as Fred. I'm the one who drove Toni into another man's arms, robbed Lorene of all she treasured in the world.

Fred sat down on the deck and looked up at Scott through red eyes. "I loved her, and I failed her."

Scott placed a reassuring hand on his friend's shoulder. "Go below and get warm, Fred."

Vic walked over carrying rain slickers, a bottle of brandy, and some water glasses. He poured a generous portion of brandy into one and stuck it in Fred's hand. Fred took it, sipped once, and started to cry.

Erin was in the *Nellie J*'s galley digging around for coffee when Scott found her again. "About Brice," she said. "You knew he lied about the artifacts?"

"Yes," Scott said.

Unhappiness filled her face. "I wanted to find out. That's why I went over there. It seemed so odd—the fake in Victoria, that the others would be authentic. I'm not the expert Brice is, but I could tell when I looked. The work was crude, very unlike the one Mrs. McDonald showed us in Victoria." She set the coffeepot under the water tap and filled it. "What do you think it means about Brice?"

"I imagine he purchased some of Owen's pieces and knew Owen was replacing them with fakes."

"You think he lied because he feared he'd be dragged in?"

"It could be something like that."

"To cover up. A man like him!" She shook her head in bewilderment. "Will it have to come out? It could damage his reputation very badly."

"Depends. If it was an innocent purchase, an honest mistake, maybe not. But if he was helping Owen launder drug money, they'll throw the book at him."

She nodded understanding and went back to the stove and the coffee.

Fifteen minutes passed while they waited in the cold, the wind blowing the rain in a soft spray across the decks. This nightmare wasn't over yet, and with Leroy's delay, the tension grew.

Vic looked off across the bay. "Leroy said the bust would be 'round here somewhere. What you think, Doc?"

"Battleship Island is my guess. Gives them a clear shot into Canada if anything goes wrong. What bothers me, Lorene was racing here to warn them."

"You're thinking they should be here by now."

"Where they going with it?" Davey wondered.

"Transfer to fast boats, more drops, maybe to the fishermen."

"They been transferring coke and hash off Iceberg for months," Vic said.

Scott looked sharply at his friend. "How do you know that?"

"Me and Billy put it together. Some of the boats"—Vic and Billy exchanged amused glances—"not just the Indians, been coming up with big profits."

Davey agreed. "Anyone who says he's making a killing this season is a liar. Not on fish, he's not."

"A liar or a drug pusher," Billy added bitterly. "The kids've been getting it from somewhere."

"I don't think they'll be going to Iceberg tonight. Not after Marilyn blew the whistle on it," Scott said.

"Hey, Doc, is that why they knocked her off?" Georgie asked.

Scott thought of the look on Lorene's face when Fred danced with Marilyn. Had Marilyn's tendency to talk too much been the reason? "It played a part." He hadn't told any of them about Lorene and the killings, only about her role in the drug operation. He imagined they guessed the rest and, thinking of

Fred, still sitting alone on the *Mollie O* refusing all efforts at communication, saw no useful purpose in discussing it. Scott was grateful.

Erin came on deck to refill the coffee cups and told Scott she'd managed to reach Al on the radio. Georgie, standing by the reel, said he thought he saw the sheriff's patrol boat coming through Davison. Erin went to find Fred.

Leroy stepped off his Whaler onto the *Nellie J*. He accepted the story of Lorene with a fatalistic lift of his shoulders and quickly moved to the problem at hand. The key members of the drug-smuggling ring were yet to be rounded up, and catching them with the goods, a vital part of shutting them down, would not be easy. They looked anxiously at each other.

"You and Harold aren't going alone on this deal, are you, Sheriff?"

Leroy wore his usual noncommittal face. "Treasury boys are coming in by chopper any minute now. More of my men are driving from Friday. Won't be long."

"What about the drug runners?" Georgie asked.

"Word is they left Friday Harbor fifteen minutes ago."

Scott looked at his watch. "They should be rounding Davison Head in ten minutes."

"That's the way I figure it," Leroy said.

Vic, who'd come out of Korea with a Silver Star and two oak-leaf clusters, laughed. "C'mon, Sheriff, loosen up. You and Harold can't go alone, and you can't wait, and we're here."

They all wanted to go, each for his own reason. For Scott, to expiate guilt; for the others, maybe it answered their frustrations or maybe it was to pay back those from among their own who'd violated a trust. Vic pointed out that the sheriff's patrol boat would be spotted right away, but that the skiff, lightweight aluminum and sturdy, would be less suspicious, less likely to alert the drug runners. Vic scored with this point. Leroy inspected the darkened skies. "Wonder where the hell they got to?"

Off Davison Head a light flickered from a small boat heading west, toward Battleship Island. They watched Leroy anxiously for his answer. Leroy gave in, exacting the promise that they'd all back off as soon as the treasury officers arrived. Scott, Billy, and Davey would go with Vic and Leroy in Vic's skiff, get just close enough to spot them, and alert the chopper. Harold would follow in the Whaler, lead the chopper in. Georgie, Fred, and the rest of the crews would stay aboard the boats with Erin, and alert the deputies when they arrived. Georgie didn't like it.

"Stop bitching," Vic said as his men lowered the skiff. "Too many would slow us down."

"What about him?" Georgie pointed to Fred, who'd come onto the *Nellie J* and was just waking up to what was going on.

"I'm going," Fred said, setting his lips grimly.

Scott was going to argue that Fred was in too highly an emotional state, that he might not act rationally, and a lot of other reasons that boiled down to the same thing. But one look at Fred's face, and he knew none of it would be of any use. Vic shrugged. "Let's get going."

Vic threw the throttle forward, and the skiff exploded on the sea. Scott looked back at Erin, who was huddled next to Georgie, and grinned at her. But Erin wasn't smiling.

"We'll head him off going around McCracken Point," Vic said.

Leroy nodded. His hand rested on the big Colt .38 strapped to his side. Scott didn't know much about how the drug-smuggling operation worked, but he had an idea. In this case, two small boats meeting in the dark of night, one to make the drop, the other to pick up the goods and beat it to the next transfer point, on land or to another boat. Scott imagined the one running the university craft was a student, someone recruited by Lorene, maybe when she'd worked on one of her community projects, like the University Dropout Rehabilitation Center. But who was piloting the receiving craft? A onetime hireling with a fast boat, or a regular? Or, the thought flashed in his mind, someone who knew more about the operation than that, who'd been in it all along. Scott's arm and leg muscles tensed up in anticipation.

The wind and rain eased, and the big diesel put out a

thundering rumble as the skiff closed in on Henry Island. Leroy didn't like it.

"What's the matter?"

"With that wind dying, they might hear our engine."

"And they'll see a boatload of drunk fishermen joyriding."

Leroy wasn't reassured.

"Want I should slow down?"

"Can't chance that either. I guess our best hope is surprise."

Vic nodded and threw the throttle wide open. The skiff wasn't meant for speed or crowds. She was a working boat—no soft spots, just bare metal and a seat for the helmsman. They bounced around in its big metal insides, each bounce cutting into legs and elbows, jarring insides. Bruised and sore, Scott struggled to his knees and got a hold on the gunwales as Vic ran mercilessly on through the passage between Pearl and Henry. No one complained.

From the opening he cut around the point and struck a course south and west. Battleship Island, named for its resemblance to a battleship when viewed from the strait, was an undeveloped state park with a small beach at low tide and a rocky headland on its south side. Vic aimed for the south, hoping to take cover behind the headland and approach the drug runners from their blind side. It wasn't a bad plan, and Vic did a good job maneuvering around the rocks. He tucked her up against a reef on the lee side of Battleship just as the university boat poked its nose out of Speiden.

"We'll wait here until he clears Barren Island," Vic said.

Leroy nodded and looked anxiously into the empty sky. Still no sign of the chopper, and Scott knew what Leroy was thinking. Would they arrive in time for the transfer, and, if not, could a skiffload of amateurs handle the situation? Dare they move in against men who quite likely had guns and were sure to be desperate enough to try anything?

The university boat, small and speedy, reached the island and began flashing its lights across the open water. The answering flash came from behind Bell Rock and put a beacon of light up the slot like the floods from an ocean liner.

"He doesn't see us," Davey said, a nervous tremor in his voice.

Vic took the skiff around the reef, and they caught a full view of the small runabout hanging alongside a seaplane, a plane just like the one off Campbell River. The possible became the probable—Charlie and Jerry. Vic's hand hovered on the throttle, and Scott began counting off seconds.

Leroy looked fretfully at the sky. Whatever else they were, these drug smugglers weren't amateurs. If given too much time they'd make their transfer and be on their way. The plane, of course, could take off, be out of range in seconds. Another problem also presented itself. If the skiff reached them before they could take off, they would surely dump the evidence, and without the proof Leroy and the treasury people wouldn't have a case. Without backup from the sky, it was risky to go ahead, but if they didn't move they risked losing everything. They watched and waited.

A wave splashed over the bow and hosed them down. Leroy gave the signal. Vic gunned it. They vaulted out from the rocks like an overfed whale. It was a sloppy operation from beginning to end, but the thundering rumble of the wind drowned the noise of the diesel, allowed them time to spring their surprise. Vic nearly ran the small plane down with the skiff, slammed against a pontoon, and quickly threw a line around the struts, rendering the plane helpless. A good deal of scurrying and swearing followed. The student on the runabout panicked and jumped overboard, floundering in the waves. Davey fished him out. He was a frightened boy of nineteen or twenty. Leroy put a warning shot over the nose of the plane. Panic spread.

"This is the law. Come out with your arms raised."

Bullets zinged off the metal sides of the skiff.

"Jee-sus," Davey murmured.

A distant rumble shook the skies, and the chopper moved down on them. Harold pulled up in the patrol boat, and the plane door flew open and one of its occupants pitched a silver object into the water. The splash was followed by another. The guns! Scott feared what would go next. Overhead, the deafening clatter of the chopper made its presence felt in a terrifying way. The pilot burst out of the plane, hands raised, and surrendered himself into Leroy's hands. His companion, the short, stocky one, the one called Charlie, hesitated at the door, holding something.

"Hey," Billy shouted, "he's going to dump the stuff."

Fred, who'd maintained a robotlike presence during the run, suddenly came alive. He leaped onto the pontoon, shot up the strut, and dove through the plane's open door like the entire line of the Chicago Bears. Charlie went down, the stuff still in his hands. Fearful for Fred, Scott followed through the cabin door. Fred had Charlie pinned between the cockpit seat and the instrument panel and was pounding on him as he might attack a punching bag. It was a different Fred—eyes glazed over, jaw set—who beat on Charlie with a merciless barrage of lefts and rights, hard chops that made meat of Charlie's face, pounded the wind out of his lungs. All the rage and frustration of Fred's nightmare erupted in those blows. It wasn't much of a struggle from Charlie's point of view. He held his hands in front of his face, trying to protect himself against angry fists that found their mark anyway, and blood started flowing all over the place. Fred kept it up, not stopping, for if he had, he would have seen that Charlie was already a lump of raw flesh with not an ounce of fight left in him. Scott pulled on Fred's arms and dragged him to the open door. Fred was breathing hard and still had fire in his eyes.

"He's had enough, Fred."

Fred stared dumbly at the thoroughly beaten Charlie and nodded, and he and Scott pulled Charlie and the bag of cocaine to the door and into Leroy's waiting hands. Leroy took one look at Charlie's puffed-up face and swore as Fred stumbled back onto the skiff, drooping badly. He'd expended every last ounce of energy in the attack on Charlie. Leroy loaded them all up into the Whaler—the pilot, Charlie, and the student. Only Scott knew there was still one left.

Scott climbed into the plane. The slender, bone-tough gunman, the one called Jerry, backed up behind the luggage racks, his hands in front of his face, his knees tucked under his chin. Scott took a step toward him.

"Get away from me!"

The toughness was gone from the voice. Fred's brutal assault on his partner had removed any thought of resistance. It had also tempered Scott's own desire for revenge. Something else, however, began to tick off in Scott's head, an idea that had begun when he'd seen it was the same two from the *Pilgrim*. These two weren't ordinary lackeys. They'd killed the treasury man and quite possibly Owen as well, probably pumped shot into Marilyn's dead body to cover up for Lorene's own work.

Now, the one with all the mouth on the beach that night cowered under the racks. In his present state, scared out of his wits, he presented an opportunity. If properly enticed, he might tell what he knew about the drug ring that had spread its network through the islands. Lorene wasn't the only one. There had to be someone else—a lieutenant maybe, even a general. Leroy was busy on the Whaler. There was no one standing over them to see. No one to stop Scott as he wrapped his fingers around Jerry's neck and held him to the floor.

"You're choking me," Jerry whimpered. "Let me go. I know my rights."

"You killed three people. That takes away all rights."

"I didn't . . . wasn't me. I didn't kill the T-man. Charlie . . . Charlie did it."

"And Owen?"

"The bitch—she told us to do it. It was the bitch."

"I'm not interested in her. I want to know about the other one. I want a name. Who were you taking this stuff to? Who's the one you answer to besides Lorene Chapman?"

Jerry's face screwed up. "Don't know what you're talking about."

Scott's fingers tightened around Jerry's neck, squeezed the cords until Jerry's eyes started to bulge. "I can shut off the carotid artery this way. You'll be dead in an instant, and no one will ever know it wasn't an accident."

"Uk, " Jerry croaked.

Scott pressed harder. Jerry tried to yell, but couldn't. How far dared he go with it? Scott wondered. Where was the point of no return? Scott thought of Toni and Marilyn and Billie's kids and Prissie. He squeezed another notch. Jerry made a sound. No words came out. Scott let go. Jerry choked wildly, fighting for air. "Who?" Scott said fiercely, pressing on the vocal chords again. "Give me a name."

"Ran . . . Randall," Jerry gasped, spitting up bile. "Brice Ran . . . dall."

Twenty-Four

Scott felt a deep ache as Fred piled into the chopper with Lorene for her last trip to the mainland. There was no way to help, nothing to be done. Only time could help his friend.

The light still burned in Al's window when they drove up in Leroy's wagon. Out on the pass the waters were settling down. A piece of moon found its way out of the black layers of cloud and cast a golden glow over Goose Island. Erin called out a soft "Good night" to Leroy as she and Scott slipped out of the patrol car. Leroy waved the one-arm salute and rolled quietly back onto the road, headed toward town and, Scott hoped, a well-earned night's sleep without the television cameramen and the rest of the Seattle media that had poured onto the island by plane and chopper to record the now famed drug bust.

They woke Al from a sound sleep in his chair, but he was far too anxious to learn what had happened to be annoyed. The questions tumbled one after another without pause. It had gone smoothly enough, Scott told Al. Leroy had turned Charlie and Jerry over to the treasury boys along with Bob Delaney, who was already indicating a willingness to testify as a material witness to the drug-laundering business, which he'd been in up to his neck.

Al wasn't surprised about Brice. "I read not long ago he was having trouble with one of his buildings that couldn't pass code. He was being sued all over the place. Catches up with them. What I don't understand is Lorene. She came from a wealthy family. Why would she mess around with the drug business?"

Scott replied. "From what Cynthia told me, her parents lost

most of their money, and Lorene had this obsession that Fred only hung around because of her inheritance."

"You mean Fred didn't know she was broke? He thought all the money she was raking in from the drug operation came from her trust?"

"That's it."

"But I thought Fred did pretty well in commodities."

"I think he does, but he's up and down, a natural-born gambler. Some people love living on the edge. Fred is one of those."

Al frowned at Erin. "Which reminds me, why the blue blazes did you go with Lorene on that boat?"

"It seems stupid now, but it started out innocently enough. She asked me to drive her over to the boat, said she had to retrieve a coffeepot and that we could have a chance to chat." Erin's cheeks pinked in the firelight. "We'd been having a pleasant conversation."

"You told her about the masks?"

"A good deal more than that, I'm afraid. I never in the world guessed. She was a friend of yours, and I assumed—"

"There's no way you could have known."

"Anyway, I could see she wanted company, and there was something so lonely about her. Then when we reached the boat she started undoing the lines, and before I knew it, we were on our way. I didn't get really alarmed until I saw she was actually going out in the storm, and after we were under way she started saying wild things, accusing me of coming on to Fred, and . . ." Erin shook her head, remembering. "I knew then she was quite crazy. I had the weirdest idea she thought I was someone else."

"I'm sure she did," Scott said.

Puzzled, Erin started to say something. Al interrupted. "How did those hired gunmen happen to operate a ship carrying university students?"

Scott explained about Preston Fields and how he'd fallen into the mess.

"Poor Pres," Erin said.

"Poor Pres, my eye!" Al delivered a stern lecture on faculty ethics, and stopped finally when he thought of another question. "What about the necklace and the masks? What was that all about?"

"The masks are simple. Owen and Randall bought and sold the artifacts to launder the drug money. It's a pretty good way to drop a lot of cash unnoticed, and the value of art fluctuates just like diamonds or gold or land. They buy a collection of African art at auction for cash and then when they sell it again it's clean. Same thing with the land, running it through Canada with dummy companies. They probably had a number of such maneuvers with fishing boats, oil leases, who knows what all."

"Why the fakes?"

"Owen wanted to conceal what they were doing."

Al was still puzzled. "I can see why Lorene was afraid Erin would ruin everything, but why did she kill Owen?"

"You know Owen. He was the kind who couldn't pass up an extra buck, and he knew something no one else knew, that it was Lorene who'd put drugs into Toni's drink the night of Randall's party celebrating the opening of the Center Mall. There I'm a little unsure, but my guess is Lorene drove Toni to the ferry landing, put the Mercedes in gear, and —"

Erin drew in her breath. "Oh, no! She was jealous of Toni, too."

"But why did they break into your place?" Al asked.

"Lorene put them up to that, too. They were after Toni's appointment book, which undoubtedly had Toni's notation about meeting Lorene. Or Lorene was afraid it did, and she feared sooner or later someone would see and figure it out." Scott didn't tell them about Toni and Fred or that Owen had found out about their affair. "Lorene imagined all kinds of things in the last year."

"Mmm," Al said, but nothing more.

Erin had another concern. "Was Brice Randall involved in the murders?"

"I doubt it. My guess is that when Brice received that call from Leroy about the masks, he panicked, told Leroy they were valuable when he knew they were fakes. I think he hoped to switch his collection back and cover up the lie, not very smart for a smart operator like him."

"What about the people who own the *Pilgrim*?"

"Camstar? Their dummy company. It may have connections with some international drug money as well. I tried to track it down, but found only the subsidiary they used in their land deals, which makes me think they're tied up in foreign trusts. I imagine our treasury men will have to unravel it. All I know for a fact is that Owen was an officer, a front man. Brice and Lorene were too smart for that."

Al's eyelids began to droop. "You still haven't explained about the necklace."

"Or how the mask turned up in Victoria."

"I suppose Jerry and Charlie were doing a little free-lancing."

"I guess that's the size of it, all right." Al yawned again.

Scott rose from his chair. "I'll leave you now and let you both get some sleep."

"See you tomorrow," Al mumbled sleepily, shuffling off to the bedroom.

Erin trapped Scott at the door. "You're not telling all you know," she accused with a smile.

She was standing close, and the sweet scent of her perfume wafted between them. He kissed her, a long lingering kiss, held her tight until he felt her lips tremble and she was kissing him back. When he let her go there was no confusion in her eyes. She knew as well as he that it had not been a brotherly kiss, and that whatever direction this would take them, they were no longer just friends. "Good night," he whispered.

As he walked home it all came as clear as the moon lighting the path in front of him. He would go back to his surgical practice. Ralph had known all along that he'd need time to sort things out, but that he'd come back to what he knew best. He suspected Erin had known that, too. He wasn't sure how long he'd be able to tolerate it—the rules, the forms, the screeners poring over his records, telling him how to treat his patients—but he knew Erin would understand that, too, that it would always be that way between them—understanding, everything shared, all the things that had been missing between him and Toni. Scott looked across the rippling seas in front of his house and felt an inner peace he hadn't known in a long time.

Scott was pouring himself a bowl of breakfast cereal when Dandy announced an early-morning visitor. Somehow Scott wasn't surprised to see Vic standing on the doorstep, looking unhappy. "C'mon in, Vic. Good show last night."

"Yeah," Vic said, but there was no cheer in his voice or his eyes.

"Coffee?"

"Can't stay." Vic said, not moving out of the doorway.

"Come in, at least, and tell me what's bugging you."

Shrugging, Vic walked in, followed Scott into the kitchen, settled himself on a stool, and watched while Scott proceeded to fill up the coffeepot. "Don't know how to tell you this," he said.

"Then don't."

"Nope. Time to square things."

"If you don't think last night did that—"

"You don't know what I got to tell you. You don't know what a damn fool thing I did."

Scott plugged in the coffeepot and turned to look into his friend's worried face. "You mean like taking the mask and the necklace from Owen's house and trying to peddle it in Victoria? Is that the damn fool thing you're referring to?"

Vic's mouth gaped. "How the hell did you know that?"

"You went there the night of the murder."

Vic nodded dumbly. "I wanted to have it out with Owen. He lost me a pile on the fish-buyer deal, and I was going to wring it out of him. Trouble was, he was dead when I got there."

"And you didn't call the sheriff?"

"I was going to, and then I got to thinking how it might look, me with such damn good reason to want the son of a bitch dead. I started to go, and it suddenly hit me that that bastard screwed me out of two hundred thousand bucks, and now I'd never get it back."

"So you took the mask and the necklace? You could've taken a lot more."

"All I wanted was some of what Owen cost me." He shook his head morosely. "But the mask turned out to be as phony as Owen."

"What about the necklace?"

"That's why I came." Vic reached into his jacket pocket and pulled out a long gold chain and handed it to Scott.

The links of elephant hair and gold fell into a heavy snakelike coil in Scott's hand. Scott examined the interlocking twists of bright gold, but he already knew from its weight that it was the one authentic piece in Owen's collection. "I have to tell you, Vic. This piece *is* worth something."

Vic shook his head in disgust. "I don't give a shit. It's not worth the gut ache it's cost me, I can tell you that. All I want to know is, what do I do with it now?"

Scott studied his friend's unhappy face. Vic had paid a dear price for his indiscretion. Some would say he'd paid a greater price than was due. "Mmm," Scott said. "Do you trust me?"

"What kind of dumb question is that?"

"I mean, do you trust this to me?"

"I was a damn fool—you know that, Doc—but I don't see myself going up on murder charges for lifting a pile of African junk. Don't much like the idea of landing in the slammer either. But those are the horrors of war, I suppose." He shook his head and looked glum again.

"You may not have to if you leave it to me and keep your mouth shut."

Vic left like a man with a giant burden removed.

In the sheriff's office, Leroy laid the necklace in front of him on his desk and studied it. "You trying to tell me you found this thing on one of those two clowns last night and you're just returning it now?"

"That's right," Scott said, staring back into the sheriff's doubting eyes. "Everything was happening so fast I forgot about it."

Leroy leaned back in the swivel chair and contemplated the ceiling. "Okay," he said finally. "I'll buy it. Now you can deliver a message for me. Tell your friends thanks. I couldn't have done it last night without them."

"Vic and the boys will be pleased to hear that."

Leroy's lips played one of those half-smiles. "Yes, it was Vic I was thinking about."

The End